THREE NOVELS OF

Ernest Hemingway

Books by Ernest Hemingway

THE ENDURING HEMINGWAY

THE NICK ADAMS STORIES

ISLANDS IN THE STREAM

THE FIFTH COLUMN AND FOUR STORIES
    OF THE SPANISH CIVIL WAR

BY-LINE: ERNEST HEMINGWAY

A MOVEABLE FEAST

THREE NOVELS

THE SNOWS OF KILIMANJARO AND OTHER STORIES

THE HEMINGWAY READER

THE OLD MAN AND THE SEA

ACROSS THE RIVER AND INTO THE TREES

FOR WHOM THE BELL TOLLS

THE SHORT STORIES OF ERNEST HEMINGWAY

TO HAVE AND HAVE NOT

GREEN HILLS OF AFRICA

WINNER TAKE NOTHING

DEATH IN THE AFTERNOON

IN OUR TIME

A FAREWELL TO ARMS

MEN WITHOUT WOMEN

THE SUN ALSO RISES

THE TORRENTS OF SPRING

THREE NOVELS OF ERNEST HEMINGWAY

The Sun Also Rises

WITH AN INTRODUCTION BY
MALCOLM COWLEY

A Farewell to Arms

WITH AN INTRODUCTION BY
ROBERT PENN WARREN

The Old Man and the Sea

WITH AN INTRODUCTION BY
CARLOS BAKER

CHARLES SCRIBNER'S SONS

NEW YORK

5 7 9 11 13 15 17 19 F/P 20 18 16 14 12 10 8 6
Printed in the United States of America
Library of Congress Catalog Card Number 62-9455
ISBN 0-684-15612-1

CONTENTS

INTRODUCTION TO

The Sun Also Rises

BY MALCOLM COWLEY

INTRODUCTION

"Commencing with the Simplest Things"

AT THE end of December, 1921, when Hemingway was twenty-two years old and newly married, he came to Paris for a second visit. The first, in May, 1918, had lasted only until he picked up a Red Cross ambulance, which he drove in convoy to the Italian front. There he had been gravely wounded early in July, and he had spent three months in and out of military hospitals. After his return to Chicago he had written many stories and poems and had even started a novel, but he had so far published nothing over his own name except in high-school papers and in the weekly magazine of the Toronto *Star*. He now planned to finish out his apprenticeship as a writer, and the second visit—interrupted by four unhappy months in Toronto—would last for nearly seven years. His apprenticeship, however, would end spectacularly in 1926, with the publication of *The Sun Also Rises*.

In these days when many things have ended, it is a melancholy pleasure to go back over the records of that era when everything was starting, for Hemingway and others, and when almost anything seemed possible. He came to Paris with letters of introduction from Sherwood Anderson, whom he had known well in Chicago, and also with a roving commission from the Toronto *Star* to write color stories, for which he would be paid at space rates if the stories were printed. In those days such commissions were easy to obtain, since they did not obligate a newspaper to spend money, and usually they led to nothing but a few rejected or grudgingly printed manuscripts. Hemingway's stories were good enough to feature, and they quickly led to definite assignments, with travel expenses.

Suddenly elevated to the position of staff reporter and authorized to send cables—but not too many of them—Hemingway was dispatched to the Genoa Economic Conference in March, 1922, to the Near East in September, for the last days of the Greco-Turkish War, and to Lausanne at the end of November, for the peace conference that followed. He also worked for Hearst's International News Service on the last two of those assignments, earning while he learned. In Asia Minor he studied the Greek retreat as if it were a laboratory experiment in warfare. At Lausanne he studied the mechanics of international relations, with the help of barside lectures from William Bolitho, already famous as a correspondent. In both places he studied the curious language known as cabelese, in which every word has to do the work of six or seven. At three dollars a word he would put a message something like this on the wires: KEMAL INSWARDS UNBURNED SMYRNA GUILTY GREEKS. The translation appearing in the Hearst papers would be: "Mustapha Kemal in an exclusive interview today with the correspondent of the International News Service [KEMAL INSWARDS] denied vehemently that the Turkish forces had any part in the burning of Smyrna [UNBURNED SMYRNA]. The city, Kemal stated, was fired by incendiaries in the troops of the Greek rear guard before the first Turkish patrols entered the city [GUILTY GREEKS]."

Cabelese was an exercise in omitting everything that can be

taken for granted. It contributed to Hemingway's literary method, just as the newspaper assignments contributed to his subject matter. Going back over the records, one is astonished to find how much he learned during that first year abroad. He said afterwards that "A great enough writer seems to be born with knowledge. But he really is not; he has only been born with the ability to learn in a quicker ratio to the passage of time than other men and without conscious application, and with an intelligence to accept or reject what is already presented as knowledge." Hemingway had that gift to such an extent that I sometimes think of him as an instinctive student who never went to college. His motto through life was not that of Sherwood Anderson's groping adolescents, "I want to know why," but rather, "I want to know *how*"—how to write, first of all, but also how to fish, how to box, how to ski, how to act in the bull ring, how to remember his own sensations, how to nurse his talent, how to live while learning to write, and more broadly how to *live,* in the sense of mastering the rules that must be followed by anyone who wants to respect himself. Many of his stories can be read and have been read by thousands as, essentially, object lessons in practical ethics and professional decorum.

There is much more to be said about Hemingway as a lifelong student. Charles A. Fenton wrote a useful book on the subject, *The Apprenticeship of Ernest Hemingway,* but it deals only with his early training as a writer and omits his other fields of study. Besides those already mentioned, the fields would eventually include wing shooting, big-game fishing and hunting, food, wines and liquors, Italian, French, Spanish, Basque, Swahili, military geography, navigation, ballistics, and death as a natural phenomenon. He had a true student's humility, but also a student's pride and a burning wish to excel. If he did not stand high in a field of study, or did not need it in his daily life, he quickly abandoned it, as he abandoned the cello, football, bridge, tennis (except for exercise), and amateur bullfighting, for which, as he told the Old

Lady of *Death in the Afternoon,* "I was too old, too heavy and too awkward." In other fields he went on to take postgraduate work —for example in bullfighting as a spectator sport—and became an acknowledged master.

Since there were no textbooks in many of his fields, or none that could be trusted, he went straight to the best teachers. Among those under whom he studied during his first Paris year were Gertrude Stein and Ezra Pound, both friends of Hemingway but not of each other, and a cross-eyed Negro jockey from Cincinnati named Jim Winkfield.

How much he learned from his two older literary friends is the subject of a long-standing argument, but I think he learned a great deal. He listened attentively, and he had too much confidence in himself to fear, as many young writers do, that he would end as somebody's disciple. He could afford to take from others because he gave so much in return. What he gave to Miss Stein is partly revealed in his letters to her, now in the Yale Library: he helped to get her work published in the *transatlantic review* when he was helping to edit it, and having learned that she had only a bound manuscript of *The Making of Americans,* he typed long sections of it for the printer. One thing he took from her was an apparently colloquial American style, full of repeated words, prepositional phrases, and present participles, the style in which he wrote his early published stories. One thing he took from Pound—in return for trying vainly to teach him how to box—was the doctrine of the accurate image, which he applied in the "chapters" printed between the stories that went into *In Our Time;* but Hemingway also learned from him to blue-pencil most of his adjectives and adverbs. What he learned from Jim Winkfield was much simpler: it was the name of a winning horse.

I heard the story from the late Evan Shipman, poet, trotting-horse columnist, and one of Hemingway's lifelong friends. Winkfield, he told me, had won the Kentucky Derby in 1901, on His

Eminence, and again the following year, on Alan-a-Dale. By 1922 Negro jockeys were not being employed on American tracks, and Winkfield was in France training horses for Pierre Wertheimer, who had a famous stable. There is no outside audience when colts are trained in France, and there are no professional clockers at their time trials; every stable has its own secrets. At Wertheimer's stable the secret was Epinard, a sensationally promising colt with an unfashionable sire. Winkfield, who was seeing a lot of Hemingway, told him that Epinard was going to run his first race at Deauville that summer. Having borrowed all the money he could, Hemingway laid it on Epinard's nose.

That wasn't his only big day at the track. In June of the same year—writing from Milan, where he said that most of the races were fixed—he reported to Gertrude Stein that he had picked seventeen winners out of twenty-one starts. Most of his winnings went into the bank, for he already planned to stop working for newspapers. Miss Stein had something to do with the decision. "If you keep on doing newspaper work," she told him, "you will never see things, you will only see words, and that will not do— that is, of course, if you intend to be a writer."

Hemingway had never intended to be anything else, but writing every day was a luxury he still couldn't afford. The *Star,* impressed by a series of articles he had lately submitted on the French occupation of the Ruhr, offered him a job in the home office at a top reporter's salary, for those days, of $125 a week. In September, 1923, he left for Toronto with the intention of working two years and saving enough money to finish a novel. Soon he came into conflict with Harry C. Hindmarsh, then assistant managing editor of the *Star,* who tried to break his spirit with what seems to have been a series of nagging persecutions. Hemingway resigned explosively at the end of December, and the following month he was back in Paris, resolved to starve if he must but write for himself.

II

Those were the days when young American writers regarded Paris as a necessary stage in their educations and the only place in the world where they could meet others who were doing serious work. They came to Paris by scores and later by hundreds, crowding the boat trains and pouring through the Gare Saint-Lazare like stampeding Herefords. They took rooms in disreputable hotels on the Left Bank, then hurried off to the Café du Dôme, where they remained for most of the night and other nights as well. After months or a year they usually decided that Paris wasn't the best place for working after all, and they grandly moved south to the Riviera, Majorca, Capri, or wherever they could write a book without interruptions. But they came back with the book half started, and especially in the long June evenings one could see them outside the Dôme, in noisy groups at the tables covered with saucers, or sitting alone and recognizable not only by their simple bulk, as compared with the French, but also by the uneasy glance with which they searched for an acquaintance willing to read an unfinished manuscript or lend them fifty francs to carry them over until the next check came from home.

Some of the young writers were already known and were soon to become famous: in Paris at the time were E. E. Cummings, John Dos Passos, John Peale Bishop, Kay Boyle, Scott Fitzgerald, Glenway Wescott, Louis Bromfield, Robert M. Coates, and Archibald MacLeish, to mention only a few. Hemingway knew all of these and was a close friend of three or four, but it was a younger group that specially looked up to him. The group was composed of writers then in the process of being "discovered," which is to say that they were getting their first stories or poems printed in little magazines that bloomed and disappeared like wildflowers; at least a brace of new talents was discovered in every issue of every new magazine. Running over a list of names some years ago, I found that many of the group had gone into business or teaching, that others were dead, like Shipman and John Herrmann—not even bullfighters have a higher mortality rate than unread writers—and that still others, then including Morley Callaghan, were writing well but in comparative obscurity while waiting to be discovered again.

You couldn't say that Hemingway was a leader among them, because he didn't belong to the group, but they were proud to be seen with him. He seldom appeared at the Dôme except in the early morning for coffee. It was an event of the evening when he passed the café, tall, broad, and handsome, usually wearing a patched jacket and sneakers, and often walking on the balls of his feet like a boxer. Arms waved in greeting from the sidewalk tables, and friends ran out to urge him to sit down with them. "The occasions were charming little scenes, as if spontaneous even though repeated," says Nathan Asch, who remembers those days. "In view of the whole terrace, Hemingway would be striding toward the Montparnasse railroad station, his mind seemingly busy with the mechanics of someone's arrival or departure, and he wouldn't quite recognize whoever greeted him. Then suddenly his beautiful smile appeared that made those watching him also smile; and with a will and an eagerness he put out his hands and warmly greeted his acquaintance, who, overcome by this reception, simply glowed; and who returned with Hem to the table as if with an overwhelming prize."

"No, I have no criticism to make of Hem's conduct," said another veteran of the Paris years. "I do think it's a crazy situation, though, that the elimination was so brutal, that of all the writers in Paris then, Hem is holding the world by the handle and everybody else is either obscure or dead. But you can't blame it on Hem."

What distinguished him from the young writers at the sidewalk tables, now obscure or dead, was of course his greater talent, but it was also his studious habit of mind and his willingness to work harder than any of the others. "He was gay, he was sentimental," Lincoln Steffens said of him, "but he was always at work." Once when they were dining at a Chinese restaurant in Paris, he insisted to Mrs. Steffens that anyone could write. "You can," he told her, feinting as if to give her a left to the jaw, for he was always shadow-boxing in those days. "It's hell. It takes it all out of you; it nearly kills you; but you can do it. Anybody can. Even you can, Stef. . . . I haven't done it yet, but I will." He seemed to think, Steffens reported, "that writing was a matter of honesty and labor, and maybe it is, utter honesty and hard labor."

Hemingway had met Steffens at the Lausanne Conference and had shown him some of his dispatches from the Near East. Steffens wanted to see more of his work, and Hemingway asked his wife, Hadley, to send it on from Paris. That was just before Christmas, 1922. Hadley packed his manuscripts in a suitcase and carried it herself, because she was afraid they would be lost if she sent them by express. At the Gare de Lyon in Paris, she left the compartment for a moment to get a drink of water, and the suitcase was stolen. It contained everything he had written and saved until that time—an unfinished novel, eighteen stories, thirty poems—and it was never recovered. There was a little salvage. *Poetry* had accepted six poems, the *Cosmopolitan* had rejected a story, "My Old Man," which was then in the mail, and lying on his desk was another story, "Up in Michigan." For the rest, all the early work that he valued was irretrievably lost.

It was a disaster for Hemingway, but in some ways a fortunate one. With his early work destroyed as if by fire, he could start from the beginning and build another structure on new lines. "I was trying to learn to write," he says on the second page of *Death in the Afternoon,* in a passage referring to those months, "commencing with the simplest things." That last phrase is almost unique in its mixture of humility and hard-headedness. I have known many apprentice writers, but not one other who was willing, at twenty-three, to put aside everything he had learned or accomplished and start again with the simplest things.

Hemingway studied writing in Paris as if he were studying geometry without a textbook and inventing theorems as he went along. He accepted as a postulate that the function of any literary work is to evoke some particular emotion from the reader; but how could that best be done? Most writers were content to describe an emotion as it was felt by themselves or their heroes, in hopes that the reader would be moved by it, but this was a method that made him the mere auditor of someone else's fear or longing or rage. Hemingway wanted to make his readers feel the emotion directly—not as if they were being told about an event, but as if they were taking part in it. The best way to produce this effect, he decided as a first theorem, was to set down exactly, in their proper sequence, the sights, sounds, touches, tastes, and smells that had produced an emotion he remembered feeling. Then, without auctorial comments and without ever saying that he or his hero had been frightened, sad, or angry, he could make the reader feel the emotion for himself.

"I was trying to write then," he says in that same passage of *Death in the Afternoon,* "and I found the greatest difficulty, aside from knowing truly what you really felt, rather than what you were supposed to feel, and had been taught to feel, was to put down what really happened in action; what the actual things were which produced the emotion that you experienced. In writing for a newspaper you told what happened and, with one trick and another, you communicated the emotion aided by the element of timeliness which gives a certain emotion to any account of something that has happened on that day; but the real thing, the sequence of motion and fact which made the emotion and which would be as valid in a year or in ten years or, with luck and if you stated it purely enough, always, was beyond me and I was working very hard to try to get it."

That often quoted passage suggests a whole system of practical aesthetics—not the loftiest one, not one to which Hemingway would always confine himself, but a sound system within its self-imposed limitations and an excellent guide for any young writer. Hemingway is suggesting, in substance, that a piece of writing might be regarded as a machine for producing a particular effect, and that its capacity for producing the effect should be permanent. "When you describe something that has happened that day," he would say elsewhere, "the timeliness makes people see it in their own imaginations. A month later that element of time is gone and your account would be flat and they would not see in their minds nor remember it." Good writing, as Ezra Pound was already saying, is "news that *stays* news." It can stay news if it has achieved certain definite qualities, that is, if it is absolutely honest —a virtue that depends on "knowing truly what you really felt, rather than what you were supposed to feel, and had been taught to feel"—and if it presents "the real thing, the sequence of motion and fact which made the emotion." But a writer's luck, or unconscious, also plays a part in the process, and the real thing had to be stated "purely enough" if it is to remain valid through the years.

"Purely enough," for Hemingway, meant without tricks of any sort, without conventionally emotive language, and with a bare minimum of adjectives and adverbs. It also meant that the permanent work had to be written like cabelese, with everything omitted that the reader could take for granted, and with each detail so carefully selected that it did the work of six or seven. One of Hemingway's early studies was the art of omission. "If a writer of prose knows enough about what he is writing about," he says in another chapter of *Death in the Afternoon*, "he may omit things that he knows and the reader, if the writer is writing truly enough, will have a feeling of those things as strongly as though the writer had stated them. The dignity of movement of an ice-berg is due to only one-eighth of it being above water."

That sort of dignity is difficult to attain, and Hemingway "was working very hard to try to get it." With his talent for methodology, for the *how*, he thought it could best be achieved, at the beginning, in very short pieces. The first ones he wrote after starting again with the simplest things were the vignettes, or "chapters," that would later be printed in italics between the stories in the first of his books to be issued by a New York publisher, *In Our Time*. Much earlier six of the "chapters," all those he had finished at the moment, appeared in the April, 1923, issue of the *Little Review*. One of these was the paragraph that afterwards became "Chapter II," the one beginning "Minarets stuck up in the rain out of Adrianople across the mud flats." Perhaps it was the very first work in his new manner, and it exists in three separate versions, with a complicated history of changes that Charles A. Fenton has studied at length.

The earliest version consists of the first three paragraphs of a story that Hemingway cabled to the *Star* from Adrianople on October 20, 1922. It was not written in cabelese, as it would have been if he were sending it to the International News Service, and it was a masterly piece of reporting. Lincoln Steffens, who read it at Lausanne in December, recollected much of it ten years later when writing the last chapters of his *Autobiography*. The paragraphs, however, were not in Hemingway's new manner. In their total length of 241 words there were no less than thirty adjectives, and some of these were compound words like "never-ending" and "muddy-flanked." There were also signposts to guide the reader toward having the proper emotions, that is, there were charged words and phrases like "ghastly," "in horror," and "to keep off the driving rain." These "tricks," as Hemingway called them, were permissible and even necessary in a newspaper story designed to produce its effect at a single hasty glance.

In the second version, the one that Hemingway published in the *Little Review*, all the guideposts to emotion have disappeared and so have most of the adjectives. Some of the descriptive details have also been omitted, in order to bring the others into sharper focus. The process of sharpening and tightening the prose while suppressing even the implied comments of the author continued for a long time, and the results of it appear in the third and almost final version. This is the one included in a very short booklet published in France in 1924 and bearing the same title as Hemingway's first book-length collection of stories: *in our time,* but in this case without capital letters. The version reads:

Minarets stuck up in the rain out of Adrianople across the mud flats. The carts were jammed for thirty miles along the Karagatch road. Water buffalo and cattle were hauling the carts through the mud. No end and no beginning. Just carts loaded with everything they owned. The old men and women, soaked through, walked along keeping the cattle moving. The Maritza was running yellow almost up to the bridge. Carts were jammed solid on the bridge with camels bobbing along through them. Greek cavalry herded along the procession. Women and kids were in the carts crouched with mattresses, mirrors, sewing machines, bundles. There was a woman having a kid with a young girl holding a blanket over her and crying. Scared sick looking at it. It rained all through the evacuation.

Here the "chapter," as it is now called, has been shortened to 131 words, or only half the length of the newspaper version. There are only ten descriptive adjectives instead of thirty, and every one of them is simple and definite. Four of the adjectives—"loaded," "soaked," "crouched," and "scared"—are past participles and have somewhat the effect of verbs in the passive voice: the right effect, since the refugees are the passive subjects of action. There are also ten present participles, three of which occur in the same sentence: ". . . *having* a kid with a young girl *holding* a blanket over her and *crying.*" They give a sense of action that continues under our eyes. This use, and sometimes abuse, of present participles was one of the habits that Hemingway had probably acquired from Gertrude Stein, along with a fondness for prepositional phrases used in series ("*in* the rain *out of* Adrianople *across* the mud flats") and a distrust of relative clauses. All the sentences are short, averaging only ten words. (Incidentally this is not a characteristic of Hemingway's later prose, in which there are sentences almost as long as Faulkner's.) Three sentences have been stripped of their verbs, and the others without exception are simple and declarative.

There were further changes, if slight ones, in 1925 when the Adrianople "chapter" was included in the much longer American *In Our Time* (with the capitalized title), and again in 1930 when the book was reissued by Scribner's. Did the changes work, taken as a whole? To expand the question, what effects did Hemingway produce on his readers as a result of his patient revisions in this and the other brief "chapters," sixteen in all, that were written during the six months after he lost his manuscripts? I think the effects on sympathetic and attentive readers, at first a minority, were close to those he had planned to produce. Other readers blamed Hemingway, insensitively, for being tough and insensitive. But the attentive ones were moved, though they seldom knew why, and they felt they were seeing events for themselves instead of just hearing about them. They felt that the exaggeratedly simple and awkward-looking style made everything seem authentic; and they also felt that the "chapters" had an impact that was not in proportion to their size, as if part of it depended on words that went unspoken. Written without tricks—except the great ones of understatement and omission—those very brief works proved to be news that stayed news. They have exerted a permanent influence even on writers who turned against Hemingway, and they brought about something like a revolution in American prose fiction.

Hemingway himself wrote no more "chapters" after his return from Toronto in 1924. Instead he went on to the second stage in his program, which consisted in writing stories. He began by applying the methods developed in his vignettes, but this time, instead of merely presenting a scene, he included some of the events leading up to it, in strict chronological sequence. He also included dialogue, for which he had an instinctively fine ear. But simple chronology, or narrative sequence, was the principal element that distinguished the stories from the "chapters," and Hemingway displayed an extraordinary gift for putting first things first, second things second, and for stopping short of what other writers would regard as the climax in order to let the reader go on for himself. That explains the power of suggestion of early stories like "Cat in the Rain"; the climax is on the next page after the end.

In discussing the purely technical aspects of Hemingway's early work, I have omitted what he calls the element of luck. He had that too, in the shape of an unusually rich unconscious and a stock of subject matter, both giving him an advantage over two of his teachers. Ezra Pound had only two closely related subjects at the time, art and the life of art. Gertrude Stein's principal subject was herself. Hemingway's subject was also himself, or his inner world, but that self had a passion for acquiring knowledge and for rushing forward to meet external challenges, so that his inner world already included a broad and highly colored segment of the outer world. He was a very complicated young man at twenty-six, with something close to a genius for simplification. Many readers felt that his stories were completely new in American fiction. Shortly after *In Our Time* appeared in New York, Alfred Harcourt, an astute publisher who would have liked to have issued the book, said in a letter to Louis Bromfield, "Hemingway's first novel might rock the country." The letter was sent to Paris in the late autumn of 1925, at a time when Hemingway had reached a third stage in his career. Having learned how to write stories, he was then revising a hastily written draft of *The Sun Also Rises*.

III

I don't mean to suggest that Hemingway was spending all of his time at his desk. He boxed regularly at a Paris gymnasium. He played a good deal of tennis with, among others, Ezra Pound, Bill Bullitt, and Harold Loeb, the former publisher of *Broom,* who had been a middle-weight wrestler at Princeton. By this time Hemingway had acquired a wide circle of friends, or rather a number of nonintersecting circles composed respectively of tennis friends, boxing friends, racetrack friends, newspaper friends, and older and younger writing friends. Some of the younger ones he published in the two issues of the *transatlantic review* that he edited while Ford Madox Ford, its founder and publisher, was in New York. Some other friends joined with him one summer to rent a trout stream in the Black Forest. He spent several winters skiing at a little town called Schruns, in the Vorarlberg, where he was once offered the job of skiing instructor.

One is again surprised to find how much he learned in those years and how quickly he reached a professional level in most of his fields of study. At one time he was a prizefight manager, with a little stable of boxers that included Larry Gaines, a Negro heavyweight from Toronto who later beat Max Schmeling in one of Schmeling's early fights. That business career ended on a famous evening when Hemingway jumped into the ring to save a young boxer from being killed in a fixed fight, and, with a water bottle, knocked out Francis Charles, the middleweight champion of France. After that he abandoned French boxing as a crooked sport and devoted more and more attention to the bullfights in Spain.

I can't find a record of the first bullfight he saw, but in 1923 he was in Pamplona for the *feria* of San Fermin, which lasted always from July 6 to July 12. In 1924 he was back with Donald Ogden Stewart, already a successful humorist, and both men took part in the amateur bullfights that were held each morning. Hemingway returned to Paris very excited, with photographs of the big pepper-and-salt bull that had carried him across the arena on its horns, after breaking Stewart's ribs. In 1925 he was back in Pamplona for another fiesta and another adventure with the bulls; but first he had made a trout-fishing expedition to the Irati River with his wife and Don Stewart and Bill Smith, a friend he had known since his Michigan days. Construction work on a dam had ruined the fishing and they didn't catch a trout.

The fiesta was in some ways even less successful. The group in Pamplona, besides the fishermen, included Harold Loeb, Patrick Guthrie, who was an English remittance man, and his friend Lady Duff Twysden, who was believed to be the heroine of Michael Arlen's immensely popular novel, *The Girl in the Green Hat*. Usually she did wear a floppy-brimmed green felt hat, but she was more widely known for her love affairs and her capacity for holding liquor. Everybody drank a great deal at the fiesta and almost everybody quarreled. "Some fiesta," said Harold Loeb, who later described it in his memoirs. Things went better at the bull ring, where the principal attraction was Nino de la Palma, then in his first season as a matador. Awarded the ear of the last bull he killed, to great applause, he presented it to Hadley Hemingway, who wrapped it in a handkerchief and took it back to the hotel.

Hemingway and his wife went on to Madrid and then to Valencia. There on July 21, which was his twenty-sixth birthday, he started to write *The Sun Also Rises*, exactly nine days after some of the events that would be described (and considerably revised) in the novel. One of his early theorems was that the background of an experience should be presented truly, "the way it was," but that the story should be "made up," so as to become truer than what actually happened. Work on the novel continued uninterruptedly in Madrid, San Sebastian, Hendaye, and Paris, where the first draft was finished on September 6, after forty-eight working days. "I knew nothing about writing a novel when I started it," Hemingway said many years later, "and so wrote too fast and each day to the point of complete exhaustion. So the first draft was very bad. I wrote it in six weeks and I had to rewrite it completely. But in the rewriting I learned much."

Before setting to work on the revision, he put the manuscript aside for nearly three months to season. It was during this interval that he wrote a book-length satire, *The Torrents of Spring*, in a little more than a week. He went back to the novel in December, while he was skiing at Schruns, and worked hard on it during the next two months. In February, 1926, he made a hasty trip to New York, had an interview with Maxwell Perkins of Scribner's, and signed a contract for both the satire (to be published first) and the novel. Work on the latter continued during March and included a great deal of ruthless cutting, which amounted in the end to forty thousand words. Most of them were deleted from the first or Paris section of the manuscript. A final draft, consisting of eighty thousand words, went to the typist on April 1 and was published on October 22. *The Sun Also Rises* did not rock the country, but it received a number of hat-in-the-air reviews, and it soon became a handbook of conduct for the new generation. That winter an observer in Greenwich Village noted that many of the younger writers had already begun to talk, walk, and shadow-box like Hemingway, when they weren't flourishing capes in front of an imaginary bull.

I have read the book so often, for pleasure and professionally, that it is hard for me now to make fresh observations about it. One thing I notice more clearly than before is its technique, which once again reveals Hemingway's systematic or studentlike cast of mind and his habit of always starting with the simple before moving to the complex. In writing this first novel he applied the principles developed in his vignettes, along with others developed in his stories. Once again, as he went on to another stage, his work incorporated a new element besides its greater length. Whereas each of his stories had dealt with one or two persons, or three at the most, his novel deals with the rather complicated relations among a *group* of persons. That might even lead to a general description of the novel—any novel—as a literary form: it is a long but unified narrative, designed to be read at more than one sitting, which presents a situation affecting a group of characters and leading to a change in their relations.

The situation in the background of *The Sun Also Rises* is the Great War, in which most of the characters have served and in which some of them have been physically or morally wounded. All the characters except the matador, Pedro Romero, have lost their original code of values. Feeling the loss, they are now trying to live by a simpler code—essentially that of soldiers on furlough— and it is this effort which unites them as a group. "I told you he was one of us," Lady Brett says of Count Mippipopolous after he has unashamedly stripped off his shirt and shown them where an arrow had passed completely through his body. The unashamedness, the wound, and the courage it suggests are all things they have in common. The war in which they served has deadened some of their feelings, has left them capable of enjoying only the simplest and strongest pleasures, and has also given them an attitude of resigned acceptance toward all sorts of disasters, including those caused by their own follies. Robert Cohn, however, has never been wounded and has never learned to be resigned; therefore he refuses to let Brett go, fights with his rivals for her, including Romero, and is cast out of the group. Romero is their simple-minded saint. Brett is almost on the point of permanently corrupting him, but she obeys another article of the code and draws back. "You know, it makes one feel rather good deciding not to be a bitch," she says. "It's sort of what we have instead of God."

The Sun Also Rises is not, as I have heard it called, Heming-

way's best novel. After all it is his first, and there are signs in it
of his struggle to master a new medium. In spite of the forty
thousand words deleted from the manuscript, there are still some
details that do not seem essential, as notably in the street-by-street
accounts of Jake Barnes's wanderings through Paris. There are
also a few obvious guideposts for the reader, as when Jake says of
Robert Cohn that "he was not so simple" after coming back from
New York, "and he was not so nice." Although Cohn's fight with
Romero is the physical climax of the action, it is reported at second
hand—by Mike Campbell, who has heard the story from Brett,
who was the only witness of the fight—instead of being presented
before our eyes. More serious than these technical flaws, there
is the sort of timeliness that is always in danger of going stale.
Brett was a pathetic brave figure for her time, but the pathos has
been cheapened by thousands of imitation Bretts in life and fiction.
Bill Gorton's remarks are not so bright now as they once seemed.
"You're an expatriate," he tells Jake ironically. "You've lost touch
with the soil. You get precious. Fake European standards have
ruined you. . . . You hang around cafés." In 1926 one felt that he
was making exactly the right rejoinder to dozens of newspaper
editorials then fresh in the public mind; in the 1960's these have
been forgotten.

Not everything changes. After one has mentioned these wrinkles
and scars revealed by age, how much of the novel seems as
marvelously fresh as when it first appeared! Count Mippipopolous,
his wound, and his champagne; the old couple from Montana on
their first trip abroad; the busload of Basque peasants; the whole
beautiful episode of the fishing trip in the mountains, in the harsh
sunlight, and then by contrast the dark streets of Pamplona
crowded with *riau-riau* dancers, who formed a circle round Brett
as if she were a revered witch—as indeed she was, and as Jake
in a way was the wounded Fisher King ruling over a sterile land

—in all this there is nothing that has gone bad and not a word to be changed after so many years. It is all carved in stone, bigger and truer than life, and it is the work of a man who, having ended his busy term of apprenticeship, was already a master at twenty-six.

MALCOLM COWLEY

The Sun Also Rises

THIS BOOK IS FOR HADLEY

AND FOR JOHN HADLEY NICANOR

"You are all a lost generation."

—GERTRUDE STEIN *in conversation*

"One generation passeth away, and another generation cometh; but the earth abideth forever. . . The sun also ariseth, and the sun goeth down, and hasteth to the place where he arose. . . The wind goeth toward the south, and turneth about unto the north; it whirleth about continually, and the wind returneth again according to his circuits. . . All the rivers run into the sea; yet the sea is not full; unto the place from whence the rivers come, thither they return again."

—*Ecclesiastes*

BOOK I

CHAPTER I

ROBERT COHN was once middleweight boxing champion of Princeton. Do not think that I am very much impressed by that as a boxing title, but it meant a lot to Cohn. He cared nothing for boxing, in fact he disliked it, but he learned it painfully and thoroughly to counteract the feeling of inferiority and shyness he had felt on being treated as a Jew at Princeton. There was a certain inner comfort in knowing he could knock down anybody who was snooty to him, although, being very shy and a thoroughly nice boy, he never fought except in the gym. He was Spider Kelly's star pupil. Spider Kelly taught all his young gentlemen to box like featherweights, no matter whether they weighed one hundred and five or two hundred and five pounds. But it seemed to fit Cohn. He was really very fast. He was so good that Spider promptly overmatched him and got his nose permanently flattened. This increased Cohn's distaste for boxing, but it gave him a certain satisfaction of some strange sort, and it certainly improved his nose. In his last year at Princeton he read too much and took to wearing spectacles. I never met any one of his class who remem-

bered him. They did not even remember that he was middleweight boxing champion.

I mistrust all frank and simple people, especially when their
stories hold together, and I always had a suspicion that perhaps
Robert Cohn had never been middleweight boxing champion,
and that perhaps a horse had stepped on his face, or that maybe
his mother had been frightened or seen something, or that he had,
maybe, bumped into something as a young child, but I finally had
somebody verify the story from Spider Kelly. Spider Kelly not only
remembered Cohn. He had often wondered what had become of
him.

Robert Cohn was a member, through his father, of one of the
richest Jewish families in New York, and through his mother of
one of the oldest. At the military school where he prepped for
Princeton, and played a very good end on the football team, no
one had made him race-conscious. No one had ever made him feel
he was a Jew, and hence any different from anybody else, until
he went to Princeton. He was a nice boy, a friendly boy, and very
shy, and it made him bitter. He took it out in boxing, and he
came out of Princeton with painful self-consciousness and the flattened nose, and was married by the first girl who was nice to him.
He was married five years, had three children, lost most of the
fifty thousand dollars his father left him, the balance of the estate
having gone to his mother, hardened into a rather unattractive
mould under domestic unhappiness with a rich wife; and just
when he had made up his mind to leave his wife she left him
and went off with a miniature-painter. As he had been thinking
for months about leaving his wife and had not done it because it
would be too cruel to deprive her of himself, her departure was a
very healthful shock.

The divorce was arranged and Robert Cohn went out to the
Coast. In California he fell among literary people and, as he still

had a little of the fifty thousand left, in a short time he was backing a review of the Arts. The review commenced publication in Carmel, California, and finished in Provincetown, Massachusetts. By that time Cohn, who had been regarded purely as an angel, and whose name had appeared on the editorial page merely as a member of the advisory board, had become the sole editor. It was his money and he discovered he liked the authority of editing. He was sorry when the magazine became too expensive and he had to give it up.

By that time, though, he had other things to worry about. He had been taken in hand by a lady who hoped to rise with the magazine. She was very forceful, and Cohn never had a chance of not being taken in hand. Also he was sure that he loved her. When this lady saw that the magazine was not going to rise, she became a little disgusted with Cohn and decided that she might as well get what there was to get while there was still something available, so she urged that they go to Europe, where Cohn could write. They came to Europe, where the lady had been educated, and stayed three years. During these three years, the first spent in travel, the last two in Paris, Robert Cohn had two friends, Braddocks and myself. Braddocks was his literary friend. I was his tennis friend.

The lady who had him, her name was Frances, found toward the end of the second year that her looks were going, and her attitude toward Robert changed from one of careless possession and exploitation to the absolute determination that he should marry her. During this time Robert's mother had settled an allowance on him, about three hundred dollars a month. During two years and a half I do not believe that Robert Cohn looked at another woman. He was fairly happy, except that, like many people living in Europe, he would rather have been in America, and he had discovered writing. He wrote a novel, and it was not really such a

bad novel as the critics later called it, although it was a very poor
novel. He read many books, played bridge, played tennis, and
boxed at a local gymnasium.

I first became aware of his lady's attitude toward him one night
after the three of us had dined together. We had dined at
l'Avenue's and afterward went to the Café de Versailles for coffee.
We had several *fines* after the coffee, and I said I must be going.
Cohn had been talking about the two of us going off somewhere
on a weekend trip. He wanted to get out of town and get in a
good walk. I suggested we fly to Strasbourg and walk up to Saint
Odile, or somewhere or other in Alsace. "I know a girl in Strasbourg who can show us the town," I said.

Somebody kicked me under the table. I thought it was acci-
dental and went on: "She's been there two years and knows everything there is to know about the town. She's a swell girl."

I was kicked again under the table and, looking, saw Frances,
Robert's lady, her chin lifting and her face hardening.

"Hell," I said, "why go to Strasbourg? We could go up to Bruges,
or to the Ardennes."

Cohn looked relieved. I was not kicked again. I said good-night
and went out. Cohn said he wanted to buy a paper and would walk
to the corner with me. "For God's sake," he said, "why did you
say that about that girl in Strasbourg for? Didn't you see Frances?"

"No, why should I? If I know an American girl that lives in
Strasbourg what the hell is it to Frances?"

"It doesn't make any difference. Any girl. I couldn't go, that
would be all."

"Don't be silly."

"You don't know Frances. Any girl at all. Didn't you see the way
she looked?"

"Oh, well," I said, "let's go to Senlis."

"Don't get sore."

"I'm not sore. Senlis is a good place and we can stay at the Grand Cerf and take a hike in the woods and come home."

"Good, that will be fine."

"Well, I'll see you to-morrow at the courts," I said.

"Good-night, Jake," he said, and started back to the café.

"You forgot to get your paper," I said.

"That's so." He walked with me up to the kiosque at the corner. "You are not sore, are you, Jake?" He turned with the paper in his hand.

"No, why should I be?"

"See you at tennis," he said. I watched him walk back to the café holding his paper. I rather liked him and evidently she led him quite a life.

CHAPTER II

THAT winter Robert Cohn went over to America with his novel, and it was accepted by a fairly good publisher. His going made an awful row I heard, and I think that was where Frances lost him, because several women were nice to him in New York, and when he came back he was quite changed. He was more enthusiastic about America than ever, and he was not so simple, and he was not so nice. The publishers had praised his novel pretty highly and it rather went to his head. Then several women had put themselves out to be nice to him, and his horizons had all shifted. For four years his horizon had been absolutely limited to his wife. For three years, or almost three years, he had never seen beyond Frances. I am sure he had never been in love in his life.

He had married on the rebound from the rotten time he had in college, and Frances took him on the rebound from his discovery that he had not been everything to his first wife. He was not in love yet but he realized that he was an attractive quantity to women, and that the fact of a woman caring for him and wanting to live with him was not simply a divine miracle. This changed him so that he was not so pleasant to have around. Also, playing for higher stakes than he could afford in some rather steep bridge games with his New York connections, he had held cards and won several hundred dollars. It made him rather vain of his bridge game, and he talked several times of how a man could always make a living at bridge if he were ever forced to.

Then there was another thing. He had been reading W. H. Hudson. That sounds like an innocent occupation, but Cohn had read and reread "The Purple Land." "The Purple Land" is a very sinister book if read too late in life. It recounts splendid imaginary amorous adventures of a perfect English gentleman in an intensely romantic land, the scenery of which is very well described. For a man to take it at thirty-four as a guide-book to what life holds is about as safe as it would be for a man of the same age to enter Wall Street direct from a French convent, equipped with a complete set of the more practical Alger books. Cohn, I believe, took every word of "The Purple Land" as literally as though it had been an R. G. Dun report. You understand me, he made some reservations, but on the whole the book to him was sound. It was all that was needed to set him off. I did not realize the extent to which it had set him off until one day he came into my office.

"Hello, Robert," I said. "Did you come in to cheer me up?"

"Would you like to go to South America, Jake?" he asked.

"No."

"Why not?"

"I don't know. I never wanted to go. Too expensive. You can see all the South Americans you want in Paris anyway."

"They're not the real South Americans."

"They look awfully real to me."

I had a boat train to catch with a week's mail stories, and only half of them written.

"Do you know any dirt?" I asked.

"No."

"None of your exalted connections getting divorces?"

"No; listen, Jake. If I handled both our expenses, would you go to South America with me?"

"Why me?"

"You can talk Spanish. And it would be more fun with two of us."

"No," I said, "I like this town and I go to Spain in the summer-time."

"All my life I've wanted to go on a trip like that," Cohn said. He sat down. "I'll be too old before I can ever do it."

"Don't be a fool," I said. "You can go anywhere you want. You've got plenty of money."

"I know. But I can't get started."

"Cheer up," I said. "All countries look just like the moving pictures."

But I felt sorry for him. He had it badly.

"I can't stand it to think my life is going so fast and I'm not really living it."

"Nobody ever lives their life all the way up except bull-fighters."

"I'm not interested in bull-fighters. That's an abnormal life. I want to go back in the country in South America. We could have a great trip."

"Did you ever think about going to British East Africa to shoot?"

"No, I wouldn't like that."

"I'd go there with you."

"No; that doesn't interest me."

"That's because you never read a book about it. Go on and read a book all full of love affairs with the beautiful shiny black princesses."

"I want to go to South America."

He had a hard, Jewish, stubborn streak.

"Come on down-stairs and have a drink."

"Aren't you working?"

"No," I said. We went down the stairs to the café on the ground floor. I had discovered that was the best way to get rid of friends. Once you had a drink all you had to say was: "Well, I've got to get back and get off some cables," and it was done. It is very important to discover graceful exits like that in the newspaper business, where it is such an important part of the ethics that you should never seem to be working. Anyway, we went down-stairs to the bar and had a whiskey and soda. Cohn looked at the bottles in bins around the wall. "This is a good place," he said.

"There's a lot of liquor," I agreed.

"Listen, Jake," he leaned forward on the bar. "Don't you ever get the feeling that all your life is going by and you're not taking advantage of it? Do you realize you've lived nearly half the time you have to live already?"

"Yes, every once in a while."

"Do you know that in about thirty-five years more we'll be dead?"

"What the hell, Robert," I said. "What the hell."

"I'm serious."

"It's one thing I don't worry about," I said.

"You ought to."

"I've had plenty to worry about one time or other. I'm through worrying."

"Well, I want to go to South America."

"Listen, Robert, going to another country doesn't make any difference. I've tried all that. You can't get away from yourself by moving from one place to another. There's nothing to that."

"But you've never been to South America."

"South America hell! If you went there the way you feel now it would be exactly the same. This is a good town. Why don't you start living your life in Paris?"

"I'm sick of Paris, and I'm sick of the Quarter."

"Stay away from the Quarter. Cruise around by yourself and see what happens to you."

"Nothing happens to me. I walked alone all one night and nothing happened except a bicycle cop stopped me and asked to see my papers."

"Wasn't the town nice at night?"

"I don't care for Paris."

So there you were. I was sorry for him, but it was not a thing you could do anything about, because right away you ran up against the two stubbornnesses: South America could fix it and he did not like Paris. He got the first idea out of a book, and I suppose the second came out of a book too.

"Well," I said, "I've got to go up-stairs and get off some cables."

"Do you really have to go?"

"Yes, I've got to get these cables off."

"Do you mind if I come up and sit around the office?"

"No, come on up."

He sat in the outer room and read the papers, and the Editor and Publisher and I worked hard for two hours. Then I sorted out the carbons, stamped on a by-line, put the stuff in a couple of big manila envelopes and rang for a boy to take them to the Gare St. Lazare. I went out into the other room and there was Robert Cohn asleep in the big chair. He was asleep with his head on his arms. I did not like to wake him up, but I wanted to lock the office and shove off. I put my hand on his shoulder. He shook his head. "I can't do it," he said, and put his head deeper into his arms. "I can't do it. Nothing will make me do it."

"Robert," I said, and shook him by the shoulder. He looked up. He smiled and blinked.

"Did I talk out loud just then?"

"Something. But it wasn't clear."

"God, what a rotten dream!"

"Did the typewriter put you to sleep?"

"Guess so. I didn't sleep all last night."

"What was the matter?"

"Talking," he said.

I could picture it. I have a rotten habit of picturing the bedroom scenes of my friends. We went out to the Café Napolitain to have an *apéritif* and watch the evening crowd on the Boulevard.

CHAPTER III

It was a warm spring night and I sat at a table on the terrace of the Napolitain after Robert had gone, watching it get dark and the electric signs come on, and the red and green stop-and-go traffic-signal, and the crowd going by, and the horse-cabs clippety-clopping along at the edge of the solid taxi traffic, and the *poules* going by, singly and in pairs, looking for the evening meal. I watched a good-looking girl walk past the table and watched her go up the street and lost sight of her, and watched another, and then saw the first one coming back again. She went by once more and I caught her eye, and she came over and sat down at the table. The waiter came up.

"Well, what will you drink?" I asked.

"Pernod."

"That's not good for little girls."

"Little girl yourself. Dites garçon, un pernod."

"A pernod for me, too."

"What's the matter?" she asked. "Going on a party?"

"Sure. Aren't you?"

"I don't know. You never know in this town."

"Don't you like Paris?"

"No."

"Why don't you go somewhere else?"

"Isn't anywhere else."

"You're happy, all right."

"Happy, hell!"

Pernod is greenish imitation absinthe. When you add water it turns milky. It tastes like licorice and it has a good uplift, but it drops you just as far. We sat and drank it, and the girl looked sullen.

"Well," I said, "are you going to buy me a dinner?"

She grinned and I saw why she made a point of not laughing. With her mouth closed she was a rather pretty girl. I paid for the saucers and we walked out to the street. I hailed a horse-cab and the driver pulled up at the curb. Settled back in the slow, smoothly rolling *fiacre* we moved up the Avenue de l'Opéra, passed the locked doors of the shops, their windows lighted, the Avenue broad and shiny and almost deserted. The cab passed the New York *Herald* bureau with the window full of clocks.

"What are all the clocks for?" she asked.

"They show the hour all over America."

"Don't kid me."

We turned off the Avenue up the Rue des Pyramides, through the traffic of the Rue de Rivoli, and through a dark gate into the Tuileries. She cuddled against me and I put my arm around her. She looked up to be kissed. She touched me with one hand and I put her hand away.

"Never mind."

"What's the matter? You sick?"

"Yes."

"Everybody's sick. I'm sick, too."

We came out of the Tuileries into the light and crossed the Seine and then turned up the Rue des Saints Pères.

"You oughtn't to drink pernod if you're sick."

"You neither."

"It doesn't make any difference with me. It doesn't make any difference with a woman."

"What are you called?"

"Georgette. How are you called?"

"Jacob."

"That's a Flemish name."

"American too."

"You're not Flamand?"

"No, American."

"Good, I detest Flamands."

By this time we were at the restaurant. I called to the *cocher* to stop. We got out and Georgette did not like the looks of the place. "This is no great thing of a restaurant."

"No," I said. "Maybe you would rather go to Foyot's. Why don't you keep the cab and go on?"

I had picked her up because of a vague sentimental idea that it would be nice to eat with some one. It was a long time since I had dined with a *poule*, and I had forgotten how dull it could be. We went into the restaurant, passed Madame Lavigne at the desk and into a little room. Georgette cheered up a little under the food.

"It isn't bad here," she said. "It isn't chic, but the food is all right."

"Better than you eat in Liège."

"Brussels, you mean."

We had another bottle of wine and Georgette made a joke. She smiled and showed all her bad teeth, and we touched glasses.

"You're not a bad type," she said. "It's a shame you're sick. We get on well. What's the matter with you, anyway?"

"I got hurt in the war," I said.

"Oh, that dirty war."

We would probably have gone on and discussed the war and agreed that it was in reality a calamity for civilization, and perhaps would have been better avoided. I was bored enough. Just then from the other room some one called: "Barnes! I say, Barnes! Jacob Barnes!"

"It's a friend calling me," I explained, and went out.

There was Braddocks at a big table with a party: Cohn, Frances Clyne, Mrs. Braddocks, several people I did not know.

"You're coming to the dance, aren't you?" Braddocks asked.

"What dance?"

"Why, the dancings. Don't you know we've revived them?" Mrs. Braddocks put in.

"You must come, Jake. We're all going," Frances said from the end of the table. She was tall and had a smile.

"Of course, he's coming," Braddocks said. "Come in and have coffee with us, Barnes."

"Right."

"And bring your friend," said Mrs. Braddocks laughing. She was a Canadian and had all their easy social graces.

"Thanks, we'll be in," I said. I went back to the small room.

"Who are your friends?" Georgette asked.

"Writers and artists."

"There are lots of those on this side of the river."

"Too many."

"I think so. Still, some of them make money."

"Oh, yes."

We finished the meal and the wine. "Come on," I said. "We're going to have coffee with the others."

Georgette opened her bag, made a few passes at her face as she looked in the little mirror, re-defined her lips with the lip-stick, and straightened her hat.

"Good," she said.

We went into the room full of people and Braddocks and the men at his table stood up.

"I wish to present my fiancée, Mademoiselle Georgette Leblanc," I said. Georgette smiled that wonderful smile, and we shook hands all round.

"Are you related to Georgette Leblanc, the singer?" Mrs. Braddocks asked.

"Connais pas," Georgette answered.

"But you have the same name," Mrs. Braddocks insisted cordially.

"No," said Georgette. "Not at all. My name is Hobin."

"But Mr. Barnes introduced you as Mademoiselle Georgette Leblanc. Surely he did," insisted Mrs. Braddocks, who in the excitement of talking French was liable to have no idea what she was saying.

"He's a fool," Georgette said.

"Oh, it was a joke, then," Mrs. Braddocks said.

"Yes," said Georgette. "To laugh at."

"Did you hear that, Henry?" Mrs. Braddocks called down the table to Braddocks. "Mr. Barnes introduced his fiancée as Mademoiselle Leblanc, and her name is actually Hobin."

"Of course, darling. Mademoiselle Hobin, I've known her for a very long time."

"Oh, Mademoiselle Hobin," Frances Clyne called, speaking French very rapidly and not seeming so proud and astonished as Mrs. Braddocks at its coming out really French. "Have you been in Paris long? Do you like it here? You love Paris, do you not?"

"Who's she?" Georgette turned to me. "Do I have to talk to her?"

She turned to Frances, sitting smiling, her hands folded, her head poised on her long neck, her lips pursed ready to start talking again.

"No, I don't like Paris. It's expensive and dirty."

"Really? I find it so extraordinarily clean. One of the cleanest cities in all Europe."

"I find it dirty."

"How strange! But perhaps you have not been here very long."

"I've been here long enough."

"But it does have nice people in it. One must grant that."

Georgette turned to me. "You have nice friends."

Frances was a little drunk and would have liked to have kept it up but the coffee came, and Lavigne with the liqueurs, and after that we all went out and started for Braddocks's dancing-club.

The dancing-club was a *bal musette* in the Rue de la Montagne Sainte Geneviève. Five nights a week the working people of the Pantheon quarter danced there. One night a week it was the dancing-club. On Monday nights it was closed. When we arrived it was quite empty, except for a policeman sitting near the door, the wife of the proprietor back of the zinc bar, and the proprietor himself. The daughter of the house came downstairs as we went in. There were long benches, and tables ran across the room, and at the far end a dancing-floor.

"I wish people would come earlier," Braddocks said. The daughter came up and wanted to know what we would drink. The proprietor got up on a high stool beside the dancing-floor and began to play the accordion. He had a string of bells around one of his ankles and beat time with his foot as he played. Every one danced. It was hot and we came off the floor perspiring.

"My God," Georgette said. "What a box to sweat in!"

"It's hot."

"Hot, my God!"

"Take off your hat."

"That's a good idea."

Some one asked Georgette to dance, and I went over to the bar. It was really very hot and the accordion music was pleasant in the hot night. I drank a beer, standing in the doorway and getting the cool breath of wind from the street. Two taxis were coming down the steep street. They both stopped in front of the Bal. A crowd of young men, some in jerseys and some in their shirt-sleeves, got out. I could see their hands and newly washed, wavy hair in the light from the door. The policeman standing by the door looked at me and smiled. They came in. As they went in, under the light I saw white hands, wavy hair, white faces, grimacing, gesturing, talking. With them was Brett. She looked very lovely and she was very much with them.

One of them saw Georgette and said: "I do declare. There is an actual harlot. I'm going to dance with her, Lett. You watch me."

The tall dark one, called Lett, said: "Don't you be rash."

The wavy blond one answered: "Don't you worry, dear." And with them was Brett.

I was very angry. Somehow they always made me angry. I know they are supposed to be amusing, and you should be tolerant, but I wanted to swing on one, any one, anything to shatter that superior, simpering composure. Instead, I walked down the street and had a beer at the bar at the next Bal. The beer was not good and I had a worse cognac to take the taste out of my mouth. When I came back to the Bal there was a crowd on the floor and Georgette was dancing with the tall blond youth, who danced big-hippily, carrying his head on one side, his eyes lifted as he danced. As soon as the music stopped another one of them asked her to dance. She had been taken up by them. I knew then that they would all dance with her. They are like that.

I sat down at a table. Cohn was sitting there. Frances was dancing. Mrs. Braddocks brought up somebody and introduced him as Robert Prentiss. He was from New York by way of Chicago, and was a rising new novelist. He had some sort of an English accent. I asked him to have a drink.

"Thanks so much," he said, "I've just had one."

"Have another."

"Thanks, I will then."

We got the daughter of the house over and each had a *fine à l'eau*.

"You're from Kansas City, they tell me," he said.

"Yes."

"Do you find Paris amusing?"

"Yes."

"Really?"

I was a little drunk. Not drunk in any positive sense but just enough to be careless.

"For God's sake," I said, "yes. Don't you?"

"Oh, how charmingly you get angry," he said. "I wish I had that faculty."

I got up and walked over toward the dancing-floor. Mrs. Braddocks followed me. "Don't be cross with Robert," she said. "He's still only a child, you know."

"I wasn't cross," I said. "I just thought perhaps I was going to throw up."

"Your fiancée is having a great success," Mrs. Braddocks looked out on the floor where Georgette was dancing in the arms of the tall, dark one, called Lett.

"Isn't she?" I said.

"Rather," said Mrs. Braddocks.

Cohn came up. "Come on, Jake," he said, "have a drink." We walked over to the bar. "What's the matter with you? You seem all worked up over something?"

"Nothing. This whole show makes me sick is all."

Brett came up to the bar.

"Hello, you chaps."

"Hello, Brett," I said. "Why aren't you tight?"

"Never going to get tight any more. I say, give a chap a brandy and soda."

She stood holding the glass and I saw Robert Cohn looking at her. He looked a great deal as his compatriot must have looked when he saw the promised land. Cohn, of course, was much younger. But he had that look of eager, deserving expectation.

Brett was damned good-looking. She wore a slipover jersey sweater and a tweed skirt, and her hair was brushed back like a boy's. She started all that. She was built with curves like the hull of a racing yacht, and you missed none of it with that wool jersey.

"It's a fine crowd you're with, Brett," I said.

"Aren't they lovely? And you, my dear. Where did you get it?"

"At the Napolitain."

"And have you had a lovely evening?"

"Oh, priceless," I said.

Brett laughed. "It's wrong of you, Jake. It's an insult to all of us. Look at Frances there, and Jo."

This for Cohn's benefit.

"It's in restraint of trade," Brett said. She laughed again.

"You're wonderfully sober," I said.

"Yes. Aren't I? And when one's with the crowd I'm with, one can drink in such safety, too."

The music started and Robert Cohn said: "Will you dance this with me, Lady Brett?"

Brett smiled at him. "I've promised to dance this with Jacob," she laughed. "You've a hell of a biblical name, Jake."

"How about the next?" asked Cohn.

"We're going," Brett said. "We've a date up at Montmartre."

Dancing, I looked over Brett's shoulder and saw Cohn, standing at the bar, still watching her.

"You've made a new one there," I said to her.

"Don't talk about it. Poor chap. I never knew it till just now."

"Oh, well," I said. "I suppose you like to add them up."

"Don't talk like a fool."

"You do."

"Oh, well. What if I do?"

"Nothing," I said. We were dancing to the accordion and some one was playing the banjo. It was hot and I felt happy. We passed close to Georgette dancing with another one of them.

"What possessed you to bring her?"

"I don't know, I just brought her."

"You're getting damned romantic."

"No, bored."

"Now?"

"No, not now."

"Let's get out of here. She's well taken care of."

"Do you want to?"

"Would I ask you if I didn't want to?"

We left the floor and I took my coat off a hanger on the wall and put it on. Brett stood by the bar. Cohn was talking to her. I stopped at the bar and asked them for an envelope. The patronne found one. I took a fifty-franc note from my pocket, put it in the envelope, sealed it, and handed it to the patronne.

"If the girl I came with asks for me, will you give her this?" I said. "If she goes out with one of those gentlemen, will you save this for me?"

"C'est entendu, Monsieur," the patronne said. "You go now? So early?"

"Yes," I said.

We started out the door. Cohn was still talking to Brett. She said good night and took my arm. "Good night, Cohn," I said. Outside in the street we looked for a taxi.

"You're going to lose your fifty francs," Brett said.

"Oh, yes."

"No taxis."

"We could walk up to the Pantheon and get one."

"Come on and we'll get a drink in the pub next door and send for one."

"You wouldn't walk across the street."

"Not if I could help it."

We went into the next bar and I sent a waiter for a taxi.

"Well," I said, "we're out away from them."

We stood against the tall zinc bar and did not talk and looked at each other. The waiter came and said the taxi was outside. Brett pressed my hand hard. I gave the waiter a franc and we went out. "Where should I tell him?" I asked.

"Oh, tell him to drive around."

I told the driver to go to the Parc Montsouris, and got in, and slammed the door. Brett was leaning back in the corner, her eyes closed. I got in and sat beside her. The cab started with a jerk.

"Oh, darling, I've been so miserable," Brett said.

CHAPTER IV

THE taxi went up the hill, passed the lighted square, then on into the dark, still climbing, then levelled out onto a dark street behind St. Etienne du Mont, went smoothly down the asphalt, passed the trees and the standing bus at the Place de la Contrescarpe, then turned onto the cobbles of the Rue Mouffetard. There were lighted bars and late open shops on each side of the street. We were sitting apart and we jolted close together going down the old street. Brett's hat was off. Her head was back. I saw her face in the lights from the open shops, then it was dark, then I saw her face clearly as we came out on the Avenue des Gobelins. The street was torn up and men were working on the car-tracks by the light of acetylene flares. Brett's face was white and the long line of her neck showed in the bright light of the flares. The street was dark again and I kissed her. Our lips were tight together and then she turned away and pressed against the corner of the seat, as far away as she could get. Her head was down.

"Don't touch me," she said. "Please don't touch me."

"What's the matter?"

"I can't stand it."

"Oh, Brett."

"You mustn't. You must know. I can't stand it, that's all. Oh, darling, please understand!"

"Don't you love me?"

"Love you? I simply turn all to jelly when you touch me."

"Isn't there anything we can do about it?"

She was sitting up now. My arm was around her and she was leaning back against me, and we were quite calm. She was looking into my eyes with that way she had of looking that made you wonder whether she really saw out of her own eyes. They would look on and on after every one else's eyes in the world would have stopped looking. She looked as though there were nothing on earth she would not look at like that, and really she was afraid of so many things.

"And there's not a damn thing we could do," I said.

"I don't know," she said. "I don't want to go through that hell again."

"We'd better keep away from each other."

"But, darling, I have to see you. It isn't all that you know."

"No, but it always gets to be."

"That's my fault. Don't we pay for all the things we do, though?"

She had been looking into my eyes all the time. Her eyes had different depths, sometimes they seemed perfectly flat. Now you could see all the way into them.

"When I think of the hell I've put chaps through. I'm paying for it all now."

"Don't talk like a fool," I said. "Besides, what happened to me is supposed to be funny. I never think about it."

"Oh, no. I'll lay you don't."

"Well, let's shut up about it."

"I laughed about it too, myself, once." She wasn't looking at me. "A friend of my brother's came home that way from Mons. It seemed like a hell of a joke. Chaps never know anything, do they?"

"No," I said. "Nobody ever knows anything."

I was pretty well through with the subject. At one time or another I had probably considered it from most of its various angles, including the one that certain injuries or imperfections are a subject of merriment while remaining quite serious for the person possessing them.

"It's funny," I said. "It's very funny. And it's a lot of fun, too, to be in love."

"Do you think so?" her eyes looked flat again.

"I don't mean fun that way. In a way it's an enjoyable feeling."

"No," she said. "I think it's hell on earth."

"It's good to see each other."

"No. I don't think it is."

"Don't you want to?"

"I have to."

We were sitting now like two strangers. On the right was the Parc Montsouris. The restaurant where they have the pool of live trout and where you can sit and look out over the park was closed and dark. The driver leaned his head around.

"Where do you want to go?" I asked. Brett turned her head away.

"Oh, go to the Select."

"Café Select," I told the driver. "Boulevard Montparnasse." We drove straight down, turning around the Lion de Belfort that guards the passing Montrouge trams. Brett looked straight ahead. On the Boulevard Raspail, with the lights of Montparnasse in sight, Brett said: "Would you mind very much if I asked you to do something?"

"Don't be silly."

"Kiss me just once more before we get there."

When the taxi stopped I got out and paid. Brett came out putting on her hat. She gave me her hand as she stepped down. Her hand was shaky. "I say, do I look too much of a mess?" She pulled her man's felt hat down and started in for the bar. Inside, against the bar and at tables, were most of the crowd who had been at the dance.

"Hello, you chaps," Brett said. "I'm going to have a drink."

"Oh, Brett! Brett!" the little Greek portrait-painter, who called himself a duke, and whom everybody called Zizi, pushed up to her. "I got something fine to tell you."

"Hello, Zizi," Brett said.

"I want you to meet a friend," Zizi said. A fat man came up.

"Count Mippipopolous, meet my friend Lady Ashley."

"How do you do?" said Brett.

"Well, does your Ladyship have a good time here in Paris?" asked Count Mippipopolous, who wore an elk's tooth on his watch-chain.

"Rather," said Brett.

"Paris is a fine town all right," said the count. "But I guess you have pretty big doings yourself over in London."

"Oh, yes," said Brett. "Enormous."

Braddocks called to me from a table. "Barnes," he said, "have a drink. That girl of yours got in a frightful row."

"What about?"

"Something the patronne's daughter said. A corking row. She was rather splendid, you know. Showed her yellow card and demanded the patronne's daughter's too. I say it was a row."

"What finally happened?"

"Oh, some one took her home. Not a bad-looking girl. Wonderful command of the idiom. Do stay and have a drink."

"No," I said. "I must shove off. Seen Cohn?"

"He went home with Frances," Mrs. Braddock put in.

"Poor chap, he looks awfully down," Braddocks said.

"I dare say he is," said Mrs. Braddocks.

"I have to shove off," I said. "Good night."

I said good night to Brett at the bar. The count was buying champagne. "Will you take a glass of wine with us, sir?" he asked.

"No. Thanks awfully. I have to go."

"Really going?" Brett asked.

"Yes," I said. "I've got a rotten headache."

"I'll see you to-morrow?"

"Come in at the office."

"Hardly."

"Well, where will I see you?"

"Anywhere around five o'clock."

"Make it the other side of town then."

"Good. I'll be at the Crillon at five."

"Try and be there," I said.

"Don't worry," Brett said. "I've never let you down, have I?"

"Heard from Mike?"

"Letter to-day."

"Good night, sir," said the count.

I went out onto the sidewalk and walked down toward the Boulevard St. Michel, passed the tables of the Rotonde, still crowded, looked across the street at the Dome, its tables running out to the edge of the pavement. Some one waved at me from a table, I did not see who it was and went on. I wanted to get home. The Boulevard Montparnasse was deserted. Lavigne's was closed tight, and they were stacking the tables outside the Closerie des Lilas. I passed Ney's statue standing among the new-leaved chestnut-trees in the arc-light. There was a faded purple wreath leaning against the base. I stopped and read the inscription: from the Bonapartist Groups, some date; I forget. He looked very fine, Marshal Ney in his top-boots, gesturing with his sword among the green new horse-chestnut leaves. My flat was just across the street, a little way down the Boulevard St. Michel.

There was a light in the concierge's room and I knocked on the door and she gave me my mail. I wished her good night and went up-stairs. There were two letters and some papers. I looked at them under the gas-light in the dining-room. The letters were from the States. One was a bank statement. It showed a balance of $2432.60. I got out my check-book and deducted four checks drawn since the first of the month, and discovered I had a balance of $1832.60. I wrote this on the back of the statement. The other letter was a wedding announcement. Mr. and Mrs. Aloysius Kirby announce the marriage of their daughter Katherine—I knew neither the girl nor the man she was marrying. They must be circularizing the town. It was a funny name. I felt sure I could remember anybody with a name like Aloysius. It was a good Catholic name. There was a crest on the announcement. Like Zizi the Greek duke. And that count. The count was funny. Brett had a title, too. Lady Ashley. To hell with Brett. To hell with you, Lady Ashley.

I lit the lamp beside the bed, turned off the gas, and opened the wide windows. The bed was far back from the windows, and I sat with the windows open and undressed by the bed. Outside a night train, running on the street-car tracks, went by carrying vegetables to the markets. They were noisy at night when you could not sleep. Undressing, I looked at myself in the mirror of the big armoire beside the bed. That was a typically French way to furnish a room. Practical, too, I suppose. Of all the ways to be wounded. I suppose it was funny. I put on my pajamas and got into bed. I had the two bull-fight papers, and I took their wrappers off. One was orange. The other yellow. They would both have the same news, so whichever I read first would spoil the other. *Le Toril* was the better paper, so I started to read it. I read it all the way through, including the Petite Correspondance and the Cornigrams. I blew out the lamp. Perhaps I would be able to sleep.

My head started to work. The old grievance. Well, it was a rotten way to be wounded and flying on a joke front like the Italian. In the Italian hospital we were going to form a society. It had a funny name in Italian. I wonder what became of the others, the Italians. That was in the Ospedale Maggiore in Milano, Padiglione Ponte. The next building was the Padiglione Zonda. There was a statue of Ponte, or maybe it was Zonda. That was where the liaison colonel came to visit me. That was funny. That was about the first funny thing. I was all bandaged up. But they had told him about it. Then he made that wonderful speech: "You, a foreigner, an Englishman" (any foreigner was an Englishman) "have given more than your life." What a speech! I would like to have it illuminated to hang in the office. He never laughed. He was putting himself in my place, I guess. "Che mala fortuna! Che mala fortuna!"

I never used to realize it, I guess. I try and play it along and just not make trouble for people. Probably I never would have had any trouble if I hadn't run into Brett when they shipped me to England. I suppose she only wanted what she couldn't have. Well, people were that way. To hell with people. The Catholic Church had an awfully good way of handling all that. Good advice, anyway. Not to think about it. Oh, it was swell advice. Try and take it sometime. Try and take it.

I lay awake thinking and my mind jumping around. Then I couldn't keep away from it, and I started to think about Brett and all the rest of it went away. I was thinking about Brett and my mind stopped jumping around and started to go in sort of smooth waves. Then all of a sudden I started to cry. Then after a while it was better and I lay in bed and listened to the heavy trams go by and way down the street, and then I went to sleep.

I woke up. There was a row going on outside. I listened and I thought I recognized a voice. I put on a dressing-gown and went to the door. The concierge was talking down-stairs. She was very angry. I heard my name and called down the stairs.

"Is that you, Monsieur Barnes?" the concierge called.

"Yes. It's me."

"There's a species of woman here who's waked the whole street up. What kind of a dirty business at this time of night! She says she must see you. I've told her you're asleep."

Then I heard Brett's voice. Half asleep I had been sure it was Georgette. I don't know why. She could not have known my address.

"Will you send her up, please?"

Brett came up the stairs. I saw she was quite drunk. "Silly thing to do," she said. "Make an awful row. I say, you weren't asleep, were you?"

"What did you think I was doing?"

"Don't know. What time is it?"

I looked at the clock. It was half-past four. "Had no idea what hour it was," Brett said. "I say, can a chap sit down? Don't be cross, darling. Just left the count. He brought me here."

"What's he like?" I was getting brandy and soda and glasses.

"Just a little," said Brett. "Don't try and make me drunk. The count? Oh, rather. He's quite one of us."

"Is he a count?"

"Here's how. I rather think so, you know. Deserves to be, any-how. Knows hell's own amount about people. Don't know where he got it all. Owns a chain of sweetshops in the States."

She sipped at her glass.

"Think he called it a chain. Something like that. Linked them all up. Told me a little about it. Damned interesting. He's one of us, though. Oh, quite. No doubt. One can always tell."

She took another drink.

"How do I buck on about all this? You don't mind, do you? He's putting up for Zizi, you know."

"Is Zizi really a duke, too?"

"I shouldn't wonder. Greek, you know. Rotten painter. I rather liked the count."

"Where did you go with him?"

"Oh, everywhere. He just brought me here now. Offered me ten thousand dollars to go to Biarritz with him. How much is that in pounds?"

"Around two thousand."

"Lot of money. I told him I couldn't do it. He was awfully nice about it. Told him I knew too many people in Biarritz."

Brett laughed.

"I say, you are slow on the up-take," she said. I had only sipped my brandy and soda. I took a long drink.

"That's better. Very funny," Brett said. "Then he wanted me to go to Cannes with him. Told him I knew too many people in Cannes. Monte Carlo. Told him I knew too many people in Monte Carlo. Told him I knew too many people everywhere. Quite true, too. So I asked him to bring me here."

She looked at me, her hand on the table, her glass raised. "Don't look like that," she said. "Told him I was in love with you. True, too. Don't look like that. He was damn nice about it. Wants to drive us out to dinner to-morrow night. Like to go?"

"Why not?"

"I'd better go now."

"Why?"

"Just wanted to see you. Damned silly idea. Want to get dressed and come down? He's got the car just up the street."

"The count?"

"Himself. And a chauffeur in livery. Going to drive me around and have breakfast in the Bois. Hampers. Got it all at Zelli's. Dozen bottles of Mumms. Tempt you?"

"I have to work in the morning," I said. "I'm too far behind you now to catch up and be any fun."

"Don't be an ass."

"Can't do it."

"Right. Send him a tender message?"

"Anything. Absolutely."

"Good night, darling."

"Don't be sentimental."

"You make me ill."

We kissed good night and Brett shivered. "I'd better go," she said. "Good night, darling."

"You don't have to go."

"Yes."

We kissed again on the stairs and as I called for the cordon the concierge muttered something behind her door. I went back upstairs and from the open window watched Brett walking up the street to the big limousine drawn up to the curb under the arc-light. She got in and it started off. I turned around. On the table was an empty glass and a glass half-full of brandy and soda. I took them both out to the kitchen and poured the half-full glass down the sink. I turned off the gas in the dining-room, kicked off my slippers sitting on the bed, and got into bed. This was Brett, that I had felt like crying about. Then I thought of her walking up the street and stepping into the car, as I had last seen her, and of course in a little while I felt like hell again. It is awfully easy to be hard-boiled about everything in the daytime, but at night it is another thing.

CHAPTER V

In the morning I walked down the Boulevard to the rue Soufflot for coffee and brioche. It was a fine morning. The horse-chestnut trees in the Luxembourg gardens were in bloom. There was the pleasant early-morning feeling of a hot day. I read the papers with the coffee and then smoked a cigarette. The flower-women were coming up from the market and arranging their daily stock. Students went by going up to the law school, or down to the Sorbonne. The Boulevard was busy with trams and people going to work. I got on an S bus and rode down to the Madeleine, standing on the back platform. From the Madeleine I walked along the Boulevard des Capucines to the Opéra, and up to my office. I passed the man with the jumping frogs and the man with the boxer toys. I stepped aside to avoid walking into the thread with which his girl assistant manipulated the boxers. She was standing looking away, the thread in her folded hands. The man was urging two tourists to buy. Three more tourists had stopped and were watching. I walked on behind a man who was pushing a roller that printed the name CINZANO on the sidewalk in damp

35

letters. All along people were going to work. It felt pleasant to be going to work. I walked across the avenue and turned in to my office.

Up-stairs in the office I read the French morning papers, smoked, and then sat at the typewriter and got off a good morning's work. At eleven o'clock I went over to the Quai d'Orsay in a taxi and went in and sat with about a dozen correspondents, while the foreign-office mouthpiece, a young Nouvelle Revue Française diplomat in horn-rimmed spectacles, talked and answered questions for half an hour. The President of the Council was in Lyons making a speech, or, rather he was on his way back. Several people asked questions to hear themselves talk and there were a couple of questions asked by news service men who wanted to know the answers. There was no news. I shared a taxi back from the Quai d'Orsay with Woolsey and Krum.

"What do you do nights, Jake?" asked Krum. "I never see you around."

"Oh, I'm over in the Quarter."

"I'm coming over some night. The Dingo. That's the great place, isn't it?"

"Yes. That, or this new dive, The Select."

"I've meant to get over," said Krum. "You know how it is, though, with a wife and kids."

"Playing any tennis?" Woolsey asked.

"Well, no," said Krum. "I can't say I've played any this year. I've tried to get away, but Sundays it's always rained, and the courts are so damned crowded."

"The Englishmen all have Saturday off," Woolsey said.

"Lucky beggars," said Krum. "Well, I'll tell you. Some day I'm not going to be working for an agency. Then I'll have plenty of time to get out in the country."

"That's the thing to do. Live out in the country and have a little car."

"I've been thinking some about getting a car next year."

I banged on the glass. The chauffeur stopped. "Here's my street," I said. "Come in and have a drink."

"Thanks, old man," Krum said. Woolsey shook his head. "I've got to file that line he got off this morning."

I put a two-franc piece in Krum's hand.

"You're crazy, Jake," he said. "This is on me."

"It's all on the office, anyway."

"Nope. I want to get it."

I waved good-by. Krum put his head out. "See you at the lunch on Wednesday."

"You bet."

I went to the office in the elevator. Robert Cohn was waiting for me. "Hello, Jake," he said. "Going out to lunch?"

"Yes. Let me see if there is anything new."

"Where will we eat?"

"Anywhere."

I was looking over my desk. "Where do you want to eat?"

"How about Wetzel's? They've got good hors d'œuvres."

In the restaurant we ordered hors d'œuvres and beer. The sommelier brought the beer, tall, beaded on the outside of the steins, and cold. There were a dozen different dishes of hors d'œuvres.

"Have any fun last night?" I asked.

"No. I don't think so."

"How's the writing going?"

"Rotten. I can't get this second book going."

"That happens to everybody."

"Oh, I'm sure of that. It gets me worried, though."

"Thought any more about going to South America?"

"I mean that."

"Well, why don't you start off?"

"Frances."

"Well," I said, "take her with you."

"She wouldn't like it. That isn't the sort of thing she likes. She likes a lot of people around."

"Tell her to go to hell."

"I can't. I've got certain obligations to her."

He shoved the sliced cucumbers away and took a pickled herring.

"What do you know about Lady Brett Ashley, Jake?"

"Her name's Lady Ashley. Brett's her own name. She's a nice girl," I said. "She's getting a divorce and she's going to marry Mike Campbell. He's over in Scotland now. Why?"

"She's a remarkably attractive woman."

"Isn't she?"

"There's a certain quality about her, a certain fineness. She seems to be absolutely fine and straight."

"She's very nice."

"I don't know how to describe the quality," Cohn said. "I suppose it's breeding."

"You sound as though you liked her pretty well."

"I do. I shouldn't wonder if I were in love with her."

"She's a drunk," I said. "She's in love with Mike Campbell, and she's going to marry him. He's going to be rich as hell some day."

"I don't believe she'll ever marry him."

"Why not?"

"I don't know. I just don't believe it. Have you known her a long time?"

"Yes," I said. "She was a V. A. D. in a hospital I was in during the war."

"She must have been just a kid then."

"She's thirty-four now."

"When did she marry Ashley?"

"During the war. Her own true love had just kicked off with the dysentery."

"You talk sort of bitter."

"Sorry. I didn't mean to. I was just trying to give you the facts."

"I don't believe she would marry anybody she didn't love."

"Well," I said. "She's done it twice."

"I don't believe it."

"Well," I said, "don't ask me a lot of fool questions if you don't like the answers."

"I didn't ask you that."

"You asked me what I knew about Brett Ashley."

"I didn't ask you to insult her."

"Oh, go to hell."

He stood up from the table his face white, and stood there white and angry behind the little plates of hors d'œuvres.

"Sit down," I said. "Don't be a fool."

"You've got to take that back."

"Oh, cut out the prep-school stuff."

"Take it back."

"Sure. Anything. I never heard of Brett Ashley. How's that?"

"No. Not that. About me going to hell."

"Oh, don't go to hell," I said. "Stick around. We're just starting lunch."

Cohn smiled again and sat down. He seemed glad to sit down. What the hell would he have done if he hadn't sat down? "You say such damned insulting things, Jake."

"I'm sorry. I've got a nasty tongue. I never mean it when I say nasty things."

"I know it," Cohn said. "You're really about the best friend I have, Jake."

God help you, I thought. "Forget what I said," I said out loud. "I'm sorry."

"It's all right. It's fine. I was just sore for a minute."

"Good. Let's get something else to eat."

After we finished the lunch we walked up to the Café de la Paix and had coffee. I could feel Cohn wanted to bring up Brett again, but I held him off it. We talked about one thing and another, and I left him to come to the office.

CHAPTER VI

At five o'clock I was in the Hotel Crillon waiting for Brett. She was not there, so I sat down and wrote some letters. They were not very good letters but I hoped their being on Crillon stationery would help them. Brett did not turn up, so about quarter to six I went down to the bar and had a Jack Rose with George the barman. Brett had not been in the bar either, and so I looked for her upstairs on my way out, and took a taxi to the Café Select. Crossing the Seine I saw a string of barges being towed empty down the current, riding high, the bargemen at the sweeps as they came toward the bridge. The river looked nice. It was always pleasant crossing bridges in Paris.

The taxi rounded the statue of the inventor of the semaphore engaged in doing same, and turned up the Boulevard Raspail, and I sat back to let that part of the ride pass. The Boulevard Raspail always made dull riding. It was like a certain stretch on the P.L.M. between Fontainebleau and Montereau that always made me feel bored and dead and dull until it was over. I suppose it is some association of ideas that makes those dead places in a journey. There are other streets in Paris as ugly as the Boulevard Raspail.

It is a street I do not mind walking down at all. But I cannot stand to ride along it. Perhaps I had read something about it once. That was the way Robert Cohn was about all of Paris. I wondered where Cohn got that incapacity to enjoy Paris. Possibly from Mencken. Mencken hates Paris, I believe. So many young men get their likes and dislikes from Mencken.

The taxi stopped in front of the Rotonde. No matter what café in Montparnasse you ask a taxi-driver to bring you to from the right bank of the river, they always take you to the Rotonde. Ten years from now it will probably be the Dome. It was near enough, anyway. I walked past the sad tables of the Rotonde to the Select. There were a few people inside at the bar, and outside, alone, sat Harvey Stone. He had a pile of saucers in front of him, and he needed a shave.

"Sit down," said Harvey, "I've been looking for you."

"What's the matter?"

"Nothing. Just looking for you."

"Been out to the races?"

"No. Not since Sunday."

"What do you hear from the States?"

"Nothing. Absolutely nothing."

"What's the matter?"

"I don't know. I'm through with them. I'm absolutely through with them."

He leaned forward and looked me in the eye.

"Do you want to know something, Jake?"

"Yes."

"I haven't had anything to eat for five days."

I figured rapidly back in my mind. It was three days ago that Harvey had won two hundred francs from me shaking poker dice in the New York Bar.

"What's the matter?"

"No money. Money hasn't come," he paused. "I tell you it's

strange, Jake. When I'm like this I just want to be alone. I want
to stay in my own room. I'm like a cat."

I felt in my pocket.

"Would a hundred help you any, Harvey?"

"Yes."

"Come on. Let's go and eat."

"There's no hurry. Have a drink."

"Better eat."

"No. When I get like this I don't care whether I eat or not."

We had a drink. Harvey added my saucer to his own pile.

"Do you know Mencken, Harvey?"

"Yes. Why?"

"What's he like?"

"He's all right. He says some pretty funny things. Last time I
had dinner with him we talked about Hoffenheimer. 'The trouble
is,' he said, 'he's a garter snapper.' That's not bad."

"That's not bad."

"He's through now," Harvey went on. "He's written about all
the things he knows, and now he's on all the things he doesn't
know."

"I guess he's all right," I said. "I just can't read him."

"Oh, nobody reads him now," Harvey said, "except the people
that used to read the Alexander Hamilton Institute."

"Well," I said. "That was a good thing, too."

"Sure," said Harvey. So we sat and thought deeply for a while.

"Have another port?"

"All right," said Harvey.

"There comes Cohn," I said. Robert Cohn was crossing the
street.

"That moron," said Harvey. Cohn came up to our table.

"Hello, you bums," he said.

"Hello, Robert," Harvey said. "I was just telling Jake here that
you're a moron."

"What do you mean?"

"Tell us right off. Don't think. What would you rather do if you could do anything you wanted?"

Cohn started to consider.

"Don't think. Bring it right out."

"I don't know," Cohn said. "What's it all about, anyway?"

"I mean what would you rather do. What comes into your head first. No matter how silly it is."

"I don't know," Cohn said. "I think I'd rather play football again with what I know about handling myself, now."

"I misjudged you," Harvey said. "You're not a moron. You're only a case of arrested development."

"You're awfully funny, Harvey," Cohn said. "Some day somebody will push your face in."

Harvey Stone laughed. "You think so. They won't, though. Because it wouldn't make any difference to me. I'm not a fighter."

"It would make a difference to you if anybody did it."

"No, it wouldn't. That's where you make your big mistake. Because you're not intelligent."

"Cut it out about me."

"Sure," said Harvey. "It doesn't make any difference to me. You don't mean anything to me."

"Come on, Harvey," I said. "Have another porto."

"No," he said. "I'm going up the street and eat. See you later, Jake."

He walked out and up the street. I watched him crossing the street through the taxis, small, heavy, slowly sure of himself in the traffic.

"He always gets me sore," Cohn said. "I can't stand him."

"I like him," I said. "I'm fond of him. You don't want to get sore at him."

"I know it," Cohn said. "He just gets on my nerves."

"Write this afternoon?"

"No. I couldn't get it going. It's harder to do than my first book. I'm having a hard time handling it."

The sort of healthy conceit that he had when he returned from America early in the spring was gone. Then he had been sure of his work, only with these personal longings for adventure. Now the sureness was gone. Somehow I feel I have not shown Robert Cohn clearly. The reason is that until he fell in love with Brett, I never heard him make one remark that would, in any way, detach him from other people. He was nice to watch on the tennis-court, he had a good body, and he kept it in shape; he handled his cards well at bridge, and he had a funny sort of undergraduate quality about him. If he were in a crowd nothing he said stood out. He wore what used to be called polo shirts at school, and may be called that still, but he was not professionally youthful. I do not believe he thought about his clothes much. Externally he had been formed at Princeton. Internally he had been moulded by the two women who had trained him. He had a nice, boyish sort of cheerfulness that had never been trained out of him, and I probably have not brought it out. He loved to win at tennis. He probably loved to win as much as Lenglen, for instance. On the other hand, he was not angry at being beaten. When he fell in love with Brett his tennis game went all to pieces. People beat him who had never had a chance with him. He was very nice about it.

Anyhow, we were sitting on the terrace of the Café Select, and Harvey Stone had just crossed the street.

"Come on up to the Lilas," I said.

"I have a date."

"What time?"

"Frances is coming here at seven-fifteen."

"There she is."

Frances Clyne was coming toward us from across the street. She was a very tall girl who walked with a great deal of movement. She waved and smiled. We watched her cross the street.

"Hello," she said, "I'm so glad you're here, Jake. I've been wanting to talk to you."

"Hello, Frances," said Cohn. He smiled.

"Why, hello, Robert. Are you here?" She went on, talking rapidly. "I've had the darndest time. This one"—shaking her head at Cohn—"didn't come home for lunch."

"I wasn't supposed to."

"Oh, I know. But you didn't say anything about it to the cook. Then I had a date myself, and Paula wasn't at her office. I went to the Ritz and waited for her, and she never came, and of course I didn't have enough money to lunch at the Ritz——"

"What did you do?"

"Oh, went out, of course." She spoke in a sort of imitation joyful manner. "I always keep my appointments. No one keeps theirs, nowadays. I ought to know better. How are you, Jake, anyway?"

"Fine."

"That was a fine girl you had at the dance, and then went off with that Brett one."

"Don't you like her?" Cohn asked.

"I think she's perfectly charming. Don't you?"

Cohn said nothing.

"Look, Jake. I want to talk with you. Would you come over with me to the Dome? You'll stay here, won't you, Robert? Come on, Jake."

We crossed the Boulevard Montparnasse and sat down at a table. A boy came up with the *Paris Times,* and I bought one and opened it.

"What's the matter, Frances?"

"Oh, nothing," she said, "except that he wants to leave me."

"How do you mean?"

"Oh, he told every one that we were going to be married, and I told my mother and every one, and now he doesn't want to do it."

"What's the matter?"

"He's decided he hasn't lived enough. I knew it would happen when he went to New York."

She looked up, very bright-eyed and trying to talk inconsequentially.

"I wouldn't marry him if he doesn't want to. Of course I wouldn't. I wouldn't marry him now for anything. But it does seem to me to be a little late now, after we've waited three years, and I've just gotten my divorce."

I said nothing.

"We were going to celebrate so, and instead we've just had scenes. It's so childish. We have dreadful scenes, and he cries and begs me to be reasonable, but he says he just can't do it."

"It's rotten luck."

"I should say it is rotten luck. I've wasted two years and a half on him now. And I don't know now if any man will ever want to marry me. Two years ago I could have married anybody I wanted, down at Cannes. All the old ones that wanted to marry somebody chic and settle down were crazy about me. Now I don't think I could get anybody."

"Sure, you could marry anybody."

"No, I don't believe it. And I'm fond of him, too. And I'd like to have children. I always thought we'd have children."

She looked at me very brightly. "I never liked children much, but I don't want to think I'll never have them. I always thought I'd have them and then like them."

"He's got children."

"Oh, yes. He's got children, and he's got money, and he's got a rich mother, and he's written a book, and nobody will publish my stuff, nobody at all. It isn't bad, either. And I haven't got any money at all. I could have had alimony, but I got the divorce the quickest way."

She looked at me again very brightly.

"It isn't right. It's my own fault and it's not, too. I ought to have known better. And when I tell him he just cries and says he can't marry. Why can't he marry? I'd be a good wife. I'm easy to get along with. I leave him alone. It doesn't do any good."

"It's a rotten shame."

"Yes, it is a rotten shame. But there's no use talking about it, is there? Come on, let's go back to the café."

"And of course there isn't anything I can do."

"No. Just don't let him know I talked to you. I know what he wants." Now for the first time she dropped her bright, terribly cheerful manner. "He wants to go back to New York alone, and be there when his book comes out so when a lot of little chickens like it. That's what he wants."

"Maybe they won't like it. I don't think he's that way. Really."

"You don't know him like I do, Jake. That's what he wants to do. I know it. I know it. That's why he doesn't want to marry. He wants to have a big triumph this fall all by himself."

"Want to go back to the café?"

"Yes. Come on."

We got up from the table—they had never brought us a drink —and started across the street toward the Select, where Cohn sat smiling at us from behind the marble-topped table.

"Well, what are you smiling at?" Frances asked him. "Feel pretty happy?"

"I was smiling at you and Jake with your secrets."

"Oh, what I've told Jake isn't any secret. Everybody will know it soon enough. I only wanted to give Jake a decent version."

"What was it? About your going to England?"

"Yes, about my going to England. Oh, Jake! I forgot to tell you. I'm going to England."

"Isn't that fine!"

"Yes, that's the way it's done in the very best families. Robert's sending me. He's going to give me two hundred pounds and then

I'm going to visit friends. Won't it be lovely? The friends don't know about it, yet."

She turned to Cohn and smiled at him. He was not smiling now.

"You were only going to give me a hundred pounds, weren't you, Robert? But I made him give me two hundred. He's really very generous. Aren't you, Robert?"

I do not know how people could say such terrible things to Robert Cohn. There are people to whom you could not say insulting things. They give you a feeling that the world would be destroyed, would actually be destroyed before your eyes, if you said certain things. But here was Cohn taking it all. Here it was, all going on right before me, and I did not even feel an impulse to try and stop it. And this was friendly joking to what went on later.

"How can you say such things, Frances?" Cohn interrupted.

"Listen to him. I'm going to England. I'm going to visit friends. Ever visit friends that didn't want you? Oh, they'll have to take me, all right. 'How do you do, my dear? Such a long time since we've seen you. And how is your dear mother?' Yes, how is my dear mother? She put all her money into French war bonds. Yes, she did. Probably the only person in the world that did. 'And what about Robert?' or else very careful talking around Robert. 'You must be most careful not to mention him, my dear. Poor Frances has had a most unfortunate experience.' Won't it be fun, Robert? Don't you think it will be fun, Jake?"

She turned to me with that terribly bright smile. It was very satisfactory to her to have an audience for this.

"And where are you going to be, Robert? It's my own fault, all right. Perfectly my own fault. When I made you get rid of your little secretary on the magazine I ought to have known you'd get rid of me the same way. Jake doesn't know about that. Should I tell him?"

"Shut up, Frances, for God's sake."

"Yes, I'll tell him. Robert had a little secretary on the magazine. Just the sweetest little thing in the world, and he thought she was wonderful, and then I came along and he thought I was pretty wonderful, too. So I made him get rid of her, and he had brought her to Provincetown from Carmel when he moved the magazine, and he didn't even pay her fare back to the coast. All to please me. He thought I was pretty fine, then. Didn't you, Robert?

"You mustn't misunderstand, Jake, it was absolutely platonic with the secretary. Not even platonic. Nothing at all, really. It was just that she was so nice. And he did that just to please me. Well, I suppose that we that live by the sword shall perish by the sword. Isn't that literary, though? You want to remember that for your next book, Robert.

"You know Robert is going to get material for a new book. Aren't you, Robert? That's why he's leaving me. He's decided I don't film well. You see, he was so busy all the time that we were living together, writing on this book, that he doesn't remember anything about us. So now he's going out and get some new material. Well, I hope he gets something frightfully interesting.

"Listen, Robert, dear. Let me tell you something. You won't mind, will you? Don't have scenes with your young ladies. Try not to. Because you can't have scenes without crying, and then you pity yourself so much you can't remember what the other person's said. You'll never be able to remember any conversations that way. Just try and be calm. I know it's awfully hard. But remember, it's for literature. We all ought to make sacrifices for literature. Look at me. I'm going to England without a protest. All for literature. We must all help young writers. Don't you think so, Jake? But you're not a young writer. Are you, Robert? You're thirty-four. Still, I suppose that is young for a great writer. Look at Hardy. Look at Anatole France. He just died a little while ago. Robert doesn't think he's any good, though. Some of his

French friends told him. He doesn't read French very well himself. He wasn't a good writer like you are, was he, Robert? Do you think he ever had to go and look for material? What do you suppose he said to his mistresses when he wouldn't marry them? I wonder if he cried, too? Oh, I've just thought of something." She put her gloved hand up to her lips. "I know the real reason why Robert won't marry me, Jake. It's just come to me. They've sent it to me in a vision in the Café Select. Isn't it mystic? Some day they'll put a tablet up. Like at Lourdes. Do you want to hear, Robert? I'll tell you. It's so simple. I wonder why I never thought about it. Why, you see, Robert's always wanted to have a mistress, and if he doesn't marry me, why, then he's had one. She was his mistress for over two years. See how it is? And if he marries me, like he's always promised he would, that would be the end of all the romance. Don't you think that's bright of me to figure that out? It's true, too. Look at him and see if it's not. Where are you going, Jake?"

"I've got to go in and see Harvey Stone a minute."

Cohn looked up as I went in. His face was white. Why did he sit there? Why did he keep on taking it like that?

As I stood against the bar looking out I could see them through the window. Frances was talking on to him, smiling brightly, looking into his face each time she asked: "Isn't it so, Robert?" Or maybe she did not ask that now. Perhaps she said something else. I told the barman I did not want anything to drink and went out through the side door. As I went out the door I looked back through the two thicknesses of glass and saw them sitting there. She was still talking to him. I went down a side street to the Boulevard Raspail. A taxi came along and I got in and gave the driver the address of my flat.

CHAPTER VII

As I started up the stairs the concierge knocked on the glass of the door of her lodge, and as I stopped she came out. She had some letters and a telegram.

"Here is the post. And there was a lady here to see you."

"Did she leave a card?"

"No. She was with a gentleman. It was the one who was here last night. In the end I find she is very nice."

"Was she with a friend of mine?"

"I don't know. He was never here before. He was very large. Very, very large. She was very nice. Very, very nice. Last night she was, perhaps, a little—" She put her head on one hand and rocked it up and down. "I'll speak perfectly frankly, Monsieur Barnes. Last night I found her not so gentille. Last night I formed another idea of her. But listen to what I tell you. She is très, très gentille. She is of very good family. It is a thing you can see."

"They did not leave any word?"

"Yes. They said they would be back in an hour."

"Send them up when they come."

"Yes, Monsieur Barnes. And that lady, that lady there is some one. An eccentric, perhaps, but quelqu'une, quelqu'une!"

The concierge, before she became a concierge, had owned a drink-selling concession at the Paris race-courses. Her life-work lay in the pelouse, but she kept an eye on the people of the pesage, and she took great pride in telling me which of my guests were well brought up, which were of good family, who were sportsmen, a French word pronounced with the accent on the men. The only trouble was that people who did not fall into any of those three categories were very liable to be told there was no one home, chez Barnes. One of my friends, an extremely underfed-looking painter, who was obviously to Madame Duzinell neither well brought up, of good family, nor a sportsman, wrote me a letter asking if I could get him a pass to get by the concierge so he could come up and see me occasionally in the evenings.

I went up to the flat wondering what Brett had done to the concierge. The wire was a cable from Bill Gorton, saying he was arriving on the *France*. I put the mail on the table, went back to the bedroom, undressed and had a shower. I was rubbing down when I heard the door-bell pull. I put on a bathrobe and slippers and went to the door. It was Brett. Back of her was the count. He was holding a great bunch of roses.

"Hello, darling," said Brett. "Aren't you going to let us in?"

"Come on. I was just bathing."

"Aren't you the fortunate man. Bathing."

"Only a shower. Sit down, Count Mippipopolous. What will you drink?"

"I don't know whether you like flowers, sir," the count said, "but I took the liberty of just bringing these roses."

"Here, give them to me." Brett took them. "Get me some water in this, Jake." I filled the big earthenware jug with water in the kitchen, and Brett put the roses in it, and placed them in the centre of the dining-room table.

"I say. We have had a day."

"You don't remember anything about a date with me at the Crillon?"

"No. Did we have one? I must have been blind."

"You were quite drunk, my dear," said the count.

"Wasn't I, though? And the count's been a brick, absolutely."

"You've got hell's own drag with the concierge now."

"I ought to have. Gave her two hundred francs."

"Don't be a damned fool."

"His," she said, and nodded at the count.

"I thought we ought to give her a little something for last night. It was very late."

"He's wonderful," Brett said. "He remembers everything that's happened."

"So do you, my dear."

"Fancy," said Brett. "Who'd want to? I say, Jake, *do* we get a drink?"

"You get it while I go in and dress. You know where it is."

"Rather."

While I dressed I heard Brett put down glasses and then a siphon, and then heard them talking. I dressed slowly, sitting on the bed. I felt tired and pretty rotten. Brett came in the room, a glass in her hand, and sat on the bed.

"What's the matter, darling? Do you feel rocky?"

She kissed me coolly on the forehead.

"Oh, Brett, I love you so much."

"Darling," she said. Then: "Do you want me to send him away?"

"No. He's nice."

"I'll send him away."

"No, don't."

"Yes, I'll send him away."

"You can't just like that."

"Can't I, though? You stay here. He's mad about me, I tell you."

She was gone out of the room. I lay face down on the bed. I was having a bad time. I heard them talking but I did not listen. Brett came in and sat on the bed.

"Poor old darling." She stroked my head.

"What did you say to him?" I was lying with my face away from her. I did not want to see her.

"Sent him for champagne. He loves to go for champagne."

Then later: "Do you feel better, darling? Is the head any better?"

"It's better."

"Lie quiet. He's gone to the other side of town."

"Couldn't we live together, Brett? Couldn't we just live together?"

"I don't think so. I'd just *tromper* you with everybody. You couldn't stand it."

"I stand it now."

"That would be different. It's my fault, Jake. It's the way I'm made."

"Couldn't we go off in the country for a while?"

"It wouldn't be any good. I'll go if you like. But I couldn't live quietly in the country. Not with my own true love."

"I know."

"Isn't it rotten? There isn't any use my telling you I love you."

"You know I love you."

"Let's not talk. Talking's all bilge. I'm going away from you, and then Michael's coming back."

"Why are you going away?"

"Better for you. Better for me."

"When are you going?"

"Soon as I can."

"Where?"

"San Sebastian."

"Can't we go together?"

"No. That would be a hell of an idea after we'd just talked it out."

"We never agreed."

"Oh, you know as well as I do. Don't be obstinate, darling."

"Oh, sure," I said. "I know you're right. I'm just low, and when I'm low I talk like a fool."

I sat up, leaned over, found my shoes beside the bed and put them on. I stood up.

"Don't look like that, darling."

"How do you want me to look?"

"Oh, don't be a fool. I'm going away to-morrow."

"To-morrow?"

"Yes. Didn't I say so? I am."

"Let's have a drink, then. The count will be back."

"Yes. He should be back. You know he's extraordinary about buying champagne. It means any amount to him."

We went into the dining-room. I took up the brandy bottle and poured Brett a drink and one for myself. There was a ring at the bell-pull. I went to the door and there was the count. Behind him was the chauffeur carrying a basket of champagne.

"Where should I have him put it, sir?" asked the count.

"In the kitchen," Brett said.

"Put it in there, Henry," the count motioned. "Now go down and get the ice." He stood looking after the basket inside the kitchen door. "I think you'll find that's very good wine," he said. "I know we don't get much of a chance to judge good wine in the States now, but I got this from a friend of mine that's in the business."

"Oh, you always have some one in the trade," Brett said.

"This fellow raises the grapes. He's got thousands of acres of them."

"What's his name?" asked Brett. "Veuve Cliquot?"

"No," said the count. "Mumms. He's a baron."

"Isn't it wonderful," said Brett. "We all have titles. Why haven't you a title, Jake?"

"I assure you, sir," the count put his hand on my arm. "It never does a man any good. Most of the time it costs you money."

"Oh, I don't know. It's damned useful sometimes," Brett said.

"I've never known it to do me any good."

"You haven't used it properly. I've had hell's own amount of credit on mine."

"Do sit down, count," I said. "Let me take that stick."

The count was looking at Brett across the table under the gaslight. She was smoking a cigarette and flicking the ashes on the rug. She saw me notice it. "I say, Jake, I don't want to ruin your rugs. Can't you give a chap an ash-tray?"

I found some ash-trays and spread them around. The chauffeur came up with a bucket full of salted ice. "Put two bottles in it, Henry," the count called.

"Anything else, sir?"

"No. Wait down in the car." He turned to Brett and to me. "We'll want to ride out to the Bois for dinner?"

"If you like," Brett said. "I couldn't eat a thing."

"I always like a good meal," said the count.

"Should I bring the wine in, sir?" asked the chauffeur.

"Yes. Bring it in, Henry," said the count. He took out a heavy pigskin cigar-case and offered it to me. "Like to try a real American cigar?"

"Thanks," I said. "I'll finish the cigarette."

He cut off the end of his cigar with a gold cutter he wore on one end of his watch-chain.

"I like a cigar to really draw," said the count. "Half the cigars you smoke don't draw."

He lit the cigar, puffed at it, looking across the table at Brett. "And when you're divorced, Lady Ashley, then you won't have a title."

"No. What a pity."

"No," said the count. "You don't need a title. You got class all over you."

"Thanks. Awfully decent of you."

"I'm not joking you," the count blew a cloud of smoke. "You got the most class of anybody I ever seen. You got it. That's all."

"Nice of you," said Brett. "Mummy would be pleased. Couldn't you write it out, and I'll send it in a letter to her."

"I'd tell her, too," said the count. "I'm not joking you. I never joke people. Joke people and you make enemies. That's what I always say."

"You're right," Brett said. "You're terribly right. I always joke people and I haven't a friend in the world. Except Jake here."

"You don't joke him."

"That's it."

"Do you, now?" asked the count. "Do you joke him?"

Brett looked at me and wrinkled up the corners of her eyes.

"No," she said. "I wouldn't joke him."

"See," said the count. "You don't joke him."

"This is a hell of a dull talk," Brett said. "How about some of that champagne?"

The count reached down and twirled the bottles in the shiny bucket. "It isn't cold, yet. You're always drinking, my dear. Why don't you just talk?"

"I've talked too ruddy much. I've talked myself all out to Jake."

"I should like to hear you really talk, my dear. When you talk to me you never finish your sentences at all."

"Leave 'em for you to finish. Let any one finish them as they like."

"It is a very interesting system," the count reached down and gave the bottles a twirl. "Still I would like to hear you talk some time."

"Isn't he a fool?" Brett asked.

"Now," the count brought up a bottle. "I think this is cool."

I brought a towel and he wiped the bottle dry and held it up. "I like to drink champagne from magnums. The wine is better but it would have been too hard to cool." He held the bottle, looking at it. I put out the glasses.

"I say. You might open it," Brett suggested.

"Yes, my dear. Now I'll open it."

It was amazing champagne.

"I say that is wine," Brett held up her glass. "We ought to toast something. 'Here's to royalty.'"

"This wine is too good for toast-drinking, my dear. You don't want to mix emotions up with a wine like that. You lose the taste."

Brett's glass was empty.

"You ought to write a book on wines, count," I said.

"Mr. Barnes," answered the count, "all I want out of wines is to enjoy them."

"Let's enjoy a little more of this," Brett pushed her glass forward. The count poured very carefully. "There, my dear. Now you enjoy that slowly, and then you can get drunk."

"Drunk? Drunk?"

"My dear, you are charming when you are drunk."

"Listen to the man."

"Mr. Barnes," the count poured my glass full. "She is the only lady I have ever known who was as charming when she was drunk as when she was sober."

"You haven't been around much, have you?"

"Yes, my dear. I have been around very much. I have been around a very great deal."

"Drink your wine," said Brett. "We've all been around. I dare say Jake here has seen as much as you have."

"My dear, I am sure Mr. Barnes has seen a lot. Don't think I don't think so, sir. I have seen a lot, too."

"Of course you have, my dear," Brett said. "I was only ragging."

"I have been in seven wars and four revolutions," the count said.

"Soldiering?" Brett asked.

"Sometimes, my dear. And I have got arrow wounds. Have you ever seen arrow wounds?"

"Let's have a look at them."

The count stood up, unbuttoned his vest, and opened his shirt. He pulled up the undershirt onto his chest and stood, his chest black, and big stomach muscles bulging under the light.

"You see them?"

Below the line where his ribs stopped were two raised white welts. "See on the back where they come out." Above the small of the back were the same two scars, raised as thick as a finger.

"I say. Those are something."

"Clean through."

The count was tucking in his shirt.

"Where did you get those?" I asked.

"In Abyssinia. When I was twenty-one years old."

"What were you doing?" asked Brett. "Were you in the army?"

"I was on a business trip, my dear."

"I told you he was one of us. Didn't I?" Brett turned to me. "I love you, count. You're a darling."

"You make me very happy, my dear. But it isn't true."

"Don't be an ass."

"You see, Mr. Barnes, it is because I have lived very much that now I can enjoy everything so well. Don't you find it like that?"

"Yes. Absolutely."

"I know," said the count. "That is the secret. You must get to know the values."

"Doesn't anything ever happen to your values?" Brett asked.

"No. Not any more."

"Never fall in love?"

"Always," said the count. "I am always in love."

"What does that do to your values?"

"That, too, has got a place in my values."

"You haven't any values. You're dead, that's all."

"No, my dear. You're not right. I'm not dead at all."

We drank three bottles of the champagne and the count left the basket in my kitchen. We dined at a restaurant in the Bois. It was a good dinner. Food had an excellent place in the count's values. So did wine. The count was in fine form during the meal. So was Brett. It was a good party.

"Where would you like to go?" asked the count after dinner. We were the only people left in the restaurant. The two waiters were standing over against the door. They wanted to go home.

"We might go up on the hill," Brett said. "Haven't we had a splendid party?"

The count was beaming. He was very happy.

"You are very nice people," he said. He was smoking a cigar again. "Why don't you get married, you two?"

"We want to lead our own lives," I said.

"We have our careers," Brett said. "Come on. Let's get out of this."

"Have another brandy," the count said.

"Get it on the hill."

"No. Have it here where it is quiet."

"You and your quiet," said Brett. "What is it men feel about quiet?"

"We like it," said the count. "Like you like noise, my dear."

"All right," said Brett. "Let's have one."

"Sommelier!" the count called.

"Yes, sir."

"What is the oldest brandy you have?"

"Eighteen eleven, sir."

"Bring us a bottle."

"I say. Don't be ostentatious. Call him off, Jake."

"Listen, my dear. I get more value for my money in old brandy than in any other antiquities."

"Got many antiquities?"

"I got a houseful."

Finally we went up to Montmartre. Inside Zelli's it was crowded, smoky, and noisy. The music hit you as you went in. Brett and I danced. It was so crowded we could barely move. The nigger drummer waved at Brett. We were caught in the jam, dancing in one place in front of him.

"Hahre you?"

"Great."

"Thaats good."

He was all teeth and lips.

"He's a great friend of mine," Brett said. "Damn good drummer."

The music stopped and we started toward the table where the count sat. Then the music started again and we danced. I looked at the count. He was sitting at the table smoking a cigar. The music stopped again.

"Let's go over."

Brett started toward the table. The music started and again we danced, tight in the crowd.

"You are a rotten dancer, Jake. Michael's the best dancer I know."

"He's splendid."

"He's got his points."

"I like him," I said. "I'm damned fond of him."

"I'm going to marry him," Brett said. "Funny. I haven't thought about him for a week."

"Don't you write him?"

"Not I. Never write letters."

"I'll bet he writes to you."

"Rather. Damned good letters, too."

"When are you going to get married?"

"How do I know? As soon as we can get the divorce. Michael's trying to get his mother to put up for it."

"Could I help you?"

"Don't be an ass. Michael's people have loads of money."

The music stopped. We walked over to the table. The count stood up.

"Very nice," he said. "You looked very, very nice."

"Don't you dance, count?" I asked.

"No. I'm too old."

"Oh, come off it," Brett said.

"My dear, I would do it if I would enjoy it. I enjoy to watch you dance."

"Splendid," Brett said. "I'll dance again for you some time. I say. What about your little friend, Zizi?"

"Let me tell you. I support that boy, but I don't want to have him around."

"He is rather hard."

"You know I think that boy's got a future. But personally I don't want him around."

"Jake's rather the same way."

"He gives me the willys."

"Well," the count shrugged his shoulders. "About his future you can't ever tell. Anyhow, his father was a great friend of my father."

"Come on. Let's dance." Brett said.

We danced. It was crowded and close.

"Oh, darling," Brett said, "I'm so miserable."

I had that feeling of going through something that has all happened before. "You were happy a minute ago."

The drummer shouted: "You can't two time——"

"It's all gone."

"What's the matter?"

"I don't know. I just feel terribly."

". . . . ." the drummer chanted. Then turned to his sticks.

"Want to go?"

I had the feeling as in a nightmare of it all being something repeated, something I had been through and that now I must go through again.

". . . . ." the drummer sang softly.

"Let's go," said Brett. "You don't mind."

". . . . ." the drummer shouted and grinned at Brett.

"All right," I said. We got out from the crowd. Brett went to the dressing-room.

"Brett wants to go," I said to the count. He nodded. "Does she? That's fine. You take the car. I'm going to stay here for a while, Mr. Barnes."

We shook hands.

"It was a wonderful time," I said. "I wish you would let me get this." I took a note out of my pocket.

"Mr. Barnes, don't be ridiculous," the count said.

Brett came over with her wrap on. She kissed the count and put her hand on his shoulder to keep him from standing up. As we went out the door I looked back and there were three girls at his table. We got into the big car. Brett gave the chauffeur the address of her hotel.

"No, don't come up," she said at the hotel. She had rung and the door was unlatched.

"Really?"

"No. Please."

"Good night, Brett," I said. "I'm sorry you feel rotten."

"Good night, Jake. Good night, darling. I won't see you again."
We kissed standing at the door. She pushed me away. We kissed
again. "Oh, don't!" Brett said.

She turned quickly and went into the hotel. The chauffeur
drove me around to my flat. I gave him twenty francs and he
touched his cap and said: "Good night, sir," and drove off. I rang
the bell. The door opened and I went up-stairs and went to bed.

BOOK II

CHAPTER VIII

I DID not see Brett again until she came back from San Sebastian. One card came from her from there. It had a picture of the Concha, and said: "Darling. Very quiet and healthy. Love to all the chaps. BRETT."

Nor did I see Robert Cohn again. I heard Frances had left for England and I had a note from Cohn saying he was going out in the country for a couple of weeks, he did not know where, but that he wanted to hold me to the fishing-trip in Spain we had talked about last winter. I could reach him always, he wrote, through his bankers.

Brett was gone, I was not bothered by Cohn's troubles, I rather enjoyed not having to play tennis, there was plenty of work to do, I went often to the races, dined with friends, and put in some extra time at the office getting things ahead so I could leave it in charge of my secretary when Bill Gorton and I should shove off to Spain the end of June. Bill Gorton arrived, put up a couple of days at the flat and went off to Vienna. He was very cheerful and said the States were wonderful. New York was wonderful. There had been a grand theatrical season and a whole crop of great young light heavyweights. Any one of them was a good prospect to grow up, put on weight and trim Dempsey. Bill was very happy. He had made a lot of money on his last book, and was going to make a lot more. We had a good time while he was in Paris, and then he went off to Vienna. He was coming back in three weeks and we would leave for Spain to get in some fishing and go to the fiesta at Pamplona. He wrote that Vienna was wonderful. Then a card from Budapest: "Jake, Budapest is wonderful." Then I got a wire: "Back on Monday."

Monday evening he turned up at the flat. I heard his taxi stop and went to the window and called to him; he waved and started up-stairs carrying his bags. I met him on the stairs, and took one of the bags.

"Well," I said, "I hear you had a wonderful trip."

"Wonderful," he said. "Budapest is absolutely wonderful."

"How about Vienna?"

"Not so good, Jake. Not so good. It seemed better than it was."

"How do you mean?" I was getting glasses and a siphon.

'Tight, Jake. I was tight."

"That's strange. Better have a drink."

Bill rubbed his forehead. "Remarkable thing," he said. "Don't know how it happened. Suddenly it happened."

"Last long?"

"Four days, Jake. Lasted just four days."

"Where did you go?"

"Don't remember. Wrote you a post-card. Remember that perfectly."

"Do anything else?"

"Not so sure. Possible."

"Go on. Tell me about it."

"Can't remember. Tell you anything I could remember."

"Go on. Take that drink and remember."

"Might remember a little," Bill said. "Remember something about a prize-fight. Enormous Vienna prize-fight. Had a nigger in it. Remember the nigger perfectly."

"Go on."

"Wonderful nigger. Looked like Tiger Flowers, only four times as big. All of a sudden everybody started to throw things. Not me. Nigger'd just knocked local boy down. Nigger put up his glove. Wanted to make a speech. Awful noble-looking nigger. Started to make a speech. Then local white boy hit him. Then he knocked white boy cold. Then everybody commenced to throw chairs. Nigger went home with us in our car. Couldn't get his clothes. Wore my coat. Remember the whole thing now. Big sporting evening."

"What happened?"

"Loaned the nigger some clothes and went around with him to try and get his money. Claimed nigger owed them money on account of wrecking hall. Wonder who translated? Was it me?"

"Probably it wasn't you."

"You're right. Wasn't me at all. Was another fellow. Think we called him the local Harvard man. Remember him now. Studying music."

"How'd you come out?"

"Not so good, Jake. Injustice everywhere. Promoter claimed nigger promised let local boy stay. Claimed nigger violated contract. Can't knock out Vienna boy in Vienna. 'My God, Mister Gorton,' said nigger, 'I didn't do nothing in there for forty minutes but try and let him stay. That white boy musta ruptured himself swinging at me. I never did hit him.'"

"Did you get any money?"

"No money, Jake. All we could get was nigger's clothes. Somebody took his watch, too. Splendid nigger. Big mistake to have come to Vienna. Not so good, Jake. Not so good."

"What became of the nigger?"

"Went back to Cologne. Lives there. Married. Got a family. Going to write me a letter and send me the money I loaned him. Wonderful nigger. Hope I gave him the right address."

"You probably did."

"Well, anyway, let's eat," said Bill. "Unless you want me to tell you some more travel stories."

"Go on."

"Let's eat."

We went down-stairs and out onto the Boulevard St. Michel in the warm June evening.

"Where will we go?"

"Want to eat on the island?"

"Sure."

We walked down the Boulevard. At the juncture of the Rue Denfert-Rochereau with the Boulevard is a statue of two men in flowing robes.

"I know who they are." Bill eyed the monument. "Gentlemen who invented pharmacy. Don't try and fool me on Paris."

We went on.

"Here's a taxidermist's," Bill said. "Want to buy anything? Nice stuffed dog?"

"Come on," I said. "You're pie-eyed."

"Pretty nice stuffed dogs," Bill said. "Certainly brighten up your flat."

"Come on."

"Just one stuffed dog. I can take 'em or leave 'em alone. But listen, Jake. Just one stuffed dog."

"Come on."

"Mean everything in the world to you after you bought it. Simple exchange of values. You give them money. They give you a stuffed dog."

"We'll get one on the way back."

"All right. Have it your own way. Road to hell paved with un-bought stuffed dogs. Not my fault."

We went on.

"How'd you feel that way about dogs so sudden?"

"Always felt that way about dogs. Always been a great lover of stuffed animals."

We stopped and had a drink.

"Certainly like to drink," Bill said. "You ought to try it some times, Jake."

"You're about a hundred and forty-four ahead of me."

"Ought not to daunt you. Never be daunted. Secret of my success. Never been daunted. Never been daunted in public."

"Where were you drinking?"

"Stopped at the Crillon. George made me a couple of Jack Roses. George's a great man. Know the secret of his success? Never been daunted."

"You'll be daunted after about three more pernods."

"Not in public. If I begin to feel daunted I'll go off by myself. I'm like a cat that way."

"When did you see Harvey Stone?"

"At the Crillon. Harvey was just a little daunted. Hadn't eaten for three days. Doesn't eat any more. Just goes off like a cat. Pretty sad."

"He's all right."

"Splendid. Wish he wouldn't keep going off like a cat, though. Makes me nervous."

"What'll we do to-night?"

"Doesn't make any difference. Only let's not get daunted. Suppose they got any hard-boiled eggs here? If they had hard-boiled eggs here we wouldn't have to go all the way down to the island to eat."

"Nix," I said. "We're going to have a regular meal."

"Just a suggestion," said Bill. "Want to start now?"

"Come on."

We started on again down the Boulevard. A horse-cab passed us. Bill looked at it.

"See that horse-cab? Going to have that horse-cab stuffed for you for Christmas. Going to give all my friends stuffed animals. I'm a nature-writer."

A taxi passed, some one in it waved, then banged for the driver to stop. The taxi backed up to the curb. In it was Brett.

"Beautiful lady," said Bill. "Going to kidnap us."

"Hullo!" Brett said. "Hullo!"

"This is Bill Gorton. Lady Ashley."

Brett smiled at Bill. "I say I'm just back. Haven't bathed even. Michael comes in to-night."

"Good. Come on and eat with us, and we'll all go to meet him."

"Must clean myself."

"Oh, rot! Come on."

"Must bathe. He doesn't get in till nine."

"Come and have a drink, then, before you bathe."

"Might do that. Now you're not talking rot."

We got in the taxi. The driver looked around.

"Stop at the nearest bistro," I said.

"We might as well go to the Closerie," Brett said. "I can't drink these rotten brandies."

"Closerie des Lilas."

Brett turned to Bill.

"Have you been in this pestilential city long?"

"Just got in to-day from Budapest."

"How was Budapest?"

"Wonderful. Budapest was wonderful."

"Ask him about Vienna."

"Vienna," said Bill, "is a strange city."

"Very much like Paris," Brett smiled at him, wrinkling the corners of her eyes.

"Exactly," Bill said. "Very much like Paris at this moment."

"You *have* a good start."

Sitting out on the terraces of the Lilas Brett ordered a whiskey and soda, I took one, too, and Bill took another pernod.

"How are you, Jake?"

"Great," I said. "I've had a good time."

Brett looked at me. "I was a fool to go away," she said. "One's an ass to leave Paris."

"Did you have a good time?"

"Oh, all right. Interesting. Not frightfully amusing."

"See anybody?"

"No, hardly anybody. I never went out."

"Didn't you swim?"

"No. Didn't do a thing."

"Sounds like Vienna," Bill said.

Brett wrinkled up the corners of her eyes at him.

"So that's the way it was in Vienna."

"It was like everything in Vienna."

Brett smiled at him again.

"You've a nice friend, Jake."

"He's all right," I said. "He's a taxidermist."

"That was in another country," Bill said. "And besides all the animals were dead."

"One more," Brett said, "and I must run. Do send the waiter for a taxi."

"There's a line of them. Right out in front."

"Good."

We had the drink and put Brett into her taxi.

"Mind you're at the Select around ten. Make him come. Michael will be there."

"We'll be there," Bill said. The taxi started and Brett waved.

"Quite a girl," Bill said. "She's damned nice. Who's Michael?"

"The man she's going to marry."

"Well, well," Bill said. "That's always just the stage I meet anybody. What'll I send them? Think they'd like a couple of stuffed race-horses?"

"We better eat."

"Is she really Lady something or other?" Bill asked in the taxi on our way down to the Ile Saint Louis.

"Oh, yes. In the stud-book and everything."

"Well, well."

We ate dinner at Madame Lecomte's restaurant on the far side of the island. It was crowded with Americans and we had to stand up and wait for a place. Some one had put it in the American Women's Club list as a quaint restaurant on the Paris quais as yet untouched by Americans, so we had to wait forty-five minutes for a table. Bill had eaten at the restaurant in 1918, and right after the armistice, and Madame Lecomte made a great fuss over seeing him.

"Doesn't get us a table, though," Bill said. "Grand woman, though."

We had a good meal, a roast chicken, new green beans, mashed potatoes, a salad, and some apple-pie and cheese.

"You've got the world here all right," Bill said to Madame Lecomte. She raised her hand. "Oh, my God!"

"You'll be rich."

"I hope so."

After the coffee and a *fine* we got the bill, chalked up the same as ever on a slate, that was doubtless one of the "quaint" features. paid it, shook hands, and went out.

"You never come here any more, Monsieur Barnes," Madame Lecomte said.

"Too many compatriots."

"Come at lunch-time. It's not crowded then."

"Good. I'll be down soon."

We walked along under the trees that grew out over the river on the Quai d'Orléans side of the island. Across the river were the broken walls of old houses that were being torn down.

"They're going to cut a street through."

"They would," Bill said.

We walked on and circled the island. The river was dark and a bateau mouche went by, all bright with lights, going fast and quiet up and out of sight under the bridge. Down the river was Notre Dame squatting against the night sky. We crossed to the left bank of the Seine by the wooden foot-bridge from the Quai de Bethune, and stopped on the bridge and looked down the river at Notre Dame. Standing on the bridge the island looked dark, the houses were high against the sky, and the trees were shadows.

"It's pretty grand," Bill said. "God, I love to get back."

We leaned on the wooden rail of the bridge and looked up the river to the lights of the big bridges. Below the water was smooth and black. It made no sound against the piles of the bridge. A man and a girl passed us. They were walking with their arms around each other.

We crossed the bridge and walked up the Rue du Cardinal Lemoine. It was steep walking, and we went all the way up to the Place Contrescarpe. The arc-light shone through the leaves of the trees in the square, and underneath the trees was an S bus ready to start. Music came out of the door of the Negre Joyeux. Through the window of the Café Aux Amateurs I saw the long zinc bar. Outside on the terrace working people were drinking. In the open kitchen of the Amateurs a girl was cooking potato-chips in oil. There was an iron pot of stew. The girl ladled some onto a plate for an old man who stood holding a bottle of red wine in one hand.

"Want to have a drink?"

"No," said Bill. "I don't need it."

We turned to the right off the Place Contrescarpe, walking along smooth narrow streets with high old houses on both sides. Some of the houses jutted out toward the street. Others were cut back. We came onto the Rue du Pot de Fer and followed it along until it brought us to the rigid north and south of the Rue Saint Jacques and then walked south, past Val de Grâce, set back behind the courtyard and the iron fence, to the Boulevard du Port Royal.

"What do you want to do?" I asked. "Go up to the café and see Brett and Mike?"

"Why not?"

We walked along Port Royal until it became Montparnasse, and then on past the Lilas, Lavigne's, and all the little cafés, Damoy's, crossed the street to the Rotonde, past its lights and tables to the Select.

Michael came toward us from the tables. He was tanned and healthy-looking.

"Hel-lo, Jake," he said. "Hel-lo! Hel-lo! How are you, old lad?"

"You look very fit, Mike."

"Oh, I am. I'm frightfully fit. I've done nothing but walk. Walk all day long. One drink a day with my mother at tea."

Bill had gone into the bar. He was standing talking with Brett, who was sitting on a high stool, her legs crossed. She had no stockings on.

"It's good to see you, Jake," Michael said. "I'm a little tight you know. Amazing, isn't it? Did you see my nose?"

There was a patch of dried blood on the bridge of his nose.

"An old lady's bags did that," Mike said. "I reached up to help her with them and they fell on me."

Brett gestured at him from the bar with her cigarette-holder and wrinkled the corners of her eyes.

"An old lady," said Mike. "Her bags *fell* on me. Let's go in and see Brett. I say, she is a piece. You *are* a lovely lady, Brett. Where did you get that hat?"

"Chap bought it for me. Don't you like it?"

"It's a dreadful hat. Do get a good hat."

"Oh, we've so much money now," Brett said. "I say, haven't you met Bill yet? You *are* a lovely host, Jake."

She turned to Mike. "This is Bill Gorton. This drunkard is Mike Campbell. Mr. Campbell is an undischarged bankrupt."

"Aren't I, though? You know I met my ex-partner yesterday in London. Chap who did me in."

"What did he say?"

"Bought me a drink. I thought I might as well take it. I say, Brett, you *are* a lovely piece. Don't you think she's beautiful?"

"Beautiful. With this nose?"

"It's a lovely nose. Go on, point it at me. Isn't she a lovely piece?"

"Couldn't we have kept the man in Scotland?"

"I say, Brett, let's turn in early."

"Don't be indecent, Michael. Remember there are ladies at this bar."

"Isn't she a lovely piece? Don't you think so, Jake?"

"There's a fight to-night," Bill said. "Like to go?"

"Fight," said Mike. "Who's fighting?"

"Ledoux and somebody."

"He's very good, Ledoux," Mike said. "I'd like to see it, rather'—he was making an effort to pull himself together—"but I can't go. I had a date with this thing here. I say, Brett, do get a new hat."

Brett pulled the felt hat down far over one eye and smiled out from under it. "You two run along to the fight. I'll have to be taking Mr. Campbell home directly."

"I'm not tight," Mike said. "Perhaps just a little. I say, Brett, you are a lovely piece."

"Go on to the fight," Brett said. "Mr. Campbell's getting difficult. What are these outbursts of affection, Michael?"

"I say, you are a lovely piece."

We said good night. "I'm sorry I can't go," Mike said. Brett laughed. I looked back from the door. Mike had one hand on the bar and was leaning toward Brett, talking. Brett was looking at im quite coolly, but the corners of her eyes were smiling.

Outside on the pavement I said: "Do you want to go to the fight?"

"Sure," said Bill. "If we don't have to walk."

"Mike was pretty excited about his girl friend," I said in the taxi.

"Well," said Bill. "You can't blame him such a hell of a lot."

CHAPTER IX

The Ledoux-Kid Francis fight was the night of the 20th of June. It was a good fight. The morning after the fight I had a letter from Robert Cohn, written from Hendaye. He was having a very quiet time, he said, bathing, playing some golf and much bridge. Hendaye had a splendid beach, but he was anxious to start on the fishing-trip. When would I be down? If I would buy him a double-tapered line he would pay me when I came down.

That same morning I wrote Cohn from the office that Bill and I would leave Paris on the 25th unless I wired him otherwise, and would meet him at Bayonne, where we could get a bus over the mountains to Pamplona. The same evening about seven o'clock I stopped in at the Select to see Michael and Brett. They were not there, and I went over to the Dingo. They were inside sitting at the bar.

"Hello, darling." Brett put out her hand.

"Hello, Jake," Mike said. "I understand I was tight last night."

"Weren't you, though," Brett said. "Disgraceful business."

"Look," said Mike, "when do you go down to Spain? Would you mind if we came down with you?"

"It would be grand."

"You wouldn't mind, really? I've been at Pamplona, you know. Brett's mad to go. You're sure we wouldn't just be a bloody ruisance?"

"Don't talk like a fool."

"I'm a little tight, you know. I wouldn't ask you like this if I weren't. You're sure you don't mind?"

"Oh, shut up, Michael," Brett said. "How can the man say he'd mind now? I'll ask him later."

"But you don't mind, do you?"

"Don't ask that again unless you want to make me sore. Bill and I go down on the morning of the 25th."

"By the way, where is Bill?" Brett asked.

"He's out at Chantilly dining with some people."

"He's a good chap."

"Splendid chap," said Mike. "He is, you know."

"You don't remember him," Brett said.

"I do. Remember him perfectly. Look, Jake, we'll come down the night of the 25th. Brett can't get up in the morning."

"Indeed not!"

"If our money comes and you're sure you don't mind."

"It will come, all right. I'll see to that."

"Tell me what tackle to send for."

"Get two or three rods with reels, and lines, and some flies."

"I won't fish," Brett put in.

"Get two rods, then, and Bill won't have to buy one."

"Right," said Mike. "I'll send a wire to the keeper."

"Won't it be splendid," Brett said. "Spain! We *will* have fun."

"The 25th. When is that?"

"Saturday."

"We *will* have to get ready."

"I say," said Mike, "I'm going to the barber's."

"I must bathe," said Brett. "Walk up to the hotel with me, Jake. Be a good chap."

"We *have* got the loveliest hotel," Mike said. "I think it's a brothel!"

"We left our bags here at the Dingo when we got in, and they asked us at this hotel if we wanted a room for the afternoon only. Seemed frightfully pleased we were going to stay all night."

"I believe it's a brothel," Mike said. "And *I* should know."

"Oh, shut it and go and get your hair cut."

Mike went out. Brett and I sat on at the bar.

"Have another?"

"Might."

"I needed that," Brett said.

We walked up the Rue Delambre.

"I haven't seen you since I've been back," Brett said.

"No."

"How *are* you, Jake?"

"Fine."

Brett looked at me. "I say," she said, "is Robert Cohn going on this trip?"

"Yes. Why?"

"Don't you think it will be a bit rough on him?"

"Why should it?"

"Who did you think I went down to San Sebastian with?"

"Congratulations," I said.

We walked along.

"What did you say that for?"

"I don't know. What would you like me to say?"

We walked along and turned a corner.

"He behaved rather well, too. He gets a little dull."

"Does he?"

"I rather thought it would be good for him."

"You might take up social service."

"Don't be nasty."

"I won't."

"Didn't you really know?"

"No," I said. "I guess I didn't think about it."

"Do you think it will be too rough on him?"

"That's up to him," I said. "Tell him you're coming. He can always not come."

"I'll write him and give him a chance to pull out of it."

I did not see Brett again until the night of the 24th of June.

"Did you hear from Cohn?"

"Rather. He's keen about it."

"My God!"

"I thought it was rather odd myself."

"Says he can't wait to see me."

"Does he think you're coming alone?"

"No. I told him we were all coming down together. Michael and all."

"He's wonderful."

"Isn't he?"

They expected their money the next day. We arranged to meet at Pamplona. They would go directly to San Sebastian and take the train from there. We would all meet at the Montoya in Pamplona. If they did not turn up on Monday at the latest we would go on ahead up to Burguete in the mountains, to start fishing. There was a bus to Burguete. I wrote out an itinerary so they could follow us.

Bill and I took the morning train from the Gare d'Orsay. It was a lovely day, not too hot, and the country was beautiful from the start. We went back into the diner and had breakfast. Leaving the dining-car I asked the conductor for tickets for the first service.

"Nothing until the fifth."

"What's this?"

There were never more than two servings of lunch on that train, and always plenty of places for both of them.

"They're all reserved," the dining-car conductor said. "There will be a fifth service at three-thirty."

"This is serious," I said to Bill.

"Give him ten francs."

"Here," I said. "We want to eat in the first service."

The conductor put the ten francs in his pocket.

"Thank you," he said. "I would advise you gentlemen to get some sandwiches. All the places for the first four services were reserved at the office of the company."

"You'll go a long way, brother," Bill said to him in English. "I suppose if I'd given you five francs you would have advised us to jump off the train."

"*Comment?*"

"Go to hell!" said Bill. "Get the sandwiches made and a bottle of wine. You tell him, Jake."

"And send it up to the next car." I described where we were.

In our compartment were a man and his wife and their young son.

"I suppose you're Americans, aren't you?" the man asked. "Having a good trip?"

"Wonderful," said Bill.

"That's what you want to do. Travel while you're young. Mother and I always wanted to get over, but we had to wait a while."

"You could have come over ten years ago, if you'd wanted to," the wife said. "What you always said was: 'See America first!' I will say we've seen a good deal, take it one way and another."

"Say, there's plenty of Americans on this train," the husband said. "They've got seven cars of them from Dayton, Ohio. They've been on a pilgrimage to Rome, and now they're going down to Biarritz and Lourdes."

"So, that's what they are. Pilgrims. Goddam Puritans," Bill said.

"What part of the States you boys from?"

"Kansas City," I said. "He's from Chicago."

"You both going to Biarritz?"

"No. We're going fishing in Spain."

"Well, I never cared for it, myself. There's plenty that do out where I come from, though. We got some of the best fishing in the State of Montana. I've been out with the boys, but I never cared for it any."

"Mighty little fishing you did on them trips," his wife said.

He winked at us.

"You know how the ladies are. If there's a jug goes along, or a case of beer, they think it's hell and damnation."

"That's the way men are," his wife said to us. She smoothed her comfortable lap. "I voted against prohibition to please him, and because I like a little beer in the house, and then he talks that way. It's a wonder they ever find any one to marry them."

"Say," said Bill, "do you know that gang of Pilgrim Fathers have cornered the dining-car until half past three this afternoon?"

"How do you mean? They can't do a thing like that."

"You try and get seats."

"Well, mother, it looks as though we better go back and get another breakfast."

She stood up and straightened her dress.

"Will you boys keep an eye on our things? Come on, Hubert."

They all three went up to the wagon restaurant. A little while after they were gone a steward went through announcing the first service, and pilgrims, with their priests, commenced filing down the corridor. Our friend and his family did not come back. A waiter passed in the corridor with our sandwiches and the bottle of Chablis, and we called him in.

"You're going to work to-day," I said.

He nodded his head. "They start now, at ten-thirty."

"When do we eat?"

"Huh! When do I eat?"

He left two glasses for the bottle, and we paid him for the sandwiches and tipped him.

"I'll get the plates," he said, "or bring them with you."

We ate the sandwiches and drank the Chablis and watched the country out of the window. The grain was just beginning to ripen and the fields were full of poppies. The pastureland was green, and there were fine trees, and sometimes big rivers and chateaux off in the trees.

At Tours we got off and bought another bottle of wine, and when we got back in the compartment the gentleman from Montana and his wife and his son, Hubert, were sitting comfortably.

"Is there good swimming in Biarritz?" asked Hubert.

"That boy's just crazy till he can get in the water," his mother said. "It's pretty hard on youngsters travelling."

"There's good swimming," I said. "But it's dangerous when it's rough."

"Did you get a meal?" Bill asked.

"We sure did. We set right there when they started to come in, and they must have just thought we were in the party. One of the waiters said something to us in French, and then they just sent three of them back."

"They thought we were snappers, all right," the man said. "It certainly shows you the power of the Catholic Church. It's a pity you boys ain't Catholics. You could get a meal, then, all right."

"I am," I said. "That's what makes me so sore."

Finally at a quarter past four we had lunch. Bill had been rather difficult at the last. He buttonholed a priest who was coming back with one of the returning streams of pilgrims.

"When do us Protestants get a chance to eat, father?"

"I don't know anything about it. Haven't you got tickets?"

"It's enough to make a man join the Klan," Bill said. The priest looked back at him.

Inside the dining-car the waiters served the fifth successive table d'hôte meal. The waiter who served us was soaked through. His white jacket was purple under the arms.

"He must drink a lot of wine."

"Or wear purple undershirts."

"Let's ask him."

"No. He's too tired."

The train stopped for half an hour at Bordeaux and we went out through the station for a little walk. There was not time to get in to the town. Afterward we passed through the Landes and watched the sun set. There were wide fire-gaps cut through the pines, and you could look up them like avenues and see wooded hills way off. About seven-thirty we had dinner and watched the country through the open window in the diner. It was all sandy pine country full of heather. There were little clearings with houses in them, and once in a while we passed a sawmill. It got dark and we could feel the country hot and sandy and dark outside of the window, and about nine o'clock we got into Bayonne. The man and his wife and Hubert all shook hands with us. The were going on to LaNegresse to change for Biarritz.

"Well, I hope you have lots of luck," he said.

"Be careful about those bull-fights."

"Maybe we'll see you at Biarritz," Hubert said.

We got off with our bags and rod-cases and passed through the dark station and out to the lights and the line of cabs and hotel buses. There, standing with the hotel runners, was Robert Cohn. He did not see us at first. Then he started forward.

"Hello, Jake. Have a good trip?"

"Fine," I said. "This is Bill Gorton."

"How are you?"

"Come on," said Robert. "I've got a cab." He was a little near-sighted. I had never noticed it before. He was looking at Bill, trying to make him out. He was shy, too.

"We'll go up to my hotel. It's all right. It's quite nice."

We got into the cab, and the cabman put the bags up on the seat beside him and climbed up and cracked his whip, and we drove over the dark bridge and into the town.

"I'm awfully glad to meet you," Robert said to Bill. "I've heard so much about you from Jake and I've read your books. Did you get my line, Jake?"

The cab stopped in front of the hotel and we all got out and went in. It was a nice hotel, and the people at the desk were very cheerful, and we each had a good small room.

CHAPTER X

ιN the morning it was bright, and they were sprinkling the streets of the town, and we all had breakfast in a café. Bayonne is a nice town. It is like a very clean Spanish town and it is on a big river. Already, so early in the morning, it was very hot on the bridge across the river. We walked out on the bridge and then took a walk through the town.

I was not at all sure Mike's rods would come from Scotland in time, so we hunted a tackle store and finally bought a rod for Bill up-stairs over a drygoods store. The man who sold the tackle was out, and we had to wait for him to come back. Finally he came in, and we bought a pretty good rod cheap, and two landing-nets.

We went out into the street again and took a look at the cathedral. Cohn made some remark about it being a very good example of something or other, I forget what. It seemed like a nice cathedral, nice and dim, like Spanish churches. Then we went up past the old fort and out to the local Syndicat d'Initiative office, where the bus was supposed to start from. There they told us the bus service did not start until the 1st of July. We found out

at the tourist office what we ought to pay for a motor-car to
Pamplona and hired one at a big garage just around the corner
from the Municipal Theatre for four hundred francs. The car was
to pick us up at the hotel in forty minutes, and we stopped at the
café on the square where we had eaten breakfast, and had a beer.
It was hot, but the town had a cool, fresh, early-morning smell and
it was pleasant sitting in the café. A breeze started to blow, and
you could feel that the air came from the sea. There were pigeons
out in the square, and the houses were a yellow, sun-baked color,
and I did not want to leave the café. But we had to go to the
hotel to get our bags packed and pay the bill. We paid for the
beers, we matched and I think Cohn paid, and went up to the
hotel. It was only sixteen francs apiece for Bill and me, with ten
per cent added for the service, and we had the bags sent down
and waited for Robert Cohn. While we were waiting I saw a
cockroach on the parquet floor that must have been at least three
inches long. I pointed him out to Bill and then put my shoe on
him. We agreed he must have just come in from the garden. It
was really an awfully clean hotel.

Cohn came down, finally, and we all went out to the car. It
was a big, closed car, with a driver in a white duster with blue
collar and cuffs, and we had him put the back of the car down.
He piled in the bags and we started off up the street and out of
the town. We passed some lovely gardens and had a good look
back at the town, and then we were out in the country, green and
rolling, and the road climbing all the time. We passed lots of
Basques with oxen, or cattle, hauling carts along the road, and
nice farmhouses, low roofs, and all white-plastered. In the Basque
country the land all looks very rich and green and the houses and
villages look well-off and clean. Every village had a pelota court
and on some of them kids were playing in the hot sun. There
were signs on the walls of the churches saying it was forbidden
to play pelota against them, and the houses in the villages had

red tiled roofs, and then the road turned off and commenced to climb and we were going way up close along a hillside, with a valley below and hills stretched off back toward the sea. You couldn't see the sea. It was too far away. You could see only hills and more hills, and you knew where the sea was.

We crossed the Spanish frontier. There was a little stream and a bridge, and Spanish carabineers, with patent-leather Bonaparte hats, and short guns on their backs, on one side, and on the other fat Frenchmen in kepis and mustaches. They only opened one bag and took the passports in and looked at them. There was a general store and inn on each side of the line. The chauffeur had to go in and fill out some papers about the car and we got out and went over to the stream to see if there were any trout. Bill tried to talk some Spanish to one of the carabineers, but it did not go very well. Robert Cohn asked, pointing with his finger, if there were any trout in the stream, and the carabineer said yes, but not many.

I asked him if he ever fished, and he said no, that he didn't care for it.

Just then an old man with long, sunburned hair and beard, and clothes that looked as though they were made of gunny-sacking, came striding up to the bridge. He was carrying a long staff, and he had a kid slung on his back, tied by the four legs, the head hanging down.

The carabineer waved him back with his sword. The man turned without saying anything, and started back up the white road into Spain.

"What's the matter with the old one?" I asked.

"He hasn't got any passport."

I offered the guard a cigarette. He took it and thanked me.

"What will he do?" I asked.

The guard spat in the dust.

"Oh, he'll just wade across the stream."

"Do you have much smuggling?"

"Oh," he said, "they go through."

The chauffeur came out, folding up the papers and putting them in the inside pocket of his coat. We all got in the car and it started up the white dusty road into Spain. For a while the country was much as it had been; then, climbing all the time, we crossed the top of a Col, the road winding back and forth on itself, and then it was really Spain. There were long brown mountains and a few pines and far-off forests of beech-trees on some of the mountainsides. The road went along the summit of the Col and then dropped down, and the driver had to honk, and slow up, and turn out to avoid running into two donkeys that were sleeping in the road. We came down out of the mountains and through an oak forest, and there were white cattle grazing in the forest. Down below there were grassy plains and clear streams, and then we crossed a stream and went through a gloomy little village, and started to climb again. We climbed up and up and crossed another high Col and turned along it, and the road ran down to the right, and we saw a whole new range of mountains off to the south, all brown and baked-looking and furrowed in strange shapes.

After a while we came out of the mountains, and there were trees along both sides of the road, and a stream and ripe fields of grain, and the road went on, very white and straight ahead, and then lifted to a little rise, and off on the left was a hill with an old castle, with buildings close around it and a field of grain going right up to the walls and shifting in the wind. I was up in front with the driver and I turned around. Robert Cohn was asleep, but Bill looked and nodded his head. Then we crossed a wide plain, and there was a big river off on the right shining in the sun from between the line of trees, and away off you could see the plateau of Pamplona rising out of the plain, and the walls of the city, and the great brown cathedral, and the broken skyline of the other churches. In back of the plateau were the mountains, and every way you looked there were other mountains, and ahead the road stretched out white across the plain going toward Pamplona.

We came into the town on the other side of the plateau, the road slanting up steeply and dustily with shade-trees on both sides, and then levelling out through the new part of town they are building up outside the old walls. We passed the bull-ring, high and white and concrete-looking in the sun, and then came into the big square by a side street and stopped in front of the Hotel Montoya.

The driver helped us down with the bags. There was a crowd of kids watching the car, and the square was hot, and the trees were green, and the flags hung on their staffs, and it was good to get out of the sun and under the shade of the arcade that runs all the way around the square. Montoya was glad to see us, and shook hands and gave us good rooms looking out on the square, and then we washed and cleaned up and went down-stairs in the dining-room for lunch. The driver stayed for lunch, too, and afterward we paid him and he started back to Bayonne.

There are two dining-rooms in the Montoya. One is up-stairs on the second floor and looks out on the square. The other is down one floor below the level of the square and has a door that opens on the back street that the bulls pass along when they run through the streets early in the morning on their way to the ring. It is always cool in the down-stairs dining-room and we had a very good lunch. The first meal in Spain was always a shock with the hors d'œuvres, an egg course, two meat courses, vegetables, salad, and dessert and fruit. You have to drink plenty of wine to get it all down. Robert Cohn tried to say he did not want any of the second meat course, but we would not interpret for him, and so the waitress brought him something else as a replacement, a plate of cold meats, I think. Cohn had been rather nervous ever since we had met at Bayonne. He did not know whether we knew Brett had been with him at San Sebastian, and it made him rather awkward.

"Well," I said, "Brett and Mike ought to get in to-night."

"I'm not sure they'll come," Cohn said.

"Why not?" Bill said. "Of course they'll come."

"They're always late," I said.

"I rather think they're not coming," Robert Cohn said.

He said it with an air of superior knowledge that irritated both of us.

"I'll bet you fifty pesetas they're here to-night," Bill said. He always bets when he is angered, and so he usually bets foolishly.

"I'll take it," Cohn said. "Good. You remember it, Jake. Fifty pesetas."

"I'll remember it myself," Bill said. I saw he was angry and wanted to smooth him down.

"It's a sure thing they'll come," I said. "But maybe not to-night."

"Want to call it off?" Cohn asked.

"No. Why should I? Make it a hundred if you like."

"All right. I'll take that."

"That's enough," I said. "Or you'll have to make a book and give me some of it."

"I'm satisfied," Cohn said. He smiled. "You'll probably win it back at bridge, anyway."

"You haven't got it yet," Bill said.

We went out to walk around under the arcade to the Café Iruña for coffee. Cohn said he was going over and get a shave.

"Say," Bill said to me, "have I got any chance on that bet?"

"You've got a rotten chance. They've never been on time anywhere. If their money doesn't come it's a cinch they won't get in to-night."

"I was sorry as soon as I opened my mouth. But I had to call him. He's all right, I guess, but where does he get this inside stuff? Mike and Brett fixed it up with us about coming down here."

I saw Cohn coming over across the square.

"Here he comes."

"Well, let him not get superior and Jewish."

"The barber shop's closed," Cohn said. "It's not open till four."

We had coffee at the Iruña, sitting in comfortable wicker chairs looking out from the cool of the arcade at the big square. After a while Bill went to write some letters and Cohn went over to the barber-shop. It was still closed, so he decided to go up to the hotel and get a bath, and I sat out in front of the café and then went for a walk in the town. It was very hot, but I kept on the shady side of the streets and went through the market and had a good time seeing the town again. I went to the Ayuntamiento and found the old gentleman who subscribes for the bull-fight tickets for me every year, and he had gotten the money I sent him from Paris and renewed my subscriptions, so that was all set. He was the archivist, and all the archives of the town were in his office. That has nothing to do with the story. Anyway, his office had a green baize door and a big wooden door, and when I went out I left him sitting among the archives that covered all the walls, and I shut both the doors, and as I went out of the building into the street the porter stopped me to brush off my coat.

"You must have been in a motor-car," he said.

The back of the collar and the upper part of the shoulders were gray with dust.

"From Bayonne."

"Well, well," he said. "I knew you were in a motor-car from the way the dust was." So I gave him two copper coins.

At the end of the street I saw the cathedral and walked up toward it. The first time I ever saw it I thought the façade was ugly but I liked it now. I went inside. It was dim and dark and the pillars went high up, and there were people praying, and it smelt of incense, and there were some wonderful big windows. I knelt and started to pray and prayed for everybody I thought of, Brett and Mike and Bill and Robert Cohn and myself, and all the bull-fighters, separately for the ones I liked, and lumping all the rest, then I prayed for myself again, and while I was praying for myself I found I was getting sleepy, so I prayed that the bull-fights would be good, and that it would be a fine fiesta, and that we would get some fishing. I wondered if there was anything else I might pray for, and I thought I would like to have some money, so I prayed that I would make a lot of money, and then I started to think how I would make it, and thinking of making money reminded me of the count, and I started wondering about where he was, and regretting I hadn't seen him since that night in Montmartre, and about something funny Brett told me about him, and as all the time I was kneeling with my forehead on the wood in front of me, and was thinking of myself as praying, I was a little ashamed, and regretted that I was such a rotten Catholic, but realized there was nothing I could do about it, at least for a while, and maybe never, but that anyway it was a grand religion, and I only wished I felt religious and maybe I would the next time; and then I was out in the hot sun on the steps of the cathedral, and the forefingers and the thumb of my right hand were still damp, and I felt them dry in the sun. The sunlight was hot and hard, and I crossed over beside some buildings, and walked back along side-streets to the hotel.

At dinner that night we found that Robert Cohn had taken a bath, had had a shave and a haircut and a shampoo, and something put on his hair afterward to make it stay down. He was nervous, and I did not try to help him any. The train was due in at nine o'clock from San Sebastian, and, if Brett and Mike were coming, they would be on it. At twenty minutes to nine we were not half through dinner. Robert Cohn got up from the table and said he would go to the station. I said I would go with him, just to devil him. Bill said he would be damned if he would leave his dinner. I said we would be right back.

We walked to the station. I was enjoying Cohn's nervousness. I hoped Brett would be on the train. At the station the train was late, and we sat on a baggage-truck and waited outside in the dark. I have never seen a man in civil life as nervous as Robert Cohn—nor as eager. I was enjoying it. It was lousy to enjoy it, but I felt lousy. Cohn had a wonderful quality of bringing out the worst in anybody.

After a while we heard the train-whistle way off below on the other side of the plateau, and then we saw the headlight coming up the hill. We went inside the station and stood with a crowd of people just back of the gates, and the train came in and stopped, and everybody started coming out through the gates.

They were not in the crowd. We waited till everybody had gone through and out of the station and gotten into buses, or taken cabs, or were walking with their friends or relatives through the dark into the town.

"I knew they wouldn't come," Robert said. We were going back to the hotel.

"I thought they might," I said.

Bill was eating fruit when we came in and finishing a bottle of wine.

"Didn't come, eh?"

"No."

"Do you mind if I give you that hundred pesetas in the morning, Cohn?" Bill asked. "I haven't changed any money here yet."

"Oh, forget about it," Robert Cohn said. "Let's bet on something else. Can you bet on bull-fights?"

"You could," Bill said, "but you don't need to."

"It would be like betting on the war," I said. "You don't need any economic interest."

"I'm very curious to see them," Robert said.

Montoya came up to our table. He had a telegram in his hand. "It's for you." He handed it to me.

It read: "Stopped night San Sebastian."

"It's from them," I said. I put it in my pocket. Ordinarily I should have handed it over.

"They've stopped over in San Sebastian," I said. "Send their regards to you."

Why I felt that impulse to devil him I do not know. Of course I do know. I was blind, unforgivingly jealous of what had happened to him. The fact that I took it as a matter of course did not alter that any. I certainly did hate him. I do not think I ever really hated him until he had that little spell of superiority at lunch—that and when he went through all that barbering. So I put the telegram in my pocket. The telegram came to me, anyway.

"Well," I said. "We ought to pull out on the noon bus for Burguete. They can follow us if they get in to-morrow night."

There were only two trains up from San Sebastian, an early morning train and the one we had just met.

"That sounds like a good idea," Cohn said.

"The sooner we get on the stream the better."

"It's all one to me when we start," Bill said. "The sooner the better."

We sat in the Iruña for a while and had coffee and then took a little walk out to the bull-ring and across the field and under the trees at the edge of the cliff and looked down at the river in the dark, and I turned in early. Bill and Cohn stayed out in the café quite late, I believe, because I was asleep when they came in.

In the morning I bought three tickets for the bus to Burguete. It was scheduled to leave at two o'clock. There was nothing earlier. I was sitting over at the Iruña reading the papers when I saw Robert Cohn coming across the square. He came up to the table and sat down in one of the wicker chairs.

"This is a comfortable café," he said. "Did you have a good night, Jake?"

"I slept like a log."

"I didn't sleep very well. Bill and I were out late, too."

"Where were you?"

"Here. And after it shut we went over to that other café. The old man there speaks German and English."

"The Café Suizo."

"That's it. He seems like a nice old fellow. I think it's a better café than this one."

"It's not so good in the daytime," I said. "Too hot. By the way, I got the bus tickets."

"I'm not going up to-day. You and Bill go on ahead."

"I've got your ticket."

"Give it to me. I'll get the money back."

"It's five pesetas."

Robert Cohn took out a silver five-peseta piece and gave it to me.

"I ought to stay," he said. "You see I'm afraid there's some sort of misunderstanding."

"Why," I said. "They may not come here for three or four days now if they start on parties at San Sebastian."

"That's just it," said Robert. "I'm afraid they expected to meet me at San Sebastian, and that's why they stopped over."

"What makes you think that?"

"Well, I wrote suggesting it to Brett."

"Why in hell didn't you stay there and meet them, then?" I started to say, but I stopped. I thought that idea would come to him by itself, but I do not believe it ever did.

He was being confidential now and it was giving him pleasure to be able to talk with the understanding that I knew there was something between him and Brett.

"Well, Bill and I will go up right after lunch," I said.

"I wish I could go. We've been looking forward to this fishing all winter." He was being sentimental about it. "But I ought to stay. I really ought. As soon as they come I'll bring them right up."

"Let's find Bill."

"I want to go over to the barber-shop."

"See you at lunch."

I found Bill up in his room. He was shaving.

"Oh, yes, he told me all about it last night," Bill said. "He's a great little confider. He said he had a date with Brett at San Sebastian."

"The lying bastard!"

"Oh, no," said Bill. "Don't get sore. Don't get sore at this stage of the trip. How did you ever happen to know this fellow, anyway?"

"Don't rub it in."

Bill looked around, half-shaved, and then went on talking into the mirror while he lathered his face.

"Didn't you send him with a letter to me in New York last winter? Thank God, I'm a travelling man. Haven't you got some more Jewish friends you could bring along?" He rubbed his chin with his thumb, looked at it, and then started scraping again.

"You've got some fine ones yourself."

"Oh, yes. I've got some darbs. But not alongside of this Robert Cohn. The funny thing is he's nice, too. I like him. But he's just so awful."

"He can be damn nice."

"I know it. That's the terrible part."

I laughed.

"Yes. Go on and laugh," said Bill. "You weren't out with him last night until two o'clock."

"Was he very bad?"

"Awful. What's all this about him and Brett, anyway? Did she ever have anything to do with him?"

He raised his chin up and pulled it from side to side.

"Sure. She went down to San Sebastian with him."

"What a damn-fool thing to do. Why did she do that?"

"She wanted to get out of town and she can't go anywhere alone. She said she thought it would be good for him."

"What bloody-fool things people do. Why didn't she go off with some of her own people? Or you?"—he slurred that over— "or me? Why not me?" He looked at his face carefully in the glass, put a big dab of lather on each cheek-bone. "It's an honest face. It's a face any woman would be safe with."

"She'd never seen it."

"She should have. All women should see it. It's a face that ought to be thrown on every screen in the country. Every woman ought to be given a copy of this face as she leaves the altar. Mothers should tell their daughters about this face. My son"—he pointed the razor at me—"go west with this face and grow up with the country."

He ducked down to the bowl, rinsed his face with cold water, put on some alcohol, and then looked at himself carefully in the glass, pulling down his long upper lip.

"My God!" he said, "isn't it an awful face?"

He looked in the glass.

"And as for this Robert Cohn," Bill said, "he makes me sick, and he can go to hell, and I'm damn glad he's staying here so we won't have him fishing with us."

"You're damn right."

"We're going trout-fishing. We're going trout-fishing in the Irati River, and we're going to get tight now at lunch on the wine of the country, and then take a swell bus ride."

"Come on. Let's go over to the Iruña and start," I said.

CHAPTER XI

It was baking hot in the square when we came out after lunch with our bags and the rod-case to go to Burguete. People were on top of the bus, and others were climbing up a ladder. Bill went up and Robert sat beside Bill to save a place for me, and I went back in the hotel to get a couple of bottles of wine to take with us. When I came out the bus was crowded. Men and women were sitting on all the baggage and boxes on top, and the women all had their fans going in the sun. It certainly was hot. Robert climbed down and I fitted into the place he had saved on the one wooden seat that ran across the top.

Robert Cohn stood in the shade of the arcade waiting for us to start. A Basque with a big leather wine-bag in his lap lay across the top of the bus in front of our seat, leaning back against our legs. He offered the wine-skin to Bill and to me, and when I tipped it up to drink he imitated the sound of a klaxon motor-horn so well and so suddenly that I spilled some of the wine, and everybody laughed. He apologized and made me take another drink. He made the klaxon again a little later, and it fooled me the second time. He was very good at it. The Basques liked it. The man next to Bill was talking to him in Spanish and Bill was not getting it, so he offered the man one of the bottles of wine. The man waved it away. He said it was too hot and he had drunk too much at lunch. When Bill offered the bottle the second time he took a long drink, and then the bottle went all over that part of the bus. Every one took a drink very politely, and then they made us cork it up and put it away. They all wanted us to drink from their leather wine-bottles. They were peasants going up into the hills.

Finally, after a couple more false klaxons, the bus started, and Robert Cohn waved good-by to us, and all the Basques waved good-by to him. As soon as we started out on the road outside of town it was cool. It felt nice riding high up and close under the trees. The bus went quite fast and made a good breeze, and as we went out along the road with the dust powdering the trees and down the hill, we had a fine view, back through the trees, of the town rising up from the bluff above the river. The Basque lying against my knees pointed out the view with the neck of the wine-bottle, and winked at us. He nodded his head.

"Pretty nice, eh?"

"These Basques are swell people," Bill said.

The Basque lying against my legs was tanned the color of saddle-leather. He wore a black smock like all the rest. There were wrinkles in his tanned neck. He turned around and offered his wine-bag to Bill. Bill handed him one of our bottles. The Basque wagged a forefinger at him and handed the bottle back, slapping in the cork with the palm of his hand. He shoved the wine-bag up.

"Arriba! Arriba!" he said. "Lift it up."

Bill raised the wine-skin and let the stream of wine spurt out and into his mouth, his head tipped back. When he stopped drinking and tipped the leather bottle down a few drops ran down his chin.

"No! No!" several Basques said. "Not like that." One snatched the bottle away from the owner, who was himself about to give a demonstration. He was a young fellow and he held the wine-bottle at full arms' length and raised it high up, squeezing the leather bag with his hand so the stream of wine hissed into his mouth. He held the bag out there, the wine making a flat, hard trajectory into his mouth, and he kept on swallowing smoothly and regularly.

"Hey!" the owner of the bottle shouted. "Whose wine is that?"

The drinker waggled his little finger at him and smiled at us with his eyes. Then he bit the stream off sharp, made a quick lift with the wine-bag and lowered it down to the owner. He winked at us. The owner shook the wine-skin sadly.

We passed through a town and stopped in front of the posada, and the driver took on several packages. Then we started on again, and outside the town the road commenced to mount. We were going through farming country with rocky hills that sloped down into the fields. The grain-fields went up the hillsides. Now as we went higher there was a wind blowing the grain. The road was white and dusty, and the dust rose under the wheels and hung in the air behind us. The road climbed up into the hills and left the rich grain-fields below. Now there were only patches of grain on the bare hillsides and on each side of the water-courses. We turned sharply out to the side of the road to give room to pass to a long string of six mules, following one after the other, hauling a high-hooded wagon loaded with freight. The wagon and the mules were covered with dust. Close behind was another string of mules and another wagon. This was loaded with lumber, and the arriero driving the mules leaned back and put on the thick wooden brakes as we passed. Up here the country was quite barren and the hills were rocky and hard-baked clay furrowed by the rain.

We came around a curve into a town, and on both sides opened out a sudden green valley. A stream went through the centre of the town and fields of grapes touched the houses.

The bus stopped in front of a posada and many of the passengers got down, and a lot of the baggage was unstrapped from the roof from under the big tarpaulins and lifted down. Bill and I got down and went into the posada. There was a low, dark room with saddles and harness, and hay-forks made of white wood, and clusters of canvas rope-soled shoes and hams and slabs of bacon and white garlics and long sausages hanging from the roof. It was cool and dusky, and we stood in front of a long wooden counter with two women behind it serving drinks. Behind them were shelves stacked with supplies and goods.

We each had an aguardiente and paid forty centimes for the two drinks. I gave the woman fifty centimes to make a tip, and she gave me back the copper piece, thinking I had misunderstood the price.

Two of our Basques came in and insisted on buying a drink. So they bought a drink and then we bought a drink, and then they slapped us on the back and bought another drink. Then we bought, and then we all went out into the sunlight and the heat, and climbed back on top of the bus. There was plenty of room now for every one to sit on the seat, and the Basque who had been lying on the tin roof now sat between us. The woman who had been serving drinks came out wiping her hands on her apron and talked to somebody inside the bus. Then the driver came out swinging two flat leather mail-pouches and climbed up, and everybody waving we started off.

The road left the green valley at once, and we were up in the hills again. Bill and the wine-bottle Basque were having a conversation. A man leaned over from the other side of the seat and asked in English: "You're American?"

"Sure."

"I been there," he said. "Forty years ago."

He was an old man, as brown as the others, with the stubble of a white beard.

"How was it?"

"What you say?"

"How was America?"

"Oh, I was in California. It was fine."

"Why did you leave?"

"What you say?"

"Why did you come back here?"

"Oh! I come back to get married. I was going to go back but my wife she don't like to travel. Where you from?"

"Kansas City."

"I been there," he said. "I been in Chicago, St. Louis, Kansas City, Denver, Los Angeles, Salt Lake City."

He named them carefully.

"How long were you over?"

"Fifteen years. Then I come back and got married."

"Have a drink?"

"All right," he said. "You can't get this in America, eh?"

"There's plenty if you can pay for it."

"What you come over here for?"

"We're going to the fiesta at Pamplona."

"You like the bull-fights?"

"Sure. Don't you?"

"Yes," he said. "I guess I like them."

Then after a little:

"Where you go now?"

"Up to Burguete to fish."

"Well," he said, "I hope you catch something."

He shook hands and turned around to the back seat again. The other Basques had been impressed. He sat back comfortably and smiled at me when I turned around to look at the country. But the effort of talking American seemed to have tired him. He did not say anything after that.

The bus climbed steadily up the road. The country was barren and rocks stuck up through the clay. There was no grass beside the road. Looking back we could see the country spread out below. Far back the fields were squares of green and brown on the hillsides. Making the horizon were the brown mountains. They were strangely shaped. As we climbed higher the horizon kept changing. As the bus ground slowly up the road we could see other mountains coming up in the south. Then the road came over the crest, flattened out, and went into a forest. It was a forest of cork oaks, and the sun came through the trees in patches, and there were cattle grazing back in the trees. We went through the forest and the road came out and turned along a rise of land, and out ahead of us was a rolling green plain, with dark mountains beyond it. These were not like the brown, heat-baked mountains we had left behind. These were wooded and there were clouds coming down from them. The green plain stretched off. It was cut by fences and the white of the road showed through the trunks of a double line of trees that crossed the plain toward the north. As we came to the edge of the rise we saw the red roofs and white houses of Burguete ahead strung out on the plain, and away off on the shoulder of the first dark mountain was the gray metal-sheathed roof of the monastery of Roncesvalles.

"There's Roncevaux," I said.

"Where?"

"Way off there where the mountain starts."

"It's cold up here," Bill said.

"It's high," I said. "It must be twelve hundred metres."

"It's awful cold," Bill said.

The bus levelled down onto the straight line of road that ran to Burguete. We passed a crossroads and crossed a bridge over a stream. The houses of Burguete were along both sides of the road. There were no side-streets. We passed the church and the school-yard, and the bus stopped. We got down and the driver handed down our bags and the rod-case. A carabineer in his cocked hat and yellow leather cross-straps came up.

"What's in there?" he pointed to the rod-case.

I opened it and showed him. He asked to see our fishing permits and I got them out. He looked at the date and then waved us on

"Is that all right?" I asked.

"Yes. Of course."

We went up the street, past the whitewashed stone houses, families sitting in their doorways watching us, to the inn.

The fat woman who ran the inn came out from the kitchen and shook hands with us. She took off her spectacles, wiped them, and put them on again. It was cold in the inn and the wind was starting to blow outside. The woman sent a girl up-stairs with us to show the room. There were two beds, a washstand, a clothes-chest, and a big, framed steel-engraving of Nuestra Señora de Roncesvalles. The wind was blowing against the shutters. The room was on the north side of the inn. We washed, put on sweaters, and came down-stairs into the dining-room. It had a stone floor, low ceiling, and was oak-panelled. The shutters were all up and it was so cold you could see your breath.

"My God!" said Bill. "It can't be this cold to-morrow. I'm not going to wade a stream in this weather."

There was an upright piano in the far corner of the room beyond the wooden tables and Bill went over and started to play.

"I got to keep warm," he said.

I went out to find the woman and ask her how much the room and board was. She put her hands under her apron and looked away from me.

"Twelve pesetas."

"Why, we only paid that in Pamplona."

She did not say anything, just took off her glasses and wiped them on her apron.

"That's too much," I said. "We didn't pay more than that at a big hotel."

"We've put in a bathroom."

"Haven't you got anything cheaper?"

"Not in the summer. Now is the big season."

We were the only people in the inn. Well, I thought, it's only a few days.

"Is the wine included?"

"Oh, yes."

"Well," I said. "It's all right."

I went back to Bill. He blew his breath at me to show how cold it was, and went on playing. I sat at one of the tables and looked at the pictures on the wall. There was one panel of rabbits, dead, one of pheasants, also dead, and one panel of dead ducks. The panels were all dark and smoky-looking. There was a cupboard full of liqueur bottles. I looked at them all. Bill was still playing. "How about a hot rum punch?" he said. "This isn't going to keep me warm permanently."

I went out and told the woman what a rum punch was and how to make it. In a few minutes a girl brought a stone pitcher, steaming, into the room. Bill came over from the piano and we drank the hot punch and listened to the wind.

"There isn't too much rum in that."

I went over to the cupboard and brought the rum bottle and poured a half-tumblerful into the pitcher.

"Direct action," said Bill. "It beats legislation."

The girl came in and laid the table for supper.

"It blows like hell up here," Bill said.

The girl brought in a big bowl of hot vegetable soup and the wine. We had fried trout afterward and some sort of a stew and a big bowl full of wild strawberries. We did not lose money on the wine, and the girl was shy but nice about bringing it. The old woman looked in once and counted the empty bottles.

After supper we went up-stairs and smoked and read in bed to keep warm. Once in the night I woke and heard the wind blowing. It felt good to be warm and in bed.

CHAPTER XII

WHEN I woke in the morning I went to the window and looked out. It had cleared and there were no clouds on the mountains. Outside under the window were some carts and an old diligence, the wood of the roof cracked and split by the weather. It must have been left from the days before the motor-buses. A goat hopped up on one of the carts and then to the roof of the diligence. He jerked his head at the other goats below and when I waved at him he bounded down.

Bill was still sleeping, so I dressed, put on my shoes outside in the hall, and went down-stairs. No one was stirring down-stairs, so I unbolted the door and went out. It was cool outside in the early morning and the sun had not yet dried the dew that had come when the wind died down. I hunted around in the shed behind the inn and found a sort of mattock, and went down toward the stream to try and dig some worms for bait. The stream was clear and shallow but it did not look trouty. On the grassy bank where it was damp I drove the mattock into the earth and loosened a chunk of sod. There were worms underneath. They slid out of sight as I lifted the sod and I dug carefully and got a good many. Digging at the edge of the damp ground I filled two empty tobacco-tins with worms and sifted dirt onto them. The goats watched me dig.

When I went back into the inn the woman was down in the kitchen, and I asked her to get coffee for us, and that we wanted a lunch. Bill was awake and sitting on the edge of the bed.

"I saw you out of the window," he said. "Didn't want to interrupt you. What were you doing? Burying your money?"

"You lazy bum!"

"Been working for the common good? Splendid. I want you to do that every morning."

"Come on," I said. "Get up."

"What? Get up? I never get up."

He climbed into bed and pulled the sheet up to his chin.

"Try and argue me into getting up."

I went on looking for the tackle and putting it all together in the tackle-bag.

"Aren't you interested?" Bill asked.

"I'm going down and eat."

"Eat? Why didn't you say eat? I thought you just wanted me to get up for fun. Eat? Fine. Now you're reasonable. You go out and dig some more worms and I'll be right down."

"Oh, go to hell!"

"Work for the good of all." Bill stepped into his underclothes. "Show irony and pity."

I started out of the room with the tackle-bag, the nets, and the rod-case.

"Hey! come back!"

I put my head in the door.

"Aren't you going to show a little irony and pity?"

I thumbed my nose.

"That's not irony."

As I went down-stairs I heard Bill singing, "Irony and Pity. When you're feeling . . . Oh, Give them Irony and Give them Pity. Oh, give them Irony. When they're feeling . . . Just a little irony. Just a little pity . . ." He kept on singing until he came down-stairs. The tune was: "The Bells are Ringing for Me and my Gal." I was reading a week-old Spanish paper.

"What's all this irony and pity?"

"What? Don't you know about Irony and Pity?"

"No. Who got it up?"

"Everybody. They're mad about it in New York. It's just like the Fratellinis used to be."

The girl came in with the coffee and buttered toast. Or, rather, it was bread toasted and buttered.

"Ask her if she's got any jam," Bill said. "Be ironical with her."

"Have you got any jam?"

"That's not ironical. I wish I could talk Spanish."

The coffee was good and we drank it out of big bowls. The girl brought in a glass dish of raspberry jam.

"Thank you."

"Hey! that's not the way," Bill said. "Say something ironical. Make some crack about Primo de Rivera."

"I could ask her what kind of a jam they think they've gotten into in the Riff."

"Poor," said Bill. "Very poor. You can't do it. That's all. You don't understand irony. You have no pity. Say something pitiful."

"Robert Cohn."

"Not so bad. That's better. Now why is Cohn pitiful? Be ironic."

He took a big gulp of coffee.

"Aw, hell!" I said. "It's too early in the morning."

"There you go. And you claim you want to be a writer, too. You're only a newspaper man. An expatriated newspaper man.

You ought to be ironical the minute you get out of bed. You ought
to wake up with your mouth full of pity."

"Go on," I said. "Who did you get this stuff from?"

"Everybody. Don't you read? Don't you ever see anybody?
You know what you are? You're an expatriate. Why don't you
live in New York? Then you'd know these things. What do you
want me to do? Come over here and tell you every year?"

"Take some more coffee," I said.

"Good. Coffee is good for you. It's the caffeine in it. Caffeine,
we are here. Caffeine puts a man on her horse and a woman in
his grave. You know what's the trouble with you? You're an
expatriate. One of the worst type. Haven't you heard that? Nobody that ever left their own country ever wrote anything worth
printing. Not even in the newspapers."

He drank the coffee.

"You're an expatriate. You've lost touch with the soil. You get
precious. Fake European standards have ruined you. You drink
yourself to death. You become obsessed by sex. You spend all your
time talking, not working. You are an expatriate, see? You hang
around cafés."

"It sounds like a swell life," I said. "When do I work?"

"You don't work. One group claims women support you. Another group claims you're impotent."

"No," I said. "I just had an accident."

"Never mention that," Bill said. "That's the sort of thing that
can't be spoken of. That's what you ought to work up into a
mystery. Like Henry's bicycle."

He had been going splendidly, but he stopped. I was afraid he
thought he had hurt me with that crack about being impotent. I
wanted to start him again.

"It wasn't a bicycle," I said. "He was riding horseback."

"I heard it was a tricycle."

"Well," I said. "A plane is sort of like a tricycle. The joystick works the same way."

"But you don't pedal it."

"No," I said, "I guess you don't pedal it."

"Let's lay off that," Bill said.

"All right. I was just standing up for the tricycle."

"I think he's a good writer, too," Bill said. "And you're a hell of a good guy. Anybody ever tell you you were a good guy?"

"I'm not a good guy."

"Listen. You're a hell of a good guy, and I'm fonder of you than anybody on earth. I couldn't tell you that in New York. It'd mean I was a faggot. That was what the Civil War was about. Abraham Lincoln was a faggot. He was in love with General Grant. So was Jefferson Davis. Lincoln just freed the slaves on a bet. The Dred Scott case was framed by the Anti-Saloon League. Sex explains it all. The Colonel's Lady and Judy O'Grady are Lesbians under their skin."

He stopped.

"Want to hear some more?"

"Shoot," I said.

"I don't know any more. Tell you some more at lunch."

"Old Bill," I said.

"You bum!"

We packed the lunch and two bottles of wine in the rucksack, and Bill put it on. I carried the rod-case and the landing-nets slung over my back. We started up the road and then went across a meadow and found a path that crossed the fields and went toward the woods on the slope of the first hill. We walked across the fields on the sandy path. The fields were rolling and grassy and the grass was short from the sheep grazing. The cattle were up in the hills. We heard their bells in the woods.

The path crossed a stream on a foot-log. The log was surfaced off, and there was a sapling bent across for a rail. In the flat pool beside the stream tadpoles spotted the sand. We went up a steep bank and across the rolling fields. Looking back we saw Burguete, white houses and red roofs, and the white road with a truck going along it and the dust rising.

Beyond the fields we crossed another faster-flowing stream. A sandy road led down to the ford and beyond into the woods. The path crossed the stream on another foot-log below the ford, and joined the road, and we went into the woods.

It was a beech wood and the trees were very old. Their roots bulked above the ground and the branches were twisted. We walked on the road between the thick trunks of the old beeches and the sunlight came through the leaves in light patches on the grass. The trees were big, and the foliage was thick but it was not gloomy. There was no undergrowth, only the smooth grass, very green and fresh, and the big gray trees well spaced as though it were a park.

"This is country," Bill said.

The road went up a hill and we got into thick woods, and the road kept on climbing. Sometimes it dipped down but rose again steeply. All the time we heard the cattle in the woods. Finally, the road came out on the top of the hills. We were on the top of the height of land that was the highest part of the range of wooded hills we had seen from Burguete. There were wild strawberries growing on the sunny side of the ridge in a little clearing in the trees.

Ahead the road came out of the forest and went along the shoulder of the ridge of hills. The hills ahead were not wooded, and there were great fields of yellow gorse. Way off we saw the steep bluffs, dark with trees and jutting with gray stone, that marked the course of the Irati River.

"We have to follow this road along the ridge, cross these hills, go through the woods on the far hills, and come down to the Irati valley," I pointed out to Bill.

"That's a hell of a hike."

"It's too far to go and fish and come back the same day, comfortably."

"Comfortably. That's a nice word. We'll have to go like hell to get there and back and have any fishing at all."

It was a long walk and the country was very fine, but we were tired when we came down the steep road that led out of the wooded hills into the valley of the Rio de la Fabrica.

The road came out from the shadow of the woods into the hot sun. Ahead was a river-valley. Beyond the river was a steep hill. There was a field of buckwheat on the hill. We saw a white house under some trees on the hillside. It was very hot and we stopped under some trees beside a dam that crossed the river.

Bill put the pack against one of the trees and we jointed up the rods, put on the reels, tied on leaders, and got ready to fish.

"You're sure this thing has trout in it?" Bill asked.

"It's full of them."

"I'm going to fish a fly. You got any McGintys?"

"There's some in there."

"You going to fish bait?"

"Yeah. I'm going to fish the dam here."

"Well, I'll take the fly-book, then." He tied on a fly. "Where'd I better go? Up or down?"

"Down is the best. They're plenty up above, too."

Bill went down the bank.

"Take a worm can."

"No, I don't want one. If they won't take a fly I'll just flick it around."

Bill was down below watching the stream.

"Say," he called up against the noise of the dam. "How about putting the wine in that spring up the road?"

"All right," I shouted. Bill waved his hand and started down the stream. I found the two wine-bottles in the pack, and carried them up the road to where the water of a spring flowed out of an iron pipe. There was a board over the spring and I lifted it and, knocking the corks firmly into the bottles, lowered them down into the water. It was so cold my hand and wrist felt numbed. I put back the slab of wood, and hoped nobody would find the wine.

I got my rod that was leaning against the tree, took the bait-can and landing-net, and walked out onto the dam. It was built to provide a head of water for driving logs. The gate was up, and I sat on one of the squared timbers and watched the smooth apron of water before the river tumbled into the falls. In the white water at the foot of the dam it was deep. As I baited up, a trout shot up out of the white water into the falls and was carried down. Before I could finish baiting, another trout jumped at the falls, making the same lovely arc and disappearing into the water that was thundering down. I put on a good-sized sinker and dropped into the white water close to the edge of the timbers of the dam.

I did not feel the first trout strike. When I started to pull up I felt that I had one and brought him, fighting and bending the rod almost double, out of the boiling water at the foot of the falls, and swung him up and onto the dam. He was a good trout, and I banged his head against the timber so that he quivered out straight, and then slipped him into my bag.

While I had him on, several trout had jumped at the falls. As soon as I baited up and dropped in again I hooked another and brought him in the same way. In a little while I had six. They were all about the same size. I laid them out, side by side, all their heads pointing the same way, and looked at them. They were beautifully colored and firm and hard from the cold water. It was a hot day, so I slit them all and shucked out the insides, gills and all, and tossed them over across the river. I took the trout ashore, washed them in the cold, smoothly heavy water above the dam, and then picked some ferns and packed them all in the bag, three trout on a layer of ferns, then another layer of ferns, then three more trout, and then covered them with ferns. They looked nice in the ferns, and now the bag was bulky, and I put it in the shade of the tree.

It was very hot on the dam, so I put my worm-can in the shade with the bag, and got a book out of the pack and settled down under the tree to read until Bill should come up for lunch.

It was a little past noon and there was not much shade, but I sat against the trunk of two of the trees that grew together, and read. The book was something by A. E. W. Mason, and I was reading a wonderful story about a man who had been frozen in the Alps and then fallen into a glacier and disappeared, and his bride was going to wait twenty-four years exactly for his body to come out on the moraine, while her true love waited too, and they were still waiting when Bill came up.

"Get any?" he asked. He had his rod and his bag and his net all in one hand, and he was sweating. I hadn't heard him come up, because of the noise from the dam.

"Six. What did you get?"

Bill sat down, opened up his bag, laid a big trout on the grass. He took out three more, each one a little bigger than the last, and laid them side by side in the shade from the tree. His face was sweaty and happy.

"How are yours?"

"Smaller."

"Let's see them."

"They're packed."

"How big are they really?"

"They're all about the size of your smallest."

"You're not holding out on me?"

"I wish I were."

"Get them all on worms?"

"Yes."

"You lazy bum!"

Bill put the trout in the bag and started for the river, swinging the open bag. He was wet from the waist down and I knew he must have been wading the stream.

I walked up the road and got out the two bottles of wine. They were cold. Moisture beaded on the bottles as I walked back to the trees. I spread the lunch on a newspaper, and uncorked one of the bottles and leaned the other against a tree. Bill came up drying his hands, his bag plump with ferns.

"Let's see that bottle," he said. He pulled the cork, and tipped up the bottle and drank. "Whew! That makes my eyes ache."

"Let's try it."

The wine was icy cold and tasted faintly rusty.

"That's not such filthy wine," Bill said.

"The cold helps it," I said.

We unwrapped the little parcels of lunch.

"Chicken."

"There's hard-boiled eggs."

"Find any salt?"

"First the egg," said Bill. "Then the chicken. Even Bryan could see that."

"He's dead. I read it in the paper yesterday."

"No. Not really?"

"Yes. Bryan's dead."

Bill laid down the egg he was peeling.

"Gentlemen," he said, and unwrapped a drumstick from a piece of newspaper. "I reverse the order. For Bryan's sake. As a tribute to the Great Commoner. First the chicken; then the egg."

"Wonder what day God created the chicken?"

"Oh," said Bill, sucking the drumstick, "how should we know? We should not question. Our stay on earth is not for long. Let us rejoice and believe and give thanks."

"Eat an egg."

Bill gestured with the drumstick in one hand and the bottle of wine in the other.

"Let us rejoice in our blessings. Let us utilize the fowls of the air. Let us utilize the product of the vine. Will you utilize a little, brother?"

"After you, brother."

Bill took a long drink.

"Utilize a little, brother," he handed me the bottle. "Let us not doubt, brother. Let us not pry into the holy mysteries of the hencoop with simian fingers. Let us accept on faith and simply say —I want you to join with me in saying— What shall we say, brother?" He pointed the drumstick at me and went on. "Let me tell you. We will say, and I for one am proud to say—and I want you to say with me, on your knees, brother. Let no man be ashamed to kneel here in the great out-of-doors. Remember the woods were God's first temples. Let us kneel and say: 'Don't eat that, Lady—that's Mencken.'"

"Here," I said. "Utilize a little of this."

We uncorked the other bottle.

"What's the matter?" I said. "Didn't you like Bryan?"

"I loved Bryan," said Bill. "We were like brothers."

"Where did you know him?"

"He and Mencken and I all went to Holy Cross together."

"And Frankie Fritsch."

"It's a lie. Frankie Fritsch went to Fordham."

"Well," I said, "I went to Loyola with Bishop Manning."

"It's a lie," Bill said. "I went to Loyola with Bishop Manning myself."

"You're cock-eyed," I said.

"On wine?"

"Why not?"

"It's the humidity," Bill said. "They ought to take this damn humidity away."

"Have another shot."

"Is this all we've got?"

"Only the two bottles."

"Do you know what you are?" Bill looked at the bottle affectionately.

"No," I said.

"You're in the pay of the Anti-Saloon League."

"I went to Notre Dame with Wayne B. Wheeler."

"It's a lie," said Bill. "I went to Austin Business College with Wayne B. Wheeler. He was class president."

"Well," I said, "the saloon must go."

"You're right there, old classmate," Bill said. "The saloon must go, and I will take it with me."

"You're cock-eyed."

"On wine?"

"On wine."

"Well, maybe I am."

"Want to take a nap?"

"All right."

We lay with our heads in the shade and looked up into the trees.

"You asleep?"

"No," Bill said. "I was thinking."

I shut my eyes. It felt good lying on the ground.

"Say," Bill said, "what about this Brett business?"

"What about it?"

"Were you ever in love with her?"

"Sure."

"For how long?"

"Off and on for a hell of a long time."

"Oh, hell!" Bill said. "I'm sorry, fella."

"It's all right," I said. "I don't give a damn any more."

"Really?"

"Really. Only I'd a hell of a lot rather not talk about it."

"You aren't sore I asked you?"

"Why the hell should I be?"

"I'm going to sleep," Bill said. He put a newspaper over hi face.

"Listen, Jake," he said, "are you really a Catholic?"

"Technically."

"What does that mean?"

"I don't know."

"All right, I'll go to sleep now," he said. "Don't keep me awake by talking so much."

I went to sleep, too. When I woke up Bill was packing the rucksack. It was late in the afternoon and the shadow from the trees was long and went out over the dam. I was stiff from sleeping on the ground.

"What did you do? Wake up?" Bill asked. "Why didn't you spend the night?" I stretched and rubbed my eyes.

"I had a lovely dream," Bill said. "I don't remember what it was about, but it was a lovely dream."

"I don't think I dreamt."

"You ought to dream," Bill said. "All our biggest business men have been dreamers. Look at Ford. Look at President Coolidge. Look at Rockefeller. Look at Jo Davidson."

I disjointed my rod and Bill's and packed them in the rod-case. I put the reels in the tackle-bag. Bill had packed the rucksack and we put one of the trout-bags in. I carried the other.

"Well," said Bill, "have we got everything?"

"The worms."

"Your worms. Put them in there."

He had the pack on his back and I put the worm-cans in one
of the outside flap pockets.

"You got everything now?"

I looked around on the grass at the foot of the elm-trees.

"Yes."

We started up the road into the woods. It was a long walk
home to Burguete, and it was dark when we came down across the
fields to the road, and along the road between the houses of the
town, their windows lighted, to the inn.

We stayed five days at Burguete and had good fishing. The
nights were cold and the days were hot, and there was always a
breeze even in the heat of the day. It was hot enough so that it
felt good to wade in a cold stream, and the sun dried you when
you came out and sat on the bank. We found a stream with a
pool deep enough to swim in. In the evenings we played three-
handed bridge with an Englishman named Harris, who had
walked over from Saint Jean Pied de Port and was stopping at
the inn for the fishing. He was very pleasant and went with us
twice to the Irati River. There was no word from Robert Cohn
nor from Brett and Mike.

CHAPTER XIII

ONE morning I went down to breakfast and the Englishman, Harris, was already at the table. He was reading the paper through spectacles. He looked up and smiled.

"Good morning," he said. "Letter for you. I stopped at the post and they gave it me with mine."

The letter was at my place at the table, leaning against a coffee-cup. Harris was reading the paper again. I opened the letter. It had been forwarded from Pamplona. It was dated San Sebastian, Sunday:

DEAR JAKE,

We got here Friday, Brett passed out on the train, so brought her here for 3 days rest with old friends of ours. We go to Montoya Hotel Pamplona Tuesday, arriving at I don't know what hour. Will you send a note by the bus to tell us what to do to rejoin you all on Wednesday. All our love and sorry to be late, but Brett was really done in and will be quite all right by Tues. and is practically so now. I know her so well and try to look after her but it's not so easy. Love to all the chaps,

MICHAEL.

"What day of the week is it?" I asked Harris.

"Wednesday, I think. Yes, quite. Wednesday. Wonderful how one loses track of the days up here in the mountains."

"Yes. We've been here nearly a week."

"I hope you're not thinking of leaving?"

"Yes. We'll go in on the afternoon bus, I'm afraid."

"What a rotten business. I had hoped we'd all have another go at the Irati together."

"We have to go *into* Pamplona. We're meeting people there."

"What rotten luck for me. We've had a jolly time here at Burguete."

"Come on in to Pamplona. We can play some bridge there, and there's going to be a damned fine fiesta."

"I'd like to. Awfully nice of you to ask me. I'd best stop on here, though. I've not much more time to fish."

"You want those big ones in the Irati."

"I say, I do, you know. They're enormous trout there."

"I'd like to try them once more."

"Do. Stop over another day. Be a good chap."

"We really have to get into town," I said.

"What a pity."

After breakfast Bill and I were sitting warming in the sun on a bench out in front of the inn and talking it over. I saw a girl coming up the road from the centre of the town. She stopped in front of us and took a telegram out of the leather wallet that hung against her skirt.

"Por ustedes?"

I looked at it. The address was: "Barnes, Burguete."

"Yes. It's for us."

She brought out a book for me to sign, and I gave her a couple of coppers. The telegram was in Spanish: "Vengo Jueves Cohn."

I handed it to Bill.

"What does the word Cohn mean?" he asked.

"What a lousy telegram!" I said. "He could send ten words for the same price. 'I come Thursday'. That gives you a lot of dope, doesn't it?"

"It gives you all the dope that's of interest to Cohn."

"We're going in, anyway," I said. "There's no use trying to move Brett and Mike out here and back before the fiesta. Should we answer it?"

"We might as well," said Bill. "There's no need for us to be snooty."

We walked up to the post-office and asked for a telegraph blank.

"What will we say?" Bill asked.

"'Arriving to-night.' That's enough."

We paid for the message and walked back to the inn. Harris was there and the three of us walked up to Roncesvalles. We went through the monastery.

"It's a remarkable place," Harris said, when we came out. "But you know I'm not much on those sort of places."

"Me either," Bill said.

"It's a remarkable place, though," Harris said. "I wouldn't not have seen it. I'd been intending coming up each day."

"It isn't the same as fishing, though, is it?" Bill asked. He liked Harris.

"I say not."

We were standing in front of the old chapel of the monastery.

"Isn't that a pub across the way?" Harris asked. "Or do my eyes deceive me?"

"It has the look of a pub," Bill said.

"It looks to me like a pub," I said.

"I say," said Harris, "let's utilize it." He had taken up utilizing from Bill.

We had a bottle of wine apiece. Harris would not let us pay.

He talked Spanish quite well, and the innkeeper would not take our money.

"I say. You don't know what it's meant to me to have you chaps up here."

"We've had a grand time, Harris."

Harris was a little tight.

"I say. Really you don't know how much it means. I've not had much fun since the war."

"We'll fish together again, some time. Don't you forget it, Harris."

"We must. We *have* had such a jolly good time."

"How about another bottle around?"

"Jolly good idea," said Harris.

"This is mine," said Bill. "Or we don't drink it."

"I wish you'd let me pay for it. It *does* give me pleasure, you know."

"This is going to give me pleasure," Bill said.

The innkeeper brought in the fourth bottle. We had kept the same glasses. Harris lifted his glass.

"I say. You know this does utilize well."

Bill slapped him on the back.

"Good old Harris."

"I say. You know my name isn't really Harris. It's Wilson Harris. All one name. With a hyphen, you know."

"Good old Wilson-Harris," Bill said. "We call you Harris because we're so fond of you."

"I say, Barnes. You don't know what this all means to me."

"Come on and utilize another glass," I said.

"Barnes. Really, Barnes, you can't know. That's all."

"Drink up, Harris."

We walked back down the road from Roncesvalles with Harris between us. We had lunch at the inn and Harris went with us to the bus. He gave us his card, with his address in London and his club and his business address, and as we got on the bus he handed us each an envelope. I opened mine and there were a dozen flies in it. Harris had tied them himself. He tied all his own flies.

"I say, Harris—" I began.

"No, no!" he said. He was climbing down from the bus. "They're not first-rate flies at all. I only thought if you fished them some time it might remind you of what a good time we had."

The bus started. Harris stood in front of the post-office. He waved. As we started along the road he turned and walked back toward the inn.

"Say, wasn't that Harris nice?" Bill said.

"I think he really did have a good time."

"Harris? You bet he did."

"I wish he'd come into Pamplona."

"He wanted to fish."

"Yes. You couldn't tell how English would mix with each other, anyway."

"I suppose not."

We got into Pamplona late in the afternoon and the bus stopped in front of the Hotel Montoya. Out in the plaza they were stringing electric-light wires to light the plaza for the fiesta. A few kids came up when the bus stopped, and a customs officer for the town made all the people getting down from the bus open their bundles on the sidewalk. We went into the hotel and on the stairs I met Montoya. He shook hands with us, smiling in his embarrassed way.

"Your friends are here," he said.

"Mr. Campbell?"

"Yes. Mr. Cohn and Mr. Campbell and Lady Ashley."

He smiled as though there were something I would hear about.

"When did they get in?"

"Yesterday. I've saved you the rooms you had."

"That's fine. Did you give Mr. Campbell the room on the plaza?"

"Yes. All the rooms we looked at."

"Where are our friends now?"

"I think they went to the pelota."

"And how about the bulls?"

Montoya smiled. "To-night," he said. "To-night at seven o'clock they bring in the Villar bulls, and to-morrow come the Miuras. Do you all go down?"

"Oh, yes. They've never seen a desencajonada."

Montoya put his hand on my shoulder.

"I'll see you there."

He smiled again. He always smiled as though bull-fighting were a very special secret between the two of us; a rather shocking but really very deep secret that we knew about. He always smiled as though there were something lewd about the secret to outsiders, but that it was something that we understood. It would not do to expose it to people who would not understand.

"Your friend, is he aficionado, too?" Montoya smiled at Bill.

"Yes. He came all the way from New York to see the San Fermines."

"Yes?" Montoya politely disbelieved. "But he's not aficionado like you."

He put his hand on my shoulder again embarrassedly.

"Yes," I said. "He's a real aficionado."

"But he's not aficionado like you are."

Aficion means passion. An aficionado is one who is passionate about the bull-fights. All the good bull-fighters stayed at Montoya's hotel; that is, those with aficion stayed there. The commercial bull-fighters stayed once, perhaps, and then did not come back. The good ones came each year. In Montoya's room were their photographs. The photographs were dedicated to Juanito Montoya or to his sister. The photographs of bull-fighters Montoya had really believed in were framed. Photographs of bull-fighters who had been without aficion Montoya kept in a drawer of his desk. They often had the most flattering inscriptions. But they did not mean anything. One day Montoya took them all out and dropped them in the waste-basket. He did not want them around.

We often talked about bulls and bull-fighters. I had stopped at the Montoya for several years. We never talked for very long at a time. It was simply the pleasure of discovering what we each felt. Men would come in from distant towns and before they left Pamplona stop and talk for a few minutes with Montoya about bulls. These men were aficionados. Those who were aficionados could always get rooms even when the hotel was full. Montoya introduced me to some of them. They were always very polite at first, and it amused them very much that I should be an American. Somehow it was taken for granted that an American could not have aficion. He might simulate it or confuse it with excitement, but he could not really have it. When they saw that I had aficion, and there was no password, no set questions that could bring it out, rather it was a sort of oral spiritual examination with the questions always a little on the defensive and never apparent, there was this same embarrassed putting the hand on the shoulder, or a "Buen hombre." But nearly always there was the actual touching. It seemed as though they wanted to touch you to make it certain.

Montoya could forgive anything of a bull-fighter who had aficion. He could forgive attacks of nerves, panic, bad unexplainable actions, all sorts of lapses. For one who had aficion he could forgive anything. At once he forgave me all my friends. Without his ever saying anything they were simply a little something shameful between us, like the spilling open of the horses in bull fighting.

Bill had gone up-stairs as we came in, and I found him washing and changing in his room.

"Well," he said, "talk a lot of Spanish?"

"He was telling me about the bulls coming in tonight."

"Let's find the gang and go down."

"All right. They'll probably be at the café."

"Have you got tickets?"

"Yes. I got them for all the unloadings."

"What's it like?" He was pulling his cheek before the glass, looking to see if there were unshaved patches under the line of the jaw.

"It's pretty good," I said. "They let the bulls out of the cages one at a time, and they have steers in the corral to receive them and keep them from fighting, and the bulls tear in at the steers and the steers run around like old maids trying to quiet them down."

"Do they ever gore the steers?"

"Sure. Sometimes they go right after them and kill them."

"Can't the steers do anything?"

"No. They're trying to make friends."

"What do they have them in for?"

"To quiet down the bulls and keep them from breaking their horns against the stone walls, or goring each other."

"Must be swell being a steer."

We went down the stairs and out of the door and walked across the square toward the café Iruña. There were two lonely looking ticket-houses standing in the square. Their windows, marked SOL, SOL Y SOMBRA, and SOMBRA, were shut. They would not open until the day before the fiesta.

Across the square the white wicker tables and chairs of the Iruña extended out beyond the Arcade to the edge of the street. I looked for Brett and Mike at the tables. There they were. Brett

and Mike and Robert Cohn. Brett was wearing a Basque beret.
So was Mike. Robert Cohn was bare-headed and wearing his spectacles. Brett saw us coming and waved. Her eyes crinkled up as
we came up to the table.

"Hello, you chaps!" she called.

Brett was happy. Mike had a way of getting an intensity of
feeling into shaking hands. Robert Cohn shook hands because we
were back.

"Where the hell have you been?" I asked.

"I brought them up here," Cohn said.

"What rot," Brett said. "We'd have gotten here earlier if you
hadn't come."

"You'd never have gotten here."

"What rot! You chaps are brown. Look at Bill."

"Did you get good fishing?" Mike asked. "We wanted to join
you."

"It wasn't bad. We missed you."

"I wanted to come," Cohn said, "but I thought I ought to bring
them."

"You bring us. What rot."

"Was it really good?" Mike asked. "Did you take many?"

"Some days we took a dozen apiece. There was an Englishman
up there."

"Named Harris," Bill said. "Ever know him, Mike? He was in
the war, too."

"Fortunate fellow," Mike said. "What times we had. How I
wish those dear days were back."

"Don't be an ass."

"Were you in the war, Mike?" Cohn asked.

"Was I not."

"He was a very distinguished soldier," Brett said. "Tell them
about the time your horse bolted down Piccadilly."

"I'll not. I've told that four times."

"You never told me," Robert Cohn said.

"I'll not tell that story. It reflects discredit on me."

"Tell them about your medals."

"I'll not. That story reflects great discredit on me."

"What story's that?"

"Brett will tell you. She tells all the stories that reflect discredit on me."

"Go on. Tell it, Brett."

"Should I?"

"I'll tell it myself."

"What medals have you got, Mike?"

"I haven't got any medals."

"You must have some."

"I suppose I've the usual medals. But I never sent in for them. One time there was this wopping big dinner and the Prince of Wales was to be there, and the cards said medals will be worn. So naturally I had no medals, and I stopped at my tailor's and he was impressed by the invitation, and I thought that's a good piece of business, and I said to him: 'You've got to fix me up with some medals.' He said: 'What medals, sir?' And I said: 'Oh, any medals. Just give me a few medals.' So he said: 'What medals *have* you, sir?' And I said: 'How should I know?' Did he think I spent all my time reading the bloody gazette? 'Just give me a good lot. Pick them out yourself.' So he got me some medals, you know, miniature medals, and handed me the box, and I put it in my pocket and forgot it. Well, I went to the dinner, and it was the night they'd shot Henry Wilson, so the Prince didn't come and the King didn't come, and no one wore any medals, and all these coves were busy taking off their medals, and I had mine in my pocket."

He stopped for us to laugh.

"Is that all?"

"That's all. Perhaps I didn't tell it right."

"You didn't," said Brett. "But no matter."

We were all laughing.

"Ah, yes," said Mike. "I know now. It was a damn dull dinner, and I couldn't stick it, so I left. Later on in the evening I found the box in my pocket. What's this? I said. Medals? Bloody military medals? So I cut them all off their backing—you know, they put them on a strip—and gave them all around. Gave one to each girl. Form of souvenir. They thought I was hell's own shakes of a soldier. Give away medals in a night club. Dashing fellow."

"Tell the rest," Brett said.

"Don't you think that was funny?" Mike asked. We were all laughing. "It was. I swear it was. Any rate, my tailor wrote me and wanted the medals back. Sent a man around. Kept on writing for months. Seems some chap had left them to be cleaned. Frightfully military cove. Set hell's own store by them." Mike paused. "Rotten luck for the tailor," he said.

"You don't mean it," Bill said. "I should think it would have been grand for the tailor."

"Frightfully good tailor. Never believe it to see me now," Mike said. "I used to pay him a hundred pounds a year just to keep him quiet. So he wouldn't send me any bills. Frightful blow to him when I went bankrupt. It was right after the medals. Gave his letters rather a bitter tone."

"How did you go bankrupt?" Bill asked.

"Two ways," Mike said. "Gradually and then suddenly."

"What brought it on?"

"Friends," said Mike. "I had a lot of friends. False friends. Then I had creditors, too. Probably had more creditors than anybody in England."

"Tell them about in the court," Brett said.

"I don't remember," Mike said. "I was just a little tight."

"Tight!" Brett exclaimed. "You were blind!"

"Extraordinary thing," Mike said. "Met my former partner the other day. Offered to buy me a drink."

"Tell them about your learned counsel," Brett said.

"I will not," Mike said. "My learned counsel was blind, too. I say this is a gloomy subject. Are we going down and see these bulls unloaded or not?"

"Let's go down."

We called the waiter, paid, and started to walk through the town. I started off walking with Brett, but Robert Cohn came up and joined her on the other side. The three of us walked along, past the Ayuntamiento with the banners hung from the balcony, down past the market and down past the steep street that led to the bridge across the Arga. There were many people walking to go and see the bulls, and carriages drove down the hill and across the bridge, the drivers, the horses, and the whips rising above the walking people in the street. Across the bridge we turned up a road to the corrals. We passed a wine-shop with a sign in the window: Good Wine 30 Centimes A Liter.

"That's where we'll go when funds get low," Brett said.

The woman standing in the door of the wine-shop looked at us as we passed. She called to some one in the house and three girls came to the window and stared. They were staring at Brett.

At the gate of the corrals two men took tickets from the people that went in. We went in through the gate. There were trees inside and a low, stone house. At the far end was the stone wall of the corrals, with apertures in the stone that were like loopholes running all along the face of each corral. A ladder led up to the top of the wall, and people were climbing up the ladder and spreading down to stand on the walls that separated the two corrals. As we came up the ladder, walking across the grass under the trees, we passed the big, gray painted cages with the bulls in them. There was one bull in each travelling-box. They had come by train from a bull-breeding ranch in Castile, and had been un-loaded off flat-cars at the station and brought up here to be let out of their cages into the corrals. Each cage was stencilled with the name and the brand of the bull-breeder.

We climbed up and found a place on the wall looking down into the corral. The stone walls were whitewashed, and there was straw on the ground and wooden feed-boxes and water-troughs set against the wall.

"Look up there," I said.

Beyond the river rose the plateau of the town. All along the old walls and ramparts people were standing. The three lines of fortifications made three black lines of people. Above the walls there were heads in the windows of the houses. At the far end of the plateau boys had climbed into the trees.

"They must think something is going to happen," Brett said.

"They want to see the bulls."

Mike and Bill were on the other wall across the pit of the corral. They waved to us. People who had come late were standing be-hind us, pressing against us when other people crowded them.

"Why don't they start?" Robert Cohn asked.

A single mule was hitched to one of the cages and dragged it up against the gate in the corral wall. The men shoved and lifted it with crowbars into position against the gate. Men were stand-ing on the wall ready to pull up the gate of the corral and then the gate of the cage. At the other end of the corral a gate opened and two steers came in, swaying their heads and trotting, their lean flanks swinging. They stood together at the far end, their heads toward the gate where the bull would enter.

"They don't look happy," Brett said.

The men on top of the wall leaned back and pulled up the door of the corral. Then they pulled up the door of the cage.

I leaned way over the wall and tried to see into the cage. It was dark. Some one rapped on the cage with an iron bar. Inside something seemed to explode. The bull, striking into the wood from side to side with his horns, made a great noise. Then I saw a dark muzzle and the shadow of horns, and then, with a clattering on the wood in the hollow box, the bull charged and came out into the corral, skidding with his forefeet in the straw as he stopped, his head up, the great hump of muscle on his neck swollen tight, his body muscles quivering as he looked up at the crowd on the stone walls. The two steers backed away against the wall, their heads sunken, their eyes watching the bull.

The bull saw them and charged. A man shouted from behind one of the boxes and slapped his hat against the planks, and the bull, before he reached the steer, turned, gathered himself and charged where the man had been, trying to reach him behind the planks with a half-dozen quick, searching drives with the right horn.

"My God, isn't he beautiful?" Brett said. We were looking right down on him.

"Look how he knows how to use his horns," I said. 'He's got a left and a right just like a boxer."

"Not really?"

"You watch."

"It goes too fast."

"Wait. There'll be another one in a minute."

They had backed up another cage into the entrance. In the far corner a man, from behind one of the plank shelters, attracted the bull, and while the bull was facing away the gate was pulled up and a second bull came out into the corral.

He charged straight for the steers and two men ran out from behind the planks and shouted, to turn him. He did not change his direction and the men shouted: "Hah! Hah! Toro!" and waved their arms; the two steers turned sideways to take the shock, and the bull drove into one of the steers.

"Don't look," I said to Brett. She was watching, fascinated.

"Fine," I said. "If it doesn't buck you."

"I saw it," she said. "I saw him shift from his left to his right horn."

"Damn good!"

The steer was down now, his neck stretched out, his head twisted, he lay the way he had fallen. Suddenly the bull left off and made for the other steer which had been standing at the far end, his head swinging, watching it all. The steer ran awkwardly and the bull caught him, hooked him lightly in the flank, and then turned away and looked up at the crowd on the walls, his crest of muscle rising. The steer came up to him and made as though to nose at him and the bull hooked perfunctorily. The next time he nosed at the steer and then the two of them trotted over to the other bull.

When the next bull came out, all three, the two bulls and the steer, stood together, their heads side by side, their horns against the newcomer. In a few minutes the steer picked the new bull up, quieted him down, and made him one of the herd. When the last two bulls had been unloaded the herd were all together.

The steer who had been gored had gotten to his feet and stood against the stone wall. None of the bulls came near him, and he did not attempt to join the herd.

We climbed down from the wall with the crowd, and had a last look at the bulls through the loopholes in the wall of the corral. They were all quiet now, their heads down. We got a carriage outside and rode up to the café. Mike and Bill came in half an hour later. They had stopped on the way for several drinks.

We were sitting in the café.

"That's an extraordinary business." Brett said.

"Will those last ones fight as well as the first?" Robert Cohn asked. "They seemed to quiet down awfully fast."

"They all know each other," I said. "They're only dangerous when they're alone, or only two or three of them together."

"What do you mean, dangerous?" Bill said. "They all looked dangerous to me."

"They only want to kill when they're alone. Of course, if you went in there you'd probably detach one of them from the herd, and he'd be dangerous."

"That's too complicated," Bill said. "Don't you ever detach me from the herd, Mike."

"I say," Mike said, "they *were* fine bulls, weren't they? Did you see their horns?"

"Did I not," said Brett. "I had no idea what they were like."

"Did you see the one hit that steer?" Mike asked. "That was extraordinary."

"It's no life being a steer," Robert Cohn said.

"Don't you think so?" Mike said. "I would have thought you'd loved being a steer, Robert."

"What do you mean, Mike?"

"They lead such a quiet life. They never say anything and they're always hanging about so."

We were embarrassed. Bill laughed. Robert Cohn was angry. Mike went on talking.

"I should think you'd love it. You'd never have to say a word. Come on, Robert. Do say something. Don't just sit there."

"I said something, Mike. Don't you remember? About the steers."

"Oh, say something more. Say something funny. Can't you see we're all having a good time here?"

"Come off it, Michael. You're drunk," Brett said.

"I'm not drunk. I'm quite serious. *Is* Robert Cohn going to follow Brett around like a steer all the time?"

"Shut up, Michael. Try and show a little breeding."

"Breeding be damned. Who has any breeding, anyway, except the bulls? Aren't the bulls lovely? Don't you like them, Bill? Why don't you say something, Robert? Don't sit there looking like a bloody funeral. What if Brett did sleep with you? She's slept with lots of better people than you."

"Shut up," Cohn said. He stood up. "Shut up, Mike."

"Oh, don't stand up and act as though you were going to hit me. That won't make any difference to me. Tell me, Robert. Why do you follow Brett around like a poor bloody steer? Don't you know you're not wanted? I know when I'm not wanted. Why don't you know when you're not wanted? You came down to San Sebastian where you weren't wanted, and followed Brett around like a bloody steer. Do you think that's right?"

"Shut up. You're drunk."

"Perhaps I am drunk. Why aren't you drunk? Why don't you ever get drunk, Robert? You know you didn't have a good time at San Sebastian because none of our friends would invite you on any of the parties. You can't blame them hardly. Can you? I asked them to. They wouldn't do it. You can't blame them, now. Can you? Now, answer me. Can you blame them?"

"Go to hell, Mike."

"I can't blame them. Can you blame them? Why do you follow Brett around? Haven't you any manners? How do you think it makes *me* feel?"

"You're a splendid one to talk about manners," Brett said. "You've such lovely manners."

"Come on, Robert," Bill said.

"What do you follow her around for?"

Bill stood up and took hold of Cohn.

"Don't go," Mike said. "Robert Cohn's going to buy a drink."

Bill went off with Cohn. Cohn's face was sallow. Mike went on talking. I sat and listened for a while. Brett looked disgusted.

"I say, Michael, you might not be such a bloody ass," she interrupted. "I'm not saying he's not right, you know." She turned to me.

The emotion left Mike's voice. We were all friends together.

"I'm not so damn drunk as I sounded," he said.

"I know you're not," Brett said.

"We're none of us sober," I said.

"I didn't say anything I didn't mean."

"But you put it so badly," Brett laughed.

"He was an ass, though. He came down to San Sebastian where he damn well wasn't wanted. He hung around Brett and just *looked* at her. It made me damned well sick."

"He did behave very badly," Brett said.

"Mark you. Brett's had affairs with men before. She tells me all about everything. She gave me this chap Cohn's letters to read. I wouldn't read them."

"Damned noble of you."

"No, listen, Jake. Brett's gone off with men. But they weren't ever Jews, and they didn't come and hang about afterward."

"Damned good chaps," Brett said. "It's all rot to talk about it. Michael and I understand each other."

"She gave me Robert Cohn's letters. I wouldn't read them."

"You wouldn't read any letters, darling. You wouldn't read mine."

"I can't read letters," Mike said. "Funny, isn't it?"

"You can't read anything."

"No. You're wrong there. I read quite a bit. I read when I'm at home."

"You'll be writing next," Brett said. "Come on, Michael. Dc buck up. You've got to go through with this thing now. He's here Don't spoil the fiesta."

"Well, let him behave, then."

"He'll behave. I'll tell him."

"You tell him, Jake. Tell him either he must behave or get out."

"Yes," I said, "it would be nice for me to tell him."

"Look, Brett. Tell Jake what Robert calls you. That *is* perfect, you know."

"Oh, no. I can't."

"Go on. We're all friends. Aren't we all friends, Jake?"

"I can't tell him. It's too ridiculous."

"I'll tell him."

"You won't, Michael. Don't be an ass."

"He calls her Circe," Mike said. "He claims she turns men into swine. Damn good. I wish I were one of these literary chaps."

"He'd be good, you know," Brett said. "He writes a good letter."

"I know," I said. "He wrote me from San Sebastian."

"That was nothing," Brett said. "He can write a damned amusing letter."

"She made me write that. She was supposed to be ill."

"I damned well was, too."

"Come on," I said, "we must go in and eat."

"How should I meet Cohn?" Mike said.

"Just act as though nothing had happened."

"It's quite all right with me," Mike said. "I'm not embarrassed."

"If he says anything, just say you were tight."

"Quite. And the funny thing is I think I was tight."

"Come on," Brett said. "Are these poisonous things paid for? I must bathe before dinner."

We walked across the square. It was dark and all around the square were the lights from the cafés under the arcades. We walked across the gravel under the trees to the hotel.

They went up-stairs and I stopped to speak with Montoya.

"Well, how did you like the bulls?" he asked.

"Good. They were nice bulls."

"They're all right"—Montoya shook his head—"but they're not too good."

"What didn't you like about them?"

"I don't know. They just didn't give me the feeling that they were so good."

"I know what you mean."

"They're all right."

"Yes. They're all right."

"How did your friends like them?"

"Fine."

"Good," Montoya said.

I went up-stairs. Bill was in his room standing on the balcony looking out at the square. I stood beside him.

"Where's Cohn?"

"Up-stairs in his room."

"How does he feel?"

"Like hell, naturally. Mike was awful. He's terrible when he's tight."

"He wasn't so tight."

"The hell he wasn't. I know what we had before we came to the café."

"He sobered up afterward."

"Good. He was terrible. I don't like Cohn, God knows, and I think it was a silly trick for him to go down to San Sebastian, but nobody has any business to talk like Mike."

"How'd you like the bulls?"

"Grand. It's grand the way they bring them out."

"To-morrow come the Miuras."

"When does the fiesta start?"

"Day after to-morrow."

"We've got to keep Mike from getting so tight. That kind of stuff is terrible."

"We'd better get cleaned up for supper."

"Yes. That will be a pleasant meal."

"Won't it?"

As a matter of fact, supper was a pleasant meal. Brett wore a black, sleeveless evening dress. She looked quite beautiful. Mike acted as though nothing had happened. I had to go up and bring Robert Cohn down. He was reserved and formal, and his face was still taut and sallow, but he cheered up finally. He could not stop looking at Brett. It seemed to make him happy. It must have been pleasant for him to see her looking so lovely, and know he had been away with her and that every one knew it. They could not take that away from him. Bill was very funny. So was Michael. They were good together.

It was like certain dinners I remember from the war. There was much wine, an ignored tension, and a feeling of things coming that you could not prevent happening. Under the wine I lost the disgusted feeling and was happy. It seemed they were all such nice people.

CHAPTER XIV

I DO not know what time I got to bed. I remember undressing, putting on a bathrobe, and standing out on the balcony. I knew I was quite drunk, and when I came in I put on the light over the head of the bed and started to read. I was reading a book by Turgenieff. Probably I read the same two pages over several times. It was one of the stories in "A Sportsman's Sketches." I had read it before, but it seemed quite new. The country became very clear and the feeling of pressure in my head seemed to loosen. I was very drunk and I did not want to shut my eyes because the room would go round and round. If I kept on reading that feeling would pass.

I heard Brett and Robert Cohn come up the stairs. Cohn said good night outside the door and went on up to his room. I heard Brett go into the room next door. Mike was already in bed. He had come in with me an hour before. He woke as she came in, and they talked together. I heard them laugh. I turned off the light and tried to go to sleep. It was not necessary to read any more. I could shut my eyes without getting the wheeling sensation. But I could not sleep. There is no reason why because it is dark you should look at things differently from when it is light. The hell there isn't!

I figured that all out once, and for six months I never slept with the electric light off. That was another bright idea. To hell with women, anyway. To hell with you. Brett Ashley.

Women made such swell friends. Awfully swell. In the first place, you had to be in love with a woman to have a basis of friendship. I had been having Brett for a friend. I had not been thinking about her side of it. I had been getting something for nothing. That only delayed the presentation of the bill. The bill always came. That was one of the swell things you could count on.

I thought I had paid for everything. Not like the woman pays and pays and pays. No idea of retribution or punishment. Just exchange of values. You gave up something and got something else. Or you worked for something. You paid some way for everything that was any good. I paid my way into enough things that I liked, so that I had a good time. Either you paid by learning about them, or by experience, or by taking chances, or by money. Enjoying living was learning to get your money's worth and knowing when you had it. You could get your money's worth. The world was a good place to buy in. It seemed like a fine philosophy. In five years, I thought, it will seem just as silly as all the other fine philosophies I've had.

Perhaps that wasn't true, though. Perhaps as you went along you did learn something. I did not care what it was all about. All I wanted to know was how to live in it. Maybe if you found out how to live in it you learned from that what it was all about.

I wished Mike would not behave so terribly to Cohn, though. Mike was a bad drunk. Brett was a good drunk. Bill was a good drunk. Cohn was never drunk. Mike was unpleasant after he passed a certain point. I liked to see him hurt Cohn. I wished he would not do it, though, because afterward it made me disgusted at myself. That was morality; things that made you disgusted afterward. No, that must be immorality. That was a large statement. What a lot of bilge I could think up at night. What rot, I could hear Brett say it. What rot! When you were with English you got into the habit of using English expressions in your thinking The English spoken language—the upper classes, anyway—must have fewer words than the Eskimo. Of course I didn't know anything about the Eskimo. Maybe the Eskimo was a fine language. Say the Cherokee. I didn't know anything about the Cherokee, either. The English talked with inflected phrases. One phrase to mean everything. I liked them, though. I liked the way they talked. Take Harris. Still Harris was not the upper classes.

I turned on the light again and read. I read the Turgenieff. I knew that now, reading it in the oversensitized state of my mind after much too much brandy, I would remember it somewhere, and afterward it would seem as though it had really happened to me. I would always have it. That was another good thing you paid for and then had. Some time along toward daylight I went to sleep.

The next two days in Pamplona were quiet, and there were no more rows. The town was getting ready for the fiesta. Workmen put up the gate-posts that were to shut off the side streets when the bulls were released from the corrals and came running through the streets in the morning on their way to the ring. The workmen dug holes and fitted in the timbers, each timber numbered for its regular place. Out on the plateau beyond the town employees of the bull-ring exercised picador horses, galloping them stiff-legged on the hard, sun-baked fields behind the bull-ring. The big gate of the bull-ring was open, and inside the amphitheatre was being swept. The ring was rolled and sprinkled, and carpenters replaced weakened or cracked planks in the barrera.

Standing at the edge of the smooth rolled sand you could look up in the empty stands and see old women sweeping out the boxes.

Outside, the fence that led from the last street of the town to the entrance of the bull-ring was already in place and made a long pen; the crowd would come running down with the bulls behind them on the morning of the day of the first bull-fight. Out across the plain, where the horse and cattle fair would be, some gypsies had camped under the trees. The wine and aguardiente sellers were putting up their booths. One booth advertised ANIS DEL TORO. The cloth sign hung against the planks in the hot sun. In the big square that was the centre of the town there was no change yet. We sat in the white wicker chairs on the terrasse of the café and watched the motor-buses come in and unload peasants from the country coming in to the market, and we watched the buses fill up and start out with peasants sitting with their saddle-bags full of the things they had bought in the town. The tall gray motor-buses were the only life of the square except for the pigeons and the man with a hose who sprinkled the gravelled square and watered the streets.

In the evening was the paseo. For an hour after dinner every one, all the good-looking girls, the officers from the garrison, all the fashionable people of the town, walked in the street on one side of the square while the café tables filled with the regular after-dinner crowd.

During the morning I usually sat in the café and read the Madrid papers and then walked in the town or out into the country. Sometimes Bill went along. Sometimes he wrote in his room. Robert Cohn spent the mornings studying Spanish or trying to get a shave at the barber-shop. Brett and Mike never got up until noon. We all had a vermouth at the café. It was a quiet life and no one was drunk. I went to church a couple of times, once with Brett. She said she wanted to hear me go to confession, but I told

her that not only was it impossible but it was not as interesting
as it sounded, and, besides, it would be in a language she did not
know. We met Cohn as we came out of church, and although it
was obvious he had followed us, yet he was very pleasant and nice,
and we all three went for a walk out to the gypsy camp, and Brett
had her fortune told.

It was a good morning, there were high white clouds above the
mountains. It had rained a little in the night and it was fresh and
cool on the plateau, and there was a wonderful view. We all felt
good and we felt healthy, and I felt quite friendly to Cohn. You
could not be upset about anything on a day like that.

That was the last day before the fiesta.

CHAPTER XV

At noon of Sunday, the 6th of July, the fiesta exploded. There is no other way to describe it. People had been coming in all day from the country, but they were assimilated in the town and you did not notice them. The square was as quiet in the hot sun as on any other day. The peasants were in the outlying wine-shops. There they were drinking, getting ready for the fiesta. They had come in so recently from the plains and the hills that it was necessary that they make their shifting in values gradually. They could not start in paying café prices. They got their money's worth in the wine-shops. Money still had a definite value in hours worked and bushels of grain sold. Late in the fiesta it would not matter what they paid, nor where they bought.

Now on the day of the starting of the fiesta of San Fermin they had been in the wine-shops of the narrow streets of the town since early morning. Going down the streets in the morning on the way to mass in the cathedral, I heard them singing through the open doors of the shops. They were warming up. There were

many people at the eleven o'clock mass. San Fermin is also a
religious festival.

I walked down the hill from the cathedral and up the street to
the café on the square. It was a little before noon. Robert Cohn
and Bill were sitting at one of the tables. The marble-topped tables
and the white wicker chairs were gone. They were replaced by
cast-iron tables and severe folding chairs. The café was like a
battleship stripped for action. To-day the waiters did not leave you
alone all morning to read without asking if you wanted to order
something. A waiter came up as soon as I sat down.

"What are you drinking?" I asked Bill and Robert.

"Sherry," Cohn said.

"Jerez," I said to the waiter.

Before the waiter brought the sherry the rocket that announced
the fiesta went up in the square. It burst and there was a gray
ball of smoke high up above the Theatre Gayarre, across on the
other side of the plaza. The ball of smoke hung in the sky like a
shrapnel burst, and as I watched, another rocket came up to it,
trickling smoke in the bright sunlight. I saw the bright flash as it
burst and another little cloud of smoke appeared. By the time the
second rocket had burst there were so many people in the arcade,
that had been empty a minute before, that the waiter, holding the
bottle high up over his head, could hardly get through the crowd
to our table. People were coming into the square from all sides,
and down the street we heard the pipes and the fifes and the
drums coming. They were playing the *riau-riau* music, the pipes
shrill and the drums pounding, and behind them came the men
and boys dancing. When the fifers stopped they all crouched down
in the street, and when the reed-pipes and the fifes shrilled, and
the flat, dry, hollow drums tapped it out again, they all went up in
the air dancing. In the crowd you saw only the heads and shoulders
of the dancers going up and down.

In the square a man, bent over, was playing on a reed-pipe, and a crowd of children were following him shouting, and pulling at his clothes. He came out of the square, the children following him, and piped them past the café and down a side street. We saw his blank pockmarked face as he went by, piping, the children close behind him shouting and pulling at him.

"He must be the village idiot," Bill said. "My God! look at that!"

Down the street came dancers. The street was solid with dancers, all men. They were all dancing in time behind their own fifers and drummers. They were a club of some sort, and all wore workmen's blue smocks, and red handkerchiefs around their necks, and carried a great banner on two poles. The banner danced up and down with them as they came down surrounded by the crowd.

"Hurray for Wine! Hurray for the Foreigners!" was painted on the banner.

"Where are the foreigners?" Robert Cohn asked.

"We're the foreigners," Bill said.

All the time rockets were going up. The café tables were all full now. The square was emptying of people and the crowd was filling the cafés.

"Where's Brett and Mike?" Bill asked.

"I'll go and get them," Cohn said.

"Bring them here."

The fiesta was really started. It kept up day and night for seven days. The dancing kept up, the drinking kept up, the noise went on. The things that happened could only have happened during a fiesta. Everything became quite unreal finally and it seemed as though nothing could have any consequences. It seemed out of place to think of consequences during the fiesta. All during the fiesta you had the feeling, even when it was quiet, that you had to

shout any remark to make it heard. It was the same feeling about
any action. It was a fiesta and it went on for seven days.

That afternoon was the big religious procession. San Fermin
was translated from one church to another. In the procession were
all the dignitaries, civil and religious. We could not see them because the crowd was too great. Ahead of the formal procession
and behind it danced the *riau-riau* dancers. There was one mass
of yellow shirts dancing up and down in the crowd. All we could
see of the procession through the closely pressed people that
crowded all the side streets and curbs were the great giants, cigar-
store Indians, thirty feet high, Moors, a King and Queen, whirling
and waltzing solemnly to the *riau-riau*.

They were all standing outside the chapel where San Fermin
and the dignitaries had passed in, leaving a guard of soldiers, the
giants, with the men who danced in them standing beside their
resting frames, and the dwarfs moving with their whacking blad-
ders through the crowd. We started inside and there was a smell
of incense and people filing back into the church, but Brett was
stopped just inside the door because she had no hat, so we went
out again and along the street that ran back from the chapel into
town. The street was lined on both sides with people keeping
their place at the curb for the return of the procession. Some
dancers formed a circle around Brett and started to dance. They
wore big wreaths of white garlics around their necks. They took
Bill and me by the arms and put us in the circle. Bill started to
dance, too. They were all chanting. Brett wanted to dance but
they did not want her to. They wanted her as an image to dance
around. When the song ended with the sharp *riau-riau!* they
rushed us into a wine-shop.

We stood at the counter. They had Brett seated on a wine-
cask. It was dark in the wine-shop and full of men singing, hard-
voiced singing. Back of the counter they drew the wine from

casks. I put down money for the wine, but one of the men picked it up and put it back in my pocket.

"I want a leather wine-bottle," Bill said.

"There's a place down the street," I said. "I'll go get a couple."

The dancers did not want me to go out. Three of them were sitting on the high wine-cask beside Brett, teaching her to drink out of the wine-skins. They had hung a wreath of garlics around her neck. Some one insisted on giving her a glass. Somebody was teaching Bill a song. Singing it into his ear. Beating time on Bill's back.

I explained to them that I would be back. Outside in the street I went down the street looking for the shop that made leather wine-bottles. The crowd was packed on the sidewalks and many of the shops were shuttered, and I could not find it. I walked as far as the church, looking on both sides of the street. Then I asked a man and he took me by the arm and led me to it. The shutters were up but the door was open.

Inside it smelled of fresh tanned leather and hot tar. A man was stencilling completed wine-skins. They hung from the roof in bunches. He took one down, blew it up, screwed the nozzle tight, and then jumped on it.

"See! It doesn't leak."

"I want another one, too. A big one."

He took down a big one that would hold a gallon or more, from the roof. He blew it up, his cheeks puffing ahead of the wine-skin, and stood on the bota holding on to a chair.

"What are you going to do? Sell them in Bayonne?"

"No. Drink out of them."

He slapped me on the back.

"Good man. Eight pesetas for the two. The lowest price."

The man who was stencilling the new ones and tossing them into a pile stopped.

"It's true," he said. "Eight pesetas is cheap."

I paid and went out and along the street back to the wine-shop. It was darker than ever inside and very crowded. I did not see Brett and Bill, and some one said they were in the back room. At the counter the girl filled the two wine-skins for me. One held two litres. The other held five litres. Filling them both cost three pesetas sixty centimos. Some one at the counter, that I had never seen before, tried to pay for the wine, but I finally paid for it myself. The man who had wanted to pay then bought me a drink. He would not let me buy one in return, but said he would take a rinse of the mouth from the new wine-bag. He tipped the big five-litre bag up and squeezed it so the wine hissed against the back of his throat.

"All right," he said, and handed back the bag.

In the back room Brett and Bill were sitting on barrels surrounded by the dancers. Everybody had his arms on everybody else's shoulders, and they were all singing. Mike was sitting at a table with several men in their shirt-sleeves, eating from a bowl of tuna fish, chopped onions and vinegar. They were all drinking wine and mopping up the oil and vinegar with pieces of bread.

"Hello, Jake. Hello!" Mike called. "Come here. I want you to meet my friends. We're all having an hors-d'œuvre."

I was introduced to the people at the table. They supplied their names to Mike and sent for a fork for me.

"Stop eating their dinner, Michael," Brett shouted from the wine-barrels.

"I don't want to eat up your meal," I said when some one handed me a fork.

"Eat," he said. "What do you think it's here for?"

I unscrewed the nozzle of the big wine-bottle and handed it around. Every one took a drink, tipping the wine-skin at arm's length.

Outside, above the singing, we could hear the music of the procession going by.

"Isn't that the procession?" Mike asked.

"Nada," some one said. "It's nothing. Drink up. Lift the bottle."

"Where did they find you?" I asked Mike.

"Some one brought me here," Mike said. "They said you were here."

"Where's Cohn?"

"He's passed out," Brett called. "They've put him away somewhere."

"Where is he?"

"I don't know."

"How should we know," Bill said. "I think he's dead."

"He's not dead," Mike said. "I know he's not dead. He's just passed out on Anis del Mono."

As he said Anis del Mono one of the men at the table looked up, brought out a bottle from inside his smock, and handed it to me.

"No," I said. "No, thanks!"

"Yes. Yes. Arriba! Up with the bottle!"

I took a drink. It tasted of licorice and warmed all the way. I could feel it warming in my stomach.

"Where the hell is Cohn?"

"I don't know," Mike said. "I'll ask. Where is the drunken comrade?" he asked in Spanish.

"You want to see him?"

"Yes," I said.

"Not me," said Mike. "This gent."

The Anis del Mono man wiped his mouth and stood up.

"Come on."

In a back room Robert Cohn was sleeping quietly on some wine-casks. It was almost too dark to see his face. They had covered him with a coat and another coat was folded under his head. Around his neck and on his chest was a big wreath of twisted garlics.

"Let him sleep," the man whispered. "He's all right."

Two hours later Cohn appeared. He came into the front room still with the wreath of garlics around his neck. The Spaniards shouted when he came in. Cohn wiped his eyes and grinned.

"I must have been sleeping," he said.

"Oh, not at all," Brett said.

"You were only dead," Bill said.

"Aren't we going to go and have some supper?" Cohn asked.

"Do you want to eat?"

"Yes. Why not? I'm hungry."

"Eat those garlics, Robert," Mike said. "I say. Do eat those garlics."

Cohn stood there. His sleep had made him quite all right.

"Do let's go and eat," Brett said. "I must get a bath."

"Come on," Bill said. "Let's translate Brett to the hotel."

We said good-bye to many people and shook hands with many people and went out. Outside it was dark.

"What time is it do you suppose?" Cohn asked.

"It's to-morrow," Mike said. "You've been asleep two days."

"No," said Cohn, "what time is it?"

"It's ten o'clock."

"What a lot we've drunk."

"You mean what a lot *we've* drunk. You went to sleep."

Going down the dark streets to the hotel we saw the sky-rockets going up in the square. Down the side streets that led to the square we saw the square solid with people, those in the centre all dancing.

It was a big meal at the hotel. It was the first meal of the prices being doubled for the fiesta, and there were several new courses After the dinner we were out in the town. I remember resolving that I would stay up all night to watch the bulls go through the streets at six o'clock in the morning, and being so sleepy that I went to bed around four o'clock. The others stayed up.

My own room was locked and I could not find the key, so I went up-stairs and slept on one of the beds in Cohn's room. The fiesta was going on outside in the night, but I was too sleepy for it to keep me awake. When I woke it was the sound of the rocket exploding that announced the release of the bulls from the corrals at the edge of town. They would race through the streets and out to the bull-ring. I had been sleeping heavily and I woke feeling I was too late. I put on a coat of Cohn's and went out on the balcony. Down below the narrow street was empty. All the balconies were crowded with people. Suddenly a crowd came down the street. They were all running, packed close together. They passed along and up the street toward the bull-ring and behind them came more men running faster, and then some stragglers who were really running. Behind them was a little bare space, and then the bulls galloping, tossing their heads up and down. It all went out of sight around the corner. One man fell, rolled to the gutter, and lay quiet. But the bulls went right on and did not notice him. They were all running together.

After they went out of sight a great roar came from the bull-ring. It kept on. Then finally the pop of the rocket that meant the bulls had gotten through the people in the ring and into the corrals. I went back in the room and got into bed. I had been standing on the stone balcony in bare feet. I knew our crowd must have all been out at the bull-ring. Back in bed, I went to sleep.

Cohn woke me when he came in. He started to undress and went over and closed the window because the people on the balcony of the house just across the street were looking in.

"Did you see the show?" I asked.

"Yes. We were all there."

"Anybody get hurt?"

"One of the bulls got into the crowd in the ring and tossed six or eight people."

"How did Brett like it?"

"It was all so sudden there wasn't any time for it to bother anybody."

"I wish I'd been up."

"We didn't know where you were. We went to your room but it was locked."

"Where did you stay up?"

"We danced at some club."

"I got sleepy," I said.

"My gosh! I'm sleepy now," Cohn said. "Doesn't this thing ever stop?"

"Not for a week."

Bill opened the door and put his head in.

"Where were you, Jake?"

"I saw them go through from the balcony. How was it?"

"Grand."

"Where you going?"

"To sleep."

No one was up before noon. We ate at tables set out under the arcade. The town was full of people. We had to wait for a table. After lunch we went over to the Iruña. It had filled up, and as the time for the bull-fight came it got fuller, and the tables were crowded closer. There was a close, crowded hum that came every day before the bull-fight. The café did not make this same noise at any other time, no matter how crowded it was. This hum went on, and we were in it and a part of it.

I had taken six seats for all the fights. Three of them were barreras, the first row at the ring-side, and three were sobrepuertos, seats with wooden backs, half-way up the amphitheatre. Mike thought Brett had best sit high up for her first time, and Cohn wanted to sit with them. Bill and I were going to sit in the barreras, and I gave the extra ticket to a waiter to sell. Bill said something to Cohn about what to do and how to look so he would not mind the horses. Bill had seen one season of bull-fights.

"I'm not worried about how I'll stand it. I'm only afraid I may be bored," Cohn said.

"You think so?"

"Don't look at the horses, after the bull hits them," I said to Brett. "Watch the charge and see the picador try and keep the bull off, but then don't look again until the horse is dead if it's been hit."

"I'm a little nervy about it," Brett said. "I'm worried whether I'll be able to go through with it all right."

"You'll be all right. There's nothing but that horse part that will bother you, and they're only in for a few minutes with each bull. Just don't watch when it's bad."

"She'll be all right," Mike said. "I'll look after her."

"I don't think you'll be bored," Bill said.

"I'm going over to the hotel to get the glasses and the wine-skin," I said. "See you back here. Don't get cock-eyed."

"I'll come along," Bill said. Brett smiled at us.

We walked around through the arcade to avoid the heat of the square.

"That Cohn gets me," Bill said. "He's got this Jewish superiority so strong that he thinks the only emotion he'll get out of the fight will be being bored."

"We'll watch him with the glasses," I said.

"Oh, to hell with him!"

"He spends a lot of time there."

"I want him to stay there."

In the hotel on the stairs we met Montoya.

"Come on," said Montoya. "Do you want to meet Pedro Romero?"

"Fine," said Bill. "Let's go see him."

We followed Montoya up a flight and down the corridor.

"He's in room number eight," Montoya explained. "He's getting dressed for the bull-fight."

Montoya knocked on the door and opened it. It was a gloomy room with a little light coming in from the window on the narrow street. There were two beds separated by a monastic partition. The electric light was on. The boy stood very straight and unsmiling in his bull-fighting clothes. His jacket hung over the back of a chair. They were just finishing winding his sash. His black hair shone under the electric light. He wore a white linen shirt and the sword-handler finished his sash and stood up and stepped back. Pedro Romero nodded, seeming very far away and dignified when we shook hands. Montoya said something about what great aficionados we were, and that we wanted to wish him luck. Romero listened very seriously. Then he turned to me. He was the best-looking boy I have ever seen.

"You go to the bull-fight," he said in English.

"You know English," I said, feeling like an idiot.

"No," he answered, and smiled.

One of three men who had been sitting on the beds came up and asked us if we spoke French. "Would you like me to interpret for you? Is there anything you would like to ask Pedro Romero?"

We thanked him. What was there that you would like to ask? The boy was nineteen years old, alone except for his sword-handler, and the three hangers-on, and the bull-fight was to commence in twenty minutes. We wished him "Mucha suerte," shook hands, and went out. He was standing, straight and handsome and altogether by himself, alone in the room with the hangers-on as we shut the door.

"He's a fine boy, don't you think so?" Montoya asked.

"He's a good-looking kid," I said.

"He looks like a torero," Montoya said. "He has the type."

"He's a fine boy."

"We'll see how he is in the ring," Montoya said.

We found the big leather wine-bottle leaning against the wall in my room, took it and the field-glasses, locked the door, and went down-stairs.

It was a good bull-fight. Bill and I were very excited about Pedro Romero. Montoya was sitting about ten places away. After Romero had killed his first bull Montoya caught my eye and nodded his head. This was a real one. There had not been a real one for a long time. Of the other two matadors, one was very fair and the other was passable. But there was no comparison with Romero, although neither of his bulls was much.

Several times during the bull-fight I looked up at Mike and Brett and Cohn, with the glasses. They seemed to be all right. Brett did not look upset. All three were leaning forward on the concrete railing in front of them.

"Let me take the glasses," Bill said.

"Does Cohn look bored?" I asked.

"That kike!"

Outside the ring, after the bull-fight was over, you could not move in the crowd. We could not make our way through but had to be moved with the whole thing, slowly, as a glacier, back to town. We had that disturbed emotional feeling that always comes after a bull-fight, and the feeling of elation that comes after a good bull-fight. The fiesta was going on. The drums pounded and the pipe music was shrill, and everywhere the flow of the crowd was broken by patches of dancers. The dancers were in a crowd, so you did not see the intricate play of the feet. All you saw was the heads and shoulders going up and down, up and down. Finally, we got out of the crowd and made for the café. The waiter saved chairs for the others, and we each ordered an absinthe and watched the crowd in the square and the dancers.

"What do you suppose that dance is?" Bill asked.

"It's a sort of jota."

"They're not all the same," Bill said. "They dance differently to all the different tunes."

"It's swell dancing."

In front of us on a clear part of the street a company of boys were dancing. The steps were very intricate and their faces were intent and concentrated. They all looked down while they danced. Their rope-soled shoes tapped and spatted on the pavement. The toes touched. The heels touched. The balls of the feet touched. Then the music broke wildly and the step was finished and they were all dancing on up the street.

"Here come the gentry," Bill said.

They were crossing the street.

"Hello, men," I said.

"Hello, gents!" said Brett. "You saved us seats? How nice."

"I say," Mike said, "that Romero what'shisname is somebody. Am I wrong?"

"Oh, isn't he lovely," Brett said. "And those green trousers."

"Brett never took her eyes off them."

"I say, I must borrow your glasses to-morrow."

"How did it go?"

"Wonderfully! Simply perfect. I say, it is a spectacle!"

"How about the horses?"

"I couldn't help looking at them."

"She couldn't take her eyes off them," Mike said. "She's an extraordinary wench."

"They do have some rather awful things happen to them," Brett said. "I couldn't look away, though."

"Did you feel all right?"

"I didn't feel badly at all."

"Robert Cohn did," Mike put in. "You were quite green, Robert."

"The first horse did bother me," Cohn said.

"You weren't bored, were you?" asked Bill.

Cohn laughed.

"No. I wasn't bored. I wish you'd forgive me that."

"It's all right," Bill said, "so long as you weren't bored."

"He didn't look bored," Mike said. "I thought he was going to be sick."

"I never felt that bad. It was just for a minute."

"*I* thought he was going to be sick. You weren't bored, were you, Robert?"

"Let up on that, Mike. I said I was sorry I said it."

"He was, you know. He was positively green."

"Oh, shove it along, Michael."

"You mustn't ever get bored at your first bull-fight, Robert," Mike said. "It might make such a mess."

"Oh, shove it along, Michael," Brett said.

"He said Brett was a sadist," Mike said. "Brett's not a sadist. She's just a lovely, healthy wench."

"Are you a sadist, Brett?" I asked.

"Hope not."

"He said Brett was a sadist just because she has a good, healthy stomach."

"Won't be healthy long."

Bill got Mike started on something else than Cohn. The waiter brought the absinthe glasses.

"Did you really like it?" Bill asked Cohn.

"No, I can't say I liked it. I think it's a wonderful show."

"Gad, yes! What a spectacle!" Brett said.

"I wish they didn't have the horse part," Cohn said.

"They're not important," Bill said. "After a while you never notice anything disgusting."

"It is a bit strong just at the start," Brett said. "There's a dreadful moment for me just when the bull starts for the horse."

"The bulls were fine," Cohn said.

"They were very good," Mike said.

"I want to sit down below, next time." Brett drank from her glass of absinthe.

"She wants to see the bull-fighters close by," Mike said.

"They are something," Brett said. "That Romero lad is just a child."

"He's a damned good-looking boy," I said. "When we were up in his room I never saw a better-looking kid."

"How old do you suppose he is?"

"Nineteen or twenty."

"Just imagine it."

The bull-fight on the second day was much better than on the first. Brett sat between Mike and me at the barrera, and Bill and Cohn went up above. Romero was the whole show. I do not think Brett saw any other bull-fighter. No one else did either, except the hard-shelled technicians. It was all Romero. There were two other matadors, but they did not count. I sat beside Brett and explained to Brett what it was all about. I told her about watching the bull, not the horse, when the bulls charged the picadors, and got her to watching the picador place the point of his pic so that she saw what it was all about, so that it became more something that was going on with a definite end, and less of a spectacle with unexplained horrors. I had her watch how Romero took the bull away from a fallen horse with his cape, and how he held him with the cape and turned him, smoothly and suavely, never wasting the bull. She saw how Romero avoided every brusque movement and saved his bulls for the last when he wanted them, not winded and discomposed but smoothly worn down. She saw how close Romero always worked to the bull, and I pointed out to her the tricks the other bull-fighters used to make it look as though they were working closely. She saw why she liked Romero's cape-work and why she did not like the others.

Romero never made any contortions, always it was straight and pure and natural in line. The others twisted themselves like corkscrews, their elbows raised, and leaned against the flanks of the bull after his horns had passed, to give a faked look of danger. Afterward, all that was faked turned bad and gave an unpleasant feeling. Romero's bull-fighting gave real emotion, because he kept the absolute purity of line in his movements and always quietly and calmly let the horns pass him close each time. He did not have to emphasize their closeness. Brett saw how something that was beautiful done close to the bull was ridiculous if it were done a little way off. I told her how since the death of Joselito all the bull-fighters had been developing a technic that simulated this appearance of danger in order to give a fake emotional feeling, while the bull-fighter was really safe. Romero had the old thing, the holding of his purity of line through the maximum of exposure, while he dominated the bull by making him realize he was unattainable, while he prepared him for the killing.

"I've never seen him do an awkward thing," Brett said.

"You won't until he gets frightened," I said.

"He'll never be frightened," Mike said. "He knows too damned much."

"He knew everything when he started. The others can't ever learn what he was born with."

"And God, what looks," Brett said.

"I believe, you know, that she's falling in love with this bull-fighter chap," Mike said.

"I wouldn't be surprised."

"Be a good chap, Jake. Don't tell her anything more about him. Tell her how they beat their old mothers."

"Tell me what drunks they are."

"Oh, frightful," Mike said. "Drunk all day and spend all their time beating their poor old mothers."

"He looks that way," Brett said.

"Doesn't he?" I said.

They had hitched the mules to the dead bull and then the whips cracked, the men ran, and the mules, straining forward, their legs pushing, broke into a gallop, and the bull, one horn up, his head on its side, swept a swath smoothly across the sand and out the red gate.

"This next is the last one."

"Not really," Brett said. She leaned forward on the barrera. Romero waved his picadors to their places, then stood, his cape against his chest, looking across the ring to where the bull would come out.

After it was over we went out and were pressed tight in the crowd.

"These bull-fights are hell on one," Brett said. "I'm limp as a rag."

"Oh, you'll get a drink," Mike said.

The next day Pedro Romero did not fight. It was Miura bulls, and a very bad bull-fight. The next day there was no bull-fight scheduled. But all day and all night the fiesta kept on.

CHAPTER XVI

In the morning it was raining. A fog had come over the mountains from the sea. You could not see the tops of the mountains. The plateau was dull and gloomy, and the shapes of the trees and the houses were changed. I walked out beyond the town to look at the weather. The bad weather was coming over the mountains from the sea.

The flags in the square hung wet from the white poles and the banners were wet and hung damp against the front of the houses, and in between the steady drizzle the rain came down and drove every one under the arcades and made pools of water in the square, and the streets wet and dark and deserted; yet the fiesta kept up without any pause. It was only driven under cover.

The covered seats of the bull-ring had been crowded with people sitting out of the rain watching the concourse of Basque and Navarrais dancers and singers, and afterward the Val Carlos dancers in their costumes danced down the street in the rain, the drums sounding hollow and damp, and the chiefs of the bands riding ahead on their big, heavy-footed horses, their costumes wet,

the horses' coats wet in the rain. The crowd was in the cafés and
the dancers came in, too, and sat, their tight-wound white legs
under the tables, shaking the water from their belled caps, and
spreading their red and purple jackets over the chairs to dry.
It was raining hard outside.

I left the crowd in the café and went over to the hotel to get
shaved for dinner. I was shaving in my room when there was a
knock on the door.

"Come in," I called.

Montoya walked in.

"How are you?" he said.

"Fine," I said.

"No bulls to-day."

"No," I said, "nothing but rain."

"Where are your friends?"

"Over at the Iruña."

Montoya smiled his embarrassed smile.

"Look," he said. "Do you know the American ambassador?"

"Yes," I said. "Everybody knows the American ambassador."

"He's here in town, now."

"Yes," I said. "Everybody's seen them."

"I've seen them, too," Montoya said. He didn't say anything. I
went on shaving.

"Sit down," I said. "Let me send for a drink."

"No, I have to go."

I finished shaving and put my face down into the bowl and
washed it with cold water. Montoya was standing there looking
more embarrassed.

"Look," he said. "I've just had a message from them at the
Grand Hotel that they want Pedro Romero and Marcial Lalanda
to come over for coffee to-night after dinner."

"Well," I said, "it can't hurt Marcial any."

"Marcial has been in San Sebastian all day. He drove over in a car this morning with Marquez. I don't think they'll be back to-night."

Montoya stood embarrassed. He wanted me to say something.

"Don't give Romero the message," I said.

"You think so?"

"Absolutely."

Montoya was very pleased.

"I wanted to ask you because you were an American," he said.

"That's what I'd do."

"Look," said Montoya. "People take a boy like that. They don't know what he's worth. They don't know what he means. Any foreigner can flatter him. They start this Grand Hotel business, and in one year they're through."

"Like Algabeno," I said.

"Yes, like Algabeno."

"They're a fine lot," I said. "There's one American woman down here now that collects bull-fighters."

"I know. They only want the young ones."

"Yes," I said. "The old ones get fat."

"Or crazy like Gallo."

"Well," I said, "it's easy. All you have to do is not give him the message."

"He's such a fine boy," said Montoya. "He ought to stay with his own people. He shouldn't mix in that stuff."

"Won't you have a drink?" I asked.

"No," said Montoya, "I have to go." He went out.

I went down-stairs and out the door and took a walk around through the arcades around the square. It was still raining. I looked in at the Iruña for the gang and they were not there, so I walked on around the square and back to the hotel. They were eating dinner in the down-stairs dining-room.

They were well ahead of me and it was no use trying to catch them. Bill was buying shoe-shines for Mike. Bootblacks opened the street door and each one Bill called over and started to work on Mike.

"This is the eleventh time my boots have been polished," Mike said. "I say, Bill is an ass."

The bootblacks had evidently spread the report. Another came in.

"Limpia botas?" he said to Bill.

"No," said Bill. "For this Señor."

The bootblack knelt down beside the one at work and started on Mike's free shoe that shone already in the electric light.

"Bill's a yell of laughter," Mike said.

I was drinking red wine, and so far behind them that I felt a little uncomfortable about all this shoe-shining. I looked around the room. At the next table was Pedro Romero. He stood up when I nodded, and asked me to come over and meet a friend. His table was beside ours, almost touching. I met the friend, a Madrid bull-fight critic, a little man with a drawn face. I told Romero how much I liked his work, and he was very pleased. We talked Spanish and the critic knew a little French. I reached to our table for my wine-bottle, but the critic took my arm. Romero laughed.

"Drink here," he said in English.

He was very bashful about his English, but he was really very pleased with it, and as we went on talking he brought out words he was not sure of, and asked me about them. He was anxious to know the English for *Corrida de toros*, the exact translation. Bull-fight he was suspicious of. I explained that bull-fight in Spanish was the *lidia* of a *toro*. The Spanish word *corrida* means in English the running of bulls—the French translation is *Course de taureaux*. The critic put that in. There is no Spanish word for bull-fight.

Pedro Romero said he had learned a little English in Gibraltar. He was born in Ronda. That is not far above Gibraltar. He started bull-fighting in Malaga in the bull-fighting school there. He had only been at it three years. The bull-fight critic joked him about the number of *Malagueño* expressions he used. He was nineteen years old, he said. His older brother was with him as a banderillero, but he did not live in this hotel. He lived in a smaller hotel with the other people who worked for Romero. He asked me how many times I had seen him in the ring. I told him only three. It was really only two, but I did not want to explain after I had made the mistake.

"Where did you see me the other time? In Madrid?"

"Yes," I lied. I had read the accounts of his two appearances in Madrid in the bull-fight papers, so I was all right.

"The first or the second time?"

"The first."

"I was very bad," he said. "The second time I was better. You remember?" He turned to the critic.

He was not at all embarrassed. He talked of his work as something altogether apart from himself. There was nothing conceited or braggartly about him.

"I like it very much that you like my work," he said. "But you haven't seen it yet. To-morrow, if I get a good bull, I will try and show it to you."

When he said this he smiled, anxious that neither the bull-fight critic nor I would think he was boasting.

"I am anxious to see it," the critic said. "I would like to be convinced."

"He doesn't like my work much." Romero turned to me. He was serious.

The critic explained that he liked it very much, but that so far it had been incomplete.

"Wait till to-morrow, if a good one comes out."

"Have you seen the bulls for to-morrow?" the critic asked me.

"Yes. I saw them unloaded."

Pedro Romero leaned forward.

"What did you think of them?"

"Very nice," I said. "About twenty-six arrobas. Very short horns. Haven't you seen them?"

"Oh, yes," said Romero.

"They won't weigh twenty-six arrobas," said the critic.

"No," said Romero.

"They've got bananas for horns," the critic said.

"You call them bananas?" asked Romero. He turned to me and smiled. "*You* wouldn't call them bananas?"

"No," I said. "They're horns all right."

"They're very short," said Pedro Romero. "Very, very short. Still, they aren't bananas."

"I say, Jake," Brett called from the next table, "you *have* deserted us."

"Just temporarily," I said. "We're talking bulls."

"You *are* superior."

"Tell him that bulls have no balls," Mike shouted. He was drunk.

Romero looked at me inquiringly.

"Drunk," I said. "Borracho! Muy borracho!"

"You might introduce your friends," Brett said. She had not stopped looking at Pedro Romero. I asked them if they would like to have coffee with us. They both stood up. Romero's face was very brown. He had very nice manners.

I introduced them all around and they started to sit down, but there was not enough room, so we all moved over to the big table by the wall to have coffee. Mike ordered a bottle of Fundador and glasses for everybody. There was a lot of drunken talking.

"Tell him I think writing is lousy," Bill said. "Go on, tell him. Tell him I'm ashamed of being a writer."

Pedro Romero was sitting beside Brett and listening to her.

"Go on. Tell him!" Bill said.

Romero looked up smiling.

"This gentleman," I said, "is a writer."

Romero was impressed. "This other one, too," I said, pointing at Cohn.

"He looks like Villalta," Romero said, looking at Bill. "Rafael, doesn't he look like Villalta?"

"I can't see it," the critic said.

"Really," Romero said in Spanish. "He looks a lot like Villalta. What does the drunken one do?"

"Nothing."

"Is that why he drinks?"

"No. He's waiting to marry this lady."

"Tell him bulls have no balls!" Mike shouted, very drunk, from the other end of the table.

"What does he say?"

"He's drunk."

"Jake," Mike called. "Tell him bulls have no balls!"

"You understand?" I said.

"Yes."

I was sure he didn't, so it was all right.

"Tell him Brett wants to see him put on those green pants."

"Pipe down, Mike."

"Tell him Brett is dying to know how he can get into those pants."

"Pipe down."

During this Romero was fingering his glass and talking with Brett. Brett was talking French and he was talking Spanish and a little English, and laughing.

Bill was filling the glasses.

"Tell him Brett wants to come into——"

"Oh, pipe down, Mike, for Christ's sake!"

Romero looked up smiling. "Pipe down! I know that," he said.

Just then Montoya came into the room. He started to smile at me, then he saw Pedro Romero with a big glass of cognac in his hand, sitting laughing between me and a woman with bare shoulders, at a table full of drunks. He did not even nod.

Montoya went out of the room. Mike was on his feet proposing a toast. "Let's all drink to—" he began. "Pedro Romero," I said. Everybody stood up. Romero took it very seriously, and we touched glasses and drank it down, I rushing it a little because Mike was trying to make it clear that that was not at all what he was going to drink to. But it went off all right, and Pedro Romero shook hands with every one and he and the critic went out together.

"My God! he's a lovely boy," Brett said. "And how I would love to see him get into those clothes. He must use a shoe-horn."

"I started to tell him," Mike began. "And Jake kept interrupting me. Why do you interrupt me? Do you think you talk Spanish better than I do?"

"Oh, shut up, Mike! Nobody interrupted you."

"No, I'd like to get this settled." He turned away from me. "Do you think you amount to something, Cohn? Do you think you belong here among us? People who are out to have a good time? For God's sake don't be so noisy, Cohn!"

"Oh, cut it out, Mike," Cohn said.

"Do you think Brett wants you here? Do you think you add to the party? Why don't you say something?"

"I said all I had to say the other night, Mike."

"I'm not one of you literary chaps." Mike stood shakily and leaned against the table. "I'm not clever. But I do know when I'm not wanted. Why don't you see when you're not wanted, Cohn? Go away. Go away, for God's sake. Take that sad Jewish face away. Don't you think I'm right?"

He looked at us.

"Sure," I said. "Let's all go over to the Iruña."

"No. Don't you think I'm right? I love that woman."

"Oh, don't start that again. Do shove it along, Michael," Brett said.

"Don't you think I'm right, Jake?"

Cohn still sat at the table. His face had the sallow, yellow look it got when he was insulted, but somehow he seemed to be enjoying it. The childish, drunken heroics of it. It was his affair with a lady of title.

"Jake," Mike said. He was almost crying. "You know I'm right. Listen, you!" He turned to Cohn: "Go away! Go away now!"

"But I won't go, Mike," said Cohn.

"Then I'll make you!" Mike started toward him around the table. Cohn stood up and took off his glasses. He stood waiting, his face sallow, his hands fairly low, proudly and firmly waiting for the assault, ready to do battle for his lady love.

I grabbed Mike. "Come on to the café," I said. "You can't hit him here in the hotel."

"Good!" said Mike. "Good idea!"

We started off. I looked back as Mike stumbled up the stairs and saw Cohn putting his glasses on again. Bill was sitting at the table pouring another glass of Fundador. Brett was sitting looking straight ahead at nothing.

Outside on the square it had stopped raining and the moon was trying to get through the clouds. There was a wind blowing. The military band was playing and the crowd was massed on the far side of the square where the fireworks specialist and his son were trying to send up fire balloons. A balloon would start up jerkily, on a great bias, and be torn by the wind or blown against the houses of the square. Some fell into the crowd. The magnesium flared and the fireworks exploded and chased about in the crowd. There was no one dancing in the square. The gravel was too wet.

Brett came out with Bill and joined us. We stood in the crowd and watched Don Manuel Orquito, the fireworks king, standing on a little platform, carefully starting the balloons with sticks, standing above the heads of the crowd to launch the balloons off into the wind. The wind brought them all down, and Don Manuel Orquito's face was sweaty in the light of his complicated fireworks that fell into the crowd and charged and chased, sputtering and cracking, between the legs of the people. The people shouted as each new luminous paper bubble careened, caught fire, and fell.

"They're razzing Don Manuel," Bill said.

"How do you know he's Don Manuel?" Brett said.

"His name's on the programme. Don Manuel Orquito, the pirotecnico of esta ciudad."

"Globos illuminados," Mike said. "A collection of globos illuminados. That's what the paper said."

The wind blew the band music away.

"I say, I wish one would go up," Brett said. "That Don Manuel chap is furious."

"He's probably worked for weeks fixing them to go off, spelling out 'Hail to San Fermin,'" Bill said.

"Globos illuminados," Mike said. "A bunch of bloody globos illuminados."

"Come on," said Brett. "We can't stand here."

"Her ladyship wants a drink," Mike said.

"How you know things," Brett said.

Inside, the café was crowded and very noisy. No one noticed us come in. We could not find a table. There was a great noise going on.

"Come on, let's get out of here," Bill said.

Outside the paseo was going in under the arcade. There were some English and Americans from Biarritz in sport clothes scattered at the tables. Some of the women stared at the people going by with lorgnons. We had acquired, at some time, a friend of Bill's from Biarritz. She was staying with another girl at the Grand Hotel. The other girl had a headache and had gone to bed.

"Here's the pub," Mike said. It was the Bar Milano, a small, tough bar where you could get food and where they danced in the back room. We all sat down at a table and ordered a bottle of Fundador. The bar was not full. There was nothing going on.

"This is a hell of a place," Bill said.

"It's too early."

"Let's take the bottle and come back later," Bill said. "I don't want to sit here on a night like this."

"Let's go and look at the English," Mike said. "I love to look at the English."

"They're awful," Bill said. "Where did they all come from?"

"They come from Biarritz," Mike said. "They come to see the last day of the quaint little Spanish fiesta."

"I'll festa them," Bill said.

"You're an extraordinarily beautiful girl." Mike turned to Bill's friend. "When did you come here?"

"Come off it, Michael."

"I say, she *is* a lovely girl. Where have I been? Where have I been looking all this while? You're a lovely thing. *Have* we met? Come along with me and Bill. We're going to festa the English."

"I'll festa them," Bill said. "What the hell are they doing at this fiesta?"

"Come on," Mike said. "Just us three. We're going to festa the bloody English. I hope you're not English? I'm Scotch. I hate the English. I'm going to festa them. Come on, Bill."

Through the window we saw them, all three arm in arm, going toward the café. Rockets were going up in the square.

"I'm going to sit here," Brett said.

"I'll stay with you," Cohn said.

"Oh, don't!" Brett said. "For God's sake, go off somewhere. Can't you see Jake and I want to talk?"

"I didn't," Cohn said. "I thought I'd sit here because I felt a little tight."

"What a hell of a reason for sitting with any one. If you're tight, go to bed. Go on to bed."

"Was I rude enough to him?" Brett asked. Cohn was gone. "My God! I'm so sick of him!"

"He doesn't add much to the gayety."

"He depresses me so."

"He's behaved very badly."

"Damned badly. He had a chance to behave so well."

"He's probably waiting just outside the door now."

"Yes. He would. You know I do know how he feels. He can't believe it didn't mean anything."

"I know."

"Nobody else would behave as badly. Oh, I'm so sick of the whole thing. And Michael. Michael's been lovely, too."

"It's been damned hard on Mike."

"Yes. But he didn't need to be a swine."

"Everybody behaves badly," I said. "Give them the proper chance."

"You wouldn't behave badly." Brett looked at me.

"I'd be as big an ass as Cohn," I said.

"Darling, don't let's talk a lot of rot."

"All right. Talk about anything you like."

"Don't be difficult. You're the only person I've got, and I feel rather awful to-night."

"You've got Mike."

"Yes, Mike. Hasn't he been pretty?"

"Well," I said, "it's been damned hard on Mike, having Cohn around and seeing him with you."

"Don't I know it, darling? Please don't make me feel any worse than I do."

Brett was nervous as I had never seen her before. She kept looking away from me and looking ahead at the wall.

"Want to go for a walk?"

"Yes. Come on."

I corked up the Fundador bottle and gave it to the bartender.

"Let's have one more drink of that," Brett said. "My nerves are rotten."

We each drank a glass of the smooth amontillado brandy.

"Come on," said Brett.

As we came out the door I saw Cohn walk out from under the arcade.

"He *was* there," Brett said.

"He can't be away from you."

"Poor devil!"

"I'm not sorry for him. I hate him, myself."

"I hate him, too," she shivered. "I hate his damned suffering."

We walked arm in arm down the side street away from the crowd and the lights of the square. The street was dark and wet, and we walked along it to the fortifications at the edge of town. We passed wine-shops with light coming out from their doors onto the black, wet street, and sudden bursts of music.

"Want to go in?"

"No."

We walked out across the wet grass and onto the stone wall of the fortifications. I spread a newspaper on the stone and Brett sat down. Across the plain it was dark, and we could see the mountains. The wind was high up and took the clouds across the moon. Below us were the dark pits of the fortifications. Behind were the trees and the shadow of the cathedral, and the town silhouetted against the moon.

"Don't feel bad," I said.

"I feel like hell," Brett said. "Don't let's talk."

We looked out at the plain. The long lines of trees were dark in the moonlight. There were the lights of a car on the road climbing the mountain. Up on the top of the mountain we saw the lights of the fort. Below to the left was the river. It was high from the rain, and black and smooth. Trees were dark along the banks. We sat and looked out. Brett stared straight ahead. Suddenly she shivered.

"It's cold."

"Want to walk back?"

"Through the park."

We climbed down. It was clouding over again. In the park it was dark under the trees.

"Do you still love me, Jake?"

"Yes," I said.

"Because I'm a goner," Brett said.

"How?"

"I'm a goner. I'm mad about the Romero boy. I'm in love with him, I think."

"I wouldn't be if I were you."

"I can't help it. I'm a goner. It's tearing me all up inside."

"Don't do it."

"I can't help it. I've never been able to help anything."

"You ought to stop it."

"How can I stop it? I can't stop things. Feel that?"

Her hand was trembling.

"I'm like that all through."

"You oughtn't to do it."

"I can't help it. I'm a goner now, anyway. Don't you see the difference?"

"No."

"I've got to do something. I've got to do something I really want to do. I've lost my self-respect."

"You don't have to do that."

"Oh, darling, don't be difficult. What do you think it's meant to have that damned Jew about, and Mike the way he's acted?"

"Sure."

"I can't just stay tight all the time."

"No."

"Oh, darling, please stay by me. Please stay by me and see me through this."

"Sure."

"I don't say it's right. It is right though for me. God knows, I've never felt such a bitch."

"What do you want me to do?"

"Come on," Brett said. "Let's go and find him."

Together we walked down the gravel path in the park in the dark, under the trees and then out from under the trees and past the gate into the street that led into town.

Pedro Romero was in the café. He was at a table with other bull-fighters and bull-fight critics. They were smoking cigars. When we came in they looked up. Romero smiled and bowed. We sat down at a table half-way down the room.

"Ask him to come over and have a drink."

"Not yet. He'll come over."

"I can't look at him."

"He's nice to look at," I said.

"I've always done just what I wanted."

"I know."

"I do feel such a bitch."

"Well," I said.

"My God!" said Brett, "the things a woman goes through."

"Yes?"

"Oh, I do feel such a bitch."

I looked across at the table. Pedro Romero smiled. He said something to the other people at his table, and stood up He came over to our table. I stood up and we shook hands.

"Won't you have a drink?"

"You must have a drink with me," he said. He seated himself, asking Brett's permission without saying anything. He had very nice manners. But he kept on smoking his cigar. It went well with his face.

"You like cigars?" I asked.

"Oh, yes. I always smoke cigars."

It was part of his system of authority. It made him seem older. I noticed his skin. It was clear and smooth and very brown. There was a triangular scar on his cheek-bone. I saw he was watching Brett. He felt there was something between them. He must have felt it when Brett gave him her hand. He was being very careful. I think he was sure, but he did not want to make any mistake.

"You fight to-morrow?" I said.

"Yes," he said. "Algabeno was hurt to-day in Madrid. Did you hear?"

"No," I said. "Badly?"

He shook his head.

"Nothing. Here," he showed his hand. Brett reached out and spread the fingers apart.

"Oh!" he said in English, "you tell fortunes?"

"Sometimes. Do you mind?"

"No. I like it." He spread his hand flat on the table. "Tell me I live for always, and be a millionaire."

He was still very polite, but he was surer of himself. "Look," he said, "do you see any bulls in my hand?"

He laughed. His hand was very fine and the wrist was small.

"There are thousands of bulls," Brett said. She was not at all nervous now. She looked lovely.

"Good," Romero laughed. "At a thousand duros apiece," he said to me in Spanish. "Tell me some more."

"It's a good hand," Brett said. "I think he'll live a long time."

"Say it to me. Not to your friend."

"I said you'd live a long time."

"I know it," Romero said. "I'm never going to die."

I tapped with my finger-tips on the table. Romero saw it. He shook his head.

"No. Don't do that. The bulls are my best friends."

I translated to Brett.

"You kill your friends?" she asked.

"Always," he said in English, and laughed. "So they don't kill me." He looked at her across the table.

"You know English well."

"Yes," he said. "Pretty well, sometimes. But I must not let anybody know. It would be very bad, a torero who speaks English."

"Why?" asked Brett.

"It would be bad. The people would not like it. Not yet."

"Why not?"

"They would not like it. Bull-fighters are not like that."

"What are bull-fighters like?"

He laughed and tipped his hat down over his eyes and changed the angle of his cigar and the expression of his face.

"Like at the table," he said. I glanced over. He had mimicked exactly the expression of Nacional. He smiled, his face natural again. "No. I must forget English."

"Don't forget it, yet," Brett said.

"No?"

"No."

"All right."

He laughed again.

"I would like a hat like that," Brett said.

"Good. I'll get you one."

"Right. See that you do."

"I will. I'll get you one to-night."

I stood up. Romero rose, too.

"Sit down," I said. "I must go and find our friends and bring them here."

He looked at me. It was a final look to ask if it were understood. It was understood all right.

"Sit down," Brett said to him. "You must teach me Spanish."

He sat down and looked at her across the table. I went out. The hard-eyed people at the bull-fighter table watched me go. It was not pleasant. When I came back and looked in the café, twenty minutes later, Brett and Pedro Romero were gone. The coffee-glasses and our three empty cognac-glasses were on the table. A waiter came with a cloth and picked up the glasses and mopped off the table.

CHAPTER XVII

Outside the Bar Milano I found Bill and Mike and Edna. Edna was the girl's name.

"We've been thrown out," Edna said.

"By the police," said Mike. "There's some people in there that don't like me."

"I've kept them out of four fights," Edna said. "You've got to help me."

Bill's face was red.

"Come back in, Edna," he said. "Go on in there and dance with Mike."

"It's silly," Edna said. "There'll just be another row."

"Damned Biarritz swine," Bill said.

"Come on," Mike said. "After all, it's a pub. They can't occupy a whole pub."

"Good old Mike," Bill said. "Damned English swine come here and insult Mike and try and spoil the fiesta."

"They're so bloody," Mike said. "I hate the English."

"They can't insult Mike," Bill said. "Mike is a swell fellow.

They can't insult Mike. I won't stand it. Who cares if he is a damn bankrupt?" His voice broke.

"Who cares?" Mike said. "I don't care. Jake doesn't care. Do *you* care?"

"No," Edna said. "Are you a bankrupt?"

"Of course I am. You don't care, do you, Bill?"

Bill put his arm around Mike's shoulder.

"I wish to hell I was a bankrupt. I'd show those bastards."

"They're just English," Mike said. "It never makes any difference what the English say."

"The dirty swine," Bill said. "I'm going to clean them out."

"Bill," Edna looked at me. "Please don't go in again, Bill. They're so stupid."

"That's it," said Mike. "They're stupid. I knew that was what it was."

"They can't say things like that about Mike," Bill said.

"Do you know them?" I asked Mike.

"No. I never saw them. They say they know me."

"I won't stand it," Bill said.

"Come on. Let's go over to the Suizo," I said.

"They're a bunch of Edna's friends from Biarritz," Bill said.

"They're simply stupid," Edna said.

"One of them's Charley Blackman, from Chicago," Bill said.

"I was never in Chicago," Mike said.

Edna started to laugh and could not stop.

"Take me away from here," she said, "you bankrupts."

"What kind of a row was it?" I asked Edna. We were walking across the square to the Suizo. Bill was gone.

"I don't know what happened, but some one had the police called to keep Mike out of the back room. There were some people that had known Mike at Cannes. What's the matter with Mike?"

"Probably he owes them money," I said. "That's what people usually get bitter about."

In front of the ticket-booths out in the square there were two lines of people waiting. They were sitting on chairs or crouched on the ground with blankets and newspapers around them. They were waiting for the wickets to open in the morning to buy tickets for the bull-fight. The night was clearing and the moon was out. Some of the people in the line were sleeping.

At the Café Suizo we had just sat down and ordered Fundador when Robert Cohn came up.

"Where's Brett?" he asked.

"I don't know."

"She was with you."

"She must have gone to bed."

"She's not."

"I don't know where she is."

His face was sallow under the light. He was standing up.

"Tell me where she is."

"Sit down," I said. "I don't know where she is."

"The hell you don't!"

"You can shut your face."

"Tell me where Brett is."

"I'll not tell you a damn thing."

"You know where she is."

"If I did I wouldn't tell you."

"Oh, go to hell, Cohn," Mike called from the table. "Brett's gone off with the bull-fighter chap. They're on their honeymoon."

"You shut up."

"Oh, go to hell!" Mike said languidly.

"Is that where she is?" Cohn turned to me.

"Go to hell!"

"She was with you. Is that where she is?"

"Go to hell!"

"I'll make you tell me"—he stepped forward—"you damned pimp."

I swung at him and he ducked. I saw his face duck sideways in the light. He hit me and I sat down on the pavement. As I started to get on my feet he hit me twice. I went down backward under a table. I tried to get up and felt I did not have any legs. I felt I must get on my feet and try and hit him. Mike helped me up. Some one poured a carafe of water on my head. Mike had an arm around me, and I found I was sitting on a chair. Mike was pulling at my ears.

"I say, you were cold," Mike said.

"Where the hell were you?"

"Oh, I was around."

"You didn't want to mix in it?"

"He knocked Mike down, too," Edna said.

"He didn't knock me out," Mike said. "I just lay there."

"Does this happen every night at your fiestas?" Edna asked. "Wasn't that Mr. Cohn?"

"I'm all right," I said. "My head's a little wobbly."

There were several waiters and a crowd of people standing around.

"Vaya!" said Mike. "Get away. Go on."

The waiters moved the people away.

"It was quite a thing to watch," Edna said. "He must be a boxer."

"He is."

"I wish Bill had been here," Edna said. "I'd like to have seen Bill knocked down, too. I've always wanted to see Bill knocked down. He's so big."

"I was hoping he would knock down a waiter," Mike said, "and get arrested. I'd like to see Mr. Robert Cohn in jail."

"No," I said.

"Oh, no," said Edna. "You don't mean that."

"I do, though," Mike said. "I'm not one of these chaps likes being knocked about. I never play games, even."

Mike took a drink.

"I never liked to hunt, you know. There was always the danger of having a horse fall on you. How do you feel, Jake?"

"All right."

"You're nice," Edna said to Mike. "Are you really a bankrupt?"

"I'm a tremendous bankrupt," Mike said. "I owe money to everybody. Don't you owe any money?"

"Tons."

"I owe everybody money," Mike said. "I borrowed a hundred pesetas from Montoya to-night."

"The hell you did," I said.

"I'll pay it back," Mike said. "I always pay everything back."

"That's why you're a bankrupt, isn't it?" Edna said.

I stood up. I had heard them talking from a long way away. It all seemed like some bad play.

"I'm going over to the hotel," I said. Then I heard them talking about me.

"Is he all right?" Edna asked.

"We'd better walk with him."

"I'm all right," I said. "Don't come. I'll see you all later."

I walked away from the café. They were sitting at the table. I looked back at them and at the empty tables. There was a waiter sitting at one of the tables with his head in his hands.

Walking across the square to the hotel everything looked new and changed. I had never seen the trees before. I had never seen the flagpoles before, nor the front of the theatre. It was all different. I felt as I felt once coming home from an out-of-town football game. I was carrying a suitcase with my football things in it, and I walked up the street from the station in the town I had lived in all my life and it was all new. They were raking the lawns and burning leaves in the road, and I stopped for a long time and watched. It was all strange. Then I went on, and my feet seemed to be a long way off, and everything seemed to come from a long way off, and I could hear my feet walking a great distance away. I had been kicked in the head early in the game. It was like that crossing the square. It was like that going up the stairs in the hotel. Going up the stairs took a long time, and I had the feeling that I was carrying my suitcase. There was a light in the room. Bill came out and met me in the hall.

"Say," he said, "go up and see Cohn. He's been in a jam, and he's asking for you."

"The hell with him."

"Go on. Go on up and see him."

I did not want to climb another flight of stairs.

"What are you looking at me that way for?"

"I'm not looking at you. Go on up and see Cohn. He's in bad shape."

"You were drunk a little while ago," I said.

"I'm drunk now," Bill said. "But you go up and see Cohn. He wants to see you."

"All right," I said. It was just a matter of climbing more stairs. I went on up the stairs carrying my phantom suitcase. I walked down the hall to Cohn's room. The door was shut and I knocked.

"Who is it?"

"Barnes."

"Come in, Jake."

I opened the door and went in, and set down my suitcase. There was no light in the room. Cohn was lying, face down, on the bed in the dark.

"Hello, Jake."

"Don't call me Jake."

I stood by the door. It was just like this that I had come home. Now it was a hot bath that I needed. A deep, hot bath, to lie back in.

"Where's the bathroom?" I asked.

Cohn was crying. There he was, face down on the bed, crying

He had on a white polo shirt, the kind he'd worn at Princeton.

"I'm sorry, Jake. Please forgive me."

"Forgive you, hell."

"Please forgive me, Jake."

I did not say anything. I stood there by the door.

"I was crazy. You must see how it was."

"Oh, that's all right."

"I couldn't stand it about Brett."

"You called me a pimp."

I did not care. I wanted a hot bath. I wanted a hot bath in deep water.

"I know. Please don't remember it. I was crazy."

"That's all right."

He was crying. His voice was funny. He lay there in his white shirt on the bed in the dark. His polo shirt.

"I'm going away in the morning."

He was crying without making any noise.

"I just couldn't stand it about Brett. I've been through hell, Jake. It's been simply hell. When I met her down here Brett treated me as though I were a perfect stranger. I just couldn't stand it. We lived together at San Sebastian. I suppose you know it. I can't stand it any more."

He lay there on the bed.

"Well," I said, "I'm going to take a bath."

"You were the only friend I had, and I loved Brett so."

"Well," I said, "so long."

"I guess it isn't any use," he said. "I guess it isn't any damn use."

"What?"

"Everything. Please say you forgive me, Jake."

"Sure," I said. "It's all right."

"I felt so terribly. I've been through such hell, Jake. Now everything's gone. Everything."

"Well," I said, "so long. I've got to go."

He rolled over, sat on the edge of the bed, and then stood up.

"So long, Jake," he said. "You'll shake hands, won't you?"

"Sure. Why not?"

We shook hands. In the dark I could not see his face very well.

"Well," I said, "see you in the morning."

"I'm going away in the morning."

"Oh, yes," I said.

I went out. Cohn was standing in the door of the room.

"Are you all right, Jake?" he asked.

"Oh, yes," I said. "I'm all right."

I could not find the bathroom. After a while I found it. There was a deep stone tub. I turned on the taps and the water would not run. I sat down on the edge of the bath-tub. When I got up to go I found I had taken off my shoes. I hunted for them and found them and carried them down-stairs. I found my room and went inside and undressed and got into bed.

I woke with a headache and the noise of the bands going by in the street. I remembered I had promised to take Bill's friend Edna to see the bulls go through the street and into the ring. I dressed and went down-stairs and out into the cold early morning. People were crossing the square, hurrying toward the bull-ring Across the square were the two lines of men in front of the ticket-booths. They were still waiting for the tickets to go on sale at seven o'clock. I hurried across the street to the café. The waiter told me that my friends had been there and gone.

"How many were they?"

"Two gentlemen and a lady."

That was all right. Bill and Mike were with Edna. She had been afraid last night they would pass out. That was why I was to be sure to take her. I drank the coffee and hurried with the other people toward the bull-ring. I was not groggy now. There

was only a bad headache. Everything looked sharp and clear, and
the town smelt of the early morning.

The stretch of ground from the edge of the town to the bull-
ring was muddy. There was a crowd all along the fence that led
to the ring, and the outside balconies and the top of the bull-ring
were solid with people. I heard the rocket and I knew I could not
get into the ring in time to see the bulls come in, so I shoved
through the crowd to the fence. I was pushed close against the
planks of the fence. Between the two fences of the runway the
police were clearing the crowd along. They walked or trotted on
into the bull-ring. Then people commenced to come running. A
drunk slipped and fell. Two policemen grabbed him and rushed
him over to the fence. The crowd were running fast now. There
was a great shout from the crowd, and putting my head through
between the boards I saw the bulls just coming out of the street
into the long running pen. They were going fast and gaining on
the crowd. Just then another drunk started out from the fence
with a blouse in his hands. He wanted to do capework with the
bulls. The two policemen tore out, collared him, one hit him with
a club, and they dragged him against the fence and stood flattened out against the fence as the last of the crowd and the bulls
went by. There were so many people running ahead of the bulls
that the mass thickened and slowed up going through the gate
into the ring, and as the bulls passed, galloping together, heavy,
muddy-sided, horns swinging, one shot ahead, caught a man in
the running crowd in the back and lifted him in the air. Both the
man's arms were by his sides, his head went back as the horn went
in, and the bull lifted him and then dropped him. The bull
picked another man running in front, but the man disappeared
into the crowd, and the crowd was through the gate and into the
ring with the bulls behind them. The red door of the ring went
shut, the crowd on the outside balconies of the bull-ring were

pressing through to the inside, there was a shout, then another shout.

The man who had been gored lay face down in the trampled mud. People climbed over the fence, and I could not see the man because the crowd was so thick around him. From inside the ring came the shouts. Each shout meant a charge by some bull into the crowd. You could tell by the degree of intensity in the shout how bad a thing it was that was happening. Then the rocket went up that meant the steers had gotten the bulls out of the ring and into the corrals. I left the fence and started back toward the town.

Back in the town I went to the café to have a second coffee and some buttered toast. The waiters were sweeping out the café and mopping off the tables. One came over and took my order.

"Anything happen at the encierro?"

"I didn't see it all. One man was badly cogido."

"Where?"

"Here." I put one hand on the small of my back and the other on my chest, where it looked as though the horn must have come through. The waiter nodded his head and swept the crumbs from the table with his cloth.

"Badly cogido," he said. "All for sport. All for pleasure."

He went away and came back with the long-handled coffee and milk pots. He poured the milk and coffee. It came out of the long spouts in two streams into the big cup. The waiter nodded his head.

"Badly cogido through the back," he said. He put the pots down on the table and sat down in the chair at the table. "A big horn wound. All for fun. Just for fun. What do you think of that?"

"I don't know."

"That's it. All for fun. Fun, you understand."

"You're not an aficionado?"

"Me? What are bulls? Animals. Brute animals." He stood up

and put his hand on the small of his back. "Right through the back. A cornada right through the back. For fun—you understand."

He shook his head and walked away, carrying the coffee-pots. Two men were going by in the street. The waiter shouted to them. They were grave-looking. One shook his head. "Muerto!" he called.

The waiter nodded his head. The two men went on. They were on some errand. The waiter came over to my table.

"You hear? Muerto. Dead. He's dead. With a horn through him. All for morning fun. Es muy flamenco."

"It's bad."

"Not for me," the waiter said. "No fun in that for me."

Later in the day we learned that the man who was killed was named Vicente Girones, and came from near Tafalla. The next day in the paper we read that he was twenty-eight years old, and had a farm, a wife, and two children. He had continued to come to the fiesta each year after he was married. The next day his wife came in from Tafalla to be with the body, and the day after there was a service in the chapel of San Fermin, and the coffin was carried to the railway-station by members of the dancing and drinking society of Tafalla. The drums marched ahead, and there was music on the fifes, and behind the men who carried the coffin walked the wife and two children. . . . Behind them marched all the members of the dancing and drinking societies of Pamplona, Estella, Tafalla, and Sanguesa who could stay over for the funeral. The coffin was loaded into the baggage-car of the train, and the widow and the two children rode, sitting, all three together, in an open third-class railway-carriage. The train started with a jerk, and then ran smoothly, going down grade around the edge of the plateau and out into the fields of grain that blew in the wind on the plain on the way to Tafalla.

The bull who killed Vicente Girones was named Bocanegra, was Number 118 of the bull-breeding establishment of Sanchez Taberno, and was killed by Pedro Romero as the third bull of that same afternoon. His ear was cut by popular acclamation and given to Pedro Romero, who, in turn, gave it to Brett, who wrapped it in a handkerchief belonging to myself, and left both ear and hand-kerchief, along with a number of Muratti cigarette-stubs, shoved far back in the drawer of the bed-table that stood beside her bed in the Hotel Montoya, in Pamplona.

Back in the hotel, the night watchman was sitting on a bench inside the door. He had been there all night and was very sleepy. He stood up as I came in. Three of the waitresses came in at the same time. They had been to the morning show at the bull-ring. They went up-stairs laughing. I followed them up-stairs and went into my room. I took off my shoes and lay down on the bed. The window was open onto the balcony and the sunlight was bright in the room. I did not feel sleepy. It must have been half past three o'clock when I had gone to bed and the bands had waked me at six. My jaw was sore on both sides. I felt it with my thumb and fingers. That damn Cohn. He should have hit somebody the first time he was insulted, and then gone away. He was so sure that Brett loved him. He was going to stay, and true love would conquer all. Some one knocked on the door.

"Come in."

It was Bill and Mike. They sat down on the bed.

"Some encierro," Bill said. "Some encierro."

"I say, weren't you there?" Mike asked. "Ring for some beer, Bill."

"What a morning!" Bill said. He mopped off his face. "My God! what a morning! And here's old Jake. Old Jake, the human punching-bag."

"What happened inside?"

"Good God!" Bill said, "what happened, Mike?"

"There were these bulls coming in," Mike said. "Just ahead of them was the crowd, and some chap tripped and brought the whole lot of them down."

"And the bulls all came in right over them," Bill said.

"I heard them yell."

"That was Edna," Bill said.

"Chaps kept coming out and waving their shirts."

"One bull went along the barrera and hooked everybody over."

"They took about twenty chaps to the infirmary," Mike said.

"What a morning!" Bill said. "The damn police kept arresting chaps that wanted to go and commit suicide with the bulls."

"The steers took them in, in the end," Mike said.

"It took about an hour."

"It was really about a quarter of an hour," Mike objected.

"Oh, go to hell," Bill said. "You've been in the war. It was two hours and a half for me."

"Where's that beer?" Mike asked.

"What did you do with the lovely Edna?"

"We took her home just now. She's gone to bed."

"How did she like it?"

"Fine. We told her it was just like that every morning."

"She was impressed," Mike said.

"She wanted us to go down in the ring, too," Bill said. "She likes action."

"I said it wouldn't be fair to my creditors," Mike said.

"What a morning," Bill said. "And what a night!"

"How's your jaw, Jake?" Mike asked.

"Sore," I said.

Bill laughed.

"Why didn't you hit him with a chair?"

"You can talk," Mike said. "He'd have knocked you out, too.

I never saw him hit me. I rather think I saw him just before, and then quite suddenly I was sitting down in the street, and Jake was lying under a table."

"Where did he go afterward?" I asked.

"Here she is," Mike said. "Here's the beautiful lady with the beer."

The chambermaid put the tray with the beer-bottles and glasses down on the table.

"Now bring up three more bottles," Mike said.

"Where did Cohn go after he hit me?" I asked Bill.

"Don't you know about that?" Mike was opening a beer-bottle. He poured the beer into one of the glasses, holding the glass close to the bottle.

"Really?" Bill asked.

"Why he went in and found Brett and the bull-fighter chap in the bull-fighter's room, and then he massacred the poor, bloody bull-fighter."

"No."

"Yes."

"What a night!" Bill said.

"He nearly killed the poor, bloody bull-fighter. Then Cohn wanted to take Brett away. Wanted to make an honest woman of her, I imagine. Damned touching scene."

He took a long drink of the beer.

"He is an ass."

"What happened?"

"Brett gave him what for. She told him off. I think she was rather good."

"I'll bet she was," Bill said.

"Then Cohn broke down and cried, and wanted to shake hands with the bull-fighter fellow. He wanted to shake hands with Brett, too."

"I know. He shook hands with me."

"Did he? Well, they weren't having any of it. The bull-fighter fellow was rather good. He didn't say much, but he kept getting up and getting knocked down again. Cohn couldn't knock him out. It must have been damned funny."

"Where did you hear all this?"

"Brett. I saw her this morning."

"What happened finally?"

"It seems the bull-fighter fellow was sitting on the bed. He'd been knocked down about fifteen times, and he wanted to fight some more. Brett held him and wouldn't let him get up. He was weak, but Brett couldn't hold him, and he got up. Then Cohn said he wouldn't hit him again. Said he couldn't do it. Said it would be wicked. So the bull-fighter chap sort of rather staggered over to him. Cohn went back against the wall.

" 'So you won't hit me?'

" 'No,' said Cohn. 'I'd be ashamed to.'

"So the bull-fighter fellow hit him just as hard as he could in the face, and then sat down on the floor. He couldn't get up, Brett said. Cohn wanted to pick him up and carry him to the bed. He said if Cohn helped him he'd kill him, and he'd kill him anyway this morning if Cohn wasn't out of town. Cohn was crying, and Brett had told him off, and he wanted to shake hands. I've told you that before."

"Tell the rest," Bill said.

"It seems the bull-fighter chap was sitting on the floor. He was waiting to get strength enough to get up and hit Cohn again. Brett wasn't having any shaking hands, and Cohn was crying and telling her how much he loved her, and she was telling him not to be a ruddy ass. Then Cohn leaned down to shake hands with the bull-fighter fellow. No hard feelings, you know. All for forgiveness. And the bull-fighter chap hit him in the face again."

"That's quite a kid," Bill said.

"He ruined Cohn," Mike said. "You know I don't think Cohn will ever want to knock people about again."

"When did you see Brett?"

"This morning. She came in to get some things. She's looking after this Romero lad."

He poured out another bottle of beer.

"Brett's rather cut up. But she loves looking after people. That's how we came to go off together. She was looking after me."

"I know," I said.

"I'm rather drunk," Mike said. "I think I'll *stay* rather drunk. This is all awfully amusing, but it's not too pleasant. It's not too pleasant for me."

He drank off the beer.

"I gave Brett what for, you know. I said if she would go about with Jews and bull-fighters and such people, she must expect trouble." He leaned forward. "I say, Jake, do you mind if I drink that bottle of yours? She'll bring you another one."

"Please," I said. "I wasn't drinking it, anyway."

Mike started to open the bottle. "Would you mind opening it?" I pressed up the wire fastener and poured it for him.

"You know," Mike went on, "Brett was rather good. She's always rather good. I gave her a fearful hiding about Jews and bull-fighters, and all those sort of people, and do you know what she said: 'Yes. I've had such a hell of a happy life with the British aristocracy!'"

He took a drink.

"That was rather good. Ashley, chap she got the title from, was a sailor, you know. Ninth baronet. When he came home he wouldn't sleep in a bed. Always made Brett sleep on the floor. Finally, when he got really bad, he used to tell her he'd kill her. Always slept with a loaded service revolver. Brett used to take the shells out when he'd gone to sleep. She hasn't had an absolutely happy life, Brett. Damned shame, too. She enjoys things so."

He stood up. His hand was shaky.

"I'm going in the room. Try and get a little sleep."

He smiled.

"We go too long without sleep in these fiestas. I'm going to start now and get plenty of sleep. Damn bad thing not to get sleep. Makes you frightfully nervy."

"We'll see you at noon at the Iruña," Bill said.

Mike went out the door. We heard him in the next room.

He rang the bell and the chambermaid came and knocked at the door.

"Bring up half a dozen bottles of beer and a bottle of Fundador," Mike told her.

"Si, Señorito."

"I'm going to bed," Bill said. "Poor old Mike. I had a hell of a row about him last night."

"Where? At that Milano place?"

"Yes. There was a fellow there that had helped pay Brett and Mike out of Cannes, once. He was damned nasty."

"I know the story."

"I didn't. Nobody ought to have a right to say things about Mike."

"That's what makes it bad."

"They oughtn't to have any right. I wish to hell they didn't have any right. I'm going to bed."

"Was anybody killed in the ring?"

"I don't think so. Just badly hurt."

"A man was killed outside in the runway."

"Was there?" said Bill.

CHAPTER XVIII

At noon we were all at the café. It was crowded. We were eating shrimps and drinking beer. The town was crowded. Every street was full. Big motor-cars from Biarritz and San Sebastian kept driving up and parking around the square. They brought people for the bull-fight. Sight-seeing cars came up, too. There was one with twenty-five Englishwomen in it. They sat in the big, white car and looked through their glasses at the fiesta. The dancers were all quite drunk. It was the last day of the fiesta.

The fiesta was solid and unbroken, but the motor-cars and tourist-cars made little islands of onlookers. When the cars emptied, the onlookers were absorbed into the crowd. You did not see them again except as sport clothes, odd-looking at a table among the closely packed peasants in black smocks. The fiesta absorbed even the Biarritz English so that you did not see them unless you passed close to a table. All the time there was music in the street. The drums kept on pounding and the pipes were going. Inside the cafés men with their hands gripping the table, or on each other's shoulders, were singing the hard-voiced singing.

"Here comes Brett," Bill said.

I looked and saw her coming through the crowd in the square, walking, her head up, as though the fiesta were being staged in her honor, and she found it pleasant and amusing.

"Hello, you chaps!" she said. "I say, I *have* a thirst."

"Get another big beer," Bill said to the waiter.

"Shrimps?"

"Is Cohn gone?" Brett asked.

"Yes," Bill said. "He hired a car."

The beer came. Brett started to lift the glass mug and her hand shook. She saw it and smiled, and leaned forward and took a long sip.

"Good beer."

"Very good," I said. I was nervous about Mike. I did not think he had slept. He must have been drinking all the time, but he seemed to be under control.

"I heard Cohn had hurt you, Jake," Brett said.

"No. Knocked me out. That was all."

"I say, he did hurt Pedro Romero," Brett said. "He hurt him most badly."

"How is he?"

"He'll be all right. He won't go out of the room."

"Does he look badly?"

"Very. He was really hurt. I told him I wanted to pop out and see you chaps for a minute."

"Is he going to fight?"

"Rather. I'm going with you, if you don't mind."

"How's your boy friend?" Mike asked. He had not listened to anything that Brett had said.

"Brett's got a bull-fighter," he said. "She had a Jew named Cohn, but he turned out badly."

Brett stood up.

"I am not going to listen to that sort of rot from you, Michael."

"How's your boy friend?"

"Damned well," Brett said. "Watch him this afternoon."

"Brett's got a bull-fighter," Mike said. "A beautiful, bloody bull-fighter."

"Would you mind walking over with me? I want to talk to you, Jake."

"Tell him all about your bull-fighter," Mike said. "Oh, to hell with your bull-fighter!" He tipped the table so that all the beers and the dish of shrimps went over in a crash.

"Come on," Brett said. "Let's get out of this."

In the crowd crossing the square I said: "How is it?"

"I'm not going to see him after lunch until the fight. His people come in and dress him. They're very angry about me, he says."

Brett was radiant. She was happy. The sun was out and the day was bright.

"I feel altogether changed," Brett said. "You've no idea, Jake."

"Anything you want me to do?"

"No, just go to the fight with me."

"We'll see you at lunch?"

"No. I'm eating with him."

We were standing under the arcade at the door of the hotel. They were carrying tables out and setting them up under the arcade.

"Want to take a turn out to the park?" Brett asked. "I don't want to go up yet. I fancy he's sleeping."

We walked along past the theatre and out of the square and along through the barracks of the fair, moving with the crowd between the lines of booths. We came out on a cross-street that led to the Paseo de Sarasate. We could see the crowd walking there, all the fashionably dressed people. They were making the turn at the upper end of the park.

"Don't let's go there," Brett said. "I don't want staring at just now."

We stood in the sunlight. It was hot and good after the rain and the clouds from the sea.

"I hope the wind goes down," Brett said. "It's very bad for him."

"So do I."

"He says the bulls are all right."

"They're good."

"Is that San Fermin's?"

Brett looked at the yellow wall of the chapel.

"Yes. Where the show started on Sunday."

"Let's go in. Do you mind? I'd rather like to pray a little for him or something."

We went in through the heavy leather door that moved very lightly. It was dark inside. Many people were praying. You saw them as your eyes adjusted themselves to the half-light. We knelt at one of the long wooden benches. After a little I felt Brett stiffen beside me, and saw she was looking straight ahead.

"Come on," she whispered throatily. "Let's get out of here. Makes me damned nervous."

Outside in the hot brightness of the street Brett looked up at the tree-tops in the wind. The praying had not been much of a success.

"Don't know why I get so nervy in church," Brett said. "Never does me any good."

We walked along.

"I'm damned bad for a religious atmosphere," Brett said. "I've the wrong type of face."

"You know," Brett said, "I'm not worried about him at all. I just feel happy about him."

"Good."

"I wish the wind would drop, though."

"It's liable to go down by five o'clock."

"Let's hope."

"You might pray," I laughed.

"Never does me any good. I've never gotten anything I prayed for. Have you?"

"Oh, yes."

"Oh, rot," said Brett. "Maybe it works for some people, though You don't look very religious, Jake."

"I'm pretty religious."

"Oh, rot," said Brett. "Don't start proselyting to-day. To-day's going to be bad enough as it is."

It was the first time I had seen her in the old happy, careless way since before she went off with Cohn. We were back again in front of the hotel. All the tables were set now, and already several were filled with people eating.

"Do look after Mike," Brett said. "Don't let him get too bad."

"Your frients haff gone up-stairs," the German maitre d'hôtel said in English. He was a continual eavesdropper. Brett turned to him:

"Thank you, so much. Have you anything else to say?"

"No, *ma'am*."

"Good," said Brett.

"Save us a table for three," I said to the German. He smiled his dirty little pink-and-white smile.

"Iss madam eating here?"

"No," Brett said.

"Den I think a tabul for two will be enuff."

"Don't talk to him," Brett said. "Mike must have been in bad shape," she said on the stairs. We passed Montoya on the stairs. He bowed and did not smile.

"I'll see you at the café," Brett said. "Thank you, so much, Jake."

We had stopped at the floor our rooms were on. She went straight down the hall and into Romero's room. She did not knock. She simply opened the door, went in, and closed it behind her.

I stood in front of the door of Mike's room and knocked. There was no answer. I tried the knob and it opened. Inside the room was in great disorder. All the bags were opened and clothing was strewn around. There were empty bottles beside the bed. Mike lay on the bed looking like a death mask of himself. He opened his eyes and looked at me.

"Hello, Jake," he said very slowly. "I'm getting a lit tle sleep. I've want ed a lit tle sleep for a long time."

"Let me cover you over."

"No. I'm quite warm."

"Don't go. I have n't got ten to sleep yet."

"You'll sleep, Mike. Don't worry, boy."

"Brett's got a bull-fighter," Mike said. "But her Jew has gone away."

He turned his head and looked at me.

"Damned good thing, what?"

"Yes. Now go to sleep, Mike. You ought to get some sleep."

"I'm just start ing. I'm go ing to get a lit tle sleep."

He shut his eyes. I went out of the room and turned the door to quietly. Bill was in my room reading the paper.

"See Mike?"

"Yes."

"Let's go and eat."

"I won't eat down-stairs with that German head waiter. He was damned snotty when I was getting Mike up-stairs."

"He was snotty to us, too."

"Let's go out and eat in the town."

We went down the stairs. On the stairs we passed a girl coming up with a covered tray.

"There goes Brett's lunch," Bill said.

"And the kid's," I said.

Outside on the terrace under the arcade the German head waiter came up. His red cheeks were shiny. He was being polite.

"I haff a tabul for two for you gentlemen." he said.

"Go sit at it," Bill said. We went on out across the street.

We ate at a restaurant in a side street off the square. They were all men eating in the restaurant. It was full of smoke and drinking and singing. The food was good and so was the wine. We did not talk much. Afterward we went to the café and watched the fiesta come to the boiling-point. Brett came over soon after lunch. She said she had looked in the room and that Mike was asleep.

When the fiesta boiled over and toward the bull-ring we went with the crowd. Brett sat at the ringside between Bill and me. Directly below us was the callejon, the passageway between the stands and the red fence of the barrera. Behind us the concrete stands filled solidly. Out in front, beyond the red fence, the sand of the ring was smooth-rolled and yellow. It looked a little heavy from the rain, but it was dry in the sun and firm and smooth. The sword-handlers and bull-ring servants came down the callejon carrying on their shoulders the wicker baskets of fighting capes and muletas. They were bloodstained and compactly folded and packed in the baskets. The sword-handlers opened the heavy leather sword-cases so the red wrapped hilts of the sheaf of swords showed as the leather case leaned against the fence. They unfolded the dark-stained red flannel of the muletas and fixed batons in them to spread the stuff and give the matador something to hold. Brett watched it all. She was absorbed in the professional details.

"He's his name stencilled on all the capes and muletas," she said. "Why do they call them muletas?"

"I don't know."

"I wonder if they ever launder them."

"I don't think so. It might spoil the color."

"The blood must stiffen them," Bill said.

"Funny," Brett said. "How one doesn't mind the blood."

Below in the narrow passage of the callejon the sword-handlers arranged everything. All the seats were full. Above, all the boxes were full. There was not an empty seat except in the President's box. When he came in the fight would start. Across the smooth sand, in the high doorway that led into the corrals, the bull-fighters were standing, their arms furled in their capes, talking, waiting for the signal to march in across the arena. Brett was watching them with the glasses.

"Here, would you like to look?"

I looked through the glasses and saw the three matadors. Romero was in the centre, Belmonte on his left, Marcial on his right. Back of them were their people, and behind the bande-rilleros, back in the passageway and in the open space of the corral, I saw the picadors. Romero was wearing a black suit. His tricornered hat was low down over his eyes. I could not see his face clearly under the hat, but it looked badly marked. He was looking straight ahead. Marcial was smoking a cigarette guard-edly, holding it in his hand. Belmonte looked ahead, his face wan and yellow, his long wolf jaw out. He was looking at nothing. Neither he nor Romero seemed to have anything in common with the others. They were all alone. The President came in; there was handclapping above us in the grand stand, and I handed the glasses to Brett. There was applause. The music started. Brett looked through the glasses.

"Here, take them," she said.

Through the glasses I saw Belmonte speak to Romero. Marcial straightened up and dropped his cigarette, and, looking straight ahead, their heads back, their free arms swinging, the three mata-dors walked out. Behind them came all the procession, opening out, all striding in step, all the capes furled, everybody with free arms swinging, and behind rode the picadors, their pics rising like lances. Behind all came the two trains of mules and the bull-ring servants. The matadors bowed, holding their hats on, before the President's box, and then came over to the barrera below us.

Pedro Romero took off his heavy gold-brocaded cape and handed it over the fence to his sword-handler. He said something to the sword-handler. Close below us we saw Romero's lips were puffed, both eyes were discolored. His face was discolored and swollen. The sword-handler took the cape, looked up at Brett, and came over to us and handed up the cape.

"Spread it out in front of you," I said.

Brett leaned forward. The cape was heavy and smoothly stiff with gold. The sword-handler looked back, shook his head, and said something. A man beside me leaned over toward Brett.

"He doesn't want you to spread it," he said. "You should fold it and keep it in your lap."

Brett folded the heavy cape.

Romero did not look up at us. He was speaking to Belmonte. Belmonte had sent his formal cape over to some friends. He looked across at them and smiled, his wolf smile that was only with the mouth. Romero leaned over the barrera and asked for the water-jug. The sword-handler brought it and Romero poured water over the percale of his fighting-cape, and then scuffed the lower folds in the sand with his slippered foot.

"What's that for?" Brett asked.

"To give it weight in the wind."

"His face looks bad," Bill said.

"He feels very badly," Brett said. "He should be in bed."

The first bull was Belmonte's. Belmonte was very good. But because he got thirty thousand pesetas and people had stayed in line all night to buy tickets to see him, the crowd demanded that he should be more than very good. Belmonte's great attraction is working close to the bull. In bull-fighting they speak of the terrain of the bull and the terrain of the bull-fighter. As long as a bull-fighter stays in his own terrain he is comparatively safe. Each time he enters into the terrain of the bull he is in great danger. Belmonte, in his best days, worked always in the terrain of the bull. This way he gave the sensation of coming tragedy. People went to the corrida to see Belmonte, to be given tragic sensations, and perhaps to see the death of Belmonte. Fifteen years ago they said if you wanted to see Belmonte you should go quickly, while he was still alive. Since then he has killed more than a thousand bulls. When he retired the legend grew up about how his bullfighting had been, and when he came out of retirement the public were disappointed because no real man could work as close to the bulls as Belmonte was supposed to have done, not, of course, even Belmonte.

Also Belmonte imposed conditions and insisted that his bulls should not be too large, nor too dangerously armed with horns, and so the element that was necessary to give the sensation of tragedy was not there, and the public, who wanted three times as much from Belmonte, who was sick with a fistula, as Belmonte had ever been able to give, felt defrauded and cheated, and Belmonte's jaw came further out in contempt, and his face turned yellower, and he moved with greater difficulty as his pain increased, and finally the crowd were actively against him, and he was utterly contemptuous and indifferent. He had meant to have a great afternoon, and instead it was an afternoon of sneers, shouted insults, and finally a volley of cushions and pieces of bread and vegetables, thrown down at him in the plaza where he had had his greatest triumphs. His jaw only went further out. Sometimes he turned to smile that toothed, long-jawed, lipless smile when he was called something particularly insulting, and always the pain that any movement produced grew stronger and stronger, until finally his yellow face was parchment color, and after his second bull was dead and the throwing of bread and cushions was over, after he had saluted the President with the same wolf-jawed smile and contemptuous eyes, and handed his sword over the barrera to be wiped, and put back in its case, he passed through into the callejon and leaned on the barrera below us, his head on his arms, not seeing, not hearing anything, only going through his pain. When he looked up, finally, he asked for a drink of water. He swallowed a little, rinsed his mouth, spat the water, took his cape, and went back into the ring.

Because they were against Belmonte the public were for Romero. From the moment he left the barrera and went toward the bull they applauded him. Belmonte watched Romero, too, watched him always without seeming to. He paid no attention to Marcial. Marcial was the sort of thing he knew all about. He had come out of retirement to compete with Marcial, knowing it was a competition gained in advance. He had expected to compete with Marcial and the other stars of the decadence of bull-fighting, and he knew that the sincerity of his own bull-fighting would be so set off by the false æsthetics of the bull-fighters of the decadent period that he would only have to be in the ring. His return from retirement had been spoiled by Romero. Romero did always, smoothly, calmly, and beautifully, what he, Belmonte, could only bring himself to do now sometimes. The crowd felt it, even the people from Biarritz, even the American ambassador saw it, finally. It was a competition that Belmonte would not enter because it would lead only to a bad horn wound or death. Belmonte was no longer well enough. He no longer had his greatest moments in the bull-ring. He was not sure that there were any great moments. Things were not the same and now life only came in flashes. He had flashes of the old greatness with his bulls, but they were not of value because he had discounted them in advance when he had picked the bulls out for their safety, getting out of a motor and leaning on a fence, looking over at the herd on the ranch of his friend the bull-breeder. So he had two small, manageable bulls without much horns, and when he felt the greatness again coming, just a little of it through the pain that was always with him, it had been discounted and sold in advance, and it did not give him a good feeling. It was the greatness, but it did not make bull-fighting wonderful to him any more.

Pedro Romero had the greatness. He loved bull-fighting, and I think he loved the bulls, and I think he loved Brett. Everything of which he could control the locality he did in front of her all that afternoon. Never once did he look up. He made it stronger that way, and did it for himself, too, as well as for her. Because he did not look up to ask if it pleased he did it all for himself inside, and it strengthened him, and yet he did it for her, too. But he did not do it for her at any loss to himself. He gained by it all through the afternoon.

His first "quite" was directly below us. The three matadors take the bull in turn after each charge he makes at a picador. Belmonte was the first. Marcial was the second. Then came Romero. The three of them were standing at the left of the horse. The picador, his hat down over his eyes, the shaft of his pic angling sharply toward the bull, kicked in the spurs and held them and with the reins in his left hand walked the horse forward toward the bull. The bull was watching. Seemingly he watched the white horse, but really he watched the triangular steel point of the pic. Romero, watching, saw the bull start to turn his head. He did not want to charge. Romero flicked his cape so the color caught the bull's eye. The bull charged with the reflex, charged, and found not the flash of color but a white horse, and a man leaned far over the horse, shot the steel point of the long hickory shaft into the hump of muscle on the bull's shoulder, and pulled his horse sideways as he pivoted on the pic, making a wound, enforcing the iron into the bull's shoulder, making him bleed for Belmonte.

The bull did not insist under the iron. He did not really want to get at the horse. He turned and the group broke apart and Romero was taking him out with his cape. He took him out softly and smoothly, and then stopped and, standing squarely in front of the bull, offered him the cape. The bull's tail went up and he charged, and Romero moved his arms ahead of the bull, wheeling, his feet firmed. The dampened, mud-weighted cape swung open and full as a sail fills, and Romero pivoted with it just ahead of the bull. At the end of the pass they were facing each other again. Romero smiled. The bull wanted it again, and Romero's cape filled again, this time on the other side. Each time he let the bull pass so close that the man and the bull and the cape that filled and pivoted ahead of the bull were all one sharply etched mass. It was all so slow and so controlled. It was as though he were rocking the bull to sleep. He made four veronicas like that, and finished with a half-veronica that turned his back on the bull and came away toward the applause, his hand on his hip, his cape on his arm, and the bull watching his back going away.

In his own bulls he was perfect. His first bull did not see well. After the first two passes with the cape Romero knew exactly how bad the vision was impaired. He worked accordingly. It was not brilliant bull-fighting. It was only perfect bull-fighting. The crowd wanted the bull changed. They made a great row. Nothing very fine could happen with a bull that could not see the lures, but the President would not order him replaced.

"Why don't they change him?" Brett asked.

"They've paid for him. They don't want to lose their money."

"It's hardly fair to Romero."

"Watch how he handles a bull that can't see the color."

"It's the sort of thing I don't like to see."

It was not nice to watch if you cared anything about the person who was doing it. With the bull who could not see the colors of the capes, or the scarlet flannel of the muleta, Romero had to make the bull consent with his body. He had to get so close that the bull saw his body, and would start for it, and then shift the bull's charge to the flannel and finish out the pass in the classic manner. The Biarritz crowd did not like it. They thought Romero was afraid, and that was why he gave that little sidestep each time as he transferred the bull's charge from his own body to the flannel. They preferred Belmonte's imitation of himself or Marcial's imitation of Belmonte. There were three of them in the row behind us.

"What's he afraid of the bull for? The bull's so dumb he only goes after the cloth."

"He's just a young bull-fighter. He hasn't learned it yet."

"But I thought he was fine with the cape before."

"Probably he's nervous now."

Out in the centre of the ring, all alone, Romero was going on with the same thing, getting so close that the bull could see him plainly, offering the body, offering it again a little closer, the bull watching dully, then so close that the bull thought he had him, offering again and finally drawing the charge and then, just before the horns came, giving the bull the red cloth to follow with that little, almost imperceptible, jerk that so offended the critical judgment of the Biarritz bull-fight experts.

"He's going to kill now," I said to Brett. "The bull's still strong. He wouldn't wear himself out."

Out in the centre of the ring Romero profiled in front of the bull, drew the sword out from the folds of the muleta, rose on his toes, and sighted along the blade. The bull charged as Romero charged. Romero's left hand dropped the muleta over the bull's muzzle to blind him, his left shoulder went forward between the horns as the sword went in, and for just an instant he and the bull were one, Romero way out over the bull, the right arm extended high up to where the hilt of the sword had gone in between the bull's shoulders. Then the figure was broken. There was a little jolt as Romero came clear, and then he was standing, one hand up, facing the bull, his shirt ripped out from under his sleeve, the white blowing in the wind, and the bull, the red sword hilt tight between his shoulders, his head going down and his legs settling.

"There he goes," Bill said.

Romero was close enough so the bull could see him. His hand still up, he spoke to the bull. The bull gathered himself, then his head went forward and he went over slowly, then all over, suddenly, four feet in the air.

They handed the sword to Romero, and carrying it blade down, the muleta in his other hand, he walked over to in front of the President's box, bowed, straightened, and came over to the barrera and handed over the sword and muleta.

"Bad one," said the sword-handler.

"He made me sweat," said Romero. He wiped off his face. The sword-handler handed him the water-jug. Romero wiped his lips. It hurt him to drink out of the jug. He did not look up at us.

Marcial had a big day. They were still applauding him when Romero's last bull came in. It was the bull that had sprinted out and killed the man in the morning running.

During Romero's first bull his hurt face had been very noticeable. Everything he did showed it. All the concentration of the awkwardly delicate working with the bull that could not see well brought it out. The fight with Cohn had not touched his spirit but his face had been smashed and his body hurt. He was wiping all that out now. Each thing that he did with this bull wiped that out a little cleaner. It was a good bull, a big bull, and with horns, and it turned and recharged easily and surely. He was what Romero wanted in bulls.

When he had finished his work with the muleta and was ready to kill, the crowd made him go on. They did not want the bull killed yet, they did not want it to be over. Romero went on. It was like a course in bull-fighting. All the passes he linked up, all completed, all slow, templed and smooth. There were no tricks and no mystifications. There was no brusqueness. And each pass as it reached the summit gave you a sudden ache inside. The crowd did not want it ever to be finished.

The bull was squared on all four feet to be killed, and Romero killed directly below us. He killed not as he had been forced to by the last bull, but as he wanted to. He profiled directly in front of the bull, drew the sword out of the folds of the muleta and sighted along the blade. The bull watched him. Romero spoke to the bull and tapped one of his feet. The bull charged and Romero waited for the charge, the muleta held low, sighting along the blade, his feet firm. Then without taking a step forward, he became one with the bull, the sword was in high between the shoulders, the bull had followed the low-swung flannel, that disappeared as Romero lurched clear to the left, and it was over. The bull tried to go forward, his legs commenced to settle, he swung from side to side, hesitated, then went down on his knees, and Romero's older brother leaned forward behind him and drove a short knife into the bull's neck at the base of the horns. The first time he missed. He drove the knife in again, and the bull went over, twitching and rigid. Romero's brother, holding the bull's horn in one hand, the knife in the other, looked up at the President's box. Handkerchiefs were waving all over the bull-ring. The President looked down from the box and waved his handkerchief. The brother cut the notched black ear from the dead bull and trotted over with it to Romero. The bull lay heavy and black on the sand, his tongue out. Boys were running toward him from all parts of the arena, making a little circle around him. They were starting to dance around the bull.

Romero took the ear from his brother and held it up toward the President. The President bowed and Romero, running to get ahead of the crowd, came toward us. He leaned up against the barrera and gave the ear to Brett. He nodded his head and smiled. The crowd were all about him. Brett held down the cape.

"You liked it?" Romero called.

Brett did not say anything. They looked at each other and smiled. Brett had the ear in her hand.

"Don't get bloody," Romero said, and grinned. The crowd wanted him. Several boys shouted at Brett. The crowd was the boys, the dancers, and the drunks. Romero turned and tried to get through the crowd. They were all around him trying to lift him and put him on their shoulders. He fought and twisted away, and started running, in the midst of them, toward the exit. He did not want to be carried on people's shoulders. But they held him and lifted him. It was uncomfortable and his legs were spraddled and his body was very sore. They were lifting him and all running toward the gate. He had his hand on somebody's shoulder. He looked around at us apologetically. The crowd, running, went out the gate with him.

We all three went back to the hotel. Brett went upstairs. Bill and I sat in the down-stairs dining-room and ate some hard-boiled eggs and drank several bottles of beer. Belmonte came down in his street clothes with his manager and two other men. They sat at the next table and ate. Belmonte ate very little. They were leaving on the seven o'clock train for Barcelona. Belmonte wore a blue-striped shirt and a dark suit, and ate soft-boiled eggs. The others ate a big meal. Belmonte did not talk. He only answered questions.

Bill was tired after the bull-fight. So was I. We both took a bull-fight very hard. We sat and ate the eggs and I watched Belmonte and the people at his table. The men with him were tough-looking and businesslike.

"Come on over to the café," Bill said. "I want an absinthe."

It was the last day of the fiesta. Outside it was beginning to be cloudy again. The square was full of people and the fireworks experts were making up their set pieces for the night and covering them over with beech branches. Boys were watching. We passed stands of rockets with long bamboo stems. Outside the café there was a great crowd. The music and the dancing were going on. The giants and the dwarfs were passing.

"Where's Edna?" I asked Bill.

"I don't know."

We watched the beginning of the evening of the last night of the fiesta. The absinthe made everything seem better. I drank it without sugar in the dripping glass, and it was pleasantly bitter.

"I feel sorry about Cohn," Bill said. "He had an awful time."

"Oh, to hell with Cohn," I said.

"Where do you suppose he went?"

"Up to Paris."

"What do you suppose he'll do?"

"Oh, to hell with him."

"What do you suppose he'll do?"

"Pick up with his old girl, probably."

"Who was his old girl?"

"Somebody named Frances."

We had another absinthe.

"When do you go back?" I asked.

"To-morrow."

After a little while Bill said: "Well, it was a swell fiesta."

"Yes," I said; "something doing all the time."

"You wouldn't believe it. It's like a wonderful nightmare."

"Sure," I said. "I'd believe anything. Including nightmares."

"What's the matter? Feel low?"

"Low as hell."

"Have another absinthe. Here, waiter! Another absinthe for this señor."

"I feel like hell," I said.

"Drink that," said Bill. "Drink it slow."

It was beginning to get dark. The fiesta was going on. I began to feel drunk but I did not feel any better.

"How do you feel?"

"I feel like hell."

"Have another?"

"It won't do any good."

"Try it. You can't tell; maybe this is the one that gets it. Hey, waiter! Another absinthe for this señor!"

I poured the water directly into it and stirred it instead of letting it drip. Bill put in a lump of ice. I stirred the ice around with a spoon in the brownish, cloudy mixture.

"How is it?"

"Fine."

"Don't drink it fast that way. It will make you sick."

I set down the glass. I had not meant to drink it fast.

"I feel tight."

"You ought to."

"That's what you wanted, wasn't it?"

"Sure. Get tight. Get over your damn depression."

"Well, I'm tight. Is that what you want?"

"Sit down."

"I won't sit down," I said. "I'm going over to the hotel."

I was very drunk. I was drunker than I ever remembered having been. At the hotel I went up-stairs. Brett's door was open. I put my head in the room. Mike was sitting on the bed. He waved a bottle.

"Jake," he said. "Come in, Jake."

I went in and sat down. The room was unstable unless I looked at some fixed point.

"Brett, you know. She's gone off with the bull-fighter chap."

"No."

"Yes. She looked for you to say good-bye. They went on the seven o'clock train."

"Did they?"

"Bad thing to do," Mike said. "She shouldn't have done it."

"No."

"Have a drink? Wait while I ring for some beer."

"I'm drunk," I said. "I'm going in and lie down."

"Are you blind? I was blind myself."

"Yes," I said, "I'm blind."

"Well, bung-o," Mike said. "Get some sleep, old Jake."

I went out the door and into my own room and lay on the bed. The bed went sailing off and I sat up in bed and looked at the wall to make it stop. Outside in the square the fiesta was going on. It did not mean anything. Later Bill and Mike came in to get me to go down and eat with them. I pretended to be asleep.

"He's asleep. Better let him alone."

"He's blind as a tick," Mike said. They went out.

I got up and went to the balcony and looked out at the dancing in the square. The world was not wheeling any more. It was just very clear and bright, and inclined to blur at the edges. I washed, brushed my hair. I looked strange to myself in the glass, and went down-stairs to the dining-room.

"Here he is!" said Bill. "Good old Jake! I knew you wouldn't pass out."

"Hello, you old drunk," Mike said.

"I got hungry and woke up."

"Eat some soup," Bill said.

The three of us sat at the table, and it seemed as though about six people were missing.

BOOK III

CHAPTER XIX

In the morning it was all over. The fiesta was finished. I woke about nine o'clock, had a bath, dressed, and went down-stairs. The square was empty and there were no people on the streets. A few children were picking up rocket-sticks in the square. The cafés were just opening and the waiters were carrying out the comfortable white wicker chairs and arranging them around the marble-topped tables in the shade of the arcade. They were sweeping the streets and sprinkling them with a hose.

I sat in one of the wicker chairs and leaned back comfortably. The waiter was in no hurry to come. The white-paper announcements of the unloading of the bulls and the big schedules of special trains were still up on the pillars of the arcade. A waiter wearing a blue apron came out with a bucket of water and a cloth, and commenced to tear down the notices, pulling the paper off in strips and washing and rubbing away the paper that stuck to the stone. The fiesta was over.

I drank a coffee and after a while Bill came over. I watched him come walking across the square. He sat down at the table and ordered a coffee.

"Well," he said, "it's all over."

"Yes," I said. "When do you go?"

"I don't know. We better get a car, I think. Aren't you going back to Paris?"

"No. I can stay away another week. I think I'll go to San Sebastian."

"I want to get back."

"What's Mike going to do?"

"He's going to Saint Jean de Luz."

"Let's get a car and all go as far as Bayonne. You can get the train up from there to-night."

"Good. Let's go after lunch."

"All right. I'll get the car."

We had lunch and paid the bill. Montoya did not come near us. One of the maids brought the bill. The car was outside. The chauffeur piled and strapped the bags on top of the car and put them in beside him in the front seat and we got in. The car went out of the square, along through the side streets, out under the trees and down the hill and away from Pamplona. It did not seem like a very long ride. Mike had a bottle of Fundador. I only took a couple of drinks. We came over the mountains and out of Spain and down the white roads and through the overfoliaged, wet, green, Basque country, and finally into Bayonne. We left Bill's baggage at the station, and he bought a ticket to Paris. His train left at seven-ten. We came out of the station. The car was standing out in front.

"What shall we do about the car?" Bill asked.

"Oh, bother the car," Mike said. "Let's just keep the car with us."

"All right," Bill said. "Where shall we go?"

"Let's go to Biarritz and have a drink."

"Old Mike the spender," Bill said.

We drove in to Biarritz and left the car outside a very Ritz place. We went into the bar and sat on high stools and drank a whiskey and soda.

"That drink's mine," Mike said.

"Let's roll for it."

So we rolled poker dice out of a deep leather dice-cup. Bill was out first roll. Mike lost to me and handed the bartender a hundred-franc note. The whiskeys were twelve francs apiece. We had another round and Mike lost again. Each time he gave the bartender a good tip. In a room off the bar there was a good jazz band playing. It was a pleasant bar. We had another round. I went out on the first roll with four kings. Bill and Mike rolled. Mike won the first roll with four jacks. Bill won the second. On the final roll Mike had three kings and let them stay. He handed the dice-cup to Bill. Bill rattled them and rolled, and there were three kings, an ace, and a queen.

"It's yours, Mike," Bill said. "Old Mike, the gambler."

"I'm so sorry," Mike said. "I can't get it."

"What's the matter?"

"I've no money," Mike said. "I'm stony. I've just twenty francs. Here, take twenty francs."

Bill's face sort of changed.

"I just had enough to pay Montoya. Damned lucky to have it, too."

"I'll cash you a check," Bill said.

"That's damned nice of you, but you see I can't write checks."

"What are you going to do for money?"

"Oh, some will come through. I've two weeks allowance should be here. I can live on tick at this pub in Saint Jean."

"What do you want to do about the car?" Bill asked me. "Do you want to keep it on?"

"It doesn't make any difference. Seems sort of idiotic."

"Come on, let's have another drink," Mike said.

"Fine. This one is on me," Bill said. "Has Brett any money?" He turned to Mike.

"I shouldn't think so. She put up most of what I gave to old Montoya."

"She hasn't any money with her?" I asked.

"I shouldn't think so. She never has any money. She gets five hundred quid a year and pays three hundred and fifty of it in interest to Jews."

"I suppose they get it at the source," said Bill.

"Quite. They're not really Jews. We just call them Jews. They're Scotsmen, I believe."

"Hasn't she any at all with her?" I asked.

"I hardly think so. She gave it all to me when she left."

"Well," Bill said, "we might as well have another drink."

"Damned good idea," Mike said. "One never gets anywhere by discussing finances."

"No," said Bill. Bill and I rolled for the next two rounds. Bill lost and paid. We went out to the car.

"Anywhere you'd like to go, Mike?" Bill asked.

"Let's take a drive. It might do my credit good. Let's drive about a little."

"Fine. I'd like to see the coast. Let's drive down toward Hendaye."

"I haven't any credit along the coast."

"You can't ever tell," said Bill.

We drove out along the coast road. There was the green of the headlands, the white, red-roofed villas, patches of forest, and the ocean very blue with the tide out and the water curling far out along the beach. We drove through Saint Jean de Luz and passed through villages farther down the coast. Back of the rolling country we were going through we saw the mountains we had come over from Pamplona. The road went on ahead. Bill looked at his watch. It was time for us to go back. He knocked on the glass and told the driver to turn around. The driver backed the car out into the grass to turn it. In back of us were the woods, below a stretch of meadow, then the sea.

At the hotel where Mike was going to stay in Saint Jean we stopped the car and he got out. The chauffeur carried in his bags. Mike stood by the side of the car.

"Good-bye, you chaps," Mike said. "It was a damned fine fiesta."

"So long, Mike," Bill said.

"I'll see you around," I said.

"Don't worry about money," Mike said. "You can pay for the car, Jake, and I'll send you my share."

"So long, Mike."

"So long, you chaps. You've been damned nice."

We all shook hands. We waved from the car to Mike. He stood in the road watching. We got to Bayonne just before the train left. A porter carried Bill's bags in from the consigne. I went as far as the inner gate to the tracks.

"So long, fella," Bill said.

"So long, kid!"

"It was swell. I've had a swell time."

"Will you be in Paris?"

"No, I have to sail on the 17th. So long, fella!"

"So long, old kid!"

He went in through the gate to the train. The porter went ahead with the bags. I watched the train pull out. Bill was at one of the windows. The window passed, the rest of the train passed, and the tracks were empty. I went outside to the car.

"How much do we owe you?" I asked the driver. The price to Bayonne had been fixed at a hundred and fifty pesetas.

"Two hundred pesetas."

"How much more will it be if you drive me to San Sebastian on your way back?"

"Fifty pesetas."

"Don't kid me."

"Thirty-five pesetas."

"It's not worth it," I said. "Drive me to the Hotel Panier Fleuri."

At the hotel I paid the driver and gave him a tip. The car was powdered with dust. I rubbed the rod-case through the dust. It seemed the last thing that connected me with Spain and the fiesta. The driver put the car in gear and went down the street. I watched it turn off to take the road to Spain. I went into the hotel and they gave me a room. It was the same room I had slept in when Bill and Cohn and I were in Bayonne. That seemed a very long time ago. I washed, changed my shirt, and went out in the town.

At a newspaper kiosque I bought a copy of the New York Herald and sat in a café to read it. It felt strange to be in France again. There was a safe, suburban feeling. I wished I had gone up to Paris with Bill, except that Paris would have meant more fiesta-ing. I was through with fiestas for a while. It would be quiet in San Sebastian. The season does not open there until August. I could get a good hotel room and read and swim. There was a fine beach there. There were wonderful trees along the promenade above the beach, and there were many children sent down with their nurses before the season opened. In the evening there would be band concerts under the trees across from the Café Marinas. I could sit in the Marinas and listen.

"How does one eat inside?" I asked the waiter. Inside the café was a restaurant.

"Well. Very well. One eats very well."

"Good."

I went in and ate dinner. It was a big meal for France but it seemed very carefully apportioned after Spain. I drank a bottle of wine for company. It was a Château Margaux. It was pleasant to be drinking slowly and to be tasting the wine and to be drinking alone. A bottle of wine was good company. Afterward I had coffee. The waiter recommended a Basque liqueur called Izzarra. He brought in the bottle and poured a liqueur-glass full. He said Izzarra was made of the flowers of the Pyrenees. The veritable flowers of the Pyrenees. It looked like hair-oil and smelled like Italian *strega*. I told him to take the flowers of the Pyrenees away and bring me a *vieux marc*. The *marc* was good. I had a second *marc* after the coffee.

The waiter seemed a little offended about the flowers of the Pyrenees, so I overtipped him. That made him happy. It felt comfortable to be in a country where it is so simple to make people happy. You can never tell whether a Spanish waiter will thank you. Everything is on such a clear financial basis in France. It is the simplest country to live in. No one makes things complicated by becoming your friend for any obscure reason. If you want people to like you you have only to spend a little money. I spent a little money and the waiter liked me. He appreciated my valuable qualities. He would be glad to see me back. I would dine there again some time and he would be glad to see me, and would want me at his table. It would be a sincere liking because it would have a sound basis. I was back in France.

Next morning I tipped every one a little too much at the hotel to make more friends, and left on the morning train for San Sebastian. At the station I did not tip the porter more than I should because I did not think I would ever see him again. I only wanted a few good French friends in Bayonne to make me welcome in case I should come back there again. I knew that if they remembered me their friendship would be loyal.

At Irun we had to change trains and show passports. I hated to leave France. Life was so simple in France. I felt I was a fool to be going back into Spain. In Spain you could not tell about anything. I felt like a fool to be going back into it, but I stood in line with my passport, opened my bags for the customs, bought a ticket, went through a gate, climbed onto the train, and after forty minutes and eight tunnels I was at San Sebastian.

Even on a hot day San Sebastian has a certain early-morning quality. The trees seem as though their leaves were never quite dry. The streets feel as though they had just been sprinkled. It is always cool and shady on certain streets on the hottest day. I went to a hotel in the town where I had stopped before, and they gave me a room with a balcony that opened out above the roofs of the town. There was a green mountainside beyond the roofs.

I unpacked my bags and stacked my books on the table beside the head of the bed, put out my shaving things, hung up some clothes in the big armoire, and made up a bundle for the laundry. Then I took a shower in the bathroom and went down to lunch. Spain had not changed to summer-time, so I was early. I set my watch again. I had recovered an hour by coming to San Sebastian.

As I went into the dining-room the concierge brought me a police bulletin to fill out. I signed it and asked him for two telegraph forms, and wrote a message to the Hotel Montoya, telling them to forward all mail and telegrams for me to this address. I calculated how many days I would be in San Sebastian and then wrote out a wire to the office asking them to hold mail, but forward all wires for me to San Sebastian for six days. Then I went in and had lunch.

After lunch I went up to my room, read a while, and went to sleep. When I woke it was half past four. I found my swimming-suit, wrapped it with a comb in a towel, and went down-stairs and walked up the street to the Concha. The tide was about half-way out. The beach was smooth and firm, and the sand yellow. I went into a bathing-cabin, undressed, put on my suit, and walked across the smooth sand to the sea. The sand was warm under bare feet. There were quite a few people in the water and on the beach. Out beyond where the headlands of the Concha almost met to form the harbor there was a white line of breakers and the open sea. Although the tide was going out, there were a few slow rollers. They came in like undulations in the water, gathered weight of water, and then broke smoothly on the warm sand. I waded out. The water was cold. As a roller came I dove, swam out under water, and came to the surface with all the chill gone. I swam out to the raft, pulled myself up, and lay on the hot planks. A boy and girl were at the other end. The girl had undone the top strap of her bathing-suit and was browning her back. The boy lay face downward on the raft and talked to her. She laughed at things he said, and turned her brown back in the sun. I lay on the raft in the sun until I was dry. Then I tried several dives. I dove deep once, swimming down to the bottom. I swam with my eyes open and it was green and dark. The raft made a dark shadow. I came out of water beside the raft, pulled up, dove once more, holding it for length, and then swam ashore. I lay on the beach until I was dry, then went into the bathing-cabin, took off my suit, sloshed myself with fresh water, and rubbed dry.

I walked around the harbor under the trees to the casino, and then up one of the cool streets to the Café Marinas. There was an orchestra playing inside the café and I sat out on the terrace and enjoyed the fresh coolness in the hot day, and had a glass of lemon-juice and shaved ice and then a long whiskey and soda. I sat in front of the Marinas for a long time and read and watched the people, and listened to the music.

Later when it began to get dark, I walked around the harbor and out along the promenade, and finally back to the hotel for supper. There was a bicycle-race on, the Tour du Pays Basque, and the riders were stopping that night in San Sebastian. In the dining-room, at one side, there was a long table of bicycle-riders, eating with their trainers and managers. They were all French and Belgians, and paid close attention to their meal, but they were having a good time. At the head of the table were two good-looking French girls, with much Rue du Faubourg Montmartre chic. I could not make out whom they belonged to. They all spoke in slang at the long table and there were many private jokes and some jokes at the far end that were not repeated when the girls asked to hear them. The next morning at five o'clock the race resumed with the last lap, San Sebastian-Bilbao. The bicycle-riders drank much wine, and were burned and browned by the sun. They did not take the race seriously except among themselves. They had raced among themselves so often that it did not make much difference who won. Especially in a foreign country. The money could be arranged.

The man who had a matter of two minutes lead in the race had an attack of boils, which were very painful. He sat on the small of his back. His neck was very red and the blond hairs were sunburned. The other riders joked him about his boils. He tapped on the table with his fork.

"Listen," he said, "to-morrow my nose is so tight on the handle-bars that the only thing touches those boils is a lovely breeze."

One of the girls looked at him down the table, and he grinned and turned red. The Spaniards, they said, did not know how to pedal.

I had coffee out on the terrasse with the team manager of one of the big bicycle manufacturers. He said it had been a very pleasant race, and would have been worth watching if Bottechia had not abandoned it at Pamplona. The dust had been bad, but in Spain the roads were better than in France. Bicycle road-racing was the only sport in the world, he said. Had I ever followed the Tour de France? Only in the papers. The Tour de France was the greatest sporting event in the world. Following and organizing the road races had made him know France. Few people know France. All spring and all summer and all fall he spent on the road with bicycle road-racers. Look at the number of motor-cars now that followed the riders from town to town in a road race. It

was a rich country and more *sportif* every year. It would be the
most *sportif* country in the world. It was bicycle road-racing did it.
That and football. He knew France. *La France Sportive*. He knew
road-racing. We had a cognac. After all, though, it wasn't bad to
get back to Paris. There is only one Paname. In all the world,
that is. Paris is the town the most *sportif* in the world. Did I know
the *Chope de Negre?* Did I not. I would see him there some
time. I certainly would. We would drink another *fine* together.
We certainly would. They started at six o'clock less a quarter in
the morning. Would I be up for the depart? I would certainly try
to. Would I like him to call me? It was very interesting. I would
leave a call at the desk. He would not mind calling me. I could
not let him take the trouble. I would leave a call at the desk. We
said good-bye until the next morning.

In the morning when I awoke the bicycle-riders and their following cars had been on the road for three hours. I had coffee
and the papers in bed and then dressed and took my bathing-suit
down to the beach. Everything was fresh and cool and damp in
the early morning. Nurses in uniform and in peasant costume
walked under the trees with children. The Spanish children were
beautiful. Some bootblacks sat together under a tree talking to a
soldier. The soldier had only one arm. The tide was in and there
was a good breeze and a surf on the beach.

I undressed in one of the bath-cabins, crossed the narrow line
of beach and went into the water. I swam out, trying to swim
through the rollers, but having to dive sometimes. Then in the
quiet water I turned and floated. Floating I saw only the sky, and
felt the drop and lift of the swells. I swam back to the surf and
coasted in, face down, on a big roller, then turned and swam,
trying to keep in the trough and not have a wave break over me.
It made me tired, swimming in the trough, and I turned and
swam out to the raft. The water was buoyant and cold. It felt as
though you could never sink. I swam slowly, it seemed like a long

swim with the high tide, and then pulled up on the raft and sat, dripping, on the boards that were becoming hot in the sun. I looked around at the bay, the old town, the casino, the line of trees along the promenade, and the big hotels with their white porches and gold-lettered names. Off on the right, almost closing the harbor, was a green hill with a castle. The raft rocked with the motion of the water. On the other side of the narrow gap that led into the open sea was another high headland. I thought I would like to swim across the bay but I was afraid of cramp.

I sat in the sun and watched the bathers on the beach. They looked very small. After a while I stood up, gripped with my toes on the edge of the raft as it tipped with my weight, and dove cleanly and deeply, to come up through the lightening water, blew the salt water out of my head, and swam slowly and steadily in to shore.

After I was dressed and had paid for the bath-cabin, I walked back to the hotel. The bicycle-racers had left several copies of *L'Auto* around, and I gathered them up in the reading-room and took them out and sat in an easy chair in the sun to read about and catch up on French sporting life. While I was sitting there the concierge came out with a blue envelope in his hand.

"A telegram for you, sir."

I poked my finger along under the fold that was fastened down, spread it open, and read it. It had been forwarded from Paris:

> COULD YOU COME HOTEL MONTANA MADRID
> AM RATHER IN TROUBLE BRETT.

I tipped the concierge and read the message again. A postman was coming along the sidewalk. He turned in the hotel. He had a big moustache and looked very military. He came out of the hotel again. The concierge was just behind him.

"Here's another telegram for you, sir."

"Thank you," I said.

I opened it. It was forwarded from Pamplona.

> COULD YOU COME HOTEL MONTANA MADRID
> AM RATHER IN TROUBLE BRETT.

The concierge stood there waiting for another tip, probably.

"What time is there a train for Madrid?"

"It left at nine this morning. There is a slow train at eleven, and the Sud Express at ten to-night."

"Get me a berth on the Sud Express. Do you want the money now?"

"Just as you wish," he said. "I will have it put on the bill."

"Do that."

Well, that meant San Sebastian all shot to hell. I suppose, vaguely, I had expected something of the sort. I saw the concierge standing in the doorway.

"Bring me a telegram form, please."

He brought it and I took out my fountain-pen and printed:

> LADY ASHLEY HOTEL MONTANA MADRID
> ARRIVING SUD EXPRESS TOMORROW LOVE
> JAKE.

That seemed to handle it. That was it. Send a girl off with one man. Introduce her to another to go off with him. Now go and bring her back. And sign the wire with love. That was it all right. I went in to lunch.

I did not sleep much that night on the Sud Express. In the morning I had breakfast in the dining-car and watched the rock and pine country between Avila and Escorial. I saw the Escorial out of the window, gray and long and cold in the sun, and did not give a damn about it. I saw Madrid come up over the plain, a compact white sky-line on the top of a little cliff away off across the sun-hardened country.

The Norte station in Madrid is the end of the line. All trains

finish there. They don't go on anywhere. Outside were cabs and
taxis and a line of hotel runners. It was like a country town. I took
a taxi and we climbed up through the gardens, by the empty
palace and the unfinished church on the edge of the cliff, and on
up until we were in the high, hot, modern town. The taxi coasted
down a smooth street to the Puerta del Sol, and then through the
traffic and out into the Carrera San Jeronimo. All the shops had
their awnings down against the heat. The windows on the sunny
side of the street were shuttered. The taxi stopped at the curb. I
saw the sign HOTEL MONTANA on the second floor. The taxi-driver
carried the bags in and left them by the elevator. I could not make
the elevator work, so I walked up. On the second floor up was a
cut brass sign: HOTEL MONTANA. I rang and no one came to the
door. I rang again and a maid with a sullen face opened the door.

"Is Lady Ashley here?" I asked.

She looked at me dully.

"Is an Englishwoman here?"

She turned and called some one inside. A very fat woman
came to the door. Her hair was gray and stiffly oiled in scallops
around her face. She was short and commanding.

"Muy buenos," I said. "Is there an Englishwoman here? I
would like to see this English lady."

"Muy buenos. Yes, there is a female English. Certainly you can
see her if she wishes to see you."

"She wishes to see me."

"The chica will ask her."

"It is very hot."

"It is very hot in the summer in Madrid."

"And how cold in winter."

"Yes, it is very cold in winter."

Did I want to stay myself in person in the Hotel Montana?

Of that as yet I was undecided, but it would give me pleasure if my bags were brought up from the ground floor in order that they might not be stolen. Nothing was ever stolen in the Hotel Montana. In other fondas, yes. Not here. No. The personages of this establishment were rigidly selectioned. I was happy to hear it. Nevertheless I would welcome the upbringal of my bags.

The maid came in and said that the female English wanted to see the male English now, at once.

"Good," I said. "You see. It is as I said."

"Clearly."

I followed the maid's back down a long, dark corridor. At the end she knocked on a door.

"Hello," said Brett. "Is it you, Jake?"

"It's me."

"Come in. Come in."

I opened the door. The maid closed it after me. Brett was in bed. She had just been brushing her hair and held the brush in her hand. The room was in that disorder produced only by those who have always had servants.

"Darling!" Brett said.

I went over to the bed and put my arms around her. She kissed me, and while she kissed me I could feel she was thinking of something else. She was trembling in my arms. She felt very small.

"Darling! I've had such a hell of a time."

"Tell me about it."

"Nothing to tell. He only left yesterday. I made him go."

"Why didn't you keep him?"

"I don't know. It isn't the sort of thing one does. I don't think I hurt him any."

"You were probably damn good for him."

"He shouldn't be living with any one. I realized that right away."

"No."

"Oh, hell!" she said, "let's not talk about it. Let's never talk about it."

"All right."

"It was rather a knock his being ashamed of me. He was ashamed of me for a while, you know."

"No."

"Oh, yes. They ragged him about me at the café, I guess. He wanted me to grow my hair out. Me, with long hair. I'd look so like hell."

"It's funny."

"He said it would make me more womanly. I'd look a fright."

"What happened?"

"Oh, he got over that. He wasn't ashamed of me long."

"What was it about being in trouble?"

"I didn't know whether I could make him go, and I didn't have a sou to go away and leave him. He tried to give me a lot of money, you know. I told him I had scads of it. He knew that was a lie. I couldn't take his money, you know."

"No."

"Oh, let's not talk about it. There were some funny things, though. Do give me a cigarette."

I lit the cigarette.

"He learned his English as a waiter in Gib."

"Yes."

"He wanted to marry me, finally."

"Really?"

"Of course. I can't even marry Mike."

"Maybe he thought that would make him Lord Ashley."

"No. It wasn't that. He really wanted to marry me. So I couldn't go away from him, he said. He wanted to make it sure I could never go away from him. After I'd gotten more womanly, of course."

"You ought to feel set up."

"I do. I'm all right again. He's wiped out that damned Cohn."

"Good."

"You know I'd have lived with him if I hadn't seen it was bad for him. We got along damned well."

"Outside of your personal appearance."

"Oh, he'd have gotten used to that."

She put out the cigarette.

"I'm thirty-four, you know. I'm not going to be one of these bitches that ruins children."

"No."

"I'm not going to be that way. I feel rather good, you know. I feel rather set up."

"Good."

She looked away. I thought she was looking for another cigarette. Then I saw she was crying. I could feel her crying. Shaking and crying. She wouldn't look up. I put my arms around her.

"Don't let's ever talk about it. Please don't let's ever talk about it."

"Dear Brett."

"I'm going back to Mike." I could feel her crying as I held her close. "He's so damned nice and he's so awful. He's my sort of thing."

She would not look up. I stroked her hair. I could feel her shaking.

"I won't be one of those bitches," she said. "But, oh, Jake, please let's never talk about it."

We left the Hotel Montana. The woman who ran the hotel would not let me pay the bill. The bill had been paid.

"Oh, well. Let it go," Brett said. "It doesn't matter now."

We rode in a taxi down to the Palace Hotel, left the bags, arranged for berths on the Sud Express for the night, and went into the bar of the hotel for a cocktail. We sat on high stools at the bar while the barman shook the Martinis in a large nickelled shaker.

"It's funny what a wonderful gentility you get in the bar of a big hotel," I said.

"Barmen and jockeys are the only people who are polite any more."

"No matter how vulgar a hotel is, the bar is always nice."

"It's odd."

"Bartenders have always been fine."

"You know," Brett said, "it's quite true. He is only nineteen. Isn't it amazing?"

We touched the two glasses as they stood side by side on the bar. They were coldly beaded. Outside the curtained window was the summer heat of Madrid.

"I like an olive in a Martini," I said to the barman.

"Right you are, sir. There you are."

"Thanks."

"I should have asked, you know."

The barman went far enough up the bar so that he would not hear our conversation. Brett had sipped from the Martini as it stood, on the wood. Then she picked it up. Her hand was steady enough to lift it after that first sip.

"It's good. Isn't it a nice bar?"

"They're all nice bars."

"You know I didn't believe it at first. He was born in 1905. I was in school in Paris, then. Think of that."

"Anything you want me to think about it?"

"Don't be an ass. *Would* you buy a lady a drink?"

"We'll have two more Martinis."

"As they were before, sir?"

"They were very good." Brett smiled at him.

"Thank you, ma'am."

"Well, bung-o," Brett said.

"Bung-o!"

"You know," Brett said, "he'd only been with two women be-fore. He never cared about anything but bull-fighting."

"He's got plenty of time."

"I don't know. He thinks it was me. Not the show in general."

"Well, it was you."

"Yes. It was me."

"I thought you weren't going to ever talk about it."

"How can I help it?"

"You'll lose it if you talk about it."

"I just talk around it. You know I feel rather damned good, Jake."

"You should."

"You know it makes one feel rather good deciding not to be a bitch."

"Yes."

"It's sort of what we have instead of God."

"Some people have God," I said. "Quite a lot."

"He never worked very well with me."

"Should we have another Martini?"

The barman shook up two more Martinis and poured them out into fresh glasses.

"Where will we have lunch?" I asked Brett. The bar was cool. You could feel the heat outside through the window.

"Here?" asked Brett.

"It's rotten here in the hotel. Do you know a place called Botin's?" I asked the barman.

"Yes, sir. Would you like to have me write out the address?"

"Thank you."

We lunched up-stairs at Botin's. It is one of the best restaurants in the world. We had roast young suckling pig and drank *rioja alta*. Brett did not eat much. She never ate much. I ate a very big meal and drank three bottles of *rioja alta*.

"How do you feel, Jake?" Brett asked. "My God! what a meal you've eaten."

"I feel fine. Do you want a dessert?"

"Lord, no."

Brett was smoking.

"You like to eat, don't you?" she said.

"Yes." I said. "I like to do a lot of things."

"What do you like to do?"

"Oh," I said, "I like to do a lot of things. Don't you want a dessert?"

"You asked me that once," Brett said.

"Yes," I said. "So I did. Let's have another bottle of *rioja alta*."

"It's very good."

"You haven't drunk much of it," I said.

"I have. You haven't seen."

"Let's get two bottles," I said. The bottles came. I poured a little in my glass, then a glass for Brett, then filled my glass. We touched glasses.

"Bung-o!" Brett said. I drank my glass and poured out another. Brett put her hand on my arm.

"Don't get drunk, Jake," she said. "You don't have to."

"How do you know?"

"Don't," she said. "You'll be all right."

"I'm not getting drunk," I said. "I'm just drinking a little wine. I like to drink wine."

"Don't get drunk," she said. "Jake, don't get drunk."

"Want to go for a ride?" I said. "Want to ride through the town?"

"Right," Brett said. "I haven't seen Madrid. I should see Madrid."

"I'll finish this," I said.

Down-stairs we came out through the first-floor dining-room to the street. A waiter went for a taxi. It was hot and bright. Up the street was a little square with trees and grass where there were taxis parked. A taxi came up the street, the waiter hanging out at the side. I tipped him and told the driver where to drive, and got in beside Brett. The driver started up the street. I settled back Brett moved close to me. We sat close against each other. I put my arm around her and she rested against me comfortably. It was very hot and bright, and the houses looked sharply white. We turned out onto the Gran Via.

"Oh, Jake," Brett said, "we could have had such a damned good time together."

Ahead was a mounted policeman in khaki directing traffic. He raised his baton. The car slowed suddenly pressing Brett against me.

"Yes," I said. "Isn't it pretty to think so?"

THE END

INTRODUCTION TO

A Farewell to Arms

BY ROBERT PENN WARREN

INTRODUCTION

In May, 1929, in *Scribner's Magazine,* the first installment of *A Farewell to Arms* appeared. The novel was completed in the issue of October, and was published in book form the same year. Ernest Hemingway was already regarded, by a limited literary public, as a writer of extraordinary freshness and power, as one of the makers, indeed, of a new American fiction. *A Farewell to Arms* more than justified the early enthusiasm of the connoisseurs for Hemingway, and extended his reputation from them to the public at large. Its great importance was at once acknowledged, and its reputation has survived through the changing fashions and interests of passing years.

What was the immediate cause of its appeal? It told a truth about the First World War, and a truth about the generation who had fought the war and whose lives, because of the war, had been wrenched from the expected pattern and the old values. Other writers had told or were to tell similar truths about this war. John Dos Passos in *Three Soldiers,* E. E. Cummings in *The Enormous Room,* William Faulkner in *Soldier's Pay,* Maxwell Anderson and

Laurence Stallings in *What Price Glory?* All these writers had presented the pathos and endurance and gallantry of the individual caught and mangled in the great anonymous mechanism of a modern war fought for reasons that the individual could not understand, found insufficient to justify the event, or believed to be no reasons at all. And *A Farewell to Arms* was not the first book to record the plight of the men and women who, because of the war, had been unable to come to terms with life in the old way. Hemingway himself in *The Sun Also Rises*, of 1926, had given the picture of the dislocated life of young English and American expatriates in the bars of Paris, the "lost generation," as the phrase from Gertrude Stein defined them. But before that F. Scott Fitzgerald, who had been no nearer to the war than an officers' training camp, had written of the lost generation. For the young people about whom Fitzgerald wrote, even when they were not veterans and even when their love stories were enacted in parked cars, fraternity houses, and country clubs and not in the cafés and hotels of Paris, were like Hemingway's expatriates under the shadow of the war and were groping to find some satisfaction in a world from which the old values had been withdrawn. Hemingway's expatriates had turned their backs on the glitter of the Great Boom of the 1920's, and Fitzgerald's young men were usually drawn to the romance of wealth and indulgence, but this difference is superficial. If Hemingway's young men begin by repudiating the Great Boom, Fitzgerald's young men end with disappointment in what even success has to offer. "All the sad young men" of Fitzgerald—to take the title of one of his collections of stories—and the "lost generation" of Hemingway are seekers for landmarks and bearings in a terrain for which the maps have been mislaid.

A Farewell to Arms, which appeared ten years after the First World War and on the eve of the collapse of the Great Boom, seemed to sum up and bring to focus an inner meaning of the decade being finished. It worked thus, not because it disclosed the end results that the life of the decade was producing—the discontents and disasters that were beginning to be noticed even by unreflective people—but because it cut back to the beginning of the process, to the moment that had held within itself the explanation of the subsequent process. Those who had grown up in the war, or in the shadow of the war, could look back nostalgically, as it were, to the lost moment of innocence of motive and purity of emotion. If those things had been tarnished or manhandled by the later business of living, they had, at least, existed, and on a grand scale. If they had been tarnished or manhandled, it was not through the fault of the individual who looked back to see the image of the old simple and heroic self in Frederick or Catherine, but through the impersonal grindings of the great machine of the universe. *A Farewell to Arms* served, in a way, as the great romantic alibi for a generation, and for those who aped and emulated that generation. It showed how cynicism or disillusionment, failure of spirit or the worship of material success, debauchery or despair, might have been grounded in heroism, simplicity, and fidelity that had met unmerited defeat. The early tragedy could cast a kind of flattering and extenuating afterglow over what had come later. The battlefields of *A Farewell to Arms* explained the bars of *The Sun Also Rises*—and explained the young Krebs, of the story "Soldier's Home," who came back home to a Middle-Western town to accept his own slow disintegration.

This is not said in disparagement of *A Farewell to Arms*. It is, after all, a compliment to the hypnotic force of the book. For the hypnotic force of the book was felt from the first, and it is not unusual for such a book to be relished by its first readers for superficial reasons and not for the essential virtues that may engage those who come to it later.

In accounting for the immediate appeal of *A Farewell to Arms*, the history of the author himself is of some importance. In so far as the reader knew about Ernest Hemingway in 1929, he knew about a young man who seemed to typify in his own experience the central experience of his generation. Behind the story of *A Farewell to Arms* and his other books there was the shadow of his own story that could stamp his fiction with the authenticity of a document and, for the more impressionable, with the value of a revelation. He could give an ethic and a technique for living, even in the face of defeat or frustration, and yet his own story was the story that we have always loved: the American success story.

He was born in Oak Park, Illinois, in the Middle West, that region that it was fashionable to condemn (after Mencken and Sinclair Lewis) as romanceless, but, with its Main Streets and Winesburg, Ohio's, became endowed, paradoxically enough, with the romance of the American average. His father was a physician. There were two boys and four girls in the family. In the summers the family lived in northern Michigan, where there were Indians, and where lake, streams, and forests gave boyhood pursuits their appropriate setting. In the winters he went to school in Oak Park. He played football in high school, ran away from home, returned and, in 1917, graduated. After graduation he was for a short time a reporter on the *Kansas City Star*, but the war was on and he went to Italy as a volunteer ambulance driver. He was wounded and decorated, and after his recovery served in the Italian army as a soldier. For a time after the war he was a foreign correspondent for the *Toronto Star*, in the Near East.

In the years after the war Hemingway set about learning, quite consciously and with rigorous self-discipline, the craft and art of writing. During most of his apprenticeship he lived in Paris, one of the great number of expatriates who were drawn to the artistic capital of the world to learn to be writers, painters, sculptors, or dancers, or simply to enjoy on a low monetary exchange the freedom of life away from American or British conventions. "Young America," writes Ford Madox Ford, the eminent English novelist and then editor of the *transatlantic review*, "from the limitless prairies leapt, released, on Paris. They stampeded with the madness of colts when you let down the slip-rails between dried pasture and green. The noise of their advancing drowned all sounds. Their innumerable forms hid the very trees on the boulevards. Their perpetual motion made you dizzy." And of Hemingway himself: "He was presented to me by Ezra* and Bill Bird and had rather the aspect of an Eton-Oxford, huskyish young captain of a midland regiment of His Britannic Majesty. . . . Into that animated din would drift Hemingway, balancing on the point of his toes, feinting at my head with hands as large as hams and relating sinister stories of Paris landlords. He told them with singularly choice words in a slow voice."†

The originality and force of Hemingway's early stories, published in little magazines, and in limited editions in France, were recognized from the first by many who made their acquaintance. The seeds of his later work were in those stories of *In Our Time,* concerned chiefly with scenes of inland American life and a boy's growing awareness of that life in contrast to vivid flashes of the disorder and brutality of the war years and the immediate post-war years in Europe. There are both contrast and continuity between the two elements of *In Our Time.* There is the contrast between the lyric rendering of one aspect of the boyhood world and the realistic rendering of the world of war, but there is also a continuity because in the boyhood world there are recurring intimations of the blackness into which experience can lead even in the peaceful setting of Michigan.

With the publication of *The Sun Also Rises,* in 1926, Hemingway's work reached a wider audience, and at the same time defined more clearly the line his genius was to follow and his role as one of the spokesmen for a generation. But *A Farewell to Arms* gave him his first substantial popular success and established his reputa-

---

* Ezra Pound, the American poet. William Bird published in Paris, in 1924, his second book, the original version of *In Our Time.*

† Introduction to the Modern Library edition of *A Farewell to Arms.*

tion. It was a brilliant and compelling novel; it provided the great alibi; it crowned the success story of the American boy from the Middle West, who had hunted and fished, played football in high school, been a newspaper reporter, gone to war and been wounded and decorated, wandered exotic lands as a foreign correspondent, lived the free life of the Latin Quarter of Paris, and, at the age of thirty, written a best seller—athlete, sportsman, correspondent, soldier, adventurer, and author.

II

It would be possible and even profitable to discuss *A Farewell to Arms* in isolation from Hemingway's other work. But Hemingway was a peculiarly personal writer, and for all the apparent objectivity and self-suppression in his method as a writer, his work forms a continuous whole to an uncommon degree. One part explains and interprets another part. It is true that there have been changes between early and late work, that there has been an increasing self-consciousness, that attitudes and methods that in the beginning were instinctive and simple have become calculated and elaborated. But the best way to understand one of his books is, nevertheless, to compare it with both earlier and later pieces and seek to discern motives and methods that underlie all of his work.

Perhaps the simplest way into the whole question is to consider what kind of world Hemingway wrote about. A writer may write about his special world merely because he happens to know that world, but he may also write about that special world because it best dramatizes for him the issues and questions that are his fundamental concerns—because, in other words, that special world has a kind of symbolic significance for him. There is often—if we discount mere literary fashion and imitation—an inner and necessary reason for the writer's choice of his characters and situations. What situations and characters did Hemingway write about?

They are usually violent. There is the hard-drinking and sexually promiscuous world of *The Sun Also Rises;* the chaotic and brutal world of war as in *A Farewell to Arms, For Whom the Bell Tolls,* many of the inserted sketches of *In Our Time,* the play *The Fifth Column,* and some of the stories; the world of sport, as in "Fifty Grand," "My Old Man," "The Undefeated," "The Snows of Kilimanjaro"; the world of crime as in "The Killers," "The Gambler, the Nun, and the Radio," and *To Have and Have Not.* Even when the situation of a story does not fall into one of these categories, it usually involves a desperate risk, and behind it is the shadow of ruin, physical or spiritual. As for the typical characters, they are usually tough men, experienced in the hard worlds they inhabit, and not obviously given to emotional display or sensitive shrinking, men like Rinaldi or Frederick Henry of *A Farewell to Arms,* Robert Jordan of *For Whom the Bell Tolls,* Harry Morgan of *To Have and Have Not,* the big-game hunter of "The Snows of Kilimanjaro," the old bullfighter of "The Undefeated," or the pugilist of "Fifty Grand." Or if the typical character is not of this seasoned order, he is a very young man, or boy, first entering the violent world and learning his first adjustment to it.

We have said that the shadow of ruin is behind the typical Hemingway situation. The typical character faces defeat or death. But out of defeat or death the character usually manages to salvage something. And here we discover Hemingway's special interest in such situations and such characters. His heroes are not defeated except upon their own terms. They are not squealers, welchers, compromisers, or cowards, and when they confront defeat they realize that the stance they take, the stoic endurance, the stiff upper lip mean a kind of victory. If they are to be defeated they are defeated upon their own terms; some of them have even courted their defeat; and certainly they have maintained, even in the practical defeat, an ideal of themselves, some definition of how a man should behave, formulated or unformulated, by which they have lived. They represent some notion of a code, some notion of honor, that makes a man a man, and that distinguishes him from people who merely follow their random impulses and who are, by consequence, "messy."

In case after case, we can illustrate this "principle of sportsmanship," as one critic has called it,* at the center of a story or novel. Robert Jordan, in *For Whom the Bell Tolls,* is somehow happy as he lies, wounded, behind the machine gun that is to cover the escape of his friends and his sweetheart from Franco's Fascists. The old bullfighter, in "The Undefeated," continues his incompetent fight even under the jeers and hoots of the crowd until the bull is dead and he himself is mortally hurt. Francis Macomber, the rich young sportsman who goes lion-hunting in "The Short, Happy Life of Francis Macomber," and who has funked it and bolted before a wounded lion, at last learns the lesson that the code of the hunter demands that he go into the bush after an animal he has wounded. Brett, the heroine of *The Sun Also Rises,* gives up Romero, the young bullfighter with whom she is in love, because she knows she will ruin him, and her tight-lipped remark to Jake, the newspaper man who is the narrator of the novel, might almost serve as the motto of Hemingway's work: "You know it makes one feel rather good deciding not to be a bitch."

It is the discipline of the code that makes man human, a sense of style or good form. This applies not only in isolated, dramatic cases such as those listed above, but is a more pervasive thing that can give meaning, partially at least, to the confusions of living. The discipline of the soldier, the form of the athlete, the gameness of the sportsman, the technique of an artist can give some sense of the human order, and can achieve a moral significance. And here we see how Hemingway's concern with war and sport crosses his concern with literary style. If a writer can get the kind of style at which Hemingway professes, in *Green Hills of Africa,* to aim, then

---

* Edmund Wilson, "Hemingway: Gauge of Morale," in *The Wound and the Bow,* Houghton Mifflin Co.

"nothing else matters. It is more important than anything else he can do." It is more important because, ultimately, it is a moral achievement. And no doubt for this reason, as well as for the reason of Henry James's concern with cruxes of a moral code, he is, as he says in *Green Hills of Africa,* an admirer of the work of Henry James, the devoted stylist.

But to return to the subject of Hemingway's world: the code and the discipline are important because they can give meaning to life that otherwise seems to have no meaning or justification. In other words, in a world without supernatural sanctions, in the God-abandoned world of modernity, man can realize an ideal meaning only in so far as he can define and maintain the code. The effort to define and maintain the code, however limited and imperfect it may be, is the characteristically human effort and provides the tragic or pitiful human story. Hemingway's attitude on this point is much like that of Robert Louis Stevenson as Stevenson states it in one of his essays, "Pulvis et Umbra":

Poor soul, here for so little, cast among so many hardships, filled with desires so incommensurate and so inconsistent, savagely surrounded, savagely descended, irremediably condemned to prey upon his fellow lives: who should have blamed him had he been of a piece with his destiny and a being merely barbarous? And we look and behold him instead, filled with imperfect virtues . . . an ideal of decency, to which he would rise if it were possible; a limit of shame, below which, if it be possible, he will not stoop. . . . Man is indeed marked for failure in his effort to do right. But where the best consistently miscarry how tenfold more remarkable that all should continue to strive; and surely we should find it both touching and inspiriting, that in a field from which success is banished, our race should not cease to labor. . . . It matters not where we look, under what climate we observe him, in what stage of society, in what depth of ignorance, burthened with what erroneous morality; by campfires in Assiniboia, the snow powdering his shoulders, the wind plucking his blanket, as he sits, passing the ceremonial calumet and uttering his grave opinions like a Roman senator; on ships at sea, a man inured to hardship and vile pleasures, his brightest hope a fiddle in a tavern and a bedizened trull who sells herself to rob him, and he for all that, simple, innocent, cheerful, kindly like a child, constant to toil, brave to drown, for others; . . . in the brothel, the discard of society, living mainly on strong drink, fed with affronts, a fool, a thief, the comrade of thieves, and even here keeping the point of honor and the touch of pity, often repaying the world's scorn with service, often standing firm upon a scruple, and at a certain cost, rejecting riches:—everywhere some virtue cherished or affected, everywhere some decency of thought or carriage, everywhere the ensign of man's ineffectual goodness! . . . under every circumstance of failure, without hope, without help, without thanks, still obscurely fighting the lost fight of virtue, still clinging, in the brothel or on the scaffold, to some rag of honor, the poor jewel of their souls! They may seek to escape, and yet they cannot; it is not alone their privilege and glory, but their doom; they are condemned to some nobility. . . .

Hemingway's code is more rigorous than Stevenson's and perhaps he finds fewer devoted to it, but like Stevenson he can find his characteristic hero and characteristic story among the discards of society, and like Stevenson is aware of the touching irony of that fact. But for the moment the important thing in the parallel is that, for Stevenson, the world in which this drama of pitiful aspiration and stoic endurance is played out, is apparently a violent and meaningless world—"our rotary island loaded with predatory life and more drenched with blood . . . than ever mutinied ship, scuds through space."

Neither Hemingway nor Stevenson invented this world. It had already appeared in literature before their time, and that is a way of saying that this cheerless vision had already begun to trouble men. It is the world we find pictured (and denied) in Tennyson's "In Memoriam"—the world in which human conduct is a product of "dying Nature's earth and lime." It is the world pictured (and not denied) in Hardy and Housman, a world that seems to be presided over by blind Doomsters (if by anybody), as Hardy put it in his poem "Hap," or made by some brute and blackguard (if by anybody), as Housman put it in his poem "The Chestnut Casts

Its Flambeaux." It is the world of Zola or Dreiser or Conrad or Faulkner. It is the world of, to use Bertrand Russell's phrase, "secular hurryings through space." It is the God-abandoned world, the world of Nature-as-all. We know where the literary men got this picture. They got it from the scientists of the nineteenth century. This is Hemingway's world, too, the world with nothing at center.

Over against this particular version of the naturalistic view of the world, there was, of course, an argument for Divine Intelligence and a Divine purpose, an argument that based itself on the beautiful system of nature, on natural law. The closely knit order of the natural world, so the argument ran, implies a Divine Intelligence. But if one calls Hemingway's attention to the fact that the natural world is a world of order, his reply is on record in a story called "A Natural History of the Dead." There he quotes from the traveller Mungo Park, who, naked and starving in an African desert, observed a beautiful little moss-flower and meditated thus:

Can the Being who planted, watered, and brought to perfection, in this obscure part of the world, a thing which appears of so small importance, look with unconcern upon the situation and suffering of creatures formed after his own image? Surely not. Reflections like these would not allow me to despair: I started up and, disregarding both hunger and fatigue, travelled forward, assured that relief was at hand; and I was not disappointed.

And Hemingway continues:

With a disposition to wonder and adore in like manner, as Bishop Stanley says [the author of *A Familiar History of Birds*], can any branch of Natural History be studied without increasing that faith, love and hope which we also, everyone of us, need in our journey through the wilderness of life? Let us therefore see what inspiration we may derive from the dead.

Then Hemingway presents the picture of a modern battlefield, where the bloated and decaying bodies give a perfect example of the natural order of chemistry—but scarcely an argument for faith, hope, and love. That picture is his answer to the argument that the order of nature implies meaning in the world.

In one of the stories, "A Clean, Well-Lighted Place," we find the best description of this world that underlies Hemingway's world of violent action. In the early stages of the story we see an old man sitting late in a Spanish café. Two waiters are speaking of him.

> "Last week he tried to commit suicide," one waiter said.
> "Why?"
> "He was in despair."
> "What about?"
> "Nothing."
> "How do you know it was nothing?"
> "He has plenty of money."

The despair beyond plenty of money—or beyond all the other gifts of the world: its nature becomes a little clearer at the end of the story when the older of the two waiters is left alone, reluctant too to leave the clean, well-lighted place:

> Turning off the electric light he continued the conversation with himself. It is the light of course but it is necessary that the place be clean and pleasant. You do not want music. Certainly you do not want music. Nor can you stand before a bar with dignity although that is all that is provided for these hours. What did he fear? It was not fear or dread. It was a nothing that he knew too well. It was all a nothing and a man was nothing too. It was only that and light was all it needed and a certain cleanness and order. Some lived in it and never felt it but he knew it all was nada y pues nada y nada y pues nada.* Our nada who art in nada, nada be thy name thy kingdom nada thy will be nada in nada as it is in nada. Give us this nada our daily nada and nada us our nada as we nada our nadas and nada us not into nada but deliver us from nada; pues nada. Hail nothing full of nothing, nothing is with thee. He smiled and stood before a bar with a shining steam pressure coffee machine.
> "What's yours?" asked the barman.
> "Nada."

* nada y pues nada, etc.: nothing and after that nothing, etc.

At the end the old waiter is ready to go home:

Now, without thinking further, he would go home to his room. He would lie in bed and finally, with daylight, he would go to sleep. After all, he said to himself, it is probably only insomnia. Many must have it.

And the sleepless man—the man obsessed by death, by the meaninglessness of the world, by nothingness, by nada—is one of the recurring symbols in the work of Hemingway. In this phase Hemingway is a religious writer. The despair beyond plenty of money, the despair that makes a sleeplessness beyond insomnia, is the despair felt by a man who hungers for the sense of order and assurance that men seem to find in religious faith, but who cannot find grounds for his faith.

Another recurring symbol, we have said, is the violent man. But the sleepless man and the violent man are not contradictory but complementary symbols. They represent phases of the same question, the same hungering for meaning in the world. The sleepless man is the man brooding upon nada, upon chaos, upon Nature-as-all. (For Nature-as-all equals moral chaos; even its bulls and lions and kudu are not admired by Hemingway as creatures of conscious self-discipline; their courage has a meaning only in so far as it symbolizes human courage.) The violent man is the man taking an action appropriate to the realization of the fact of nada. He is, in other words, engaged in the effort to discover human values in a naturalistic world.

Before we proceed with this line of discussion, it might be asked, "Why does Hemingway feel that the quest necessarily involves violence?" Now, at one level, the answer to this question would involve the whole matter of the bias toward violence in modern literature. But let us take it in its more immediate reference. The typical Hemingway hero is the man aware, or in the process of becoming aware, of nada. Death is the great nada. Therefore whatever code or creed the hero gets must, to be good, stick even in the face of death. It has to be good in the bull-ring or on the battlefield and not merely in the study or lecture room. In fact, Hemingway is anti-intellectual, and has a great contempt for any type of solution arrived at without the testings of immediate experience.

So aside from the question of a dramatic sense that would favor violence, and aside from the mere matter of personal temperament (for Hemingway describes himself on more than one occasion as obsessed by death), the presentation of violence is appropriate in his work because death is the great nada. In taking violent risks man confronts in dramatic terms the issue of nada that is implicit in all of Hemingway's world.

But to return to our general line of discussion. There are two aspects to this violence that is involved in the quest of the Hemingway hero, two aspects that seem to represent an ambivalent attitude toward nature.

First, there is the conscious sinking into nature, as we may call it. On this line of reasoning we would find something like this: if there is at center only nada, then the only sure compensation in life, the only reality, is gratification of appetite, the relish of sensation.

Continually in the stories and novels one finds such sentences as this from *Green Hills of Africa*: ". . . drinking this, the first one of the day, the finest one there is, and looking at the thick bush we passed in the dark, feeling the cool wind of the night and smelling the good smell of Africa, I was altogether happy." What is constantly interesting in such sentences is the fact that happiness, a notion that we traditionally connect with a complicated state of being, with notions of virtue, of achievement, etc., is here equated with a set of merely agreeable sensations. For instance, in "Cross-Country Snow," one of the boys, George, says to the other, Nick, who in story after story is a sort of shadow of Hemingway himself, "Maybe we'll never go skiing again, Nick." And Nick replies, "We've got to. It isn't worth while if you can't." The sensations of skiing are the end of life. Or in another story, "Big Two-Hearted

River: Part II," a story that is full of the sensation-as-happiness theme, we find this remark about Nick, who has been wading in a trout stream: "Nick climbed out onto the meadow and stood, water running down his trousers and out of his shoes, his shoes squelchy. He went over and sat on the logs. He did not want to rush his sensations any." The careful relish of sensation—that is what counts, always.

This intense awareness of the world of the senses is, of course, one of the things that made the early work of Hemingway seem, upon its first impact, so fresh and pure. Physical nature is nowhere rendered with greater vividness than in his work, and probably his only competitors in this department of literature are William Faulkner, among the modern, and Henry David Thoreau, among the older American writers. The meadows, forests, lakes, and trout streams of America, and the arid, sculpturesque mountains of Spain, appear with astonishing immediacy, and immediacy not dependent upon descriptive flourishes. But not only the appearance of landscape is important; a great deal of the freshness comes from the discrimination of sensation, the coldness of water in the "squelchy" shoes after wading, the tangy smell of dry sagebrush, the "cleanly" smell of grease and oil on a field piece.* Hemingway's appreciation of the aesthetic qualities of the physical world is important, but a peculiar poignancy is implicit in the rendering of those qualities; the beauty of the physical world is a background for the human predicament, and the very relishing of the beauty is merely a kind of desperate and momentary compensation possible in the midst of the predicament.

This careful relishing of the world of the senses comes to a climax in drinking and sex. Drink is the "giant-killer," the weapon against man's thought of nada. And so is sex, for that matter, though when sexual attraction achieves the status of love, the proc-

---

* Commented on by Ford Madox Ford in his introduction to the Modern Library edition of *A Farewell to Arms*.

ess is one that attempts to achieve a meaning rather than to forget meaninglessness in the world. In terms of drinking and sex, the typical Hemingway hero is a man of monel-metal stomach and Homeric prowess in the arts of love. And the typical situation is love, with some drinking, against the background of nada—of civilization gone to pot, or war, or death—as we get it in all of the novels in one form or another, and in many of the stories.

It is important to remember, however, that the sinking into nature, even at the level of drinking and mere sexuality, is a self-conscious act. It is not the random gratification of appetite. We see this quite clearly in *The Sun Also Rises* in the contrast between Cohn, who is merely a random dabbler in the world of sensation, who is merely trying to amuse himself, and the initiates like Jake and Brett, who are aware of the nada at the center of things and whose dissipations, therefore, have a philosophical significance. The initiate in Hemingway's world raises the gratification of appetite to the level of a cult and a discipline.

The cult of sensation, as we have already indicated, passes over very readily into the cult of true love, for the typical love story is presented primarily in terms of the cult of sensation. (*A Farewell to Arms*, as we shall see when we come to a detailed study of that novel, is closely concerned with this transition.) Even in the cult of true love it is the moment that counts, and the individual. There is never any past or future to the love stories and the lovers are always isolated, not moving in an ordinary human society within its framework of obligations. The notion of the cult—a secret cult composed of those who have been initiated into the secret of nada—is constantly played up. In *A Farewell to Arms*, for instance, Catherine and Frederick are, quite consciously, two against the world, a world that is, literally as well as figuratively, an alien world. The peculiar relationship between Frederick and the priest takes on a new significance if viewed in terms of the secret cult. We shall come to this topic later, but for the moment we can say that the priest is a priest of Divine Love, the subject about which he and Frederick converse in the hospital, and that Frederick himself is a kind of priest, one of the initiate in the end, of the cult of profane love. This same pattern of two against the world with an understanding confidante or interpreter, reappears in *For Whom the Bell Tolls*—with Pilar, the gipsy woman who understands "love," substituting for the priest of *A Farewell to Arms*.

The initiates of the cult of love are those who are aware of nada, but their effort, as members of the cult, is to find a meaning to put in place of the nada. That is, there is an attempt to make the relationship of love take on a religious significance in so far as it can give meaning to life. This general topic is not new with the work of Hemingway. It is one of the literary themes of the nineteenth century—and has, as a matter of fact, a longer history than that.

If the cult of love arises from and states itself in the language of the cult of sensation, it is an extension of the sinking-into-nature aspect of the typical Hemingway violence; but in so far as it involves a discipline and a search for a "faith," it leads us to the second aspect of the typical violence.

The violence, although in its first aspect it represents a sinking into nature, at the same time, in its second aspect, represents a conquest of nature, and of nada in man. It represents such a conquest, not because of the fact of violence, but because the violence appears in terms of a discipline, a style, and a code. It is, as we have already seen, in terms of a self-imposed discipline that the heroes make one gallant, though limited, effort to redeem the incoherence of the world: they attempt to impose some form upon the disorder of their lives, the technique of the bullfighter or sportsman, the discipline of the soldier, the fidelity of the lover, or even the code of the gangster, which, though brutal and apparently dehumanizing, has its own ethic. (Ole Anderson, in "The Killers," is willing to take his medicine without whining, and even recognizes some necessity and justice in his plight. Or the dying Mexican, in "The Gambler, the Nun, and the Radio," refuses to squeal despite the detective's argument: "One can, with honor, denounce one's assailant.")

If it is said that Frederick in *A Farewell to Arms* does not, when he deserts, exhibit the discipline of the soldier, the answer is simple: his obligation has been constantly presented as an obligation to the men in his immediate command, and he and the men in his command have never recognized an obligation to the total war—they recognize no meaning in the war and are bound together only by a squad sense and by their immediate respect for each other; when Frederick is separated from his men his obligation is gone. His true obligation then becomes the fidelity to Catherine.

The discipline, the form, is never quite capable of subduing the world, but fidelity to it is part of the gallantry of defeat. By fidelity to it the hero manages to keep one small place "clean" and "well-lighted," and manages to retain, or achieve for one last moment, his dignity. As the old Spanish waiter muses, there should be a "clean, well-lighted place" where one could keep one's dignity at the late hour.

We have said earlier that the typical Hemingway character is tough and, apparently, insensitive. But only apparently, for the fidelity to a code, to the discipline, may be the index to a sensitivity that allows the characters to see, at moments, their true plight. At times, and usually at times of stress, it is the tough man in the Hemingway world, the disciplined man, who is actually aware of pathos or tragedy. The individual toughness (which may be taken to be the private discipline demanded by the world) may find itself in conflict with the natural human reaction; but the Hemingway hero, though he may be aware of the claims of the natural reaction, the spontaneous human emotion, cannot surrender to it because he knows that the only way to hold on to the definition of himself, to "honor" or "dignity," is to maintain the discipline, the code. For example, when pity appears in the Hemingway world—as in "The Pursuit Race"—it does not appear in its maximum but in its minimum manifestation.

What this means in terms of style and method is the use of understatement. This understatement, stemming from the contrast between the sensitivity and the superimposed discipline, is a constant aspect of the work, an aspect that was caught in a cartoon in the *New Yorker*. The cartoon showed a brawny, muscle-knotted forearm and a hairy hand that clutched a rose. It was entitled "The Soul of Ernest Hemingway." Just as there is a margin of victory in the defeat of the Hemingway characters, so there is a little margin of sensitivity in their brutal and apparently insensitive world. Hence we have the ironical circumstance—a central circumstance in creating the pervasive irony of Hemingway's work—that the revelation of the values characteristic of his work arises from the most unpromising people and the most unpromising situations—the little streak of poetry or pathos in "The Pursuit Race," "The Killers," "My Old Man," "A Clean, Well-Lighted Place," or "The Undefeated." We have a perfect example of it in the last-named story. After the defeat of the old bullfighter, who is lying wounded on an operating table, Zurito, the picador, is about to cut off the old fellow's pigtail, the mark of his profession. But when the wounded man starts up, despite his pain, and says, "You couldn't do a thing like that," Zurito says, "I was joking." Zurito becomes aware that, after all, the old bullfighter is, in a way, undefeated, and deserves to die with his coleta on.

This locating of the poetic, the pathetic, or the tragic in the unpromising person or situation is not unique with Hemingway. It is something with which we are acquainted in a great deal of our literature since the Romantic Movement. The sensibility is played down, and an anti-romantic surface sheathes the work; the point is in the contrast. The impulse that led Hemingway to the simple character is akin to the one that drew Wordsworth to the same choice. Wordsworth felt that his unsophisticated peasants were more honest in their responses than the cultivated man, and were therefore more poetic. Instead of Wordsworth's peasant we have in Hemingway's work the bullfighter, the soldier, the revolutionist, the sportsman, and the gangster; instead of Wordsworth's children we have the young men like Nick, the person just on the verge of being initiated into the world. There are, of course, differences between the approach of Wordsworth and that of Hemingway, but there is little difference on the point of marginal sensibility. In one sense, both are anti-intellectual, and in such poems as "Resolution and Independence" or "Michael" one finds even closer ties.

I have just indicated a similarity between Wordsworth and Hemingway on the grounds of a romantic anti-intellectualism. But with Hemingway it is far more profound and radical than with Wordsworth. All we have to do to see the difference is to put Wordsworth's Preface to the *Lyrical Ballads* over against any number of passages from Hemingway. The intellectualism of the eighteenth century had merely put a veil of stereotyped language over the world and a veil of snobbism over a large area of human experience. That is Wordsworth's indictment. But Hemingway's indictment of the intellectualism of the past is that it wound up in the mire and blood of 1914 to 1918; that it was a pack of lies leading to death. We can put over against the Preface of Wordsworth, a passage from *A Farewell to Arms*:

I was always embarrassed by the words sacred, glorious, and sacrifice and the expression in vain. We had heard them, sometimes standing in the rain almost out of earshot, so that only the shouted words came through, and had read them, on proclamations that were slapped up by billposters over other proclamations, now for a long time, and I had seen nothing sacred, and the things that were glorious had no glory and the sacrifices were like the stockyards at Chicago if nothing was done with the meat except to bury it. There were many words that you could not stand to hear and finally only the names of places had dignity.

. . . Abstract words such as glory, honor, courage, or hallow were obscene beside the concrete names of villages, the numbers of roads, the names of rivers, the numbers of regiments and the dates.

I do not mean to say that the general revolution in style, and the revolt against the particular intellectualism of the nineteenth century was a result of the First World War. As a matter of fact, that revolt was going on long before the war, but for Hemingway, and for many others, the war gave the situation a peculiar depth and urgency.

Perhaps we might scale the matter thus: Wordsworth was a revolutionist—he truly had a new view of the world—but his revolutionary view left great tracts of the world untouched; the Church of England, for instance. Arnold and Tennyson, a generation or so later, though not revolutionists themselves, are much more profoundly stirred by the revolutionary situation than ever Wordsworth was; that is, the area of the world involved in the debate was for them greater. Institutions are called into question in a more fundamental way. But they managed to hang on to their English God and their English institutions. With Hardy, the area of disturbance has grown greater, and what can be salvaged is much less. He, like the earlier Victorians, had a strong sense of community to sustain him in the face of the universe that was for him, as not finally for Arnold and Tennyson, unfriendly, or at least neutral and Godless. But his community underlay institutions. It was a human communion that, as a matter of fact, was constantly being violated by institutions. Their violation of it is, in fact, a constant source of subject matter and a constant spring of irony. Nevertheless Hardy could refer to himself as a meliorist. He could not keep company with Wordsworth or Tennyson or Arnold; and when Hardy, having been elected an Honorary Fellow of Magdalene College, Cambridge, was to be formally admitted, the Master, Doctor Donaldson (as we know from A. C. Benson's *Diary*) was much afraid that Hardy might dislike the religious service.

The occasion, however, went off very well, even though Hardy, after impressing the Master with his knowledge of ecclesiastical music, did remark, "Of course it's only a sentiment to me now." Hardy listened to a sermon by the Archdeacon of Zanzibar, who declared that God was "a God of *desire*—who both hated and loved —not a mild or impersonal force." But even though Hardy could not accept the God of the Bishop of Zanzibar, he still had faith in the constructive power of the secret community.

Now in Hemingway we see something very like Hardy's secret community, but one much smaller, one whose definition has become much more specialized. Its members are those who know the code. They recognize each other, they know the password and the secret grip, but they are few in number, and each is set off against the world like a wounded lion ringed round by waiting hyenas (*Green Hills of Africa* gives us the hyena symbol—the animal whose death is comic because it is all hideously "appetite": wounded, it eats its own intestines). Furthermore, this secret community is not constructive; Hemingway is no meliorist. In fact, there are hints that somewhere in the back of his mind, and in behind his work, there is a kind of Spenglerian view of history: our civilization is running down. We get this most explicitly in *Green Hills of Africa*:

A continent ages quickly once we come. The natives live in harmony with it. But the foreigner destroys, cuts down the trees, drains the water, so that the water supply is altered and in a short time the soil, once the sod is turned under, is cropped out and, next, it starts to blow away as it has blown away in every old country and as I had seen it start to blow in Canada. The earth gets tired of being exploited. A country wears out quickly unless man puts back in it all his residue and that of all his beasts. When he quits using beasts and uses machines, the earth defeats him quickly. The machine can't reproduce, nor does it fertilize the soil, and it eats what he cannot raise. A country was made to be as we found it. We are the intruders and after we are dead we may have ruined it but it will still be there and we don't know what the next changes are. I suppose they all end up like Mongolia.

I would come back to Africa but not to make a living from it. . . .
But I would come back to where it pleased me to live; to really live.
Not just let my life pass. Our people went to America because that
was the place for them to go then. It had been a good country and we
had made a bloody mess of it and I would go, now, somewhere else
as we had always had the right to go somewhere else and as we had
always gone. You could always come back. Let the others come to
America who did not know that they had come too late. Our people
had seen it at its best and fought for it when it was well worth fighting
for. Now I would go somewhere else.

This is the most explicit statement, but the view is implicit in
case after case. The general human community, the general human
project, has gone to pot. There is only the little secret community
of, paradoxically enough, individualists who have resigned from the
general community, and who are strong enough to live without any
of the illusions, lies, and big words of the herd. At least, this is the
case up to the novel *To Have and Have Not,* which appeared in
1937. In that novel and in *For Whom the Bell Tolls* Hemingway
attempts to bring his individualistic hero back to society, to give
him a common stake with the fate of other men.

But to return to the matter of Wordsworth and Hemingway.
What in Wordsworth is merely simple or innocent is in Hemingway violent: the gangster or bullfighter replaces the leech-gatherer
or the child. Hemingway's world is a more disordered world, and
the sensibility of his characters is more ironically in contrast with
their world. The most immediate consideration here is the playing
down of the sensibility as such, the sheathing of it in the code of
toughness. Gertrude Stein's tribute is here relevant: "Hemingway
is the shyest and proudest and sweetest-smelling storyteller of my
reading." But this shyness manifests itself in the irony. In this, of
course, Hemingway's irony corresponds to the Byronic irony. But
the relation to Byron is even more fundamental. The pity is only
valid when it is wrung from the man who has been seasoned by
experience. Therefore a premium is placed on the fact of violent

experience. The "dumb ox" character, commented on by Wyndham Lewis,* represents the Wordsworthian peasant; the character with the code of the tough guy, the initiate, the man cultivating honor, gallantry, and recklessness, represents the Byronic aristocrat.

The failures of Hemingway, like his successes, are rooted in this situation. The successes occur in those instances where Hemingway accepts the essential limitations of his premises, that is, when there is an equilibrium between the dramatization and the characteristic Hemingway "point," when the system of ironies and understatements is coherent. On the other hand, the failures occur when we feel that Hemingway has not respected the limitations of his premises; that is, when the dramatization seems to be "rigged" and the violence, therefore, merely theatrical. The characteristic irony, or understatement, in such cases, seems to be too self-conscious. For example, let us glance at Hemingway's most spectacular failure, *To Have and Have Not*. The point of the novel is based on the contrast between the smuggler and the rich owners of the yachts along the quay. But the irony is essentially an irony without any center of reference. It is superficial, for, as a critic in the *Partisan Review*† indicated, the only difference between the smuggler and the rich is that the rich were successful in their buccaneering. The revelation that comes to the smuggler dying in his launch—"a man alone ain't got no . . . chance"—is a meaningless revelation, for it has no reference to the actual dramatization. It is, finally, a failure in intellectual analysis of the situation.

There is, I believe, a good chance that *For Whom the Bell Tolls* will turn out to be not Hemingway's best novel—an honor I should reserve for *A Farewell to Arms*—primarily because in this most ambitious of the novels Hemingway does not accept the limitations of his premises. I do not mean to imply that it is on a level with *To*

* "The Dumb Ox, A Study of Ernest Hemingway," *American Review*, June, 1934.
† "The Social Muse and the Great Kudu," by Philip Rahv, *Partisan Review*, December, 1937.

Have and Have Not. There is a subtler irony in the later novel. I have pointed out that the irony in *To Have and Have Not* is that of the contrast between the smuggler and the rich in the yachts along the pier; that is, it is a simple irony, in direct line with the ostensible surface direction of the story. But the irony in *For Whom the Bell Tolls* runs counter to the ostensible surface direction of the story. As surface, we have a conflict between the forces of light and the forces of darkness, freedom versus fascism, etc. Hero and heroine are clearly and completely and romantically aligned on the side of light. We are prepared to see the fascist atrocities and the general human kindness of the Loyalists. It happens to work out the other way. The scene of horror is the massacre by the Loyalists, not by the Fascists. Again, in the attack on El Sordo's hill by the Fascists, we are introduced to a young Fascist lieutenant, whose bosom friend is killed in the attack. We are suddenly given this little human glimpse—against the grain of the surface. But this incident, we discover later, is preparation for the very end of the novel. We leave the hero lying wounded, preparing to cover the retreat of his friends. The man who is over the sights of the machine gun as the book ends is the Fascist lieutenant, whom we have been made to know as a man not as a monster. This general ironical conditioning of the overt story line is reflected also in the attitude of Anselmo, who kills but cannot believe in killing. In other words, the irony here is much more functional, and more complicated, than·that of the other novel mentioned; the irony affirms that the human values may transcend the party lines.

Much has been said to the effect that *To Have and Have Not* and *For Whom the Bell Tolls* represent a basic change of point of view, an enlargement of what I have called the secret community. Now no doubt that is the intention behind both books, but the temper of both books, the good one and the bad one, is the old temper, the cast of characters is the old cast, and the assumptions lying far below the explicit intention are the old assumptions.

The monotony and self-imitation, into which Hemingway's work sometimes falls is again an effect of a failure in dramatization. Hemingway, apparently, can dramatize his "point" in only one basic situation and with only one set of characters. He has, as we have seen, only two key characters, with certain variations from them by way of contrast or counterpoint. His best women characters, by the way, are those who must nearly approximate the men; that is, they embody the masculine virtues and point of view characteristic of Hemingway's work.

But the monotony is not merely a monotony deriving from the characters as types; it derives, rather, from the limitations of the author's sensibility, which seems to come alive in only one issue. A more flexible sensibility, one capable of making nicer discriminations, might discover great variety in such key characters and situations. But Hemingway's successes are due, in part at least, to the close coordination that he sometimes achieves between the character and situation, on the one hand, and the sensibility as it reflects itself in the style, on the other hand.

The style characteristically is simple, even to the point of monotony. The characteristic sentence is simple, or compound; and if compound, there is no implied subtlety in the coordination of the clauses. The paragraph structure is, characteristically, based on simple sequence. There is an obvious relation between this style and the characters and situations with which the author is concerned—a relation of dramatic decorum. (There are, on the other hand, examples, especially in the novels, of other, more fluent, lyrical effects, but even here this fluency is founded on the conjunction *and*; it is a rhythmical and not a logical fluency. And the lyrical quality is simply a manifestation of that marginal sensibility, as can be demonstrated by an analysis of the occasions on which it appears.)

But there is a more fundamental aspect of the question, an aspect that involves not the sensibility of the characters but the sensibility of the author. The short, simple rhythms, the succession of coordinate clauses, the general lack of subordination—all suggest a dislocated and ununified world. The figures who live in this world live a sort of hand-to-mouth existence perceptually, and conceptually they hardly live at all. Subordination implies some exercise of discrimination—the sifting of reality through the intellect. But in Hemingway we see a Romantic anti-intellectualism.

In Wordsworth, too, we see this strain of anti-intellectualism. He too wishes to clear away the distorting sophistications of the intellect, and to keep his eye on the object. The formulations of the intellect create the "veil of familiarity" that he would clear away. His mode, too, was to take unpromising material and reveal in it the lyric potentiality. He, too, was interested in the margin of sensibility. He, too, wished to respect the facts, and could have understood Hemingway's rejection of the big abstract words in favor of "the concrete names of villages, the numbers of roads, the names of rivers, the numbers of regiments and the dates."

The passage from *A Farewell to Arms* from which the above quotation comes is, of course, the passage most commonly used to explain the attitude behind Hemingway's style. But we can put with it other passages of a similar import, and best of all a sentence from the story "Soldier's Home." Krebs, the boy who has been through the war and who comes back home to find himself cut off from life, had "acquired the nausea in regard to experience that is the result of untruth or exaggeration." He is a casualty, not of bullet or bayonet, but of the big, abstract words. Hemingway's style is, in a way, an attempt to provide an antidote for that "nausea."

III

A Farewell to Arms is a love story. It is a compelling story at the merely personal level, but it is much more compelling and significant when we see the figures of the lovers silhouetted against the flame-streaked blackness of war, of a collapsing world, of nada.

For there is a story behind the love story. That story is the quest for meaning and certitude in a world that seems to offer nothing of the sort. It is, in a sense, a religious book; if it does not offer a religious solution it is nevertheless conditioned by the religious problem.

The very first scene of the book, though seemingly casual, is important if we are to understand the deeper motivations of the story. It is the scene at the officers' mess where the captain baits the priest. "Priest every night five against one," the captain explains to Frederick. But Frederick, we see in this and later scenes, takes no part in the baiting. There is a bond between him and the priest, a bond that they both recognize. This becomes clear when, after the officers have advised Frederick where he should go on his leave to find the best girls, the priest turns to him and says that he would like to have him to go to Abruzzi, his own province:

"There is good hunting. You would like the people and though it is cold it is clear and dry. You could stay with my family. My father is a famous hunter."
"Come on," said the captain. "We go whorehouse before it shuts."
"Goodnight," I said to the priest.
"Goodnight," he said.

In this preliminary contrast between the officers, who invite the hero to go to the brothel, and the priest, who invites him to go to the cold, clear, dry country, we have in its simplest form the issue of the novel.

Frederick does go with the officers that night, and on his leave he does go to the cities, "to the smoke of cafés and nights when the room whirled and you needed to look at the wall to make it stop, nights in bed, drunk, when you knew that that was all there was, and the strange excitement of waking and not knowing who it was with you, and the world all unreal in the dark and so exciting that you must resume again unknowing and not caring in the night, sure that this was all and all and all and not caring." Frederick, at the opening of the novel, lives in the world of random and meaningless appetite, knowing that it is all and all and all, or thinking that he knows that. But behind that there is a dissatisfaction and disgust. Upon his return from his leave, sitting in the officers' mess, he tries to tell the priest how he is sorry that he had not gone to the clear, cold, dry country—the priest's home, which takes on the shadowy symbolic significance of another kind of life, another view of the world. The priest had always known that other country.

He had always known what I did not know and what, when I learned it, I was always able to forget. But I did not know that then, although I learned it later.

What Frederick learns later is the story behind the love story of the book.

But this theme is not merely stated at the opening of the novel and then absorbed into the action. It appears later, at crucial points, to define the line of meaning in the action. When, for example, Frederick is wounded, the priest visits him in the hospital. Their conversation makes even plainer the religious background of the novel. The priest has said that he would like to go back after the war to the Abruzzi. He continues:

"It does not matter. But there in my country it is understood that a man may love God. It is not a dirty joke."
"I understand."
He looked at me and smiled.
"You understand but you do not love God."
"No."
"You do not love Him at all?" he asked.
"I am afraid of Him in the night sometimes."
"You should love Him."
"I don't love much."
"Yes," he said. "You do. What you tell me about in the nights.

That is not love. That is only passion and lust. When you love you wish to do things for. You wish to sacrifice for. You wish to serve."

"I don't love."

"You will. I know you will. Then you will be happy."

We have here two important items. First, there is the definition of Frederick as the sleepless man, the man haunted by nada. Second, at this stage in the novel, the end of Book I, the true meaning of the love story with Catherine has not yet been defined. It is still at the level of appetite. The priest's role is to indicate the next stage of the story, the discovery of the true nature of love, the "wish to do things for." And he accomplishes this by indicating a parallel between secular love and Divine love, a parallel which implies Frederick's quest for meaning and certitude. And to emphasize further this idea, Frederick, after the priest leaves, muses on the high, clean country of the Abruzzi, the priest's home that has already been endowed with the symbolic significance of the religious view of the world.

In the middle of Book II (chapter xviii), in which the love story begins to take on the significance that the priest had predicted, the point is indicated by a bit of dialogue between the lovers.

"Couldn't we be married privately some way? Then if anything happened to me or if you had a child."

"There's no way to be married except by church or state. We are married privately. You see, darling, it would mean everything to me if I had any religion. But I haven't any religion."

"You gave me the Saint Anthony."

"That was for luck. Some one gave it to me."

"Then nothing worries you?"

"Only being sent away from you. You're my religion. You're all I've got."

Again, toward the end of Book IV (chapter xxxv), just before Frederick and Catherine make their escape into Switzerland, Frederick is talking with a friend, the old Count Greffi, who has just said that he thought H. G. Wells's novel *Mr. Britling Sees It Through* a very good study of the English middle-class soul. But Frederick twists the word *soul* into another meaning.

"I don't know about the soul."
"Poor boy. We none of us know about the soul. Are you *Croyant?*"
"At night."

Later in the same conversation the Count returns to the topic:

"And if you ever become devout pray for me if I am dead. I am asking several of my friends to do that. I had expected to become devout myself but it has not come." I thought he smiled sadly but I could not tell. He was so old and his face was very wrinkled, so that a smile used so many lines that all gradations were lost.
"I might become very devout," I said. "Anyway, I will pray for you."
"I had always expected to become devout. All my family died very devout. But somehow it does not come."
"It's too early."
"Maybe it is too late. Perhaps I have outlived my religious feeling."
"My own comes only at night."
"Then too you are in love. Do not forget that is a religious feeling."

So here we find, again, Frederick defined as the sleepless man, and the relation established between secular love and Divine love.

In the end, with the death of Catherine, Frederick discovers that the attempt to find a substitute for universal meaning in the limited meaning of the personal relationship is doomed to failure. It is doomed because it is liable to all the accidents of a world in which human beings are like the ants running back and forth on a log burning in a campfire and in which death is, as Catherine says just before her own death, "just a dirty trick." But this is not to deny the value of the effort, or to deny the value of the discipline, the code, the stoic endurance, the things that make it true —or half true—that "nothing ever happens to the brave."

This question of the characteristic discipline takes us back to the beginning of the book, and to the context from which Frederick's effort arises. We have already mentioned the contrast between the officers of the mess and the priest. It is a contrast based on the man who is aware of the issue of meaning in life and those who are unaware of it, who give themselves over to the mere flow of acci- dent, the contrast between the disciplined and the undisciplined. But the contrast is not merely between the priest and the officers. Frederick's friend, the surgeon Rinaldi, is another who is on the same "side" of the contrast as the priest. He may go to the brothel with his brother officers, he may even bait the priest a little, but his personal relationship with Frederick indicates his affiliations; he is one of the initiate. Furthermore, he has the discipline of his profession, and, as we have seen, in the Hemingway world, the discipline that seems to be merely technical, the style of the artist or the form of the athlete or bullfighter, may be an index to a moral value. "Already," Rinaldi says, "I am only happy when I am working." (Already the seeking of pleasure in sensation is inadequate for Rinaldi.) This point appears more sharply in the remarks about the doctor who first attends to Frederick's wounded leg. He is incompetent and does not wish to take the responsi- bility for a decision.

> Before he came back three doctors came into the room. I have noticed that doctors who fail in the practice of medicine have a tendency to seek one another's company and aid in consultation. A doctor who cannot take out your appendix properly will recommend to you a doctor who will be unable to remove your tonsils with success. These were three such doctors.

In contrast with them there is Doctor Valentini, who is competent, who is willing to take responsibility, and who, as a kind of mark of his role, speaks the same lingo, with the same bantering, ironical tone, as Rinaldi—the tone that is the mark of the initiate.

So we have the world of the novel divided into two groups, the initiate and the uninitiate, the aware and the unaware, the dis- ciplined and the undisciplined. In the first group are Frederick, Catherine, Rinaldi, Valentini, Count Greffi, the old man who cut the paper silhouettes "for pleasure," and Passini, Manera, and the other ambulance men in Frederick's command. In the second group are the officers of the mess, the incompetent doctors, the "legitimate hero" Ettore, and the "patriots"—all the people who do not know what is really at stake, who are deluded by the big words, who do not have the discipline. They are the messy people, the people who surrender to the flow and illusion of things. It is this second group who provide the context of the novel, and more especially the context from which Frederick moves toward his final complete awareness.

The final awareness means, as we have said, that the individual is thrown back upon his private discipline and his private capacity to endure. The hero cuts himself off from the herd, the confused world, which symbolically appears as the routed army at Caporetto. And, as Malcolm Cowley has pointed out,* the plunge into the flooded Tagliamento, when Frederick escapes from the battle police, has the significance of a rite. By this "baptism" Frederick is reborn into another world; he comes out into the world of the man alone, no longer supported by and involved in society.

---

* Introduction to the *Portable Hemingway*, The Viking Press. In this general connection one may consider the strategic advantage that Hemingway has in that it is the Italian army from which his hero deserts. If his hero had, for instance, deserted from the American army, the American reader's resistance to accepting the act would have been much greater—the reader's own immediate loyalties, etc., would have been betrayed by Frederick's act. And by the same token the resistance to the symbolic meaning of the act—the resigning from society—would have been much greater. The reader is led to accept the act because the desertion is from a "foreign" army. The point is indicated in a passage of dialogue between Frederick and Catherine. Frederick complains that he doesn't want them to have to live in secret and on the run like criminals.
"I feel like a criminal. I've deserted from the army."
"Darling, *please* be sensible. It's not deserting from the army. It's only the Italian army."
It may be objected that since Hemingway himself saw service on the Italian front it is only natural that his story should be laid there and that by consequence the fact has no symbolic significance and no significance as fictional strategy. But the fact that circumstances of personal history dictated the setting of the story does not prevent the author from seizing on and using the advantages inherent in the situation.

Anger was washed away in the river along with my obligation. Although that ceased when the carabiniere put his hands on my collar. I would like to have had the uniform off although I did not care much about the outward forms. I had taken off the stars, but that was for convenience. It was no point of honor. I was not against them. I was through. I wished them all the luck. There were the good ones, and the brave ones, and the calm ones and the sensible ones, and they deserved it. But it was not my show any more and I wished this bloody train would get to Maestre and I would eat and stop thinking.

So Frederick, by a decision, does what the boy Nick* does as the result of the accident of a wound. He makes a "separate peace." And from the waters of the flooded Tagliamento arises the Hemingway hero in his purest form, with human history and obligation washed away, ready to enact the last phase of his appropriate drama, and learn from his inevitable defeat the lesson of lonely fortitude.

IV

This is not the time to attempt to give a final appraisal of Hemingway's work as a whole or even of this particular novel—if there is ever a time for a "final" appraisal. But we may touch on some of the objections which have been brought against his work.

First, there is the objection that his work is immoral or dirty or disgusting. This objection appeared in various quarters against *A Farewell to Arms* at the time of its first publication. For instance, Robert Herrick, himself a respected novelist, wrote that if suppression were to be justified at all it would be justified in this case. He said that the book had no significance, was merely a "lustful indulgence," and smelled of the "boudoir," and summarized his view by calling it "garbage." † That objection has, for the most part, died out, but its echoes can still be occasionally heard, and now and then at rare intervals some bigot or high-minded but uninstructed moralist will object to the inclusion of *A Farewell to Arms*

---

* *In Our Time,* chapter vi.
† "What Is Dirt?" *Bookman,* November, 1929.

in a college course. The answer to such an objection is fundamentally an answer to the charge that the book has no meaning. The answer would seek to establish the fact that the book does deal seriously with a moral and philosophical issue, which, for better or worse, does exist in the modern world in substantially the terms presented by Hemingway. This means that the book, even if it does not end with a solution that is generally acceptable, still embodies a moral effort and is another document of the human effort to achieve ideal values. As for the bad effect it may have on some readers, the best answer is perhaps to be found in a quotation from Thomas Hardy, who is now sanctified but whose most famous novels, *Tess of the D'Urbervilles* and *Jude the Obscure,* once suffered the attacks of the dogmatic moralists, and one of whose books was burned by a bishop:

Of the effects of such sincere presentation on weak minds, when the courses of the characters are not exemplary and the rewards and punishments ill adjusted to deserts, it is not our duty to consider too closely. A novel which does moral injury to a dozen imbeciles, and has bracing results upon intellects of normal vigor, can justify its existence; and probably a novel was never written by the purest-minded author for which there could not be found some moral invalid or other whom it was capable of harming.*

Second, there is the objection that Hemingway's work, especially of the period before *To Have and Have Not,* has no social relevance, that it is off the main stream of modern life, and that it has no concern with the economic structure of society. Critics who hold this general view regard Hemingway, like Joseph Conrad and perhaps like Henry James, as an exotic. There are several possible lines of retort to this objection. One line is well stated in the following passage if we substitute the name of Hemingway for Conrad:

Thus it is no reproach to Conrad that he does not concern himself at all with the economic and social background underlying human

* "The Profitable Reading of Fiction," in *Life and Art, Essays, Notes and Letters.*

relationships in modern civilization, for he never sets out to study those relationships. The Marxists cannot accuse him of cowardice or falsification, because in this case the charge is not relevant [though it might be relevant to *To Have and Have Not* or to *For Whom the Bell Tolls*]. That, from the point of view of the man with a theory, there are accidents in history, no one can deny. And if a writer chooses to discuss those accidents rather than the events which follow the main stream of historical causation, the economic, or other, determinist can only shrug his shoulder and maintain that these events are less instructive to the students than are the major events which he chooses to study; but he cannot accuse the writer of falsehood or distortion.†

That much is granted by one of the ablest critics of the group who would find Hemingway an exotic. But a second line of retort would fix on the word *instructive* in the foregoing passage, and would ask what kind of instruction, if any, is to be expected of fiction, as fiction. Is the kind of instruction expected of fiction in direct competition, at the same level, with the kind of instruction offered in Political Science I or Economics II? If that is the case, then out with Shakespeare and Keats and in with Upton Sinclair.

Perhaps *instruction* is not a relevant word, after all, for this case. This is a very thorny and debatable question, but it can be ventured that what good fiction gives us is the stimulation of a powerful image of human nature trying to fulfill itself, and not instruction in an abstract sense. The economic and political man are important aspects of human nature and may well constitute part of the *materials* of fiction. But the economic and political man are not the complete man and other concerns may still be important enough to engage worthily the attention of a writer—such concerns as love, death, courage, the point of honor, and the moral scruple. A man does not only have to live with other men in terms of economic and political arrangements; he has to live with them in terms of moral arrangements, and he has to live with himself, he has to define himself. It can truly be said that these concerns are all interrelated in fact, but it might be dangerously dogmatic to insist that

† David Daiches, "Joseph Conrad," in *Fiction in the Modern World.*

a writer should not bring one aspect into sharp, dramatic focus.

And it might be dangerously dogmatic to insist that Hemingway's ideas are not relevant to modern life. The mere fact that they exist and have stirred a great many people is a testimony to their relevance. Or to introduce a variation on that theme, it might be dogmatic to object to his work on the ground that he has few basic ideas. The history of literature seems to show that good artists may have very few *basic* ideas. They may have many ideas, but the ideas do not lead a life of democratic give-and-take, of genial camaraderie. No, there are usually one or two basic, obsessive ones. Like the religious reformer Savonarola, the artist may say: *"Le mie cose erano poche e grandi"*—my ideas were few and grand. And the ideas of the artist are grand because they are intensely felt, intensely realized—not because, by objective standards, by public, statistical standards, "important." No, that kind of public, statistical importance may be a condition of their being grand but is not of the special essence of their grandeur. (Perhaps not even the condition—perhaps the grandeur inheres in the fact that the artistic work shows us a parable of meaning—how idea is felt and how passion becomes idea through order.)

An artist may need few basic ideas, but in assessing his work we must introduce another criterion in addition to that of intensity. We must introduce the criterion of area. An artist's basic ideas do not operate in splendid isolation; to a greater or lesser degree, they prove themselves by their conquest of other ideas. Or again differently, the focus is a focus of experience, and the area of experience involved gives us another criterion of condition, the criterion of area. Perhaps an example would be helpful here. We have said that Hemingway is concerned with the scruple of honor, that this is a basic idea in his work. But we find that he applies this idea to a relatively small area of experience. In fact, we never see a story in which the issue involves the problem of definition of the scruple, nor do we ever see a story in which honor calls for a slow, grinding, day-to-day conquest of nagging difficulties. In other words, the idea is submitted to the test of a relatively small area of experience, to experience of a hand-picked sort, and to characters of a limited range.

But within that range, within the area in which he finds congenial material and in which competing ideas do not intrude themselves too strongly, Hemingway's expressive capacity is very powerful and the degree of intensity is very great. He is concerned not to report variety of human nature or human situation, or to analyze the forces operating in society, but to communicate a certain feeling about, a certain attitude toward, a special issue. That is, he is essentially a lyric rather than a dramatic writer, and for the lyric writer virtue depends upon the intensity with which the personal vision is rendered rather than upon the creation of a variety of characters whose visions are in conflict among themselves. And though Hemingway has not given—and never intended to give— a documented diagnosis of our age, he has given us one of the most compelling symbols of a personal response to our age.

ROBERT PENN WARREN

A Farewell to Arms

TO G. A. PFEIFFER

BOOK ONE

CHAPTER I

In the late summer of that year we lived in a house in a village that looked across the river and the plain to the mountains. In the bed of the river there were pebbles and boulders, dry and white in the sun, and the water was clear and swiftly moving and blue in the channels. Troops went by the house and down the road and the dust they raised powdered the leaves of the trees. The trunks of the trees too were dusty and the leaves fell early that year and we saw the troops marching along the road and the dust rising and leaves, stirred by the breeze, falling and the soldiers marching and afterward the road bare and white except for the leaves.

The plain was rich with crops; there were many orchards of fruit trees and beyond the plain the mountains were brown and bare. There was fighting in the mountains and at night we could see the flashes from the artillery. In the dark it was like summer lightning, but the nights were cool and there was not the feeling of a storm coming.

Sometimes in the dark we heard the troops marching under the window and guns going past pulled by motor-tractors. There was much traffic at night and many mules on the roads with boxes of ammunition on each side of their pack-saddles and gray motor trucks that carried men, and other trucks with loads covered with canvas that moved slower in the traffic. There were big guns too that passed in the day drawn by tractors, the long barrels of the guns covered with green branches and green leafy branches and vines laid over the tractors. To the north we could look across a valley and see a forest of chestnut trees and behind it another mountain on this side of the river. There was fighting for that mountain too, but it was not successful, and in the fall when the rains came the leaves all fell from the chestnut trees and the branches were bare and the trunks black with rain. The vineyards were thin and bare-branched too and all the country wet and brown and dead with the autumn. There were mists over the river and clouds on the mountain and the trucks splashed mud on the road and the troops were muddy and wet in their capes; their rifles were wet and under their capes the two leather cartridge-boxes on the front of the belts, gray leather boxes heavy with the packs of clips of thin, long 6.5 mm. cartridges, bulged forward under the capes so that the men, passing on the road, marched as though they were six months gone with child.

There were small gray motor cars that passed going very fast; usually there was an officer on the seat with the driver and more officers in the back seat. They splashed more mud than the camions even and if one of the officers in the back was very small and sitting between two generals, he himself so small that you could not see his face but only the top of his cap and his narrow back, and if the car went especially fast it was probably the King. He lived in Udine and came out in this way nearly every day to see how things were going, and things went very badly.

At the start of the winter came the permanent rain and with the rain came the cholera. But it was checked and in the end only seven thousand died of it in the army.

CHAPTER II

The next year there were many victories. The mountain that was beyond the valley and the hillside where the chestnut forest grew was captured and there were victories beyond the plain on the plateau to the south and we crossed the river in August and lived in a house in Gorizia that had a fountain and many thick shady trees in a walled garden and a wistaria vine purple on the side of the house. Now the fighting was in the next mountains beyond and was not a mile away. The town was very nice and our house was very fine. The river ran behind us and the town had been captured very handsomely but the mountains beyond it could not be taken and I was very glad the Austrians seemed to want to come back to the town some time, if the war should end, because they did not bombard it to destroy it but only a little in a military way. People lived on in it and there were hospitals and cafés and artillery up side streets and two bawdy houses, one for troops and one for officers, and with the end of the summer, the cool nights, the fighting in the mountains beyond the town, the shell-marked iron of the railway bridge, the smashed tunnel by the river where the fighting had been, the trees around the square and the long avenue of trees that led to the square; these with there being girls in the town, the King passing in his motor car, sometimes now seeing his face and little long necked body and gray beard like a goat's chin tuft; all these with the sudden interiors of houses that had lost a wall through shelling, with plaster and rubble in their gardens and sometimes in the street, and the whole thing going well on the Carso made the fall very different from the last fall when we had been in the country. The war was changed too.

The forest of oak trees on the mountain beyond the town was gone. The forest had been green in the summer when we had come into the town but now there were the stumps and the broken trunks and the ground torn up, and one day at the end of the fall when I was out where the oak forest had been I saw a cloud coming over the mountain. It came very fast and the sun went a dull yellow and then everything was gray and the sky was covered and the cloud came on down the mountain and suddenly we were in it and it was snow. The snow slanted across the wind, the bare ground was covered, the stumps of trees projected, there was snow on the guns and there were paths in the snow going back to the latrines behind trenches.

Later, below in the town, I watched the snow falling, looking out of the window of the bawdy house, the house for officers, where I sat with a friend and two glasses drinking a bottle of Asti, and, looking out at the snow falling slowly and heavily, we knew it was all over for that year. Up the river the mountains had not been taken; none of the mountains beyond the river had been taken. That was all left for next year. My friend saw the priest from our mess going by in the street, walking carefully in the slush, and pounded on the window to attract his attention. The priest looked up. He saw us and smiled. My friend motioned for him to come in. The priest shook his head and went on. That night in the mess after the spaghetti course, which every one ate very quickly and seriously, lifting the spaghetti on the fork until the loose strands hung clear then lowering it into the mouth, or else using a continuous lift and sucking into the mouth, helping ourselves to wine from the grass-covered gallon flask; it swung in a metal cradle and you pulled the neck of the flask down with the forefinger and the wine, clear red, tannic and lovely, poured out into the glass held with the same hand; after this course, the captain commenced picking on the priest.

The priest was young and blushed easily and wore a uniform like the rest of us but with a cross in dark red velvet above the left breast pocket of his gray tunic. The captain spoke pidgin Italian for my doubtful benefit, in order that I might understand perfectly, that nothing should be lost.

"Priest to-day with girls," the captain said looking at the priest and at me. The priest smiled and blushed and shook his head. This captain baited him often.

"Not true?" asked the captain. "To-day I see priest with girls."

"No," said the priest. The other officers were amused at the baiting.

"Priest not with girls," went on the captain. "Priest never with girls," he explained to me. He took my glass and filled it, looking at my eyes all the time, but not losing sight of the priest.

"Priest every night five against one." Every one at the table laughed. "You understand? Priest every night five against one." He made a gesture and laughed loudly. The priest accepted it as a joke.

"The Pope wants the Austrians to win the war," the major said. "He loves Franz Joseph. That's where the money comes from. I am an atheist."

"Did you ever read the 'Black Pig'?" asked the lieutenant. "I will get you a copy. It was that which shook my faith."

"It is a filthy and vile book," said the priest. "You do not really like it."

"It is very valuable," said the lieutenant. "It tells you about those priests. You will like it," he said to me. I smiled at the priest and he smiled back across the candle-light. "Don't you read it," he said.

"I will get it for you," said the lieutenant.

"All thinking men are atheists," the major said. "I do not believe in the Free Masons however."

"I believe in the Free Masons," the lieutenant said. "It is a noble organization." Some one came in and as the door opened I could see the snow falling.

"There will be no more offensive now that the snow has come," I said.

"Certainly not," said the major. "You should go on leave. You should go to Rome, Naples, Sicily——"

"He should visit Amalfi," said the lieutenant. "I will write you cards to my family in Amalfi. They will love you like a son."

"He should go to Palermo."

"He ought to go to Capri."

"I would like you to see Abruzzi and visit my family at Capracotta," said the priest.

"Listen to him talk about the Abruzzi. There's more snow there than here. He doesn't want to see peasants. Let him go to centres of culture and civilization."

"He should have fine girls. I will give you the addresses of places in Naples. Beautiful young girls—accompanied by their mothers. Ha! Ha! Ha!" The captain spread his hand open, the thumb up and fingers outspread as when you make shadow pictures. There was a shadow from his hand on the wall. He spoke again in pidgin Italian. "You go away like this," he pointed to the thumb, "and come back like this," he touched the little finger. Every one laughed.

"Look," said the captain. He spread the hand again. Again the candle-light made its shadows on the wall. He started with the upright thumb and named in their order the thumb and four fingers, "soto-tenente (the thumb), tenente (first finger), capitano (next finger), maggiore (next to the little finger), and tenente-colonello (the little finger). You go away soto-tenente! You come back soto-colonello!" They all laughed. The captain was having a great success with finger games. He looked at the priest and shouted, "Every night priest five against one!" They all laughed again.

"You must go on leave at once," the major said.

"I would like to go with you and show you things," the lieutenant said.

"When you come back bring a phonograph."

"Bring good opera disks."

"Bring Caruso."

"Don't bring Caruso. He bellows."

"Don't you wish you could bellow like him?"

"He bellows. I say he bellows!"

"I would like you to go to Abruzzi," the priest said. The others were shouting. "There is good hunting. You would like the people and though it is cold it is clear and dry. You could stay with my family. My father is a famous hunter."

"Come on," said the captain. "We go whorehouse before it shuts."

"Good-night," I said to the priest.

"Good-night," he said.

CHAPTER III

When I came back to the front we still lived in that town. There were many more guns in the country around and the spring had come. The fields were green and there were small green shoots on the vines, the trees along the road had small leaves and a breeze came from the sea. I saw the town with the hill and the old castle above it in a cup in the hills with the mountains beyond, brown mountains with a little green on their slopes. In the town there were more guns, there were some new hospitals, you met British men and sometimes women, on the street, and a few more houses had been hit by shell fire. It was warm and like the spring and I walked down the alleyway of trees, warmed from the sun on the wall, and found we still lived in the same house and that it all looked the same as when I had left it. The door was open, there was a soldier sitting on a bench outside in the sun, an ambulance was waiting by the side door and inside the door, as I went in, there was the smell of marble floors and hospital. It was all as I had left it except that now it was spring. I looked in the door of the big room and saw the major sitting at his desk, the window open and the sunlight coming into the room. He did not see me and I did not know whether to go in and report or go upstairs first and clean up. I decided to go on upstairs.

The room I shared with the lieutenant Rinaldi looked out on the courtyard. The window was open, my bed was made up with blankets and my things hung on the wall, the gas mask in an oblong tin can, the steel helmet on the same peg. At the foot of the bed was my flat trunk, and my winter boots, the leather shiny with oil, were on the trunk. My Austrian sniper's rifle with its blued octagon barrel and the lovely dark walnut, cheek-fitted, *schutzen* stock, hung over the two beds. The telescope that fitted it was, I remembered, locked in the trunk. The lieutenant, Rinaldi, lay asleep on the other bed. He woke when he heard me in the room and sat up.

"Ciaou!" he said. "What kind of time did you have?"

"Magnificent."

We shook hands and he put his arm around my neck and kissed me.

"Oughf," I said.

"You're dirty," he said. "You ought to wash. Where did you go and what did you do? Tell me everything at once."

"I went everywhere. Milan, Florence, Rome, Naples, Villa San Giovanni, Messina, Taormina——"

"You talk like a time-table. Did you have any beautiful adventures?"

"Yes."

"Where?"

"Milano, Firenze, Roma, Napoli——"

"That's enough. Tell me really what was the best."

"In Milano."

"That was because it was first. Where did you meet her? In the Cova? Where did you go? How did you feel? Tell me everything at once. Did you stay all night?"

"Yes."

"That's nothing. Here now we have beautiful girls. New girls never been to the front before."

"Wonderful."

"You don't believe me? We will go now this afternoon and see. And in the town we have beautiful English girls. I am now in love with Miss Barkley. I will take you to call. I will probably marry Miss Barkley."

"I have to get washed and report. Doesn't anybody work now?"

"Since you are gone we have nothing but frostbites, chilblains, jaundice, gonorrhea, self-inflicted wounds, pneumonia and hard and soft chancres. Every week some one gets wounded by rock fragments. There are a few real wounded. Next week the war starts again. Perhaps it start again. They say so. Do you think I would do right to marry Miss Barkley—after the war of course?"

"Absolutely," I said and poured the basin full of water.

"To-night you will tell me everything," said Rinaldi. "Now I must go back to sleep to be fresh and beautiful for Miss Barkley."

I took off my tunic and shirt and washed in the cold water in the basin. While I rubbed myself with a towel I looked around the room and out the window and at Rinaldi lying with his eyes closed on the bed. He was good-looking, was my age, and he came from Amalfi. He loved being a surgeon and we were great friends. While I was looking at him he opened his eyes.

"Have you any money?"

"Yes."

"Loan me fifty lire."

I dried my hands and took out my pocket-book from the inside of my tunic hanging on the wall. Rinaldi took the note, folded it without rising from the bed and slid it in his breeches pocket. He smiled, "I must make on Miss Barkley the impression of a man of sufficient wealth. You are my great and good friend and financial protector."

"Go to hell," I said.

That night at the mess I sat next to the priest and he was disappointed and suddenly hurt that I had not gone to the Abruzzi. He had written to his father that I was coming and they had made preparations. I myself felt as badly as he did and could not understand why I had not gone. It was what I had wanted to do and I tried to explain how one thing had led to another and finally he saw it and understood that I had really wanted to go and it was almost all right. I had drunk much wine and afterward coffee and Strega and I explained, winefully, how we did not do the things we wanted to do; we never did such things.

We two were talking while the others argued. I had wanted to go to Abruzzi. I had gone to no place where the roads were frozen and hard as iron, where it was clear cold and dry and the snow was dry and powdery and hare-tracks in the snow and the peasants took off their hats and called you Lord and there was good hunting. I had gone to no such place but to the smoke of cafés and nights when the room whirled and you needed to look at the wall to make it stop, nights in bed, drunk, when you knew that that was all there was, and the strange excitement of waking and not knowing who it was with you, and the world all unreal in the dark and so exciting that you must resume again unknowing and not caring in the night, sure that this was all and all and all and not caring. Suddenly to care very much and to sleep to wake with it sometimes morning and all that had been there gone and everything sharp and hard and clear and sometimes a dispute about the cost. Sometimes still pleasant and fond and warm and breakfast and lunch. Sometimes all niceness gone and glad to get out on the street but always another day starting and then another night. I tried to tell about the night and the difference between the night and the day and how the night was better unless the day was very clean and cold and I could not tell it; as I cannot tell it now. But if you have had it you know. He had not had it but he understood that I had really wanted to go to the Abruzzi but had not gone and we were still friends, with many tastes alike, but with the difference between us. He had always known what I did not know and what, when I learned it, I was always able to forget. But I did not know that then, although I learned it later. In the meantime we were all at the mess, the meal was finished, and the argument went on. We two stopped talking and the captain shouted, "Priest not happy. Priest not happy without girls."

"I am happy," said the priest.

"Priest not happy. Priest wants Austrians to win the war," the captain said. The others listened. The priest shook his head.

"No," he said.

"Priest wants us never to attack. Don't you want us never to attack?"

"No. If there is a war I suppose we must attack."

"Must attack. Shall attack!"

The priest nodded.

"Leave him alone," the major said. "He's all right."

"He can't do anything about it anyway," the captain said. We all got up and left the table.

CHAPTER IV

The battery in the next garden woke me in the morning and I saw the sun coming through the window and got out of the bed. I went to the window and looked out. The gravel paths were moist and the grass was wet with dew. The battery fired twice and the air came each time like a blow and shook the window and made the front of my pajamas flap. I could not see the guns but they were evidently firing directly over us. It was a nuisance to have them there but it was a comfort that they were no bigger. As I looked out at the garden I heard a motor truck starting on the road. I dressed, went downstairs, had some coffee in the kitchen and went out to the garage.

Ten cars were lined up side by side under the long shed. They were top-heavy, blunt-nosed ambulances, painted gray and built like moving-vans. The mechanics were working on one out in the yard. Three others were up in the mountains at dressing stations.

"Do they ever shell that battery?" I asked one of the mechanics.

"No, Signor Tenente. It is protected by the little hill."

"How's everything?"

"Not so bad. This machine is no good but the others march."
He stopped working and smiled. "Were you on permission?"

"Yes."

He wiped his hands on his jumper and grinned. "You have a good time?" The others all grinned too.

"Fine," I said. "What's the matter with this machine?"

"It's no good. One thing after another."

"What's the matter now?"

"New rings."

I left them working, the car looking disgraced and empty with the engine open and parts spread on the work bench, and went in under the shed and looked at each of the cars. They were moderately clean, a few freshly washed, the others dusty. I looked at the tires carefully, looking for cuts or stone bruises. Everything seemed in good condition. It evidently made no difference whether I was there to look after things or not. I had imagined that the condition of the cars, whether or not things were obtainable, the smooth functioning of the business of removing wounded and sick from the dressing stations, hauling them back from the mountains to the clearing station and then distributing them to the hospitals named on their papers, depended to a considerable extent on myself. Evidently it did not matter whether I was there or not.

"Has there been any trouble getting parts?" I asked the sergeant mechanic.

"No, Signor Tenente."

"Where is the gasoline park now?"

"At the same place."

"Good," I said and went back to the house and drank another bowl of coffee at the mess table. The coffee was a pale gray and sweet with condensed milk. Outside the window it was a lovely spring morning. There was that beginning of a feeling of dryness in the nose that meant the day would be hot later on. That day I visited the posts in the mountains and was back in town late in the afternoon.

The whole thing seemed to run better while I was away. The offensive was going to start again I heard. The division for which we worked were to attack at a place up the river and the major told me that I would see about the posts for during the attack. The attack would cross the river up above the narrow gorge and spread up the hillside. The posts for the cars would have to be as near the river as they could get and keep covered. They would, of course, be selected by the infantry but we were supposed to work it out. It was one of those things that gave you a false feeling of soldiering.

I was very dusty and dirty and went up to my room to wash. Rinaldi was sitting on the bed with a copy of Hugo's English grammar. He was dressed, wore his black boots, and his hair shone.

"Splendid," he said when he saw me. "You will come with me to see Miss Barkley."

"No."

"Yes. You will please come and make me a good impression on her."

"All right. Wait till I get cleaned up."

"Wash up and come as you are."

I washed, brushed my hair and we started.

"Wait a minute," Rinaldi said. "Perhaps we should have a drink." He opened his trunk and took out a bottle.

"Not Strega," I said.

"No. Grappa."

"All right."

He poured two glasses and we touched them, first fingers extended. The grappa was very strong.

"Another?"

"All right," I said. We drank the second grappa, Rinaldi put away the bottle and we went down the stairs. It was hot walking through the town but the sun was starting to go down and it was very pleasant. The British hospital was a big villa built by Germans before the war. Miss Barkley was in the garden. Another nurse was with her. We saw their white uniforms through the trees and walked toward them. Rinaldi saluted. I saluted too but more moderately.

"How do you do?" Miss Barkley said. "You're not an Italian, are you?"

"Oh, no."

Rinaldi was talking with the other nurse. They were laughing.

"What an odd thing—to be in the Italian army."

"It's not really the army. It's only the ambulance."

"It's very odd though. Why did you do it?"

"I don't know," I said. "There isn't always an explanation for everything."

"Oh, isn't there? I was brought up to think there was."

"That's awfully nice."

"Do we have to go on and talk this way?"

"No," I said.

"That's a relief. Isn't it?"

"What is the stick?" I asked. Miss Barkley was quite tall. She wore what seemed to me to be a nurse's uniform, was blonde and had a tawny skin and gray eyes. I thought she was very beautiful. She was carrying a thin rattan stick like a toy riding-crop, bound in leather.

"It belonged to a boy who was killed last year."

"I'm awfully sorry."

"He was a very nice boy. He was going to marry me and he was killed in the Somme."

"It was a ghastly show."

"Were you there?"

"No."

"I've heard about it," she said. "There's not really any war of that sort down here. They sent me the little stick. His mother sent it to me. They returned it with his things."

"Had you been engaged long?"

"Eight years. We grew up together."

"And why didn't you marry?"

"I don't know," she said. "I was a fool not to. I could have given him that anyway. But I thought it would be bad for him."

"I see."

"Have you ever loved any one?"

"No," I said.

We sat down on a bench and I looked at her.

"You have beautiful hair," I said.

"Do you like it?"

"Very much."

"I was going to cut it all off when he died."

"No."

"I wanted to do something for him. You see I didn't care about the other thing and he could have had it all. He could have had anything he wanted if I would have known. I would have married him or anything. I know all about it now. But then he wanted to go to war and I didn't know."

I did not say anything.

"I didn't know about anything then. I thought it would be worse for him. I thought perhaps he couldn't stand it and then of course he was killed and that was the end of it."

"I don't know."

"Oh, yes," she said. "That's the end of it."

We looked at Rinaldi talking with the other nurse.

"What is her name?"

"Ferguson. Helen Ferguson. Your friend is a doctor, isn't he?"

"Yes. He's very good."

"That's splendid. You rarely find any one any good this close to the front. This is close to the front, isn't it?"

"Quite."

"It's a silly front," she said. "But it's very beautiful. Are they going to have an offensive?"

"Yes."

"Then we'll have to work. There's no work now."

"Have you done nursing long?"

"Since the end of 'fifteen. I started when he did. I remember having a silly idea he might come to the hospital where I was. With a sabre cut, I suppose, and a bandage around his head. Or shot through the shoulder. Something picturesque."

"This is the picturesque front," I said.

"Yes," she said. "People can't realize what France is like. If they did, it couldn't all go on. He didn't have a sabre cut. They blew him all to bits."

I didn't say anything.

"Do you suppose it will always go on?"

"No."

"What's to stop it?"

"It will crack somewhere."

"We'll crack. We'll crack in France. They can't go on doing things like the Somme and not crack."

"They won't crack here," I said.

"You think not?"

"No. They did very well last summer."

"They may crack," she said. "Anybody may crack."

"The Germans too."

"No," she said. "I think not."

We went over toward Rinaldi and Miss Ferguson.

"You love Italy?" Rinaldi asked Miss Ferguson in English.

"Quite well."

"No understand," Rinaldi shook his head.

"Abbastanza bene," I translated. He shook his head.

"That is not good. You love England?"

"Not too well. I'm Scotch, you see."

Rinaldi looked at me blankly.

"She's Scotch, so she loves Scotland better than England," I said in Italian.

"But Scotland is England."

I translated this for Miss Ferguson.

"Pas encore," said Miss Ferguson.

"Not really?"

"Never. We do not like the English."

"Not like the English? Not like Miss Barkley?"

"Oh, that's different. You mustn't take everything so literally."

After a while we said good-night and left. Walking home Rinaldi said, "Miss Barkley prefers you to me. That is very clear. But the little Scotch one is very nice."

"Very," I said. I had not noticed her. "You like her?"

"No," said Rinaldi.

CHAPTER V

The next afternoon I went to call on Miss Barkley again. She was not in the garden and I went to the side door of the villa where the ambulances drove up. Inside I saw the head nurse, who said Miss Barkley was on duty—"there's a war on, you know."

I said I knew.

"You're the American in the Italian army?" she asked.

"Yes, ma'am."

"How did you happen to do that? Why didn't you join up with us?"

"I don't know," I said. "Could I join now?"

"I'm afraid not now. Tell me. Why did you join up with the Italians?"

"I was in Italy," I said, "and I spoke Italian."

"Oh," she said. "I'm learning it. It's beautiful language."

"Somebody said you should be able to learn it in two weeks."

"Oh, I'll not learn it in two weeks. I've studied it for months now. You may come and see her after seven o'clock if you wish. She'll be off then. But don't bring a lot of Italians."

"Not even for the beautiful language?"

"No. Nor for the beautiful uniforms."

"Good evening," I said.

"A rivederci, Tenente."

"A rivederla." I saluted and went out. It was impossible to salute foreigners as an Italian, without embarrassment. The Italian salute never seemed made for export.

The day had been hot. I had been up the river to the bridgehead at Plava. It was there that the offensive was to begin. It had been impossible to advance on the far side the year before because there was only one road leading down from the pass to the pontoon bridge and it was under machine-gun and shell fire for nearly a mile. It was not wide enough either to carry all the transport for an offensive and the Austrians could make a shambles out of it. But the Italians had crossed and spread out a little way on the far side to hold about a mile and a half on the Austrian side of the river. It was a nasty place and the Austrians should not have let them hold it. I suppose it was mutual tolerance because the Austrians still kept a bridgehead further down the river. The Austrian trenches were above on the hillside only a few yards from the Italian lines. There had been a little town but it was all rubble. There was what was left of a railway station and a smashed permanent bridge that could not be repaired and used because it was in plain sight.

I went along the narrow road down toward the river, left the car at the dressing station under the hill, crossed the pontoon bridge, which was protected by a shoulder of the mountain, and went through the trenches in the smashed-down town and along the edge of the slope. Everybody was in the dugouts. There were racks of rockets standing to be touched off to call for help from the artillery or to signal with if the telephone wires were cut. It was quiet, hot and dirty. I looked across the wire at the Austrian lines.

Nobody was in sight. I had a drink with a captain that I knew in one of the dugouts and went back across the bridge.

A new wide road was being finished that would go over the mountain and zig-zag down to the bridge. When this road was finished the offensive would start. It came down through the forest in sharp turns. The system was to bring everything down the new road and take the empty trucks, carts and loaded ambulances and all returning traffic up the old narrow road. The dressing station was on the Austrian side of the river under the edge of the hill and stretcher-bearers would bring the wounded back across the pontoon bridge. It would be the same when the offensive started. As far as I could make out the last mile or so of the new road where it started to level out would be able to be shelled steadily by the Austrians. It looked as though it might be a mess. But I found a place where the cars would be sheltered after they passed that last bad-looking bit and could wait for the wounded to be brought across the pontoon bridge. I would have liked to drive over the new road but it was not yet finished. It looked wide and well made with a good grade and the turns looked very impressive where you could see them through openings in the forest on the mountain side. The cars would be all right with their good metal-to-metal brakes and anyway, coming down, they would not be loaded. I drove back up the narrow road.

Two carabinieri held the car up. A shell had fallen and while we waited three others fell up the road. They were seventy-sevens and came with a whishing rush of air, a hard bright burst and flash and then gray smoke that blew across the road. The carabinieri waved us to go on. Passing where the shells had landed I avoided the small broken places and smelled the high explosive and the smell of blasted clay and stone and freshly shattered flint. I drove back to Gorizia and our villa and, as I said, went to call on Miss Barkley, who was on duty.

At dinner I ate very quickly and left for the villa where the British had their hospital. It was really very large and beautiful and there were fine trees in the grounds. Miss Barkley was sitting on a bench in the garden. Miss Ferguson was with her. They seemed glad to see me and in a little while Miss Ferguson excused herself and went away.

"I'll leave you two," she said. "You get along very well without me."

"Don't go, Helen," Miss Barkley said.

"I'd really rather. I must write some letters."

"Good-night," I said.

"Good-night, Mr. Henry."

"Don't write anything that will bother the censor."

"Don't worry. I only write about what a beautiful place we live in and how brave the Italians are."

"That way you'll be decorated."

"That will be nice. Good-night, Catherine."

"I'll see you in a little while," Miss Barkley said. Miss Ferguson walked away in the dark.

"She's nice," I said.

"Oh, yes, she's very nice. She's a nurse."

"Aren't you a nurse?"

"Oh, no. I'm something called a V. A. D. We work very hard but no one trusts us."

"Why not?"

"They don't trust us when there's nothing going on. When there is really work they trust us."

"What is the difference?"

"A nurse is like a doctor. It takes a long time to be. A V. A. D. is a short cut."

"I see."

"The Italians didn't want women so near the front. So we're all on very special behavior. We don't go out."

"I can come here though."

"Oh, yes. We're not cloistered."

"Let's drop the war."

"It's very hard. There's no place to drop it."

"Let's drop it anyway."

"All right."

We looked at each other in the dark. I thought she was very beautiful and I took her hand. She let me take it and I held it and put my arm around under her arm.

"No," she said. I kept my arm where it was.

"Why not?"

"No."

"Yes," I said. "Please." I leaned forward in the dark to kiss her and there was a sharp stinging flash. She had slapped my face hard. Her hand had hit my nose and eyes, and tears came in my eyes from the reflex.

"I'm so sorry," she said. I felt I had a certain advantage.

"You were quite right."

"I'm dreadfully sorry," she said. "I just couldn't stand the nurse's-evening-off aspect of it. I didn't mean to hurt you. I did hurt you, didn't I?"

She was looking at me in the dark. I was angry and yet certain, seeing it all ahead like the movies in a chess game.

"You did exactly right," I said. "I don't mind at all."

"Poor man."

"You see I've been leading a sort of a funny life. And I never even talk English. And then you are so very beautiful." I looked at her.

"You don't need to say a lot of nonsense. I said I was sorry. We do get along."

"Yes," I said. "And we have gotten away from the war."

She laughed. It was the first time I had ever heard her laugh. I watched her face.

"You are sweet," she said.

"No, I'm not."

"Yes. You are a dear. I'd be glad to kiss you if you don't mind."

I looked in her eyes and put my arm around her as I had before and kissed her. I kissed her hard and held her tight and tried to open her lips; they were closed tight. I was still angry and as I held her suddenly she shivered. I held her close against me and could feel her heart beating and her lips opened and her head went back against my hand and then she was crying on my shoulder.

"Oh, darling," she said. "You will be good to me, won't you?"

What the hell, I thought. I stroked her hair and patted her shoulder. She was crying.

"You will, won't you?" She looked up at me. "Because we're going to have a strange life."

After a while I walked with her to the door of the villa and she went in and I walked home. Back at the villa I went upstairs to the room. Rinaldi was lying on his bed. He looked at me.

"So you make progress with Miss Barkley?"

"We are friends."

"You have that pleasant air of a dog in heat."

I did not understand the word.

"Of a what?"

He explained.

"You," I said, "have that pleasant air of a dog who——"

"Stop it," he said. "In a little while we would say insulting things." He laughed.

"Good-night," I said.

"Good-night, little puppy."

I knocked over his candle with the pillow and got into bed in the dark.

Rinaldi picked up the candle, lit it and went on reading.

CHAPTER VI

I was away for two days at the posts. When I got home it was too late and I did not see Miss Barkley until the next evening. She was not in the garden and I had to wait in the office of the hospital until she came down. There were many marble busts on painted wooden pillars along the walls of the room they used for an office. The hall too, that the office opened on, was lined with them. They had the complete marble quality of all looking alike. Sculpture had always seemed a dull business—still, bronzes looked like something. But marble busts all looked like a cemetery. There was one fine cemetery though—the one at Pisa. Genoa was the place to see the bad marbles. This had been the villa of a very wealthy German and the busts must have cost him plenty. I wondered who had done them and how much he got. I tried to make out whether they were members of the family or what; but they were all uniformly classical. You could not tell anything about them.

I sat on a chair and held my cap. We were supposed to wear steel helmets even in Gorizia but they were uncomfortable and too bloody theatrical in a town where the civilian inhabitants had not been evacuated. I wore one when we went up to the posts and carried an English gas mask. We were just beginning to get some of them. They were a real mask. Also we were required to wear an automatic pistol; even doctors and sanitary officers. I felt it against the back of the chair. You were liable to arrest if you did not have one worn in plain sight. Rinaldi carried a holster stuffed with toilet paper. I wore a real one and felt like a gunman until I practised firing it. It was an Astra 7.65 caliber with a short barrel and it jumped so sharply when you let it off that there was no question of hitting anything. I practised with it, holding below the target and trying to master the jerk of the ridiculous short barrel until I could hit within a yard of where I aimed at twenty paces and then the ridiculousness of carrying a pistol at all came over me and I soon forgot it and carried it flopping against the small of my back with no feeling at all except a vague sort of shame when I met English-speaking people. I sat now in the chair and an orderly of some sort looked at me disapprovingly from behind a desk while I looked at the marble floor, the pillars with the marble busts, and the frescoes on the wall and waited for Miss Barkley. The frescoes were not bad. Any frescoes were good when they started to peel and flake off.

I saw Catherine Barkley coming down the hall, and stood up. She did not seem tall walking toward me but she looked very lovely.

"Good-evening, Mr. Henry," she said.

"How do you do?" I said. The orderly was listening behind the desk.

"Shall we sit here or go out in the garden?"

"Let's go out. It's much cooler."

I walked behind her out into the garden, the orderly looking after us. When we were out on the gravel drive she said, "Where have you been?"

"I've been out on post."

"You couldn't have sent me a note?"

"No," I said. "Not very well. I thought I was coming back."

"You ought to have let me know, darling."

We were off the driveway, walking under the trees. I took her hands, then stopped and kissed her.

"Isn't there anywhere we can go?"

"No," she said. "We have to just walk here. You've been away a long time."

"This is the third day. But I'm back now."

She looked at me, "And you do love me?"

"Yes."

"You did say you loved me, didn't you?"

"Yes," I lied. "I love you." I had not said it before.

"And you call me Catherine?"

"Catherine." We walked on a way and were stopped under a tree.

"Say, 'I've come back to Catherine in the night.'"

"I've come back to Catherine in the night."

"Oh, darling, you have come back, haven't you?"

"Yes."

"I love you so and it's been awful. You won't go away?"

"No. I'll always come back."

"Oh, I love you so. Please put your hand there again."

"It's not been away." I turned her so I could see her face when I kissed her and I saw that her eyes were shut. I kissed both her shut eyes. I thought she was probably a little crazy. It was all right if she was. I did not care what I was getting into. This was better than going every evening to the house for officers where the girls climbed all over you and put your cap on backward as a sign of affection between their trips upstairs with brother officers. I knew I did not love Catherine Barkley nor had any idea of loving her. This was a game, like bridge, in which you said things instead of playing cards. Like bridge you had to pretend you were playing for money or playing for some stakes. Nobody had mentioned what the stakes were. It was all right with me.

"I wish there was some place we could go," I said. I was experiencing the masculine difficulty of making love very long standing up.

"There isn't any place," she said. She came back from wherever she had been.

"We might sit there just for a little while."

We sat on the flat stone bench and I held Catherine Barkley's hand. She would not let me put my arm around her.

"Are you very tired?" she asked.

"No."

She looked down at the grass.

"This is a rotten game we play, isn't it?"

"What game?"

"Don't be dull."

"I'm not, on purpose."

"You're a nice boy," she said. "And you play it as well as you know how. But it's a rotten game."

"Do you always know what people think?"

"Not always. But I do with you. You don't have to pretend you love me. That's over for the evening. Is there anything you'd like to talk about?"

"But I do love you."

"Please let's not lie when we don't have to. I had a very fine little show and I'm all right now. You see I'm not mad and I'm not gone off. It's only a little sometimes."

I pressed her hand, "Dear Catherine."

"It sounds very funny now—Catherine. You don't pronounce it very much alike. But you're very nice. You're a very good boy."

"That's what the priest said."

"Yes, you're very good. And you will come and see me?"

"Of course."

"And you don't have to say you love me. That's all over for a while." She stood up and put out her hand. "Good-night."

I wanted to kiss her.

"No," she said. "I'm awfully tired."

"Kiss me, though," I said.

"I'm awfully tired, darling."

"Kiss me."

"Do you want to very much?"

"Yes."

We kissed and she broke away suddenly. "No. Good-night, please, darling." We walked to the door and I saw her go in and down the hall. I liked to watch her move. She went on down the hall. I went on home. It was a hot night and there was a good deal going on up in the mountains. I watched the flashes on San Gabriele.

I stopped in front of the Villa Rossa. The shutters were up but it was still going on inside. Somebody was singing. I went on home. Rinaldi came in while I was undressing.

"Ah, ha!" he said. "It does not go so well. Baby is puzzled."

"Where have you been?"

"At the Villa Rossa. It was very edifying, baby. We all sang. Where have you been?"

"Calling on the British."

"Thank God I did not become involved with the British."

CHAPTER VII

I came back the next afternoon from our first mountain post and stopped the car at the *smistimento* where the wounded and sick were sorted by their papers and the papers marked for the different hospitals. I had been driving and I sat in the car and the driver took the papers in. It was a hot day and the sky was very bright and blue and the road was white and dusty. I sat in the high seat of the Fiat and thought about nothing. A regiment went by in the road and I watched them pass. The men were hot and sweating. Some wore their steel helmets but most of them carried them slung from their packs. Most of the helmets were too big and came down almost over the ears of the men who wore them. The officers all wore helmets; better-fitting helmets. It was half of the brigata Basilicata. I identified them by their red and white striped collar mark. There were stragglers going by long after the regiment had passed—men who could not keep up with their platoons. They were sweaty, dusty and tired. Some looked pretty bad. A soldier came along after the last of the stragglers. He was walking with a limp. He stopped and sat down beside the road. I got down and went over.

"What's the matter?"

He looked at me, then stood up.

"I'm going on."

"What's the trouble?"

" —— the war."

"What's wrong with your leg?"

"It's not my leg. I got a rupture."

"Why don't you ride with the transport?" I asked. "Why don't you go to the hospital?"

"They won't let me. The lieutenant said I slipped the truss on purpose."

"Let me feel it."

"It's way out."

"Which side is it on?"

"Here."

I felt it.

"Cough," I said.

"I'm afraid it will make it bigger. It's twice as big as it was this morning."

"Sit down," I said. "As soon as I get the papers on these wounded I'll take you along the road and drop you with your medical officers."

"He'll say I did it on purpose."

"They can't do anything," I said. "It's not a wound. You've had it before, haven't you?"

"But I lost the truss."

"They'll send you to a hospital."

"Can't I stay here, Tenente?"

"No, I haven't any papers for you."

The driver came out of the door with the papers for the wounded in the car.

"Four for 105. Two for 132," he said. They were hospitals beyond the river.

"You drive," I said. I helped the soldier with the rupture up on the seat with us.

"You speak English?" he asked.

"Sure."

"How you like this goddam war?"

"Rotten."

"I say it's rotten. Jesus Christ, I say it's rotten."

"Were you in the States?"

"Sure. In Pittsburgh. I knew you was an American."

"Don't I talk Italian good enough?"

"I knew you was an American all right."

"Another American," said the driver in Italian looking at the hernia man.

"Listen, lootenant. Do you have to take me to that regiment?"

"Yes."

"Because the captain doctor knew I had this rupture. I threw away the goddam truss so it would get bad and I wouldn't have to go to the line again."

"I see."

"Couldn't you take me no place else?"

"If it was closer to the front I could take you to a first medical post. But back here you've got to have papers."

"If I go back they'll make me get operated on and then they'll put me in the line all the time."

I thought it over.

"You wouldn't want to go in the line all the time, would you?" he asked.

"No."

"Jesus Christ, ain't this a goddam war?"

"Listen," I said. "You get out and fall down by the road and get a bump on your head and I'll pick you up on our way back and take you to a hospital. We'll stop by the road here, Aldo." We stopped at the side of the road. I helped him down.

"I'll be right here, lieutenant," he said.

"So long," I said. We went on and passed the regiment about a mile ahead, then crossed the river, cloudy with snow-water and running fast through the spiles of the bridge, to ride along the road across the plain and deliver the wounded at the two hospitals. I drove coming back and went fast with the empty car to find the man from Pittsburgh. First we passed the regiment, hotter and slower than ever: then the stragglers. Then we saw a horse ambulance stopped by the road. Two men were lifting the hernia man to put him in. They had come back for him. He shook his head at me. His helmet was off and his forehead was bleeding below the hair line. His nose was skinned and there was dust on the bloody patch and dust in his hair.

"Look at the bump, lieutenant!" he shouted. "Nothing to do. They come back for me."

When I got back to the villa it was five o'clock and I went out where we washed the cars, to take a shower. Then I made out my report in my room, sitting in my trousers and an undershirt in front of the open window. In two days the offensive was to start and I would go with the cars to Plava. It was a long time since I had written to the States and I knew I should write but I had let it go so long that it was almost impossible to write now. There was nothing to write about. I sent a couple of army Zona di Guerra post-cards, crossing out everything except, I am well. That should handle them. Those post-cards would be very fine in America; strange and mysterious. This was a strange and mysterious war zone but I supposed it was quite well run and grim compared to other wars with the Austrians. The Austrian army was created to give Napoleon victories; any Napoleon. I wished we had a Napoleon, but instead we had Il Generale Cadorna, fat and prosperous and Vittorio Emmanuele, the tiny man with the long thin neck and the goat beard. Over on the right they had the Duke of

Aosta. Maybe he was too good-looking to be a great general but he looked like a man. Lots of them would have liked him to be king. He looked like a king. He was the King's uncle and commanded the third army. We were in the second army. There were some British batteries up with the third army. I had met two gunners from that lot, in Milan. They were very nice and we had a big evening. They were big and shy and embarrassed and very appreciative together of anything that happened. I wish that I was with the British. It would have been much simpler. Still I would probably have been killed. Not in this ambulance business. Yes, even in the ambulance business. British ambulance drivers were killed sometimes. Well, I knew I would not be killed. Not in this war. It did not have anything to do with me. It seemed no more dangerous to me myself than war in the movies. I wished to God it was over though. Maybe it would finish this summer. Maybe the Austrians would crack. They had always cracked in other wars. What was the matter with this war? Everybody said the French were through. Rinaldi said that the French had mutinied and troops marched on Paris. I asked him what happened and he said, "Oh, they stopped them." I wanted to go to Austria without war. I wanted to go to the Black Forest. I wanted to go to the Hartz Mountains. Where were the Hartz Mountains anyway? They were fighting in the Carpathians. I did not want to go there anyway. It might be good though. I could go to Spain if there was no war. The sun was going down and the day was cooling off. After supper I would go and see Catherine Barkley. I wish she were here now. I wished I were in Milan with her. I would like to eat at the Cova and then walk down the Via Manzoni in the hot evening and cross over and turn off along the canal and go to the hotel with Catherine Barkley. Maybe she would. Maybe she would pretend that I was her boy that was killed and we would go in the front door and the porter would take off his cap and I would stop at the concierge's desk and ask for the key and she would stand by the elevator and then we would get in the elevator and it would go up very slowly clicking at all the floors and then our floor and the boy would open the door and stand there and she would step out and I would step out and we would walk down the hall and I would put the key in the door and open it and go in and then take down the telephone and ask them to send a bottle of capri bianca in a silver bucket full of ice and you would hear the ice against the pail coming down the corridor and the boy would knock and I would say leave it outside the door please. Because we would not wear any clothes because it was so hot and the window open and the swallows flying over the roofs of the houses and when it was dark afterward and you went to the window very small bats hunting over the houses and close down over the trees and we would drink the capri and the door locked and it hot and only a sheet and the whole night and we would both love each other all night in the hot night in Milan. That was how it ought to be. I would eat quickly and go and see Catherine Barkley.

They talked too much at the mess and I drank wine because to-night we were not all brothers unless I drank a little and talked with the priest about Archbishop Ireland who was, it seemed, a noble man and with whose injustice, the injustices he had received and in which I participated as an American, and of which I had never heard, I feigned acquaintance. It would have been impolite not to have known something of them when I had listened to such a splendid explanation of their causes which were, after all, it seemed, misunderstandings. I thought he had a fine name and he came from Minnesota which made a lovely name: Ireland of Minnesota, Ireland of Wisconsin, Ireland of Michigan. What made it pretty was that it sounded like Island. No that wasn't it. There was more to it than that. Yes, father. That is true, father. Perhaps, father. No, father. Well, maybe yes, father. You know more about it than I do, father. The priest was good but dull. The officers were not good but dull. The King was good but dull. The wine was bad but not dull. It took the enamel off your teeth and left it on the roof of your mouth.

"And the priest was locked up," Rocca said, "because they found the three per cent bonds on his person. It was in France of course. Here they would never have arrested him. He denied all knowledge of the five per cent bonds. This took place at Béziers. I was there and reading of it in the paper, went to the jail and asked to see the priest. It was quite evident he had stolen the bonds."

"I don't believe a word of this," Rinaldi said.

"Just as you like," Rocca said. "But I am telling it for our priest here. It is very informative. He is a priest; he will appreciate it."

The priest smiled. "Go on," he said. "I am listening."

"Of course some of the bonds were not accounted for but the priest had all of the three per cent bonds and several local obligations, I forget exactly what they were. So I went to the jail, now this is the point of the story, and I stood outside his cell and I said as though I were going to confession, 'Bless me, father, for you have sinned.' "

There was great laughter from everybody.

"And what did he say?" asked the priest. Rocca ignored this and went on to explain the joke to me. "You see the point, don't you?" It seemed it was a very funny joke if you understood it properly. They poured me more wine and I told the story about the English private soldier who was placed under the shower bath. Then the major told the story of the eleven Czecho-slovaks and the Hungarian corporal. After some more wine I told the story of the jockey who found the penny. The major said there was an Italian story something like that about the duchess who could not sleep at night. At this point the priest left and I told the story about the travelling salesman who arrived at five o'clock in the morning at Marseilles when the mistral was blowing. The major said he had heard a report that I could drink. I denied this. He said it was true and by the corpse of Bacchus we would test whether it was true or not. Not Bacchus, I said. Not Bacchus. Yes, Bacchus, he said. I should drink cup for cup and glass for glass with Bassi, Fillipo Vincenza. Bassi said no that was no test because he had already drunk twice as much as I. I said that was a foul lie and, Bacchus or no Bacchus, Fillipo Vincenza Bassi or Bassi Fillippo Vicenza had never touched a drop all evening and what was his name anyway? He said was my name Frederico Enrico or Enrico Federico? I said let the best man win, Bacchus barred, and the major started us with red wine in mugs. Half-way through the wine I did not want any more. I remembered where I was going.

"Bassi wins," I said. "He's a better man than I am. I have to go."

"He does really," said Rinaldi. "He has a rendezvous. I know all about it."

"I have to go."

"Another night," said Bassi. "Another night when you feel stronger." He slapped me on the shoulder. There were lighted candles on the table. All the officers were very happy. "Good-night, gentlemen," I said.

Rinaldi went out with me. We stood outside the door on the patch and he said, "You better not go up there drunk."

"I'm not drunk, Rinin. Really."

"You'd better chew some coffee."

"Nonsense."

"I'll get some, baby. You walk up and down." He came back with a handful of roasted coffee beans. "Chew those, baby, and God be with you."

"Bacchus," I said.

"I'll walk down with you."

"I'm perfectly all right."

We walked along together through the town and I chewed the coffee. At the gate of the driveway that led up to the British villa, Rinaldi said good-night.

"Good-night," I said. "Why don't you come in?"

He shook his head. "No," he said. "I like the simpler pleasures."

"Thank you for the coffee beans."

"Nothing, baby. Nothing."

I started down the driveway. The outlines of the cypresses that lined it were sharp and clear. I looked back and saw Rinaldi standing watching me and waved to him.

I sat in the reception hall of the villa, waiting for Catherine Barkley to come down. Some one was coming down the hallway. I stood up, but it was not Catherine. It was Miss Ferguson.

"Hello," she said. "Catherine asked me to tell you she was sorry she couldn't see you this evening."

"I'm so sorry. I hope she's not ill."

"She's not awfully well."

"Will you tell her how sorry I am?"

"Yes, I will."

"'Do you think it would be any good to try and see her to-morrow?"

"Yes, I do."

"Thank you very much," I said. "Good-night."

I went out the door and suddenly I felt lonely and empty. I had treated seeing Catherine very lightly, I had gotten somewhat drunk and had nearly forgotten to come but when I could not see her there I was feeling lonely and hollow.

CHAPTER VIII

The next afternoon we heard there was to be an attack up the river that night and that we were to take four cars there. Nobody knew anything about it although they all spoke with great positiveness and strategical knowledge. I was riding in the first car and as we passed the entry to the British hospital I told the driver to stop. The other cars pulled up. I got out and told the driver to go on and that if we had not caught up to them at the junction of the road to Cormons to wait there. I hurried up the driveway and inside the reception hall I asked for Miss Barkley.

"She's on duty."

"Could I see her just for a moment?"

They sent an orderly to see and she came back with him.

"I stopped to ask if you were better. They told me you were on duty, so I asked to see you."

"I'm quite well," she said, "I think the heat knocked me over yesterday."

"I have to go."

"I'll just step out the door a minute."

"And you're all right?" I asked outside.

"Yes, darling. Are you coming to-night?"

"No. I'm leaving now for a show up above Plava."

"A show?"

"I don't think it's anything."

"And you'll be back?"

"To-morrow."

She was unclasping something from her neck. She put it in my hand. "It's a Saint Anthony," she said. "And come to-morrow night."

"You're not a Catholic, are you?"

"No. But they say a Saint Anthony's very useful."

"I'll take care of him for you. Good-by."

"No," she said, "not good-by."

"All right."

"Be a good boy and be careful. No, you can't kiss me here. You can't."

"All right."

I looked back and saw her standing on the steps. She waved and I kissed my hand and held it out. She waved again and then I was out of the driveway and climbing up into the seat of the ambulance and we started. The Saint Anthony was in a little white metal capsule. I opened the capsule and spilled him out into my hand.

"Saint Anthony?" asked the driver.

"Yes."

"I have one." His right hand left the wheel and opened a button on his tunic and pulled it out from under his shirt.

"See?"

I put my Saint Anthony back in the capsule, spilled the thin gold chain together and put it all in my breast pocket.

"You don't wear him?"

"No."

"It's better to wear him. That's what it's for."

"All right," I said. I undid the clasp of the gold chain and put it around my neck and clasped it. The saint hung down on the outside of my uniform and I undid the throat of my tunic, unbuttoned the shirt collar and dropped him in under the shirt. I felt him in his metal box against my chest while we drove. Then I forgot about him. After I was wounded I never found him. Some one probably got it at one of the dressing stations.

We drove fast when we were over the bridge and soon we saw the dust of the other cars ahead down the road. The road curved and we saw the three cars looking quite small, the dust rising from the wheels and going off through the trees. We caught them and passed them and turned off on a road that climbed up into the hills. Driving in convoy is not unpleasant if you are the first car and I settled back in the seat and watched the country. We were in the foot-hills on the near side of the river and as the road mounted there were the high mountains off to the north with snow still on the tops. I looked back and saw the three cars all climbing, spaced by the interval of their dust. We passed a long column of loaded mules, the drivers walking along beside the mules wearing red fezzes. They were bersaglieri.

Beyond the mule train the road was empty and we climbed through the hills and then went down over the shoulder of a long hill into a river-valley. There were trees along both sides of the road and through the right line of trees I saw the river, the water clear, fast and shallow. The river was low and there were stretches of sand and pebbles with a narrow channel of water and sometimes the water spread like a sheen over the pebbly bed. Close to the bank I saw deep pools, the water blue like the sky. I saw arched stone bridges over the river where tracks turned off from the road and we passed stone farmhouses with pear trees candela-braed against their south walls and low stone walls in the fields. The road went up the valley a long way and then we turned off and commenced to climb into the hills again. The road climbed steeply going up and back and forth through chestnut woods to level finally along a ridge. I could look down through the woods and see, far below, with the sun on it, the line of the river that separated the two armies. We went along the rough new military road that followed the crest of the ridge and I looked to the north at the two ranges of mountains, green and dark to the snow-line and then white and lovely in the sun. Then, as the road mounted along the ridge, I saw a third range of mountains, higher snow mountains, that looked chalky white and furrowed, with strange planes, and then there were mountains far off beyond all these that you could hardly tell if you really saw. Those were all the Austrians' mountains and we had nothing like them. Ahead there was a rounded turn-off in the road to the right and looking down I could see the road dropping through the trees. There were troops on this road and motor trucks and mules with mountain guns and as we went down, keeping to the side, I could see the river far down below, the line of ties and rails running along it, the old bridge where the railway crossed to the other side and across, under a hill beyond the river, the broken houses of the little town that was to be taken.

It was nearly dark when we came down and turned onto the main road that ran beside the river.

CHAPTER IX

The road was crowded and there were screens of corn-stalk and straw matting on both sides and matting over the top so that it was like the entrance at a circus or a native village. We drove slowly in this matting-covered tunnel and came out onto a bare cleared space where the railway station had been. The road here was below the level of the river bank and all along the side of the sunken road there were holes dug in the bank with infantry in them. The sun was going down and looking up along the bank as we drove I saw the Austrian observation balloons above the hills on the other side dark against the sunset. We parked the cars beyond a brickyard. The ovens and some deep holes had been equipped as dressing stations. There were three doctors that I knew. I talked with the major and learned that when it should start and our cars should be loaded we would drive them back along the screened road and up to the main road along the ridge where there would be a post and other cars to clear them. He hoped the road would not jam. It was a one-road show. The road was screened because it was in sight of the Austrians across the river. Here at the brickyard we were sheltered from rifle or machine-gun fire by the river bank. There was one smashed bridge across the river. They were going to put over another bridge when the bombardment started and some troops were to cross at the shallows up above at the bend of the river. The major was a little man with upturned mustaches. He had been in the war in Libya and wore two wound-stripes. He said that if the thing went well he would see that I was decorated. I said I hoped it would go well but that he was too kind. I asked him if there was a big dugout where the drivers could stay and he sent a soldier to show me. I went with him and found the dugout, which was very good. The drivers were pleased with it and I left them there. The major asked me to have a drink with him and two other officers. We drank rum and it was very friendly. Outside it was getting dark. I asked what time the attack was to be and they said as soon as it was dark. I went back to the drivers. They were sitting in the dugout talking and when I came in they stopped. I gave them each a package of cigarettes, Macedonias, loosely packed cigarettes that spilled tobacco and needed to have the ends twisted before you smoked them. Manera lit his lighter and passed it around. The lighter was shaped like a Fiat radiator. I told them what I had heard.

"Why didn't we see the post when we came down?" Passini asked.

"It was just beyond where we turned off."

"That road will be a dirty mess," Manera said.

"They'll shell the —— out of us."

"Probably."

"What about eating, lieutenant? We won't get a chance to eat after this thing starts."

"I'll go and see now," I said.

"You want us to stay here or can we look around?"

"Better stay here."

I went back to the major's dugout and he said the field kitchen would be along and the drivers could come and get their stew. He would loan them mess tins if they did not have them. I said I thought they had them. I went back and told the drivers I would get them as soon as the food came. Manera said he hoped it would come before the bombardment started. They were silent until I went out. They were all mechanics and hated the war.

I went out to look at the cars and see what was going on and then came back and sat down in the dugout with the four drivers. We sat on the ground with our backs against the wall and smoked. Outside it was nearly dark. The earth of the dugout was warm and dry and I let my shoulders back against the wall, sitting on the small of my back, and relaxed.

"Who goes to the attack?" asked Gavuzzi.

"Bersaglieri."

"All bersaglieri?"

"I think so."

"There aren't enough troops here for a real attack."

"It is probably to draw attention from where the real attack will be."

"Do the men know that who attack?"

"I don't think so."

"Of course they don't," Manera said. "They wouldn't attack if they did."

"Yes, they would," Passini said. "Bersaglieri are fools."

"They are brave and have good discipline," I said.

"They are big through the chest by measurement, and healthy. But they are still fools."

"The granatieri are tall," Manera said. This was a joke. They all laughed.

"Were you there, Tenente, when they wouldn't attack and they shot every tenth man?"

"No."

"It is true. They lined them up afterward and took every tenth man. Carabinieri shot them."

"Carabinieri," said Passini and spat on the floor. "But those grenadiers; all over six feet. They wouldn't attack."

"If everybody would not attack the war would be over," Manera said.

"It wasn't that way with the granatieri. They were afraid. The officers all came from such good families."

"Some of the officers went alone."

"A sergeant shot two officers who would not get out."

"Some troops went out."

"Those that went out were not lined up when they took the tenth men."

"One of those shot by the carabinieri is from my town," Passini said. "He was a big smart tall boy to be in the granatieri. Always in Rome. Always with the girls. Always with the carabinieri." He laughed. "Now they have a guard outside his house with a bayonet and nobody can come to see his mother and father and sisters and his father loses his civil rights and cannot even vote. They are all without law to protect them. Anybody can take their property."

"If it wasn't that that happens to their families nobody would go to the attack."

"Yes. Alpini would. These V. E. soldiers would. Some bersaglieri."

"Bersaglieri have run too. Now they try to forget it."

"You should not let us talk this way, Tenente. Evviva l'esercito," Passini said sarcastically.

"I know how you talk," I said. "But as long as you drive the cars and behave——"

"——and don't talk so other officers can hear," Manera finished.

"I believe we should get the war over," I said. "It would not finish it if one side stopped fighting. It would only be worse if we stopped fighting."

"It could not be worse," Passini said respectfully. "There is nothing worse than war."

"Defeat is worse."

"I do not believe it," Passini said still respectfully. "What is defeat? You go home."

"They come after you. They take your home. They take your sisters."

"I don't believe it," Passini said. "They can't do that to everybody. Let everybody defend his home. Let them keep their sisters in the house."

"They hang you. They come and make you be a soldier again. Not in the auto-ambulance, in the infantry."

"They can't hang every one."

"An outside nation can't make you be a soldier," Manera said. "At the first battle you all run."

"Like the Tchecos."

"I think you do not know anything about being conquered and so you think it is not bad."

"Tenente," Passini said. "We understand you let us talk. Listen. There is nothing as bad as war. We in the auto-ambulance cannot even realize at all how bad it is. When people realize how bad it is they cannot do anything to stop it because they go crazy. There are some people who never realize. There are people who are afraid of their officers. It is with them the war is made."

"I know it is bad but we must finish it."

"It doesn't finish. There is no finish to a war."

"Yes there is."

Passini shook his head.

"War is not won by victory. What if we take San Gabriele? What if we take the Carso and Monfalcone and Trieste? Where are we then? Did you see all the far mountains to-day? Do you think we could take all them too? Only if the Austrians stop fighting. One side must stop fighting. Why don't we stop fighting? If they come down into Italy they will get tired and go away. They have their own country. But no, instead there is a war."

"You're an orator."

"We think. We read. We are not peasants. We are mechanics. But even the peasants know better than to believe in a war. Everybody hates this war."

"There is a class that controls a country that is stupid and does not realize anything and never can. That is why we have this war."

"Also they make money out of it."

"Most of them don't," said Passini. "They are too stupid. They do it for nothing. For stupidity."

"We must shut up," said Manera. "We talk too much even for the Tenente."

"He likes it," said Passini. "We will convert him."

"But now we will shut up," Manera said.

"Do we eat yet, Tenente?" Gavuzzi asked.

"I will go and see," I said. Gordini stood up and went outside with me.

"Is there anything I can do, Tenente? Can I help in any way?" He was the quietest one of the four. "Come with me if you want," I said, "and we'll see."

It was dark outside and the long light from the search-lights was moving over the mountains. There were big search-lights on that front mounted on camions that you passed sometimes on the roads at night, close behind the lines, the camion stopped a little off the road, an officer directing the light and the crew scared. We crossed the brickyard, and stopped at the main dressing station. There was a little shelter of green branches outside over the entrance and in the dark the night wind rustled the leaves dried by the sun. Inside there was a light. The major was at the telephone sitting on a box. One of the medical captains said the attack had been put forward an hour. He offered me a glass of cognac. I looked at the board tables, the instruments shining in the light, the basins and the stoppered bottles. Gordini stood behind me. The major got up from the telephone.

"It starts now," he said. "It has been put back again."

I looked outside, it was dark and the Austrian search-lights were moving on the mountains behind us. It was quiet for a moment still, then from all the guns behind us the bombardment started.

"Savoia," said the major.

"About the soup, major," I said. He did not hear me. I repeated it.

"It hasn't come up."

A big shell came in and burst outside in the brickyard. Another burst and in the noise you could hear the smaller noise of the brick and dirt raining down.

"What is there to eat?"

"We have a little pasta asciutta," the major said.

"I'll take what you can give me."

The major spoke to an orderly who went out of sight in the back and came back with a metal basin of cold cooked macaroni. I handed it to Gordini.

"Have you any cheese?"

The major spoke grudgingly to the orderly who ducked back into the hole again and came out with a quarter of a white cheese.

"Thank you very much," I said.

"You'd better not go out."

Outside something was set down beside the entrance. One of the two men who had carried it looked in.

"Bring him in," said the major. "What's the matter with you? Do you want us to come outside and get him?"

The two stretcher-bearers picked up the man under the arms and by the legs and brought him in.

"Slit the tunic," the major said.

He held a forceps with some gauze in the end. The two captains took off their coats. "Get out of here," the major said to the two stretcher-bearers.

"Come on," I said to Gordini.

"You better wait until the shelling is over," the major said over his shoulder.

"They want to eat," I said.

"As you wish."

Outside we ran across the brickyard. A shell burst short near the river bank. Then there was one that we did not hear coming until the sudden rush. We both went flat and with the flash and bump of the burst and the smell heard the singing off of the fragments and the rattle of falling brick. Gordini got up and ran for the dug-out. I was after him, holding the cheese, its smooth surface covered with brick dust. Inside the dugout were the three drivers sitting against the wall, smoking.

"Here, you patriots," I said.

"How are the cars?" Manera asked.

"All right."

"Did they scare you, Tenente?"

"You're damned right," I said.

I took out my knife, opened it, wiped off the blade and pared off the dirty outside surface of the cheese. Gavuzzi handed me the basin of macaroni.

"Start in to eat, Tenente."

"No," I said. "Put it on the floor. We'll all eat."

"There are no forks."

"What the hell," I said in English.

I cut the cheese into pieces and laid them on the macaroni.

"Sit down to it," I said. They sat down and waited. I put thumb and fingers into the macaroni and lifted. A mass loosened.

"Lift it high, Tenente."

I lifted it to arm's length and the strands cleared. I lowered it into the mouth, sucked and snapped in the ends, and chewed, then took a bite of cheese, chewed, and then a drink of the wine. It tasted of rusty metal. I handed the canteen back to Passini.

"It's rotten," he said. "It's been in there too long. I had it in the car."

They were all eating, holding their chins close over the basin, tipping their heads back, sucking in the ends. I took another mouthful and some cheese and a rinse of wine. Something landed outside that shook the earth.

"Four hundred twenty or minnenwerfer," Gavuzzi said.

"There aren't any four hundred twenties in the mountains," I said.

"They have big Skoda guns. I've seen the holes."

"Three hundred fives."

We went on eating. There was a cough, a noise like a railway engine starting and then an explosion that shook the earth again.

"This isn't a deep dugout," Passini said.

"That was a big trench mortar."

"Yes, sir."

I ate the end of my piece of cheese and took a swallow of wine. Through the other noise I heard a cough, then came the chuh-chuh-chuh-chuh—then there was a flash, as when a blast-furnace door is swung open, and a roar that started white and went red and on and on in a rushing wind. I tried to breathe but my breath would not come and I felt myself rush bodily out of myself and out and out and out and all the time bodily in the wind. I went out swiftly, all of myself, and I knew I was dead and that it had all been a mistake to think you just died. Then I floated, and instead of going on I felt myself slide back. I breathed and I was back. The ground was torn up and in front of my head there was a splintered beam of wood. In the jolt of my head I heard somebody crying. I thought somebody was screaming. I tried to move but I could not move. I heard the machine-guns and rifles firing across the river and all along the river. There was a great splashing and I saw the star-shells go up and burst and float whitely and rockets going up and heard the bombs, all this in a moment, and then I heard close to me some one saying "Mama Mia! Oh, mama Mia!" I pulled and twisted and got my legs loose finally and turned around and touched him. It was Passini and when I touched him he screamed. His legs were toward me and I saw in the dark and the light that they were both smashed above the knee. One leg was gone and the other was held by tendons and part of the trouser and the stump twitched and jerked as though it were not connected. He bit his arm and moaned, "Oh mama mia, mama Mia," then, "Dio te salve, Maria. Dio te salve, Maria. Oh Jesus shoot me Christ shoot me mama mia mama Mia oh purest lovely Mary shoot me. Stop it. Stop it. Stop it. Oh Jesus lovely Mary stop it. Oh oh oh oh," then choking, "Mama mama mia." Then he was quiet, biting his arm, the stump of his leg twitching.

"Porta feriti!" I shouted holding my hands cupped. "Porta feriti!" I tried to get closer to Passini to try to put a tourniquet on the legs but I could not move. I tried again and my legs moved a little. I could pull backward along with my arms and elbows. Passini was quiet now. I sat beside him, undid my tunic and tried to rip the tail of my shirt. It would not rip and I bit the edge of the cloth to start it. Then I thought of his puttees. I had on wool stockings but Passini wore puttees. All the drivers wore puttees but Passini had only one leg. I unwound the puttee and while I was doing it I saw there was no need to try and make a tourniquet because he was dead already. I made sure he was dead. There were three others to locate. I sat up straight and as I did so something inside my head moved like the weights on a doll's eyes and it hit me inside in back of my eyeballs. My legs felt warm and wet and my shoes were wet and warm inside. I knew that I was hit and leaned over and put my hand on my knee. My knee wasn't there. My hand went in and my knee was down on my shin. I wiped my hand on my shirt and another floating light came very slowly down and I looked at my leg and was very afraid. Oh, God, I said, get me out of here. I knew, however, that there had been three others. There were four drivers. Passini was dead. That left three. Some one took hold of me under the arms and somebody else lifted my legs.

"There are three others," I said. "One is dead."

"It's Manera. We went for a stretcher but there wasn't any. How are you, Tenente?"

"Where is Gordini and Gavuzzi?"

"Gordini's at the post getting bandaged. Gavuzzi has your legs. Hold on to my neck, Tenente. Are you badly hit?"

"In the leg. How is Gordini?"

"He's all right. It was a big trench mortar shell."

"Passini's dead."

"Yes. He's dead."

A shell fell close and they both dropped to the ground and dropped me. "I'm sorry, Tenente," said Manera. "Hang onto my neck."

"If you drop me again."

"It was because we were scared."

"Are you unwounded?"

"We are both wounded a little."

"Can Gordini drive?"

"I don't think so."

They dropped me once more before we reached the post.

"You sons of bitches," I said.

"I am sorry, Tenente," Manera said. "We won't drop you again."

Outside the post a great many of us lay on the ground in the dark. They carried wounded in and brought them out. I could see the light come out from the dressing station when the curtain opened and they brought some one in or out. The dead were off to one side. The doctors were working with their sleeves up to their shoulders and were red as butchers. There were not enough stretchers. Some of the wounded were noisy but most were quiet. The wind blew the leaves in the bower over the door of the dressing station and the night was getting cold. Stretcher-bearers came in all the time, put their stretchers down, unloaded them and went away. As soon as I got to the dressing station Manera brought a medical sergeant out and he put bandages on both my legs. He said there was so much dirt blown into the wound that there had not been much hemorrhage. They would take me as soon as possible. He went back inside. Gordini could not drive, Manera said. His shoulder was smashed and his head was hurt. He had not felt bad but now the shoulder had stiffened. He was sitting up beside one of the brick walls. Manera and Gavuzzi each went off with a load of wounded. They could drive all right. The British had come with three ambulances and they had two men on each ambulance. One of their drivers came over to me, brought by Gordini who looked very white and sick. The Britisher leaned over.

"Are you hit badly?" he asked. He was a tall man and wore steel-rimmed spectacles.

"In the legs."

"It's not serious I hope. Will you have a cigarette?"

"Thanks."

"They tell me you've lost two drivers."

"Yes. One killed and the fellow that brought you."

"What rotten luck. Would you like us to take the cars?"

"That's what I wanted to ask you."

"We'd take quite good care of them and return them to the villa. 206 aren't you?"

"Yes."

"It's a charming place. I've seen you about. They tell me you're an American."

"Yes."

"I'm English."

"No!"

"Yes, English. Did you think I was Italian? There were some Italians with one of our units."

"It would be fine if you would take the cars," I said.

"We'll be most careful of them," he straightened up. "This chap of yours was very anxious for me to see you." He patted Gordini on the shoulder. Gordini winced and smiled. The Englishman broke into voluble and perfect Italian. "Now everything is arranged. I've seen your Tenente. We will take over the two cars. You won't worry now." He broke off, "I must do something about getting you out of here. I'll see the medical wallahs. We'll take you back with us."

He walked across to the dressing station, stepping carefully among the wounded. I saw the blanket open, the light came out and he went in.

"He will look after you, Tenente," Gordini said.

"How are you, Franco?"

"I am all right." He sat down beside me. In a moment the blanket in front of the dressing station opened and two stretcher-bearers came out followed by the tall Englishman. He brought them over to me.

"Here is the American Tenente," he said in Italian.

"I'd rather wait," I said. "There are much worse wounded than me. I'm all right."

"Come, come," he said. "Don't be a bloody hero." Then in Italian: "Lift him very carefully about the legs. His legs are very painful. He is the legitimate son of President Wilson." They picked me up and took me into the dressing room. Inside they were operating on all the tables. The little major looked at us furious. He recognized me and waved a forceps.

"Ça va bien?"

"Ça va."

"I have brought him in," the tall Englishman said in Italian. "The only son of the American Ambassador. He can be here until you are ready to take him. Then I will take him with my first load." He bent over me. "I'll look up their adjutant to do your papers and it will all go much faster." He stooped to go under the doorway and went out. The major was unhooking the forceps now, dropping them in a basin. I followed his hands with my eyes. Now he was bandaging. Then the stretcher-bearers took the man off the table.

"I'll take the American Tenente," one of the captains said. They lifted me onto the table. It was hard and slippery. There were many strong smells, chemical smells and the sweet smell of blood. They took off my trousers and the medical captain commenced dictating to the sergeant-adjutant while he worked, "Multiple superficial wounds of the left and right thigh and left and right knee and right foot. Profound wounds of right knee and foot. Lacerations of the scalp (he probed—Does that hurt?—Christ, yes!) with possible fracture of the skull. Incurred in the line of duty. That's what keeps you from being court-martialled for self-inflicted wounds," he said. "Would you like a drink of brandy? How did you run into this thing anyway? What were you trying to do? Commit suicide? Antitetanus please, and mark a cross on both legs. Thank you. I'll clean this up a little, wash it out, and put on a dressing. Your blood coagulates beautifully."

The adjutant, looking up from the paper, "What inflicted the wounds?"

The medical captain, "What hit you?"

Me, with the eyes shut, "A trench mortar shell."

The captain, doing things that hurt sharply and severing tissue—"Are you sure?"

Me—trying to lie still and feeling my stomach flutter when the flesh was cut, "I think so."

Captain doctor—(interested in something he was finding),

"Fragments of enemy trench-mortar shell. Now I'll probe for some of this if you like but it's not necessary. I'll paint all this and— Does that sting? Good, that's nothing to how it will feel later. The pain hasn't started yet. Bring him a glass of brandy. The shock dulls the pain; but this is all right, you have nothing to worry about if it doesn't infect and it rarely does now. How is your head?"

"Good Christ!" I said.

"Better not drink too much brandy then. If you've got a fracture you don't want inflammation. How does that feel?"

Sweat ran all over me.

"Good Christ!" I said.

"I guess you've got a fracture all right. I'll wrap you up and don't bounce your head around." He bandaged, his hands moving very fast and the bandage coming taut and sure. "All right, good luck and Vive la France."

"He's an American," one of the other captains said.

"I thought you said he was a Frenchman. He talks French," the captain said. "I've known him before. I always thought he was French." He drank a half tumbler of cognac. "Bring on something serious. Get some more of that Antitetanus." The captain waved to me. They lifted me and the blanket-flap went across my face as we went out. Outside the sergeant-adjutant knelt down beside me where I lay, "Name?" he asked softly. "Middle name? First name? Rank? Where born? What class? What corps?" and so on. "I'm sorry for your head, Tenente. I hope you feel better. I'm sending you now with the English ambulance."

"I'm all right," I said. "Thank you very much." The pain that the major had spoken about had started and all that was happening was without interest or relation. After a while the English ambulance came up and they put me onto a stretcher and lifted the stretcher up to the ambulance level and shoved it in. There was another stretcher by the side with a man on it whose nose I could see, waxy-looking, out of the bandages. He breathed very heavily.

There were stretchers lifted and slid into the slings above. The tall English driver came around and looked in, "I'll take it very easily," he said. "I hope you'll be comfy." I felt the engine start, felt him climb up into the front seat, felt the brake come off and the clutch go in, then we started. I lay still and let the pain ride.

As the ambulance climbed along the road, it was slow in the traffic, sometimes it stopped, sometimes it backed on a turn, then finally it climbed quite fast. I felt something dripping. At first it dropped slowly and regularly, then it pattered into a stream. I shouted to the driver. He stopped the car and looked in through the hole behind his seat.

"What is it?"

"The man on the stretcher over me has a hemorrhage."

"We're not far from the top. I wouldn't be able to get the stretcher out alone." He started the car. The stream kept on. In the dark I could not see where it came from the canvas overhead. I tried to move sideways so that it did not fall on me. Where it had run down under my shirt it was warm and sticky. I was cold and my leg hurt so that it made me sick. After a while the stream from the stretcher above lessened and started to drip again and I heard and felt the canvas above move as the man on the stretcher settled more comfortably.

"How is he?" the Englishman called back. "We're almost up."

"He's dead I think," I said.

The drops fell very slowly, as they fall from an icicle after the sun has gone. It was cold in the car in the night as the road climbed. At the post on the top they took the stretcher out and put another in and we went on.

CHAPTER X

In the ward at the field hospital they told me a visitor was coming to see me in the afternoon. It was a hot day and there were many flies in the room. My orderly had cut paper into strips and tied the strips to a stick to make a brush that swished the flies away. I watched them settle on the ceiling. When he stopped swishing and fell asleep they came down and I blew them away and finally covered my face with my hands and slept too. It was very hot and when I woke my legs itched. I waked the orderly and he poured mineral water on the dressings. That made the bed damp and cool. Those of us that were awake talked across the ward. The afternoon was a quiet time. In the morning they came to each bed in turn, three men nurses and a doctor and picked you up out of bed and carried you into the dressing room so that the beds could be made while we were having our wounds dressed. It was not a pleasant trip to the dressing room and I did not know until later that beds could be made with men in them. My orderly had finished pouring water and the bed felt cool and lovely and I was telling him where to scratch on the soles of my feet against the itching when one of the doctors brought in Rinaldi. He came in very fast and bent down over the bed and kissed me. I saw he wore gloves.

"How are you, baby? How do you feel? I bring you this—" It was a bottle of cognac. The orderly brought a chair and he sat down, "and good news. You will be decorated. They want to get you the medaglia d'argento but perhaps they can get only the bronze."

"What for?"

"Because you are gravely wounded. They say if you can prove you did any heroic act you can get the silver. Otherwise it will be the bronze. Tell me exactly what happened. Did you do any heroic act?"

"No," I said. "I was blown up while we were eating cheese."

"Be serious. You must have done something heroic either before or after. Remember carefully."

"I did not."

"Didn't you carry anybody on your back? Gordini says you carried several people on your back but the medical major at the first post declares it is impossible. He had to sign the proposition for the citation."

"I didn't carry anybody. I couldn't move."

"That doesn't matter," said Rinaldi.

He took off his gloves.

"I think we can get you the silver. Didn't you refuse to be medically aided before the others?"

"Not very firmly."

"That doesn't matter. Look how you are wounded. Look at your valorous conduct in asking to go always to the first line. Besides, the operation was successful."

"Did they cross the river all right?"

"Enormously. They take nearly a thousand prisoners. It's in the bulletin. Didn't you see it?"

"No."

"I'll bring it to you. It is a successful coup de main."

"How is everything?"

"Splendid. We are all splendid. Everybody is proud of you. Tell me just exactly how it happened. I am positive you will get the silver. Go on tell me. Tell me all about it." He paused and thought. "Maybe you will get an English medal too. There was an English there. I'll go and see him and ask if he will recommend you. He ought to be able to do something. Do you suffer much? Have a drink. Orderly, go get a corkscrew. Oh you should see what I did in the removal of three metres of small intestine and better now than ever. It is one for *The Lancet*. You do me a translation and I will send it to *The Lancet*. Every day I am better. Poor dear baby, how do you feel? Where is that damn corkscrew? You are so brave and quiet I forget you are suffering." He slapped his gloves on the edge of the bed.

"Here is the corkscrew, Signor Tenente," the orderly said.

"Open the bottle. Bring a glass. Drink that, baby. How is your poor head? I looked at your papers. You haven't any fracture. That major at the first post was a hog-butcher. I would take you and never hurt you. I never hurt anybody. I learn how to do it. Every day I learn to do things smoother and better. You must forgive me for talking so much, baby. I am very moved to see you badly wounded. There, drink that. It's good. It cost fifteen lire. It ought to be good. Five stars. After I leave here I'll go see that English and he'll get you an English medal."

"They don't give them like that."

"You are so modest. I will send the liaison officer. He can handle the English."

"Have you seen Miss Barkley?"

"I will bring her here. I will go now and bring her here."

"Don't go," I said. "Tell me about Gorizia. How are the girls?"

"There are no girls. For two weeks now they haven't changed

them. I don't go there any more. It is disgraceful. They aren't girls; they are old war comrades."

"You don't go at all?"

"I just go to see if there is anything new. I stop by. They all ask for you. It is a disgrace that they should stay so long that they become friends."

"Maybe girls don't want to go to the front any more."

"Of course they do. They have plenty of girls. It is just bad administration. They are keeping them for the pleasure of dug-out hiders in the rear."

"Poor Rinaldi," I said. "All alone at the war with no new girls."

Rinaldi poured himself another glass of the cognac.

"I don't think it will hurt you, baby. You take it."

I drank the cognac and felt it warm all the way down. Rinaldi poured another glass. He was quieter now. He held up the glass. "To your valorous wounds. To the silver medal. Tell me, baby, when you lie here all the time in the hot weather don't you get excited?"

"Sometimes."

"I can't imagine lying like that. I would go crazy."

"You are crazy."

"I wish you were back. No one to come in at night from adventures. No one to make fun of. No one to lend me money. No blood brother and roommate. Why do you get yourself wounded?"

"You can make fun of the priest."

"That priest. It isn't me that makes fun of him. It is the captain. I like him. If you must have a priest have that priest. He's coming to see you. He makes big preparations."

"I like him."

"Oh, I knew it. Sometimes I think you and he are a little that way. You know."

"No, you don't."

"Yes, I do sometimes. A little that way like the number of the first regiment of the Brigata Ancona."

"Oh, go to hell."

He stood up and put on his gloves.

"Oh I love to tease you, baby. With your priest and your English girl, and really you are just like me underneath."

"No, I'm not."

"Yes, we are. You are really an Italian. All fire and smoke and nothing inside. You only pretend to be American. We are brothers and we love each other."

"Be good while I'm gone," I said.

"I will send Miss Barkley. You are better with her without me. You are purer and sweeter."

"Oh, go to hell."

"I will send her. Your lovely cool goddess. English goddess. My God what would a man do with a woman like that except worship her? What else is an Englishwoman good for?"

"You are an ignorant foul-mouthed dago."

"A what?"

"An ignorant wop."

"Wop. You are a frozen-faced . . . wop."

"You are ignorant. Stupid." I saw that word pricked him and kept on. "Uninformed. Inexperienced, stupid from inexperience."

"Truly? I tell you something about your good women. Your goddesses. There is only one difference between taking a girl who has always been good and a woman. With a girl it is painful. That's all I know." He slapped the bed with his glove. "And you never know if the girl will really like it."

"Don't get angry."

"I'm not angry. I just tell you, baby, for your own good. To save you trouble."

"That's the only difference?"

"Yes. But millions of fools like you don't know it."

"You were sweet to tell me."

"We won't quarrel, baby. I love you too much. But don't be a fool."

"No. I'll be wise like you."

"Don't be angry, baby. Laugh. Take a drink. I must go, really."

"You're a good old boy."

"Now you see. Underneath we are the same. We are war brothers. Kiss me good-by."

"You're sloppy."

"No. I am just more affectionate."

I felt his breath come toward me. "Good-by. I come to see you again soon." His breath went away. "I won't kiss you if you don't want. I'll send your English girl. Good-by, baby. The cognac is under the bed. Get well soon."

He was gone.

CHAPTER XI

It was dusk when the priest came. They had brought the soup and afterward taken away the bowls and I was lying looking at the rows of beds and out the window at the tree-top that moved a little in the evening breeze. The breeze came in through the window and it was cooler with the evening. The flies were on the ceiling now and on the electric light bulbs that hung on wires. The lights were only turned on when some one was brought in at night or when something was being done. It made me feel very young to have the dark come after the dusk and then remain. It was like being put to bed after early supper. The orderly came down between the beds and stopped. Some one was with him. It was the priest. He stood there small, brown-faced, and embarrassed.

"How do you do?" he asked. He put some packages down by the bed, on the floor.

"All right, father."

He sat down in the chair that had been brought for Rinaldi and looked out of the window embarrassedly. I noticed his face looked very tired.

"I can only stay a minute," he said. "It is late."

"It's not late. How is the mess?"

He smiled. "I am still a great joke," he sounded tired too. "Thank God they are all well.

"I am so glad you are all right," he said. "I hope you don't suffer." He seemed very tired and I was not used to seeing him tired.

"Not any more."

"I miss you at the mess."

"I wish I were there. I always enjoyed our talking."

"I brought you a few little things," he said. He picked up the packages. "This is mosquito netting. This is a bottle of vermouth. You like vermouth? These are English papers."

"Please open them."

He was pleased and undid them. I held the mosquito netting in my hands. The vermouth he held up for me to see and then put it on the floor beside the bed. I held up one of the sheaf of English papers. I could read the headlines by turning it so the half-light from the window was on it. It was *The News of the World*.

"The others are illustrated," he said.

"It will be a great happiness to read them. Where did you get them?"

"I sent for them to Mestre. I will have more."

"You were very good to come, father. Will you drink a glass of vermouth?"

"Thank you. You keep it. It's for you."

"No, drink a glass."

"All right. I will bring you more then."

The orderly brought the glasses and opened the bottle. He broke off the cork and the end had to be shoved down into the bottle. I could see the priest was disappointed but he said, "That's all right. It's no matter."

"Here's to your health, father."

"To your better health."

Afterward he held the glass in his hand and we looked at one another. Sometimes we talked and were good friends but to-night it was difficult.

"What's the matter, father? You seem very tired."

"I am tired but I have no right to be."

"It's the heat."

"No. This is only the spring. I feel very low."

"You have the war disgust."

"No. But I hate the war."

"I don't enjoy it," I said. He shook his head and looked out of the window.

"You do not mind it. You do not see it. You must forgive me. I know you are wounded."

"That is an accident."

"Still even wounded you do not see it. I can tell. I do not see it myself but I feel it a little."

"When I was wounded we were talking about it. Passini was talking."

The priest put down the glass. He was thinking about something else.

"I know them because I am like they are," he said.

"You are different though."

"But really I am like they are."

"The officers don't see anything."

"Some of them do. Some are very delicate and feel worse than any of us."

"They are mostly different."

"It is not education or money. It is something else. Even if they had education or money men like Passini would not wish to be officers. I would not be an officer."

"You rank as an officer. I am an officer."

"I am not really. You are not even an Italian. You are a foreigner. But you are nearer the officers than you are to the men."

"What is the difference?"

"I cannot say it easily. There are people who would make war. In this country there are many like that. There are other people who would not make war."

"But the first ones make them do it."

"Yes."

"And I help them."

"You are a foreigner. You are a patriot."

"And the ones who would not make war? Can they stop it?"

"I do not know."

He looked out of the window again. I watched his face.

"Have they ever been able to stop it?"

"They are not organized to stop things and when they get organized their leaders sell them out."

"Then it's hopeless?"

"It is never hopeless. But sometimes I cannot hope. I try always to hope but sometimes I cannot."

"Maybe the war will be over."

"I hope so."

"What will you do then?"

"If it is possible I will return to the Abruzzi."

His brown face was suddenly very happy.

"You love the Abruzzi?"

"Yes, I love it very much."

"You ought to go there then."

"I would be too happy. If I could live there and love God and serve Him."

"And be respected," I said.

"Yes and be respected. Why not?"

"No reason not. You should be respected."

"It does not matter. But there in my country it is understood that a man may love God. It is not a dirty joke."

"I understand."

He looked at me and smiled.

"You understand but you do not love God."

"No."

"You do not love Him at all?" he asked.

"I am afraid of Him in the night sometimes."

"You should love Him."

"I don't love much."

"Yes," he said. "You do. What you tell me about in the nights. That is not love. That is only passion and lust. When you love you wish to do things for. You wish to sacrifice for. You wish to serve."

"I don't love."

"You will. I know you will. Then you will be happy."

"I'm happy. I've always been happy."

"It is another thing. You cannot know about it unless you have it."

"Well," I said. "If I ever get it I will tell you."

"I stay too long and talk too much." He was worried that he really did.

"No. Don't go. How about loving women? If I really loved some woman would it be like that?"

"I don't know about that. I never loved any woman."

"What about your mother?"

"Yes, I must have loved my mother."

"Did you always love God?"

"Ever since I was a little boy."

"Well," I said. I did not know what to say. "You are a fine boy," I said.

"I am a boy," he said. "But you call me father."

"That's politeness."

He smiled.

"I must go, really," he said. "You do not want me for anything?" he asked hopefully.

"No. Just to talk."

"I will take your greetings to the mess."

"Thank you for the many fine presents."

"Nothing."

"Come and see me again."

"Yes. Good-by," he patted my hand.

"So long," I said in dialect.

"Ciaou," he repeated.

It was dark in the room and the orderly, who had sat by the foot of the bed, got up and went out with him. I liked him very much and I hoped he would get back to the Abruzzi some time. He had a rotten life in the mess and he was fine about it but I thought how he would be in his own country. At Capracotta, he had told me, there were trout in the stream below the town. It was forbidden to play the flute at night. When the young men serenaded only the flute was forbidden. Why, I had asked. Because it was bad for the girls to hear the flute at night. The peasants all called you "Don" and when you met them they took off their hats. His father hunted every day and stopped to eat at the houses of peasants. They were always honored. For a foreigner to hunt he must present a certificate that he had never been arrested. There were bears on the Gran Sasso D'Italia but it was a long way. Aquila was a fine town. It was cool in the summer at night and the spring in Abruzzi was the most beautiful in Italy. But what was lovely was the fall to go hunting through the chestnut woods. The birds were all good because they fed on grapes and you never took a lunch because the peasants were always honored if you would eat with them at their houses. After a while I went to sleep.

CHAPTER XII

The room was long with windows on the right-hand side and a door at the far end that went into the dressing room. The row of beds that mine was in faced the windows and another row, under the windows, faced the wall. If you lay on your left side you could see the dressing-room door. There was another door at the far end that people sometimes came in by. If any one were going to die they put a screen around the bed so you could not see them die, but only the shoes and puttees of doctors and men nurses showed under the bottom of the screen and sometimes at the end there would be whispering. Then the priest would come out from behind the screen and afterward the men nurses would go back behind the screen to come out again carrying the one who was dead with a blanket over him down the corridor between the beds and some one folded the screen and took it away.

That morning the major in charge of the ward asked me if I felt that I could travel the next day. I said I could. He said then they would ship me out early in the morning. He said I would be better off making the trip now before it got too hot.

When they lifted you up out of bed to carry you into the dressing room you could look out of the window and see the new graves in the garden. A soldier sat outside the door that opened onto the garden making crosses and painting on them the names, rank, and regiment of the men who were buried in the garden. He also ran errands for the ward and in his spare time made me a cigarette lighter out of an empty Austrian rifle cartridge. The doctors were very nice and seemed very capable. They were anxious to ship me to Milan where there were better X-ray facilities and where, after the operation, I could take mechano-therapy. I wanted to go to Milan too. They wanted to get us all out and back as far as possible because all the beds were needed for the offensive, when it should start.

The night before I left the field hospital Rinaldi came in to see me with the major from our mess. They said that I would go to an American hospital in Milan that had just been installed. Some American ambulance units were to be sent down and this hospital would look after them and any other Americans on service in Italy. There were many in the Red Cross. The States had declared war on Germany but not on Austria.

The Italians were sure America would declare war on Austria too and they were very excited about any Americans coming down, even the Red Cross. They asked me if I thought President Wilson would declare war on Austria and I said it was only a matter of days. I did not know what we had against Austria but it seemed logical that they should declare war on her if they did on Germany. They asked me if we would declare war on Turkey. I said that was doubtful. Turkey, I said, was our national bird but the joke translated so badly and they were so puzzled and suspicious that I said yes, we would probably declare war on Turkey. And on Bulgaria? We had drunk several glasses of brandy and I said yes by God on Bulgaria too and on Japan. But, they said, Japan is an ally of England. You can't trust the bloody English. The Japanese want Hawaii, I said. Where is Hawaii? It is in the Pacific Ocean. Why do the Japanese want it? They don't really want it, I said. That is all talk. The Japanese are a wonderful little people fond of dancing and light wines. Like the French, said the major. We will get Nice and Savoia from the French. We will get Corsica and all the Adriatic coast-line, Rinaldi said. Italy will return to the splendors of Rome, said the major. I don't like Rome, I said. It is hot and full of fleas. You don't like Rome? Yes, I love Rome. Rome is the mother of nations. I will never forget Romulus suckling the Tiber. What? Nothing. Let's all go to Rome. Let's go to Rome to-night and never come back. Rome is a beautiful city, said the major. The mother and father of nations, I said. Roma is feminine, said Rinaldi. It cannot be the father. Who is the father, then, the Holy Ghost? Don't blaspheme. I wasn't blaspheming, I was asking for information. You are drunk, baby. Who made me drunk? I made you drunk, said the major. I made you drunk because I love you and because America is in the war. Up to the hilt, I said. You go away in the morning, baby, Rinaldi said. To Rome, I said. No, to Milan. To Milan, said the major, to the Crystal Palace, to the Cova, to Campari's, to Biffi's, to the galleria. You lucky boy. To the Gran Italia, I said, where I will borrow money from George. To the Scala, said Rinaldi. You will go to the Scala. Every night, I said. You won't be able to afford it every night, said the major.

The tickets are very expensive. I will draw a sight draft on my grandfather, I said. A what? A sight draft. He has to pay or I go to jail. Mr. Cunningham at the bank does it. I live by sight drafts. Can a grandfather jail a patriotic grandson who is dying that Italy may live? Live the American Garibaldi, said Rinaldi. Viva the sight drafts, I said. We must be quiet, said the major. Already we have been asked many times to be quiet. Do you go to-morrow really, Federico? He goes to the American hospital I tell you, Rinaldi said. To the beautiful nurses. Not the nurses with beards of the field hospital. Yes, yes, said the major, I know he goes to the American hospital. I don't mind their beards, I said. If any man wants to raise a beard let him. Why don't you raise a beard, Signor Maggiore? It could not go in a gas mask. Yes it could. Anything can go in a gas mask. I've vomited into a gas mask. Don't be so loud, baby, Rinaldi said. We all know you have been at the front. Oh, you fine baby, what will I do while you are gone? We must go, said the major. This becomes sentimental. Listen, I have a surprise for you. Your English. You know? The English you go to see every night at their hospital? She is going to Milan too. She goes with another to be at the American hospital. They had not got nurses yet from America. I talked to-day with the head of their riparto. They have too many women here at the front. They send some back. How do you like that, baby? All right. Yes? You go to live in a big city and have your English there to cuddle you. Why don't I get wounded? Maybe you will, I said. We must go, said the major. We drink and make noise and disturb Federico. Don't go. Yes, we must go. Good-by. Good luck. Many things. Ciaou. Ciaou. Ciaou. Come back quickly, baby. Rinaldi kissed me. You smell of lysol. Good-by, baby. Good-by. Many things. The major patted my shoulder. They tiptoed out. I found I was quite drunk but went to sleep.

The next day in the morning we left for Milan and arrived forty-eight hours later. It was a bad trip. We were sidetracked for a long time this side of Mestre and children came and peeked in. I got a little boy to go for a bottle of cognac but he came back and said he could only get grappa. I told him to get it and when it came I gave him the change and the man beside me and I got drunk and slept until past Vicenza where I woke up and was very sick on the floor. It did not matter because the man on that side had been very sick on the floor several times before. Afterward I thought I could not stand the thirst and in the yards outside of Verona I called to a soldier who was walking up and down beside the train and he got me a drink of water. I woke Georgetti, the other boy who was drunk, and offered him some water. He said to pour it on his shoulder and went back to sleep. The soldier would not take the penny I offered him and brought me a pulpy orange. I sucked on that and spit out the pith and watched the soldier pass up and down past a freight-car outside and after a while the train gave a jerk and started.

BOOK TWO

CHAPTER XIII

We got into Milan early in the morning and they unloaded us in the freight yard. An ambulance took me to the American hospital. Riding in the ambulance on a stretcher I could not tell what part of town we were passing through but when they unloaded the stretcher I saw a market-place and an open wine shop with a girl sweeping out. They were watering the street and it smelled of the early morning. They put the stretcher down and went in. The porter came out with them. He had gray mustaches, wore a doorman's cap and was in his shirt sleeves. The stretcher would not go into the elevator and they discussed whether it was better to lift me off the stretcher and go up in the elevator or carry the stretcher up the stairs. I listened to them discussing it. They decided on the elevator. They lifted me from the stretcher. "Go easy," I said. "Take it softly."

In the elevator we were crowded and as my legs bent the pain was very bad. "Straighten out the legs," I said.

"We can't, Signor Tenente. There isn't room." The man who said this had his arm around me and my arm was around his neck.

His breath came in my face metallic with garlic and red wine.

"Be gentle," the other man said.

"Son of a bitch who isn't gentle!"

"Be gentle I say," the man with my feet repeated.

I saw the doors of the elevator closed, and the grill shut and the fourth-floor button pushed by the porter. The porter looked worried. The elevator rose slowly.

"Heavy?" I asked the man with the garlic.

"Nothing," he said. His face was sweating and he grunted. The elevator rose steadily and stopped. The man holding the feet opened the door and stepped out. We were on a balcony. There were several doors with brass knobs. The man carrying the feet pushed a button that rang a bell. We heard it inside the doors. No one came. Then the porter came up the stairs.

"Where are they?" the stretcher-bearers asked.

"I don't know," said the porter. "They sleep down stairs."

"Get somebody."

The porter rang the bell, then knocked on the door, then he opened the door and went in. When he came back there was an elderly woman wearing glasses with him. Her hair was loose and half-falling and she wore a nurse's dress.

"I can't understand," she said. "I can't understand Italian."

"I can speak English," I said. "They want to put me somewhere."

"None of the rooms are ready. There isn't any patient expected." She tucked at her hair and looked at me near-sightedly.

"Show them any room where they can put me."

"I don't know," she said. "There's no patient expected. I couldn't put you in just any room."

"Any room will do," I said. Then to the porter in Italian, "Find an empty room."

"They are all empty," said the porter. "You are the first patient." He held his cap in his hand and looked at the elderly nurse.

"For Christ's sweet sake take me to some room." The pain

had gone on and on with the legs bent and I could feel it going in and out of the bone. The porter went in the door, followed by the gray-haired woman, then came hurrying back. "Follow me," he said. They carried me down a long hallway and into a room with drawn blinds. It smelled of new furniture. There was a bed and a big wardrobe with a mirror. They laid me down on the bed.

"I can't put on sheets," the woman said. "The sheets are locked up."

I did not speak to her. "There is money in my pocket," I said to the porter. "In the buttoned-down pocket." The porter took out the money. The two stretcher-bearers stood beside the bed holding their caps. "Give them five lire apiece and five lire for yourself. My papers are in the other pocket. You may give them to the nurse."

The stretcher-bearers saluted and said thank you. "Good-by," I said. "And many thanks." They saluted again and went out.

"Those papers," I said to the nurse, "describe my case and the treatment already given."

The woman picked them up and looked at them through her glasses. There were three papers and they were folded. "I don't know what to do," she said. "I can't read Italian. I can't do anything without the doctor's orders." She commenced to cry and put the papers in her apron pocket. "Are you an American?" she asked crying.

"Yes. Please put the papers on the table by the bed."

It was dim and cool in the room. As I lay on the bed I could see the big mirror on the other side of the room but could not see what it reflected. The porter stood by the bed. He had a nice face and was very kind.

"You can go," I said to him. "You can go too," I said to the nurse. "What is your name?"

"Mrs. Walker."

"You can go, Mrs. Walker. I think I will go to sleep."

I was alone in the room. It was cool and did not smell like a hospital. The mattress was firm and comfortable and I lay without moving, hardly breathing, happy in feeling the pain lessen. After a while I wanted a drink of water and found the bell on a cord by the bed and rang it but nobody came. I went to sleep.

When I woke I looked around. There was sunlight coming in through the shutters. I saw the big armoire, the bare walls, and two chairs. My legs in the dirty bandages, stuck straight out in the bed. I was careful not to move them. I was thirsty and I reached for the bell and pushed the button. I heard the door open and looked and it was a nurse. She looked young and pretty.

"Good-morning," I said.

"Good-morning," she said and came over to the bed. "We haven't been able to get the doctor. He's gone to Lake Como. No one knew there was a patient coming. What's wrong with you anyway?"

"I'm wounded. In the legs and feet and my head is hurt."

"What's your name?"

"Henry. Frederic Henry."

"I'll wash you up. But we can't do anything to the dressings until the doctor comes."

"Is Miss Barkley here?"

"No. There's no one by that name here."

"Who was the woman who cried when I came in?"

The nurse laughed. "That's Mrs. Walker. She was on night duty and she'd been asleep. She wasn't expecting any one."

While we were talking she was undressing me, and when I was undressed, except for the bandages, she washed me, very gently and smoothly. The washing felt very good. There was a bandage on my head but she washed all around the edge.

"Where were you wounded?"

"On the Isonze north of Plava."

"Where is that?"

"North of Gorizia."

I could see that none of the places meant anything to her.

"Do you have a lot of pain?"

"No. Not much now."

She put a thermometer in my mouth.

"The Italians put it under the arm," I said.

"Don't talk."

When she took the thermometer out she read it and then shook it.

"What's the temperature?"

"You're not supposed to know that."

"Tell me what it is."

"It's almost normal."

"I never have any fever. My legs are full of old iron too."

"What do you mean?"

"They're full of trench-mortar fragments, old screws and bed-springs and things."

She shook her head and smiled.

"If you had any foreign bodies in your legs they would set up an inflammation and you'd have fever."

"All right," I said. "We'll see what comes out."

She went out of the room and came back with the old nurse of the early morning. Together they made the bed with me in it. That was new to me and an admirable proceeding.

"Who is in charge here?"

"Miss Van Campen."

"How many nurses are there?"

"Just us two."

"Won't there be more?"

"Some more are coming."

"When will they get here?"

"I don't know. You ask a great many questions for a sick boy."

"I'm not sick," I said. "I'm wounded."

They had finished making the bed and I lay with a clean smooth sheet under me and another sheet over me. Mrs. Walker went out and came back with a pajama jacket. They put that on me and I felt very clean and dressed.

"You're awfully nice to me," I said. The nurse called Miss Gage giggled. "Could I have a drink of water?" I asked.

"Certainly. Then you can have breakfast."

"I don't want breakfast. Can I have the shutters opened please?"

The light had been dim in the room and when the shutters were opened it was bright sunlight and I looked out on a balcony and beyond were the tile roofs of houses and chimneys. I looked out over the tiled roofs and saw white clouds and the sky very blue.

"Don't you know when the other nurses are coming?"

"Why? Don't we take good care of you?"

"You're very nice."

"Would you like to use the bedpan?"

"I might try."

They helped me and held me up but it was not any use. Afterward I lay and looked out the open doors onto the balcony.

"When does the doctor come?"

"When he gets back. We've tried to telephone to Lake Como for him."

"Aren't there any other doctors?"

"He's the doctor for the hospital."

Miss Gage brought a pitcher of water and a glass. I drank three glasses and then they left me and I looked out the window a while and went back to sleep. I ate some lunch and in the afternoon Miss Van Campen, the superintendent, came up to see me. She did not like me and I did not like her. She was small and neatly suspicious and too good for her position. She asked many questions and seemed to think it was somewhat disgraceful that I was with the Italians.

"Can I have wine with the meals?" I asked her.

"Only if the doctor prescribes it."

"I can't have it until he comes?"

"Absolutely not."

"You plan on having him come eventually?"

"We've telephoned him at Lake Como."

She went out and Miss Gage came back.

"Why were you rude to Miss Van Campen?" she asked after she had done something for me very skilfully.

"I didn't mean to be. But she was snooty."

"She said you were domineering and rude."

"I wasn't. But what's the idea of a hospital without a doctor?"

"He's coming. They've telephoned for him to Lake Como."

"What does he do there? Swim?"

"No. He has a clinic there."

"Why don't they get another doctor?"

"Hush. Hush. Be a good boy and he'll come."

I sent for the porter and when he came I told him in Italian to get me a bottle of Cinzano at the wine shop, a fiasco of chianti and the evening papers. He went away and brought them wrapped in newspaper, unwrapped them and, when I asked him to, drew the corks and put the wine and vermouth under the bed. They left me alone and I lay in bed and read the papers awhile, the news from the front, and the list of dead officers with their decorations and then reached down and brought up the bottle of Cinzano and held it straight up on my stomach, the cool glass against my stomach, and took little drinks making rings on my stomach from holding the bottle there between drinks, and watched it get dark outside over the roofs of the town. The swallows circled around and I watched them and the night-hawks flying above the roofs and drank the Cinzano. Miss Gage brought up a glass with some egg-nog in it. I lowered the vermouth bottle to the other side of the bed when she came in.

"Miss Van Campen had some sherry put in this," she said. "You shouldn't be rude to her. She's not young and this hospital is a big responsibility for her. Mrs. Walker's too old and she's no use to her."

"She's a splendid woman," I said. "Thank her very much."

"I'm going to bring your supper right away."

"That's all right," I said. "I'm not hungry."

When she brought the tray and put it on the bed table I thanked her and ate a little of the supper. Afterward it was dark outside and I could see the beams of the search-lights moving in the sky. I watched for a while and then went to sleep. I slept heavily except once I woke sweating and scared and then went back to sleep trying to stay outside of my dream. I woke for good long before it was light and heard roosters crowing and stayed on awake until it began to be light. I was tired and once it was really light I went back to sleep again.

CHAPTER XIV

It was bright sunlight in the room when I woke. I thought I was back at the front and stretched out in bed. My legs hurt me and I looked down at them still in the dirty bandages, and seeing them knew where I was. I reached up for the bell-cord and pushed the button. I heard it buzz down the hall and then some one coming on rubber soles along the hall. It was Miss Gage and she looked a little older in the bright sunlight and not so pretty.

"Good-morning," she said. "Did you have a good night?"

"Yes. Thanks very much," I said. "Can I have a barber?"

"I came in to see you and you were asleep with this in the bed with you."

She opened the armoire door and held up the vermouth bottle. It was nearly empty. "I put the other bottle from under the bed in there too," she said. "Why didn't you ask me for a glass?"

"I thought maybe you wouldn't let me have it."

"I'd have had some with you."

"You're a fine girl."

"It isn't good for you to drink alone," she said. "You mustn't do it."

"All right."

"Your friend Miss Barkley's come," she said.

"Really?"

"Yes. I don't like her."

"You will like her. She's awfully nice."

She shook her head. "I'm sure she's fine. Can you move just a little to this side? That's fine. I'll clean you up for breakfast." She washed me with a cloth and soap and warm water. "Hold your shoulder up," she said. "That's fine."

"Can I have the barber before breakfast?"

"I'll send the porter for him." She went out and came back. "He's gone for him," she said and dipped the cloth she held in the basin of water.

The barber came with the porter. He was a man of about fifty with an upturned mustache. Miss Gage was finished with me and went out and the barber lathered my face and shaved. He was very solemn and refrained from talking.

"What's the matter? Don't you know any news?" I asked.

"What news?"

"Any news. What's happened in the town?"

"It is time of war," he said. "The enemy's ears are everywhere."

I looked up at him. "Please hold your face still," he said and went on shaving. "I will tell nothing."

"What's the matter with you?" I asked.

"I am an Italian. I will not communicate with the enemy."

I let it go at that. If he was crazy, the sooner I could get out from under the razor the better. Once I tried to get a good look at him. "Beware," he said. "The razor is sharp."

I paid him when it was over and tipped him half a lira. He returned the coins.

"I will not. I am not at the front. But I am an Italian."

"Get the hell out of here."

"With your permission," he said and wrapped his razors in newspaper. He went out leaving the five copper coins on the table beside the bed. I rang the bell. Miss Gage came in. "Would you ask the porter to come please?"

"All right."

The porter came in. He was trying to keep from laughing.

"Is that barber crazy?"

"No, signorino. He made a mistake. He doesn't understand very well and he thought I said you were an Austrian officer."

"Oh," I said.

"Ho ho ho," the porter laughed. "He was funny. One move from you he said and he would have—" he drew his forefinger across his throat.

"Ho ho ho," he tried to keep from laughing. "When I tell him you were not an Austrian. Ho ho ho."

"Ho ho ho," I said bitterly. "How funny if he would cut my throat. Ho ho ho."

"No, signorino. No, no. He was so frightened of an Austrian. Ho ho ho."

"Ho ho ho," I said. "Get out of here."

He went out and I heard him laughing in the hall. I heard some one coming down the hallway. I looked toward the door. It was Catherine Barkley.

She came in the room and over to the bed.

"Hello, darling," she said. She looked fresh and young and very beautiful. I thought I had never seen any one so beautiful.

"Hello," I said. When I saw her I was in love with her. Everything turned over inside of me. She looked toward the door, saw there was no one, then she sat on the side of the bed and leaned over and kissed me. I pulled her down and kissed her and felt her heart beating.

"You sweet," I said. "Weren't you wonderful to come here?"

"It wasn't very hard. It may be hard to stay."

"You've got to stay," I said. "Oh, you're wonderful." I was crazy about her. I could not believe she was really there and held her tight to me.

"You mustn't," she said. "You're not well enough."

"Yes, I am. Come on."

"No. You're not strong enough."

"Yes. I am. Yes. Please."

"You do love me?"

"I really love you. I'm crazy about you. Come on please."

"Feel our hearts beating."

"I don't care about our hearts. I want you. I'm just mad about you."

"You really love me?"

"Don't keep on saying that. Come on. Please. Please, Catherine."

"All right but only for a minute."

"All right," I said. "Shut the door."

"You can't. You shouldn't."

"Come on. Don't talk. Please come on."

Catherine sat in a chair by the bed. The door was open into the hall. The wildness was gone and I felt finer than I had ever felt.

She asked, "Now do you believe I love you?"

"Oh, you're lovely," I said. "You've got to stay. They can't send you away. I'm crazy in love with you."

"We'll have to be awfully careful. That was just madness. We can't do that."

"We can at night."

"We'll have to be awfully careful. You'll have to be careful in front of other people."

"I will."

"You'll have to be. You're sweet. You do love me, don't you?"

"Don't say that again. You don't know what that does to me."

"I'll be careful then. I don't want to do anything more to you. I have to go now, darling, really."

"Come back right away."

"I'll come when I can."

"Good-by."

"Good-by, sweet."

She went out. God knows I had not wanted to fall in love with her. I had not wanted to fall in love with any one. But God knows I had and I lay on the bed in the room of the hospital in Milan and all sorts of things went through my head but I felt wonderful and finally Miss Gage came in.

"The doctor's coming," she said. "He telephoned from Lake Como."

"When does he get here?"

"He'll be here this afternoon."

CHAPTER XV

Nothing happened until afternoon. The doctor was a thin quiet little man who seemed disturbed by the war. He took out a number of small steel splinters from my thighs with delicate and refined distaste. He used a local anæsthetic called something or other "snow," which froze the tissue and avoided pain until the probe, the scalpel or the forceps got below the frozen portion. The anæsthetized area was clearly defined by the patient and after a time the doctor's fragile delicacy was exhausted and he said it would be better to have an X-ray. Probing was unsatisfactory, he said.

The X-ray was taken at the Ospedale Maggiore and the doctor who did it was excitable, efficient and cheerful. It was arranged by holding up the shoulders, that the patient should see personally some of the larger foreign bodies through the machine. The plates were to be sent over. The doctor requested me to write in his pocket notebook, my name, and regiment and some sentiment. He declared that the foreign bodies were ugly, nasty, brutal. The Austrians were sons of bitches. How many had I killed? I had not killed any but I was anxious to please—and I said I had killed plenty. Miss Gage was with me and the doctor put his arm around her and said she was more beautiful than Cleopatra. Did she understand that? Cleopatra the former queen of Egypt. Yes, by God she was. We returned to the little hospital in the ambulance and after a while and much lifting I was upstairs and in bed again. The plates came that afternoon, the doctor had said by God he would have them that afternoon and he did. Catherine Barkley showed them to me. They were in red envelopes and she took them out of the envelopes and held them up to the light and we both looked.

"That's your right leg," she said, then put the plate back in the envelope. "This is your left."

"Put them away," I said, "and come over to the bed."

"I can't," she said. "I just brought them in for a second to show you."

She went out and I lay there. It was a hot afternoon and I was sick of lying in bed. I sent the porter for the papers, all the papers he could get.

Before he came back three doctors came into the room. I have noticed that doctors who fail in the practice of medicine have a tendency to seek one another's company and aid in consultation. A doctor who cannot take out your appendix properly will recommend to you a doctor who will be unable to remove your tonsils with success. These were three such doctors.

"This is the young man," said the house doctor with the delicate hands.

"How do you do?" said the tall gaunt doctor with the beard. The third doctor, who carried the X-ray plates in their red envelopes, said nothing.

"Remove the dressings?" questioned the bearded doctor.

"Certainly. Remove the dressings, please, nurse," the house doctor said to Miss Gage. Miss Gage removed the dressings. I looked down at the legs. At the field hospital they had the look of not too freshly ground hamburger steak. Now they were crusted and the knee was swollen and discolored and the calf sunken but there was no pus.

"Very clean," said the house doctor. "Very clean and nice."

"Um," said the doctor with the beard. The third doctor looked over the house doctor's shoulder.

"Please move the knee," said the bearded doctor.

"I can't."

"Test the articulation?" the bearded doctor questioned. He had a stripe beside the three stars on his sleeve. That meant he was a first captain.

"Certainly," the house doctor said. Two of them took hold of my right leg very gingerly and bent it.

"That hurts," I said.

"Yes. Yes. A little further, doctor."

"That's enough. That's as far as it goes," I said.

"Partial articulation," said the first captain. He straightened up. "May I see the plates again, please, doctor?" The third doctor handed him one of the plates. "No. The left leg, please."

"That is the left leg, doctor."

"You are right. I was looking from a different angle." He returned the plate. The other plate he examined for some time. "You see, doctor?" he pointed to one of the foreign bodies which showed spherical and clear against the light. They examined the plate for some time.

"Only one thing I can say," the first captain with the beard said. "It is a question of time. Three months, six months probably."

"Certainly the synovial fluid must re-form."

"Certainly. It is a question of time. I could not conscientiously open a knee like that before the projectile was encysted."

"I agree with you, doctor."

"Six months for what?" I asked.

"Six months for the projectile to encyst before the knee can be opened safely."

"I don't believe it," I said.

"Do you want to keep your knee, young man?"

"No," I said.

"What?"

"I want it cut off," I said, "so I can wear a hook on it."

"What do you mean? A hook?"

"He is joking," said the house doctor. He patted my shoulder very delicately. "He wants to keep his knee. This is a very brave young man. He has been proposed for the silver medal of valor."

"All my felicitations," said the first captain. He shook my hand. "I can only say that to be on the safe side you should wait at least six months before opening such a knee. You are welcome of course to another opinion."

"Thank you very much," I said. "I value your opinion."

The first captain looked at his watch.

"We must go," he said. "All my best wishes."

"All my best wishes and many thanks," I said. I shook hands with the third doctor. "Capitano Varini—Tenente Enry," and they all three went out of the room.

"Miss Gage," I called. She came in. "Please ask the house doctor to come back a minute."

He came in holding his cap and stood by the bed. "Did you wish to see me?"

"Yes. I can't wait six months to be operated on. My God, doctor, did you ever stay in bed six months?"

"You won't be in bed all the time. You must first have the wounds exposed to the sun. Then afterward you can be on crutches."

"For six months and then have an operation?"

"That is the safe way. The foreign bodies must be allowed to encyst and the synovial fluid will re-form. Then it will be safe to open up the knee."

"Do you really think yourself I will have to wait that long?"

"That is the safe way."

"Who is that first captain?"

"He is a very excellent surgeon of Milan."

"He's a first captain, isn't he?"

"Yes, but he is an excellent surgeon."

"I don't want my leg fooled with by a first captain. If he was any good he would be made a major. I know what a first captain is, doctor."

"He is an excellent surgeon and I would rather have his judgment than any surgeon I know."

"Could another surgeon see it?"

"Certainly if you wish. But I would take Dr. Varella's opinion myself."

"Could you ask another surgeon to come and see it?"

"I will ask Valentini to come."

"Who is he?"

"He is a surgeon of the Ospedale Maggiore."

"Good. I appreciate it very much. You understand, doctor, I couldn't stay in bed six months."

"You would not be in bed. You would first take a sun cure. Then you could have light exercise. Then when it was encysted we would operate."

"But I can't wait six months."

The doctor spread his delicate fingers on the cap he held and smiled. "You are in such a hurry to get back to the front?"

"Why not?"

"It is very beautiful," he said. "You are a noble young man." He stooped over and kissed me very delicately on the forehead. "I will send for Valentini. Do not worry and excite yourself. Be a good boy."

"Will you have a drink?" I asked.

"No thank you. I never drink alcohol."

"Just have one." I rang for the porter to bring glasses.

"No. No thank you. They are waiting for me."

"Good-by," I said.

"Good-by."

Two hours later Dr. Valentini came into the room. He was in a great hurry and the points of his mustache stood straight up. He was a major, his face was tanned and he laughed all the time.

"How did you do it, this rotten thing?" he asked. "Let me see the plates. Yes. Yes. That's it. You look healthy as a goat. Who's the pretty girl? Is she your girl? I thought so. Isn't this a bloody war? How does that feel? You are a fine boy. I'll make you better than new. Does that hurt? You bet it hurts. How they love to hurt you, these doctors. What have they done for you so far? Can't that girl talk Italian? She should learn. What a lovely girl. I could teach her. I will be a patient here myself. No, but I will do all your maternity work free. Does she understand that? She will make you a fine boy. A fine blonde like she is. That's fine. That's all right. What a lovely girl. Ask her if she eats supper with me. No I won't take her away from you. Thank you. Thank you very much, Miss. That's all."

"That's all I want to know." He patted me on the shoulder. "Leave the dressings off."

"Will you have a drink, Dr. Valentini?"

"A drink? Certainly. I will have ten drinks. Where are they?"

"In the armoire. Miss Barkley will get the bottle."

"Cheery oh. Cheery oh to you, Miss. What a lovely girl. I will bring you better cognac than that." He wiped his mustache.

"When do you think it can be operated on?"

"To-morrow morning. Not before. Your stomach must be emptied. You must be washed out. I will see the old lady downstairs and leave instructions. Good-by. I see you to-morrow. I'll bring you

better cognac than that. You are very comfortable here. Good-by.
Until to-morrow. Get a good sleep. I'll see you early." He waved
from the doorway, his mustaches went straight up, his brown face
was smiling. There was a star in a box on his sleeve because he
was a major.

CHAPTER XVI

That night a bat flew into the room through the open door that led onto the balcony and through which we watched the night over the roofs of the town. It was dark in our room except for the small light of the night over the town and the bat was not frightened but hunted in the room as though he had been outside. We lay and watched him and I do not think he saw us because we lay so still. After he went out we saw a searchlight come on and watched the beam move across the sky and then go off and it was dark again. A breeze came in the night and we heard the men of the anti-aircraft gun on the next roof talking. It was cool and they were putting on their capes. I worried in the night about some one coming up but Catherine said they were all asleep. Once in the night we went to sleep and when I woke she was not there but I heard her coming along the hall and the door opened and she came back to the bed and said it was all right she had been downstairs and they were all asleep. She had been outside Miss Van Campen's door and heard her breathing in her sleep. She brought crackers and we ate them and drank some vermouth. We were very hungry but she said that would all have to be gotten out of me in the morning. I went to sleep again in the morning when it was light and when I was awake I found she was gone again. She came in looking fresh and lovely and sat on the bed and the sun rose while I had the thermometer in my mouth and we smelled the dew on the roofs and then the coffee of the men at the gun on the next roof.

"I wish we could go for a walk," Catherine said. "I'd wheel you if we had a chair."

"How would I get into the chair?"

"We'd do it."

"We could go out to the park and have breakfast outdoors." I looked out the open doorway.

"What we'll really do," she said, "is get you ready for your friend Dr. Valentini."

"I thought he was grand."

"I didn't like him as much as you did. But I imagine he's very good."

"Come back to bed, Catherine. Please," I said.

"I can't. Didn't we have a lovely night?"

"And can you be on night duty to-night?"

"I probably will. But you won't want me."

"Yes, I will."

"No, you won't. You've never been operated on. You don't know how you'll be."

"I'll be all right."

"You'll be sick and I won't be anything to you."

"Come back then now."

"No," she said. "I have to do the chart, darling, and fix you up."

"You don't really love me or you'd come back again."

"You're such a silly boy." She kissed me. "That's all right for the chart. Your temperature's always normal. You've such a lovely temperature."

"You've got a lovely everything."

"Oh no. You have the lovely temperature. I'm awfully proud of your temperature."

"Maybe all our children will have fine temperatures."

"Our children will probably have beastly temperatures."

"What do you have to do to get me ready for Valentini?"

"Not much. But quite unpleasant."

"I wish you didn't have to do it."

"I don't. I don't want any one else to touch you. I'm silly. I get furious if they touch you."

"Even Ferguson?"

"Especially Ferguson and Gage and the other, what's her name?"

"Walker?"

"That's it. They've too many nurses here now. There must be some more patients or they'll send us away. They have four nurses now."

"Perhaps there'll be some. They need that many nurses. It's quite a big hospital."

"I hope some will come. What would I do if they sent me away? They will unless there are more patients."

"I'd go too."

"Don't be silly. You can't go yet. But get well quickly, darling, and we will go somewhere."

"And then what?"

"Maybe the war will be over. It can't always go on."

"I'll get well," I said. "Valentini will fix me."

"He should with those mustaches. And, darling, when you're going under the ether just think about something else—not us. Because people get very blabby under an anæsthetic."

"What should I think about?"

"Anything. Anything but us. Think about your people. Or even any other girl."

"No."

"Say your prayers then. That ought to create a splendid impression."

"Maybe I won't talk."

"That's true. Often people don't talk."

"I won't talk."

"Don't brag, darling. Please don't brag. You're so sweet and you don't have to brag."

"I won't talk a word."

"Now you're bragging, darling. You know you don't need to brag. Just start your prayers or poetry or something when they tell you to breathe deeply. You'll be lovely that way and I'll be so proud of you. I'm very proud of you anyway. You have such a lovely temperature and you sleep like a little boy with your arm around the pillow and think it's me. Or is it some other girl? Some fine Italian girl?"

"It's you."

"Of course it's me. Oh I do love you and Valentini will make you a fine leg. I'm glad I don't have to watch it."

"And you'll be on night duty to-night."

"Yes. But you won't care."

"You wait and see."

"There, darling. Now you're all clean inside and out. Tell me. How many people have you ever loved?"

"Nobody."

"Not me even?"

"Yes, you."

"How many others really?"

"None."

"How many have you—how do you say it?—stayed with?"

"None."

"You're lying to me."

"Yes."

"It's all right. Keep right on lying to me. That's what I want you to do. Were they pretty?"

"I never stayed with any one."

"That's right. Were they very attractive?"

"I don't know anything about it."

"You're just mine. That's true and you've never belonged to any one else. But I don't care if you have. I'm not afraid of them. But don't tell me about them. When a man stays with a girl when does she say how much it costs?"

"I don't know."

"Of course not. Does she say she loves him? Tell me that. I want to know that."

"Yes. If he wants her to."

"Does he say he loves her? Tell me please. It's important."

"He does if he wants to."

"But you never did? Really?"

"No."

"Not really. Tell me the truth."

"No," I lied.

"You wouldn't," she said. "I knew you wouldn't. Oh, I love you, darling."

Outside the sun was up over the roofs and I could see the points of the cathedral with the sunlight on them. I was clean inside and outside and waiting for the doctor.

"And that's it?" Catherine said. "She says just what he wants her to?"

"Not always."

"But I will. I'll say just what you wish and I'll do what you wish and then you will never want any other girls, will you?" She looked at me very happily. "I'll do what you want and say what you want and then I'll be a great success, won't I?"

"Yes."

"What would you like me to do now that you're all ready?"

"Come to the bed again."

"All right. I'll come."

"Oh, darling, darling, darling," I said.

"You see," she said. "I do anything you want."

"You're so lovely."

"I'm afraid I'm not very good at it yet."

"You're lovely."

"I want what you want. There isn't any me any more. Just what you want."

"You sweet."

"I'm good. Aren't I good? You don't want any other girls, do you?"

"No."

"You see? I'm good. I do what you want."

CHAPTER XVII

When I was awake after the operation I had not been away. You do not go away. They only choke you. It is not like dying it is just a chemical choking so you do not feel, and afterward you might as well have been drunk except that when you throw up nothing comes but bile and you do not feel better afterward. I saw sandbags at the end of the bed. They were on pipes that came out of the cast. After a while I saw Miss Gage and she said, "How is it now?"

"Better," I said.

"He did a wonderful job on your knee."

"How long did it take?"

"Two hours and a half."

"Did I say anything silly?"

"Not a thing. Don't talk. Just be quiet."

I was sick and Catherine was right. It did not make any difference who was on night duty.

There were three other patients in the hospital now, a thin boy in the Red Cross from Georgia with malaria, a nice boy, also thin, from New York, with malaria and jaundice, and a fine boy who had tried to unscrew the fuse-cap from a combination shrapnel and high explosive shell for a souvenir. This was a shrapnel shell used by the Austrians in the mountains with a nose-cap which went on after the burst and exploded on contact.

Catherine Barkley was greatly liked by the nurses because she would do night duty indefinitely. She had quite a little work with the malaria people, the boy who had unscrewed the nose-cap was a friend of ours and never rang at night, unless it was necessary but between the times of working we were together. I loved her very much and she loved me. I slept in the daytime and we wrote notes during the day when we were awake and sent them by Ferguson. Ferguson was a fine girl. I never learned anything about her except that she had a brother in the Fifty-Second Division and a brother in Mesopotamia and she was very good to Catherine Barkley.

"Will you come to our wedding, Fergy?" I said to her once.

"You'll never get married."

"We will."

"No you won't."

"Why not?"

"You'll fight before you'll marry."

"We never fight."

"You've time yet."

"We don't fight."

"You'll die then. Fight or die. That's what people do. They don't marry."

I reached for her hand. "Don't take hold of me," she said. "I'm not crying. Maybe you'll be all right you two. But watch out you don't get her in trouble. You get her in trouble and I'll kill you."

"I won't get her in trouble."

"Well watch out then. I hope you'll be all right. You have a good time."

"We have a fine time."

"Don't fight then and don't get her into trouble."

"I won't."

"Mind you watch out. I don't want her with any of these war babies."

"You're a fine girl, Fergy."

"I'm not. Don't try to flatter me. How does your leg feel?"

"Fine."

"How is your head?" She touched the top of it with her fingers. It was sensitive like a foot that had gone to sleep. "It's never bothered me."

"A bump like that could make you crazy. It never bothers you?"

"No."

"You're a lucky young man. Have you the letter done? I'm going down."

"It's here," I said.

"You ought to ask her not to do night duty for a while. She's getting very tired."

"All right. I will."

"I want to do it but she won't let me. The others are glad to let her have it. You might give her just a little rest."

"All right."

"Miss Van Campen spoke about you sleeping all the forenoons."

"She would."

"It would be better if you let her stay off nights a little while."

"I want her to."

"You do not. But if you would make her I'd respect you for it."

"I'll make her."

"I don't believe it." She took the note and went out. I rang the bell and in a little while Miss Gage came in.

"What's the matter?"

"I just wanted to talk to you. Don't you think Miss Barkley

ought to go off night duty for a while? She looks awfully tired. Why does she stay on so long?"

Miss Gage looked at me.

"I'm a friend of yours," she said. "You don't have to talk to me like that."

"What do you mean?"

"Don't be silly. Was that all you wanted?"

"Do you want a vermouth?"

"All right. Then I have to go." She got out the bottle from the armoire and brought a glass.

"You take the glass," I said. "I'll drink out of the bottle."

"Here's to you," said Miss Gage.

"What did Van Campen say about me sleeping late in the mornings?"

"She just jawed about it. She calls you our privileged patient."

"To hell with her."

"She isn't mean," Miss Gage said. "She's just old and cranky. She never liked you."

"No."

"Well, I do. And I'm your friend. Don't forget that."

"You're awfully damned nice."

"No. I know who you think is nice. But I'm your friend. How does your leg feel?"

"Fine."

"I'll bring some cold mineral water to pour over it. It must itch under the cast. It's hot outside."

"You're awful nice."

"Does it itch much?"

"No. It's fine."

"I'll fix those sandbags better." She leaned over. "I'm your friend."

"I know you are."

"No you don't. But you will some day."

Catherine Barkley took three nights off night duty and then she came back on again. It was as though we met again after each of us had been away on a long journey.

CHAPTER XVIII

We had a lovely time that summer. When I could go out we rode in a carriage in the park. I remember the carriage, the horse going slowly, and up ahead the back of the driver with his varnished high hat, and Catherine Barkley sitting beside me. If we let our hands touch, just the side of my hand touching hers, we were excited. Afterward when I could get around on crutches we went to dinner at Biffi's or the Gran Italia and sat at the tables outside on the floor of the galleria. The waiters came in and out and there were people going by and candles with shades on the tablecloths and after we decided that we liked the Gran Italia best, George, the headwaiter, saved us a table. He was a fine waiter and we let him order the meal while we looked at the people, and the great galleria in the dusk, and each other. We drank dry white capri iced in a bucket; although we tried many of the other wines, fresa, barbera and the sweet white wines. They had no wine waiter because of the war and George would smile ashamedly when I asked about wines like fresa.

"If you imagine a country that makes a wine because it tastes like strawberries," he said.

"Why shouldn't it?" Catherine asked. "It sounds splendid."

"You try it, lady," said George, "if you want to. But let me bring a little bottle of margaux for the Tenente."

"I'll try it too, George."

"Sir, I can't recommend you to. It doesn't even taste like strawberries."

"It might," said Catherine. "It would be wonderful if it did."

"I'll bring it," said George, "and when the lady is satisfied I'll take it away."

It was not much of a wine. As he said, it did not even taste like strawberries. We went back to capri. One evening I was short of money and George loaned me a hundred lire. "That's all right, Tenente," he said. "I know how it is. I know how a man gets short. If you or the lady need money I've always got money."

After dinner we walked through the galleria, past the other restaurants and the shops with their steel shutters down, and stopped at the little place where they sold sandwiches; ham and lettuce sandwiches and anchovy sandwiches made of very tiny brown glazed rolls and only about as long as your finger. They were to eat in the night when we were hungry. Then we got into an open carriage outside the galleria in front of the cathedral and rode to the hospital. At the door of the hospital the porter came out to help with the crutches. I paid the driver, and then we rode upstairs in the elevator. Catherine got off at the lower floor where the nurses lived and I went on up and went down the hall on crutches to my room; sometimes I undressed and got into bed and sometimes I sat out on the balcony with my leg up on another chair and watched the swallows over the roofs and waited for Catherine. When she came upstairs it was as though she had been away on a long trip and I went along the hall with her on the crutches and carried the basins and waited outside the doors, or went in with her; it depending on whether they were friends of ours or not, and when she had done all there was to be done we sat out on the balcony outside my room. Afterward I went to bed and when they were all asleep and she was sure they would not call she came in. I loved to take her hair down and she sat on the bed and kept very still, except suddenly she would dip down to kiss me while I was doing it, and I would take out the pins and lay them on the sheet and it would be loose and I would watch her while she kept very still and then take out the last two pins and it would all come down and she would drop her head and we would both be inside of it, and it was the feeling of inside a tent or behind a falls.

She had wonderfully beautiful hair and I would lie sometimes and watch her twisting it up in the light that came in the open door and it shone even in the night as water shines sometimes just before it is really daylight. She had a lovely face and body and lovely smooth skin too. We would be lying together and I would touch her cheeks and her forehead and under her eyes and her chin and throat with the tips of my fingers and say, "Smooth as piano keys," and she would stroke my chin with her finger and say, "Smooth as emery paper and very hard on piano keys."

"Is it rough?"

"No, darling. I was just making fun of you."

It was lovely in the nights and if we could only touch each other we were happy. Besides all the big times we had many small ways of making love and we tried putting thoughts in the other one's head while we were in different rooms. It seemed to work sometimes but that was probably because we were thinking the same thing anyway.

We said to each other that we were married the first day she had come to the hospital and we counted months from our wedding day. I wanted to be really married but Catherine said that if we were they would send her away and if we merely started on the formalities they would watch her and would break us up. We

would have to be married under Italian law and the formalities
were terrific. I wanted us to be married really because I worried
about having a child if I thought about it, but we pretended to
ourselves we were married and did not worry much and I suppose
I enjoyed not being married, really. I know one night we talked
about it and Catherine said, "But, darling, they'd send me away."

"Maybe they wouldn't."

"They would. They'd send me home and then we would be apart
until after the war."

"I'd come on leave."

"You couldn't get to Scotland and back on a leave. Besides, I
won't leave you. What good would it do to marry now? We're really
married. I couldn't be any more married."

"I only wanted to for you."

"There isn't any me. I'm you. Don't make up a separate me."

"I thought girls always wanted to be married."

"They do. But, darling, I am married. I'm married to you. Don't
I make you a good wife?"

"You're a lovely wife."

"You see, darling, I had one experience of waiting to be married."

"I don't want to hear about it."

"You know I don't love any one but you. You shouldn't mind
because some one else loved me."

"I do."

"You shouldn't be jealous of some one who's dead when you
have everything."

"No, but I don't want to hear about it."

"Poor darling. And I know you've been with all kinds of girls
and it doesn't matter to me."

"Couldn't we be married privately some way? Then if anything
happened to me or if you had a child."

"There's no way to be married except by church or state. We are married privately. You see, darling, it would mean everything to me if I had any religion. But I haven't any religion."

"You gave me the Saint Anthony."

"That was for luck. Some one gave it to me."

"Then nothing worries you?"

"Only being sent away from you. You're my religion. You're all I've got."

"All right. But I'll marry you the day you say."

"Don't talk as though you had to make an honest woman of me, darling. I'm a very honest woman. You can't be ashamed of something if you're only happy and proud of it. Aren't you happy?"

"But you won't ever leave me for some one else."

"No, darling. I won't ever leave you for some one else. I suppose all sorts of dreadful things will happen to us. But you don't have to worry about that."

"I don't. But I love you so much and you did love some one else before."

"And what happened to him?"

"He died."

"Yes and if he hadn't I wouldn't have met you. I'm not unfaithful, darling. I've plenty of faults but I'm very faithful. You'll be sick of me I'll be so faithful."

"I'll have to go back to the front pretty soon."

"We won't think about that until you go. You see I'm happy, darling, and we have a lovely time. I haven't been happy for a long time and when I met you perhaps I was nearly crazy. Perhaps I was crazy. But now we're happy and we love each other. Do let's please just be happy. You are happy, aren't you? Is there anything I do you don't like? Can I do anything to please you? Would you like me to take down my hair? Do you want to play?"

"Yes and come to bed."

"All right. I'll go and see the patients first."

CHAPTER XIX

The summer went that way. I do not remember much about the days, except that they were hot and that there were many victories in the papers. I was very healthy and my legs healed quickly so that it was not very long after I was first on crutches before I was through with them and walking with a cane. Then I started treatments at the Ospedale Maggiore for bending the knees, mechanical treatments, baking in a box of mirrors with violet rays, massage, and baths. I went over there afternoons and afterward stopped at the café and had a drink and read the papers. I did not roam around the town; but wanted to get home to the hospital from the café. All I wanted was to see Catherine. The rest of the time I was glad to kill. Mostly I slept in the mornings, and in the afternoons, sometimes, I went to the races, and late to the mechanotherapy treatments. Sometimes I stopped in at the Anglo-American Club and sat in a deep leather-cushioned chair in front of the window and read the magazines. They would not let us go out together when I was off crutches because it was unseemly for a nurse to be seen unchaperoned with a patient who did not look as though he needed attendance, so we were not together much in the afternoons. Although sometimes we could go out to dinner if Ferguson went along. Miss Van Campen had accepted the status that we were great friends because she got a great amount of work out of Catherine. She thought Catherine came from very good people and that prejudiced her in her favor finally. Miss Van Campen admired family very much and came from an excellent family herself. The hospital was quite busy, too, and that kept her occupied. It was a hot summer and I knew many people in Milan but always was anxious to get back home to the hospital as soon as the afternoon was over. At the front they were advancing on the Carso, they had taken Kuk across from Plava and were taking the Bainsizza plateau. The West front did not sound so good. It looked as though the war were going on for a long time. We were in the war now but I thought it would take a year to get any great amount of troops over and train them for combat. Next year would be a bad year, or a good year maybe. The Italians were using up an awful amount of men. I did not see how it could go on. Even if they took all the Bainsizza and Monte San Gabriele there were plenty of mountains beyond for the Austrians. I had seen them. All the highest mountains were beyond. On the Carso they were going forward but there were marshes and swamps down by the sea. Napoleon would have whipped the Austrians on the plains. He never would have fought them in the mountains. He would have let them come down and whipped them around Verona. Still nobody was whipping any one on the Western front. Perhaps wars weren't won any more. Maybe they went on forever. Maybe it was another Hundred Years' War. I put the paper back on the rack and left the club. I went down the steps carefully and walked up the Via Manzoni. Outside the Gran Hotel I met old Meyers and his wife getting out of a carriage. They were coming back from the races. She was a big-busted woman in black satin. He was short and old, with a white mustache and walked flat-footed with a cane.

"How do you do? How do you do?" She shook hands. "Hello," said Meyers.

"How were the races?"

"Fine. They were just lovely. I had three winners."

"How did you do?" I asked Meyers.

"All right. I had a winner."

"I never know how he does," Mrs. Meyers said. "He never tells me."

"I do all right," Meyers said. He was being cordial. "You ought to come out." While he talked you had the impression that he was not looking at you or that he mistook you for some one else.

"I will," I said.

"I'm coming up to the hospital to see you," Mrs. Meyers said. "I have some things for my boys. You're all my boys. You certainly are my dear boys."

"They'll be glad to see you."

"Those dear boys. You too. You're one of my boys."

"I have to get back," I said.

"You give my love to all those dear boys. I've got lots of things to bring. I've some fine marsala and cakes."

"Good-by," I said. "They'll be awfully glad to see you."

"Good-by," said Meyers. "You come around to the galleria. You know where my table is. We're all there every afternoon." I went on up the street. I wanted to buy something at the Cova to take to Catherine. Inside, at the Cova, I bought a box of chocolate and while the girl wrapped it up I walked over to the bar. There were a couple of British and some aviators. I had a martini alone, paid for it, picked up the box of chocolate at the outside counter and walked on home toward the hospital. Outside the little bar up the street from the Scala there were some people I knew, a vice-consul, two fellows who studied singing, and Ettore Moretti, an Italian from San Francisco who was in the Italian army. I had a drink with them. One of the singers was named Ralph Simmons, and he was singing under the name of Enrico DelCredo. I never knew how well he could sing but he was always on the point of something very big happening. He was fat and looked shopworn around the nose and mouth as though he had hayfever. He had come back from singing in Piacenza. He had sung Tosca and it had been wonderful.

"Of course you've never heard me sing," he said.

"When will you sing here?"

"I'll be at the Scala in the fall."

"I'll bet they throw the benches at you," Ettore said. "Did you hear how they threw the benches at him in Modena?"

"It's a damned lie."

"They threw the benches at him," Ettore said. "I was there. I threw six benches myself."

"You're just a wop from Frisco."

"He can't pronounce Italian," Ettore said. "Everywhere he goes they throw the benches at him."

"Piacenza's the toughest house to sing in the north of Italy," the other tenor said. "Believe me that's a tough little house to sing." This tenor's name was Edgar Saunders, and he sang under the name of Edouardo Giovanni.

"I'd like to be there to see them throw the benches at you," Ettore said. "You can't sing Italian."

"He's a nut," said Edgar Saunders. "All he knows how to say is throw benches."

"That's all they know how to do when you two sing," Ettore said. "Then when you go to America you'll tell about your triumphs at the Scala. They wouldn't let you get by the first note at the Scala."

"I'll sing at the Scala," Simmons said. "I'm going to sing Tosca in October."

"We'll go, won't we, Mac?" Ettore said to the vice-consul. "They'll need somebody to protect them."

"Maybe the American army will be there to protect them," the vice-consul said. "Do you want another drink, Simmons? You want a drink, Saunders?"

"All right," said Saunders.

"I hear you're going to get the silver medal," Ettore said to me. "What kind of citation you going to get?"

"I don't know. I don't know I'm going to get it."

"You're going to get it. Oh boy, the girls at the Cova will think you're fine then. They'll all think you killed two hundred Austrians or captured a whole trench by yourself. Believe me, I got to work for my decorations."

"How many have you got, Ettore?" asked the vice-consul.

"He's got everything," Simmons said. "He's the boy they're running the war for."

"I've got the bronze twice and three silver medals," said Ettore. "But the papers on only one have come through."

"What's the matter with the others?" asked Simmons.

"The action wasn't successful," said Ettore. "When the action isn't successful they hold up all the medals."

"How many times have you been wounded, Ettore?"

"Three times bad. I got three wound stripes. See?" He pulled his sleeve around. The stripes were parallel silver lines on a black background sewed to the cloth of the sleeve about eight inches below the shoulder.

"You got one too," Ettore said to me. "Believe me they're fine to have. I'd rather have them than medals. Believe me, boy, when you get three you've got something. You only get one for a wound that puts you three months in the hospital."

"Where were you wounded, Ettore?" asked the vice-consul.

Ettore pulled up his sleeve. "Here," he showed the deep smooth red scar. "Here on my leg. I can't show you that because I got puttees on; and in the foot. There's dead bone in my foot that stinks right now. Every morning I take new little pieces out and it stinks all the time."

"What hit you?" asked Simmons.

"A hand-grenade. One of those potato mashers. It just blew the whole side of my foot off. You know those potato mashers?" He turned to me.

"Sure."

"I saw the son of a bitch throw it," Ettore said. "It knocked me down and I thought I was dead all right but those damn potato mashers haven't got anything in them. I shot the son of a bitch with my rifle. I always carry a rifle so they can't tell I'm an officer."

"How did he look?" asked Simmons.

"That was the only one he had," Ettore said. "I don't know why he threw it. I guess he always wanted to throw one. He never saw any real fighting probably. I shot the son of a bitch all right."

"How did he look when you shot him?" Simmons asked.

"Hell, how should I know?" said Ettore. "I shot him in the belly. I was afraid I'd miss him if I shot him in the head."

"How long have you been an officer, Ettore?" I asked.

"Two years. I'm going to be a captain. How long have you been a lieutenant?"

"Going on three years."

"You can't be a captain because you don't know the Italian language well enough," Ettore said. "You can talk but you can't read and write well enough. You got to have an education to be a captain. Why don't you go in the American army?"

"Maybe I will."

"I wish to God I could. Oh, boy, how much does a captain get, Mac?"

"I don't know exactly. Around two hundred and fifty dollars, I think."

"Jesus Christ what I could do with two hundred and fifty dollars. You better get in the American army quick, Fred. See if you can't get me in."

"All right."

"I can command a company in Italian. I could learn it in English easy."

"You'd be a general," said Simmons.

"No, I don't know enough to be a general. A general's got to know a hell of a lot. You guys think there ain't anything to war. You ain't got brains enough to be a second-class corporal."

"Thank God I don't have to be," Simmons said.

"Maybe you will if they round up all you slackers. Oh, boy, I'd like to have you two in my platoon. Mac too. I'd make you my orderly, Mac."

"You're a great boy, Ettore," Mac said. "But I'm afraid you're a militarist."

"I'll be a colonel before the war's over," Ettore said.

"If they don't kill you."

"They won't kill me." He touched the stars at his collar with his thumb and forefinger. "See me do that? We always touch our stars if anybody mentions getting killed."

"Let's go, Sim," said Saunders standing up.

"All right."

"So long," I said. "I have to go too." It was a quarter to six by the clock inside the bar. "Ciaou, Ettore."

"Ciaou, Fred," said Ettore. "That's pretty fine you're going to get the silver medal."

"I don't know I'll get it."

"You'll get it all right, Fred. I heard you were going to get it all right."

"Well, so long," I said. "Keep out of trouble, Ettore."

"Don't worry about me. I don't drink and I don't run around. I'm no boozer and whorehound. I know what's good for me."

"So long," I said. "I'm glad you're going to be promoted captain."

"I don't have to wait to be promoted. I'm going to be a captain for merit of war. You know. Three stars with the crossed swords and crown above. That's me."

"Good luck."

"Good luck. When you going back to the front?"

"Pretty soon."

"Well, I'll see you around."

"So long."

"So long. Don't take any bad nickels."

I walked on down a back street that led to a cross-cut to the hospital. Ettore was twenty-three. He had been brought up by an uncle in San Francisco and was visiting his father and mother in Torino when war was declared. He had a sister, who had been sent to America with him at the same time to live with the uncle, who would graduate from normal school this year. He was a legitimate hero who bored every one he met. Catherine could not stand him.

"We have heroes too," she said. "But usually, darling, they're much quieter."

"I don't mind him."

"I wouldn't mind him if he wasn't so conceited and didn't bore me, and bore me, and bore me."

"He bores me."

"You're sweet to say so, darling. But you don't need to. You can picture him at the front and you know he's useful but he's so much the type of boy I don't care for."

"I know."

"You're awfully sweet to know, and I try and like him but he's a dreadful, dreadful boy really."

"He said this afternoon he was going to be a captain."

"I'm glad," said Catherine. "That should please him."

"Wouldn't you like me to have some more exalted rank?"

"No, darling. I only want you to have enough rank so that we're admitted to the better restaurants."

"That's just the rank I have."

"You have a splendid rank. I don't want you to have any more rank. It might go to your head. Oh, darling, I'm awfully glad you're not conceited. I'd have married you even if you were conceited but it's very restful to have a husband who's not conceited."

We were talking softly out on the balcony. The moon was supposed to rise but there was a mist over the town and it did not come up and in a little while it started to drizzle and we came in. Outside the mist turned to rain and in a little while it was raining hard and we heard it drumming on the roof. I go up and stood at the door to see if it was raining in but it wasn't, so I left the door open.

"Who else did you see?" Catherine asked.

"Mr. and Mrs. Meyers."

"They're a strange lot."

"He's supposed to have been in the penitentiary at home. They let him out to die."

"And he lived happily in Milan forever after."

"I don't know how happily."

"Happily enough after jail I should think."

"She's bringing some things here."

"She brings splendid things. Were you her dear boy?"

"One of them."

"You are all her dear boys," Catherine said. "She prefers the dear boys. Listen to it rain."

"It's raining hard."

"And you'll always love me, won't you?"

"Yes."

"And the rain won't make any difference?"

"No."

"That's good. Because I'm afraid of the rain."

"Why?" I was sleepy. Outside the rain was falling steadily.

"I don't know, darling. I've always been afraid of the rain."

"I like it."

"I like to walk in it. But it's very hard on loving."

"I'll love you always."

"I'll love you in the rain and in the snow and in the hail and—what else is there?"

"I don't know. I guess I'm sleepy."

"Go to sleep, darling, and I'll love you no matter how it is."

"You're not really afraid of the rain are you?"

"Not when I'm with you."

"Why are you afraid of it?"

"I don't know."

"Tell me."

"Don't make me."

"Tell me."

"No."

"Tell me."

"All right. I'm afraid of the rain because sometimes I see me dead in it."

"No."

"And sometimes I see you dead in it."

"That's more likely."

"No, it's not, darling. Because I can keep you safe. I know I can. But nobody can help themselves."

"Please stop it. I don't want you to get Scotch and crazy to-night. We won't be together much longer."

"No, but I am Scotch and crazy. But I'll stop it. It's all nonsense."

"Yes it's all nonsense."

"It's all nonsense. It's only nonsense. I'm not afraid of the rain. I'm not afraid of the rain. Oh, oh, God, I wish I wasn't." She was crying. I comforted her and she stopped crying. But outside it kept on raining.

CHAPTER XX

One day in the afternoon we went to the races. Ferguson went too and Crowell Rodgers, the boy who had been wounded in the eyes by the explosion of the shell nose-cap. The girls dressed to go after lunch while Crowell and I sat on the bed in his room and read the past performances of the horses and the predictions in the racing paper. Crowell's head was bandaged and he did not care much about these races but read the racing paper constantly and kept track of all the horses for something to do. He said the horses were a terrible lot but they were all the horses we had. Old Meyers liked him and gave him tips. Meyers won on nearly every race but disliked to give tips because it brought down the prices. The racing was very crooked. Men who had been ruled off the turf everywhere else were racing in Italy. Meyers' information was good but I hated to ask him because sometimes he did not answer, and always you could see it hurt him to tell you, but he felt obligated to tell us for some reason and he hated less to tell Crowell. Crowell's eyes had been hurt, one was hurt badly, and Meyers had trouble with his eyes and so he liked Crowell. Meyers never told his wife what horses he was playing and she won or lost, mostly lost, and talked all the time.

We four drove out to San Siro in an open carriage. It was a lovely day and we drove out through the park and out along the tramway and out of town where the road was dusty. There were villas with iron fences and big overgrown gardens and ditches with water flowing and green vegetable gardens with dust on the leaves. We could look across the plain and see farmhouses and the rich green farms with their irrigation ditches and the mountains to the north. There were many carriages going into the race track and the men at the gate let us in without cards because we were in uniform. We left the carriage, bought programmes, and walked across the infield and then across the smooth thick turf of the course to the paddock. The grand-stands were old and made of wood and the betting booths were under the stands and in a row out near the stables. There was a crowd of soldiers along the fence in the infield. The paddock was fairly well filled with people and they were walking the horses around in a ring under the trees behind the grand-stand. We saw people we knew and got chairs for Ferguson and Catherine and watched the horses.

They went around, one after the other, their heads down, the grooms leading them. One horse, a purplish black, Crowell swore was dyed that color. We watched him and it seemed possible. He had only come out just before the bell rang to saddle. We looked him up in the programme from the number on the groom's arm and it was listed a black gelding named Japalac. The race was for horses that had never won a race worth one thousand lire or more. Catherine was sure his color had been changed. Ferguson said she could not tell. I thought he looked suspicious. We all agreed we ought to back him and pooled one hundred lire. The odds sheets showed he would pay thirty-five to one. Crowell went over and bought the tickets while we watched the jockeys ride around once more and then go out under the trees to the track and gallop slowly up to the turn where the start was to be.

We went up in the grand-stand to watch the race. They had no elastic barrier at San Siro then and the starter lined up all the horses, they looked very small way up the track, and then sent them off with a crack of his long whip. They came past us with the black horse well in front and on the turn he was running away from the others. I watched them on the far side with the glasses and saw the jockey fighting to hold him in but he could not hold him and when they came around the turn and into the stretch the black horse was fifteen lengths ahead of the others. He went way on up and around the turn after the finish.

"Isn't it wonderful," Catherine said. "We'll have over three thousand lire. He must be a splendid horse."

"I hope his color doesn't run," Crowell said, "before they pay off."

"He was really a lovely horse," Catherine said. "I wonder if Mr. Meyers backed him."

"Did you have the winner?" I called to Meyers. He nodded.

"I didn't," Mrs. Meyers said. "Who did you children bet on?"

"Japalac."

"Really? He's thirty-five to one!"

"We liked his color."

"I didn't. I thought he looked seedy. They told me not to back him."

"He won't **pay** much," Meyers said.

"He's marked thirty-five to one in the quotes," I said.

"He won't pay much. At the last minute," Meyers said, "they put a lot of money on him."

"Who?"

"Kempton and the boys. You'll see. He won't pay two to one."

"Then we won't get three thousand lire," Catherine said. "I don't like this crooked racing!"

"We'll get two hundred lire."

"That's nothing. That doesn't do us any good. I thought we were going to get three thousand."

"It's crooked and disgusting," Ferguson said.

"Of course," said Catherine, "if it hadn't been crooked we'd never have backed him at all. But I would have liked the three thousand lire."

"Let's go down and get a drink and see what they pay," Crowell said. We went out to where they posted the numbers and the bell rang to pay off and they put up 18.50 after Japalac to win. That meant he paid less than even money on a ten-lira bet.

We went to the bar under the grand-stand and had a whiskey and soda apiece. We ran into a couple of Italians we knew and McAdams, the vice-consul, and they came up with us when we joined the girls. The Italians were full of manners and McAdams talked to Catherine while we went down to bet again. Mr. Meyers was standing near the pari-mutuel.

"Ask him what he played," I said to Crowell.

"What are you on, Mr. Meyers?" Crowell asked. Meyers took out his programme and pointed to the number five with his pencil.

"Do you mind if we play him too?" Crowell asked.

"Go ahead. Go ahead. But don't tell my wife I gave it to you."

"Will you have a drink?" I asked.

"No thanks. I never drink."

We put a hundred lire on number five to win and a hundred to place and then had another whiskey and soda apiece. I was feeling very good and we picked up a couple more Italians, who each had a drink with us, and went back to the girls. These Italians were also very mannered and matched manners with the two we had collected before. In a little while no one could sit down. I gave the tickets to Catherine.

"What horse is it?"

"I don't know. Mr. Meyers' choice."

"Don't you even know the name?"

"No. You can find it on the programme. Number five I think."

"You have touching faith," she said. The number five won but did not pay anything. Mr. Meyers was angry.

"You have to put up two hundred lire to make twenty," he said. "Twelve lire for ten. It's not worth it. My wife lost twenty lire."

"I'll go down with you," Catherine said to me. The Italians all stood up. We went downstairs and out to the paddock.

"Do you like this?" Catherine asked.

"Yes. I guess I do."

"It's all right, I suppose," she said. "But, darling, I can't stand to see so many people."

"We don't see many."

"No. But those Meyers and the man from the bank with his wife and daughters——"

"He cashes my sight drafts," I said.

"Yes but some one else would if he didn't. Those last four boys were awful."

"We can stay out here and watch the race from the fence."

"That will be lovely. And, darling, let's back a horse we've never heard of and that Mr. Meyers won't be backing."

"All right."

We backed a horse named Light For Me that finished fourth in a field of five. We leaned on the fence and watched the horses go by, their hoofs thudding as they went past, and saw the mountains off in the distance and Milan beyond the trees and the fields.

"I feel so much cleaner," Catherine said. The horses were coming back, through the gate, wet and sweating, the jockeys quieting them and riding up to dismount under the trees.

"Wouldn't you like a drink? We could have one out here and see the horses."

"I'll get them," I said.

"The boy will bring them," Catherine said. She put her hand up and the boy came out from the Pagoda bar beside the stables. We sat down at a round iron table.

"Don't you like it better when we're alone?"

"Yes," I said.

"I felt very lonely when they were all there."

"It's grand here," I said.

"Yes. It's really a pretty course."

"It's nice."

"Don't let me spoil your fun, darling. I'll go back whenever you want."

"No," I said. "We'll stay here and have our drink. Then we'll go down and stand at the water jump for the steeplechase."

"You're awfully good to me," she said.

After we had been alone awhile we were glad to see the others again. We had a good time.

CHAPTER XXI

In September the first cool nights came, then the days were cool and the leaves on the trees in the park began to turn color and we knew the summer was gone. The fighting at the front went very badly and they could not take San Gabriele. The fighting on the Bainsizza plateau was over and by the middle of the month the fighting for San Gabriele was about over too. They could not take it. Ettore was gone back to the front. The horses were gone to Rome and there was no more racing. Crowell had gone to Rome too, to be sent back to America. There were riots twice in the town against the war and bad rioting in Turin. A British major at the club told me the Italians had lost one hundred and fifty thousand men on the Bainsizza plateau and on San Gabriele. He said they had lost forty thousand on the Carso besides. We had a drink and he talked. He said the fighting was over for the year down here and that the Italians had bitten off more than they could chew. He said the offensive in Flanders was going to the bad. If they killed men as they did this fall the Allies would be cooked in another year. He said we were all cooked but we were all right as long as we did not know it. We were all cooked. The thing was not to recognize it. The last country to realize they were cooked would win the war. We had another drink. Was I on somebody's staff? No. He was. It was all balls. We were alone in the club sitting back in one of the big leather sofas. His boots were smoothly polished dull leather. They were beautiful boots. He said it was all balls. They thought only in divisions and man-power. They all squabbled about divisions and only killed them when they got them. They were all cooked. The Germans won the victories. By God they were soldiers. The old Hun was a soldier. But they were cooked too. We were all cooked. I asked about Russia. He said they were cooked already. I'd soon see they were cooked. Then the Austrians were cooked too. If they got some Hun divisions they could do it. Did he think they would attack this fall? Of course they would. The Italians were cooked. Everybody knew they were cooked. The old Hun would come down through the Trentino and cut the railway at Vicenza and then where would the Italians be? They tried that in 'sixteen, I said. Not with Germans. Yes, I said. But they probably wouldn't do that, he said. It was too simple. They'd try something complicated and get royally cooked. I had to go, I said. I had to get back to the hospital. "Good-by," he said. Then cheerily, "Every sort of luck!" There was a great contrast between his world pessimism and personal cheeriness.

I stopped at a barber shop and was shaved and went home to the hospital. My leg was as well as it would get for a long time. I had been up for examination three days before. There were still some treatments to take before my course at the Ospedale Maggiore was finished and I walked along the side street practising not limping. An old man was cutting silhouettes under an arcade. I stopped to watch him. Two girls were posing and he cut their silhouettes together, snipping very fast and looking at them, his head on one side. The girls were giggling. He showed me the silhouettes before he pasted them on white paper and handed them to the girls.

"They're beautiful," he said. "How about you, Tenente?"

The girls went away looking at their silhouettes and laughing. They were nice-looking girls. One of them worked in the wine shop across from the hospital.

"All right," I said.

"Take your cap off."

"No. With it on."

"It will not be so beautiful," the old man said. "But," he brightened, "it will be more military."

He snipped away at the black paper, then separated the two thicknesses and pasted the profiles on a card and handed them to me.

"How much?"

"That's all right." He waved his hand. "I just made them for you."

"Please." I brought out some coppers. "For pleasure."

"No. I did them for a pleasure. Give them to your girl."

"Many thanks until we meet."

"Until I see thee."

I went on to the hospital. There were some letters, an official one, and some others. I was to have three weeks' convalescent leave and then return to the front. I read it over carefully. Well, that was that. The convalescent leave started October fourth when my course was finished. Three weeks was twenty-one days. That made October twenty-fifth. I told them I would not be in and went to the restaurant a little way up the street from the hospital for supper and read my letters and the *Corriere Della Sera* at the table. There was a letter from my grandfather, containing family news, patriotic encouragement, a draft for two hundred dollars, and a few clippings; a dull letter from the priest at our mess, a letter from a man I knew who was flying with the French and had gotten in with a wild gang and was telling about it, and a note from Rinaldi asking me how long I was going to skulk in Milano and what was all the news? He wanted me to bring him phonograph records and enclosed a list. I drank a small bottle of chianti with the meal, had a coffee afterward with a glass of cognac, finished the paper, put my letters in my pocket, left the paper on the table with the tip and went out. In my room at the hospital I undressed, put on pajamas and a dressing-gown, pulled down the curtains on the door that opened onto the balcony and sitting up in bed read Boston papers from a pile Mrs. Meyers had left for her boys at the hospital. The Chicago White Sox were winning the American League pennant and the New York Giants were leading the National League. Babe Ruth was a pitcher then playing for Boston. The papers were dull, the news was local and stale, and the war news was all old. The American news was all training camps. I was glad I wasn't in a training camp. The baseball news was all I could read and I did not have the slightest interest in it. A number of papers together made it impossible to read with interest. It was not very timely but I read at it for a while. I wondered if America really got into the war, if they would close down the major leagues. They probably wouldn't. There was still racing in Milan and the war could not be much worse. They had stopped racing in France. That was where our horse Japalac came from. Catherine was not due on duty until nine o'clock. I heard her passing along the floor when she first came on duty and once saw her pass in the hall. She went to several other rooms and finally came into mine.

"I'm late, darling," she said. "There was a lot to do. How are you?"

I told her about my papers and the leave.

"That's lovely," she said. "Where do you want to go?"

"Nowhere. I want to stay here."

"That's silly. You pick a place to go and I'll come too."

"How will you work it?"

"I don't know. But I will."

"You're pretty wonderful."

"No I'm not. But life isn't hard to manage when you've nothing to lose."

"How do you mean?"

"Nothing. I was only thinking how small obstacles seemed that once were so big."

"I should think it might be hard to manage."

"No it won't, darling. If necessary I'll simply leave. But it won't come to that."

"Where should we go?"

"I don't care. Anywhere you want. Anywhere we don't know people."

"Don't you care where we go?"

"No. I'll like any place."

She seemed upset and taut.

"What's the matter, Catherine?"

"Nothing. Nothing's the matter."

"Yes there is."

"No nothing. Really nothing."

"I know there is. Tell me, darling. You can tell me."

"It's nothing."

"Tell me."

"I don't want to. I'm afraid I'll make you unhappy or worry you."

"No it won't."

"You're sure? It doesn't worry me but I'm afraid to worry you."

"It won't if it doesn't worry you."

"I don't want to tell."

"Tell it."

"Do I have to?"

"Yes."

"I'm going to have a baby, darling. It's almost three months along. You're not worried, are you? Please please don't. You mustn't worry."

"All right."

"Is it all right?"

"Of course."

"I did everything. I took everything but it didn't make any difference."

"I'm not worried."

"I couldn't help it, darling, and I haven't worried about it. You mustn't worry or feel badly."

"I only worry about you."

"That's it. That's what you mustn't do. People have babies all the time. Everybody has babies. It's a natural thing."

"You're pretty wonderful."

"No I'm not. But you mustn't mind, darling. I'll try and not make trouble for you. I know I've made trouble now. But haven't I been a good girl until now? You never knew it, did you?"

"No."

"It will all be like that. You simply mustn't worry. I can see you're worrying. Stop it. Stop it right away. Wouldn't you like a drink, darling? I know a drink always makes you feel cheerful."

"No. I feel cheerful. And you're pretty wonderful."

"No I'm not. But I'll fix everything to be together if you pick out a place for us to go. It ought to be lovely in October. We'll have a lovely time, darling, and I'll write you every day while you're at the front."

"Where will you be?"

"I don't know yet. But somewhere splendid. I'll look after all that."

We were quiet awhile and did not talk. Catherine was sitting on the bed and I was looking at her but we did not touch each other. We were apart as when some one comes into a room and people are self-conscious. She put out her hand and took mine.

"You aren't angry are you, darling?"

"No."

"And you don't feel trapped?"

"Maybe a little. But not by you."

"I didn't mean by me. You mustn't be stupid. I meant trapped at all."

"You always feel trapped biologically."

She went away a long way without stirring or removing her hand.

" 'Always' isn't a pretty word."

"I'm sorry."

"It's all right. But you see I've never had a baby and I've never even loved any one. And I've tried to be the way you wanted and then you talk about 'always.' "

"I could cut off my tongue," I offered.

"Oh, darling!" she came back from wherever she had been. "You mustn't mind me." We were both together again and the self-consciousness was gone. "We really are the same one and we mustn't misunderstand on purpose."

"We won't."

"But people do. They love each other and they misunderstand on purpose and they fight and then suddenly they aren't the same one."

"We won't fight."

"We mustn't. Because there's only us two and in the world there's all the rest of them. If anything comes between us we're gone and then they have us."

"They won't get us," I said. "Because you're too brave. Nothing ever happens to the brave."

"They die of course."

"But only once."

"I don't know. Who said that?"

"The coward dies a thousand deaths, the brave but one?"

"Of course. Who said it?"

"I don't know."

"He was probably a coward," she said. "He knew a great deal about cowards but nothing about the brave. The brave dies perhaps two thousand deaths if he's intelligent. He simply doesn't mention them."

"I don't know. It's hard to see inside the head of the brave."

"Yes. That's how they keep that way."

"You're an authority."

"You're right, darling. That was deserved."

"You're brave."

"No," she said. "But I would like to be."

"I'm not," I said. "I know where I stand. I've been out long enough to know. I'm like a ball-player that bats two hundred and thirty and knows he's no better."

"What is a ball-player that bats two hundred and thirty? It's awfully impressive."

"It's not. It means a mediocre hitter in baseball."

"But still a hitter," she prodded me.

"I guess we're both conceited," I said. "But you are brave."

"No. But I hope to be."

"We're both brave," I said. "And I'm very brave when I've had a drink."

"We're splendid people," Catherine said. She went over to the armoire and brought me the cognac and a glass. "Have a drink, darling," she said. "You've been awfully good."

"I don't really want one."

"Take one."

"All right." I poured the water glass a third full of cognac and drank it off.

"That was very big," she said. "I know brandy is for heroes. But you shouldn't exaggerate."

"Where will we live after the war?"

"In an old people's home probably," she said. "For three years I looked forward very childishly to the war ending at Christmas. But now I look forward till when our son will be a lieutenant commander."

"Maybe he'll be a general."

"If it's an hundred years' war he'll have time to try both of the services."

"Don't you want a drink?"

"No. It always makes you happy, darling, and it only makes me dizzy."

"Didn't you ever drink brandy?"

"No, darling. I'm a very old-fashioned wife."

I reached down to the floor for the bottle and poured another drink.

"I'd better go to have a look at your compatriots," Catherine said. "Perhaps you'll read the papers until I come back."

"Do you have to go?"

"Now or later."

"All right. Now."

"I'll come back later."

"I'll have finished the papers," I said.

CHAPTER XXII

It turned cold that night and the next day it was raining. Coming home from the Ospedale Maggiore it rained very hard and I was wet when I came in. Up in my room the rain was coming down heavily outside on the balcony, and the wind blew it against the glass doors. I changed my clothing and drank some brandy but the brandy did not taste good. I felt sick in the night and in the morning after breakfast I was nauseated.

"There is no doubt about it," the house surgeon said. "Look at the whites of his eyes, Miss."

Miss Gage looked. They had me look in a glass. The whites of the eyes were yellow and it was the jaundice. I was sick for two weeks with it. For that reason we did not spend a convalescent leave together. We had planned to go to Pallanza on Lago Maggiore. It is nice there in the fall when the leaves turn. There are walks you can take and you can troll for trout in the lake. It would have been better than Stresa because there are fewer people at Pallanza. Stresa is so easy to get to from Milan that there are always people you know. There is a nice village at Pallanza and you can row out to the islands where the fishermen live and there is a restaurant on the biggest island. But we did not go.

One day while I was in bed with jaundice Miss Van Campen came in the room, opened the door into the armoire and saw the empty bottles there. I had sent a load of them down by the porter and I believe she must have seen them going out and come up to find some more. They were mostly vermouth bottles, marsala bottles, capri bottles, empty chianti flasks and a few cognac bottles. The porter had carried out the large bottles, those that had held vermouth, and the straw-covered chianti flasks, and left the brandy bottles for the last. It was the brandy bottles and a bottle shaped like a bear, which had held kümmel, that Miss Van Campen found. The bear-shaped bottle enraged her particularly. She held it up, the bear was sitting up on his haunches with his paws up, there was a cork in his glass head and a few sticky crystals at the bottom. I laughed.

"It is kümmel," I said. "The best kümmel comes in those bear-shaped bottles. It comes from Russia."

"Those are all brandy bottles, aren't they?" Miss Van Campen asked.

"I can't see them all," I said. "But they probably are."

"How long has this been going on?"

"I bought them and brought them in myself," I said. "I have had Italian officers visit me frequently and I have kept brandy to offer them."

"You haven't been drinking it yourself?" she said.

"I have also drunk it myself."

"Brandy," she said. "Eleven empty bottles of brandy and that bear liquid."

"Kümmel."

"I will send for some one to take them away. Those are all the empty bottles you have?"

"For the moment."

"And I was pitying you having jaundice. Pity is something that is wasted on you."

"Thank you."

"I suppose you can't be blamed for not wanting to go back to the front. But I should think you would try something more intelligent than producing jaundice with alcoholism."

"With what?"

"With alcoholism. You heard me say it." I did not say anything. "Unless you find something else I'm afraid you will have to go back to the front when you are through with your jaundice. I don't believe self-inflicted jaundice entitles you to a convalescent leave."

"You don't?"

"I do not."

"Have you ever had jaundice, Miss Van Campen?"

"No, but I have seen a great deal of it."

"You noticed how the patients enjoyed it?"

"I suppose it is better than the front."

"Miss Van Campen," I said, "did you ever know a man who tried to disable himself by kicking himself in the scrotum?"

Miss Van Campen ignored the actual question. She had to ignore it or leave the room. She was not ready to leave because she had disliked me for a long time and she was now cashing in.

"I have known many men to escape the front through self-inflicted wounds."

"That wasn't the question. I have seen self-inflicted wounds also. I asked you if you had ever known a man who had tried to disable himself by kicking himself in the scrotum. Because that is the nearest sensation to jaundice and it is a sensation that I believe few women have ever experienced. That was why I asked you if you had ever had the jaundice, Miss Van Campen, because—" Miss Van Campen left the room. Later Miss Gage came in.

"What did you say to Van Campen? She was furious."

"We were comparing sensations. I was going to suggest that she had never experienced childbirth——"

"You're a fool," Gage said. "She's after your scalp."

"She has my scalp," I said. "She's lost me my leave and she might try and get me court-martialled. She's mean enough."

"She never liked you," Gage said. "What's it about?"

"She says I've drunk myself into jaundice so as not to go back to the front."

"Pooh," said Gage. "I'll swear you've never taken a drink. Everybody will swear you've never taken a drink."

"She found the bottles."

"I've told you a hundred times to clear out those bottles. Where are they now?"

"In the armoire."

"Have you a suitcase?"

"No. Put them in that rucksack."

Miss Gage packed the bottles in the rucksack. "I'll give them to the porter," she said. She started for the door.

"Just a minute," Miss Van Campen said. "I'll take those bottles." She had the porter with her. "Carry them, please," she said. "I want to show them to the doctor when I make my report."

She went down the hall. The porter carried the sack. He knew what was in it.

Nothing happened except that I lost my leave.

CHAPTER XXIII

The night I was to return to the front I sent the porter down to hold a seat for me on the train when it came from Turin. The train was to leave at midnight. It was made up at Turin and reached Milan about half-past ten at night and lay in the station until time to leave. You had to be there when it came in, to get a seat. The porter took a friend with him, a machine-gunner on leave who worked in a tailor shop, and was sure that between them they could hold a place. I gave them money for platform tickets and had them take my baggage. There was a big rucksack and two musettes.

I said good-by at the hospital at about five o'clock and went out. The porter had my baggage in his lodge and I told him I would be at the station a little before midnight. His wife called me "Signorino" and cried. She wiped her eyes and shook hands and then cried again. I patted her on the back and she cried once more. She had done my mending and was a very short dumpy, happy-faced woman with white hair. When she cried her whole face went to pieces. I went down to the corner where there was a wine shop and waited inside looking out the window. It was dark outside and cold and misty. I paid for my coffee and grappa and I watched the people going by in the light from the window. I saw Catherine and knocked on the window. She looked, saw me and smiled, and I went out to meet her. She was wearing a dark blue cape and a soft felt hat. We walked along together, along the sidewalk past the wine shops, then across the market square and up the street and through the archway to the cathedral square. There were streetcar tracks and beyond them was the cathedral. It was white and wet in the mist. We crossed the tram tracks. On our left were the shops, their windows lighted, and the entrance to the galleria. There was a fog in the square and when we came close to the front of the cathedral it was very big and the stone was wet.

"Would you like to go in?"

"No," Catherine said. We walked along. There was a soldier standing with his girl in the shadow of one of the stone buttresses ahead of us and we passed them. They were standing tight up against the stone and he had put his cape around her.

"They're like us," I said.

"Nobody is like us," Catherine said. She did not mean it happily.

"I wish they had some place to go."

"It mightn't do them any good."

"I don't know. Everybody ought to have some place to go."

"They have the cathedral," Catherine said. We were past it now. We crossed the far end of the square and looked back at the cathedral. It was fine in the mist. We were standing in front of the leather goods shop. There were riding boots, a rucksack and ski boots in the window. Each article was set apart as an exhibit; the rucksack in the centre, the riding boots on one side and the ski boots on the other. The leather was dark and oiled smooth as a used saddle. The electric light made high lights on the dull oiled leather.

"We'll ski some time."

"In two months there will be ski-ing at Mürren," Catherine said.

"Let's go there."

"All right," she said. We went on past other windows and turned down a side street.

"I've never been this way."

"This is the way I go to the hospital," I said. It was a narrow street and we kept on the right-hand side. There were many people passing in the fog. There were shops and all the windows were lighted. We looked in a window at a pile of cheeses. I stopped in front of an armorer's shop.

"Come in a minute. I have to buy a gun."

"What sort of gun?"

"A pistol." We went in and I unbuttoned my belt and laid it with the empty holster on the counter. Two women were behind the counter. The women brought out several pistols.

"It must fit this," I said, opening the holster. It was a gray leather holster and I had bought it second-hand to wear in the town.

"Have they good pistols?" Catherine asked.

"They're all about the same. Can I try this one?" I asked the woman.

"I have no place now to shoot," she said. "But it is very good. You will not make a mistake with it."

I snapped it and pulled back the action. The spring was rather strong but it worked smoothly. I sighted it and snapped it again.

"It is used," the woman said. "It belonged to an officer who was an excellent shot."

"Did you sell it to him?"

"Yes."

"How did you get it back?"

"From his orderly."

"Maybe you have mine," I said. "How much is this?"

"Fifty lire. It is very cheap."

"All right. I want two extra clips and a box of cartridges."

She brought them from under the counter.

"Have you any need for a sword?" she asked. "I have some used vords very cheap."

"I'm going to the front," I said.

"Oh yes, then you won't need a sword," she said.

I paid for the cartridges and the pistol, filled the magazine and put it in place, put the pistol in my empty holster, filled the extra clips with cartridges and put them in the leather slots on the holster and then buckled on my belt. The pistol felt heavy on the belt. Still, I thought, it was better to have a regulation pistol. You could always get shells.

"Now we're fully armed," I said. "That was the one thing I had to remember to do. Some one got my other one going to the hospital."

"I hope it's a good pistol," Catherine said.

"Was there anything else?" the woman asked

"I don't believe so."

"The pistol has a lanyard," she said.

"So I noticed." The woman wanted to sell something else.

"You don't need a whistle?"

"I don't believe so."

The woman said good-by and we went out onto the sidewalk. Catherine looked in the window. The woman looked out and bowed to us.

"What are those little mirrors set in wood for?"

"They're for attracting birds. They twirl them out in the field and larks see them and come out and the Italians shoot them."

"They are an ingenious people," Catherine said. "You don't shoot larks do you, darling, in America?"

"Not especially."

We crossed the street and started to walk up the other side.

"I feel better now," Catherine said. "I felt terrible when we started."

"We always feel good when we're together."

"We always will be together."

"Yes, except that I'm going away at midnight."

"Don't think about it, darling."

We walked on up the street. The fog made the lights yellow.

"Aren't you tired?" Catherine asked.

"How about you?"

"I'm all right. It's fun to walk."

"But let's not do it too long."

"No."

We turned down a side street where there were no lights and walked in the street. I stopped and kissed Catherine. While I kissed her I felt her hand on my shoulder. She had pulled my cape around her so it covered both of us. We were standing in the street against a high wall.

"Let's go some place," I said.

"Good," said Catherine. We walked on along the street until it came out onto a wider street that was beside a canal. On the other side was a brick wall and buildings. Ahead, down the street, I saw a streetcar cross a bridge.

"We can get a cab up at the bridge," I said. We stood on the bridge in the fog waiting for a carriage. Several streetcars passed, full of people going home. Then a carriage came along but there was some one in it. The fog was turning to rain.

"We could walk or take a tram," Catherine said.

"One will be along," I said. "They go by here."

"Here one comes," she said.

The driver stopped his horse and lowered the metal sign on his meter. The top of the carriage was up and there were drops of water on the driver's coat. His varnished hat was shining in the wet. We sat back in the seat together and the top of the carriage made it dark.

"Where did you tell him to go?"

"To the station. There's a hotel across from the station where we can go."

"We can go the way we are? Without luggage?"

"Yes," I said.

It was a long ride to the station up side streets in the rain.

"Won't we have dinner?" Catherine asked. "I'm afraid I'll be hungry."

"We'll have it in our room."

"I haven't anything to wear. I haven't even a night-gown."

"We'll get one," I said and called to the driver.

"Go to the Via Manzoni and up that." He nodded and turned off to the left at the next corner. On the big street Catherine watched for a shop.

"Here's a place," she said. I stopped the driver and Catherine got out, walked across the sidewalk and went inside. I sat back in the carriage and waited for her. It was raining and I could smell the wet street and the horse steaming in the rain. She came back with a package and got in and we drove on.

"I was very extravagant, darling," she said, "but it's a fine night-gown."

At the hotel I asked Catherine to wait in the carriage while I went in and spoke to the manager. There were plenty of rooms. Then I went out to the carriage, paid the driver, and Catherine and I walked in together. The small boy in buttons carried the package. The manager bowed us toward the elevator. There was much red plush and brass. The manager went up in the elevator with us.

"Monsieur and Madame wish dinner in their rooms?"

"Yes. Will you have the menu brought up?" I said.

"You wish something special for dinner. Some game or a soufflé?"

The elevator passed three floors with a click each time, then clicked and stopped.

"What have you as game?"

"I could get a pheasant, or a woodcock."

"A woodcock," I said. We walked down the corridor. The carpet was worn. There were many doors. The manager stopped and unlocked a door and opened it.

"Here you are. A lovely room."

The small boy in buttons put the package on the table in the centre of the room. The manager opened the curtains.

"It is foggy outside," he said. The room was furnished in red plush. There were many mirrors, two chairs and a large bed with a satin coverlet. A door led to the bathroom.

"I will send up the menu," the manager said. He bowed and went out.

I went to the window and looked out, then pulled a cord that shut the thick plush curtains. Catherine was sitting on the bed, looking at the cut glass chandelier. She had taken her hat off and her hair shone under the light. She saw herself in one of the mirrors and put her hands to her hair. I saw her in three other mirrors. She did not look happy. She let her cape fall on the bed.

"What's the matter, darling?"

"I never felt like a whore before," she said. I went over to the window and pulled the curtain aside and looked out. I had not thought it would be like this.

"You're not a whore."

"I know it, darling. But it isn't nice to feel like one." Her voice was dry and flat.

"This was the best hotel we could get in," I said. I looked out the window. Across the square were the lights of the station. There were carriages going by on the street and I saw the trees in the park. The lights from the hotel shone on the wet pavement. Oh, hell, I thought, do we have to argue now?

"Come over here please," Catherine said. The flatness was all gone out of her voice. "Come over, please. I'm a good girl again." I looked over at the bed. She was smiling.

I went over and sat on the bed beside her and kissed her.

"You're my good girl."

"I'm certainly yours," she said.

After we had eaten we felt fine, and then after, we felt very happy and in a little time the room felt like our own home. My room at the hospital had been our own home and this room was our home too in the same way.

Catherine wore my tunic over her shoulders while we ate. We were very hungry and the meal was good and we drank a bottle of Capri and a bottle of St. Estephe. I drank most of it but Catherine drank some and it made her feel splendid. For dinner we had a woodcock with soufflé potatoes and purée de marron, a salad, and zabaione for dessert.

"It's a fine room," Catherine said. "It's a lovely room. We should have stayed here all the time we've been in Milan."

"It's a funny room. But it's nice."

"Vice is a wonderful thing," Catherine said. "The people who go in for it seem to have good taste about it. The red plush is really fine. It's just the thing. And the mirrors are very attractive."

"You're a lovely girl."

"I don't know how a room like this would be for waking up in the morning. But it's really a splendid room." I poured another glass of St. Estephe.

"I wish we could do something really sinful," Catherine said. "Everything we do seems so innocent and simple. I can't believe we do anything wrong."

"You're a grand girl."

"I only feel hungry. I get terribly hungry."

"You're a fine simple girl," I said.

"I am a simple girl. No one ever understood it except you."

"Once when I first met you I spent an afternoon thinking how we would go to the Hotel Cavour together and how it would be."

"That was awfully cheeky of you. This isn't the Cavour is it?"

"No. They wouldn't have taken us in there."

"They'll take us in some time. But that's how we differ, darling. I never thought about anything."

"Didn't you ever at all?"

"A little," she said.

"Oh you're a lovely girl."

I poured another glass of wine.

"I'm a very simple girl," Catherine said.

"I didn't think so at first. I thought you were a crazy girl."

"I was a little crazy. But I wasn't crazy in any complicated manner. I didn't confuse you did I, darling?"

"Wine is a grand thing," I said. "It makes you forget all the bad."

"It's lovely," said Catherine. "But it's given my father gout very badly."

"Have you a father?"

"Yes," said Catherine. "He has gout. You won't ever have to meet him. Haven't you a father?"

"No," I said. "A step-father."

"Will I like him?"

"You won't have to meet him."

"We have such a fine time," Catherine said. "I don't take any interest in anything else any more. I'm so very happy married to you."

The waiter came and took away the things. After a while we were very still and we could hear the rain. Down below on the street a motor car honked.

> " 'But at my back I always hear
> Time's wingèd chariot hurrying near,' "

I said.

"I know that poem," Catherine said. "It's by Marvell. But it's about a girl who wouldn't live with a man."

My head felt very clear and cold and I wanted to talk facts.

"Where will you have the baby?"

"I don't know. The best place I can find."

"How will you arrange it?"

"The best way I can. Don't worry, darling. We may have several babies before the war is over."

"It's nearly time to go."

"I know. You can make it time if you want."

"No."

"Then don't worry, darling. You were fine until now and now you're worrying."

"I won't. How often will you write?"

"Every day. Do they read your letters?"

"They can't read English enough to hurt any."

"I'll make them very confusing," Catherine said.

"But not too confusing."

"I'll just make them a little confusing."

"I'm afraid we have to start to go."

"All right, darling."

"I hate to leave our fine house."

"So do I."

"But we have to go."

"All right. But we're never settled in our home very long."

"We will be."

"I'll have a fine home for you when you come back."

"Maybe I'll be back right away."

"Perhaps you'll be hurt just a little in the foot."

"Or the lobe of the ear."

"No I want your ears the way they are."

"And not my feet?"

"Your feet have been hit already."

"We have to go, darling. Really."

"All right. You go first."

CHAPTER XXIV

We walked down the stairs instead of taking the elevator. The carpet on the stairs was worn. I had paid for the dinner when it came up and the waiter, who had brought it, was sitting on a chair near the door. He jumped up and bowed and I went with him into the side room and paid the bill for the room. The manager had remembered me as a friend and refused payment in advance but when he retired he had remembered to have the waiter stationed at the door so that I should not get out without paying. I suppose that had happened; even with his friends. One had so many friends in a war.

I asked the waiter to get us a carriage and he took Catherine's package that I was carrying and went out with an umbrella. Outside through the window we saw him crossing the street in the rain. We stood in the side room and looked out the window.

"How do you feel, Cat?"

"Sleepy."

"I feel hollow and hungry."

"Have you anything to eat?"

"Yes, in my musette."

I saw the carriage coming. It stopped, the horse's head hanging in the rain, and the waiter stepped out, opened his umbrella, and came toward the hotel. We met him at the door and walked out under the umbrella down the wet walk to the carriage at the curb. Water was running in the gutter.

"There is your package on the seat," the waiter said. He stood with the umbrella until we were in and I had tipped him.

"Many thanks. Pleasant journey," he said. The coachman lifted the reins and the horse started. The waiter turned away under the umbrella and went toward the hotel. We drove down the street and turned to the left, then came around to the right in front of the station. There were two carabinieri standing under the light just out of the rain. The light shone on their hats. The rain was clear and transparent against the light from the station. A porter came out from under the shelter of the station, his shoulders up against the rain.

"No," I said. "Thanks. I don't need thee."

He went back under the shelter of the archway. I turned to Catherine. Her face was in the shadow from the hood of the carriage.

"We might as well say good-by."

"I can't go in?"

"No."

"Good-by, Cat."

"Will you tell him the hospital?"

"Yes."

I told the driver the address to drive to. He nodded.

"Good-by," I said. "Take good care of yourself and young Catherine."

"Good-by, darling."

"Good-by," I said. I stepped out into the rain and the carriage started. Catherine leaned out and I saw her face in the light. She

smiled and waved. The carriage went up the street, Catherine
pointed in toward the archway. I looked, there were only the two
carabinieri and the archway. I realized she meant for me to get in
out of the rain. I went in and stood and watched the carriage turn
the corner. Then I started through the station and down the runway to the train.

The porter was on the platform looking for me. I followed him
into the train, crowding past people and along the aisle and in
through a door to where the machine-gunner sat in the corner of a
full compartment. My rucksack and musettes were above his head
on the luggage rack. There were many men standing in the corridor and the men in the compartment all looked at us when we
came in. There were not enough places in the train and every one
was hostile. The machine-gunner stood up for me to sit down.
Some one tapped me on the shoulder. I looked around. It was a
very tall gaunt captain of artillery with a red scar along his jaw. He
had looked through the glass on the corridor and then come in.

"What do you say?" I asked. I had turned and faced him. He was
taller than I and his face was very thin under the shadow of his
cap-visor and the scar was new and shiny. Every one in the compartment was looking at me.

"You can't do that," he said. "You can't have a soldier save you a
place."

"I have done it."

He swallowed and I saw his Adam's apple go up and then down.
The machine-gunner stood in front of the place. Other men looked
in through the glass. No one in the compartment said anything.

"You have no right to do that. I was here two hours before you
came."

"What do you want?"

"The seat."

"So do I."

I watched his face and could feel the whole compartment against me. I did not blame them. He was in the right. But I wanted the seat. Still no one said anything.

Oh, hell, I thought.

"Sit down, Signor Capitano," I said. The machine-gunner moved out of the way and the tall captain sat down. He looked at me. His face seemed hurt. But he had the seat. "Get my things," I said to the machine-gunner. We went out in the corridor. The train was full and I knew there was no chance of a place. I gave the porter and the machine-gunner ten lire apiece. They went down the corridor and outside on the platform looking in the windows but there were no places.

"Maybe some will get off at Brescia," the porter said.

"More will get on at Brescia," said the machine-gunner. I said good-by to them and we shook hands and they left. They both felt badly. Inside the train we were all standing in the corridor when the train started. I watched the lights of the station and the yards as we went out. It was still raining and soon the windows were wet and you could not see out. Later I slept on the floor of the corridor; first putting my pocket-book with my money and papers in it inside my shirt and trousers so that it was inside the leg of my breeches. I slept all night, waking at Brescia and Verona when more men got on the train, but going back to sleep at once. I had my head on one of the musettes and my arms around the other and I could feel the pack and they could all walk over me if they wouldn't step on me. Men were sleeping on the floor all down the corridor. Others stood holding on to the window rods or leaning against the doors. That train was always crowded.

BOOK THREE

CHAPTER XXV

Now in the fall the trees were all bare and the roads were muddy. I rode to Gorizia from Udine on a camion. We passed other camions on the road and I looked at the country. The mulberry trees were bare and the fields were brown. There were wet dead leaves on the road from the rows of bare trees and men were working on the road, tamping stone in the ruts from piles of crushed stone along the side of the road between the trees. We saw the town with a mist over it that cut off the mountains. We crossed the river and I saw that it was running high. It had been raining in the mountains. We came into the town past the factories and then the houses and villas and I saw that many more houses had been hit. On a narrow street we passed a British Red Cross ambulance. The driver wore a cap and his face was thin and very tanned. I did not know him. I got down from the camion in the big square in front of the Town Major's house, the driver handed down my rucksack and I put it on and swung on the two musettes and walked to our villa. It did not feel like a homecoming.

I walked down the damp gravel driveway looking at the villa

through the trees. The windows were all shut but the door was open. I went in and found the major sitting at a table in the bare room with maps and typed sheets of paper on the wall.

"Hello," he said. "How are you?" He looked older and drier.

"I'm good," I said. "How is everything?"

"It's all over," he said. "Take off your kit and sit down." I put my pack and the two musettes on the floor and my cap on the pack. I brought the other chair over from the wall and sat down by the desk.

"It's been a bad summer," the major said. "Are you strong now?"

"Yes."

"Did you ever get the decorations?"

"Yes. I got them fine. Thank you very much."

"Let's see them."

I opened my cape so he could see the two ribbons.

"Did you get the boxes with the medals?"

"No. Just the papers."

"The boxes will come later. That takes more time."

"What do you want me to do?"

"The cars are all away. There are six up north at Caporetto. You know Caporetto?"

"Yes," I said. I remembered it as a little white town with a campanile in a valley. It was a clean little town and there was a fine fountain in the square.

"They are working from there. There are many sick now. The fighting is over."

"Where are the others?"

"There are two up in the mountains and four still on the Bainsizza. The other two ambulance sections are in the Carso with the third army."

"What do you wish me to do?"

"You can go and take over the four cars on the Bainsizza if you like. Gino has been up there a long time. You haven't seen it up there, have you?"

"No."

"It was very bad. We lost three cars."

"I heard about it."

"Yes, Rinaldi wrote you."

"Where is Rinaldi?"

"He is here at the hospital. He has had a summer and fall of it."

"I believe it."

"It has been bad," the major said. "You couldn't believe how bad it's been. I've often thought you were lucky to be hit when you were."

"I know I was."

"Next year will be worse," the major said. "Perhaps they will attack now. They say they are to attack but I can't believe it. It is too late. You saw the river?"

"Yes. It's high already."

"I don't believe they will attack now that the rains have started. We will have the snow soon. What about your countrymen? Will there be other Americans besides yourself?"

"They are training an army of ten million."

"I hope we get some of them. But the French will hog them all. We'll never get any down here. All right. You stay here to-night and go out to-morrow with the little car and send Gino back. I'll send somebody with you that knows the road. Gino will tell you everything. They are shelling quite a little still but it is all over. You will want to see the Bainsizza."

"I'm glad to see it. I am glad to be back with you again, Signor Maggiore."

He smiled. "You are very good to say so. I am very tired of this war. If I was away I do not believe I would come back."

"Is it so bad?"

"Yes. It is so bad and worse. Go get cleaned up and find your friend Rinaldi."

I went out and carried my bags up the stairs. Rinaldi was not in the room but his things were there and I sat down on the bed and unwrapped my puttees and took the shoe off my right foot. Then I lay back on the bed. I was tired and my right foot hurt. It seemed silly to lie on the bed with one shoe off, so I sat up and unlaced the other shoe and dropped it on the floor, then lay back on the blanket again. The room was stuffy with the window closed but I was too tired to get up and open it. I saw my things were all in one corner of the room. Outside it was getting dark. I lay on the bed and thought about Catherine and waited for Rinaldi. I was going to try not to think about Catherine except at night before I went to sleep. But now I was tired and there was nothing to do, so I lay and thought about her. I was thinking about her when Rinaldi came in. He looked just the same. Perhaps he was a little thinner.

"Well, baby," he said. I sat up on the bed. He came over, sat down and put his arm around me. "Good old baby." He whacked me on the back and I held both his arms.

"Old baby," he said. "Let me see your knee."

"I'll have to take off my pants."

"Take off your pants, baby. We're all friends here. I want to see what kind of a job they did." I stood up, took off the breeches and pulled off the knee-brace. Rinaldi sat on the floor and bent the knee gently back and forth. He ran his finger along the scar; put his thumbs together over the kneecap and rocked the knee gently with his fingers.

"Is that all the articulation you have?"

"Yes."

"It's a crime to send you back. They ought to get complete articulation."

"It's a lot better than it was. It was stiff as a board."

Rinaldi bent it more. I watched his hands. He had fine surgeon's hands. I looked at the top of his head, his hair shiny and parted smoothly. He bent the knee too far.

"Ouch!" I said.

"You ought to have more treatment on it with the machines," Rinaldi said.

"It's better than it was."

"I see that, baby. This is something I know more about than you." He stood up and sat down on the bed. "The knee itself is a good job." He was through with the knee. "Tell me all about everything."

"There's nothing to tell," I said. "I've led a quiet life."

"You act like a married man," he said. "What's the matter with you?"

"Nothing," I said. "What's the matter with you?"

"This war is killing me," Rinaldi said, "I am very depressed by it." He folded his hands over his knee.

"Oh," I said.

"What's the matter? Can't I even have human impulses?"

"No. I can see you've been having a fine time. Tell me."

"All summer and all fall I've operated. I work all the time. I do everybody's work. All the hard ones they leave to me. By God, baby, I am becoming a lovely surgeon."

"That sounds better."

"I never think. No, by God, I don't think; I operate."

"That's right."

"But now, baby, it's all over. I don't operate now and I feel like hell. This is a terrible war, baby. You believe me when I say it. Now you cheer me up. Did you bring the phonograph records?"

"Yes."

They were wrapped in paper in a cardboard box in my rucksack. I was too tired to get them out.

"Don't you feel good yourself, baby?"

"I feel like hell."

"This war is terrible," Rinaldi said. "Come on. We'll both get drunk and be cheerful. Then we'll go get the ashes dragged. Then we'll feel fine."

"I've had the jaundice," I said, "and I can't get drunk."

"Oh, baby, how you've come back to me. You come back serious and with a liver. I tell you this war is a bad thing. Why did we make it anyway."

"We'll have a drink. I don't want to get drunk but we'll have a drink."

Rinaldi went across the room to the washstand and brought back two glasses and a bottle of cognac.

"It's Austrian cognac," he said. "Seven stars. It's all they captured on San Gabriele."

"Were you up there?"

"No. I haven't been anywhere. I've been here all the time operating. Look, baby, this is your old tooth-brushing glass. I kept it all the time to remind me of you."

"To remind you to brush your teeth."

"No. I have my own too. I kept this to remind me of you trying to brush away the Villa Rossa from your teeth in the morning, swearing and eating aspirin and cursing harlots. Every time I see that glass I think of you trying to clean your conscience with a toothbrush." He came over to the bed. "Kiss me once and tell me you're not serious."

"I never kiss you. You're an ape."

"I know, you are the fine good Anglo-Saxon boy. I know. You are the remorse boy, I know. I will wait till I see the Anglo-Saxon brushing away harlotry with a toothbrush."

"Put some cognac in the glass."

We touched glasses and drank. Rinaldi laughed at me.

"I will get you drunk and take out your liver and put you in a good Italian liver and make you a man again."

I held the glass for some more cognac. It was dark outside now.

Holding the glass of cognac, I went over and opened the window. The rain had stopped falling. It was colder outside and there was a mist in the trees.

"Don't throw the cognac out the window," Rinaldi said. "If you can't drink it give it to me."

"Go something yourself," I said. I was glad to see Rinaldi again. He had spent two years teasing me and I had always liked it. We understood each other very well.

"Are you married?" he asked from the bed. I was standing against the wall by the window.

"Not yet."

"Are you in love?"

"Yes."

"With that English girl?"

"Yes."

"Poor baby. Is she good to you?"

"Of course."

"I mean is she good to you practically speaking?"

"Shut up."

"I will. You will see I am a man of extreme delicacy. Does she——?"

"Rinin," I said. "Please shut up. If you want to be my friend, shut up."

"I don't *want* to be your friend, baby. I *am* your friend."

"Then shut up."

"All right."

I went over to the bed and sat down beside Rinaldi. He was holding his glass and looking at the floor.

"You see how it is, Rinin?"

"Oh, yes. All my life I encounter sacred subjects. But very few with you. I suppose you must have them too." He looked at the floor.

"You haven't any?"

"No."

"Not any?"

"No."

"I can say this about your mother and that about your sister?"

"And that about *your sister*," Rinaldi said swiftly. We both laughed.

"The old superman," I said.

"I am jealous maybe," Rinaldi said.

"No, you're not."

"I don't mean like that. I mean something else. Have you any married friends?"

"Yes," I said.

"I haven't," Rinaldi said. "Not if they love each other."

"Why not?"

"They don't like me."

"Why not?"

"I am the snake. I am the snake of reason."

"You're getting it mixed. The apple was reason."

"No, it was the snake." He was more cheerful.

"You are better when you don't think so deeply," I said.

"I love you, baby," he said. "You puncture me when I become a great Italian thinker. But I know many things I can't say. I know more than you."

"Yes. You do."

"But you will have a better time. Even with remorse you will have a better time."

"I don't think so."

"Oh, yes. That is true. Already I am only happy when I am working." He looked at the floor again.

"You'll get over that."

"No. I only like two other things; one is bad for my work and the other is over in half an hour or fifteen minutes. Sometimes less."

"Sometimes a good deal less."

"Perhaps I have improved, baby. You do not know. But there are only the two things and my work."

"You'll get other things."

"No. We never get anything. We are born with all we have and we never learn. We never get anything new. We all start complete. You should be glad not to be a Latin."

"There's no such thing as a Latin. That is 'Latin' thinking. You are so proud of your defects." Rinaldi looked up and laughed.

"We'll stop, baby. I am tired from thinking so much." He had looked tired when he came in. "It's nearly time to eat. I'm glad you're back. You are my best friend and my war brother."

"When do the war brothers eat?" I asked.

"Right away. We'll drink once more for your liver's sake."

"Like Saint Paul."

"You are inaccurate. That was wine and the stomach. Take a little wine for your stomach's sake."

"Whatever you have in the bottle," I said. "For any sake you mention."

"To your girl," Rinaldi said. He held out his glass.

"All right."

"I'll never say a dirty thing about her."

"Don't strain yourself."

He drank off the cognac. "I am pure," he said. "I am like you, baby. I will get an English girl too. As a matter of fact I knew your girl first but she was a little tall for me. A tall girl for a sister," he quoted.

"You have a lovely pure mind," I said.

"Haven't I? That's why they call me Rinaldo Purissimo."

"Rinaldo Sporchissimo."

"Come on, baby, we'll go down to eat while my mind is still pure."

I washed, combed my hair and we went down the stairs. Rinaldi was a little drunk. In the room where we ate, the meal was not quite ready.

"I'll go get the bottle," Rinaldi said. He went off up the stairs. I sat at the table and he came back with the bottle and poured us each a half tumbler of cognac.

"Too much," I said and held up the glass and sighted at the lamp on the table.

"Not for an empty stomach. It is a wonderful thing. It burns out the stomach completely. Nothing is worse for you."

"All right."

"Self-destruction day by day," Rinaldi said. "It ruins the stomach and makes the hand shake. Just the thing for a surgeon."

"You recommend it?"

"Heartily. I use no other. Drink it down, baby, and look forward to being sick."

I drank half the glass. In the hall I could hear the orderly calling. "Soup! Soup is ready!"

The major came in, nodded to us and sat down. He seemed very small at table.

"Is this all we are?" he asked. The orderly put the soup bowl down and he ladled out a plate full.

"We are all," Rinaldi said. "Unless the priest comes. If he knew Federico was here he would be here."

"Where is he?" I asked.

"He's at 307," the major said. He was busy with his soup. He wiped his mouth, wiping his upturned gray mustache carefully. "He will come I think. I called them and left word to tell him you were here."

"I miss the noise of the mess," I said.

"Yes, it's quiet," the major said.

"I will be noisy," said Rinaldi.

"Drink some wine, Enrico," said the major. He filled my glass. The spaghetti came in and we were all busy. We were finishing the

spaghetti when the priest came in. He was the same as ever, small
and brown and compact looking. I stood up and we shook hands.
He put his hand on my shoulder.

"I came as soon as I heard," he said.

"Sit down," the major said. "You're late."

"Good-evening, priest," Rinaldi said, using the English word.
They had taken that up from the priest-baiting captain, who
spoke a little English. "Good-evening, Rinaldo," the priest said.
The orderly brought him soup but he said he would start with the
spaghetti.

"How are you?" he asked me.

"Fine," I said. "How have things been?"

"Drink some wine, priest," Rinaldi said. "Take a little wine for
your stomach's sake. That's Saint Paul, you know."

"Yes I know," said the priest politely. Rinaldi filled his glass.

"That Saint Paul," said Rinaldi. "He's the one who makes all
the trouble." The priest looked at me and smiled. I could see that
the baiting did not touch him now.

"That Saint Paul," Rinaldi said. "He was a rounder and a
chaser and then when he was no longer hot he said it was no good.
When he was finished he made the rules for us who are still hot.
Isn't it true, Federico?"

The major smiled. We were eating meat stew now.

"I never discuss a Saint after dark," I said. The priest looked up
from the stew and smiled at me.

"There he is, gone over with the priest," Rinaldi said. "Where
are all the good old priest-baiters? Where is Cavalcanti? Where is
Brundi? Where is Cesare? Do I have to bait this priest alone without support?"

"He is a good priest," said the major.

"He is a good priest," said Rinaldi. "But still a priest. I try to
make the mess like the old days. I want to make Federico happy.
To hell with you, priest!"

I saw the major look at him and notice that he was drunk. His thin face was white. The line of his hair was very black against the white of his forehead.

"It's all right, Rinaldo," said the priest. "It's all right."

"To hell with you," said Rinaldi. "To hell with the whole damn business." He sat back in his chair.

"He's been under a strain and he's tired," the major said to me. He finished his meat and wiped up the gravy with a piece of bread.

"I don't give a damn," Rinaldi said to the table. "To hell with the whole business." He looked defiantly around the table, his eyes flat, his face pale.

"All right," I said. "To hell with the whole damn business."

"No, no," said Rinaldi. "You can't do it. You can't do it. I say you can't do it. You're dry and you're empty and there's nothing else. There's nothing else I tell you. Not a damned thing. I know, when I stop working."

The priest shook his head. The orderly took away the stew dish.

"What are you eating meat for?" Rinaldi turned to the priest. "Don't you know it's Friday?"

"It's Thursday," the priest said.

"It's a lie. It's Friday. You're eating the body of our Lord. It's God-meat. I know. It's dead Austrian. That's what you're eating."

"The white meat is from officers," I said, completing the old joke.

Rinaldi laughed. He filled his glass.

"Don't mind me," he said. "I'm just a little crazy."

"You ought to have a leave," the priest said.

The major shook his head at him. Rinaldi looked at the priest.

"You think I ought to have a leave?"

The major shook his head at the priest. Rinaldi was looking at the priest.

"Just as you like," the priest said. "Not if you don't want."

"To hell with you," Rinaldi said. "They try to get rid of me. Every night they try to get rid of me. I fight them off. What if I have it. Everybody has it. The whole world's got it. First," he went on, assuming the manner of a lecturer, "it's a little pimple. Then we notice a rash between the shoulders. Then we notice nothing at all. We put our faith in mercury."

"Or salvarsan," the major interrupted quietly.

"A mercurial product," Rinaldi said. He acted very elated now. "I know something worth two of that. Good old priest," he said. "You'll never get it. Baby will get it. It's an industrial accident. It's a simple industrial accident."

The orderly brought in the sweet and coffee. The dessert was a sort of black bread pudding with hard sauce. The lamp was smoking; the black smoke going close up inside the chimney.

"Bring two candles and take away the lamp," the major said. The orderly brought two lighted candles each in a saucer, and took out the lamp blowing it out. Rinaldi was quiet now. He seemed all right. We talked and after the coffee we all went out into the hall.

"You want to talk to the priest. I have to go in the town," Rinaldi said. "Good-night, priest."

"Good-night, Rinaldo," the priest said.

"I'll see you, Fredi," Rinaldi said.

"Yes," I said. "Come in early." He made a face and went out the door. The major was standing with us. "He's very tired and overworked," he said. "He thinks too he has syphilis. I don't believe it but he may have. He is treating himself for it. Good-night. You will leave before daylight, Enrico?"

"Yes."

"Good-by then," he said. "Good luck. Peduzzi will wake you and go with you."

"Good-by, Signor Maggiore."

"Good-by. They talk about an Austrian offensive but I don't believe it. I hope not. But anyway it won't be here. Gino will tell you everything. The telephone works well now."

"I'll call regularly."

"Please do. Good-night. Don't let Rinaldi drink so much brandy."

"I'll try not to."

"Good-night, priest."

"Good-night, Signor Maggiore."

He went off into his office.

CHAPTER XXVI

I went to the door and looked out. It had stopped raining but there was a mist.

"Should we go upstairs?" I asked the priest.

"I can only stay a little while."

"Come on up."

We climbed the stairs and went into my room. I lay down on Rinaldi's bed. The priest sat on my cot that the orderly had set up. It was dark in the room.

"Well," he said, "how are you really?"

"I'm all right. I'm tired to-night."

"I'm tired too, but from no cause."

"What about the war?"

"I think it will be over soon. I don't know why, but I feel it."

"How do you feel it?"

"You know how your major is? Gentle? Many people are like that now."

"I feel that way myself," I said.

"It has been a terrible summer," said the priest. He was surer of himself now than when I had gone away. "You cannot believe how it has been. Except that you have been there and you know how it can be. Many people have realized the war this summer. Officers whom I thought could never realize it realize it now."

"What will happen?" I stroked the blanket with my hand.

"I do not know but I do not think it can go on much longer."

"What will happen?"

"They will stop fighting."

"Who?"

"Both sides."

"I hope so," I said.

"You don't believe it?"

"I don't believe both sides will stop fighting at once."

"I suppose not. It is too much to expect. But when I see the changes in men I do not think it can go on."

"Who won the fighting this summer?"

"No one."

"The Austrians won," I said. "They kept them from taking San Gabriele. They've won. They won't stop fighting."

"If they feel as we feel they may stop. They have gone through the same thing."

"No one ever stopped when they were winning."

"You discourage me."

"I can only say what I think."

"Then you think it will go on and on? Nothing will ever happen?"

"I don't know. I only think the Austrians will not stop when they have won a victory. It is in defeat that we become Christian."

"The Austrians are Christians—except for the Bosnians."

"I don't mean technically Christian. I mean like Our Lord."

He said nothing.

"We are all gentler now because we are beaten. How would Our Lord have been if Peter had rescued him in the Garden?"

"He would have been just the same."

"I don't think so," I said.

"You discourage me," he said. "I believe and I pray that something will happen. I have felt it very close."

"Something may happen," I said. "But it will happen only to us. If they felt the way we do, it would be all right. But they have beaten us. They feel another way."

"Many of the soldiers have always felt this way. It is not because they were beaten."

"They were beaten to start with. They were beaten when they took them from their farms and put them in the army. That is why the peasant has wisdom, because he is defeated from the start. Put him in power and see how wise he is."

He did not say anything. He was thinking.

"Now I am depressed myself," I said. "That's why I never think about these things. I never think and yet when I begin to talk I say the things I have found out in my mind without thinking."

"I had hoped for something."

"Defeat?"

"No. Something more."

"There isn't anything more. Except victory. It may be worse."

"I hoped for a long time for victory."

"Me too."

"Now I don't know."

"It has to be one or the other."

"I don't believe in victory any more."

"I don't. But I don't believe in defeat. Though it may be better."

"What do you believe in?"

"In sleep," I said. He stood up.

"I am very sorry to have stayed so long. But I like so to talk with you."

"It is very nice to talk again. I said that about sleeping, meaning nothing."

We stood up and shook hands in the dark.

"I sleep at 307 now," he said.

"I go out on post early to-morrow."

"I'll see you when you come back."

"We'll have a walk and talk together." I walked with him to the door.

"Don't go down," he said. "It is very nice that you are back. Though not so nice for you." He put his hand on my shoulder.

"It's all right for me," I said. "Good-night."

"Good-night. Ciaou!"

"Ciaou!" I said. I was deadly sleepy.

CHAPTER XXVII

I woke when Rinaldi came in but he did not talk and I went back to sleep again. In the morning I was dressed and gone before it was light. Rinaldi did not wake when I left.

I had not seen the Bainsizza before and it was strange to go up the slope where the Austrians had been, beyond the place on the river where I had been wounded. There was a steep new road and many trucks. Beyond, the road flattened out and I saw woods and steep hills in the mist. There were woods that had been taken quickly and not smashed. Then beyond where the road was not protected by the hills it was screened by matting on the sides and over the top. The road ended in a wrecked village. The lines were up beyond. There was much artillery around. The houses were badly smashed but things were very well organized and there were signboards everywhere. We found Gino and he got us some coffee and later I went with him and met various people and saw the posts. Gino said the British cars were working further down the Bainsizza at Ravne. He had great admiration for the British. There was still a certain amount of shelling, he said, but not many wounded. There would be many sick now the rains had started. The Austrians were supposed to attack but he did not believe it. We were supposed to attack too, but they had not brought up any new troops so he thought that was off too. Food was scarce and he would be glad to get a full meal in Gorizia. What kind of supper had I had? I told him and he said that would be wonderful. He was especially impressed by the *dolce*. I did not describe it in detail, only said it was a *dolce,* and I think he believed it was something more elaborate than bread pudding.

Did I know where he was going to go? I said I didn't but that some of the other cars were at Caporetto. He hoped he would go up that way. It was a nice little place and he liked the high mountain hauling up beyond. He was a nice boy and every one seemed to like him. He said where it really had been hell was at San Gabriele and the attack beyond Lom that had gone bad. He said the Austrians had a great amount of artillery in the woods along Ternova ridge beyond and above us, and shelled the roads badly at night. There was a battery of naval guns that had gotten on his nerves. I would recognize them because of their flat trajectory. You heard the report and then the shriek commenced almost instantly. They usually fired two guns at once, one right after the other, and the fragments from the burst were enormous. He showed me one, a smoothly jagged piece of metal over a foot long. It looked like babbitting metal.

"I don't suppose they are so effective," Gino said. "But they scare me. They all sound as though they came directly for you. There is the boom, then instantly the shriek and burst. What's the use of not being wounded if they scare you to death?"

He said there were Croats in the lines opposite us now and some Magyars. Our troops were still in the attacking positions. There was no wire to speak of and no place to fall back to if there should be an Austrian attack. There were fine positions for defense along the low mountains that came up out of the plateau but nothing had been done about organizing them for defense. What did I think about the Bainsizza anyway?

I had expected it to be flatter, more like a plateau. I had not realized it was so broken up.

"Alto piano," Gino said, "but no piano."

We went back to the cellar of the house where he lived. I said I thought a ridge that flattened out on top and had a little depth would be easier and more practical to hold than a succession of small mountains. It was no harder to attack up a mountain than on the level, I argued. "That depends on the mountains," he said. "Look at San Gabriele."

"Yes," I said, "but where they had trouble was at the top where it was flat. They got up to the top easy enough."

"Not so easy," he said.

"Yes," I said, "but that was a special case because it was a fortress rather than a mountain, anyway. The Austrians had been fortifying it for years." I meant tactically speaking in a war where there was some movement a succession of mountains were nothing to hold as a line because it was too easy to turn them. You should have possible mobility and a mountain is not very mobile. Also, people always over-shoot downhill. If the flank were turned, the best men would be left on the highest mountains. I did not believe in a war in mountains. I had thought about it a lot, I said. You pinched off one mountain and they pinched off another but when something really started every one had to get down off the mountains.

What were you going to do if you had a mountain frontier? he asked.

I had not worked that out yet, I said, and we both laughed. "But," I said, "in the old days the Austrians were always whipped in the quadrilateral around Verona. They let them come down onto the plain and whipped them there."

"Yes," said Gino. "But those were Frenchmen and you can work out military problems clearly when you are fighting in somebody else's country."

"Yes," I agreed, "when it is your own country you cannot use it so scientifically."

"The Russians did, to trap Napoleon."

"Yes, but they had plenty of country. If you tried to retreat to trap Napoleon in Italy you would find yourself in Brindisi."

"A terrible place," said Gino. "Have you ever been there?"

"Not to stay."

"I am a patriot," Gino said. "But I cannot love Brindisi or Taranto."

"Do you love the Bainsizza?" I asked.

"The soil is sacred," he said. "But I wish it grew more potatoes. You know when we came here we found fields of potatoes the Austrians had planted."

"Has the food really been short?"

"I myself have never had enough to eat but I am a big eater and I have not starved. The mess is average. The regiments in the line get pretty good food but those in support don't get so much. Something is wrong somewhere. There should be plenty of food."

"The dogfish are selling it somewhere else."

"Yes, they give the battalions in the front line as much as they can but the ones in back are very short. They have eaten all the Austrians' potatoes and chestnuts from the woods. They ought to feed them better. We are big eaters. I am sure there is plenty of food. It is very bad for the soldiers to be short of food. Have you ever noticed the difference it makes in the way you think?"

"Yes," I said. "It can't win a war but it can lose one."

"We won't talk about losing. There is enough talk about losing. What has been done this summer cannot have been done in vain."

I did not say anything. I was always embarrassed by the words sacred, glorious, and sacrifice and the expression in vain. We had heard them, sometimes standing in the rain almost out of earshot, so that only the shouted words came through, and had read them, on proclamations that were slapped up by billposters over other proclamations, now for a long time, and I had seen nothing sacred, and the things that were glorious had no glory and the sacrifices were like the stockyards at Chicago if nothing was done with the meat except to bury it. There were many words that you could not stand to hear and finally only the names of places had dignity. Certain numbers were the same way and certain dates and these with the names of the places were all you could say and have them mean anything. Abstract words such as glory, honor, courage, or hallow were obscene beside the concrete names of villages, the numbers of roads, the names of rivers, the numbers of regiments and the dates. Gino was a patriot, so he said things that separated us sometimes, but he was also a fine boy and I understood his being a patriot. He was born one. He left with Peduzzi in the car to go back to Gorizia.

It stormed all that day. The wind drove down the rain and everywhere there was standing water and mud. The plaster of the broken houses was gray and wet. Late in the afternoon the rain stopped and from out number two post I saw the bare wet autumn country with clouds over the tops of the hills and the straw screening over the roads wet and dripping. The sun came out once before it went down and shone on the bare woods beyond the ridge. There were many Austrian guns in the woods on that ridge but only a few fired. I watched the sudden round puffs of shrapnel smoke in the sky above a broken farmhouse near where the line was; soft puffs with a yellow white flash in the centre. You saw the flash, then heard the crack, then saw the smoke ball distort and thin in the wind. There were many iron shrapnel balls in the rubble of the houses and on the road beside the broken house where the post was, but they did not shell near the post that afternoon. We loaded two cars and drove down the road that was screened with wet mats and the last of the sun came through in the breaks between the strips of mattings. Before we were out on the clear road behind the hill the sun was down. We went on down the clear road and as it turned a corner into the open and went into the square arched tunnel of matting the rain started again.

The wind rose in the night and at three o'clock in the morning with the rain coming in sheets there was a bombardment and the Croatians came over across the mountain meadows and through patches of woods and into the front line. They fought in the dark in the rain and a counter-attack of scared men from the second line drove them back. There was much shelling and many rockets in the rain and machine-gun and rifle fire all along the line. They did not come again and it was quieter and between the gusts of wind and rain we could hear the sound of a great bombardment far to the north.

The wounded were coming into the post, some were carried on stretchers, some walking and some were brought on the backs of men that came across the field. They were wet to the skin and all were scared. We filled two cars with stretcher cases as they came up from the cellar of the post and as I shut the door of the second car and fastened it I felt the rain on my face turn to snow. The flakes were coming heavy and fast in the rain.

When daylight came the storm was still blowing but the snow had stopped. It had melted as it fell on the wet ground and now it was raining again. There was another attack just after daylight but it was unsuccessful. We expected an attack all day but it did not come until the sun was going down. The bombardment started to the south below the long wooded ridge where the Austrian guns were concentrated. We expected a bombardment but it did not come. It was getting dark. Guns were firing from the field behind the village and the shells, going away, had a comfortable sound.

We heard that the attack to the south had been unsuccessful. They did not attack that night but we heard that they had broken through to the north. In the night word came that we were to prepare to retreat. The captain at the post told me this. He had it from the Brigade. A little while later he came from the telephone and said it was a lie. The Brigade had received orders that the line of the Bainsizza should be held no matter what happened. I asked about the break through and he said that he had heard at the Brigade that the Austrians had broken through the twenty-seventh army corps up toward Caporetto. There had been a great battle in the north all day.

"If those bastards let them through we are cooked," he said.

"It's Germans that are attacking," one of the medical officers said. The word Germans was something to be frightened of. We did not want to have anything to do with the Germans.

"There are fifteen divisions of Germans," the medical officer said. "They have broken through and we will be cut off."

"At the Brigade, they say this line is to be held. They say they have not broken through badly and that we will hold a line across the mountains from Monte Maggiore."

"Where do they hear this?"

"From the Division."

"The word that we were to retreat came from the Division."

"We work under the Army Corps," I said. "But here I work under you. Naturally when you tell me to go I will go. But get the orders straight."

"The orders are that we stay here. You clear the wounded from here to the clearing station."

"Sometimes we clear from the clearing station to the field hospitals too," I said. "Tell me, I have never seen a retreat—if there is a retreat how are all the wounded evacuated?"

"They are not. They take as many as they can and leave the rest."

"What will I take in the cars?"

"Hospital equipment."

"All right," I said.

The next night the retreat started. We heard that Germans and Austrians had broken through in the north and were coming down the mountain valleys toward Cividale and Udine. The retreat was orderly, wet and sullen. In the night, going slowly along the crowded roads we passed troops marching under the rain, guns, horses pulling wagons, mules, motor trucks, all moving away from the front. There was no more disorder than in an advance.

That night we helped empty the field hospitals that had been set up in the least ruined villages of the plateau, taking the wounded down to Plava on the river-bed: and the next day hauled all day in the rain to evacuate the hospitals and clearing station at Plava. It rained steadily and the army of the Bainsizza moved down off the plateau in the October rain and across the river where the great victories had commenced in the spring of that year. We came into Gorizia in the middle of the next day. The rain had stopped and the town was nearly empty. As we came up the street they were loading the girls from the soldiers' whorehouse into a truck. There were seven girls and they had on their hats and coats and carried small suitcases. Two of them were crying. Of the others one smiled at us and put out her tongue and fluttered it up and down. She had thick full lips and black eyes.

I stopped the car and went over and spoke to the matron. The girls from the officers' house had left early that morning, she said. Where were they going? To Conegliano, she said. The truck started. The girl with thick lips put out her tongue again at us. The matron waved. The two girls kept on crying. The others looked interestedly out at the town. I got back in the car.

"We ought to go with them," Bonello said. "That would be a good trip."

"We'll have a good trip," I said.

"We'll have a hell of a trip."

"That's what I mean," I said. We came up the drive to the villa.

"I'd like to be there when some of those tough babies climb in and try and hop them."

"You think they will?"

"Sure. Everybody in the Second Army knows that matron."

We were outside the villa.

"They call her the Mother Superior," Bonello said. "The girls are new but everybody knows her. They must have brought them up just before the retreat."

"They'll have a time."

"I'll say they'll have a time. I'd like to have a crack at them for nothing. They charge too much at that house anyway. The government gyps us."

"Take the car out and have the mechanics go over it," I said. "Change the oil and check the differential. Fill it up and then get some sleep."

"Yes, Signor Tenente."

The villa was empty. Rinaldi was gone with the hospital. The major was gone taking hospital personnel in the staff car. There was a note on the window for me to fill the cars with the material piled in the hall and to proceed to Pordenone. The mechanics were gone already. I went out back to the garage. The other two cars came in while I was there and their drivers got down. It was starting to rain again.

"I'm so —— sleepy I went to sleep three times coming here from Plava," Piani said. "What are we going to do, Tenente?"

"We'll change the oil, grease them, fill them up, then take them around in front and load up the junk they've left."

"Then do we start?"

"No, we'll sleep for three hours."

"Christ I'm glad to sleep," Bonello said. "I couldn't keep awake driving."

"How's your car, Aymo?" I asked.

"It's all right."

"Get me a monkey suit and I'll help you with the oil."

"Don't you do that, Tenente," Aymo said. "It's nothing to do. You go and pack your things."

"My things are all packed," I said. "I'll go and carry out the stuff that they left for us. Bring the cars around as soon as they're ready."

They brought the cars around to the front of the villa and we loaded them with the hospital equipment which was piled in the hallway. When it was all in, the three cars stood in line down the driveway under the trees in the rain. We went inside.

"Make a fire in the kitchen and dry your things," I said.

"I don't care about dry clothes," Piani said. "I want to sleep."

"I'm going to sleep on the major's bed," Bonello said. "I'm going to sleep where the old man corks off."

"I don't care where I sleep," Piani said.

"There are two beds in here." I opened the door.

"I never knew what was in that room," Bonello said.

"That was old fish-face's room," Piani said.

"You two sleep in there," I said. "I'll wake you."

"The Austrians will wake us if you sleep too long, Tenente," Bonello said.

"I won't oversleep," I said. "Where's Aymo?"

"He went out in the kitchen."

"Get to sleep," I said.

"I'll sleep," Piani said. "I've been asleep sitting up all day. The whole top of my head kept coming down over my eyes."

"Take your boots off," Bonello said. "That's old fish-face's bed."

"Fish-face is nothing to me." Piani lay on the bed, his muddy boots straight out, his head on his arm. I went out to the kitchen. Aymo had a fire in the stove and a kettle of water on.

"I thought I'd start some *pasta asciutta*," he said. "We'll be hungry when we wake up."

"Aren't you sleepy, Bartolomeo?"

"Not so sleepy. When the water boils I'll leave it. The fire will go down."

"You'd better get some sleep," I said. "We can eat cheese and monkey meat."

"This is better," he said. "Something hot will be good for those two anarchists. You go to sleep, Tenente."

"There's a bed in the major's room."

"You sleep there."

"No, I'm going up to my old room. Do you want a drink, Bartolomeo?"

"When we go, Tenente. Now it wouldn't do me any good."

"If you wake in three hours and I haven't called you, wake me, will you?"

"I haven't any watch, Tenente."

"There's a clock on the wall in the major's room."

"All right."

I went out then through the dining-room and the hall and up the marble stairs to the room where I had lived with Rinaldi. It was raining outside. I went to the window and looked out. It was getting dark and I saw the three cars standing in line under the trees. The trees were dripping in the rain. It was cold and the drops hung to the branches. I went back to Rinaldi's bed and lay down and let sleep take me.

We ate in the kitchen before we started. Aymo had a basin of spaghetti with onions and tinned meat chopped up in it. We sat around the table and drank two bottles of the wine that had been left in the cellar of the villa. It was dark outside and still raining. Piani sat at the table very sleepy.

"I like a retreat better than an advance," Bonello said. "On a retreat we drink barbera."

"We drink it now. To-morrow maybe we drink rainwater," Aymo said.

"To-morrow we'll be in Udine. We'll drink champagne. That's where the slackers live. Wake up, Piani! We'll drink champagne to-morrow in Udine!"

"I'm awake," Piani said. He filled his plate with the spaghetti and meat. "Couldn't you find tomato sauce, Barto?"

"There wasn't any," Aymo said.

"We'll drink champagne in Udine," Bonello said. He filled his glass with the clear red barbera.

"We may drink —— before Udine," Piani said.

"Have you eaten enough, Tenente?" Aymo asked.

"I've got plenty. Give me the bottle, Bartolomeo."

"I have a bottle apiece to take in the cars," Aymo said.

"Did you sleep at all?"

"I don't need much sleep. I slept a little."

"To-morrow we'll sleep in the king's bed," Bonello said. He was feeling very good.

"To-morrow maybe we'll sleep in——," Piani said.

"I'll sleep with the queen," Bonello said. He looked to see how I took the joke.

"You'll sleep with ——," Piani said sleepily.

"That's treason, Tenente," Bonello said. "Isn't that treason?"

"Shut up," I said. "You get too funny with a little wine." Outside it was raining hard. I looked at my watch. It was half-past nine.

"It's time to roll," I said and stood up.

"Who are you going to ride with, Tenente?" Bonello asked.

"With Aymo. Then you come. Then Piani. We'll start out on the road for Cormons."

"I'm afraid I'll go to sleep," Piani said.

"All right. I'll ride with you. Then Bonello. Then Aymo."

"That's the best way," Piani said. "Because I'm so sleepy."

"I'll drive and you sleep awhile."

"No. I can drive just so long as I know somebody will wake me up if I go to sleep."

"I'll wake you up. Put out the lights, Barto."

"You might as well leave them," Bonello said. "We've got no more use for this place."

"I have a small locker trunk in my room," I said. "Will you help take it down, Piani?"

"We'll take it," Piani said. "Come on, Aldo." He went off into the hall with Bonello. I heard them going upstairs.

"This was a fine place," Bartolomeo Aymo said. He put two bottles of wine and half a cheese into his haversack. "There won't be a place like this again. Where will they retreat to, Tenente?"

"Beyond the Tagliamento, they say. The hospital and the sector are to be at Pordenone."

"This is a better town than Pordenone."

"I don't know Pordenone," I said. "I've just been through there."

"It's not much of a place," Aymo said.

CHAPTER XXVIII

As we moved out through the town it was empty in the rain and the dark except for columns of troops and guns that were going through the main street. There were many trucks too and some carts going through on other streets and converging on the main road. When we were out past the tanneries onto the main road the troops, the motor trucks, the horse-drawn carts and the guns were in one wide slow-moving column. We moved slowly but steadily in the rain, the radiator cap of our car almost against the tailboard of a truck that was loaded high, the load covered with wet canvas. Then the truck stopped. The whole column was stopped. It started again and we went a little farther, then stopped. I got out and walked ahead, going between the trucks and carts and under the wet necks of the horses. The block was farther ahead. I left the road, crossed the ditch on a footboard and walked along the field beyond the ditch. I could see the stalled column between the trees in the rain as I went forward across from it in the field. I went about a mile. The column did not move, although, on the other side beyond the stalled vehicles I could see the troops moving. I went back to the cars. This block might extend as far as Udine. Piani was asleep over the wheel. I climbed up beside him and went to sleep too. Several hours later I heard the truck ahead of us grinding into gear. I woke Piani and we started, moving a few yards, then stopping, then going on again. It was still raining.

The column stalled again in the night and did not start. I got down and went back to see Aymo and Bonello. Bonello had two sergeants of engineers on the seat of his car with him. They stiffened when I came up.

"They were left to do something to a bridge," Bonello said. "They can't find their unit so I gave them a ride."

"With the Sir Lieutenant's permission."

"With permission," I said.

"The lieutenant is an American," Bonello said. "He'll give anybody a ride."

One of the sergeants smiled. The other asked Bonello if I was an Italian from North or South America.

"He's not an Italian. He's North American English."

The sergeants were polite but did not believe it. I left them and went back to Aymo. He had two girls on the seat with him and was sitting back in the corner and smoking.

"Barto, Barto," I said. He laughed.

"Talk to them, Tenente," he said. "I can't understand them. Hey!" he put his hand on the girl's thigh and squeezed it in a friendly way. The girl drew her shawl tight around her and pushed his hand away. "Hey!" he said. "Tell the Tenente your name and what you're doing here."

The girl looked at me fiercely. The other girl kept her eyes down. The girl who looked at me said something in a dialect I could not understand a word of. She was plump and dark and looked about sixteen.

"Sorella?" I asked and pointed at the other girl.

She nodded her head and smiled.

"All right," I said and patted her knee. I felt her stiffen away when I touched her. The sister never looked up. She looked perhaps a year younger. Aymo put his hand on the elder girl's thigh and she pushed it away. He laughed at her.

"Good man," he pointed at himself. "Good man," he pointed at me. "Don't you worry." The girl looked at him fiercely. The pair of them were like two wild birds.

"What does she ride with me for if she doesn't like me?" Aymo asked. "They got right up in the car the minute I motioned to them." He turned to the girl. "Don't worry," he said. "No danger of ——," using the vulgar word. "No place for ——." I could see she understood the word and that was all. Her eyes looked at him very scared. She pulled the shawl tight. "Car all full," Aymo said. "No danger of ——. No place for ——." Every time he said the word the girl stiffened a little. Then sitting stiffly and looking at him she began to cry. I saw her lips working and then tears came down her plump cheeks. Her sister, not looking up, took her hand and they sat there together. The older one, who had been so fierce, began to sob.

"I guess I scared her," Aymo said. "I didn't mean to scare her."

Bartolomeo brought out his knapsack and cut off two pieces of cheese. "Here," he said. "Stop crying."

The older girl shook her head and still cried, but the younger girl took the cheese and commenced to eat. After a while the younger girl gave her sister the second piece of cheese and they both ate. The older sister still sobbed a little.

"She'll be all right after a while," Aymo said.

An idea came to him. "Virgin?" he asked the girl next to him. She nodded her head vigorously. "Virgin too?" he pointed to the sister. Both the girls nodded their heads and the elder said something in dialect.

"That's all right," Bartolomeo said. "That's all right."

Both the girls seemed cheered.

I left them sitting together with Aymo sitting back in the corner and went back to Piani's car. The column of vehicles did not move but the troops kept passing alongside. It was still raining hard and I thought some of the stops in the movement of the column might be from cars with wet wiring. More likely they were from horses or men going to sleep. Still, traffic could tie up in cities when every one was awake. It was the combination of horse and motor vehicles. They did not help each other any. The peasants' carts did not help much either. Those were a couple of fine girls with Barto. A retreat was no place for two virgins. Real virgins. Probably very religious. If there were no war we would probably all be in bed. In bed I lay me down my head. Bed and board. Stiff as a board in bed. Catherine was in bed now between two sheets, over her and under her. Which side did she sleep on? Maybe she wasn't asleep. Maybe she was lying thinking about me. Blow, blow, ye western wind. Well, it blew and it wasn't the small rain but the big rain down that rained. It rained all night. You knew it rained down that rained. Look at it. Christ, that my love were in my arms and I in my bed again. That my love Catherine. That my sweet love Catherine down might rain. Blow her again to me. Well, we were in it. Every one was caught in it and the small rain would not quiet it. "Good-night, Catherine," I said out loud. "I hope you sleep well. If it's too uncomfortable, darling, lie on the other side," I said. "I'll get you some cold water. In a little while it will be morning and then it won't be so bad. I'm sorry he makes you so uncomfortable. Try and go to sleep, sweet."

I was asleep all the time, she said. You've been talking in your sleep. Are you all right?

Are you really there?

Of course I'm here. I wouldn't go away. This doesn't make any difference between us.

You're so lovely and sweet. You wouldn't go away in the night, would you?

Of course I wouldn't go away. I'm always here. I come whenever you want me.

"——," Piani said. "They've started again."

"I was dopey," I said. I looked at my watch. It was three o'clock in the morning. I reached back behind the seat for a bottle of the barbera.

"You talked out loud," Piani said.

"I was having a dream in English," I said.

The rain was slacking and we were moving along. Before daylight we were stalled again and when it was light we were at a little rise in the ground and I saw the road of the retreat stretched out far ahead, everything stationary except for the infantry filtering through. We started to move again but seeing the rate of progress in the daylight, I knew we were going to have to get off that main road some way and go across country if we ever hoped to reach Udine.

In the night many peasants had joined the column from the roads of the country and in the column there were carts loaded with household goods; there were mirrors projecting up between mattresses, and chickens and ducks tied to carts. There was a sewing-machine on the cart ahead of us in the rain. They had saved the most valuable things. On some carts the women sat huddled from the rain and others walked beside the carts keeping as close to them as they could. There were dogs now in the column, keeping under the wagons as they moved along. The road was muddy, the ditches at the side were high with water and beyond the trees that lined the road the fields looked too wet and too soggy to try to cross. I got down from the car and worked up the road a way, looking for a place where I could see ahead to find a side-road we could take across country. I knew there were many side-roads but did not want one that would lead to nothing. I could not remember them because we had always passed them bowling along in the car on the main road and they all looked much alike. Now I knew we must find one if we hoped to get through. No one knew where the Austrians were nor how things were going but I was certain that if the rain should stop and planes come over and get to work on that column that it would be all over. All that was needed was for a few men to leave their trucks or a few horses be killed to tie up completely the movement on the road.

The rain was not falling so heavily now and I thought it might clear. I went ahead along the edge of the road and when there was a small road that led off to the north between two fields with a hedge of trees on both sides, I thought that we had better take it and hurried back to the cars. I told Piani to turn off and went back to tell Bonello and Aymo.

"If it leads nowhere we can turn around and cut back in," I said.

"What about these?" Bonello asked. His two sergeants were beside him on the seat. They were unshaven but still military looking in the early morning.

"They'll be good to push," I said. I went back to Aymo and told him we were going to try it across country.

"What about my virgin family?" Aymo asked. The two girls were asleep.

"They won't be very useful," I said. "You ought to have some one that could push."

"They could go back in the car," Aymo said. "There's room in the car."

"All right if you want them," I said. "Pick up somebody with a wide back to push."

"Bersaglieri," Aymo smiled. "They have the widest backs. They measure them. How do you feel, Tenente?"

"Fine. How are you?"

"Fine. But very hungry."

"There ought to be something up that road and we will stop and eat."

"How's your leg, Tenente?"

"Fine," I said. Standing on the step and looking up ahead I could see Piani's car pulling out onto the little side-road and starting up it, his car showing through the hedge of bare branches. Bonello turned off and followed him and then Piani worked his way out and we followed the two ambulances ahead along the narrow road between hedges. It led to a farmhouse. We found Piani and Bonello stopped in the farmyard. The house was low and long with a trellis with a grape-vine over the door. There was a well in the yard and Piani was getting up water to fill his radiator. So much going in low gear had boiled it out. The farmhouse was deserted. I looked back down the road, the farmhouse was on a slight elevation above the plain, and we could see over the country, and saw the road, the hedges, the fields and the line of trees along the main road where the retreat was passing. The two sergeants were looking through the house. The girls were awake and looking at the courtyard, the well and the two big ambulances in front of the farmhouse, with three drivers at the well. One of the sergeants came out with a clock in his hand.

"Put it back," I said. He looked at me, went in the house and came back without the clock.

"Where's your partner?" I asked.

"He's gone to the latrine." He got up on the seat of the ambulance. He was afraid we would leave him.

"What about breakfast, Tenente?" Bonello asked. "We could eat something. It wouldn't take very long."

"Do you think this road going down on the other side will lead to anything?"

"Sure."

"All right. Let's eat." Piani and Bonello went in the house.

"Come on," Aymo said to the girls. He held his hand to help them down. The older sister shook her head. They were not going into any deserted house. They looked after us.

"They are difficult," Aymo said. We went into the farmhouse

together. It was large and dark, an abandoned feeling. Bonello and Piani were in the kitchen.

"There's not much to eat," Piani said. "They've cleaned it out."

Bonello sliced a big cheese on the heavy kitchen table.

"Where was the cheese?"

"In the cellar. Piani found wine too and apples."

"That's a good breakfast."

Piani was taking the wooden cork out of a big wicker-covered wine jug. He tipped it and poured a copper pan full

"It smells all right," he said. "Find some beakers, Barto."

The two sergeants came in.

"Have some cheese, sergeants," Bonello said.

"We should go," one of the sergeants said, eating his cheese and drinking a cup of wine.

"We'll go. Don't worry," Bonello said.

"An army travels on its stomach," I said.

"What?" asked the sergeant.

"It's better to eat."

"Yes. But time is precious."

"I believe the bastards have eaten already," Piani said. The sergeants looked at him. They hated the lot of us.

"You know the road?" one of them asked me.

"No," I said. They looked at each other.

"We would do best to start," the first one said.

"We are starting," I said. I drank another cup of the red wine. It tasted very good after the cheese and apple.

"Bring the cheese," I said and went out. Bonello came out carrying the great jug of wine.

"That's too big," I said. He looked at it regretfully.

"I guess it is," he said. "Give me the canteens to fill." He filled the canteens and some of the wine ran out on the stone paving of the courtyard. Then he picked up the wine jug and put it just inside the door.

"The Austrians can find it without breaking the door down," he said.

"We'll roll," I said. "Piani and I will go ahead." The two engineers were already on the seat beside Bonello. The girls were eating cheese and apples. Aymo was smoking. We started off down the narrow road. I looked back at the two cars coming and the farmhouse. It was a fine, low, solid stone house and the ironwork of the well was very good. Ahead of us the road was narrow and muddy and there was a high hedge on either side. Behind, the cars were following closely.

CHAPTER XXIX

At noon we were stuck in a muddy road about, as nearly as we could figure, ten kilometres from Udine. The rain had stopped during the forenoon and three times we had heard planes coming, seen them pass overhead, watched them go far to the left and heard them bombing on the main highroad. We had worked through a network of secondary roads and had taken many roads that were blind, but had always, by backing up and finding another road, gotten closer to Udine. Now, Aymo's car, in backing so that we might get out of a blind road, had gotten into the soft earth at the side and the wheels, spinning, had dug deeper and deeper until the car rested on its differential. The thing to do now was to dig out in front of the wheels, put in brush so that the chains could grip, and then push until the car was on the road. We were all down on the road around the car. The two sergeants looked at the car and examined the wheels. Then they started off down the road without a word. I went after them.

"Come on," I said. "Cut some brush."

"We have to go," one said.

"Get busy," I said, "and cut brush."

"We have to go," one said. The other said nothing. They were in a hurry to start. They would not look at me.

"I order you to come back to the car and cut brush," I said. The one sergeant turned. "We have to go on. In a little while you will be cut off. You can't order us. You're not our officer."

"I order you to cut brush," I said. They turned and started down the road.

"Halt," I said. They kept on down the muddy road, the hedge on either side. "I order you to halt," I called. They went a little faster. I opened up my holster, took the pistol, aimed at the one who had talked the most, and fired. I missed and they both started to run. I shot three times and dropped one. The other went through the hedge and was out of sight. I fired at him through the hedge as he ran across the field. The pistol clicked empty and I put in another clip. I saw it was too far to shoot at the second sergeant. He was far across the field, running, his head held low. I commenced to reload the empty clip. Bonello came up.

"Let me go finish him," he said. I handed him the pistol and he walked down to where the sergeant of engineers lay face down across the road. Bonello leaned over, put the pistol against the man's head and pulled the trigger. The pistol did not fire.

"You have to cock it," I said. He cocked it and fired twice. He took hold of the sergeant's legs and pulled him to the side of the road so he lay beside the hedge. He came back and handed me the pistol.

"The son of a bitch," he said. He looked toward the sergeant. "You see me shoot him, Tenente?"

"We've got to get the brush quickly," I said. "Did I hit the other one at all?"

"I don't think so," Aymo said. "He was too far away to hit with a pistol."

"The dirty scum," Piani said. We were all cutting twigs and

branches. Everything had been taken out of the car. Bonello was digging out in front of the wheels. When we were ready Aymo started the car and put it into gear. The wheels spun round throwing brush and mud. Bonello and I pushed until we could feel our joints crack. The car would not move.

"Rock her back and forth, Barto," I said.

He drove the engine in reverse, then forward. The wheels only dug in deeper. Then the car was resting on the differential again, and the wheels spun freely in the holes they had dug. I straightened up.

"We'll try her with a rope," I said.

"I don't think it's any use, Tenente. You can't get a straight pull."

"We have to try it," I said. "She won't come out any other way."

Piani's and Bonello's cars could only move straight ahead down the narrow road. We roped both cars together and pulled. The wheels only pulled sideways against the ruts.

"It's no good," I shouted. "Stop it."

Piani and Bonello got down from their cars and came back. Aymo got down. The girls were up the road about forty yards sitting on a stone wall.

"What do you say, Tenente?" Bonello asked.

"We'll dig out and try once more with the brush," I said. I looked down the road. It was my fault. I had led them up here. The sun was almost out from behind the clouds and the body of the sergeant lay beside the hedge.

"We'll put his coat and cape under," I said. Bonello went to get them. I cut brush and Aymo and Piani dug out in front and between the wheels. I cut the cape, then ripped it in two, and laid it under the wheel in the mud, then piled brush for the wheels to catch. We were ready to start and Aymo got up on the seat and started the car. The wheels spun and we pushed and pushed. But it wasn't any use.

"It's ——ed," I said. "Is there anything you want in the car, Barto?"

Aymo climbed up with Bonello, carrying the cheese and two bottles of wine and his cape. Bonello, sitting behind the wheel, was looking through the pockets of the sergeant's coat.

"Better throw the coat away," I said. "What about Barto's virgins?"

"They can get in the back," Piani said. "I don't think we are going far."

I opened the back door of the ambulance.

"Come on," I said. "Get in." The two girls climbed in and sat in the corner. They seemed to have taken no notice of the shooting. I looked back up the road. The sergeant lay in his dirty long-sleeved underwear. I got up with Piani and we started. We were going to try to cross the field. When the road entered the field I got down and walked ahead. If we could get across, there was a road on the other side. We could not get across. It was too soft and muddy for the cars. When they were finally and completely stalled, the wheels dug in to the hubs, we left them in the field and started on foot for Udine.

When we came to the road which led back toward the main highway I pointed down it to the two girls.

"Go down there," I said. "You'll meet people." They looked at me. I took out my pocket-book and gave them each a ten-lira note. "Go down there," I said, pointing. "Friends! Family!"

They did not understand but they held the money tightly and started down the road. They looked back as though they were afraid I might take the money back. I watched them go down the road, their shawls close around them, looking back apprehensively at us. The three drivers were laughing.

"How much will you give me to go in that direction, Tenente?" Bonello asked.

"They're better off in a bunch of people than alone if they catch them," I said.

"Give me two hundred lire and I'll walk straight back toward Austria," Bonello said.

"They'd take it away from you," Piani said.

"Maybe the war will be over," Aymo said. We were going up the road as fast as we could. The sun was trying to come through. Beside the road were mulberry trees. Through the trees I could see our two big moving-vans of cars stuck in the field. Piani looked back too.

"They'll have to build a road to get them out," he said.

"I wish to Christ we had bicycles," Bonello said.

"Do they ride bicycles in America?" Aymo asked.

"They used to."

"Here it is a great thing," Aymo said. "A bicycle is a splendid thing."

"I wish to Christ we had bicycles," Bonello said. "I'm no walker."

"Is that firing?" I asked. I thought I could hear firing a long way away.

"I don't know," Aymo said. He listened.

"I think so," I said.

"The first thing we will see will be the cavalry," Piani said.

"I don't think they've got any cavalry."

"I hope to Christ not," Bonello said. "I don't want to be stuck on a lance by any —— cavalry."

"You certainly shot that sergeant, Tenente," Piani said. We were walking fast.

"I killed him," Bonello said. "I never killed anybody in this war, and all my life I've wanted to kill a sergeant."

"You killed him on the sit all right," Piani said. "He wasn't flying very fast when you killed him."

"Never mind. That's one thing I can always remember. I killed that —— of a sergeant."

"What will you say in confession?" Aymo asked.

"I'll say, 'Bless me, father, I killed a sergeant.'" They all laughed.

"He's an anarchist," Piani said. "He doesn't go to church."

"Piani's an anarchist too," Bonello said.

"Are you really anarchists?" I asked.

"No, Tenente. We're socialists. We come from Imola."

"Haven't you ever been there?"

"No."

"By Christ it's a fine place, Tenente. You come there after the war and we'll show you something."

"Are you all socialists?"

"Everybody."

"Is it a fine town?"

"Wonderful. You never saw a town like that."

"How did you get to be socialists?"

"We're all socialists. Everybody is a socialist. We've always been socialists."

"You come, Tenente. We'll make you a socialist too."

Ahead the road turned off to the left and there was a little hill and, beyond a stone wall, an apple orchard. As the road went up-hill they ceased talking. We walked along together all going fast against time.

CHAPTER XXX

Later we were on a road that led to a river. There was a long line of abandoned trucks and carts on the road leading up to the bridge. No one was in sight. The river was high and the bridge had been blown up in the centre; the stone arch was fallen into the river and the brown water was going over it. We went on up the bank looking for a place to cross. Up ahead I knew there was a railway bridge and I thought we might be able to get across there. The path was wet and muddy. We did not see any troops; only abandoned trucks and stores. Along the river bank there was nothing and no one but the wet brush and muddy ground. We went up to the bank and finally we saw the railway bridge.

"What a beautiful bridge," Aymo said. It was a long plain iron bridge across what was usually a dry river-bed.

"We'd better hurry and get across before they blow it up," I said.

"There's nobody to blow it up," Piani said. "They're all gone."

"It's probably mined," Bonello said. "You cross first, Tenente."

"Listen to the anarchist," Aymo said. "Make him go first."

"I'll go," I said. "It won't be mined to blow up with one man."

"You see," Piani said. "That is brains. Why haven't you brains, anarchist?"

"If I had brains I wouldn't be here," Bonello said.

"That's pretty good, Tenente," Aymo said.

"That's pretty good," I said. We were close to the bridge now. The sky had clouded over again and it was raining a little. The bridge looked long and solid. We climbed up the embankment.

"Come one at a time," I said and started across the bridge. I watched the ties and the rails for any trip-wires or signs of explosive but I saw nothing. Down below the gaps in the ties the river ran muddy and fast. Ahead across the wet countryside I could see Udine in the rain. Across the bridge I looked back. Just up the river was another bridge. As I watched, a yellow mud-colored motor car crossed it. The sides of the bridge were high and the body of the car, once on, was out of sight. But I saw the heads of the driver, the man on the seat with him, and the two men on the rear seat. They all wore German helmets. Then the car was over the bridge and out of sight behind the trees and the abandoned vehicles on the road. I waved to Aymo who was crossing and to the others to come on. I climbed down and crouched beside the railway embankment. Aymo came down with me.

"Did you see the car?" I asked.

"No. We were watching you."

"A German staff car crossed on the upper bridge."

"A staff car?"

"Yes."

"Holy Mary."

The others came and we all crouched in the mud behind the embankment, looking across the rails at the bridge, the line of trees, the ditch and the road.

"Do you think we're cut off then, Tenente?"

"I don't know. All I know is a German staff car went along that road."

"You don't feel funny, Tenente? You haven't got strange feelings in the head?"

"Don't be funny, Bonello."

"What about a drink?" Piani asked. "If we're cut off we might as well have a drink." He unhooked his canteen and uncorked it.

"Look! Look!" Aymo said and pointed toward the road. Along the top of the stone bridge we could see German helmets moving. They were bent forward and moved smoothly, almost supernaturally, along. As they came off the bridge we saw them. They were bicycle troops. I saw the faces of the first two. They were ruddy and healthy-looking. Their helmets came low down over their foreheads and the side of their faces. Their carbines were clipped to the frame of the bicycles. Stick bombs hung handle down from their belts. Their helmets and their gray uniforms were wet and they rode easily, looking ahead and to both sides. There were two —then four in line, then two, then almost a dozen; then another dozen—then one alone. They did not talk but we could not have heard them because of the noise from the river. They were gone out of sight up the road.

"Holy Mary," Aymo said.

"They were Germans," Piani said. "Those weren't Austrians."

"Why isn't there somebody here to stop them?" I said. "Why haven't they blown the bridge up? Why aren't there machine-guns along this embankment?"

"You tell us, Tenente," Bonello said.

I was very angry.

"The whole bloody thing is crazy. Down below they blow up a little bridge. Here they leave a bridge on the main road. Where is everybody? Don't they try and stop them at all?"

"You tell us, Tenente," Bonello said. I shut up. It was none of my business; all I had to do was to get to Pordenone with three ambulances. I had failed at that. All I had to do now was get to Pordenone. I probably could not even get to Udine. The hell I couldn't. The thing to do was to be calm and not get shot or captured.

"Didn't you have a canteen open?" I asked Piani. He handed it to me. I took a long drink. "We might as well start," I said. "There's no hurry though. Do you want to eat something?"

"This is no place to stay," Bonello said.

"All right. We'll start."

"Should we keep on this side—out of sight?"

"We'd be better off on top. They may come along this bridge too. We don't want them on top of us before we see them."

We walked along the railroad track. On both sides of us stretched the wet plain. Ahead across the plain was the hill of Udine. The roofs fell away from the castle on the hill. We could see the campanile and the clock-tower. There were many mulberry trees in the fields. Ahead I saw a place where the rails were torn up. The ties had been dug out too and thrown down the embankment.

"Down! down!" Aymo said. We dropped down beside the embankment. There was another group of bicyclists passing along the road. I looked over the edge and saw them go on.

"They saw us but they went on," Aymo said.

"We'll get killed up there, Tenente," Bonello said.

"They don't want us," I said. "They're after something else. We're in more danger if they should come on us suddenly."

"I'd rather walk here out of sight," Bonello said.

"All right. We'll walk along the tracks."

"Do you think we can get through?" Aymo asked.

"Sure. There aren't very many of them yet. We'll go through in the dark."

"What was that staff car doing?"

"Christ knows," I said. We kept on up the tracks. Bonello tired of walking in the mud of the embankment and came up with the rest of us. The railway moved south away from the highway now and we could not see what passed along the road. A short bridge over a canal was blown up but we climbed across on what was left of the span. We heard firing ahead of us.

We came up on the railway beyond the canal. It went on straight toward the town across the low fields. We could see the line of the other railway ahead of us. To the north was the main road where we had seen the cyclists; to the south there was a small branch-road across the fields with thick trees on each side. I thought we had better cut to the south and work around the town that way and across country toward Campoformio and the main road to the Tagliamento. We could avoid the main line of the retreat by keeping to the secondary roads beyond Udine. I knew there were plenty of side-roads across the plain. I started down the embankment.

"Come on," I said. We would make for the side-road and work to the south of the town. We all started down the embankment. A shot was fired at us from the side-road. The bullet went into the mud of the embankment.

"Go on back," I shouted. I started up the embankment, slipping in the mud. The drivers were ahead of me. I went up the embankment as fast as I could go. Two more shots came from the thick brush and Aymo, as he was crossing the tracks, lurched, tripped and fell face down. We pulled him down on the other side and turned him over. "His head ought to be uphill," I said. Piani moved him around. He lay in the mud on the side of the embankment, his feet pointing downhill, breathing blood irregularly. The three of us squatted over him in the rain. He was hit low in the back of the neck and the bullet had ranged upward and come out under the right eye. He died while I was stopping up the two holes. Piani laid his head down, wiped at his face, with a piece of the emergency dressing, then let it alone.

"The ——," he said.

"They weren't Germans," I said. "There can't be any Germans over there."

"Italians," Piani said, using the word as an epithet, "Italiani!" Bonello said nothing. He was sitting beside Aymo, not looking at him. Piani picked up Aymo's cap where it had rolled down the embankment and put it over his face. He took out his canteen.

"Do you want a drink?" Piani handed Bonello the canteen.

"No," Bonello said. He turned to me. "That might have happened to us any time on the railway tracks."

"No," I said. "It was because we started across the field."

Bonello shook his head. "Aymo's dead," he said. "Who's dead next, Tenente? Where do we go now?"

"Those were Italians that shot," I said. "They weren't Germans."

"I suppose if they were Germans they'd have killed all of us," Bonello said.

"We are in more danger from Italians than Germans," I said. "The rear guard are afraid of everything. The Germans know what they're after."

"You reason it out, Tenente," Bonello said.

"Where do we go now?" Piani asked.

"We better lie up some place till it's dark. If we could get south we'd be all right."

"They'd have to shoot us all to prove they were right the first time," Bonello said. "I'm not going to try them."

"We'll find a place to lie up as near to Udine as we can get and then go through when it's dark."

"Let's go then," Bonello said. We went down the north side of the embankment. I looked back. Aymo lay in the mud with the angle of the embankment. He was quite small and his arms were by his side, his puttee-wrapped legs and muddy boots together, his cap over his face. He looked very dead. It was raining. I had liked him as well as any one I ever knew. I had his papers in my pocket and would write to his family. Ahead across the fields was a farmhouse. There were trees around it and the farm buildings were built against the house. There was a balcony along the second floor held up by columns.

"We better keep a little way apart," I said. "I'll go ahead." I started toward the farmhouse. There was a path across the field.

Crossing the field, I did not know but that some one would fire on us from the trees near the farmhouse or from the farmhouse itself. I walked toward it, seeing it very clearly. The balcony of the second floor merged into the barn and there was hay coming out between the columns. The courtyard was of stone blocks and all the trees were dripping with the rain. There was a big empty two-wheeled cart, the shafts tipped high up in the rain. I came to the courtyard, crossed it, and stood under the shelter of the balcony. The door of the house was open and I went in. Bonello and Piani came in after me. It was dark inside. I went back to the kitchen. There were ashes of a fire on the big open hearth. The pots hung over the ashes, but they were empty. I looked around but I could not find anything to eat.

"We ought to lie up in the barn," I said. "Do you think you could find anything to eat, Piani, and bring it up there?"

"I'll look," Piani said.

"I'll look too," Bonello said.

"All right," I said. "I'll go up and look at the barn." I found a stone stairway that went up from the stable underneath. The stable smelt dry and pleasant in the rain. The cattle were all gone, probably driven off when they left. The barn was half full of hay. There were two windows in the roof, one was blocked with boards, the other was a narrow dormer window on the north side. There was a chute so that hay might be pitched down to the cattle. Beams crossed the opening down into the main floor where the hay-carts drove in when the hay was hauled in to be pitched up. I heard the rain on the roof and smelled the hay and, when I went down, the clean smell of dried dung in the stable. We could pry a board

loose and see out of the south window down into the courtyard.
The other window looked out on the field toward the north. We
could get out of either window onto the roof and down, or go down
the hay chute if the stairs were impractical. It was a big barn and
we could hide in the hay if we heard any one. It seemed like a good
place. I was sure we could have gotten through to the south if
they had not fired on us. It was impossible that there were Germans there. They were coming from the north and down the road
from Cividale. They could not have come through from the south.
The Italians were even more dangerous. They were frightened
and firing on anything they saw. Last night on the retreat we had
heard that there had been many Germans in Italian uniforms mix-
ing with the retreat in the north. I did not believe it. That was one
of those things you always heard in the war. It was one of the
things the enemy always did to you. You did not know any one
who went over in German uniform to confuse them. Maybe they
did but it sounded difficult. I did not believe the Germans did it.
I did not believe they had to. There was no need to confuse our
retreat. The size of the army and the fewness of the roads did that.
Nobody gave any orders, let alone Germans. Still, they would shoot
us for Germans. They shot Aymo. The hay smelled good and lying
in a barn in the hay took away all the years in between. We had
lain in hay and talked and shot sparrows with an air-rifle when they
perched in the triangle cut high up in the wall of the barn. The
barn was gone now and one year they had cut the hemlock woods
and there were only stumps, dried tree-tops, branches and fireweed
where the woods had been. You could not go back. If you did not
go forward what happened? You never got back to Milan. And if
you got back to Milan what happened? I listened to the firing to
the north toward Udine. I could hear machine-gun firing. There
was no shelling. That was something. They must have gotten
some troops along the road. I looked down in the half-light of the
hay-barn and saw Piani standing on the hauling floor. He had a

long sausage, a jar of something and two bottles of wine under his arm.

"Come up," I said. "There is the ladder." Then I realized that I should help him with the things and went down. I was vague in the head from lying in the hay. I had been nearly asleep.

"Where's Bonello?" I asked.

"I'll tell you," Piani said. We went up the ladder. Up on the hay we set the things down. Piani took out his knife with the corkscrew and drew the cork on a wine bottle.

"They have sealing-wax on it," he said. "It must be good." He smiled.

"Where's Bonello?" I asked.

Piani looked at me.

"He went away, Tenente," he said. "He wanted to be a prisoner."

I did not say anything.

"He was afraid we would get killed."

I held the bottle of wine and did not say anything.

"You see we don't believe in the war anyway, Tenente."

"Why didn't you go?" I asked.

"I did not want to leave you."

"Where did he go?"

"I don't know, Tenente. He went away."

"All right," I said. "Will you cut the sausage?"

Piani looked at me in the half-light.

"I cut it while we were talking," he said. We sat in the hay and ate the sausage and drank the wine. It must have been wine they had saved for a wedding. It was so old that it was losing its color.

"You look out of this window, Luigi," I said. "I'll go look out the other window."

We had each been drinking out of one of the bottles and I took my bottle with me and went over and lay flat on the hay and looked out the narrow window at the wet country. I do not know what I expected to see but I did not see anything except the fields and the bare mulberry trees and the rain falling. I drank the wine and it did not make me feel good. They had kept it too long and it had gone to pieces and lost its quality and color. I watched it get dark outside; the darkness came very quickly. It would be a black night with the rain. When it was dark there was no use watching any more, so I went over to Piani. He was lying asleep and I did not wake him but sat down beside him for a while. He was a big man and he slept heavily. After a while I woke him and we started.

That was a very strange night. I do not know what I had expected, death perhaps and shooting in the dark and running, but nothing happened. We waited, lying flat beyond the ditch along the main road while a German battalion passed, then when they were gone we crossed the road and went on to the north. We were very close to Germans twice in the rain but they did not see us. We got past the town to the north without seeing any Italians, then after a while came on the main channels of the retreat and walked all night toward the Tagliamento. I had not realized how gigantic the retreat was. The whole country was moving, as well as the army. We walked all night, making better time than the vehicles. My leg ached and I was tired but we made good time. It seemed so silly for Bonello to have decided to be taken prisoner. There was no danger. We had walked through two armies without incident. If Aymo had not been killed there would never have seemed to be any danger. No one had bothered us when we were in plain sight along the railway. The killing came suddenly and unreasonably. I wondered where Bonello was.

"How do you feel, Tenente?" Piani asked. We were going along the side of a road crowded with vehicles and troops.

"Fine."

"I'm tired of this walking."

"Well, all we have to do is walk now. We don't have to worry."

"Bonello was a fool."

"He was a fool all right."

"What will you do about him, Tenente?"

"I don't know."

"Can't you just put him down as taken prisoner?"

"I don't know."

"You see if the war went on they would make bad trouble for his family."

"The war won't go on," a soldier said. "We're going home. The war is over."

"Everybody's going home."

"We're all going home."

"Come on, Tenente," Piani said. He wanted to get past them.

"Tenente? Who's a Tenente? *A basso gli ufficiali!* Down with the officers!"

Piani took me by the arm. "I better call you by your name," he said. "They might try and make trouble. They've shot some officers." We worked up past them.

"I won't make a report that will make trouble for his family." I went on with our conversation.

"If the war is over it makes no difference," Piani said. "But I don't believe it's over. It's too good that it should be over."

"We'll know pretty soon," I said.

"I don't believe it's over. They all think it's over but I don't believe it."

"*Viva la Pace!*" a soldier shouted out. "We're going home!"

"It would be fine if we all went home," Piani said. "Wouldn't you like to go home?"

"Yes."

"We'll never go. I don't think it's over."

"*Andiamo a casa!*" a soldier shouted.

"They throw away their rifles," Piani said. "They take them off and drop them down while they're marching. Then they shout."

"They ought to keep their rifles."

"They think if they throw away their rifles they can't make them fight."

In the dark and the rain, making our way along the side of the road I could see that many of the troops still had their rifles. They stuck up above the capes.

"What brigade are you?" an officer called out.

"*Brigata di Pace*," some one shouted. "Peace Brigade!" The officer said nothing.

"What does he say? What does the officer say?"

"Down with the officer. *Viva la Pace!*"

"Come on," Piani said. We passed two British ambulances, abandoned in the block of vehicles.

"They're from Gorizia," Piani said. "I know the cars."

"They got further than we did."

"They started earlier."

"I wonder where the drivers are?"

"Up ahead probably."

"The Germans have stopped outside Udine," I said. "These people will all get across the river."

"Yes," Piani said. "That's why I think the war will go on."

"The Germans could come on," I said. "I wonder why they don't come on."

"I don't know. I don't know anything about this kind of war."

"They have to wait for their transport I suppose."

"I don't know," Piani said. Alone he was much gentler. When he was with the others he was a very rough talker.

"Are you married, Luigi?"

"You know I am married."

"Is that why you did not want to be a prisoner?"

"That is one reason. Are you married, Tenente?"

"No."

"Neither is Bonello."

"You can't tell anything by a man's being married. But I should think a married man would want to get back to his wife," I said. I would be glad to talk about wives.

"Yes."

"How are your feet?"

"They're sore enough."

Before daylight we reached the bank of the Tagliamento and followed down along the flooded river to the bridge where all the traffic was crossing.

"They ought to be able to hold at this river," Piani said. In the dark the flood looked high. The water swirled and it was wide. The wooden bridge was nearly three-quarters of a mile across, and the river, that usually ran in narrow channels in the wide stony bed far below the bridge, was close under the wooden planking. We went along the bank and then worked our way into the crowd that were crossing the bridge. Crossing slowly in the rain a few feet above the flood, pressed tight in the crowd, the box of an artillery caisson just head, I looked over the side and watched the river. Now that we could not go our own pace I felt very tired. There was no exhilaration in crossing the bridge. I wondered what it would be like if a plane bombed it in the daytime.

"Piani," I said.

"Here I am, Tenente." He was a little ahead in the jam. No one was talking. They were all trying to get across as soon as they could: thinking only of that. We were almost across. At the far end of the bridge there were officers and carabinieri standing on both sides flashing lights. I saw them silhouetted against the sky-line. As we came close to them I saw one of the officers point to a man in the column. A carabiniere went in after him and came out holding the man by the arm. He took him away from the road. We came almost opposite them. The officers were scrutinizing every one in the column, sometimes speaking to each other, going forward to flash a light in some one's face. They took some one else out just before we came opposite. I saw the man. He was a lieutenant-colonel. I saw the stars in the box on his sleeve as they flashed a light on him. His hair was gray and he was short and fat. The carabiniere pulled him in behind the line of officers. As we came opposite I saw one or two of them look at me. Then one pointed at me and spoke to a carabiniere. I saw the carabiniere start for me, come through the edge of the column toward me, then felt him take me by the collar.

"What's the matter with you?" I said and hit him in the face. I saw his face under the hat, upturned mustaches and blood coming down his cheek. Another one dove in toward us.

"What's the matter with you?" I said. He did not answer. He was watching a chance to grab me. I put my arm behind me to loosen my pistol.

"Don't you know you can't touch an officer?"

The other one grabbed me from behind and pulled my arm up so that it twisted in the socket. I turned with him and the other one grabbed me around the neck. I kicked his shins and got my left knee into his groin.

"Shoot him if he resists," I heard some one say.

"What's the meaning of this?" I tried to shout but my voice was not very loud. They had me at the side of the road now.

"Shoot him if he resists," an officer said. "Take him over back."

"Who are you?"

"You'll find out."

"Who are you?"

"Battle police," another officer said.

"Why don't you ask me to step over instead of having one of these airplanes grab me?"

They did not answer. They did not have to answer. They were battle police.

"Take him back there with the others," the first officer said. "You see. He speaks Italian with an accent."

"So do you, you ——," I said.

"Take him back with the others," the first officer said. They took me down behind the line of officers below the road toward a group of people in a field by the river bank. As we walked toward them shots were fired. I saw flashes of the rifles and heard the reports. We came up to the group. There were four officers standing together, with a man in front of them with a carabiniere on each side of him. A group of men were standing guarded by carabinieri. Four other carabinieri stood near the questioning officers, leaning on their carbines. They were wide-hatted carabinieri. The two who had me shoved me in with the group waiting to be questioned. I looked at the man the officers were questioning. He was the fat gray-haired little lieutenant-colonel they had taken out of the column. The questioners had all the efficiency, coldness and command of themselves of Italians who are firing and are not being fired on.

"Your brigade?"

He told them.

"Regiment?"

He told them.

"Why are you not with your regiment?"

He told them.

"Do you not know that an officer should be with his troops?"

He did.

That was all. Another officer spoke.

"It is you and such as you that have let the barbarians onto the sacred soil of the fatherland."

"I beg your pardon," said the lieutenant-colonel.

"It is because of treachery such as yours that we have lost the fruits of victory."

"Have you ever been in a retreat?" the lieutenant-colonel asked.

"Italy should never retreat."

We stood there in the rain and listened to this. We were facing the officers and the prisoner stood in front and a little to one side of us.

"If you are going to shoot me," the lieutenant-colonel said, "please shoot me at once without further questioning. The questioning is stupid." He made the sign of the cross. The officers spoke together. One wrote something on a pad of paper.

"Abandoned his troops, ordered to be shot," he said.

Two carabinieri took the lieutenant-colonel to the river bank. He walked in the rain, an old man with his hat off, a carabinieri on either side. I did not watch them shoot him but I heard the shots. They were questioning some one else. This officer too was separated from his troops. He was not allowed to make an explanation. He cried when they read the sentence from the pad of paper, and they were questioning another when they shot him. They made a point of being intent on questioning the next man while the man who had been questioned before was being shot. In this way there was obviously nothing they could do about it. I did not know whether I should wait to be questioned or make a break now. I was obviously a German in Italian uniform. I saw how their minds worked; if they had minds and if they worked. They were all young men and they were saving their country. The second army was being re-formed beyond the Tagliamento. They were executing officers of the rank of major and above who were separated from their troops. They were also dealing summarily with German agitators in Italian uniform. They wore steel helmets. Only two of us had steel helmets. Some of the carabinieri had them. The other carabinieri wore the wide hat. Airplanes we called them. We stood in the rain and were taken out one at a time to be questioned and shot. So far they had shot every one they had questioned. The questioners had that beautiful detachment and devotion to stern justice of men dealing in death without being in any danger of it. They were questioning a full colonel of a line regiment. Three more officers had just been put in with us.

"Where was his regiment?"

I looked at the carabinieri. They were looking at the newcomers. The others were looking at the colonel. I ducked down, pushed between two men, and ran for the river, my head down. I tripped at the edge and went in with a splash. The water was very cold and I stayed under as long as I could. I could feel the current swirl me and I stayed under until I thought I could never come up. The minute I came up I took a breath and went down again. It was easy to stay under with so much clothing and my boots. When I came up the second time I saw a piece of timber ahead of me and reached it and held on with one hand. I kept my head behind it and did not even look over it. I did not want to see the bank. There were shots when I ran and shots when I came up the first time. I heard them when I was almost above water. There were no shots now. The piece of timber swung in the current and I held it with one hand. I looked at the bank. It seemed to be going by very fast. There was much wood in the stream. The water was very cold. We passed the brush of an island above the water. I held onto the timber with both hands and let it take me along. The shore was out of sight now.

CHAPTER XXXI

You do not know how long you are in a river when the current moves swiftly. It seems a long time and it may be very short. The water was cold and in flood and many things passed that had been floated off the banks when the river rose. I was lucky to have a heavy timber to hold on to, and I lay in the icy water with my chin on the wood, holding as easily as I could with both hands. I was afraid of cramps and I hoped we would move toward the shore. We went down the river in a long curve. It was beginning to be light enough so I could see the bushes along the shore-line. There was a brush island ahead and the current moved toward the shore. I wondered if I should take off my boots and clothes and try to swim ashore, but decided not to. I had never thought of anything but that I would reach the shore some way, and I would be in a bad position if I landed barefoot. I had to get to Mestre some way.

I watched the shore come close, then swing away, then come closer again. We were floating more slowly. The shore was very close now. I could see twigs on the willow bush. The timber swung slowly so that the bank was behind me and I knew we were in an eddy. We went slowly around. As I saw the bank again, very close now, I tried holding with one arm and kicking and swimming the timber toward the bank with the other, but I did not bring it any closer. I was afraid we would move out of the eddy and, holding with one hand, I drew up my feet so they were against the side of the timber and shoved hard toward the bank. I could see the brush, but even with my momentum and swimming as hard as I could, the current was taking me away. I thought then I would drown because of my boots, but I thrashed and fought through the water, and when I looked up the bank was coming toward me, and I kept thrashing and swimming in a heavy-footed panic until I reached it. I hung to the willow branch and did not have strength to pull myself up but I knew I would not drown now. It had never occurred to me on the timber that I might drown. I felt hollow and sick in my stomach and chest from the effort, and I held to the branches and waited. When the sick feeling was gone I pulled into the willow bushes and rested again, my arms around some brush, holding tight with my hands to the branches. Then I crawled out, pushed on through the willows and onto the bank. It was half-daylight and I saw no one. I lay flat on the bank and heard the river and the rain.

After a while I got up and started along the bank. I knew there was no bridge across the river until Latisana. I thought I might be opposite San Vito. I began to think out what I should do. Ahead there was a ditch running into the river. I went toward it. So far I had seen no one and I sat down by some bushes along the bank of the ditch and took off my shoes and emptied them of water. I took off my coat, took my wallet with my papers and my money all wet in it out of the inside pocket and then wrung the coat out. I took off my trousers and wrung them too, then my shirt and under clothing. I slapped and rubbed myself and then dressed again. I had lost my cap.

Before I put on my coat I cut the cloth stars off my sleeves and put them in the inside pocket with my money. My money was wet but was all right. I counted it. There were three thousand and some lire. My clothes felt wet and clammy and I slapped my arms to keep the circulation going. I had woven underwear and I did not think I would catch cold if I kept moving. They had taken my pistol at the road and I put the holster under my coat. I had no cape and it was cold in the rain. I started up the bank of the canal. It was daylight and the country was wet, low and dismal looking. The fields were bare and wet; a long way away I could see a campanile rising out of the plain. I came up onto a road. Ahead I saw some troops coming down the road. I limped along the side of the road and they passed me and paid no attention to me. They were a machine-gun detachment going up toward the river. I went on down the road.

That day I crossed the Venetian plain. It is a low level country and under the rain it is even flatter. Toward the sea there are salt marshes and very few roads. The roads all go along the river mouths to the sea and to cross the country you must go along the paths beside the canals. I was working across the country from the north to the south and had crossed two railway lines and many roads and finally I came out at the end of a path onto a railway line where it ran beside a marsh. It was the main line from Venice to Trieste, with a high solid embankment, a solid roadbed and double track. Down the tracks a way was a flag-station and I could see soldiers on guard. Up the line there was a bridge over a stream that flowed into the marsh. I could see a guard too at the bridge. Crossing the fields to the north I had seen a train pass on this railroad, visible a long way across the flat plain, and I thought a train might come from Portogruaro. I watched the guards and lay down on the embankment so that I could see both ways along the track. The guard at the bridge walked a way up the line toward where I lay, then turned and went back toward the bridge. I lay, and was hungry, and waited for the train. The one I had seen was so long that the engine moved it very slowly and I was sure I could get aboard it. After I had almost given up hoping for one I saw a train coming. The engine, coming straight on, grew larger slowly. I looked at the guard at the bridge. He was walking on the near side of the bridge but on the other side of the tracks. That would put him out of sight when the train passed. I watched the engine come nearer. It was working hard. I could see there were many cars. I knew there would be guards on the train, and I tried to see where they were, but, keeping out of sight, I could not. The engine was almost to where I was lying. When it came opposite, working and puffing even on the level, and I saw the engineer pass, I stood up and stepped up close to the passing cars. If the guards were watching I was a less suspicious object standing beside the track. Several closed freight-cars passed. Then I saw a low open car of the sort they call gondolas coming, covered with canvas. I stood until it had almost passed, then jumped and caught the rear hand-rods and pulled up. I crawled down between the gondola and the shelter of the high freight-car behind. I did not think any one had seen me. I was holding to the hand-rods and crouching low, my feet on the coupling. We were almost opposite the bridge. I remembered the guard. As we passed him he looked at me. He was a boy and his helmet was too big for him. I stared at him contemptuously and he looked away. He thought I had something to do with the train.

We were past. I saw him still looking uncomfortable, watching the other cars pass and I stooped to see how the canvas was fastened. It had grummets and was laced down at the edge with cord. I took out my knife, cut the cord and put my arm under. There were hard bulges under the canvas that tightened in the rain. I looked up and ahead. There was a guard on the freight-car ahead but he was looking forward. I let go of the hand-rails and ducked under the canvas. My forehead hit something that gave me a violent bump and I felt blood on my face but I crawled on in and lay flat. Then I turned around and fastened down the canvas.

I was in under the canvas with guns. They smelled cleanly of oil and grease. I lay and listened to the rain on the canvas and the clicking of the car over the rails. There was a little light came through and I lay and looked at the guns. They had their canvas jackets on. I thought they must have been sent ahead from the third army. The bump on my forehead was swollen and I stopped the bleeding by lying still and letting it coagulate, then picked away the dried blood except over the cut. It was nothing. I had no handkerchief, but feeling with my fingers I washed away where the dried blood had been, with rainwater that dripped from the canvas, and wiped it clean with the sleeve of my coat. I did not want to look conspicuous. I knew I would have to get out before they got to Mestre because they would be taking care of these guns. They had no guns to lose or forget about. I was terrifically hungry.

CHAPTER XXXII

Lying on the floor of the flat-car with the guns beside me under the canvas I was wet, cold and very hungry. Finally I rolled over and lay flat on my stomach with my head on my arms. My knee was stiff, but it had been very satisfactory. Valentini had done a fine job. I had done half the retreat on foot and swum part of the Tagliamento with his knee. It was his knee all right. The other knee was mine. Doctors did things to you and then it was not your body any more. The head was mine, and the inside of the belly. It was very hungry in there. I could feel it turn over on itself. The head was mine, but not to use, not to think with, only to remember and not too much remember.

I could remember Catherine but I knew I would get crazy if I thought about her when I was not sure yet I would see her, so I would not think about her, only about her a little, only about her with the car going slowly and clickingly, and some light through the canvas and my lying with Catherine on the floor of the car. Hard as the floor of the car to lie not thinking only feeling, having been away too long, the clothes wet and the floor moving only a little each time and lonesome inside and alone with wet clothing and hard floor for a wife.

You did not love the floor of a flat-car nor guns with canvas jackets and the smell of vaselined metal or a canvas that rain leaked through, although it is very fine under a canvas and pleasant with guns; but you loved some one else whom now you knew was not even to be pretended there; you seeing now very clearly and coldly—not so coldly as clearly and emptily. You saw emptily, lying on your stomach, having been present when one army moved back and another came forward. You had lost your cars and your men as a floorwalker loses the stock of his department in a fire. There was, however, no insurance. You were out of it now. You had no more obligation. If they shot floorwalkers after a fire in the department store because they spoke with an accent they had always had, then certainly the floorwalkers would not be expected to return when the store opened again for business. They might seek other employment; if there was any other employment and the police did not get them.

Anger was washed away in the river along with any obligation. Although that ceased when the carabiniere put his hands on my collar. I would like to have had the uniform off although I did not care much about the outward forms. I had taken off the stars, but that was for convenience. It was no point of honor. I was not against them. I was through. I wished them all the luck. There were the good ones, and the brave ones, and the calm ones and the sensible ones, and they deserved it. But it was not my show any more and I wished this bloody train would get to Mestre and I would eat and stop thinking. I would have to stop.

Piani would tell them they had shot me. They went through the pockets and took the papers of the people they shot. They would not have my papers. They might call me drowned. I wondered what they would hear in the States. Dead from wounds and other causes. Good Christ I was hungry. I wondered what had become of the priest at the mess. And Rinaldi. He was probably at Pordenone. If they had not gone further back. Well, I would never see him now. I would never see any of them now. That life was over. I did not think he had syphilis. It was not a serious disease anyway if you took it in time, they said. But he would worry. I would worry too if I had it. Any one would worry.

I was not made to think. I was made to eat. My God, yes. Eat and drink and sleep with Catherine. To-night maybe. No that was impossible. But to-morrow night, and a good meal and sheets and never going away again except together. Probably have to go damned quickly. She would go. I knew she would go. When would we go? That was something to think about. It was getting dark. I lay and thought where we would go. There were many places.

BOOK FOUR

CHAPTER XXXIII

I dropped off the train in Milan as it slowed to come into the station early in the morning before it was light. I crossed the track and came out between some buildings and down onto the street. A wine shop was open and I went in for some coffee. It smelled of early morning, of swept dust, spoons in coffee-glasses and the wet circles left by wine-glasses. The proprietor was behind the bar. Two soldiers sat at a table. I stood at the bar and drank a glass of coffee and ate a piece of bread. The coffee was gray with milk, and I skimmed the milk scum off the top with a piece of bread. The proprietor looked at me.

"You want a glass of grappa?"

"No thanks."

"On me," he said and poured a small glass and pushed it toward me. "What's happening at the front?"

"I would not know."

"They are drunk," he said, moving his hand toward the two soldiers. I could believe him. They looked drunk.

"Tell me," he said, "what is happening at the front?"

"I would not know about the front."

"I saw you come down the wall. You came off the train."

"There is a big retreat."

"I read the papers. What happens? Is it over?"

"I don't think so."

He filled the glass with grappa from a short bottle. "If you are in trouble," he said, "I can keep you."

"I am not in trouble."

"If you are in trouble stay here with me."

"Where does one stay?"

"In the building. Many stay here. Any who are in trouble stay here."

"Are many in trouble?"

"It depends on the trouble. You are a South American?"

"No."

"Speak Spanish?"

"A little."

He wiped off the bar.

"It is hard now to leave the country but in no way impossible."

"I have no wish to leave."

"You can stay here as long as you want. You will see what sort of man I am."

"I have to go this morning but I will remember the address to return."

He shook his head. "You won't come back if you talk like that. I thought you were in real trouble."

"I am in no trouble. But I value the address of a friend."

I put a ten-lira note on the bar to pay for the coffee.

"Have a grappa with me," I said.

"It is not necessary."

"Have one."

He poured the two glasses.

"Remember," he said. "Come here. Do not let other people take you in. Here you are all right."

"I am sure."

"You are sure?"

"Yes."

He was serious. "Then let me tell you one thing. Do not go about with that coat."

"Why?"

"On the sleeves it shows very plainly where the stars have been cut away. The cloth is a different color."

I did not say anything.

"If you have no papers I can give you papers."

"What papers?"

"Leave-papers."

"I have no need for papers. I have papers."

"All right," he said. "But if you need papers I can get what you wish."

"How much are such papers?"

"It depends on what they are. The price is reasonable."

"I don't need any now."

He shrugged his shoulders.

"I'm all right," I said.

When I went out he said, "Don't forget that I am your friend."

"No."

"I will see you again," he said.

"Good," I said.

Outside I kept away from the station, where there were military police, and picked up a cab at the edge of the little park. I gave the driver the address of the hospital. At the hospital I went to the porter's lodge. His wife embraced me. He shook my hand.

"You are back. You are safe."

"Yes."

"Have you had breakfast?"

"Yes."

"How are you, Tenente? How are you?" the wife asked.

"Fine."

"Won't you have breakfast with us?"

"No, thank you. Tell me is Miss Barkley here at the hospital now?"

"Miss Barkley?"

"The English lady nurse."

"His girl," the wife said. She patted my arm and smiled.

"No," the porter said. "She is away."

My heart went down. "You are sure? I mean the tall blonde English young lady."

"I am sure. She is gone to Stresa."

"When did she go?"

"She went two days ago with the other lady English."

"Good," I said. "I wish you to do something for me. Do not tell any one you have seen me. It is very important."

"I won't tell any one," the porter said. I gave him a ten-lira note. He pushed it away.

"I promise you I will tell no one," he said. "I don't want any money."

"What can we do for you, Signor Tenente?" his wife asked.

"Only that," I said.

"We are dumb," the porter said. "You will let me know anything I can do?"

"Yes," I said. "Good-by. I will see you again."

They stood in the door, looking after me.

I got into the cab and gave the driver the address of Simmons, one of the men I knew who was studying singing.

Simmons lived a long way out in the town toward the Porta Magenta. He was still in bed and sleepy when I went to see him.

"You get up awfully early, Henry," he said.

"I came in on the early train."

"What's all this retreat? Were you at the front? Will you have a cigarette? They're in that box on the table." It was a big room with a bed beside the wall, a piano over on the far side and a dresser and table. I sat on a chair by the bed. Simmons sat propped up by the pillows and smoked.

"I'm in a jam, Sim," I said.

"So am I," he said. "I'm always in a jam. Won't you smoke?"

"No," I said. "What's the procedure in going to Switzerland?"

"For you? The Italians wouldn't let you out of the country."

"Yes. I know that. But the Swiss. What will they do?"

"They intern you."

"I know. But what's the mechanics of it?"

"Nothing. It's very simple. You can go anywhere. I think you just have to report or something. Why? Are you fleeing the police?"

"Nothing definite yet."

"Don't tell me if you don't want. But it would be interesting to hear. Nothing happens here. I was a great flop at Piacenza."

"I'm awfully sorry."

"Oh yes—I went very badly. I sung well too. I'm going to try it again at the Lyrico here."

"I'd like to be there."

"You're awfully polite. You aren't in a bad mess, are you?"

"I don't know."

"Don't tell me if you don't want. How do you happen to be away from the bloody front?"

"I think I'm through with it."

"Good boy. I always knew you had sense. Can I help you any way?"

"You're awfully busy."

"Not a bit of it, my dear Henry. Not a bit of it. I'd be happy to do anything."

"You're about my size. Would you go out and buy me an outfit of civilian clothes? I've clothes but they're all at Rome."

"You did live there, didn't you? It's a filthy place. How did you ever live there?"

"I wanted to be an architect."

"That's no place for that. Don't buy clothes. I'll give you all the clothes you want. I'll fit you out so you'll be a great success. Go in that dressing room. There's a closet. Take anything you want. My dear fellow, you don't want to buy clothes."

"I'd rather buy them, Sim."

"My dear fellow, it's easier for me to let you have them than go out and buy them. Have you got a passport? You won't get far without a passport."

"Yes. I've still got my passport."

"Then get dressed, my dear fellow, and off to old Helvetia."

"It's not that simple. I have to go up to Stresa first."

"Ideal, my dear fellow. You just row a boat across. If I wasn't trying to sing, I'd go with you. I'll go yet."

"You could take up yodelling."

"My dear fellow, I'll take up yodelling yet. I really can sing though. That's the strange part."

"I'll bet you can sing."

He lay back in bed smoking a cigarette.

"Don't bet too much. But I can sing though. It's damned funny, but I can. I like to sing. Listen." He roared into "Africana," his neck swelling, the veins standing out. "I can sing," he said. "Whether they like it or not." I looked out of the window. "I'll go down and let my cab go."

"Come back up, my dear fellow, and we'll have breakfast." He stepped out of bed, stood straight, took a deep breath and commenced doing bending exercises. I went downstairs and paid off the cab.

CHAPTER XXXIV

In civilian clothes I felt a masquerader. I had been in uniform a long time and I missed the feeling of being held by your clothes. The trousers felt very floppy. I had bought a ticket at Milan for Stresa. I had also bought a new hat. I could not wear Sim's hat but his clothes were fine. They smelled of tobacco and as I sat in the compartment and looked out the window the new hat felt very new and the clothes very old. I myself felt as sad as the wet Lombard country that was outside through the window. There were some aviators in the compartment who did not think much of me. They avoided looking at me and were very scornful of a civilian my age. I did not feel insulted. In the old days I would have insulted them and picked a fight. They got off at Gallarate and I was glad to be alone. I had the paper but I did not read it because I did not want to read about the war. I was going to forget the war. I had made a separate peace. I felt damned lonely and was glad when the train got to Stresa.

At the station I had expected to see the porters from the hotels but there was no one. The season had been over a long time and no one met the train. I got down from the train with my bag, it was Sim's bag, and very light to carry, being empty except for two shirts, and stood under the roof of the station in the rain while the train went on. I found a man in the station and asked him if he knew what hotels were open. The Grand-Hôtel & des Isles Borromées was open and several small hotels that stayed open all the year. I started in the rain for the Isles Borromées carrying my bag I saw a carriage coming down the street and signalled to the driver It was better to arrive in a carriage. We drove up to the carriage entrance of the big hotel and the concierge came out with an umbrella and was very polite.

I took a good room. It was very big and light and looked out on the lake. The clouds were down over the lake but it would be beautiful with the sunlight. I was expecting my wife, I said. There was a big double bed, a *letto matrimoniale* with a satin coverlet. The hotel was very luxurious. I went down the long halls, down the wide stairs, through the rooms to the bar. I knew the barman and sat on a high stool and ate salted almonds and potato chips. The martini felt cool and clean.

"What are you doing here in *borghese?*" the barman asked after he had mixed a second martini.

"I am on leave. Convalescing-leave."

"There is no one here. I don't know why they keep the hotel open."

"Have you been fishing?"

"I've caught some beautiful pieces. Trolling this time of year you catch some beautiful pieces."

"Did you ever get the tobacco I sent?"

"Yes. Didn't you get my card?"

I laughed. I had not been able to get the tobacco. It was American pipe-tobacco that he wanted, but my relatives had stopped sending it or it was being held up. Anyway it never came.

"I'll get some somewhere," I said. "Tell me have you seen two English girls in the town? They came here day before yesterday."

"They are not at the hotel."

"They are nurses."

"I have seen two nurses. Wait a minute, I will find out where they are."

"One of them is my wife," I said. "I have come here to meet her."

"The other is my wife."

"I am not joking."

"Pardon my stupid joke," he said. "I did not understand." He went away and was gone quite a little while. I ate olives, salted almonds and potato chips and looked at myself in civilian clothes in the mirror behind the bar. The bartender came back. "They are at the little hotel near the station," he said.

"How about some sandwiches?"

"I'll ring for some. You understand there is nothing here, now there are no people."

"Isn't there really any one at all?"

"Yes. There are a few people."

The sandwiches came and I ate three and drank a couple more martinis. I had never tasted anything so cool and clean. They made me feel civilized. I had had too much red wine, bread, cheese, bad coffee and grappa. I sat on the high stool before the pleasant mahogany, the brass and the mirrors and did not think at all. The barman asked me some question.

"Don't talk about the war," I said. The war was a long way away. Maybe there wasn't any war. There was no war here. Then I realized it was over for me. But I did not have the feeling that it was really over. I had the feeling of a boy who thinks of what is happening at a certain hour at the schoolhouse from which he has played truant.

Catherine and Helen Ferguson were at supper when I came
to their hotel. Standing in the hallway I saw them at table. Catherine's face was away from me and I saw the line of her hair and
her cheek and her lovely neck and shoulders. Ferguson was talking. She stopped when I came in.

"My God," she said.

"Hello," I said.

"Why it's you!" Catherine said. Her face lighted up. She looked
too happy to believe it. I kissed her. Catherine blushed and I sat
down at the table.

"You're a fine mess," Ferguson said. "What are you doing here?
Have you eaten?"

"No." The girl who was serving the meal came in and I told
her to bring a plate for me. Catherine looked at me all the time,
her eyes happy.

"What are you doing in mufti?" Ferguson asked.

"I'm in the Cabinet."

"You're in some mess."

"Cheer up, Fergy. Cheer up just a little."

"I'm not cheered by seeing you. I know the mess you've gotten
this girl into. You're no cheerful sight to me."

Catherine smiled at me and touched me with her foot under the
table.

"No one got me in a mess, Fergy. I get in my own messes."

"I can't stand him," Ferguson said. "He's done nothing but ruin
you with his sneaking Italian tricks. Americans are worse than
Italians."

"The Scotch are such a moral people," Catherine said.

"I don't mean that. I mean his Italian sneakiness."

"Am I sneaky, Fergy?"

"You are. You're worse than sneaky. You're like a snake. A
snake with an Italian uniform: with a cape around your neck."

"I haven't got an Italian uniform now."

"That's just another example of your sneakiness. You had a love affair all summer and got this girl with child and now I suppose you'll sneak off."

I smiled at Catherine and she smiled at me.

"We'll both sneak off," she said.

"You're two of the same thing," Ferguson said. "I'm ashamed of you, Catherine Barkley. You have no shame and no honor and you're as sneaky as he is."

"Don't, Fergy," Catherine said and patted her hand. "Don't denounce me. You know we like each other."

"Take your hand away," Ferguson said. Her face was red. "If you had any shame it would be different. But you're God knows how many months gone with child and you think it's a joke and are all smiles because your seducer's come back. You've no shame and no feelings." She began to cry. Catherine went over and put her arm around her. As she stood comforting Ferguson, I could see no change in her figure.

"I don't care," Ferguson sobbed. "I think it's dreadful."

"There, there, Fergy," Catherine comforted her. "I'll be ashamed. Don't cry, Fergy. Don't cry, old Fergy."

"I'm not crying," Ferguson sobbed. "I'm not crying. Except for the awful thing you've gotten into." She looked at me. "I hate you," she said. "She can't make me not hate you. You dirty sneaking American Italian." Her eyes and nose were red with crying.

Catherine smiled at me.

"Don't you smile at him with your arm around me."

"You're unreasonable, Fergy."

"I know it," Ferguson sobbed. "You mustn't mind me, either of you. I'm so upset. I'm not reasonable. I know it. I want you both to be happy."

"We're happy," Catherine said. "You're a sweet Fergy."

Ferguson cried again. "I don't want you happy the way you are. Why don't you get married? You haven't got another wife have you?"

"No," I said. Catherine laughed.

"It's nothing to laugh about," Ferguson said. "Plenty of them have other wives."

"We'll be married, Fergy," Catherine said, "if it will please you."

"Not to please me. You should want to be married."

"We've been very busy."

"Yes. I know. Busy making babies." I thought she was going to cry again but she went into bitterness instead. "I suppose you'll go off with him now to-night?"

"Yes," said Catherine. "If he wants me."

"What about me?"

"Are you afraid to stay here alone?"

"Yes, I am."

"Then I'll stay with you."

"No, go on with him. Go with him right away. I'm sick of seeing both of you."

"We'd better finish dinner."

"No. Go right away."

"Fergy, be reasonable."

"I say get out right away. Go away both of you."

"Let's go then," I said. I was sick of Fergy.

"You do want to go. You see you want to leave me even to eat dinner alone. I've always wanted to go to the Italian lakes and this is how it is. Oh, Oh," she sobbed, then looked at Catherine and choked.

"We'll stay till after dinner," Catherine said. "And I'll not leave you alone if you want me to stay. I won't leave you alone, Fergy."

"No. No. I want you to go. I want you to go." She wiped her eyes. "I'm so unreasonable. Please don't mind me."

The girl who served the meal had been upset by all the crying. Now as she brought in the next course she seemed relieved that things were better.

That night at the hotel, in our room with the long empty hall outside and our shoes outside the door, a thick carpet on the floor of the room, outside the windows the rain falling and in the room light and pleasant and cheerful, then the light out and it exciting with smooth sheets and the bed comfortable, feeling that we had come home, feeling no longer alone, waking in the night to find the other one there, and not gone away; all other things were unreal. We slept when we were tired and if we woke the other one woke too so one was not alone. Often a man wishes to be alone and a girl wishes to be alone too and if they love each other they are jealous of that in each other, but I can truly say we never felt that. We could feel alone when we were together, alone against the others. It has only happened to me like that once. I have been alone while I was with many girls and that is the way that you can be most lonely. But we were never lonely and never afraid when we were together. I know that the night is not the same as the day: that all things are different, that the things of the night cannot be explained in the day, because they do not then exist, and the night can be a dreadful time for lonely people once their loneliness has started. But with Catherine there was almost no difference in the night except that it was an even better time. If people bring so much courage to this world the world has to kill them to break them, so of course it kills them. The world breaks every one and afterward many are strong at the broken places. But those that will not break it kills. It kills the very good and the very gentle and the very brave impartially. If you are none of these you can be sure it will kill you too but there will be no special hurry.

I remember waking in the morning. Catherine was asleep and the sunlight was coming in through the window. The rain had stopped and I stepped out of bed and across the floor to the window. Down below were the gardens, bare now but beautifully regular, the gravel paths, the trees, the stone wall by the lake and the lake in the sunlight with the mountains beyond. I stood at the window looking out and when I turned away I saw Catherine was awake and watching me.

"How are you, darling?" she said. "Isn't it a lovely day?"

"How do you feel?"

"I feel very well. We had a lovely night."

"Do you want breakfast?"

She wanted breakfast. So did I and we had it in bed, the November sunlight coming in the window, and the breakfast tray across my lap.

"Don't you want the paper? You always wanted the paper in the hospital?"

"No," I said. "I don't want the paper now."

"Was it so bad you don't want even to read about it?"

"I don't want to read about it."

"I wish I had been with you so I would know about it too."

"I'll tell you about it if I ever get it straight in my head."

"But won't they arrest you if they catch you out of uniform?"

"They'll probably shoot me."

"Then we'll not stay here. We'll get out of the country."

"I'd thought something of that."

"We'll get out. Darling, you shouldn't take silly chances. Tell me how did you come from Mestre to Milan?"

"I came on the train. I was in uniform then."

"Weren't you in danger then?"

"Not much. I had an old order of movement. I fixed the dates on it in Mestre."

"Darling, you're liable to be arrested here any time. I won't have it. It's silly to do something like that. Where would we be if they took you off?"

"Let's not think about it. I'm tired of thinking about it."

"What would you do if they came to arrest you?"

"Shoot them."

"You see how silly you are, I won't let you go out of the hotel until we leave here."

"Where are we going to go?"

"Please don't be that way, darling. We'll go wherever you say But please find some place to go right away."

"Switzerland is down the lake, we can go there."

"That will be lovely."

It was clouding over outside and the lake was darkening.

"I wish we did not always have to live like criminals," I said.

"Darling, don't be that way. You haven't lived like a criminal very long. And we never live like criminals. We're going to have a fine time."

"I feel like a criminal. I've deserted from the army."

"Darling, *please* be sensible. It's not deserting from the army. It's only the Italian army."

I laughed. "You're a fine girl. Let's get back into bed. I feel fine in bed."

A little while later Catherine said, "You don't feel like a criminal do you?"

"No," I said. "Not when I'm with you."

"You're such a silly boy," she said. "But I'll look after you. Isn't it splendid, darling, that I don't have any morning-sickness?"

"It's grand."

"You don't appreciate what a fine wife you have. But I don't care. I'll get you some place where they can't arrest you and then we'll have a lovely time."

"Let's go there right away."

"We will, darling. I'll go any place any time you wish."

"Let's not think about anything."

"All right."

CHAPTER XXXV

Catherine went along the lake to the little hotel to see Ferguson and I sat in the bar and read the papers. There were comfortable leather chairs in the bar and I sat in one of them and read until the barman came in. The army had not stood at the Tagliamento. They were falling back to the Piave. I remembered the Piave. The railroad crossed it near San Dona going up to the front. It was deep and slow there and quite narrow. Down below there were mosquito marshes and canals. There were some lovely villas. Once, before the war, going up to Cortina D'Ampezzo I had gone along it for several hours in the hills. Up there it looked like a trout stream, flowing swiftly with shallow stretches and pools under the shadow of the rocks. The road turned off from it at Cadore. I wondered how the army that was up there would come down. The barman came in.

"Count Greffi was asking for you," he said.

"Who?"

"Count Greffi. You remember the old man who was here when you were here before."

"Is he here?"

"Yes, he's here with his niece. I told him you were here. He wants you to play billiards."

"Where is he?"

"He's taking a walk."

"How is he?"

"He's younger than ever. He drank three champagne cocktails last night before dinner."

"How's his billiard game?"

"Good. He beat me. When I told him you were here he was very pleased. There's nobody here for him to play with."

Count Greffi was ninety-four years old. He had been a contemporary of Metternich and was an old man with white hair and mustache and beautiful manners. He had been in the diplomatic service of both Austria and Italy and his birthday parties were the great social event of Milan. He was living to be one hundred years old and played a smoothly fluent game of billiards that contrasted with his own ninety-four-year-old brittleness. I had met him when I had been at Stresa once before out of season and while we played billiards we drank champagne. I thought it was a splendid custom and he gave me fifteen points in a hundred and beat me.

"Why didn't you tell me he was here?"

"I forgot it."

"Who else is here?"

"No one you know. There are only six people altogether."

"What are you doing now?"

"Nothing."

"Come on out fishing."

"I could come for an hour."

"Come on. Bring the trolling line."

The barman put on a coat and we went out We went down and got a boat and I rowed while the barman sat in the stern and let out the line with a spinner and a heavy sinker on the end to troll for lake trout. We rowed along the shore, the barman holding the line in his hand and giving it occasional jerks forward. Stresa looked very deserted from the lake. There were the long rows of bare trees, the big hotels and the closed villas. I rowed across to Isola Bella and went close to the walls, where the water deepened sharply, and you saw the rock wall slanting down in the clear water, and then up and along to the fisherman's island. The sun was under a cloud and the water was dark and smooth and very cold. We did not have a strike though we saw some circles on the water from rising fish.

I rowed up opposite the fisherman's island where there were boats drawn up and men were mending nets.

"Should we get a drink?"

"All right."

I brought the boat up to the stone pier and the barman pulled in the line, coiling it on the bottom of the boat and hooking the spinner on the edge of the gunwale. I stepped out and tied the boat. We went into a little café, sat at a bare wooden table and ordered vermouth.

"Are you tired from rowing?"

"No."

"I'll row back," he said.

"I like to row."

"Maybe if you hold the line it will change the luck."

"All right."

"Tell me how goes the war."

"Rotten."

"I don't have to go. I'm too old, like Count Greffi."

"Maybe you'll have to go yet."

"Next year they'll call my class. But I won't go."

"What will you do?"

"Get out of the country. I wouldn't go to war. I was at the war once in Abyssinia. Nix. Why do you go?"

"I don't know. I was a fool."

"Have another vermouth?"

"All right."

The barman rowed back. We trolled up the lake beyond Stresa and then down not far from shore. I held the taut line and felt the faint pulsing of the spinner revolving while I looked at the dark November water of the lake and the deserted shore. The barman rowed with long strokes and on the forward thrust of the boat the line throbbed. Once I had a strike: the line hardened suddenly and jerked back. I pulled and felt the live weight of the trout and then the line throbbed again. I had missed him.

"Did he feel big?"

"Pretty big."

"Once when I was out trolling alone I had the line in my teeth and one struck and nearly took my mouth out."

"The best way is to have it over your leg," I said. "Then you feel it and don't lose your teeth."

I put my hand in the water. It was very cold. We were almost opposite the hotel now.

"I have to go in," the barman said, "to be there for eleven o'clock. L'heure du cocktail."

"All right."

I pulled in the line and wrapped it on a stick notched at each end. The barman put the boat in a little slip in the stone wall and locked it with a chain and padlock.

"Any time you want it," he said, "I'll give you the key."

"Thanks."

We went up to the hotel and into the bar. I did not want another drink so early in the morning so I went up to our room. The maid had just finished doing the room and Catherine was not back yet. I lay down on the bed and tried to keep from thinking.

When Catherine came back it was all right again. Ferguson was downstairs, she said. She was coming to lunch.

"I knew you wouldn't mind," Catherine said.

"No," I said.

"What's the matter, darling?"

"I don't know."

"I know. You haven't anything to do. All you have is me and I go away."

"That's true."

"I'm sorry, darling. I know it must be a dreadful feeling to have nothing at all suddenly."

"My life used to be full of everything," I said. "Now if you aren't with me I haven't a thing in the world."

"But I'll be with you. I was only gone for two hours. Isn't there anything you can do?"

"I went fishing with the barman."

"Wasn't it fun?"

"Yes."

"Don't think about me when I'm not here."

"That's the way I worked it at the front. But there was something to do then."

"Othello with his occupation gone," she teased.

"Othello was a nigger," I said. "Besides, I'm not jealous. I'm just so in love with you that there isn't anything else."

"Will you be a good boy and be nice to Ferguson?"

"I'm always nice to Ferguson unless she curses me."

"Be nice to her. Think how much we have and she hasn't anything."

"I don't think she wants what we have."

"You don't know much, darling, for such a wise boy."

"I'll be nice to her."

"I know you will. You're so sweet."

"She won't stay afterward, will she?"

"No. I'll get rid of her."

"And then we'll come up here."

"Of course. What do you think I want to do?"

We went downstairs to have lunch with Ferguson. She was very impressed by the hotel and the splendor of the dining-room. We had a good lunch with a couple of bottles of white capri. Count Greffi came into the dining-room and bowed to us. His niece, who looked a little like my grandmother, was with him. I told Catherine and Ferguson about him and Ferguson was very impressed. The hotel was very big and grand and empty but the food was good, the wine was very pleasant and finally the wine made us all feel very well. Catherine had no need to feel any better. She was very happy. Ferguson became quite cheerful. I felt very well myself. After lunch Ferguson went back to her hotel. She was going to lie down for a while after lunch she said.

Along late in the afternoon some one knocked on our door. "Who is it?"

"The Count Greffi wishes to know if you will play billiards with him."

I looked at my watch; I had taken it off and it was under the pillow.

"Do you have to go, darling?" Catherine whispered.

"I think I'd better." The watch was a quarter-past four o'clock. Out loud I said, "Tell the Count Greffi I will be in the billiard-room at five o'clock."

At a quarter to five I kissed Catherine good-by and went into the bathroom to dress. Knotting my tie and looking in the glass I looked strange to myself in the civilian clothes. I must remember to buy some more shirts and socks.

"Will you be away a long time?" Catherine asked. She looked lovely in the bed. "Would you hand me the brush?"

I watched her brushing her hair, holding her head so the weight of her hair all came on one side. It was dark outside and the light over the head of the bed shone on her hair and on her neck and shoulders. I went over and kissed her and held her hand with the

brush and her head sunk back on the pillow. I kissed her neck and
shoulders. I felt faint with loving her so much.

"I don't want to go away."

"I don't want you to go away."

"I won't go then."

"Yes. Go. It's only for a little while and then you'll come back."

"We'll have dinner up here."

"Hurry and come back."

I found the Count Greffi in the billiard-room. He was practising strokes, looking very fragile under the light that came down
above the billiard table. On a card table a little way beyond the
light was a silver icing-bucket with the necks and corks of
two champagne bottles showing above the ice. The Count Greffi
straightened up when I came toward the table and walked
toward me. He put out his hand, "It is such a great pleasure that
you are here. You were very kind to come to play with me."

"It was very nice of you to ask me."

"Are you quite well? They told me you were wounded on the
Isonzo. I hope you are well again."

"I'm very well. Have you been well?"

"Oh, I am always well. But I am getting old. I detect signs of
age now."

"I can't believe it."

"Yes. Do you want to know one? It is easier for me to talk
Italian. I discipline myself but I find when I am tired that it is so
much easier to talk Italian. So I know I must be getting old."

"We could talk Italian. I am a little tired, too."

"Oh, but when you are tired it will be easier for you to talk
English."

"American."

"Yes. American. You will please talk American. It is a delightful language."

"I hardly ever see Americans."

"You must miss them. One misses one's countrymen and especially one's countrywomen. I know that experience. Should we play or are you too tired?"

"I'm not really tired. I said that for a joke. What handicap will you give me?"

"Have you been playing very much?"

"None at all."

"You play very well. Ten points in a hundred?"

"You flatter me."

"Fifteen?"

"That would be fine but you will beat me."

"Should we play for a stake? You always wished to play for a stake."

"I think we'd better."

"All right. I will give you eighteen points and we will play for a franc a point."

He played a lovely game of billiards and with the handicap I was only four ahead at fifty. Count Greffi pushed a button on the wall to ring for the barman.

"Open one bottle please," he said. Then to me, "We will take a little stimulant." The wine was icy cold and very dry and good.

"Should we talk Italian? Would you mind very much? It is my weakness now."

We went on playing, sipping the wine between shots, speaking in Italian, but talking little, concentrated on the game. Count Greffi made his one hundredth point and with the handicap I was only at ninety-four. He smiled and patted me on the shoulder.

"Now we will drink the other bottle and you will tell me about the war." He waited for me to sit down.

"About anything else," I said.

"You don't want to talk about it? Good. What have you been reading?"

"Nothing." I said. "I'm afraid I am very dull."

"No. But you should read."

"What is there written in war-time?"

"There is 'Le Feu' by a Frenchman, Barbusse. There is 'Mr. Britling Sees Through It.' "

"No, he doesn't."

"What?"

"He doesn't see through it. Those books were at the hospital."

"Then you have been reading?"

"Yes, but nothing any good."

"I thought 'Mr. Britling' a very good study of the English middle-class soul."

"I don't know about the soul."

"Poor boy. We none of us know about the soul. Are you *Croyant?*"

"At night."

Count Greffi smiled and turned the glass with his fingers. "I had expected to become more devout as I grow older but somehow I haven't," he said. "It is a great pity."

"Would you like to live after death?" I asked and instantly felt a fool to mention death. But he did not mind the word.

"It would depend on the life. This life is very pleasant. I would like to live forever," he smiled. "I very nearly have."

We were sitting in the deep leather chairs, the champagne in the ice-bucket and our glasses on the table between us.

"If you ever live to be as old as I am you will find many things strange."

"You never seem old."

"It is the body that is old. Sometimes I am afraid I will break off a finger as one breaks a stick of chalk. And the spirit is no older and not much wiser."

"You are wise."

"No, that is the great fallacy; the wisdom of old men. They do not grow wise. They grow careful."

"Perhaps that is wisdom."

"It is a very unattractive wisdom. What do you value most?"

"Some one I love."

"With me it is the same. That is not wisdom. Do you value life?"

"Yes."

"So do I. Because it is all I have. And to give birthday parties," he laughed. "You are probably wiser than I am. You do not give birthday parties."

We both drank the wine.

"What do you think of the war really?" I asked.

"I think it is stupid."

"Who will win it?"

"Italy."

"Why?"

"They are a younger nation."

"Do younger nations always win wars?"

"They are apt to for a time."

"Then what happens?"

"They become older nations."

"You said you were not wise."

"Dear boy, that is not wisdom. That is cynicism."

"It sounds very wise to me."

"It's not particularly. I could quote you the examples on the other side. But it is not bad. Have we finished the champagne?"

"Almost."

"Should we drink some more? Then I must dress."

"Perhaps we'd better not now."

"You are sure you don't want more?"

"Yes." He stood up.

"I hope you will be very fortunate and very happy and very, very healthy."

"Thank you. And I hope you will live forever."

"Thank you. I have. And if you ever become devout pray for me if I am dead. I am asking several of my friends to do that. I had expected to become devout myself but it has not come." I thought he smiled sadly but I could not tell. He was so old and his face was very wrinkled, so that a smile used so many lines that all gradations were lost.

"I might become very devout," I said. "Anyway, I will pray for you."

"I had always expected to become devout. All my family died very devout. But somehow it does not come."

"It's too early."

"Maybe it is too late. Perhaps I have outlived my religious feeling."

"My own comes only at night."

"Then too you are in love. Do not forget that is a religious feeling."

"You believe so?"

"Of course." He took a step toward the table. "You were very kind to play."

"It was a great pleasure."

"We will walk up stairs together."

CHAPTER XXXVI

That night there was a storm and I woke to hear the rain lashing the window-panes. It was coming in the open window. Some one had knocked on the door. I went to the door very softly, not to disturb Catherine, and opened it. The barman stood there. He wore his overcoat and carried his wet hat.

"Can I speak to you, Tenente?"

"What's the matter?"

"It's a very serious matter."

I looked around. The room was dark. I saw the water on the floor from the window. "Come in," I said. I took him by the arm into the bathroom; locked the door and put on the light. I sat down on the edge of the bathtub.

"What's the matter, Emilio? Are you in trouble?"

"No. You are, Tenente."

"Yes?"

"They are going to arrest you in the morning."

"Yes?"

264

"I came to tell you. I was out in the town and I heard them talking in a café."

"I see."

He stood there, his coat wet, holding his wet hat and said nothing.

"Why are they going to arrest me?"

"For something about the war."

"Do you know what?"

"No. But I know that they know you were here before as an officer and now you are here out of uniform. After this retreat they arrest everybody."

I thought a minute.

"What time do they come to arrest me?"

"In the morning. I don't know the time."

"What do you say to do?"

He put his hat in the washbowl. It was very wet and had been dripping on the floor.

"If you have nothing to fear an arrest is nothing. But it is always bad to be arrested—especially now."

"I don't want to be arrested."

"Then go to Switzerland."

"How?"

"In my boat."

"There is a storm," I said.

"The storm is over. It is rough but you will be all right."

"When should we go?"

"Right away. They might come to arrest you early in the morning."

"What about our bags?"

"Get them packed. Get your lady dressed. I will take care of them."

"Where will you be?"

"I will wait here. I don't want any one to see me outside in the hall."

I opened the door, closed it, and went into the bedroom. Catherine was awake.

"What is it, darling?"

"It's all right, Cat," I said. "Would you like to get dressed right away and go in a boat to Switzerland?"

"Would you?"

"No," I said. "I'd like to go back to bed."

"What is it about?"

"The barman says they are going to arrest me in the morning."

"Is the barman crazy?"

"No."

"Then please hurry, darling, and get dressed so we can start." She sat up on the side of the bed. She was still sleepy. "Is that the barman in the bathroom?"

"Yes."

"Then I won't wash. Please look the other way, darling, and I'll be dressed in just a minute."

I saw her white back as she took off her night-gown and then I looked away because she wanted me to. She was beginning to be a little big with the child and she did not want me to see her. I dressed hearing the rain on the windows. I did not have much to put in my bag.

"There's plenty of room in my bag, Cat, if you need any."

"I'm almost packed," she said. "Darling, I'm awfully stupid, but why is the barman in the bathroom?"

"Sh—he's waiting to take our bags down."

"He's awfully nice."

"He's an old friend," I said. "I nearly sent him some pipe-tobacco once."

I looked out the open window at the dark night. I could not see the lake, only the dark and the rain but the wind was quieter.

"I'm ready, darling," Catherine said.

"All right." I went to the bathroom door. "Here are the bags, Emilio," I said. The barman took the two bags.

"You're very good to help us," Catherine said.

"That's nothing, lady," the barman said. "I'm glad to help you just so I don't get in trouble myself. Listen," he said to me. "I'll take these out the servants' stairs and to the boat. You just go out as though you were going for a walk."

"It's a lovely night for a walk," Catherine said.

"It's a bad night all right."

"I'm glad I've an umbrella," Catherine said.

We walked down the hall and down the wide thickly carpeted stairs. At the foot of the stairs by the door the porter sat behind his desk.

He looked surprised at seeing us.

"You're not going out, sir?" he said.

"Yes," I said. "We're going to see the storm along the lake."

"Haven't you got an umbrella, sir?"

"No," I said. "This coat sheds water."

He looked at it doubtfully. "I'll get you an umbrella, sir," he said. He went away and came back with a big umbrella. "It is a little big, sir," he said. I gave him a ten-lira note. "Oh you are too good, sir. Thank you very much," he said. He held the door open and we went out into the rain. He smiled at Catherine and she smiled at him. "Don't stay out in the storm," he said. "You will get wet, sir and lady." He was only the second porter, and his English was still literally translated.

"We'll be back," I said. We walked down the path under the giant umbrella and out through the dark wet gardens to the road and across the road to the trellised pathway along the lake. The wind was blowing offshore now. It was a cold, wet November wind and I knew it was snowing in the mountains. We came along past the chained boats in the slips along the quay to where the barman's boat should be. The water was dark against the stone. The barman stepped out from beside the row of trees.

"The bags are in the boat," he said.

"I want to pay you for the boat," I said.

"How much money have you?"

"Not so much."

"You send me the money later. That will be all right."

"How much?"

"What you want."

"Tell me how much."

"If you get through send me five hundred francs. You won't mind that if you get through."

"All right."

"Here are sandwiches." He handed me a package. "Everything there was in the bar. It's all here. This is a bottle of brandy and a bottle of wine." I put them in my bag. "Let me pay you for those."

"All right, give me fifty lire."

I gave it to him. "The brandy is good," he said. "You don't need to be afraid to give it to your lady. She better get in the boat." He held the boat, it rising and falling against the stone wall and I helped Catherine in. She sat in the stern and pulled her cape around her.

"You know where to go?"

"Up the lake."

"You know how far?"

"Past Luino."

"Past Luino, Cannero, Cannobio, Tranzano. You aren't in Switzerland until you come to Brissago. You have to pass Monte Tamara."

"What time is it?" Catherine asked.

"It's only eleven o'clock," I said.

"If you row all the time you ought to be there by seven o'clock in the morning."

"Is it that far?"

"It's thirty-five kilometres."

"How should we go? In this rain we need a compass."

"No. Row to Isola Bella. Then on the other side of Isola Madre go with the wind. The wind will take you to Pallanza. You will see the lights. Then go up the shore."

"Maybe the wind will change."

"No," he said. "This wind will blow like this for three days. It comes straight down from the Mattarone. There is a can to bail with."

"Let me pay you something for the boat now."

"No, I'd rather take a chance. If you get through you pay me all you can."

"All right."

"I don't think you'll get drowned."

"That's good."

"Go with the wind up the lake."

"All right." I stepped in the boat.

"Did you leave the money for the hotel?"

"Yes. In an envelope in the room."

"All right. Good luck, Tenente."

"Good luck. We thank you many times."

"You won't thank me if you get drowned."

"What does he say?" Catherine asked.

"He says good luck."

"Good luck," Catherine said. "Thank you very much."

"Are you ready?"

"Yes."

He bent down and shoved us off. I dug at the water with the oars, then waved one hand. The barman waved back deprecatingly. I saw the lights of the hotel and rowed out, rowing straight out until they were out of sight. There was quite a sea running but we were going with the wind.

CHAPTER XXXVII

1 rowed in the dark keeping the wind in my face. The rain had stopped and only came occasionally in gusts. It was very dark, and the wind was cold. I could see Catherine in the stern but I could not see the water where the blades of the oars dipped. The oars were long and there were no leathers to keep them from slipping out. I pulled, raised, leaned forward, found the water, dipped and pulled, rowing as easily as I could. I did not feather the oars because the wind was with us. I knew my hands would blister and I wanted to delay it as long as I could. The boat was light and rowed easily. I pulled it along in the dark water. I could not see, and hoped we would soon come opposite Pallanza.

We never saw Pallanza. The wind was blowing up the lake and we passed the point that hides Pallanza in the dark and never saw the lights. When we finally saw some lights much further up the lake and close to the shore it was Intra. But for a long time we did not see any lights, nor did we see the shore but rowed steadily in the dark riding with the waves. Sometimes I missed the water with the oars in the dark as a wave lifted the boat. It was quite rough;

but I kept on rowing, until suddenly we were close ashore against a point of rock that rose beside us; the waves striking against it, rushing high up, then falling back. I pulled hard on the right oar and backed water with the other and we went out into the lake again; the point was out of sight and we were going on up the lake.

"We're across the lake," I said to Catherine.

"Weren't we going to see Pallanza?"

"We've missed it."

"How are you, darling?"

"I'm fine."

"I could take the oars awhile."

"No, I'm fine."

"Poor Ferguson," Catherine said. "In the morning she'll come to the hotel and find we're gone."

"I'm not worrying so much about that," I said, "as about getting into the Swiss part of the lake before it's daylight and the custom guards see us."

"Is it a long way?"

"It's some thirty kilometres from here."

I rowed all night. Finally my hands were so sore I could hardly close them over the oars. We were nearly smashed up on the shore several times. I kept fairly close to the shore because I was afraid of getting lost on the lake and losing time. Sometimes we were so close we could see a row of trees and the road along the shore with the mountains behind. The rain stopped and the wind drove the clouds so that the moon shone through and looking back I could see the long dark point of Castagnola and the lake with white-caps and beyond, the moon on the high snow mountains. Then the clouds came over the moon again and the mountains and the lake were gone, but it was much lighter than it had been before and we could see the shore. I could see it too clearly and pulled out where they would not see the boat if there were custom guards along the

Pallanza road. When the moon came out again we could see white villas on the shore on the slopes of the mountain and the white road where it showed through the trees. All the time I was rowing.

The lake widened and across it on the shore at the foot of the mountains on the other side we saw a few lights that should be Luino. I saw a wedgelike gap between the mountains on the other shore and I thought that must be Luino. If it was we were making good time. I pulled in the oars and lay back on the seat. I was very, very tired of rowing. My arms and shoulders and back ached and my hands were sore.

"I could hold the umbrella," Catherine said. "We could sail with that with the wind."

"Can you steer?"

"I think so."

"You take this oar and hold it under your arm close to the side of the boat and steer and I'll hold the umbrella." I went back to the stern and showed her how to hold the oar. I took the big umbrella the porter had given me and sat facing the bow and opened it. It opened with a clap. I held it on both sides, sitting astride the handle hooked over the seat. The wind was full in it and I felt the boat suck forward while I held as hard as I could to the two edges. It pulled hard. The boat was moving fast.

"We're going beautifully," Catherine said. All I could see was umbrella ribs. The umbrella strained and pulled and I felt us driving along with it. I braced my feet and held back on it, then suddenly, it buckled; I felt a rib snap on my forehead, I tried to grab the top that was bending with the wind and the whole thing buckled and went inside out and I was astride the handle of an inside-out, ripped umbrella, where I had been holding a wind-filled pulling sail. I unhooked the handle from the seat, laid the umbrella in the bow and went back to Catherine for the oar. She was laughing. She took my hand and kept on laughing.

"What's the matter?" I took the oar.

"You looked so funny holding that thing."

"I suppose so."

"Don't be cross, darling. It was awfully funny. You looked about twenty feet broad and very affectionate holding the umbrella by the edges—" she choked.

"I'll row."

"Take a rest and a drink. It's a grand night and we've come a long way."

"I have to keep the boat out of the trough of the waves."

"I'll get you a drink. Then rest a little while, darling."

I held the oars up and we sailed with them. Catherine was opening the bag. She handed me the brandy bottle. I pulled the cork with my pocket-knife and took a long drink. It was smooth and hot and the heat went all through me and I felt warmed and cheerful. "It's lovely brandy," I said. The moon was under again but I could see the shore. There seemed to be another point going out a long way ahead into the lake.

"Are you warm enough, Cat?"

"I'm splendid. I'm a little stiff."

"Bail out that water and you can put your feet down."

Then I rowed and listened to the oarlocks and the dip and scrape of the bailing tin under the stern seat.

"Would you give me the bailer?" I said. "I want a drink."

"It's awful dirty."

"That's all right. I'll rinse it."

I heard Catherine rinsing it over the side. Then she handed it to me dipped full of water. I was thirsty after the brandy and the water was icy cold, so cold it made my teeth ache. I looked toward the shore. We were closer to the long point. There were lights in the bay ahead.

"Thanks," I said and handed back the tin pail.

"You're ever so welcome," Catherine said. "There's much more if you want it."

"Don't you want to eat something?"

"No. I'll be hungry in a little while. We'll save it till then."

"All right."

What looked like a point ahead was a long high headland. I went further out in the lake to pass it. The lake was much narrower now. The moon was out again and the *guardia di finanza* could have seen our boat black on the water if they had been watching.

"How are you, Cat?" I asked.

"I'm all right. Where are we?"

"I don't think we have more than about eight miles more."

"That's a long way to row, you poor sweet. Aren't you dead?"

"No. I'm all right. My hands are sore is all."

We went on up the lake. There was a break in the mountains on the right bank, a flattening-out with a low shore line that I thought must be Cannobio. I stayed a long way out because it was from now on that we ran the most danger of meeting *guardia*. There was a high dome-capped mountain on the other shore a way ahead. I was tired. It was no great distance to row but when you were out of condition it had been a long way. I knew I had to pass that mountain and go up the lake at least five miles further before we would be in Swiss water. The moon was almost down now but before it went down the sky clouded over again and it was very dark. I stayed well out in the lake, rowing awhile, then resting and holding the oars so that the wind struck the blades.

"Let me row awhile," Catherine said.

"I don't think you ought to."

"Nonsense. It would be good for me. It would keep me from being too stiff."

"I don't think you should, Cat."

"Nonsense. Rowing in moderation is very good for the pregnant lady."

"All right, you row a little moderately. I'll go back, then you come up. Hold on to both gunwales when you come up."

I sat in the stern with my coat on and the collar turned up and watched Catherine row. She rowed very well but the oars were too long and bothered her. I opened the bag and ate a couple of sandwiches and took a drink of the brandy. It made everything much better and I took another drink.

"Tell me when you're tired," I said. Then a little later, "Watch out the oar doesn't pop you in the tummy."

"If it did"—Catherine said between strokes—"life might be much simpler."

I took another drink of the brandy.

"How are you going?"

"All right."

"Tell me when you want to stop."

"All right."

I took another drink of the brandy, then took hold of the two gunwales of the boat and moved forward.

"No. I'm going beautifully."

"Go on back to the stern. I've had a grand rest."

For a while, with the brandy, I rowed easily and steadily. Then I began to catch crabs and soon I was just chopping along again with a thin brown taste of bile from having rowed too hard after the brandy.

"Give me a drink of water, will you?" I said.

"That's easy," Catherine said.

Before daylight it started to drizzle. The wind was down or we were protected by mountains that bounded the curve the lake had made. When I knew daylight was coming I settled down and rowed hard. I did not know where we were and I wanted to get

into the Swiss part of the lake. When it was beginning to be daylight we were quite close to the shore. I could see the rocky shore
and the trees.

"What's that?" Catherine said. I rested on the oars and listened.
It was a motor boat chugging out on the lake. I pulled close up to
the shore and lay quiet. The chugging came closer; then we saw
the motor boat in the rain a little astern of us. There were four
guardia di finanza in the stern, their *alpini* hats pulled down, their
cape collars turned up and their carbines slung across their backs.
They all looked sleepy so early in the morning. I could see the yellow on their hats and the yellow marks on their cape collars. The
motor boat chugged on and out of sight in the rain.

I pulled out into the lake. If we were that close to the border
I did not want to be hailed by a sentry along the road. I stayed out
where I could just see the shore and rowed on for three quarters of
an hour in the rain. We heard a motor boat once more but I kept
quiet until the noise of the engine went away across the lake.

"I think we're in Switzerland, Cat," I said.

"Really?"

"There's no way to know until we see Swiss troops."

"Or the Swiss navy."

"The Swiss navy's no joke for us. That last motor boat we heard
was probably the Swiss navy."

"If we're in Switzerland let's have a big breakfast. They have
wonderful rolls and butter and jam in Switzerland."

It was clear daylight now and a fine rain was falling. The wind
was still blowing outside up the lake and we could see the tops of
the white-caps going away from us and up the lake. I was sure we
were in Switzerland now. There were many houses back in the
trees from the shore and up the shore a way was a village with
stone houses, some villas on the hills and a church. I had been
looking at the road that skirted the shore for guards but did not

see any. The road came quite close to the lake now and I saw a soldier coming out of a café on the road. He wore a gray-green uniform and a helmet like the Germans. He had a healthy-looking face and a little toothbrush mustache. He looked at us.

"Wave to him," I said to Catherine. She waved and the soldier smiled embarrassedly and gave a wave of his hand. I eased up rowing. We were passing the waterfront of the village.

"We must be well inside the border," I said.

"We want to be sure, darling. We don't want them to turn us back at the frontier."

"The frontier is a long way back. I think this is the customs town. I'm pretty sure it's Brissago."

"Won't there be Italians there? There are always both sides at a customs town."

"Not in war-time. I don't think they let the Italians cross the frontier."

It was a nice-looking little town. There were many fishing boats along the quay and nets were spread on racks. There was a fine November rain falling but it looked cheerful and clean even with the rain.

"Should we land then and have breakfast?"

"All right."

I pulled hard on the left oar and came in close, then straightened out when we were close to the quay and brought the boat alongside. I pulled in the oars, took hold of an iron ring, stepped up on the wet stone and was in Switzerland. I tied the boat and held my hand down to Catherine.

"Come on up, Cat. It's a grand feeling."

"What about the bags?"

"Leave them in the boat."

Catherine stepped up and we were in Switzerland together.

"What a lovely country," she said.

"Isn't it grand?"

"Let's go and have breakfast!"

"Isn't it a grand country? I love the way it feels under my shoes."

"I'm so stiff I can't feel it very well. But it feels like a splendid country. Darling, do you realize we're here and out of that bloody place?"

"I do. I really do. I've never realized anything before."

"Look at the houses. Isn't this a fine square? There's a place we can get breakfast."

"Isn't the rain fine? They never had rain like this in Italy. It's cheerful rain."

"And we're here, darling! Do you realize we're here?"

We went inside the café and sat down at a clean wooden table. We were cockeyed excited. A splendid clean-looking woman with an apron came and asked us what we wanted.

"Rolls and jam and coffee," Catherine said.

"I'm sorry, we haven't any rolls in war-time."

"Bread then."

"I can make you some toast."

"All right."

"I want some eggs fried too."

"How many eggs for the gentleman?"

"Three."

"Take four, darling."

"Four eggs."

The woman went away. I kissed Catherine and held her hand very tight. We looked at each other and at the café.

"Darling, darling, isn't it lovely?"

"It's grand," I said.

"I don't mind there not being rolls," Catherine said. "I thought about them all night. But I don't mind it. I don't mind it at all."

"I suppose pretty soon they will arrest us."

"Never mind, darling. We'll have breakfast first. You won't

mind being arrested after breakfast. And then there's nothing they
can do to us. We're British and American citizens in good standing."

"You have a passport, haven't you?"

"Of course. Oh let's not talk about it. Let's be happy."

"I couldn't be any happier," I said. A fat gray cat with a tail that
lifted like a plume crossed the floor to our table and curved against
my leg to purr each time she rubbed. I reached down and stroked
her. Catherine smiled at me very happily. "Here comes the coffee,"
she said.

They arrested us after breakfast. We took a little walk through
the village then went down to the quay to get our bags. A soldier
was standing guard over the boat.

"Is this your boat?"

"Yes."

"Where do you come from?"

"Up the lake."

"Then I have to ask you to come with me."

"How about the bags?"

"You can carry the bags."

I carried the bags and Catherine walked beside me and the soldier walked along behind us to the old custom house. In the
custom house a lieutenant, very thin and military, questioned us.

"What nationality are you?"

"American and British."

"Let me see your passports."

I gave him mine and Catherine got hers out of her handbag.

He examined them for a long time.

"Why do you enter Switzerland this way in a boat?"

"I am a sportsman," I said. "Rowing is my great sport. I always
row when I get a chance."

"Why do you come here?"

"For the winter sport. We are tourists and we want to do the winter sport."

"This is no place for winter sport."

"We know it. We want to go where they have the winter sport."

"What have you been doing in Italy?"

"I have been studying architecture. My cousin has been studying art."

"Why do you leave there?"

"We want to do the winter sport. With the war going on you cannot study architecture."

"You will please stay where you are," the lieutenant said. He went back into the building with our passports.

"You're splendid, darling," Catherine said. "Keep on the same track. You want to do the winter sport."

"Do you know anything about art?"

"Rubens," said Catherine.

"Large and fat," I said.

"Titian," Catherine said.

"Titian-haired," I said. "How about Mantegna?"

"Don't ask hard ones," Catherine said. "I know him though— very bitter."

"Very bitter," I said. "Lots of nail holes."

"You see I'll make you a fine wife," Catherine said. "I'll be able to talk art with your customers."

"Here he comes," I said. The thin lieutenant came down the length of the custom house, holding our passports.

"I will have to send you into Locarno," he said. "You can get a carriage and a soldier will go in with you."

"All right," I said. "What about the boat?"

"The boat is confiscated. What have you in those bags?"

He went all through the two bags and held up the quarter-bottle of brandy. "Would you join me in a drink?" I asked.

"No thank you." He straightened up. "How much money have you?"

"Twenty-five hundred lire."

He was favorably impressed. "How much has your cousin?"

Catherine had a little over twelve hundred lire. The lieutenant was pleased. His attitude toward us became less haughty.

"If you are going for winter sports," he said, "Wengen is the place. My father has a very fine hotel at Wengen. It is open all the time."

"That's splendid," I said. "Could you give me the name?"

"I will write it on a card." He handed me the card very politely.

"The soldier will take you into Locarno. He will keep your passports. I regret this but it is necessary. I have good hopes they will give you a visa or a police permit at Locarno."

He handed the two passports to the soldier and carrying the bags we started into the village to order a carriage. "Hi," the lieutenant called to the soldier. He said something in a German dialect to him. The soldier slung his rifle on his back and picked up the bags.

"It's a great country," I said to Catherine.

"It's so practical."

"Thank you very much," I said to the lieutenant. He waved his hand.

"*Service!*" he said. We followed our guard into the village.

We drove to Locarno in a carriage with the soldier sitting on the front seat with the driver. At Locarno we did not have a bad time. They questioned us but they were polite because we had passports and money. I do not think they believed a word of the story and I thought it was silly but it was like a law-court. You did not want something reasonable, you wanted something technical and then stuck to it without explanations. But we had passports and we would spend the money. So they gave us provisional visas.

At any time this visa might be withdrawn. We were to report to the police wherever we went.

Could we go wherever we wanted? Yes. Where did we want to go?

"Where do you want to go, Cat?"

"Montreux."

"It is a very nice place," the official said. "I think you will like that place."

"Here at Locarno is a very nice place," another official said. "I am sure you would like it here very much at Locarno. Locarno is a very attractive place."

"We would like some place where there is winter sport."

"There is no winter sport at Montreux."

"I beg your pardon," the other official said. "I come from Montreux. There is very certainly winter sport on the Montreux Oberland Bernois railway. It would be false for you to deny that."

"I do not deny it. I simply said there is no winter sport at Montreux."

"I question that," the other official said. "I question that statement."

"I hold to that statement."

"I question that statement. I myself have *luge-ed* into the streets of Montreux. I have done it not once but several times. Luge-ing is certainly winter sport."

The other official turned to me.

"Is luge-ing your idea of winter sport, sir? I tell you you would be very comfortable here in Locarno. You would find the climate healthy, you would find the environs attractive. You would like it very much."

"The gentleman has expressed a wish to go to Montreux."

"What is luge-ing?" I asked.

"You see he has never even heard of luge-ing!"

That meant a great deal to the second official. He was pleased by that.

"Luge-ing," said the first official, "is tobogganing."

"I beg to differ," the other official shook his head. "I must differ again. The toboggan is very different from the luge. The toboggan is constructed in Canada of flat laths. The luge is a common sled with runners. Accuracy means something."

"Couldn't we toboggan?" I asked.

"Of course you could toboggan," the first official said. "You could toboggan very well. Excellent Canadian toboggans are sold in Montreux. Ochs Brothers sell toboggans. They import their own toboggans."

The second official turned away. "Tobogganing," he said, "requires a special *piste*. You could not toboggan into the streets of Montreux. Where are you stopping here?"

"We don't know," I said. "We just drove in from Brissago. The carriage is outside."

"You make no mistake in going to Montreux," the first official said. "You will find the climate delightful and beautiful. You will have no distance to go for winter sport."

"If you really want winter sport," the second official said, "you will go to the Engadine or to Mürren. I must protest against your being advised to go to Montreux for the winter sport."

"At Les Avants above Montreux there is excellent winter sport of every sort." The champion of Montreux glared at his colleague.

"Gentlemen," I said, "I am afraid we must go. My cousin is very tired. We will go tentatively to Montreux."

"I congratulate you," the first official shook my hand.

"I believe that you will regret leaving Locarno," the second official said. "At any rate you will report to the police at Montreux."

"There will be no unpleasantness with the police," the first official assured me. "You will find all the inhabitants extremely courteous and friendly."

"Thank you both very much," I said. "We appreciate your advice very much."

"Good-by," Catherine said. "Thank you both very much."

They bowed us to the door, the champion of Locarno a little coldly. We went down the steps and into the carriage.

"My God, darling," Catherine said. "Couldn't we have gotten away any sooner?" I gave the name of a hotel one of the officials had recommended to the driver. He picked up the reins.

"You've forgotten the army," Catherine said. The soldier was standing by the carriage. I gave him a ten-lira note. "I have no Swiss money yet," I said. He thanked me, saluted and went off. The carriage started and we drove to the hotel.

"How did you happen to pick out Montreux?" I asked Catherine. "Do you really want to go there?"

"It was the first place I could think of," she said. "It's not a bad place. We can find some place up in the mountains."

"Are you sleepy?"

"I'm asleep right now."

"We'll get a good sleep. Poor Cat, you had a long bad night."

"I had a lovely time," Catherine said. "Especially when you sailed with the umbrella."

"Can you realize we're in Switzerland?"

"No, I'm afraid I'll wake up and it won't be true."

"I am too."

"It is true, isn't it, darling? I'm not just driving down to the *stazione* in Milan to see you off."

"I hope not."

"Don't say that. It frightens me. Maybe that's where we're going."

"I'm so groggy I don't know," I said.

"Let me see your hands."

I put them out. They were both blistered raw.

"There's no hole in my side," I said.

"Don't be sacrilegious."

I felt very tired and vague in the head. The exhilaration was all gone. The carriage was going along the street.

"Poor hands," Catherine said.

"Don't touch them," I said. "By God I don't know where we are. Where are we going, driver?" The driver stopped his horse.

"To the Hotel Metropole. Don't you want to go there?"

"Yes," I said. "It's all right, Cat."

"It's all right, darling. Don't be upset. We'll get a good sleep and you won't feel groggy to-morrow."

"I get pretty groggy," I said. "It's like a comic opera to-day. Maybe I'm hungry."

"You're just tired, darling. You'll be fine." The carriage pulled up before the hotel. Some one came out to take our bags.

"I feel all right," I said. We were down on the pavement going into the hotel.

"I know you'll be all right. You're just tired. You've been up a long time."

"Anyhow we're here."

"Yes, we're really here."

We followed the boy with the bags into the hotel.

BOOK FIVE

CHAPTER XXXVIII

That fall the snow came very late. We lived in a brown wooden house in the pine trees on the side of the mountain and at night there was frost so that there was thin ice over the water in the two pitchers on the dresser in the morning. Mrs. Guttingen came into the room early in the morning to shut the windows and started a fire in the tall porcelain stove. The pine wood crackled and sparked and then the fire roared in the stove and the second time Mrs. Guttingen came into the room she brought big chunks of wood for the fire and a pitcher of hot water. When the room was warm she brought in breakfast. Sitting up in bed eating breakfast we could see the lake and the mountains across the lake on the French side. There was snow on the tops of the mountains and the lake was a gray steel-blue.

Outside, in front of the chalet a road went up the mountain. The wheel ruts and ridges were iron hard with the frost, and the road climbed steadily through the forest and up and around the mountain to where there were meadows, and barns and cabins in the meadows at the edge of the woods looking across the valley.

The valley was deep and there was a stream at the bottom that flowed down into the lake and when the wind blew across the valley you could hear the stream in the rocks.

Sometimes we went off the road and on a path through the pine forest. The floor of the forest was soft to walk on; the frost did not harden it as it did the road. But we did not mind the hardness of the road because we had nails in the soles and heels of our boots and the heel nails bit on the frozen ruts and with nailed boots it was good walking on the road and invigorating. But it was lovely walking in the woods.

In front of the house where we lived the mountain went down steeply to the little plain along the lake and we sat on the porch of the house in the sun and saw the winding of the road down the mountain-side and the terraced vineyards on the side of the lower mountain, the vines all dead now for the winter and the fields divided by stone walls, and below the vineyards the houses of the town on the narrow plain along the lake shore. There was an island with two trees on the lake and the trees looked like the double sails of a fishing-boat. The mountains were sharp and steep on the other side of the lake and down at the end of the lake was the plain of the Rhone Valley flat between the two ranges of mountains; and up the valley where the mountains cut it off was the Dent du Midi. It was a high snowy mountain and it dominated the valley but it was so far away that it did not make a shadow.

When the sun was bright we ate lunch on the porch but the rest of the time we ate upstairs in a small room with plain wooden walls and a big stove in the corner. We bought books and magazines in the town and a copy of "Hoyle" and learned many two-handed card games. The small room with the stove was our living-room. There were two comfortable chairs and a table for books and magazines and we played cards on the dining-table when it was cleared away. Mr. and Mrs. Guttingen lived downstairs and we would hear them talking sometimes in the evening and they were very happy together too. He had been a headwaiter and she had worked as maid in the same hotel and they had saved their money to buy this place. They had a son who was studying to be a headwaiter. He was at a hotel in Zurich. Downstairs there was a parlor where they sold wine and beer, and sometimes in the evening we would hear carts stop outside on the road and men come up the steps to go in the parlor to drink wine.

There was a box of wood in the hall outside the living-room and I kept up the fire from it. But we did not stay up very late. We went to bed in the dark in the big bedroom and when I was undressed I opened the windows and saw the night and the cold stars and the pine trees below the window and then got into bed as fast as I could. It was lovely in bed with the air so cold and clear and the night outside the window. We slept well and if I woke in the night I knew it was from only one cause and I would shift the feather bed over, very softly so that Catherine would not be wakened and then go back to sleep again, warm and with the new lightness of thin covers. The war seemed as far away as the football games of some one else's college. But I knew from the papers that they were still fighting in the mountains because the snow would not come.

Sometimes we walked down the mountain into Montreux. There was a path went down the mountain but it was steep and so usually we took the road and walked down on the wide hard road between fields and then below between the stone walls of the vineyards and on down between the houses of the villages along the way. There were three villages; Chernex, Fontanivent, and the other I forget. Then along the road we passed an old square-built stone château on a ledge on the side of the mountain-side with the terraced fields of vines, each vine tied to a stick to hold it up, the vines dry and brown and the earth ready for the snow and the lake down below flat and gray as steel. The road went down a long grade below the château and then turned to the right and went down very steeply and paved with cobbles, into Montreux.

We did not know any one in Montreux. We walked along beside the lake and saw the swans and the many gulls and terns that flew up when you came close and screamed while they looked down at the water. Out on the lake there were flocks of grebes, small and dark, and leaving trails in the water when they swam. In the town we walked along the main street and looked in the windows of the shops. There were many big hotels that were closed but most of the shops were open and the people were very glad to see us. There was a fine coiffeur's place where Catherine went to have her hair done. The woman who ran it was very cheerful and the only person we knew in Montreux. While Catherine was there I went up to a beer place and drank dark Munich beer and read the papers. I read the *Corriere della Sera* and the English and American papers from Paris. All the advertisements were blacked out, supposedly to prevent communication in that way with the enemy. The papers were bad reading. Everything was going very badly everywhere. I sat back in the corner with a heavy mug of dark beer and an opened glazed-paper package of pretzels and ate the pretzels for the salty flavor and the good way they made the beer taste and read about disaster. I thought Catherine would come by but she did not come, so I hung the papers back on the rack, paid for my beer and went up the street to look for her. The day was cold and dark and wintry and the stone of the houses looked cold. Catherine was still in the hairdresser's shop. The woman was waving her hair. I sat in the little booth and watched. It was exciting to watch and Catherine smiled and talked to me and my voice was a little thick from being excited. The tongs made a pleasant clicking sound and I could see Catherine in three mirrors and it was pleasant and warm in the booth. Then the woman put up Catherine's hair, and Catherine looked in the mirror and changed it a little, taking out and putting in pins; then stood up. "I'm sorry to have taken such a long time."

"Monsieur was very interested. Were you not, monsieur?" the woman smiled.

"Yes," I said.

We went out and up the street. It was cold and wintry and the wind was blowing. "Oh, darling, I love you so," I said.

"Don't we have a fine time?" Catherine said. "Look. Let's go some place and have beer instead of tea. It's very good for young Catherine. It keeps her small."

"Young Catherine," I said. "That loafer."

"She's been very good," Catherine said. "She makes very little trouble. The doctor says beer will be good for me and keep her small."

"If you keep her small enough and she's a boy, maybe he will be a jockey."

"I suppose if we really have this child we ought to get married," Catherine said. We were in the beer place at the corner table. It was getting dark outside. It was still early but the day was dark and the dusk was coming early.

"Let's get married now," I said.

"No," Catherine said. "It's too embarrassing now. I show too plainly. I won't go before any one and be married in this state."

"I wish we'd gotten married."

"I suppose it would have been better. But when could we, darling?"

"I don't know."

"I know one thing. I'm not going to be married in this splendid matronly state."

"You're not matronly."

"Oh yes, I am, darling. The hairdresser asked me if this was our first. I lied and said no, we had two boys and two girls."

"When will we be married?"

"Any time after I'm thin again. We want to have a splendid

wedding with every one thinking what a handsome young couple."

"And you're not worried?"

"Darling, why should I be worried? The only time I ever felt badly was when I felt like a whore in Milan and that only lasted seven minutes and besides it was the room furnishings. Don't I make you a good wife?"

"You're a lovely wife."

"Then don't be too technical, darling. I'll marry you as soon as I'm thin again."

"All right."

"Do you think I ought to drink another beer? The doctor said I was rather narrow in the hips and it's all for the best if we keep young Catherine small."

"What else did he say?" I was worried.

"Nothing. I have a wonderful blood-pressure, darling. He admired my blood-pressure greatly."

"What did he say about you being too narrow in the hips?"

"Nothing. Nothing at all. He said I shouldn't ski."

"Quite right."

"He said it was too late to start if I'd never done it before. He said I could ski if I wouldn't fall down."

"He's just a big-hearted joker."

"Really he was very nice. We'll have him when the baby comes."

"Did you ask him if you ought to get married?"

"No. I told him we'd been married four years. You see, darling, if I marry you I'll be an American and any time we're married under American law the child is legitimate."

"Where did you find that out?"

"In the New York *World Almanac* in the library."

"You're a grand girl."

"I'll be very glad to be an American and we'll go to America won't we, darling? I want to see Niagara Falls."

"You're a fine girl."

"There's something else I want to see but I can't remember it."

"The stockyards?"

"No. I can't remember it."

"The Woolworth building?"

"No."

"The Grand Canyon?"

"No. But I'd like to see that."

"What was it?"

"The Golden Gate! That's what I want to see. Where is the Golden Gate?"

"San Francisco."

"Then let's go there. I want to see San Francisco anyway."

"All right. We'll go there."

"Now let's go up the mountain. Should we? Can we get the M. O. B.?"

"There's a train a little after five."

"Let's get that."

"All right. I'll drink one more beer first."

When we went out to go up the street and climb the stairs to the station it was very cold. A cold wind was coming down the Rhone Valley. There were lights in the shop windows and we climbed the steep stone stairway to the upper street, then up another stairs to the station. The electric train was there waiting, all the lights on. There was a dial that showed when it left. The clock hands pointed to ten minutes after five. I looked at the station clock. It was five minutes after. As we got on board I saw the motorman and conductor coming out of the station wine-shop. We sat down and opened the window. The train was electrically heated and stuffy but fresh cold air came in through the window.

"Are you tired, Cat?" I asked.

"No. I feel splendid."

"It isn't a long ride."

"I like the ride," she said. "Don't worry about me, darling. I feel fine."

Snow did not come until three days before Christmas. We woke one morning and it was snowing. We stayed in bed with the fire roaring in the stove and watched the snow fall. Mrs. Guttingen took away the breakfast trays and put more wood in the stove. It was a big snow storm. She said it had started about midnight. I went to the window and looked out but could not see across the road. It was blowing and snowing wildly. I went back to bed and we lay and talked.

"I wish I could ski," Catherine said. "It's rotten not to be able to ski."

"We'll get a bobsled and come down the road. That's no worse for you than riding in a car."

"Won't it be rough?"

"We can see."

"I hope it won't be too rough."

"After a while we'll take a walk in the snow."

"Before lunch," Catherine said, "so we'll have a good appetite."

"I'm always hungry."

"So am I."

We went out in the snow but it was drifted so that we could not walk far. I went ahead and made a trail down to the station but when we reached there we had gone far enough. The snow was blowing so we could hardly see and we went into the little inn by the station and swept each other off with a broom and sat on a bench and had vermouths.

"It is a big storm," the barmaid said.

"Yes."

"The snow is very late this year."

"Yes."

"Could I eat a chocolate bar?" Catherine asked. "Or is it too close to lunch? I'm always hungry."

"Go on and eat one," I said.

"I'll take one with filberts," Catherine said.

"They are very good," the girl said, "I like them the best."

"I'll have another vermouth," I said.

When we came out to start back up the road our track was filled in by the snow. There were only faint indentations where the holes had been. The snow blew in our faces so we could hardly see. We brushed off and went in to have lunch. Mr. Guttingen served the lunch.

"To-morrow there will be ski-ing," he said. "Do you ski, Mr. Henry?"

"No. But I want to learn."

"You will learn very easily. My boy will be here for Christmas and he will teach you."

"That's fine. When does he come?"

"To-morrow night."

When we were sitting by the stove in the little room after lunch looking out the window at the snow coming down Catherine said, "Wouldn't you like to go on a trip somewhere by yourself, darling, and be with men and ski?"

"No. Why should I?"

"I should think sometimes you would want to see other people besides me."

"Do you want to see other people?"

"No."

"Neither do I."

"I know. But you're different. I'm having a child and that makes me contented not to do anything. I know I'm awfully stupid now and I talk too much and I think you ought to get away so you won't be tired of me."

"Do you want me to go away?"

"No. I want you to stay."

"That's what I'm going to do."

"Come over here," she said. "I want to feel the bump on your head. It's a big bump." She ran her finger over it. "Darling, would you like to grow a beard?"

"Would you like me to?"

"It might be fun. I'd like to see you with a beard."

"All right. I'll grow one. I'll start now this minute. It's a good idea. It will give me something to do."

"Are you worried because you haven't anything to do?"

"No. I like it. I have a fine life. Don't you?"

"I have a lovely life. But I was afraid because I'm big now that maybe I was a bore to you."

"Oh, Cat. You don't know how crazy I am about you."

"This way?"

"Just the way you are. I have a fine time. Don't we have a good life?"

"I do, but I thought maybe you were restless."

"No. Sometimes I wonder about the front and about people I know but I don't worry. I don't think about anything much."

"Who do you wonder about?"

"About Rinaldi and the priest and lots of people I know. But I don't think about them much. I don't want to think about the war. I'm through with it."

"What are you thinking about now?"

"Nothing."

"Yes you were. Tell me."

"I was wondering whether Rinaldi had the syphilis."

"Was that all?"

"Yes."

"Has he the syphilis?"

"I don't know."

"I'm glad you haven't. Did you ever have anything like that?"

"I had gonorrhea."

"I don't want to hear about it. Was it very painful, darling?"

"Very."

"I wish I'd had it."

"No you don't."

"I do. I wish I'd had it to be like you. I wish I'd stayed with all your girls so I could make fun of them to you."

"That's a pretty picture."

"It's not a pretty picture you having gonorrhea."

"I know it. Look at it snow now."

"I'd rather look at you. Darling, why don't you let your hair grow?"

"How grow?"

"Just grow a little longer."

"It's long enough now."

"No, let it grow a little longer and I could cut mine and we'd be just alike only one of us blonde and one of us dark."

"I wouldn't let you cut yours."

"It would be fun. I'm tired of it. It's an awful nuisance in the bed at night."

"I like it."

"Wouldn't you like it short?"

"I might. I like it the way it is."

"It might be nice short. Then we'd both be alike. Oh, darling, I want you so much I want to be you too."

"You are. We're the same one."

"I know it. At night we are."

"The nights are grand."

"I want us to be all mixed up. I don't want you to go away. I just said that. You go if you want to. But hurry right back. Why, darling, I don't live at all when I'm not with you."

"I won't ever go away," I said. "I'm no good when you're not there. I haven't any life at all any more."

"I want you to have a life. I want you to have a fine life. But we'll have it together, won't we?"

"And now do you want me to stop growing my beard or let it go on?"

"Go on. Grow it. It will be exciting. Maybe it will be done for New Year's."

"Now do you want to play chess?"

"I'd rather play with you."

"No. Let's play chess."

"And afterward we'll play?"

"Yes."

"All right."

I got out the chess-board and arranged the pieces. It was still snowing hard outside.

One time in the night I woke up and knew that Catherine was awake too. The moon was shining in the window and made shadows on the bed from the bars on the window-panes.

"Are you awake, sweetheart?"

"Yes. Can't you sleep?"

"I just woke up thinking about how I was nearly crazy when I first met you. Do you remember?"

"You were just a little crazy."

"I'm never that way any more. I'm grand now. You say grand so sweetly. Say grand."

"Grand."

"Oh, you're sweet. And I'm not crazy now. I'm just very, very, very happy."

"Go on to sleep," I said.

"All right. Let's go to sleep at exactly the same moment."

"All right."

But we did not. I was awake for quite a long time thinking about things and watching Catherine sleeping, the moonlight on her face. Then I went to sleep, too.

CHAPTER XXXIX

By the middle of January I had a beard and the winter had settled into bright cold days and hard cold nights. We could walk on the roads again. The snow was packed hard and smooth by the hay-sleds and wood-sledges and the logs that were hauled down the mountain. The snow lay over all the country, down almost to Montreux. The mountains on the other side of the lake were all white and the plain of the Rhone Valley was covered. We took long walks on the other side of the mountain to the Bains de l'Alliaz. Catherine wore hobnailed boots and a cape and carried a stick with a sharp steel point. She did not look big with the cape and we would not walk too fast but stopped and sat on logs by the roadside to rest when she was tired.

There was an inn in the trees at the Bains de l'Alliaz where the woodcutters stopped to drink, and we sat inside warmed by the stove and drank hot red wine with spices and lemon in it. They called it *glühwein* and it was a good thing to warm you and to celebrate with. The inn was dark and smoky inside and afterward when you went out the cold air came sharply into your lungs and numbed the edge of your nose as you inhaled. We looked back at the inn with light coming from the windows and the woodcutters' horses stamping and jerking their heads outside to keep warm. There was frost on the hairs of their muzzles and their breathing made plumes of frost in the air. Going up the road toward home the road was smooth and slippery for a while and the ice orange from the horses until the wood-hauling track turned off. Then the road was clean-packed snow and led through the woods, and twice coming home in the evening, we saw foxes.

It was a fine country and every time that we went out it was fun.

"You have a splendid beard now," Catherine said. "It looks just like the woodcutters'. Did you see the man with the tiny gold earrings?"

"He's a chamois hunter," I said. "They wear them because they say it makes them hear better."

"Really? I don't believe it. I think they wear them to show they are chamois hunters. Are there chamois near here?"

"Yes, beyond the Dent de Jaman."

"It was fun seeing the fox."

"When he sleeps he wraps that tail around him to keep warm."

"It must be a lovely feeling."

"I always wanted to have a tail like that. Wouldn't it be fun if we had brushes like a fox?"

"It might be very difficult dressing."

"We'd have clothes made, or live in a country where it wouldn't make any difference."

"We live in a country where nothing makes any difference. Isn't it grand how we never see any one? You don't want to see people do you, darling?"

"No."

"Should we sit here just a minute? I'm a little bit tired."

We sat close together on the logs. Ahead the road went down through the forest.

"She won't come between us, will she? The little brat."

"No. We won't let her."

"How are we for money?"

"We have plenty. They honored the last sight draft."

"Won't your family try and get hold of you now they know you're in Switzerland?"

"Probably. I'll write them something."

"Haven't you written them?"

"No. Only the sight draft."

"Thank God I'm not your family."

"I'll send them a cable."

"Don't you care anything about them?"

"I did, but we quarrelled so much it wore itself out."

"I think I'd like them. I'd probably like them very much."

"Let's not talk about them or I'll start to worry about them." After a while I said, "Let's go on if you're rested."

"I'm rested."

We went on down the road. It was dark now and the snow squeaked under our boots. The night was dry and cold and very clear.

"I love your beard," Catherine said. "It's a great success. It looks so stiff and fierce and it's very soft and a great pleasure."

"Do you like it better than without?"

"I think so. You know, darling, I'm not going to cut my hair now until after young Catherine's born. I look too big and matronly now. But after she's born and I'm thin again I'm going to cut it and then I'll be a fine new and different girl for you. We'll go together and get it cut, or I'll go alone and come and surprise you."

I did not say anything.

"You won't say I can't, will you?"

"No. I think it would be exciting."

"Oh, you're so sweet. And maybe I'd look lovely, darling, and be so thin and exciting to you and you'll fall in love with me all over again."

"Hell," I said, "I love you enough now. What do you want to do? Ruin me?"

"Yes. I want to ruin you."

"Good," I said, "that's what I want too."

CHAPTER XL

We had a fine life. We lived through the months of January and February and the winter was very fine and we were very happy. There had been short thaws when the wind blew warm and the snow softened and the air felt like spring, but always the clear hard cold had come again and the winter had returned. In March came the first break in the winter. In the night it started raining. It rained on all morning and turned the snow to slush and made the mountain-side dismal. There were clouds over the lake and over the valley. It was raining high up the mountain. Catherine wore heavy overshoes and I wore Mr. Guttingen's rubber-boots and we walked to the station under an umbrella, through the slush and the running water that was washing the ice of the roads bare, to stop at the pub before lunch for a vermouth. Outside we could hear the rain.

"Do you think we ought to move into town?"

"What do you think?" Catherine asked.

"If the winter is over and the rain keeps up it won't be fun up here. How long is it before young Catherine?"

"About a month. Perhaps a little more."

"We might go down and stay in Montreux."

"Why don't we go to Lausanne? That's where the hospital is."

"All right. But I thought maybe that was too big a town."

"We can be as much alone in a bigger town and Lausanne might be nice."

"When should we go?"

"I don't care. Whenever you want, darling. I don't want to leave here if you don't want."

"Let's see how the weather turns out."

It rained for three days. The snow was all gone now on the mountain-side below the station. The road was a torrent of muddy snow-water. It was too wet and slushy to go out. On the morning of the third day of rain we decided to go down into town.

"That is all right, Mr. Henry," Guttingen said. "You do not have to give me any notice. I did not think you would want to stay now the bad weather is come."

"We have to be near the hospital anyway on account of Madame," I said.

"I understand," he said. "Will you come back some time and stay, with the little one?"

"Yes, if you would have room."

"In the spring when it is nice you could come and enjoy it. We could put the little one and the nurse in the big room that is closed now and you and Madame could have your same room looking out over the lake."

"I'll write about coming," I said. We packed and left on the train that went down after lunch. Mr. and Mrs. Guttingen came down to the station with us and he hauled our baggage down on a sled through the slush. They stood beside the station in the rain waving good-by.

"They were very sweet," Catherine said.

"They were fine to us."

We took the train to Lausanne from Montreux. Looking out
the window toward where we had lived you could not see the
mountains for the clouds. The train stopped in Vevey, then went
on, passing the lake on one side and on the other the wet brown
fields and the bare woods and the wet houses. We came into
Lausanne and went into a medium-sized hotel to stay. It was still
raining as we drove through the streets and into the carriage entrance of the hotel. The concierge with brass keys on his lapels,
the elevator, the carpets on the floors, and the white washbowls
with shining fixtures, the brass bed and the big comfortable bedroom all seemed very great luxury after the Guttingens. The windows of the room looked out on a wet garden with a wall topped
by an iron fence. Across the street, which sloped steeply, was another hotel with a similar wall and garden. I looked out at the rain
falling in the fountain of the garden.

Catherine turned on all the lights and commenced unpacking.
I ordered a whiskey and soda and lay on the bed and read the papers I had bought at the station. It was March, 1918, and the
German offensive had started in France. I drank the whiskey and
soda and read while Catherine unpacked and moved around the
room.

"You know what I have to get, darling," she said.

"What?"

"Baby clothes. There aren't many people reach my time without
baby things."

"You can buy them."

"I know. That's what I'll do to-morrow. I'll find out what is
necessary."

"You ought to know. You were a nurse."

"But so few of the soldiers had babies in the hospitals."

"I did."

She hit me with the pillow and spilled the whiskey and soda.

"I'll order you another," she said. "I'm sorry I spilled it."

"There wasn't much left. Come on over to the bed."

"No. I have to try and make this room look like something."

"Like what?"

"Like our home."

"Hang out the Allied flags."

"Oh shut up."

"Say it again."

"Shut up."

"You say it so cautiously," I said. "As though you didn't want to offend any one."

"I don't."

"Then come over to the bed."

"All right." She came and sat on the bed. "I know I'm no fun for you, darling. I'm like a big flour-barrel."

"No you're not. You're beautiful and you're sweet."

"I'm just something very ungainly that you've married."

"No you're not. You're more beautiful all the time."

"But I will be thin again, darling."

"You're thin now."

"You've been drinking."

"Just whiskey and soda."

"There's another one coming," she said. "And then should we order dinner up here?"

"That will be good."

"Then we won't go out, will we? We'll just stay in to-night."

"And play," I said.

"I'll drink some wine," Catherine said. "It won't hurt me. Maybe we can get some of our old white capri."

"I know we can," I said. "They'll have Italian wines at a hotel this size."

The waiter knocked at the door. He brought the whiskey in a glass with ice and beside the glass on a tray a small bottle of soda.

"Thank you," I said. "Put it down there. Will you please have dinner for two brought up here and two bottles of dry white capri in ice."

"Do you wish to commence your dinner with soup?"

"Do you want soup, Cat?"

"Please."

"Bring soup for one."

"Thank you, sir." He went out and shut the door. I went back to the papers and the war in the papers and poured the soda slowly over the ice into the whiskey. I would have to tell them not to put ice in the whiskey. Let them bring the ice separately. That way you could tell how much whiskey there was and it would not suddenly be too thin from the soda. I would get a bottle of whiskey and have them bring ice and soda. That was the sensible way. Good whiskey was very pleasant. It was one of the pleasant parts of life.

"What are you thinking, darling?"

"About whiskey."

"What about whiskey?"

"About how nice it is."

Catherine made a face. "All right," she said.

We stayed at that hotel three weeks. It was not bad; the dining-room was usually empty and very often we ate in our room at night. We walked in the town and took the cogwheel railway down to Ouchy and walked beside the lake. The weather became quite warm and it was like spring. We wished we were back in the mountains but the spring weather lasted only a few days and then the cold rawness of the breaking-up of winter came again.

Catherine bought the things she needed for the baby, up in the town. I went to a gymnasium in the arcade to box for exercise. I usually went up there in the morning while Catherine stayed late in bed. On the days of false spring it was very nice, after boxing and taking a shower, to walk along the streets smelling the spring in the air and stop at a café to sit and watch the people and read the paper and drink a vermouth; then go down to the hotel and have lunch with Catherine. The professor at the boxing gymnasium wore mustaches and was very precise and jerky and went all to pieces if you started after him. But it was pleasant in the gym. There was good air and light and I worked quite hard, skipping rope, shadow-boxing, doing abdominal exercises lying on the floor in a patch of sunlight that came through the open window, and occasionally scaring the professor when we boxed. I could not shadow-box in front of the narrow long mirror at first because it looked so strange to see a man with a beard boxing. But finally I just thought it was funny. I wanted to take off the beard as soon as I started boxing but Catherine did not want me to.

Sometimes Catherine and I went for rides out in the country in a carriage. It was nice to ride when the days were pleasant and we found two good places where we could ride out to eat. Catherine could not walk very far now and I loved to ride out along the country roads with her. When there was a good day we had a splendid time and we never had a bad time. We knew the baby was very close now and it gave us both a feeling as though something were hurrying us and we could not lose any time together.

CHAPTER XLI

One morning I awoke about three o'clock hearing Catherine stirring in the bed.

"Are you all right, Cat?"

"I've been having some pains, darling."

"Regularly?"

"No, not very."

"If you have them at all regularly we'll go to the hospital."

I was very sleepy and went back to sleep. A little while later I woke again.

"Maybe you'd better call up the doctor," Catherine said. "I think maybe this is it."

I went to the phone and called the doctor. "How often are the pains coming?" he asked.

"How often are they coming, Cat?"

"I should think every quarter of an hour."

"You should go to the hospital, then," the doctor said. "I will dress and go there right away myself."

I hung up and called the garage near the station to send up a taxi. No one answered the phone for a long time. Then I finally got a man who promised to send up a taxi at once. Catherine was dressing. Her bag was all packed with the things she would need at the hospital and the baby things. Outside in the hall I rang for the elevator. There was no answer. I went downstairs. There was no one downstairs except the night-watchman. I brought the elevator up myself, put Catherine's bag in it, she stepped in and we went down. The night-watchman opened the door for us and we sat outside on the stone slabs beside the stairs down to the driveway and waited for the taxi. The night was clear and the stars were out. Catherine was very excited.

"I'm so glad it's started," she said. "Now in a little while it will be all over."

"You're a good brave girl."

"I'm not afraid. I wish the taxi would come, though."

We heard it coming up the street and saw its headlights. It turned into the driveway and I helped Catherine in and the driver put the bag up in front.

"Drive to the hospital," I said.

We went out of the driveway and started up the hill.

At the hospital we went in and I carried the bag. There was a woman at the desk who wrote down Catherine's name, age, address, relatives and religion, in a book. She said she had no religion and the woman drew a line in the space after that word. She gave her name as Catherine Henry.

"I will take you up to your room," she said. We went up in an elevator. The woman stopped it and we stepped out and followed her down a hall. Catherine held tight to my arm.

"This is the room," the woman said. "Will you please undress and get into bed? Here is a night-gown for you to wear."

"I have a night-gown," Catherine said.

"It is better for you to wear this night-gown," the woman said.

I went outside and sat on a chair in the hallway.

"You can come in now," the woman said from the doorway. Catherine was lying in the narrow bed wearing a plain, square-cut night-gown that looked as though it were made of rough sheeting. She smiled at me.

"I'm having fine pains now," she said. The woman was holding her wrist and timing the pains with a watch.

"That was a big one," Catherine said. I saw it on her face.

"Where's the doctor?" I asked the woman.

"He's lying down sleeping. He will be here when he is needed."

"I must do something for Madame, now," the nurse said. "Would you please step out again?"

I went out into the hall. It was a bare hall with two windows and closed doors all down the corridor. It smelled of hospital. I sat on the chair and looked at the floor and prayed for Catherine.

"You can come in," the nurse said. I went in.

"Hello, darling," Catherine said.

"How is it?"

"They are coming quite often now." Her face drew up. Then she smiled.

"That was a real one. Do you want to put your hand on my back again, nurse?"

"If it helps you," the nurse said.

"You go away, darling," Catherine said. "Go out and get something to eat. I may do this for a long time the nurse says."

"The first labor is usually protracted," the nurse said.

"Please go out and get something to eat," Catherine said. "I'm fine, really."

"I'll stay awhile," I said.

The pains came quite regularly, then slackened off. Catherine was very excited. When the pains were bad she called them good ones. When they started to fall off she was disappointed and ashamed.

"You go out, darling," she said. "I think you are just making me self-conscious." Her face tied up. "There. That was better. I so want to be a good wife and have this child without any foolishness. Please go and get some breakfast, darling, and then come back. I won't miss you. Nurse is splendid to me."

"You have plenty of time for breakfast," the nurse said.

"I'll go then. Good-by, sweet."

"Good-by," Catherine said, "and have a fine breakfast for me too."

"Where can I get breakfast?" I asked the nurse.

"There's a café down the street at the square," she said. "It should be open now."

Outside it was getting light. I walked down the empty street to the café. There was a light in the window. I went in and stood at the zinc bar and an old man served me a glass of white wine and a brioche. The brioche was yesterday's. I dipped it in the wine and then drank a glass of coffee.

"What do you do at this hour?" the old man asked.

"My wife is in labor at the hospital."

"So. I wish you good luck."

"Give me another glass of wine."

He poured it from the bottle slopping it over a little so some ran down on the zinc. I drank this glass, paid and went out. Outside along the street were the refuse cans from the houses waiting for the collector. A dog was nosing at one of the cans.

"What do you want?" I asked and looked in the can to see if there was anything I could pull out for him; there was nothing on top but coffee-grounds, dust and some dead flowers.

"There isn't anything, dog," I said. The dog crossed the street. I went up the stairs in the hospital to the floor Catherine was on and down the hall to her room. I knocked on the door. There was no answer. I opened the door; the room was empty, except for

Catherine's bag on a chair and her dressing-gown hanging on a hook on the wall. I went out and down the hall, looking for somebody. I found a nurse.

"Where is Madame Henry?"

"A lady has just gone to the delivery room."

"Where is it?"

"I will show you."

She took me down to the end of the hall. The door of the room was partly open. I could see Catherine lying on a table, covered by a sheet. The nurse was on one side and the doctor stood on the other side of the table beside some cylinders. The doctor held a rubber mask attached to a tube in one hand.

"I will give you a gown and you can go in," the nurse said. "Come in here, please."

She put a white gown on me and pinned it at the neck in back with a safety pin.

"Now you can go in," she said. I went into the room.

"Hello, darling," Catherine said in a strained voice. "I'm not doing much."

"You are Mr. Henry?" the doctor asked.

"Yes. How is everything going, doctor?"

"Things are going very well," the doctor said. "We came in here where it is easy to give gas for the pains."

"I want it now," Catherine said. The doctor placed the rubber mask over her face and turned a dial and I watched Catherine breathing deeply and rapidly. Then she pushed the mask away. The doctor shut off the petcock.

"That wasn't a very big one. I had a very big one a while ago. The doctor made me go clear out, didn't you, doctor?" Her voice was strange. It rose on the word doctor.

The doctor smiled.

"I want it again," Catherine said. She held the rubber tight to

her face and breathed fast. I heard her moaning a little. Then she
pulled the mask away and smiled.

"That was a big one," she said. "That was a very big one. Don't
you worry, darling. You go away. Go have another breakfast."

"I'll stay," I said.

We had gone to the hospital about three o'clock in the morning.
At noon Catherine was still in the delivery room. The pains had
slackened again. She looked very tired and worn now but she was
still cheerful.

"I'm not any good, darling," she said. "I'm so sorry. I thought I
would do it very easily. Now—there's one—" she reached out her
hand for the mask and held it over her face. The doctor moved the
dial and watched her. In a little while it was over.

"It wasn't much," Catherine said. She smiled. "I'm a fool about
the gas. It's wonderful."

"We'll get some for the home," I said.

"*There one comes,*" Catherine said quickly. The doctor turned
the dial and looked at his watch.

"What is the interval now?" I asked.

"About a minute."

"Don't you want lunch?"

"I will have something pretty soon," he said.

"You must have something to eat, doctor," Catherine said. "I'm
so sorry I go on so long. Couldn't my husband give me the gas?"

"If you wish," the doctor said. "You turn it to the numeral two."

"I see," I said. There was a marker on a dial that turned with a
handle.

"*I want it now,*" Catherine said. She held the mask tight to her
face. I turned the dial to number two and when Catherine put
down the mask I turned it off. It was very good of the doctor to let
me do something.

"Did you do it, darling?" Catherine asked. She stroked my wrist.
"Sure."

"You're so lovely." She was a little drunk from the gas.

"I will eat from a tray in the next room," the doctor said. "You
can call me any moment." While the time passed I watched him
eat, then, after a while, I saw that he was lying down and smoking
a cigarette. Catherine was getting very tired.

"Do you think I'll ever have this baby?" she asked.

"Yes, of course you will."

"I try as hard as I can. I push down but it goes away. *There it
comes. Give it to me.*"

At two o'clock I went out and had lunch. There were a few men
in the café sitting with coffee and glasses of kirsch or marc on the
tables. I sat down at a table. "Can I eat?" I asked the waiter.

"It is past time for lunch."

"Isn't there anything for all hours?"

"You can have *choucroute.*"

"Give me *choucroute* and beer."

"A demi or a bock?"

"A light demi."

The waiter brought a dish of sauerkraut with a slice of ham over
the top and a sausage buried in the hot wine-soaked cabbage. I ate
it and drank the beer. I was very hungry. I watched the people at
the tables in the café. At one table they were playing cards. Two
men at the table next me were talking and smoking. The café was
full of smoke. The zinc bar, where I had breakfasted, had three
people behind it now; the old man, a plump woman in a black
dress who sat behind a counter and kept track of everything served
to the tables, and a boy in an apron. I wondered how many children the woman had and what it had been like.

When I was through with the *choucroute* I went back to the
hospital. The street was all clean now. There were no refuse cans
out. The day was cloudy but the sun was trying to come through.

I rode upstairs in the elevator, stepped out and went down the hall to Catherine's room, where I had left my white gown. I put it on and pinned it in back at the neck. I looked in the glass and saw myself looking like a fake doctor with a beard. I went down the hall to the delivery room. The door was closed and I knocked. No one answered so I turned the handle and went in. The doctor sat by Catherine. The nurse was doing something at the other end of the room.

"Here is your husband," the doctor said.

"Oh, darling, I have the most wonderful doctor," Catherine said in a very strange voice. "He's been telling me the most wonderful story and when the pain came too badly he put me all the way out. He's wonderful. You're wonderful, doctor."

"You're drunk," I said.

"I know it." Catherine said. "But you shouldn't say it." Then "*Give it to me. Give it to me.*" She clutched hold of the mask and breathed short and deep, pantingly, making the respirator click. Then she gave a long sigh and the doctor reached with his left hand and lifted away the mask.

"That was a very big one," Catherine said. Her voice was very strange. "I'm not going to die now, darling. I'm past where I was going to die. Aren't you glad?"

"Don't you get in that place again."

"I won't. I'm not afraid of it though. I won't die, darling."

"You will not do any such foolishness," the doctor said. "You would not die and leave your husband."

"Oh, no. I won't die. I wouldn't die. It's silly to die. There it comes. *Give it to me.*"

After a while the doctor said, "You will go out, Mr. Henry, for a few moments and I will make an examination."

"He wants to see how I am doing," Catherine said. "You can come back afterward, darling, can't he, doctor?"

"Yes," said the doctor. "I will send word when he can come back."

I went out the door and down the hall to the room where Catherine was to be after the baby came. I sat in a chair there and looked at the room. I had the paper in my coat that I had bought when I went out for lunch and I read it. It was beginning to be dark outside and I turned the light on to read. After a while I stopped reading and turned off the light and watched it get dark outside. I wondered why the doctor did not send for me. Maybe it was better I was away. He probably wanted me away for a while. I looked at my watch. If he did not send for me in ten minutes I would go down anyway.

Poor, poor dear Cat. And this was the price you paid for sleeping together. This was the end of the trap. This was what people got for loving each other. Thank God for gas, anyway. What must it have been like before there were anæsthetics? Once it started, they were in the mill-race. Catherine had a good time in the time of pregnancy. It wasn't bad. She was hardly ever sick. She was not awfully uncomfortable until toward the last. So now they got her in the end. You never got away with anything. Get away hell! It would have been the same if we had been married fifty times. And what if she should die? She won't die. People don't die in childbirth nowadays. That was what all husbands thought. Yes, but what if she should die? She won't die. She's just having a bad time. The initial labor is usually protracted. She's only having a bad time. Afterward we'd say what a bad time and Catherine would say it wasn't really so bad. But what if she should die? She can't die. Yes, but what if she should die? She can't, I tell you. Don't be a fool. It's just a bad time. It's just nature giving her hell. It's only the first labor, which is almost always protracted. Yes, but what if she should die? She can't die. Why would she die? What reason is there for her to die? There's just a child that has to be born, the by-product of good nights in Milan. It makes trouble and is born

and then you look after it and get fond of it maybe. But what if she
should die? She won't die. But what if she should die? She won't.
She's all right. But what if she should die? She can't die. But
what if she should die? Hey, what about that? What if she should
die?

The doctor came into the room.

"How does it go, doctor?"

"It doesn't go," he said.

"What do you mean?"

"Just that. I made an examination—" He detailed the result of
the examination. "Since then I've waited to see. But it doesn't go."

"What do you advise?"

"There are two things. Either a high forceps delivery which can
tear and be quite dangerous besides being possibly bad for the
child, and a Cæsarean."

"What is the danger of a Cæsarean?" What if she should die!

"It should be no greater than the danger of an ordinary delivery."

"Would you do it yourself?"

"Yes. I would need possibly an hour to get things ready and to
get the people I would need. Perhaps a little less."

"What do you think?"

"I would advise a Cæsarean operation. If it were my wife I
would do a Cæsarean."

"What are the after effects?"

"There are none. There is only the scar."

"What about infection?"

"The danger is not so great as in a high forceps delivery."

"What if you just went on and did nothing?"

"You would have to do something eventually. Mrs. Henry is already losing much of her strength. The sooner we operate now the
safer."

"Operate as soon as you can," I said.

"I will go and give the instructions."

I went into the delivery room. The nurse was with Catherine who lay on the table, big under the sheet, looking very pale and tired.

"Did you tell him he could do it?" she asked.

"Yes."

"Isn't that grand. Now it will be all over in an hour. I'm almost done, darling. I'm going all to pieces. *Please give me that.* It doesn't work. *Oh, it doesn't work!*"

"Breathe deeply."

"I am. Oh, it doesn't work any more. It doesn't work!"

"Get another cylinder," I said to the nurse.

"That is a new cylinder."

"I'm just a fool, darling," Catherine said. "But it doesn't work any more." She began to cry. "Oh, I wanted so to have this baby and not make trouble, and now I'm all done and all gone to pieces and it doesn't work. Oh, darling, it doesn't work at all. I don't care if I die if it will only stop. Oh, please, darling, please make it stop. *There it comes. Oh Oh Oh!*" She breathed sobbingly in the mask. "It doesn't work. It doesn't work. It doesn't work. Don't mind me, darling. Please don't cry. Don't mind me. I'm just gone all to pieces. You poor sweet. I love you so and I'll be good again. I'll be good this time. *Can't they give me something?* If they could only give me something."

"I'll make it work. I'll turn it all the way."

"Give it to me now."

I turned the dial all the way and as she breathed hard and deep her hand relaxed on the mask. I shut off the gas and lifted the mask. She came back from a long way away.

"That was lovely, darling. Oh, you're so good to me."

"You be brave, because I can't do that all the time. It might kill you."

"I'm not brave any more, darling. I'm all broken. They've broken me. I know it now."

"Everybody is that way."

"But it's awful. They just keep it up till they break you."

"In an hour it will be over."

"Isn't that lovely? Darling, I won't die, will I?"

"No. I promise you won't."

"Because I don't want to die and leave you, but I get so tired of it and I feel I'm going to die."

"Nonsense. Everybody feels that."

"Sometimes I know I'm going to die."

"You won't. You can't."

"But what if I should?"

"I won't let you."

"Give it to me quick. *Give it to me!*"

Then afterward, "I won't die. I won't let myself die."

"Of course you won't."

"You'll stay with me?"

"Not to watch it."

"No, just to be there."

"Sure. I'll be there all the time."

"You're so good to me. There, give it to me. Give me some more. *It's not working!*"

I turned the dial to three and then four. I wished the doctor would come back. I was afraid of the numbers above two.

Finally a new doctor came in with two nurses and they lifted Catherine onto a wheeled stretcher and we started down the hall. The stretcher went rapidly down the hall and into the elevator where every one had to crowd against the wall to make room; then up, then an open door and out of the elevator and down the hall on rubber wheels to the operating room. I did not recognize the doctor with his cap and mask on. There was another doctor and more nurses.

"*They've got to give me something,*" Catherine said. "*They've got to give me something.* Oh please, doctor, give me enough to do some good!"

One of the doctors put a mask over her face and I looked through the door and saw the bright small amphitheatre of the operating room.

"You can go in the other door and sit up there," a nurse said to me. There were benches behind a rail that looked down on the white table and the lights. I looked at Catherine. The mask was over her face and she was quiet now. They wheeled the stretcher forward. I turned away and walked down the hall. Two nurses were hurrying toward the entrance to the gallery.

"It's a Cæsarean," one said. "They're going to do a Cæsarean."

The other one laughed, "We're just in time. Aren't we lucky?" They went in the door that led to the gallery.

Another nurse came along. She was hurrying too.

"You go right in there. Go right in," she said.

"I'm staying outside."

She hurried in. I walked up and down the hall. I was afraid to go in. I looked out the window. It was dark but in the light from the window I could see it was raining. I went into a room at the far end of the hall and looked at the labels on bottles in a glass case. Then I came out and stood in the empty hall and watched the door of the operating room.

A doctor came out followed by a nurse. He held something in his two hands that looked like a freshly skinned rabbit and hurried across the corridor with it and in through another door. I went down to the door he had gone into and found them in the room doing things to a new-born child. The doctor held him up for me to see. He held him by the heels and slapped him.

"Is he all right?"

"He's magnificent. He'll weigh five kilos."

I had no feeling for him. He did not seem to have anything to do with me. I felt no feeling of fatherhood.

"Aren't you proud of your son?" the nurse asked. They were washing him and wrapping him in something. I saw the little dark face and dark hand, but I did not see him move or hear him cry. The doctor was doing something to him again. He looked upset.

"No," I said. "He nearly killed his mother."

"It isn't the little darling's fault. Didn't you want a boy?"

"No," I said. The doctor was busy with him. He held him up by the feet and slapped him. I did not wait to see it. I went out in the hall. I could go in now and see. I went in the door and a little way down the gallery. The nurses who were sitting at the rail motioned for me to come down where they were. I shook my head. I could see enough where I was.

I thought Catherine was dead. She looked dead. Her face was gray, the part of it that I could see. Down below, under the light, the doctor was sewing up the great long, forcep-spread, thick-edged, wound. Another doctor in a mask gave the anæsthetic. Two nurses in masks handed things. It looked like a drawing of the Inquisition. I knew as I watched I could have watched it all, but I was glad I hadn't. I do not think I could have watched them cut, but I watched the wound closed into a high welted ridge with quick skilful-looking stitches like a cobbler's, and was glad. When the wound was closed I went out into the hall and walked up and down again. After a while the doctor came out.

"How is she?"

"She is all right. Did you watch?"

He looked tired.

"I saw you sew up. The incision looked very long."

"You thought so?"

"Yes. Will that scar flatten out?"

"Oh, yes."

After a while they brought out the wheeled stretcher and took it very rapidly down the hallway to the elevator. I went along beside it. Catherine was moaning. Downstairs they put her in the bed in her room. I sat in a chair at the foot of the bed. There was a nurse in the room. I got up and stood by the bed. It was dark in the room. Catherine put out her hand. "Hello, darling," she said. Her voice was very weak and tired.

"Hello, you sweet."

"What sort of baby was it?"

"Sh—don't talk," the nurse said.

"A boy. He's long and wide and dark."

"Is he all right?"

"Yes," I said. "He's fine."

I saw the nurse look at me strangely.

"I'm awfully tired," Catherine said. "And I hurt like hell. Are you all right, darling?"

"I'm fine. Don't talk."

"You were lovely to me. Oh, darling, I hurt dreadfully. What does he look like?"

"He looks like a skinned rabbit with a puckered-up old-man's face."

"You must go out," the nurse said. "Madame Henry must not talk."

"I'll be outside."

"Go and get something to eat."

"No. I'll be outside." I kissed Catherine. She was very gray and weak and tired.

"May I speak to you?" I said to the nurse. She came out in the hall with me. I walked a little way down the hall.

"What's the matter with the baby?" I asked.

"Didn't you know?"

"No."

"He wasn't alive."

"He was dead?"

"They couldn't start him breathing. The cord was caught around his neck or something."

"So he's dead."

"Yes. It's such a shame. He was such a fine big boy. I thought you knew."

"No," I said. "You better go back in with Madame."

I sat down on the chair in front of a table where there were nurses' reports hung on clips at the side and looked out of the window. I could see nothing but the dark and the rain falling across the light from the window. So that was it. The baby was dead. That was why the doctor looked so tired. But why had they acted the way they did in the room with him? They supposed he would come around and start breathing probably. I had no religion but I knew he ought to have been baptized. But what if he never breathed at all. He hadn't. He had never been alive. Except in Catherine. I'd felt him kick there often enough. But I hadn't for a week. Maybe he was choked all the time. Poor little kid. I wished the hell I'd been choked like that. No I didn't. Still there would not be all this dying to go through. Now Catherine would die. That was what you did. You died. You did not know what it was about. You never had time to learn. They threw you in and told you the rules and the first time they caught you off base they killed you. Or they killed you gratuitously like Aymo. Or gave you the syphilis like Rinaldi. But they killed you in the end. You could count on that. Stay around and they would kill you.

Once in camp I put a log on top of the fire and it was full of ants. As it commenced to burn, the ants swarmed out and went first toward the centre where the fire was; then turned back and ran toward the end. When there were enough on the end they fell off into the fire. Some got out, their bodies burnt and flattened, and went off not knowing where they were going. But most of them went toward the fire and then back toward the end and swarmed on the cool end and finally fell off into the fire. I remember thinking at the time that it was the end of the world and a splendid chance to be a messiah and lift the log off the fire and throw it out where the ants could get off onto the ground. But I did not do anything but throw a tin cup of water on the log, so that I would have the cup empty to put whiskey in before I added water to it. I think the cup of water on the burning log only steamed the ants.

So now I sat out in the hall and waited to hear how Catherine was. The nurse did not come out, so after a while I went to the door and opened it very softly and looked in. I could not see at first because there was a bright light in the hall and it was dark in the room. Then I saw the nurse sitting by the bed and Catherine's head on a pillow, and she was all flat under the sheet. The nurse put her finger to her lips, then stood up and came to the door.

"How is she?" I asked.

"She's all right," the nurse said. "You should go and have your supper and then come back if you wish."

I went down the hall and then down the stairs and out the door of the hospital and down the dark street in the rain to the café. It was brightly lighted inside and there were many people at the tables. I did not see a place to sit, and a waiter came up to me and took my wet coat and hat and showed me a place at a table across from an elderly man who was drinking beer and reading the evening paper. I sat down and asked the waiter what the *plat du jour* was.

"Veal stew—but it is finished."

"What can I have to eat?"

"Ham and eggs, eggs with cheese, or *choucroute*."

"I had *choucroute* this noon," I said.

"That's true," he said. "That's true. You ate *choucroute* this noon." He was a middle-aged man with a bald top to his head and his hair slicked over it. He had a kind face.

"What do you want? Ham and eggs or eggs with cheese?"

"Ham and eggs," I said, "and beer."

"A demi-blonde?"

"Yes," I said.

"I remembered," he said. "You took a demi-blonde this noon."

I ate the ham and eggs and drank the beer. The ham and eggs were in a round dish—the ham underneath and the eggs on top. It was very hot and at the first mouthful I had to take a drink of beer to cool my mouth. I was hungry and I asked the waiter for another order. I drank several glasses of beer. I was not thinking at all but read the paper of the man opposite me. It was about the break through on the British front. When he realized I was reading the back of his paper he folded it over. I thought of asking the waiter for a paper, but I could not concentrate. It was hot in the café and the air was bad. Many of the people at the tables knew one another. There were several card games going on. The waiters were busy bringing drinks from the bar to the tables. Two men came in and could find no place to sit. They stood opposite the table where I was. I ordered another beer. I was not ready to leave yet. It was too soon to go back to the hospital. I tried not to think and to be perfectly calm. The men stood around but no one was leaving, so they went out. I drank another beer. There was quite a pile of saucers now on the table in front of me. The man opposite me had taken off his spectacles, put them away in a case, folded his paper and put it in his pocket and now sat holding his liqueur glass and looking out at the room. Suddenly I knew I had to get back. I called the waiter, paid the reckoning, got into my coat, put on my hat and started out the door. I walked through the rain up to the hospital.

Upstairs I met the nurse coming down the hall.

"I just called you at the hotel," she said. Something dropped inside me.

"What is wrong?"

"Mrs. Henry has had a hemorrhage."

"Can I go in?"

"No, not yet. The doctor is with her."

"Is it dangerous?"

"It is very dangerous." The nurse went into the room and shut the door. I sat outside in the hall. Everything was gone inside of me. I did not think. I could not think. I knew she was going to die and I prayed that she would not. Don't let her die. Oh, God, please don't let her die. I'll do anything for you if you won't let her die. Please, please, please, dear God, don't let her die. Dear God, don't let her die. Please, please, please don't let her die. God please make her not die. I'll do anything you say if you don't let her die. You took the baby but don't let her die. That was all right but don't let her die. Please, please, dear God, don't let her die.

The nurse opened the door and motioned with her finger for me to come. I followed her into the room. Catherine did not look up when I came in. I went over to the side of the bed. The doctor was standing by the bed on the opposite side. Catherine looked at me and smiled. I bent down over the bed and started to cry.

"Poor darling," Catherine said very softly. She looked gray.

"You're all right, Cat," I said. "You're going to be all right."

"I'm going to die," she said; then waited and said, "I hate it."

I took her hand.

"Don't touch me," she said. I let go of her hand. She smiled. "Poor darling. You touch me all you want."

"You'll be all right, Cat. I know you'll be all right."

"I meant to write you a letter to have if anything happened, but I didn't do it."

"Do you want me to get a priest or any one to come and see you?"

"Just you," she said. Then a little later, "I'm not afraid. I just hate it."

"You must not talk so much," the doctor said.

"All right," Catherine said.

"Do you want me to do anything, Cat? Can I get you anything?"

Catherine smiled, "No." Then a little later, "You won't do our things with another girl, or say the same things, will you?"

"Never."

"I want you to have girls, though."

"I don't want them."

"You are talking too much," the doctor said. "Mr. Henry must go out. He can come back again later. You are not going to die. You must not be silly."

"All right," Catherine said. "I'll come and stay with you nights," she said. It was very hard for her to talk.

"Please go out of the room," the doctor said. "You cannot talk." Catherine winked at me, her face gray. "I'll be right outside," I said.

"Don't worry, darling," Catherine said. "I'm not a bit afraid. It's just a dirty trick."

"You dear, brave sweet."

I waited outside in the hall. I waited a long time. The nurse came to the door and came over to me. "I'm afraid Mrs. Henry is very ill," she said. "I'm afraid for her."

"Is she dead?"

"No, but she is unconscious."

It seems she had one hemorrhage after another. They couldn't stop it. I went into the room and stayed with Catherine until she died. She was unconscious all the time, and it did not take her very long to die.

Outside the room, in the hall, I spoke to the doctor, "Is there anything I can do to-night?"

"No. There is nothing to do. Can I take you to your hotel?"

"No, thank you. I am going to stay here a while."

"I know there is nothing to say. I cannot tell you——"

"No," I said. "There's nothing to say."

"Good-night," he said. "I cannot take you to your hotel?"

"No, thank you."

"It was the only thing to do," he said. "The operation proved——"

"I do not want to talk about it," I said.

"I would like to take you to your hotel."

"No, thank you."

He went down the hall. I went to the door of the room.

"You can't come in now," one of the nurses said.

"Yes I can," I said.

"You can't come in yet."

"You get out," I said. "The other one too."

But after I had got them out and shut the door and turned off the light it wasn't any good. It was like saying good-by to a statue. After a while I went out and left the hospital and walked back to the hotel in the rain.

THE END

INTRODUCTION TO

The Old Man and the Sea

BY CARLOS BAKER

INTRODUCTION

I

ON THE afternoon of July 20, 1951, the day before his fifty-second birthday, Ernest Hemingway stood at his typewriter in the large room at Finca Vigia, his Cuban establishment, writing a long letter to his publisher. He had just returned from a three-day fishing trip down the coast aboard his launch, the *Pilar*. Coming into the harbor they had bucked a line squall with rain so thick that the bow was invisible from the flying bridge. Now in the late afternoon the wind had dropped, but the rain was still streaming straight up and down as if the weather gods were determined to make up for the droughts of many previous years. Hemingway stood bulkily before the typewriter, knocking out the words. The burden of his letter was a book about the sea.

The total manuscript, he told Charles Scribner, ran to nearly two thousand pages and had been conceived in four parts. At the moment his task was the monumental Part One, which he had not touched since 1947. In a month of morning labor he had completely rewritten 179 of its 1195 pages. When that job was finished, he planned to perform a good deal of "very careful scalpel work" on another of the four sections. But the last two parts would need no cutting at all. If he should die, accidentally or otherwise, these two parts, and even the third, would be ready to publish.

Yet he did not wish to hurry. According to his doctor, his chances of living to complete the book were excellent. Still, he said, he had worked so hard in the last six months that he needed a rest and a change of climate. For weeks the temperature had stood near ninety degrees and he had permanent prickly heat. There was, moreover, the perennial harassment of hypertension. It was possible to whip your blood pressure, as he had done, by training and abstemiousness; but if you worked as hard as he had been working, it wore you down so that you might be victimized by any passing germ. He did not think that many writers could average over a thousand words a day for a four-month stretch, especially of the kind of writing which Charles Scribner had read on a recent visit. Now he would like to get the same tempo into the lengthy Part One.

The piece of writing Scribner had read during a visit to Cuba that winter concerned the lone fishing expedition of an aged man called Santiago. Ever since April, Hemingway had been surreptitiously showing it around, testing its effect on his friends, gradually assuring and reassuring himself that his personal belief in the story's moral worth and emotional impact could find support and confirmation in other minds. This process continued for another seven months. It was not in fact until March of 1952, some three weeks after Mr. Scribner's sudden death, that the editors at Charles Scribner's Sons were permitted to read the tale of Santiago.

In the letter he sent along with the typescript, Hemingway carefully noted that it was 26,531 words in length. He would not try to point out its particular "virtues or implicaciones." But he knew that it was the best writing he had ever done in his life. It was neither a short story nor a novella. It was in fact the epilogue to his long book. But that book could get along very well without an endpiece. As for the tale of Santiago, it could well stand, he thought, as an epilogue to all his writing and to all he had learned, or tried to learn, while writing and trying to live.

The Old Man and the Sea did come in the course of time to stand as the epilogue to all Hemingway's writing, not only because it was the last of his books to be published while he lived, but also because its "virtues and implicaciones" made it representative of his true forte in the writing of fiction. As the body of his work takes its provisional position in the long *galleria* of world literature, it is evident that his prime virtue lies in the ability to present physical actions which at the same time carry the "implicaciones" of symbolic actions. This is not to deny him other powers, such as the always disciplined accuracy of observation; a skill with landscape as unerring as Cézanne's; mastery of stylized dialogues and internal monologues for purposes of characterization; a moral outlook whose overtones are stoical; and the ability to communicate to his readers a golden sense of life's glamour, even when he and his readers know very well that between the peaks of power and glory lie vast flat stretches of monotony, to say nothing of the black gulfs of despair into which both the just and the unjust may inadvertently stumble. Yet Hemingway's senses are never so alert, his emotions at such a controlled pitch of intensity, his narrative talents so absolutely at his sovereign service, as when he concentrates upon a sequence of physical actions from which he expects his readers to infer a sequence of symbolic "implicaciones."

He discovered how to do it at the beginning of his mature writing life. "Out of Season," one of the three stories in his first published book, is an early example of the method at work. Yet another fishing story, *The Old Man and the Sea*, demonstrates the degree to which he had managed to develop the method after some thirty further years of effort. Between these temporal extremes stand other memorable instances—"Big Two-Hearted River," "A Clean, Well-Lighted Place," "Alpine Idyll," "The Snows of Kilimanjaro," and "The Short Happy Life of Francis Macomber," to name only a few. In spite of their variety of locale and circumstance, all of them employ a technique in which explicit events are made to convey implicit meanings without explanation, preachment, or even undue insistence upon the possible "implicaciones."

He soon learned how to use the same technique in key passages of the longer works. Anyone familiar with the novels can quickly isolate a whole series of narrative units or set pieces in which Hemingway almost visibly rolls up his sleeves, girds up his loins, gathers his powers about him, and rises to the required occasion. The length of these units, curiously consistent, usually varies from four to six thousand words—as in the climactic Romero-Belmonte bullfight of *The Sun Also Rises* or the flight of the lovers up the lake in *A Farewell to Arms*. The incident of the smuggled Chinese in *To Have and Have Not* and the crowning kudu chase of *The Green Hills of Africa* may be mentioned as units of similar length and strategic position. *For Whom the Bell Tolls* includes such nearly perfect set pieces as El Sordo's last stand on the hilltop and Jordan's successful dynamiting of the bridge. Pilar's excruciating account of the massacre of the fascists, running to roughly twelve thousand words, is the longest of the set piece units in any of the novels until we reach *The Old Man and the Sea*. At 26,531 words (by the author's laborious count) it is perhaps his most sustained attempt to unite the actual and the symbolic under one continuous narrative roof.

The brevity of the book caused him some concern. It might be impossible, he told Wallace Meyer, then his editor at Scribner's, to publish a book of this length. But he knew that in the history of publishing there had been books of this length which had enjoyed an extraordinary and continued sale. Without intending to make qualitative comparisons, said Hemingway, he could think immediately of such short and commercially successful books as *The Story of the Other Wise Man*, *A Christmas Carol*, and *The Man Without a Country*. He was sick and tired, he said, of not publishing anything. Other writers could publish short books. But he would always be considered a bum unless he came in with a *War and Peace* or a *Crime and Punishment*. It was just possible, he speculated, that people might like to handle a good non-overweight book where a man had shown what a human being could do, and something about the dignity of the human soul, without the word *soul's* being capitalized.

Having mailed in his typescript, Hemingway set out with his wife aboard the *Pilar* for a two-week "austerity vacation" down the Cuban coast. On March 16, while the launch lay at anchor off Pinar del Río province, he wrote Meyer that he was still wondering about the title. Should he try to beat it? When he got home to the source books where all the titles were, he would give the matter further thought. Usually he had a list of fifty or more. Aboard the *Pilar*, when he woke in the night, titles kept popping into his head. But the sun, coming up out of the sea, always burned them away like early mist. On the twentieth, still at sea, he confessed that he had been unable to think of a better title. In the general scheme of the several books he had called it, sometimes, "The Sea in Being." Such other titles as he had thought of seemed worthless. "The Dignity of Man" was correct but pompous. He knew that lately there had been many books with the word *sea* in their titles. One fine one was Rachel Carson's *The Sea Around Us,* and there were others in which the sea figured. But his own book was not just another book about the sea. Nor was it one in which ships contended with an angry ocean.

Despite his lingering doubts about length and title, Hemingway remained convinced of the worth of what he had written. He had told Charles Scribner that it destroyed good and able work by being placed alongside of it. Though he would try to write better, it would be hard. This was not to be construed as a rush of conceit to the head; as a professional writer he knew something about the qualities of prose. One gauge of its validity was the uncluttered cleanness of the path by which it had emerged. He had done the first draft of *The Sun Also Rises* in six weeks when he was 26 or so, he told Meyer, and when he was 51, going on 52, he had written *The Old Man and the Sea* in eight weeks and had learned enough so that he did not have to rewrite. Except for minor corrections, the book that finally appeared in September, 1952, was the same one, word for word, that he had shown his friends a year and a half earlier.

This was an unusual experience for a man accustomed to "very fine scalpel work," which often continued well into the stage of page proof. Also unusual was the length of time he permitted to elapse between his first hearing the story on which that of Santiago was based and his first attempt to give it full fictional treatment. It was his custom to set his stories down while the experiences out of which they grew were still fresh in his mind. The famous Pamplona holiday of 1925, for example, was no more than a week behind him when he started work on *The Sun Also Rises*. In the spring of 1934 he had scarcely shaken the safari dust from the heels of his hunting boots before he began to write *The Green Hills of Africa* about the previous winter's hunting in Tanganyika. His melodrama, *The Fifth Column,* was completed on location in Madrid at the height of the Spanish Civil War late in 1937. And in the spring of 1939, the Spanish capital had only recently fallen when he commenced the enormous task of writing *For Whom the Bell Tolls.* Except for *The Old Man and the Sea,* the only major novel based on events more than a year or two old at the time of composition is *A Farewell to Arms,* written in 1928-1929 when the author's wartime wounding and his love affair with an American nurse in the Milanese hospital were already ten years behind him.

The story of Santiago matured in Hemingway's mind a full fifteen years before he set it down. In the course of an article on the Gulf Stream published in *Esquire* magazine in the spring of 1936, he told of "an old man fishing alone in a skiff out of Cabanas" who hooked "a great marlin that, on the heavy sashcord handline, pulled the skiff far out to sea. Two days later the old man was picked up by fishermen 60 miles to the eastward, the head and the forward part of the marlin lashed alongside. What was left of the fish, less than half, weighed 800 pounds. The old man had stayed with him a day, a night, a day and another night while the fish swam deep and pulled the boat. When he had come up the old man had pulled the boat up on him and harpooned him. Lashed alongside the sharks had hit him and the old man had fought them out alone in the Gulf Stream in a skiff, clubbing them, stabbing at them, lunging at them with an oar until he was exhausted and the sharks had eaten all they could hold. He was crying in the boat when the fishermen picked him up, half crazy from his loss, and the sharks were still circling the boat."

In this 200-word anecdote one easily discerns the essence of Santiago's story: that inexorable and morally inexplicable process of addition and subtraction, accession and deprivation, which seems to be built into the rhythms of nature and of human life. Nor does Hemingway greatly alter the outlines of the tale when he retells it in *The Old Man and the Sea*. It is true that he rounds out the length of Santiago's voyage to a magical three days and three nights. Rather than half a fish, the fictional old man is left with nothing but the head, the tail, and the vertebral links between, as if Hemingway were remembering the theme of "Winner Take Nothing." Instead of being rescued at sea, Santiago returns alone and unaided to his native harbor and his home. Nor does he rave or cry, even though such forms of protest might be justified. In short, though the alterations are worth noticing, they are scarcely sweeping. The difference between the anecdote about the nameless fisherman and the artful implications of the story of Santiago must be looked for outside the essential shape of the story.

One of Hemingway's major additions is the boy Manolo, called Manolin, who provides a framework of human sympathy at the beginning and the end of the old man's lonely struggle. His admiration for Santiago both as man and fisherman also helps to enlarge our belief in the heroism of the undertaking, to enhance our sense of Santiago's stature to dimensions larger than life— even though, as with Melville's Captain Ahab, we know that extrinsically he is only a simple fisherman, a toiler of the sea.

To enlist our sympathy and our admiration is, however, only the lesser part of Manolo's dramatic function. For he also serves to introduce a complex theme of many strands by which Hemingway —himself the father of three sons—was steadily fascinated all his life and in particular during the period 1949-1959. This is the theme of the return, the rediscovery of things past. It involves a doubling back upon one's former paths in order to gain fresh perspectives on the relations between past and present. The process leads to confrontations of various kinds. The protagonist meets all that he formerly was in the full and simultaneous realization of all that he now is. Hemingway experimented with this theme in *Across the River and Into the Trees* where the girl Renata, whose name signifies *rebirth,* is made to embody the aging colonel's recollections of his lost youth, his first experience of Venice at a time when he was precisely the age Renata is now. It is a curious fact that in 1953, the year after *The Old Man and the Sea* was published, Hemingway undertook a double revisitation to Spain and to Africa. His most memorable meeting in Spain was with young Antonio Ordoñez, son of the bullfighter whose exploits had been celebrated in *The Sun Also Rises*. And in Africa, Hemingway chose as his gunbearer the son of that M'Cola with whom he had established so firm a friendship on safari twenty years before. So the boy Manolo serves to recall for Santiago the period of his own lost youth when he was in full possession of all his powers, and when his greatest achievements yet lay in the future rather than as now in the past.

It is therefore no accident, it is rather an aspect of Hemingway's psychological plan, that during the old man's ordeal the two sentences, "I wish the boy was here" and "I wish I had the boy," keep crossing his mind at periodic intervals. In one of the story's subtler rhythms, Santiago always manages, just after he has repeated these words, to secure a new lease on his ebbing strength, as if the consciousness of his former powers, represented by that complex of associations which he sums up simply in "the boy," could always be invoked as a psychological spur at the moments of his greatest need.

The young lions serve a similar purpose. "When I was your age," says Santiago to Manolo, "I was before the mast on a square rigged ship that ran to Africa and I have seen lions on the beaches in the evening." These lions are by way of being one of Santiago's benign obsessions. They persistently recur in his dreams. "They played like young cats in the dusk," writes Hemingway, "and he loved them as he loved the boy." In Santiago's subconscious the distant remembrance of the young lions has met and merged with the more recent image of the boy Manolo. The tensile strength of their fusion is such that they now buttress him in his old age, in the time of his suffering, and in the achievement of one more victory, however Pyrrhic, over those internal and external adversaries which he must now confront.

This wave-like motion of ebbing strength and fluent courage is one of the rhythmic devices through which Hemingway sustains the interest of his narrative. There can be little doubt that this was what he meant when he told Charles Scribner that he was trying to get "the same tempo" into the first part of his long book about the sea whose epilogue was the story of Santiago. The fundamental movement of *The Old Man and the Sea*—at least in the central account of the hooking, the capture, and the loss of the giant marlin—is not unlike the slow, majestic tempo of the groundswell of the ocean. Whenever Santiago rises to a theoretical peak of his resistance, there always follows a time of relaxation into a trough of temporary rest. The very structure of the prose, one discovers with astonishment, partakes of the rhythm of the sea, a tempo old as time and as exactly fitted to the nature and locale of the narrative as the movement of the prose at the opening of the Book of Genesis is fitted to the cosmic creation there enacted.

We have come this far without a glance at Joseph Conrad, of whose work Hemingway was an early and ardent admirer. Conrad's short story, "Youth," virtually a novella in itself, is that rare thing in Hemingway—an undoubted literary influence. Without being able to say precisely how it came about, one may assert that "Youth" exerted a powerful influential effect upon *The Old Man and the Sea* during its long gestational period. Even more than Hemingway has done, Conrad builds his story on the dramatic contrast between the points of view of young and older men. "I remember my youth," says Conrad's narrator Marlow, "and the feeling which will never come back any more—the feeling that I could last for ever, outlast the sea, the earth, and all men; . . . the triumphant conviction of strength, the heat of life in the handful of dust, the glow in the heart that every year grows dim." During the course of the disastrous voyage of the barque *Judea*, bound east for Bangkok, young Marlow is paired with the brave old ship's master, Captain Beard. "He was sixty, if a day," says Marlow. "And he had blue eyes in that old face of his, which were amazingly like a boy's with that candid expression some quite common men preserve to the end of their days by a rare internal gift of simplicity of heart and rectitude of soul." Marlow's words are equally applicable to Santiago, of whom Hemingway remarks that "everything about him was old except his eyes and they were the same color as the sea and were cheerful and undefeated." It almost goes without saying that he also shares with Marlow's captain the qualities of simplicity, rectitude, and courage in the face of extreme adversity. One recalls a remark of Archibald Henderson's, set down in 1932, that "the old demand for the incredible, the impossible, the superhuman . . . has fallen off; and the demand now is for heroes in whom we can recognize our own humanity." Whether or not Henderson's sense of the public taste fitted the situation in 1952 as in 1932, it is plain that Santiago, like Captain Beard before him, is a "quite common" man who rises to the plane of heroism as a direct result of his personal character. "Do or die" is the motto affixed to the stern timbers of the decrepit old *Judea*. It might with equal justice have been carved on the bow of Santiago's sailing skiff.

II

One feels an equal certainty that the larger "implicaciones" in Hemingway's story of old age would not have been lost on the Conrad who wrote "Youth." For it is once again the Conradian narrator Marlow who reminds us of the way in which one account of one man on one journey can extend outwards in our imaginations until it becomes a kind of paradigm for the course of all men's lives. "There are those voyages," says Marlow, beginning his account of the ill-fated *Judea*, "that seem ordered for the illustration of life, that might stand for a symbol of existence. You fight, work, sweat, nearly kill yourself, sometimes do kill yourself, trying to accomplish something—and you can't." If this is true of the *Judea*, bound for Bangkok, do or die, it is true likewise for Santiago, homeward bound for Havana, with the approaching sharks just beginning to smell the blood of the great marlin he has dominated. In such works as this of Hemingway's, we all put out to sea. The locale of the story is what used to be known as the Spanish Main. It is also, by imaginative transference, that more extensive main or mainstream where we all drift or sail, in fair or foul weather, against or with the wind, defending our prize catches, fighting off our predatory sharks, accepting our luck, good or bad, and mustering such courage as we can in the face of any challenge.

Mark Schorer was surely correct in emphasizing this parabolical aspect of the novel in a brilliant commentary written some years ago. "The true quality of fable is first of all in the style," he said, "in the degree of abstraction, which is not only in some ways Biblical but is always tending toward the proverbial rhythm. ('The setting of the sun is a difficult time for fish.') Next, it is in the simplicity of the narrative, and in the beautiful proportion (about three fourths to one fourth) of its rise and fall. Finally, of course, it is in the moral significance of the narrative, this fine story of an ancient who goes too far out, 'beyond the boundaries of permitted aspiration,' as Conrad put it—('You violated your luck when you went too far outside,' the old man thinks)—and encounters his destiny:

His choice had been to stay in the deep dark water far out beyond all snares and traps and treacheries. My choice was to go there to find him beyond all people. Beyond all people in the world. Now we are joined together and have been since noon. And no one to help either one of us.

In this isolation [Schorer continues], he wins a Conradian victory, which means destruction and triumph. We permit his martyrdom because he has earned it."

Conrad's memorable phrase about quests that carry "beyond the boundaries of permitted aspiration" suggests yet another of the possible implications of Hemingway's novel. This is the classical doctrine of *hubris*. We may speculate on the possibility that much

of the best American fiction from Melville to Faulkner and Hemingway is built (whether consciously or not) on what may be
called *the trope of too-far-out*. One thinks, for example, of Tashtego's upraised and still defiant arm as he nails the *Pequod's* flag
yet faster to the topmost spar the moment before the ship makes
its final plunge into the welter of the sea. The Japanese critic
Harada has suggested that Santiago's purpose in going too far out
is to unite "temporality with eternity." In thus overstepping the
"boundary of man's finite and limited nature," he becomes involved
with a *hubris* for which he must take the consequences. It does
not matter that the marlin itself is at least partly responsible for
pulling him too far out, nor that his act in killing the fish is merely
his obligation as a professional fisherman. For it is written into the
scheme of things that he must pay the price for this glory, and
Nemesis in the guise of sharks is therefore inevitable. Like the
Furies who haunt Orestes, says Harada, "the sharks seem to be
determined to prevent the old man from taking the prize of his
fighting out of the sacred region." They seem to resemble "mortuary divinities . . . angered by the sacrilegious attempt of the
old man to expose the unknowable face to those in the . . . finite
order." In the end, Santiago knows he has transgressed "the
boundaries of permitted aspiration." He admits to having gone
"too far out." *And what beat you?* asks one of his internal voices.
Nothing, says the second voice. *I went out too far.* Urged on by
pride, by the love of his trade, by his refusal to take continuing
bad luck as his portion, and by a resurgent belief that he might
win, Santiago made trial of the impossible. In the tragic process,
he achieved the moral triumph, the failure which was also victory.

Something of this familiar paradox of tragic literature seems
to have underlain Hemingway's decision to introduce certain
images derived from the story of the Crucifixion. These come at
intervals through the novel, but they are chiefly concentrated in
the course of the long and bitter, though also heroic, voyage home.

Allusions to Jesus Christ occur with some frequency in Hemingway's earlier works. These are always gentle, and they seem always to emphasize His powers of endurance, human courage, and the dignity of His conduct in the full sweep and magnitude of the necessary agony. The implied parallelism here is by no means inept. For Santiago's name is Spanish for Saint James, the martyred apostle who began as a simple fisherman on the Sea of Galilee. In going on to employ such other symbolic reminders as the blood on the forehead, the manual stigmata, or the ship's mast like the weight of the cross over Santiago's shoulder as he ascends, going home, his own equivalent of Calvary, Hemingway appears to be suggesting that there must be a resemblance between Jesus Christ in his human aspect as the Son of Man and those countless and nameless thousands in the history of Christianity who belong to the category of "good men," and who may accordingly, and without impiety, be seen as followers of Our Lord, whatever the professed degree of their Christian commitment. Any writer who sets out, as Hemingway did, to show "what a human being is capable of" and to prove something about "the dignity of the human soul without the word *soul* being capitalized" may end, as here, by thinking of the example of Jesus Christ. "I tried," said Hemingway, "to make a real old man, a real boy, a real sea and a real fish and real sharks. But if I made them good and true enough they would mean many things."

Many things, indeed. It has even been suggested that Hemingway's fable is wide enough to embrace all creation. According to the Italian critic Marcello Camilucci, the balanced terms of the title which worried Hemingway so much may be seen as "emblematic of the history of the world." First in the order of being is the Sea, "the face of the waters" in the Book of Genesis. It stands, says Camilucci, as a poetic image for that whole expanse of created nature whose essential mystery remains even when we have ransacked our way "through all its laws and forms." Yet at the same

time it may deliver itself "to those who make of it a path to that
love from which springs everything that makes the life of creatures
beautiful and precious." Not less important, according to Camilucci, is the second term, Man, who in Genesis is given "domin-
ion over the fish of the sea . . . and over all the earth," yet who is
"substantially disarmed" in the face of the mystery "if he attempts
to dominate instead of worshipping it."

Hemingway's engagement of this emblematic dualism, both in
his title and the pages which follow, thus gives his novel something of the enigmatic quality of wisdom-literature. By its combination of simplicity and profundity, the actual and the symbolic,
the book takes on resemblances to "those fables which have come
to us down the broad river of time,"—worn smooth as stones "by
the flow of centuries." Yet these are stones, says Camilucci, which
still carry so much fire in their veins that they gleam at night like
fallen stars along the banks of streams. Whether or not we are
quite willing to accept this view of its ultimate "implicaciones,"
The Old Man and the Sea can fittingly serve as the epilogue to
the rest of Hemingway's fiction, not only by virtue of its possibly
final position in the published canon but also, as the author himself
appeared to think, because it embodies in a stirring narrative of
courage and endurance the sum of what he had learned in the
lifelong process of writing and trying to live.

CARLOS BAKER

The Old Man and the Sea

THE OLD MAN AND THE SEA

He was an old man who fished alone in a skiff in the Gulf Stream and he had gone eighty-four days now without taking a fish. In the first forty days a boy had been with him. But after forty days without a fish the boy's parents had told him that the old man was now definitely and finally *salao*, which is the worst form of unlucky, and the boy had gone at their orders in another boat which caught three good fish the first week. It made the boy sad to see the old man come in each day with his skiff empty and he always went down to help him carry either the coiled lines or the gaff and harpoon and the sail that was furled around the mast. The sail was patched with flour sacks and, furled, it looked like the flag of permanent defeat.

The old man was thin and gaunt with deep wrinkles in the back of his neck. The brown blotches of the benevolent skin cancer the sun brings from its reflection on the tropic sea were on his cheeks. The blotches ran well down the sides of his face and his hands had the deep-creased scars from handling heavy fish on the cords. But none of these scars were fresh. They were as old as erosions in a fishless desert.

Everything about him was old except his eyes and they were the same colour as the sea and were cheerful and undefeated.

"Santiago," the boy said to him as they climbed the bank from where the skiff was hauled up. "I could go with you again. We've made some money."

The old man had taught the boy to fish and the boy loved him.

"No," the old man said. "You're with a lucky boat. Stay with them."

"But remember how you went eighty-seven days without fish and then we caught big ones every day for three weeks."

"I remember," the old man said. "I know you did not leave me because you doubted."

"It was papa made me leave. I am a boy and I must obey him."

"I know," the old man said. "It is quite normal."

"He hasn't much faith."

"No," the old man said. "But we have. Haven't we?"

"Yes," the boy said. "Can I offer you a beer on the Terrace and then we'll take the stuff home."

"Why not?" the old man said. "Between fishermen."

They sat on the Terrace and many of the fishermen made fun of the old man and he was not angry. Others, of the older fishermen, looked at him and were sad. But they did not show it and they spoke politely about the current and the depths they had drifted their lines at and the steady good weather and of what they had seen. The successful fishermen of that day were already in and had butchered their marlin out and carried them laid full length across two planks, with two men staggering at the end of each plank, to the fish house where they waited for the ice truck to carry them to the market in Havana. Those who had caught sharks had taken them to the shark factory on the other side of the cove where they were hoisted on a block and tackle, their livers removed, their fins cut off and their hides skinned out and their flesh cut into strips for salting.

When the wind was in the east a smell came across the harbour from the shark factory; but today there was only the faint edge of the odour because the wind had backed into the north and then dropped off and it was pleasant and sunny on the Terrace.

"Santiago," the boy said.

"Yes," the old man said. He was holding his glass and thinking of many years ago.

"Can I go out to get sardines for you for tomorrow?"

"No. Go and play baseball. I can still row and Rogelio will throw the net."

"I would like to go. If I cannot fish with you, I would like to serve in some way."

"You bought me a beer," the old man said. "You are already a man."

"How old was I when you first took me in a boat?"

"Five and you nearly were killed when I brought the fish in too green and he nearly tore the boat to pieces. Can you remember?"

"I can remember the tail slapping and banging and the thwart breaking and the noise of the clubbing. I can remember you throwing me into the bow where the wet coiled lines were and feeling the whole boat shiver and the noise of you clubbing him like chopping a tree down and the sweet blood smell all over me."

"Can you really remember that or did I just tell it to you?"

"I remember everything from when we first went together."

The old man looked at him with his sun-burned, confident loving eyes.

"If you were my boy I'd take you out and gamble," he said. "But you are your father's and your mother's and you are in a lucky boat."

"May I get the sardines? I know where I can get four baits too."

"I have mine left from today. I put them in salt in the box."

"Let me get four fresh ones."

"One," the old man said. His hope and his confidence had never gone. But now they were freshening as when the breeze rises.

"Two," the boy said.

"Two," the old man agreed. "You didn't steal them?"

"I would," the boy said. "But I bought these."

"Thank you," the old man said. He was too simple to wonder when he had attained humility. But he knew he had attained it and he knew it was not disgraceful and it carried no loss of true pride.

"Tomorrow is going to be a good day with this current," he said.

"Where are you going?" the boy asked.

"Far out to come in when the wind shifts. I want to be out before it is light."

"I'll try to get him to work far out," the boy said. "Then if you hook something truly big we can come to your aid."

"He does not like to work too far out."

"No," the boy said. "But I will see something that he cannot see such as a bird working and get him to come out after dolphin."

"Are his eyes that bad?"

"He is almost blind."

"It is strange," the old man said. "He never went turtle-ing. That is what kills the eyes."

"But you went turtle-ing for years off the Mosquito Coast and your eyes are good."

"I am a strange old man."

"But are you strong enough now for a truly big fish?"

"I think so. And there are many tricks."

"Let us take the stuff home," the boy said. "So I can get the cast net and go after the sardines."

They picked up the gear from the boat. The old man carried the mast on his shoulder and the boy carried the wooden box with the coiled, hard-braided brown lines, the gaff and the harpoon with its shaft. The box with the baits was under the stern of the skiff along with the club that was used to subdue the big fish when they were brought alongside. No one would steal from the old man but it was better to take the sail and the heavy lines home as the dew was bad for them and, though he was quite sure no local people would steal from him, the old man thought that a gaff and a harpoon were needless temptations to leave in a boat.

They walked up the road together to the old man's shack and went in through its open door. The old man leaned the mast with its wrapped sail against the wall and the boy put the box and the other gear beside it. The mast was nearly as long as the one room of the shack. The shack was made of the tough bud-shields of the royal palm which are called *guano* and in it there was a bed, a table, one chair, and a place on the dirt floor to cook with charcoal. On the brown walls of the flattened, overlapping leaves of the sturdy fibered *guano* there was a picture in colour of the Sacred Heart of Jesus and another of the Virgin of Cobre. These were relics of his wife. Once there had been a tinted photograph of his wife on the wall but he had taken it down because it made him too lonely to see it and it was on the shelf in the corner under his clean shirt.

"What do you have to eat?" the boy asked.

"A pot of yellow rice with fish. Do you want some?"

"No. I will eat at home. Do you want me to make the fire?"

"No. I will make it later on. Or I may eat the rice cold."

"May I take the cast net?"

"Of course."

There was no cast net and the boy remembered when they had sold it. But they went through this fiction every day. There was no pot of yellow rice and fish and the boy knew this too.

"Eighty-five is a lucky number," the old man said. "How would you like to see me bring one in that dressed out over a thousand pounds?"

"I'll get the cast net and go for sardines. Will you sit in the sun in the doorway?"

"Yes. I have yesterday's paper and I will read the baseball."

The boy did not know whether yesterday's paper was a fiction too. But the old man brought it out from under the bed.

"Perico gave it to me at the *bodega*," he explained.

"I'll be back when I have the sardines. I'll keep yours and mine together on ice and we can share them in the morning. When I come back you can tell me about the baseball."

"The Yankees cannot lose."

"But I fear the Indians of Cleveland."

"Have faith in the Yankees my son. Think of the great DiMaggio."

"I fear both the Tigers of Detroit and the Indians of Cleveland."

"Be careful or you will fear even the Reds of Cincinnati and the White Sox of Chicago."

"You study it and tell me when I come back."

"Do you think we should buy a terminal of the lottery with an eighty-five? Tomorrow is the eighty-fifth day."

"We can do that," the boy said. "But what about the eighty-seven of your great record?"

"It could not happen twice. Do you think you can find an eighty-five?"

"I can order one."

"One sheet. That's two dollars and a half. Who can we borrow that from?"

"That's easy. I can always borrow two dollars and a half."

"I think perhaps I can too. But I try not to borrow. First you borrow. Then you beg."

"Keep warm old man," the boy said. "Remember we are in September."

"The month when the great fish come," the old man said. "Anyone can be a fisherman in May."

"I go now for the sardines," the boy said.

When the boy came back the old man was asleep in the chair and the sun was down. The boy took the old army blanket off the bed and spread it over the back of the chair and over the old man's shoulders. They were strange shoulders, still powerful although very old, and the neck was still strong too and the creases did not show so much when the old man was asleep and his head fallen forward. His shirt had been patched so many times that it was like the sail and the patches were faded to many different shades by the sun. The old man's head was very old though and with his eyes closed there was no life in his face. The newspaper lay across his knees and the weight of his arm held it there in the evening breeze. He was barefooted.

The boy left him there and when he came back the old man was still asleep.

"Wake up old man," the boy said and put his hand on one of the old man's knees.

The old man opened his eyes and for a moment he was coming back from a long way away. Then he smiled.

"What have you got?" he asked.

"Supper," said the boy. "We're going to have supper."

"I'm not very hungry."

"Come on and eat. You can't fish and not eat."

"I have," the old man said getting up and taking the newspaper and folding it. Then he started to fold the blanket.

"Keep the blanket around you," the boy said. "You'll not fish without eating while I'm alive."

"Then live a long time and take care of yourself," the old man said. "What are we eating?"

"Black beans and rice, fried bananas, and some stew."

The boy had brought them in a two-decker metal container from the Terrace. The two sets of knives and forks and spoons were in his pocket with a paper napkin wrapped around each set.

"Who gave this to you?"

"Martin. The owner."

"I must thank him."

"I thanked him already," the boy said. "You don't need to thank him."

"I'll give him the belly meat of a big fish," the old man said. "Has he done this for us more than once?"

"I think so."

"I must give him something more than the belly meat then. He is very thoughtful for us."

"He sent two beers."

"I like the beer in cans best."

"I know. But this is in bottles, Hatuey beer, and I take back the bottles."

"That's very kind of you," the old man said. "Should we eat?"

"I've been asking you to," the boy told him gently. "I have not wished to open the container until you were ready."

"I'm ready now," the old man said. "I only needed time to wash."

Where did you wash? the boy thought. The village water supply was two streets down the road. I must have water here for him, the boy thought, and soap and a good towel. Why am I so thoughtless? I must get him another shirt and a jacket for the winter and some sort of shoes and another blanket.

"Your stew is excellent," the old man said.

"Tell me about the baseball," the boy asked him.

"In the American League it is the Yankees as I said," the old man said happily.

"They lost today," the boy told him.

"That means nothing. The great DiMaggio is himself again."

"They have other men on the team."

"Naturally. But he makes the difference. In the other league, between Brooklyn and Philadelphia I must take Brooklyn. But then I think of Dick Sisler and those great drives in the old park."

"There was nothing ever like them. He hits the longest ball I have ever seen."

"Do you remember when he used to come to the Terrace? I wanted to take him fishing but I was too timid to ask him. Then I asked you to ask him and you were too timid."

"I know. It was a great mistake. He might have gone with us. Then we would have that for all of our lives."

"I would like to take the great DiMaggio fishing," the old man said. "They say his father was a fisherman. Maybe he was as poor as we are and would understand."

"The great Sisler's father was never poor and he, the father, was playing in the big leagues when he was my age."

"When I was your age I was before the mast on a square rigged ship that ran to Africa and I have seen lions on the beaches in the evening."

"I know. You told me."

"Should we talk about Africa or about baseball?"

"Baseball I think," the boy said. "Tell me about the great John J. McGraw." He said *Jota* for J.

"He used to come to the Terrace sometimes too in the older days. But he was rough and harsh-spoken and difficult when he was drinking. His mind was on horses as well as baseball. At least he carried lists of horses at all times in his pocket and frequently spoke the names of horses on the telephone."

"He was a great manager," the boy said. "My father thinks he was the greatest."

"Because he came here the most times," the old man said. "If Durocher had continued to come here each year your father would think him the greatest manager."

"Who is the greatest manager, really, Luque or Mike Gonzalez?"

"I think they are equal."

"And the best fisherman is you."

"No. I know others better."

"*Qué va*," the boy said. "There are many good fishermen and some great ones. But there is only you."

"Thank you. You make me happy. I hope no fish will come along so great that he will prove us wrong."

"There is no such fish if you are still strong as you say."

"I may not be as strong as I think," the old man said. "But I know many tricks and I have resolution."

"You ought to go to bed now so that you will be fresh in the morning. I will take the things back to the Terrace."

"Good night then. I will wake you in the morning."

"You're my alarm clock," the boy said.

"Age is my alarm clock," the old man said. "Why do old men wake so early? Is it to have one longer day?"

"I don't know," the boy said. "All I know is that young boys sleep late and hard."

"I can remember it," the old man said. "I'll waken you in time."

"I do not like for him to waken me. It is as though I were inferior."

"I know."

"Sleep well old man."

The boy went out. They had eaten with no light on the table and the old man took off his trousers and went to bed in the dark. He rolled his trousers up to make a pillow, putting the newspaper inside them. He rolled himself in the blanket and slept on the other old newspapers that covered the springs of the bed.

He was asleep in a short time and he dreamed of Africa when he was a boy and the long golden beaches and the white beaches, so white they hurt your eyes, and the high capes and the great brown mountains. He lived along that coast now every night and in his dreams he heard the surf roar and saw the native boats come riding through it. He smelled the tar and oakum of the deck as he slept and he smelled the smell of Africa that the land breeze brought at morning.

Usually when he smelled the land breeze he woke up and dressed to go and wake the boy. But tonight the smell of the land breeze came very early and he knew it was too early in his dream and went on dreaming to see the white peaks of the Islands rising from the sea and then he dreamed of the different harbours and roadsteads of the Canary Islands.

He no longer dreamed of storms, nor of women, nor of great occurrences, nor of great fish, nor fights, nor contests of strength, nor of his wife. He only dreamed of places now and of the lions on the beach. They played like young cats in the dusk and he loved them as he loved the boy. He never dreamed about the boy. He simply woke, looked out the open door at the moon and unrolled his trousers and put them on. He urinated outside the shack and then went up the road to wake the boy. He was shivering with the morning cold. But he knew he would shiver himself warm and that soon he would be rowing.

The door of the house where the boy lived was unlocked and he opened it and walked in quietly with his bare feet. The boy was asleep on a cot in the first room and the old man could see him clearly with the light that came in from the dying moon. He took hold of one foot gently and held it until the boy woke and turned and looked at him. The old man nodded and the boy took his trousers from the chair by the bed and, sitting on the bed, pulled them on.

The old man went out the door and the boy came after him. He was sleepy and the old man put his arm across his shoulders and said, "I am sorry."

"*Qué va,*" the boy said. "It is what a man must do."

They walked down the road to the old man's shack and all along the road, in the dark, barefoot men were moving, carrying the masts of their boats.

When they reached the old man's shack the boy took the rolls of line in the basket and the harpoon and gaff and the old man carried the mast with the furled sail on his shoulder.

"Do you want coffee?" the boy asked.

"We'll put the gear in the boat and then get some."

They had coffee from condensed milk cans at an early morning place that served fishermen.

"How did you sleep old man?" the boy asked. He was waking up now although it was still hard for him to leave his sleep.

"Very well, Manolin," the old man said. "I feel confident today."

"So do I," the boy said. "Now I must get your sardines and mine and your fresh baits. He brings our gear himself. He never wants anyone to carry anything."

"We're different," the old man said. "I let you carry things when you were five years old."

"I know it," the boy said. "I'll be right back. Have another coffee. We have credit here."

He walked off, barefooted on the coral rocks, to the ice house where the baits were stored.

The old man drank his coffee slowly. It was all he would have all day and he knew that he should take it. For a long time now eating had bored him and he never carried a lunch. He had a bottle of water in the bow of the skiff and that was all he needed for the day.

The boy was back now with the sardines and the two baits wrapped in a newspaper and they went down the trail to the skiff, feeling the pebbled sand under their feet, and lifted the skiff and slid her into the water.

"Good luck old man."

"Good luck," the old man said. He fitted the rope lashings of the oars onto the thole pins and, leaning forward against the thrust of the blades in the water, he began to row out of the harbour in the dark. There were other boats from the other beaches going out to sea and the old man heard the dip and push of their oars even though he could not see them now the moon was below the hills. Sometimes someone would speak in a boat. But most of the boats were silent except for the dip of the oars. They spread apart after they were out of the mouth of the harbour and each one headed for the part of the ocean where he hoped to find fish. The old man knew he was going far out and he left the smell of the land behind and rowed out into the clean early morning smell of the ocean. He saw the phosphorescence of the Gulf weed in the water as he rowed over the part of the ocean that the fishermen called the great well because there was a sudden deep of seven hundred fathoms where all sorts of fish congregated because of the swirl the current made against the steep walls of the floor of the ocean. Here there were concentrations of shrimp and bait fish and sometimes schools of squid in the deepest holes and these rose close to the surface at night where all the wandering fish fed on them.

In the dark the old man could feel the morning coming and as he rowed he heard the trembling sound as flying fish left the water and the hissing that their stiff set wings made as they soared away in the darkness. He was very fond of flying fish as they were his principal friends on the ocean. He was sorry for the birds, especially the small delicate dark terns that were always flying and looking and almost never finding, and he thought, "The birds have a harder life than we do except for the robber birds and the heavy strong ones. Why did they make birds so delicate and fine as those sea swallows when the ocean can be so cruel? She is kind and very beautiful. But she can be so cruel and it comes so suddenly and such birds that fly, dipping and hunting, with their small sad voices are made too delicately for the sea."

He always thought of the sea as *la mar* which is what people call her in Spanish when they love her. Sometimes those who love her say bad things of her but they are always said as though she were a woman. Some of the younger fishermen, those who used buoys as floats for their lines and had motorboats, bought when the shark livers had brought much money, spoke of her as *el mar* which is masculine. They spoke of her as a contestant or a place or even an enemy. But the old man always thought of her as feminine and as something that gave or withheld great favours, and if she did wild or wicked things it was because she could not help them. The moon affects her as it does a woman, he thought.

He was rowing steadily and it was no effort for him since he kept well within his speed and the surface of the ocean was flat except for the occasional swirls of the current. He was letting the current do a third of the work and as it started to be light he saw he was already further out than he had hoped to be at this hour.

I worked the deep wells for a week and did nothing, he thought. Today I'll work out where the schools of bonita and albacore are and maybe there will be a big one with them.

Before it was really light he had his baits out and was drifting with the current. One bait was down forty fathoms. The second was at seventy-five and the third and fourth were down in the blue water at one hundred and one hundred and twenty-five fathoms. Each bait hung head down with the shank of the hook inside the bait fish, tied and sewed solid and all the projecting part of the hook, the curve and the point, was covered with fresh sardines. Each sardine was hooked through both eyes so that they made a half-garland on the projecting steel. There was no part of the hook that a great fish could feel which was not sweet smelling and good tasting.

The boy had given him two fresh small tunas, or albacores, which hung on the two deepest lines like plummets and, on the others, he had a big blue runner and a yellow jack that had been used before; but they were in good condition still and had the excellent sardines to give them scent and attractiveness. Each line, as thick around as a big pencil, was looped onto a green-sapped stick so that any pull or touch on the bait would make the stick dip and each line had two forty-fathom coils which could be made fast to the other spare coils so that, if it were necessary, a fish could take out over three hundred fathoms of line.

Now the man watched the dip of the three sticks over the side of the skiff and rowed gently to keep the lines straight up and down and at their proper depths. It was quite light and any moment now the sun would rise.

The sun rose thinly from the sea and the old man could see the other boats, low on the water and well in toward the shore, spread out across the current. Then the sun was brighter and the glare came on the water and then, as it rose clear, the flat sea sent it back at his eyes so that it hurt sharply and he rowed without looking into it. He looked down into the water and watched the lines that went straight down into the dark of the water. He kept them straighter than anyone did, so that at each level in the darkness of the stream there would be a bait waiting exactly where he wished it to be for any fish that swam there. Others let them drift with the current and sometimes they were at sixty fathoms when the fishermen thought they were at a hundred.

But, he thought, I keep them with precision. Only I have no luck any more. But who knows? Maybe today. Every day is a new day. It is better to be lucky. But I would rather be exact. Then when luck comes you are ready.

The sun was two hours higher now and it did not hurt his eyes so much to look into the east. There were only three boats in sight now and they showed very low and far inshore.

All my life the early sun has hurt my eyes, he thought. Yet they are still good. In the evening I can look straight into it without getting the blackness. It has more force in the evening too. But in the morning it is painful.

Just then he saw a man-of-war bird with his long black wings circling in the sky ahead of him. He made a quick drop, slanting down on his back-swept wings, and then circled again.

"He's got something," the old man said aloud. "He's not just looking."

He rowed slowly and steadily toward where the bird was circling. He did not hurry and he kept his lines straight up and down. But he crowded the current a little so that he was still fishing correctly though faster than he would have fished if he was not trying to use the bird.

The bird went higher in the air and circled again, his wings motionless. Then he dove suddenly and the old man saw flying fish spurt out of the water and sail desperately over the surface.

"Dolphin," the old man said aloud. "Big dolphin."

He shipped his oars and brought a small line from under the bow. It had a wire leader and a medium-sized hook and he baited it with one of the sardines. He let it go over the side and then made it fast to a ring bolt in the stern. Then he baited another line and left it coiled in the shade of the bow. He went back to rowing and to watching the long-winged black bird who was working, now, low over the water.

As he watched the bird dipped again slanting his wings for the dive and then swinging them wildly and ineffectually as he followed the flying fish. The old man could see the slight bulge in the water that the big dolphin raised as they followed the escaping fish. The dolphin were cutting through the water below the flight of the fish and would be in the water, driving at speed, when the fish dropped. It is a big school of dolphin, he thought. They are widespread and the flying fish have little chance. The bird has no chance. The flying fish are too big for him and they go too fast.

He watched the flying fish burst out again and again and the ineffectual movements of the bird. That school has gotten away from me, he thought. They are moving out too fast and too far. But perhaps I will pick up a stray and perhaps my big fish is around them. My big fish must be somewhere.

The clouds over the land now rose like mountains and the coast was only a long green line with the gray blue hills behind it. The water was a dark blue now, so dark that it was almost purple. As he looked down into it he saw the red sifting of the plankton in the dark water and the strange light the sun made now. He watched his lines to see them go straight down out of sight into the water and he was happy to see so much plankton because it meant fish. The strange light the sun made in the water, now that the sun was higher, meant good weather and so did the shape of the clouds over the land. But the bird was almost out of sight now and nothing showed on the surface of the water but some patches of yellow, sun-bleached Sargasso weed and the purple, formalized, iridescent, gelatinous bladder of a Portuguese man-of-war floating close beside the boat. It turned on its side and then righted itself. It floated cheerfully as a bubble with its long deadly purple filaments trailing a yard behind it in the water.

"*Agua mala,*" the man said. "You whore."

From where he swung lightly against his oars he looked down into the water and saw the tiny fish that were coloured like the trailing filaments and swam between them and under the small shade the bubble made as it drifted. They were immune to its poison. But men were not and when some of the filaments would catch on a line and rest there slimy and purple while the old man was working a fish, he would have welts and sores on his arms and hands of the sort that poison ivy or poison oak can give. But these poisonings from the *agua mala* came quickly and struck like a whiplash.

The iridescent bubbles were beautiful. But they were the falsest thing in the sea and the old man loved to see the big sea turtles eating them. The turtles saw them, approached them from the front, then shut their eyes so they were completely carapaced and ate them filaments and all. The old man loved to see the turtles eat them and he loved to walk on them on the beach after a storm and hear them pop when he stepped on them with the horny soles of his feet.

He loved green turtles and hawk-bills with their elegance and speed and their great value and he had a friendly contempt for the huge, stupid loggerheads, yellow in their armour-plating, strange in their love-making, and happily eating the Portuguese men-of-war with their eyes shut.

He had no mysticism about turtles although he had gone in turtle boats for many years. He was sorry for them all, even the great trunk backs that were as long as the skiff and weighed a ton. Most people are heartless about turtles because a turtle's heart will beat for hours after he has been cut up and butchered. But the old man thought, I have such a heart too and my feet and hands are like theirs. He ate the white eggs to give himself strength. He ate them all through May to be strong in September and October for the truly big fish.

He also drank a cup of shark liver oil each day from the big drum in the shack where many of the fishermen kept their gear. It was there for all fishermen who wanted it. Most fishermen hated the taste. But it was no worse than getting up at the hours that they rose and it was very good against all colds and grippes and it was good for the eyes.

Now the old man looked up and saw that the bird was circling again.

"He's found fish," he said aloud. No flying fish broke the surface and there was no scattering of bait fish. But as the old man watched, a small tuna rose in the air, turned and dropped head first into the water. The tuna shone silver in the sun and after he had dropped back into the water another and another rose and they were jumping in all directions, churning the water and leaping in long jumps after the bait. They were circling it and driving it.

If they don't travel too fast I will get into them, the old man thought, and he watched the school working the water white and the bird now dropping and dipping into the bait fish that were forced to the surface in their panic.

"The bird is a great help," the old man said. Just then the stern line came taut under his foot, where he had kept a loop of the line, and he dropped his oars and felt the weight of the small tuna's shivering pull as he held the line firm and commenced to haul it in. The shivering increased as he pulled in and he could see the blue back of the fish in the water and the gold of his sides before he swung him over the side and into the boat. He lay in the stern in the sun, compact and bullet shaped, his big, unintelligent eyes staring as he thumped his life out against the planking of the boat with the quick shivering strokes of his neat, fast-moving tail. The old man hit him on the head for kindness and kicked him, his body still shuddering, under the shade of the stern.

"Albacore," he said aloud. "He'll make a beautiful bait. He'll weigh ten pounds."

He did not remember when he had first started to talk aloud when he was by himself. He had sung when he was by himself in the old days and he had sung at night sometimes when he was alone steering on his watch in the smacks or in the turtle boats. He had probably started to talk aloud, when alone, when the boy had left. But he did not remember. When he and the boy fished together they usually spoke only when it was necessary. They talked at night or when they were storm-bound by bad weather. It was considered a virtue not to talk unnecessarily at sea and the old man had always considered it so and respected it. But now he said his thoughts aloud many times since there was no one that they could annoy.

"If the others heard me talking out loud they would think that I am crazy," he said aloud. "But since I am not crazy, I do not care.

And the rich have radios to talk to them in their boats and to bring them the baseball."

Now is no time to think of baseball, he thought. Now is the time to think of only one thing. That which I was born for. There might be a big one around that school, he thought. I picked up only a straggler from the albacore that were feeding. But they are working far out and fast. Everything that shows on the surface to-day travels very fast and to the north-east. Can that be the time of day? Or is it some sign of weather that I do not know?

He could not see the green of the shore now but only the tops of the blue hills that showed white as though they were snow-capped and the clouds that looked like high snow mountains above them. The sea was very dark and the light made prisms in the water. The myriad flecks of the plankton were annulled now by the high sun and it was only the great deep prisms in the blue water that the old man saw now with his lines going straight down into the water that was a mile deep.

The tuna, the fishermen called all the fish of that species tuna and only distinguished among them by their proper names when they came to sell them or to trade them for baits, were down again. The sun was hot now and the old man felt it on the back of his neck and felt the sweat trickle down his back as he rowed.

I could just drift, he thought, and sleep and put a bight of line around my toe to wake me. But today is eighty-five days and I should fish the day well.

Just then, watching his lines, he saw one of the projecting green sticks dip sharply.

"Yes," he said. "Yes," and shipped his oars without bumping the boat. He reached out for the line and held it softly between the thumb and forefinger of his right hand. He felt no strain nor weight and he held the line lightly. Then it came again. This time it was a tentative pull, not solid nor heavy, and he knew exactly what it was. One hundred fathoms down a marlin was eating the sardines that covered the point and the shank of the hook where the hand-forged hook projected from the head of the small tuna.

The old man held the line delicately, and softly, with his left hand, unleashed it from the stick. Now he could let it run through his fingers without the fish feeling any tension.

This far out, he must be huge in this month, he thought. Eat them, fish. Eat them. Please eat them. How fresh they are and you down there six hundred feet in that cold water in the dark. Make another turn in the dark and come back and eat them.

He felt the light delicate pulling and then a harder pull when a sardine's head must have been more difficult to break from the hook. Then there was nothing.

"Come on," the old man said aloud. "Make another turn. Just smell them. Aren't they lovely? Eat them good now and then there is the tuna. Hard and cold and lovely. Don't be shy, fish. Eat them."

He waited with the line between his thumb and his finger, watching it and the other lines at the same time for the fish might have swum up or down. Then came the same delicate pulling touch again.

"He'll take it," the old man said aloud. "God help him to take it."

He did not take it though. He was gone and the old man felt nothing.

"He can't have gone," he said. "Christ knows he can't have gone. He's making a turn. Maybe he has been hooked before and he remembers something of it."

Then he felt the gentle touch on the line and he was happy.

"It was only his turn," he said. "He'll take it."

He was happy feeling the gentle pulling and then he felt something hard and unbelievably heavy. It was the weight of the fish and he let the line slip down, down, down, unrolling off the first of the two reserve coils. As it went down, slipping lightly through the old man's fingers, he still could feel the great weight, though the pressure of his thumb and finger were almost imperceptible.

"What a fish," he said. "He has it sideways in his mouth now and he is moving off with it."

Then he will turn and swallow it, he thought. He did not say that because he knew that if you said a good thing it might not happen. He knew what a huge fish this was and he thought of him moving away in the darkness with the tuna held crosswise in his mouth. At that moment he felt him stop moving but the weight was still there. Then the weight increased and he gave more line. He tightened the pressure of his thumb and finger for a moment and the weight increased and was going straight down.

"He's taken it," he said. "Now I'll let him eat it well."

He let the line slip through his fingers while he reached down with his left hand and made fast the free end of the two reserve coils to the loop of the two reserve coils of the next line. Now he was ready. He had three forty-fathom coils of line in reserve now, as well as the coil he was using.

"Eat it a little more," he said. "Eat it well."

Eat it so that the point of the hook goes into your heart and kills you, he thought. Come up easy and let me put the harpoon into you. All right. Are you ready? Have you been long enough at table?

"Now!" he said aloud and struck hard with both hands, gained a yard of line and then struck again and again, swinging with each arm alternately on the cord with all the strength of his arms and the pivoted weight of his body.

Nothing happened. The fish just moved away slowly and the old man could not raise him an inch. His line was strong and made for heavy fish and he held it against his back until it was so taut that beads of water were jumping from it. Then it began to make a slow hissing sound in the water and he still held it, bracing him-

self against the thwart and leaning back against the pull. The boat
began to move slowly off toward the North-West.

The fish moved steadily and they travelled slowly on the calm
water. The other baits were still in the water but there was nothing
to be done.

"I wish I had the boy," the old man said aloud. "I'm being towed
by a fish and I'm the towing bitt. I could make the line fast. But
then he could break it. I must hold him all I can and give him line
when he must have it. Thank God he is travelling and not going
down."

What I will do if he decides to go down, I don't know. What I'll
do if he sounds and dies I don't know. But I'll do something. There
are plenty of things I can do.

He held the line against his back and watched its slant in the
water and the skiff moving steadily to the North-West.

This will kill him, the old man thought. He can't do this forever. But four hours later the fish was still swimming steadily out
to sea, towing the skiff, and the old man was still braced solidly
with the line across his back.

"It was noon when I hooked him," he said. "And I have never
seen him."

He had pushed his straw hat hard down on his head before he
hooked the fish and it was cutting his forehead. He was thirsty too
and he got down on his knees and, being careful not to jerk on the
line, moved as far into the bow as he could get and reached the
water bottle with one hand. He opened it and drank a little. Then
he rested against the bow. He rested sitting on the un-stepped mast
and sail and tried not to think but only to endure.

Then he looked behind him and saw that no land was visible.
That makes no difference, he thought. I can always come in on
the glow from Havana. There are two more hours before the sun
sets and maybe he will come up before that. If he doesn't maybe

he will come up with the moon. If he does not do that maybe he will come up with the sunrise. I have no cramps and I feel strong. It is he that has the hook in his mouth. But what a fish to pull like that. He must have his mouth shut tight on the wire. I wish I could see him. I wish I could see him only once to know what I have against me.

The fish never changed his course nor his direction all that night as far as the man could tell from watching the stars. It was cold after the sun went down and the old man's sweat dried cold on his back and his arms and his old legs. During the day he had taken the sack that covered the bait box and spread it in the sun to dry. After the sun went down he tied it around his neck so that it hung down over his back and he cautiously worked it down under the line that was across his shoulders now. The sack cushioned the line and he had found a way of leaning forward against the bow so that he was almost comfortable. The position actually was only somewhat less intolerable; but he thought of it as almost comfortable.

I can do nothing with him and he can do nothing with me, he thought. Not as long as he keeps this up.

Once he stood up and urinated over the side of the skiff and looked at the stars and checked his course. The line showed like a phosphorescent streak in the water straight out from his shoulders. They were moving more slowly now and the glow of Havana was not so strong, so that he knew the current must be carrying them to the eastward. If I lose the glare of Havana we must be going more to the eastward, he thought. For if the fish's course held true I must see it for many more hours. I wonder how the baseball came out in the grand leagues today, he thought. It would be wonderful to do this with a radio. Then he thought, think of it always. Think of what you are doing. You must do nothing stupid.

Then he said aloud, "I wish I had the boy. To help me and to see this."

No one should be alone in their old age, he thought. But it is unavoidable. I must remember to eat the tuna before he spoils in order to keep strong. Remember, no matter how little you want to, that you must eat him in the morning. Remember, he said to himself.

During the night two porpoises came around the boat and he could hear them rolling and blowing. He could tell the difference between the blowing noise the male made and the sighing blow of the female.

"They are good," he said. "They play and make jokes and love one another. They are our brothers like the flying fish."

Then he began to pity the great fish that he had hooked. He is wonderful and strange and who knows how old he is, he thought. Never have I had such a strong fish nor one who acted so strangely. Perhaps he is too wise to jump. He could ruin me by jumping or by a wild rush. But perhaps he has been hooked many times before and he knows that this is how he should make his fight. He cannot know that it is only one man against him, nor that it is an old man. But what a great fish he is and what will he bring in the market if the flesh is good. He took the bait like a male and he pulls like a male and his fight has no panic in it. I wonder if he has any plans or if he is just as desperate as I am?

He remembered the time he had hooked one of a pair of marlin. The male fish always let the female fish feed first and the hooked fish, the female, made a wild, panic-stricken, despairing fight that soon exhausted her, and all the time the male had stayed with her, crossing the line and circling with her on the surface. He had stayed so close that the old man was afraid he would cut the line with his tail which was sharp as a scythe and almost of that size and shape. When the old man had gaffed her and clubbed her, holding the rapier bill with its sandpaper edge and clubbing her across the top of her head until her colour turned to a colour almost like the backing of mirrors, and then, with the boy's aid, hoisted her aboard, the male fish had stayed by the side of the boat. Then, while the old man was clearing the lines and preparing the harpoon, the male fish jumped high into the air beside the boat to see where the female was and then went down deep, his lavender wings, that were his pectoral fins, spread wide and all his wide lavender stripes showing. He was beautiful, the old man remembered, and he had stayed.

That was the saddest thing I ever saw with them, the old man thought. The boy was sad too and we begged her pardon and butchered her promptly.

"I wish the boy was here," he said aloud and settled himself against the rounded planks of the bow and felt the strength of the great fish through the line he held across his shoulders moving steadily toward whatever he had chosen.

When once, through my treachery, it had been necessary to him to make a choice, the old man thought.

His choice had been to stay in the deep dark water far out beyond all snares and traps and treacheries. My choice was to go there to find him beyond all people. Beyond all people in the world. Now we are joined together and have been since noon. And no one to help either one of us.

Perhaps I should not have been a fisherman, he thought. But that was the thing that I was born for. I must surely remember to eat the tuna after it gets light.

Some time before daylight something took one of the baits that were behind him. He heard the stick break and the line begin to rush out over the gunwale of the skiff. In the darkness he loosened his sheath knife and taking all the strain of the fish on his left shoulder he leaned back and cut the line against the wood of the gunwale. Then he cut the other line closest to him and in the dark made the loose ends of the reserve coils fast. He worked skillfully with the one hand and put his foot on the coils to hold them as he drew his knots tight. Now he had six reserve coils of line. There were two from each bait he had severed and the two from the bait the fish had taken and they were all connected.

After it is light, he thought, I will work back to the forty-fathom bait and cut it away too and link up the reserve coils. I will have lost two hundred fathoms of good Catalan *cardel* and the hooks and leaders. That can be replaced. But who replaces this fish if I hook some fish and it cuts him off? I don't know what that fish was that took the bait just now. It could have been a marlin or a broadbill or a shark. I never felt him. I had to get rid of him too fast.

Aloud he said, "I wish I had the boy."

But you haven't got the boy, he thought. You have only yourself and you had better work back to the last line now, in the dark or not in the dark, and cut it away and hook up the two reserve coils.

So he did it. It was difficult in the dark and once the fish made a surge that pulled him down on his face and made a cut below his eye. The blood ran down his cheek a little way. But it coagulated and dried before it reached his chin and he worked his way back to the bow and rested against the wood. He adjusted the sack and carefully worked the line so that it came across a new part of his shoulders and, holding it anchored with his shoulders, he carefully felt the pull of the fish and then felt with his hand the progress of the skiff through the water.

I wonder what he made that lurch for, he thought. The wire must have slipped on the great hill of his back. Certainly his back cannot feel as badly as mine does. But he cannot pull this skiff forever, no matter how great he is. Now everything is cleared away that might make trouble and I have a big reserve of line; all that a man can ask.

"Fish," he said softly, aloud, "I'll stay with you until I am dead."

He'll stay with me too, I suppose, the old man thought and he waited for it to be light. It was cold now in the time before daylight and he pushed against the wood to be warm. I can do it as long as he can, he thought. And in the first light the line extended out and down into the water. The boat moved steadily and when the first edge of the sun rose it was on the old man's right shoulder.

"He's headed north," the old man said. The current will have set us far to the eastward, he thought. I wish he would turn with the current. That would show that he was tiring.

When the sun had risen further the old man realized that the fish was not tiring. There was only one favorable sign. The slant of the line showed he was swimming at a lesser depth. That did not necessarily mean that he would jump. But he might.

"God let him jump," the old man said. "I have enough line to handle him."

Maybe if I can increase the tension just a little it will hurt him and he will jump, he thought. Now that it is daylight let him jump so that he'll fill the sacks along his backbone with air and then he cannot go deep to die.

He tried to increase the tension, but the line had been taut up to the very edge of the breaking point since he had hooked the fish and he felt the harshness as he leaned back to pull and knew he could put no more strain on it. I must not jerk it ever, he thought. Each jerk widens the cut the hook makes and then when he does jump he might throw it. Anyway I feel better with the sun and for once I do not have to look into it.

There was yellow weed on the line but the old man knew that only made an added drag and he was pleased. It was the yellow Gulf weed that had made so much phosphorescence in the night.

"Fish," he said, "I love you and respect you very much. But I will kill you dead before this day ends."

Let us hope so, he thought.

A small bird came toward the skiff from the north. He was a warbler and flying very low over the water. The old man could see that he was very tired.

The bird made the stern of the boat and rested there. Then he flew around the old man's head and rested on the line where he was more comfortable.

"How old are you?" the old man asked the bird. "Is this your first trip?"

The bird looked at him when he spoke. He was too tired even to examine the line and he teetered on it as his delicate feet gripped it fast.

"It's steady," the old man told him. "It's too steady. You shouldn't be that tired after a windless night. What are birds coming to?"

The hawks, he thought, that come out to sea to meet them. But he said nothing of this to the bird who could not understand him anyway and who would learn about the hawks soon enough.

"Take a good rest, small bird," he said. "Then go in and take your chance like any man or bird or fish."

It encouraged him to talk because his back had stiffened in the night and it hurt truly now.

"Stay at my house if you like, bird," he said. "I am sorry I cannot hoist the sail and take you in with the small breeze that is rising. But I am with a friend."

Just then the fish gave a sudden lurch that pulled the old man down onto the bow and would have pulled him overboard if he had not braced himself and given some line.

The bird had flown up when the line jerked and the old man had not even seen him go. He felt the line carefully with his right hand and noticed his hand was bleeding.

"Something hurt him then," he said aloud and pulled back on the line to see if he could turn the fish. But when he was touching the breaking point he held steady and settled back against the strain of the line.

"You're feeling it now, fish," he said. "And so, God knows, am I."

He looked around for the bird now because he would have liked him for company. The bird was gone.

You did not stay long, the man thought. But it is rougher where you are going until you make the shore. How did I let the fish cut me with that one quick pull he made? I must be getting very stupid. Or perhaps I was looking at the small bird and thinking of him. Now I will pay attention to my work and then I must eat the tuna so that I will not have a failure of strength.

"I wish the boy were here and that I had some salt," he said aloud.

Shifting the weight of the line to his left shoulder and kneeling carefully he washed his hand in the ocean and held it there, submerged, for more than a minute watching the blood trail away and the steady movement of the water against his hand as the boat moved.

"He has slowed much," he said.

The old man would have liked to keep his hand in the salt water longer but he was afraid of another sudden lurch by the fish and he stood up and braced himself and held his hand up against the sun. It was only a line burn that had cut his flesh. But it was in the working part of his hand. He knew he would need his hands before this was over and he did not like to be cut before it started.

"Now," he said, when his hand had dried, "I must eat the small tuna. I can reach him with the gaff and eat him here in comfort."

He knelt down and found the tuna under the stern with the gaff and drew it toward him keeping it clear of the coiled lines. Holding the line with his left shoulder again, and bracing on his left hand and arm, he took the tuna off the gaff hook and put the gaff back in place. He put one knee on the fish and cut strips of dark red meat longitudinally from the back of the head to the tail. They were wedge-shaped strips and he cut them from next to the backbone down to the edge of the belly. When he had cut six strips he spread them out on the wood of the bow, wiped his knife on his trousers, and lifted the carcass of the bonito by the tail and dropped it overboard.

"I don't think I can eat an entire one," he said and drew his knife across one of the strips. He could feel the steady hard pull of the line and his left hand was cramped. It drew up tight on the heavy cord and he looked at it in disgust.

"What kind of a hand is that," he said. "Cramp then if you want. Make yourself into a claw. It will do you no good."

Come on, he thought and looked down into the dark water at the slant of the line. Eat it now and it will strengthen the hand. It is not the hand's fault and you have been many hours with the fish. But you can stay with him forever. Eat the bonito now.

He picked up a piece and put it in his mouth and chewed it slowly. It was not unpleasant.

Chew it well, he thought, and get all the juices. It would not be bad to eat with a little lime or with lemon or with salt.

"How do you feel, hand?" he asked the cramped hand that was almost as stiff as rigor mortis. "I'll eat some more for you."

He ate the other part of the piece that he had cut in two. He chewed it carefully and then spat out the skin.

"How does it go, hand? Or is it too early to know?"

He took another full piece and chewed it.

"It is a strong full-blooded fish," he thought. "I was lucky to get him instead of dolphin. Dolphin is too sweet. This is hardly sweet at all and all the strength is still in it."

There is no sense in being anything but practical though, he thought. I wish I had some salt. And I do not know whether the sun will rot or dry what is left, so I had better eat it all although I am not hungry. The fish is calm and steady. I will eat it all and then I will be ready.

"Be patient, hand," he said. "I do this for you."

I wish I could feed the fish, he thought. He is my brother. But I must kill him and keep strong to do it. Slowly and conscientiously he ate all of the wedge-shaped strips of fish.

He straightened up, wiping his hand on his trousers.

"Now," he said. "You can let the cord go, hand, and I will handle him with the right arm alone until you stop that nonsense." He put his left foot on the heavy line that the left hand had held and lay back against the pull against his back.

"God help me to have the cramp go," he said. "Because I do not know what the fish is going to do."

But he seems calm, he thought, and following his plan. But what is his plan, he thought. And what is mine? Mine I must improvise to his because of his great size. If he will jump I can kill him. But he stays down forever. Then I will stay down with him forever.

He rubbed the cramped hand against his trousers and tried to gentle the fingers. But it would not open. Maybe it will open with the sun, he thought. Maybe it will open when the strong raw tuna is digested. If I have to have it, I will open it, cost whatever it costs. But I do not want to open it now by force. Let it open by itself and come back of its own accord. After all I abused it much in the night when it was necessary to free and untie the various lines.

He looked across the sea and knew how alone he was now. But he could see the prisms in the deep dark water and the line stretching ahead and the strange undulation of the calm. The clouds were building up now for the trade wind and he looked ahead and saw a flight of wild ducks etching themselves against the sky over the water, then blurring, then etching again and he knew no man was ever alone on the sea.

He thought of how some men feared being out of sight of land in a small boat and knew they were right in the months of sudden bad weather. But now they were in hurricane months and, when there are no hurricanes, the weather of hurricane months is the best of all the year.

If there is a hurricane you always see the signs of it in the sky for days ahead, if you are at sea. They do not see it ashore because they do not know what to look for, he thought. The land must make a difference too, in the shape of the clouds. But we have no hurricane coming now.

He looked at the sky and saw the white cumulus built like friendly piles of ice cream and high above were the thin feathers of the cirrus against the high September sky.

"Light *brisa*," he said. "Better weather for me than for you, fish." His left hand was still cramped, but he was unknotting it slowly.

I hate a cramp, he thought. It is a treachery of one's own body. It is humiliating before others to have a diarrhoea from ptomaine poisoning or to vomit from it. But a cramp, he thought of it as a *calambre*, humiliates oneself especially when one is alone.

If the boy were here he could rub it for me and loosen it down from the forearm, he thought. But it will loosen up.

Then, with his right hand he felt the difference in the pull of the line before he saw the slant change in the water. Then, as he leaned against the line and slapped his left hand hard and fast against his thigh he saw the line slanting slowly upward.

"He's coming up," he said. "Come on hand. Please come on."

The line rose slowly and steadily and then the surface of the ocean bulged ahead of the boat and the fish came out. He came out unendingly and water poured from his sides. He was bright in the sun and his head and back were dark purple and in the sun the stripes on his sides showed wide and a light lavender. His sword was as long as a baseball bat and tapered like a rapier and he rose his full length from the water and then re-entered it, smoothly, like a diver and the old man saw the great scythe-blade of his tail go under and the line commenced to race out.

"He is two feet longer than the skiff," the old man said. The line was going out fast but steadily and the fish was not panicked. The old man was trying with both hands to keep the line just inside of breaking strength. He knew that if he could not slow the fish with a steady pressure the fish could take out all the line and break it.

He is a great fish and I must convince him, he thought. I must never let him learn his strength nor what he could do if he made his run. If I were him I would put in everything now and go until something broke. But, thank God, they are not as intelligent as we who kill them; although they are more noble and more able.

The old man had seen many great fish. He had seen many that weighed more than a thousand pounds and he had caught two of that size in his life, but never alone. Now alone, and out of sight of land, he was fast to the biggest fish that he had ever seen and bigger than he had ever heard of, and his left hand was still as tight as the gripped claws of an eagle.

It will uncramp though, he thought. Surely it will uncramp to help my right hand. There are three things that are brothers: the fish and my two hands. It must uncramp. It is unworthy of it to be cramped. The fish had slowed again and was going at his usual pace.

I wonder why he jumped, the old man thought. He jumped almost as though to show me how big he was. I know now, anyway, he thought. I wish I could show him what sort of man I am. But then he would see the cramped hand. Let him think I am more man than I am and I will be so. I wish I was the fish, he thought, with everything he has against only my will and my intelligence.

He settled comfortably against the wood and took his suffering as it came and the fish swam steadily and the boat moved slowly through the dark water. There was a small sea rising with the wind coming up from the east and at noon the old man's left hand was uncramped.

"Bad news for you, fish," he said and shifted the line over the sacks that covered his shoulders.

He was comfortable but suffering, although he did not admit the suffering at all.

"I am not religious," he said. "But I will say ten Our Fathers and ten Hail Marys that I should catch this fish, and I promise to make a pilgrimage to the Virgin of Cobre if I catch him. That is a promise."

He commenced to say his prayers mechanically. Sometimes he would be so tired that he could not remember the prayer and then he would say them fast so that they would come automatically. Hail Marys are easier to say than Our Fathers, he thought.

"Hail Mary full of Grace the Lord is with thee. Blessed art thou among women and blessed is the fruit of thy womb, Jesus. Holy Mary, Mother of God, pray for us sinners now and at the hour of our death. Amen." Then he added, "Blessed Virgin, pray for the death of this fish. Wonderful though he is."

With his prayers said, and feeling much better, but suffering exactly as much, and perhaps a little more, he leaned against the wood of the bow and began, mechanically, to work the fingers of his left hand.

The sun was hot now although the breeze was rising gently.

"I had better re-bait that little line out over the stern," he said. "If the fish decides to stay another night I will need to eat again and the water is low in the bottle. I don't think I can get anything but a dolphin here. But if I eat him fresh enough he won't be bad. I wish a flying fish would come on board tonight. But I have no light to attract them. A flying fish is excellent to eat raw and I would not have to cut him up. I must save all my strength now. Christ, I did not know he was so big."

"I'll kill him though," he said. "In all his greatness and his glory."

Although it is unjust, he thought. But I will show him what a man can do and what a man endures.

"I told the boy I was a strange old man," he said. "Now is when I must prove it."

The thousand times that he had proved it meant nothing. Now

he was proving it again. Each time was a new time and he never thought about the past when he was doing it.

I wish he'd sleep and I could sleep and dream about the lions, he thought. Why are the lions the main thing that is left? Don't think, old man, he said to himself. Rest gently now against the wood and think of nothing. He is working. Work as little as you can.

It was getting into the afternoon and the boat still moved slowly and steadily. But there was an added drag now from the easterly breeze and the old man rode gently with the small sea and the hurt of the cord across his back came to him easily and smoothly.

Once in the afternoon the line started to rise again. But the fish only continued to swim at a slightly higher level. The sun was on the old man's left arm and shoulder and on his back. So he knew the fish had turned east of north.

Now that he had seen him once, he could picture the fish swimming in the water with his purple pectoral fins set wide as wings and the great erect tail slicing through the dark. I wonder how much he sees at that depth, the old man thought. His eye is huge and a horse, with much less eye, can see in the dark. Once I could see quite well in the dark. Not in the absolute dark. But almost as a cat sees.

The sun and his steady movement of his fingers had uncramped his left hand now completely and he began to shift more of the strain to it and he shrugged the muscles of his back to shift the hurt of the cord a little.

"If you're not tired, fish," he said aloud, "you must be very strange."

He felt very tired now and he knew the night would come soon and he tried to think of other things. He thought of the Big Leagues, to him they were the *Gran Ligas*, and he knew that the Yankees of New York were playing the *Tigres* of Detroit.

This is the second day now that I do not know the result of the *juegos,* he thought. But I must have confidence and I must be worthy of the great DiMaggio who does all things perfectly even with the pain of the bone spur in his heel. What is a bone spur? he asked himself. *Un espuela de hueso.* We do not have them. Can it be as painful as the spur of a fighting cock in one's heel? I do not think I could endure that or the loss of the eye and of both eyes and continue to fight as the fighting cocks do. Man is not much beside the great birds and beasts. Still I would rather be that beast down there in the darkness of the sea.

"Unless sharks come," he said aloud. "If sharks come, God pity him and me."

Do you believe the great DiMaggio would stay with a fish as long as I will stay with this one? he thought. I am sure he would and more since he is young and strong. Also his father was a fisherman. But would the bone spur hurt him too much?

"I do not know," he said aloud. "I never had a bone spur."

As the sun set he remembered, to give himself more confidence, the time in the tavern at Casablanca when he had played the hand game with the great negro from Cienfuegos who was the strongest man on the docks. They had gone one day and one night with their elbows on a chalk line on the table and their forearms straight up and their hands gripped tight. Each one was trying to force the other's hand down onto the table. There was much betting and people went in and out of the room under the kerosene lights and he had looked at the arm and hand of the negro and at the negro's face. They changed the referees every four hours after the first eight so that the referees could sleep. Blood came out from under the fingernails of both his and the negro's hands and they looked each other in the eye and at their hands and forearms and the bettors went in and out of the room and sat on high chairs against the wall and watched. The walls were painted bright blue and were of wood and the lamps threw their shadows against them. The negro's shadow was huge and it moved on the wall as the breeze moved the lamps.

The odds would change back and forth all night and they fed the negro rum and lighted cigarettes for him. Then the negro, after the rum, would try for a tremendous effort and once he had the old man, who was not an old man then but was Santiago *El Campeón,* nearly three inches off balance. But the old man had raised his hand up to dead even again. He was sure then that he had the negro, who was a fine man and a great athlete, beaten. And at daylight when the bettors were asking that it be called a draw and the referee was shaking his head, he had unleashed his effort and forced the hand of the negro down and down until it rested on the wood. The match had started on a Sunday morning and ended on a Monday morning. Many of the bettors had asked for a draw because they had to go to work on the docks loading sacks of sugar or at the Havana Coal Company. Otherwise everyone would have wanted it to go to a finish. But he had finished it anyway and before anyone had to go to work.

For a long time after that everyone had called him The Champion and there had been a return match in the spring. But not much money was bet and he had won it quite easily since he had broken the confidence of the negro from Cienfuegos in the first match. After that he had a few matches and then no more. He decided that he could beat anyone if he wanted to badly enough and he decided that it was bad for his right hand for fishing. He had tried a few practice matches with his left hand. But his left hand had always been a traitor and would not do what he called on it to do and he did not trust it.

The sun will bake it out well now, he thought. It should not cramp on me again unless it gets too cold in the night. I wonder what this night will bring.

An airplane passed over head on its course to Miami and he watched its shadow scaring up the schools of flying fish.

"With so much flying fish there should be dolphin," he said, and leaned back on the line to see if it was possible to gain any on his fish. But he could not and it stayed at the hardness and water-drop shivering that preceded breaking. The boat moved ahead slowly and he watched the airplane until he could no longer see it.

It must be very strange in an airplane, he thought. I wonder what the sea looks like from that height? They should be able to see the fish well if they do not fly too high. I would like to fly very slowly at two hundred fathoms high and see the fish from above. In the turtle boats I was in the cross-trees of the mast-head and even at that height I saw much. The dolphin look greener from there and you can see their stripes and their purple spots and you can see all of the school as they swim. Why is it that all the fast-moving fish of the dark current have purple backs and usually purple stripes or spots? The dolphin looks green of course because he is really golden. But when he comes to feed, truly hungry, purple stripes show on his sides as on a marlin. Can it be anger, or the greater speed he makes that brings them out?

Just before it was dark, as they passed a great island of Sargasso weed that heaved and swung in the light sea as though the ocean were making love with something under a yellow blanket, his small line was taken by a dolphin. He saw it first when it jumped in the air, true gold in the last of the sun and bending and flapping wildly in the air. It jumped again and again in the acrobatics of its fear and he worked his way back to the stern and crouching and holding the big line with his right hand and arm, he pulled the dolphin in with his left hand, stepping on the gained line each time with his bare left foot. When the fish was at the stern, plunging and cutting from side to side in desperation, the old man leaned over the stern and lifted the burnished gold fish with its purple spots over the stern. Its jaws were working convulsively in quick bites against the hook and it pounded the bottom of the skiff with its long flat body, its tail and its head until he clubbed it across the shining golden head until it shivered and was still.

The old man unhooked the fish, rebaited the line with another sardine and tossed it over. Then he worked his way slowly back to the bow. He washed his left hand and wiped it on his trousers. Then he shifted the heavy line from his right hand to his left and washed his right hand in the sea while he watched the sun go into the ocean and the slant of the big cord.

"He hasn't changed at all," he said. But watching the movement of the water against his hand he noted that it was perceptibly slower.

"I'll lash the two oars together across the stern and that will slow him in the night," he said. "He's good for the night and so am I."

It would be better to gut the dolphin a little later to save the blood in the meat, he thought. I can do that a little later and lash the oars to make a drag at the same time. I had better keep the fish quiet now and not disturb him too much at sunset. The setting of the sun is a difficult time for all fish.

He let his hand dry in the air then grasped the line with it and eased himself as much as he could and allowed himself to be pulled forward against the wood so that the boat took the strain as much, or more, than he did.

I'm learning how to do it, he thought. This part of it anyway. Then too, remember he hasn't eaten since he took the bait and he is huge and needs much food. I have eaten the whole bonito. To-morrow I will eat the dolphin. He called it *dorado*. Perhaps I should eat some of it when I clean it. It will be harder to eat than the bonito. But, then, nothing is easy.

"How do you feel, fish?" he asked aloud. "I feel good and my left hand is better and I have food for a night and a day. Pull the boat, fish."

He did not truly feel good because the pain from the cord across his back had almost passed pain and gone into a dullness that he mistrusted. But I have had worse things than that, he thought. My hand is only cut a little and the cramp is gone from the other. My legs are all right. Also now I have gained on him in the question of sustenance.

It was dark now as it becomes dark quickly after the sun sets in September. He lay against the worn wood of the bow and rested all that he could. The first stars were out. He did not know the name of Rigel but he saw it and knew soon they would all be out and he would have all his distant friends.

"The fish is my friend too," he said aloud. "I have never seen or heard of such a fish. But I must kill him. I am glad we do not have to try to kill the stars."

Imagine if each day a man must try to kill the moon, he thought. The moon runs away. But imagine if a man each day should have to try to kill the sun? We were born lucky, he thought.

Then he was sorry for the great fish that had nothing to eat and his determination to kill him never relaxed in his sorrow for him. How many people will he feed, he thought. But are they worthy to eat him? No, of course not. There is no one worthy of eating him from the manner of his behaviour and his great dignity.

I do not understand these things, he thought. But it is good that we do not have to try to kill the sun or the moon or the stars. It is enough to live on the sea and kill our true brothers.

Now, he thought, I must think about the drag. It has its perils and its merits. I may lose so much line that I will lose him, if he makes his effort and the drag made by the oars is in place and the boat loses all her lightness. Her lightness prolongs both our suffering but it is my safety since he has great speed that he has never yet employed. No matter what passes I must gut the dolphin so he does not spoil and eat some of him to be strong.

Now I will rest an hour more and feel that he is solid and steady before I move back to the stern to do the work and make the decision. In the meantime I can see how he acts and if he shows any changes. The oars are a good trick; but it has reached the time to play for safety. He is much fish still and I saw that the hook was in the corner of his mouth and he has kept his mouth tight shut. The punishment of the hook is nothing. The punishment of hunger, and that he is against something that he does not comprehend, is everything. Rest now, old man, and let him work until your next duty comes.

He rested for what he believed to be two hours. The moon did not rise now until late and he had no way of judging the time. Nor was he really resting except comparatively. He was still bearing the pull of the fish across his shoulders but he placed his left hand on the gunwale of the bow and confided more and more of the resistance to the fish to the skiff itself.

How simple it would be if I could make the line fast, he thought. But with one small lurch he could break it. I must cushion the pull of the line with my body and at all times be ready to give line with both hands.

"But you have not slept yet, old man," he said aloud. "It is half a day and a night and now another day and you have not slept. You must devise a way so that you sleep a little if he is quiet and steady. If you do not sleep you might become unclear in the head."

I'm clear enough in the head, he thought. Too clear. I am as clear as the stars that are my brothers. Still I must sleep. They sleep and the moon and the sun sleep and even the ocean sleeps sometimes on certain days when there is no current and a flat calm.

But remember to sleep, he thought. Make yourself do it and devise some simple and sure way about the lines. Now go back and prepare the dolphin. It is too dangerous to rig the oars as a drag if you must sleep.

I could go without sleeping, he told himself. But it would be too dangerous.

He started to work his way back to the stern on his hands and knees, being careful not to jerk against the fish. He may be half asleep himself, he thought. But I do not want him to rest. He must pull until he dies.

Back in the stern he turned so that his left hand held the strain of the line across his shoulders and drew his knife from its sheath with his right hand. The stars were bright now and he saw the dolphin clearly and he pushed the blade of his knife into his head and drew him out from under the stern. He put one of his feet on the fish and slit him quickly from the vent up to the tip of his lower jaw. Then he put his knife down and gutted him with his right hand, scooping him clean and pulling the gills clear. He felt the maw heavy and slippery in his hands and he slit it open. There were two flying fish inside. They were fresh and hard and he laid them side by side and dropped the guts and the gills over the stern. They sank leaving a trail of phosphorescence in the water. The dolphin was cold and a leprous gray-white now in the starlight and the old man skinned one side of him while he held his right foot on the fish's head. Then he turned him over and skinned the other side and cut each side off from the head down to the tail.

He slid the carcass overboard and looked to see if there was any swirl in the water. But there was only the light of its slow descent. He turned then and placed the two flying fish inside the two fillets of fish and putting his knife back in its sheath, he worked his way slowly back to the bow. His back was bent with the weight of the line across it and he carried the fish in his right hand.

Back in the bow he laid the two fillets of fish out on the wood with the flying fish beside them. After that he settled the line across his shoulders in a new place and held it again with his left hand resting on the gunwale. Then he leaned over the side and washed the flying fish in the water, noting the speed of the water against his hand. His hand was phosphorescent from skinning the fish and he watched the flow of the water against it. The flow was less strong and as he rubbed the side of his hand against the planking of the skiff, particles of phosphorus floated off and drifted slowly astern.

"He is tiring or he is resting," the old man said. "Now let me get through the eating of this dolphin and get some rest and a little sleep."

Under the stars and with the night colder all the time he ate half of one of the dolphin fillets and one of the flying fish, gutted and with its head cut off.

"What an excellent fish dolphin is to eat cooked," he said. "And what a miserable fish raw. I will never go in a boat again without salt or limes."

If I had brains I would have splashed water on the bow all day and drying, it would have made salt, he thought. But then I did not hook the dolphin until almost sunset. Still it was a lack of preparation. But I have chewed it all well and I am not nauseated.

The sky was clouding over to the east and one after another the stars he knew were gone. It looked now as though he were moving into a great canyon of clouds and the wind had dropped.

"There will be bad weather in three or four days," he said. "But not tonight and not tomorrow. Rig now to get some sleep, old man, while the fish is calm and steady."

He held the line tight in his right hand and then pushed his thigh against his right hand as he leaned all his weight against the wood of the bow. Then he passed the line a little lower on his shoulders and braced his left hand on it.

My right hand can hold it as long as it is braced, he thought. If it relaxes in sleep my left hand will wake me as the line goes out. It is hard on the right hand. But he is used to punishment. Even if I sleep twenty minutes or a half an hour it is good. He lay forward cramping himself against the line with all of his body, putting all his weight onto his right hand, and he was asleep.

He did not dream of the lions but instead of a vast school of porpoises that stretched for eight or ten miles and it was in the time of their mating and they would leap high into the air and return into the same hole they had made in the water when they leaped.

Then he dreamed that he was in the village on his bed and there was a norther and he was very cold and his right arm was asleep because his head had rested on it instead of a pillow.

After that he began to dream of the long yellow beach and he saw the first of the lions come down onto it in the early dark and then the other lions came and he rested his chin on the wood of the bows where the ship lay anchored with the evening off-shore breeze and he waited to see if there would be more lions and he was happy.

The moon had been up for a long time but he slept on and the fish pulled on steadily and the boat moved into the tunnel of clouds.

He woke with the jerk of his right fist coming up against his face and the line burning out through his right hand. He had no feeling of his left hand but he braked all he could with his right and the line rushed out. Finally his left hand found the line and he leaned back against the line and now it burned his back and his left hand, and his left hand was taking all the strain and cutting badly. He looked back at the coils of line and they were feeding smoothly. Just then the fish jumped making a great bursting of the ocean and then a heavy fall. Then he jumped again and again and the boat was going fast although line was still racing out and the old man was raising the strain to breaking point and raising it to breaking point again and again. He had been pulled down tight onto the bow and his face was in the cut slice of dolphin and he could not move.

This is what we waited for, he thought. So now let us take it.

Make him pay for the line, he thought. Make him pay for it.

He could not see the fish's jumps but only heard the breaking of the ocean and the heavy splash as he fell. The speed of the line was cutting his hands badly but he had always known this would happen and he tried to keep the cutting across the calloused parts and not let the line slip into the palm nor cut the fingers.

If the boy was here he would wet the coils of line, he thought. Yes. If the boy were here. If the boy were here.

The line went out and out and out but it was slowing now and he was making the fish earn each inch of it. Now he got his head up from the wood and out of the slice of fish that his cheek had crushed. Then he was on his knees and then he rose slowly to his feet. He was ceding line but more slowly all the time. He worked back to where he could feel with his foot the coils of line that he could not see. There was plenty of line still and now the fish had to pull the friction of all that new line through the water.

Yes, he thought. And now he has jumped more than a dozen times and filled the sacks along his back with air and he cannot go down deep to die where I cannot bring him up. He will start circling soon and then I must work on him. I wonder what started him so suddenly? Could it have been hunger that made him desperate, or was he frightened by something in the night? Maybe he suddenly felt fear. But he was such a calm, strong fish and he seemed so fearless and so confident. It is strange.

"You better be fearless and confident yourself, old man," he said. "You're holding him again but you cannot get line. But soon he has to circle."

The old man held him with his left hand and his shoulders now and stooped down and scooped up water in his right hand to get the crushed dolphin flesh off of his face. He was afraid that it might nauseate him and he would vomit and lose his strength. When his face was cleaned he washed his right hand in the water over the side and then let it stay in the salt water while he watched the first light come before the sunrise. He's headed almost east, he

thought. That means he is tired and going with the current. Soon
he will have to circle. Then our true work begins.

After he judged that his right hand had been in the water long
enough he took it out and looked at it.

"It is not bad," he said. "And pain does not matter to a man."

He took hold of the line carefully so that it did not fit into any
of the fresh line cuts and shifted his weight so that he could put
his left hand into the sea on the other side of the skiff.

"You did not do so badly for something worthless," he said to his
left hand. "But there was a moment when I could not find you."

Why was I not born with two good hands? he thought. Perhaps
it was my fault in not training that one properly. But God knows
he has had enough chances to learn. He did not do so badly in the
night, though, and he has only cramped once. If he cramps
again let the line cut him off.

When he thought that he knew that he was not being clear-
headed and he thought he should chew some more of the dolphin.
But I can't, he told himself. It is better to be light-headed than to
lose your strength from nausea. And I know I cannot keep it if I
eat it since my face was in it. I will keep it for an emergency until
it goes bad. But it is too late to try for strength now through nourishment. You're stupid, he told himself. Eat the other flying fish.

It was there, cleaned and ready, and he picked it up with his left
hand and ate it chewing the bones carefully and eating all of it
down to the tail.

It has more nourishment than almost any fish, he thought. At
least the kind of strength that I need. Now I have done what I
can, he thought. Let him begin to circle and let the fight come.

The sun was rising for the third time since he had put to sea
when the fish started to circle.

He could not see by the slant of the line that the fish was circling. It was too early for that. He just felt a faint slackening of

the pressure of the line and he commenced to pull on it gently with his right hand. It tightened, as always, but just when he reached the point where it would break, line began to come in. He slipped his shoulders and head from under the line and began to pull in line steadily and gently. He used both of his hands in a swinging motion and tried to do the pulling as much as he could with his body and his legs. His old legs and shoulders pivoted with the swinging of the pulling.

"It is a very big circle," he said. "But he is circling."

Then the line would not come in any more and he held it until he saw the drops jumping from it in the sun. Then it started out and the old man knelt down and let it go grudgingly back into the dark water.

"He is making the far part of his circle now," he said. I must hold all I can, he thought. The strain will shorten his circle each time. Perhaps in an hour I will see him. Now I must convince him and then I must kill him.

But the fish kept on circling slowly and the old man was wet with sweat and tired deep into his bones two hours later. But the circles were much shorter now and from the way the line slanted he could tell the fish had risen steadily while he swam.

For an hour the old man had been seeing black spots before his eyes and the sweat salted his eyes and salted the cut over his eye and on his forehead. He was not afraid of the black spots. They were normal at the tension that he was pulling on the line. Twice, though, he had felt faint and dizzy and that had worried him.

"I could not fail myself and die on a fish like this," he said. "Now that I have him coming so beautifully, God help me endure. I'll say a hundred Our Fathers and a hundred Hail Marys. But I cannot say them now."

Consider them said, he thought. I'll say them later.

Just then he felt a sudden banging and jerking on the line he held with his two hands. It was sharp and hard-feeling and heavy.

He is hitting the wire leader with his spear, he thought. That was bound to come. He had to do that. It may make him jump though and I would rather he stayed circling now. The jumps were necessary for him to take air. But after that each one can widen the opening of the hook wound and he can throw the hook.

"Don't jump, fish," he said. "Don't jump."

The fish hit the wire several times more and each time he shook his head the old man gave up a little line.

I must hold his pain where it is, he thought. Mine does not matter. I can control mine. But his pain could drive him mad.

After a while the fish stopped beating at the wire and started circling slowly again. The old man was gaining line steadily now. But he felt faint again. He lifted some sea water with his left hand and put it on his head. Then he put more on and rubbed the back of his neck.

"I have no cramps," he said. "He'll be up soon and I can last. You have to last. Don't even speak of it."

He kneeled against the bow and, for a moment, slipped the line over his back again. I'll rest now while he goes out on the circle and then stand up and work on him when he comes in, he decided.

It was a great temptation to rest in the bow and let the fish make one circle by himself without recovering any line. But when the strain showed the fish had turned to come toward the boat, the old man rose to his feet and started the pivoting and the weaving pulling that brought in all the line he gained.

I'm tireder than I have ever been, he thought, and now the trade wind is rising. But that will be good to take him in with. I need that badly.

"I'll rest on the next turn as he goes out," he said. "I feel much better. Then in two or three turns more I will have him."

His straw hat was far on the back of his head and he sank down into the bow with the pull of the line as he felt the fish turn.

You work now, fish, he thought. I'll take you at the turn.

The sea had risen considerably. But it was a fair-weather breeze and he had to have it to get home.

"I'll just steer south and west," he said. "A man is never lost at sea and it is a long island."

It was on the third turn that he saw the fish first.

He saw him first as a dark shadow that took so long to pass under the boat that he could not believe its length.

"No," he said. "He can't be that big."

But he was that big and at the end of this circle he came to the surface only thirty yards away and the man saw his tail out of water. It was higher than a big scythe blade and a very pale lavender above the dark blue water. It raked back and as the fish swam just below the surface the old man could see his huge bulk and the purple stripes that banded him. His dorsal fin was down and his huge pectorals were spread wide.

On this circle the old man could see the fish's eye and the two gray sucking fish that swam around him. Sometimes they attached themselves to him. Sometimes they darted off. Sometimes they would swim easily in his shadow. They were each over three feet long and when they swam fast they lashed their whole bodies like eels.

The old man was sweating now but from something else besides the sun. On each calm placid turn the fish made he was gaining line and he was sure that in two turns more he would have a chance to get the harpoon in.

But I must get him close, close, close, he thought. I mustn't try for the head. I must get the heart.

"Be calm and strong, old man," he said.

On the next circle the fish's back was out but he was a little too far from the boat. On the next circle he was still too far away but he was higher out of water and the old man was sure that by gaining some more line he could have him alongside.

He had rigged his harpoon long before and its coil of light rope was in a round basket and the end was made fast to the bitt in the bow.

The fish was coming in on his circle now calm and beautiful looking and only his great tail moving. The old man pulled on him all that he could to bring him closer. For just a moment the fish turned a little on his side. Then he straightened himself and began another circle.

"I moved him," the old man said. "I moved him then."

He felt faint again now but he held on the great fish all the strain that he could. I moved him, he thought. Maybe this time I can get him over. Pull, hands, he thought. Hold up, legs. Last for me, head. Last for me. You never went. This time I'll pull him over.

But when he put all of his effort on, starting it well out before the fish came alongside and pulling with all his strength, the fish pulled part way over and then righted himself and swam away.

"Fish " the old man said. "Fish, you are going to have to die anyway. Do you have to kill me too?"

That way nothing is accomplished, he thought. His mouth was too dry to speak but he could not reach for the water now. I must get him alongside this time, he thought. I am not good for many more turns. Yes you are, he told himself. You're good for ever.

On the next turn, he nearly had him. But again the fish righted himself and swam slowly away.

You are killing me, fish, the old man thought. But you have a right to. Never have I seen a greater, or more beautiful, or a calmer or more noble thing than you, brother. Come on and kill me. I do not care who kills who.

Now you are getting confused in the head, he thought. You must keep your head clear. Keep your head clear and know how to suffer like a man. Or a fish, he thought.

"Clear up, head," he said in a voice he could hardly hear. "Clear up."

Twice more it was the same on the turns.

I do not know, the old man thought. He had been on the point of feeling himself go each time. I do not know. But I will try it once more.

He tried it once more and he felt himself going when he turned the fish. The fish righted himself and swam off again slowly with the great tail weaving in the air.

I'll try it again, the old man promised, although his hands were mushy now and he could only see well in flashes.

He tried it again and it was the same. So he thought, and he felt himself going before he started; I will try it once again.

He took all his pain and what was left of his strength and his long gone pride and he put it against the fish's agony and the fish came over onto his side and swam gently on his side, his bill almost touching the planking of the skiff and started to pass the boat, long, deep, wide, silver and barred with purple and interminable in the water.

The old man dropped the line and put his foot on it and lifted the harpoon as high as he could and drove it down with all his strength, and more strength he had just summoned, into the fish's side just behind the great chest fin that rose high in the air to the altitude of the man's chest. He felt the iron go in and he leaned on it and drove it further and then pushed all his weight after it.

Then the fish came alive, with his death in him, and rose high out of the water showing all his great length and width and all his power and his beauty. He seemed to hang in the air above the old man in the skiff. Then he fell into the water with a crash that sent spray over the old man and over all of the skiff.

The old man felt faint and sick and he could not see well. But he cleared the harpoon line and let it run slowly through his raw hands and, when he could see, he saw the fish was on his back with his silver belly up. The shaft of the harpoon was projecting at an angle from the fish's shoulder and the sea was discolouring with the red of the blood from his heart. First it was dark as a shoal in the blue water that was more than a mile deep. Then it spread like a cloud. The fish was silvery and still and floated with the waves.

The old man looked carefully in the glimpse of vision that he had. Then he took two turns of the harpoon line around the bitt in the bow and laid his head on his hands.

"Keep my head clear," he said against the wood of the bow. "I am a tired old man. But I have killed this fish which is my brother and now I must do the slave work."

Now I must prepare the nooses and the rope to lash him alongside, he thought. Even if we were two and swamped her to load him and bailed her out, this skiff would never hold him. I must prepare everything, then bring him in and lash him well and step the mast and set sail for home.

He started to pull the fish in to have him alongside so that he could pass a line through his gills and out his mouth and make his head fast alongside the bow. I want to see him, he thought, and to touch and to feel him. He is my fortune, he thought. But that is not why I wish to feel him. I think I felt his heart, he thought. When I pushed on the harpoon shaft the second time. Bring him in now and make him fast and get the noose around his tail and another around his middle to bind him to the skiff.

"Get to work, old man," he said. He took a very small drink of the water. "There is very much slave work to be done now that the fight is over."

He looked up at the sky and then out to his fish. He looked at the sun carefully. It is not much more than noon, he thought. And the trade wind is rising. The lines all mean nothing now. The boy and I will splice them when we are home.

"Come on, fish," he said. But the fish did not come. Instead he lay there wallowing now in the seas and the old man pulled the skiff up onto him.

When he was even with him and had the fish's head against the bow he could not believe his size. But he untied the harpoon rope from the bitt, passed it through the fish's gills and out his jaws, made a turn around his sword then passed the rope through the other gill, made another turn around the bill and knotted the double rope and made it fast to the bitt in the bow. He cut the rope then and went astern to noose the tail. The fish had turned silver from his original purple and silver, and the stripes showed the same pale violet colour as his tail. They were wider than a man's hand with his fingers spread and the fish's eye looked as detached as the mirrors in a periscope or as a saint in a procession.

"It was the only way to kill him," the old man said. He was feeling better since the water and he knew he would not go away and his head was clear. He's over fifteen hundred pounds the way he is, he thought. Maybe much more. If he dresses out two-thirds of that at thirty cents a pound?

"I need a pencil for that," he said. "My head is not that clear. But I think the great DiMaggio would be proud of me today. I had no bone spurs. But the hands and the back hurt truly." I wonder what a bone spur is, he thought. Maybe we have them without knowing of it.

He made the fish fast to bow and stern and to the middle thwart. He was so big it was like lashing a much bigger skiff alongside. He cut a piece of line and tied the fish's lower jaw against his bill so his mouth would not open and they would sail as cleanly as possible. Then he stepped the mast and, with the stick that was his gaff and with his boom rigged, the patched sail drew, the boat began to move, and half lying in the stern he sailed south-west.

He did not need a compass to tell him where south-west was. He only needed the feel of the trade wind and the drawing of the sail. I better put a small line out with a spoon on it and try and get something to eat and drink for the moisture. But he could not find a spoon and his sardines were rotten. So he hooked a patch of yellow gulf weed with the gaff as they passed and shook it so that the small shrimps that were in it fell onto the planking of the skiff. There were more than a dozen of them and they jumped and kicked like sand fleas. The old man pinched their heads off with his thumb and forefinger and ate them chewing up the shells and the tails. They were very tiny but he knew they were nourishing and they tasted good.

The old man still had two drinks of water in the bottle and he used half of one after he had eaten the shrimps. The skiff was sailing well considering the handicaps and he steered with the tiller under his arm. He could see the fish and he had only to look at his hands and feel his back against the stern to know that this had truly happened and was not a dream. At one time when he was feeling so badly toward the end, he had thought perhaps it was a dream. Then when he had seen the fish come out of the water and hang motionless in the sky before he fell, he was sure there was some great strangeness and he could not believe it. Then he could not see well, although now he saw as well as ever.

Now he knew there was the fish and his hands and back were no dream. The hands cure quickly, he thought. I bled them clean and the salt water will heal them. The dark water of the true gulf is the greatest healer that there is. All I must do is keep the head clear. The hands have done their work and we sail well. With his mouth shut and his tail straight up and down we sail like brothers. Then his head started to become a little unclear and he thought, is he bringing me in or am I bringing him in? If I were towing him behind there would be no question. Nor if the fish were in the skiff, with all dignity gone, there would be no question either. But they were sailing together lashed side by side and the old man thought, let him bring me in if it pleases him. I am only better than him through trickery and he meant me no harm.

They sailed well and the old man soaked his hands in the salt water and tried to keep his head clear. There were high cumulus clouds and enough cirrus above them so that the old man knew the breeze would last all night. The old man looked at the fish constantly to make sure it was true. It was an hour before the first shark hit him.

The shark was not an accident. He had come up from deep down in the water as the dark cloud of blood had settled and dispersed in the mile deep sea. He had come up so fast and absolutely without caution that he broke the surface of the blue water and was in the sun. Then he fell back into the sea and picked up the scent and started swimming on the course the skiff and the fish had taken.

Sometimes he lost the scent. But he would pick it up again, or have just a trace of it, and he swam fast and hard on the course. He was a very big Mako shark built to swim as fast as the fastest fish in the sea and everything about him was beautiful except his jaws. His back was as blue as a sword fish's and his belly was silver and his hide was smooth and handsome. He was built as a sword fish except for his huge jaws which were tight shut now as he swam fast, just under the surface with his high dorsal fin knifing through the water without wavering. Inside the closed double lip of his jaws all of his eight rows of teeth were slanted inwards. They were not the ordinary pyramid-shaped teeth of most sharks. They were shaped like a man's fingers when they are crisped like claws. They were nearly as long as the fingers of the old man and they had razor-sharp cutting edges on both sides. This was a fish built to feed on all the fishes in the sea, that were so fast and strong and well armed that they had no other enemy. Now he speeded up as he smelled the fresher scent and his blue dorsal fin cut the water.

When the old man saw him coming he knew that this was a shark that had no fear at all and would do exactly what he wished.

He prepared the harpoon and made the rope fast while he watched the shark come on. The rope was short as it lacked what he had cut away to lash the fish.

The old man's head was clear and good now and he was full of resolution but he had little hope. It was too good to last, he thought. He took one look at the great fish as he watched the shark close in. It might as well have been a dream, he thought. I cannot keep him from hitting me but maybe I can get him. *Dentuso,* he thought. Bad luck to your mother.

The shark closed fast astern and when he hit the fish the old man saw his mouth open and his strange eyes and the clicking chop of the teeth as he drove forward in the meat just above the tail. The shark's head was out of water and his back was coming out and the old man could hear the noise of skin and flesh ripping on the big fish when he rammed the harpoon down onto the shark's head at a spot where the line between his eyes intersected with the line that ran straight back from his nose. There were no such lines. There was only the heavy sharp blue head and the big eyes and the clicking, thrusting all-swallowing jaws. But that was the location of the brain and the old man hit it. He hit it with his blood mushed hands driving a good harpoon with all his strength. He hit it without hope but with resolution and complete malignancy.

The shark swung over and the old man saw his eye was not alive and then he swung over once again, wrapping himself in two loops of the rope. The old man knew that he was dead but the shark would not accept it. Then, on his back, with his tail lashing and his jaws clicking, the shark plowed over the water as a speed-boat does. The water was white where his tail beat it and three-quarters of his body was clear above the water when the rope came taut, shivered, and then snapped. The shark lay quietly for a little while on the surface and the old man watched him. Then he went down very slowly.

"He took about forty pounds," the old man said aloud. He took my harpoon too and all the rope, he thought, and now my fish bleeds again and there will be others.

He did not like to look at the fish anymore since he had been mutilated. When the fish had been hit it was as though he himself were hit.

But I killed the shark that hit my fish, he thought. And he was the biggest *dentuso* that I have ever seen. And God knows that I have seen big ones.

It was too good to last, he thought. I wish it had been a dream now and that I had never hooked the fish and was alone in bed on the newspapers.

"But man is not made for defeat," he said. "A man can be destroyed but not defeated." I am sorry that I killed the fish though, he thought. Now the bad time is coming and I do not even have the harpoon. The *dentuso* is cruel and able and strong and intelligent. But I was more intelligent than he was. Perhaps not, he thought. Perhaps I was only better armed.

"Don't think, old man," he said aloud. "Sail on this course and take it when it comes."

But I must think, he thought. Because it is all I have left. That and baseball. I wonder how the great DiMaggio would have liked the way I hit him in the brain? It was no great thing, he thought. Any man could do it. But do you think my hands were as great a handicap as the bone spurs? I cannot know. I never had anything wrong with my heel except the time the sting ray stung it when I stepped on him when swimming and paralyzed the lower leg and made the unbearable pain.

"Think about something cheerful, old man," he said. "Every minute now you are closer to home. You sail lighter for the loss of forty pounds."

He knew quite well the pattern of what could happen when

he reached the inner part of the current. But there was nothing to be done now.

"Yes there is," he said aloud. "I can lash my knife to the butt of one of the oars."

So he did that with the tiller under his arm and the sheet of the sail under his foot.

"Now," he said. "I am still an old man. But I am not unarmed."

The breeze was fresh now and he sailed on well. He watched only the forward part of the fish and some of his hope returned.

It is silly not to hope, he thought. Besides I believe it is a sin. Do not think about sin, he thought. There are enough problems now without sin. Also I have no understanding of it.

I have no understanding of it and I am not sure that I believe in it. Perhaps it was a sin to kill the fish. I suppose it was even though I did it to keep me alive and feed many people. But then everything is a sin. Do not think about sin. It is much too late for that and there are people who are paid to do it. Let them think about it. You were born to be a fisherman as the fish was born to be a fish. San Pedro was a fisherman as was the father of the great DiMaggio.

But he liked to think about all things that he was involved in and since there was nothing to read and he did not have a radio, he thought much and he kept on thinking about sin. You did not kill the fish only to keep alive and to sell for food, he thought. You killed him for pride and because you are a fisherman. You loved him when he was alive and you loved him after. If you love him, it is not a sin to kill him. Or is it more?

"You think too much, old man," he said aloud.

But you enjoyed killing the *dentuso*, he thought. He lives on the live fish as you do. He is not a scavenger nor just a moving appetite as some sharks are. He is beautiful and noble and knows no fear of anything.

"I killed him in self-defense," the old man said aloud. "And I killed him well."

Besides, he thought, everything kills everything else in some way. Fishing kills me exactly as it keeps me alive. The boy keeps me alive, he thought. I must not deceive myself too much.

He leaned over the side and pulled loose a piece of the meat of the fish where the shark had cut him. He chewed it and noted its quality and its good taste. It was firm and juicy, like meat, but it was not red. There was no stringiness in it and he knew that it would bring the highest price in the market. But there was no way to keep its scent out of the water and the old man knew that a very bad time was coming.

The breeze was steady. It had backed a little further into the north-east and he knew that meant that it would not fall off. The old man looked ahead of him but he could see no sails nor could he see the hull nor the smoke of any ship. There were only the flying fish that went up from his bow sailing away to either side and the yellow patches of gulf-weed. He could not even see a bird.

He had sailed for two hours, resting in the stern and sometimes chewing a bit of the meat from the marlin, trying to rest and to be strong, when he saw the first of the two sharks.

"*Ay*," he said aloud. There is no translation for this word and perhaps it is just a noise such as a man might make, involuntarily, feeling the nail go through his hands and into the wood.

"*Galanos*," he said aloud. He had seen the second fin now coming up behind the first and had identified them as shovel-nosed sharks by the brown, triangular fin and the sweeping movements of the tail. They had the scent and were excited and in the stupidity of their great hunger they were losing and finding the scent in their excitement. But they were closing all the time.

The old man made the sheet fast and jammed the tiller. Then he took up the oar with the knife lashed to it. He lifted it as lightly as he could because his hands rebelled at the pain. Then he opened and closed them on it lightly to loosen them. He closed them firmly so they would take the pain now and would not flinch and watched the sharks come. He could see their wide, flattened, shovel-pointed heads now and their white-tipped wide pectoral fins. They were hateful sharks, bad smelling, scavengers as well as killers, and when they were hungry they would bite at an oar or the rudder of a boat. It was these sharks that would cut the turtles' legs and flippers off when the turtles were asleep on the surface, and they would hit a man in the water, if they were hungry, even if the man had no smell of fish blood nor of fish slime on him.

"Ay," the old man said. "*Galanos*. Come on *galanos*."

They came. But they did not come as the Mako had come. One turned and went out of sight under the skiff and the old man could feel the skiff shake as he jerked and pulled on the fish. The other watched the old man with his slitted yellow eyes and then came in fast with his half circle of jaws wide to hit the fish where he had already been bitten. The line showed clearly on the top of his brown head and back where the brain joined the spinal cord and the old man drove the knife on the oar into the juncture, withdrew it, and drove it in again into the shark's yellow cat-like eyes. The shark let go of the fish and slid down, swallowing what he had taken as he died.

The skiff was still shaking with the destruction the other shark was doing to the fish and the old man let go the sheet so that the skiff would swing broadside and bring the shark out from under. When he saw the shark he leaned over the side and punched at him. He hit only meat and the hide was set hard and he barely got the knife in. The blow hurt not only his hands but his shoulder too. But the shark came up fast with his head out and the old man hit him squarely in the center of his flat-topped head as his nose came out of water and lay against the fish. The old man withdrew the blade and punched the shark exactly in the same spot again. He still hung to the fish with his jaws hooked and the old man stabbed him in his left eye. The shark still hung there.

"No?" the old man said and he drove the blade between the vertebrae and the brain. It was an easy shot now and he felt the cartilage sever. The old man reversed the oar and put the blade between the shark's jaws to open them. He twisted the blade and as the shark slid loose he said, "Go on, *galano*. Slide down a mile deep. Go see your friend, or maybe it's your mother."

The old man wiped the blade of his knife and laid down the oar. Then he found the sheet and the sail filled and he brought the skiff onto her course.

"They must have taken a quarter of him and of the best meat," he said aloud. "I wish it were a dream and that I had never hooked him. I'm sorry about it, fish. It makes everything wrong." He stopped and he did not want to look at the fish now. Drained of blood and awash he looked the colour of the silver backing of a mirror and his stripes still showed.

"I shouldn't have gone out so far, fish," he said. "Neither for you nor for me. I'm sorry, fish."

Now, he said to himself. Look to the lashing on the knife and see if it has been cut. Then get your hand in order because there still is more to come.

"I wish I had a stone for the knife," the old man said after he had checked the lashing on the oar butt. "I should have brought a stone." You should have brought many things, he thought. But you did not bring them, old man. Now is no time to think of what you do not have. Think of what you can do with what there is.

"You give me much good counsel," he said aloud. "I'm tired of it."

He held the tiller under his arm and soaked both his hands in the water as the skiff drove forward.

"God knows how much that last one took," he said. "But she's much lighter now." He did not want to think of the mutilated under-side of the fish. He knew that each of the jerking bumps of the shark had been meat torn away and that the fish now made a trail for all sharks as wide as a highway through the sea.

He was a fish to keep a man all winter, he thought. Don't think of that. Just rest and try to get your hands in shape to defend what is left of him. The blood smell from my hands means nothing now with all that scent in the water. Besides they do not bleed much. There is nothing cut that means anything. The bleeding may keep the left from cramping.

What can I think of now? he thought. Nothing. I must think of nothing and wait for the next ones. I wish it had really been a dream, he thought. But who knows? It might have turned out well.

The next shark that came was a single shovel-nose. He came like a pig to the trough if a pig had a mouth so wide that you could put your head in it. The old man let him hit the fish and then drove the knife on the oar down into his brain. But the shark jerked backwards as he rolled and the knife blade snapped.

The old man settled himself to steer. He did not even watch the big shark sinking slowly in the water, showing first life-size, then small, then tiny. That always fascinated the old man. But he did not even watch it now.

"I have the gaff now," he said. "But it will do no good. I have the two oars and the tiller and the short club."

Now they have beaten me, he thought. I am too old to club sharks to death. But I will try it as long as I have the oars and the short club and the tiller.

He put his hands in the water again to soak them. It was getting late in the afternoon and he saw nothing but the sea and the sky. There was more wind in the sky than there had been, and soon he hoped that he would see land.

"You're tired, old man," he said. "You're tired inside."

The sharks did not hit him again until just before sunset.

The old man saw the brown fins coming along the wide trail the fish must make in the water. They were not even quartering on the scent. They were headed straight for the skiff swimming side by side.

He jammed the tiller, made the sheet fast and reached under the stern for the club. It was an oar handle from a broken oar sawed off to about two and a half feet in length. He could only use it effectively with one hand because of the grip of the handle and he took good hold of it with his right hand, flexing his hand on it, as he watched the sharks come. They were both *galanos*.

I must let the first one get a good hold and hit him on the point of the nose or straight across the top of the head, he thought.

The two sharks closed together and as he saw the one nearest him open his jaws and sink them into the silver side of the fish, he raised the club high and brought it down heavy and slamming onto the top of the shark's broad head. He felt the rubbery solidity as the club came down. But he felt the rigidity of bone too and he struck the shark once more hard across the point of the nose as he slid down from the fish.

The other shark had been in and out and now came in again with his jaws wide. The old man could see pieces of the meat of the fish spilling white from the corner of his jaws as he bumped the fish and closed his jaws. He swung at him and hit only the head and the shark looked at him and wrenched the meat loose. The old man swung the club down on him again as he slipped away to swallow and hit only the heavy solid rubberiness.

"Come on, *galano*," the old man said. "Come in again."

The shark came in a rush and the old man hit him as he shut his jaws. He hit him solidly and from as high up as he could raise the club. This time he felt the bone at the base of the brain and he hit him again in the same place while the shark tore the meat loose sluggishly and slid down from the fish.

The old man watched for him to come again but neither shark showed. Then he saw one on the surface swimming in circles. He did not see the fin of the other.

I could not expect to kill them, he thought. I could have in my time. But I have hurt them both badly and neither one can feel very good. If I could have used a bat with two hands I could have killed the first one surely. Even now, he thought.

He did not want to look at the fish. He knew that half of him had been destroyed. The sun had gone down while he had been in the fight with the sharks.

"It will be dark soon," he said. "Then I should see the glow of Havana. If I am too far to the eastward I will see the lights of one of the new beaches."

I cannot be too far out now, he thought. I hope no one has been too worried. There is only the boy to worry, of course. But I am sure he would have confidence. Many of the older fishermen will worry. Many others too, he thought. I live in a good town.

He could not talk to the fish anymore because the fish had been ruined too badly. Then something came into his head.

"Half fish," he said. "Fish that you were. I am sorry that I went too far out. I ruined us both. But we have killed many sharks, you and I, and ruined many others. How many did you ever kill, old fish? You do not have that spear on your head for nothing."

He liked to think of the fish and what he could do to a shark if he were swimming free. I should have chopped the bill off to fight them with, he thought. But there was no hatchet and then there was no knife.

But if I had, and could have lashed it to an oar butt, what a weapon. Then we might have fought them together. What will you do now if they come in the night? What can you do?

"Fight them," he said. "I'll fight them until I die."

But in the dark now and no glow showing and no lights and only the wind and the steady pull of the sail he felt that perhaps he was already dead. He put his two hands together and felt the palms. They were not dead and he could bring the pain of life by simply opening and closing them. He leaned his back against the stern and knew he was not dead. His shoulders told him.

I have all those prayers I promised if I caught the fish, he thought. But I am too tired to say them now. I better get the sack and put it over my shoulders.

He lay in the stern and steered and watched for the glow to come in the sky. I have half of him, he thought. Maybe I'll have the luck to bring the forward half in. I should have some luck. No, he said. You violated your luck when you went too far outside.

"Don't be silly," he said aloud. "And keep awake and steer. You may have much luck yet."

"I'd like to buy some if there's any place they sell it," he said.

What could I buy it with? he asked himself. Could I buy it with a lost harpoon and a broken knife and two bad hands?

"You might," he said. "You tried to buy it with eighty-four days at sea. They nearly sold it to you too."

I must not think nonsense, he thought. Luck is a thing that comes in many forms and who can recognize her? I would take some though in any form and pay what they asked. I wish I could see the glow from the lights, he thought. I wish too many things. But that is the thing I wish for now. He tried to settle more comfortably to steer and from his pain he knew he was not dead.

He saw the reflected glare of the lights of the city at what must have been around ten o'clock at night. They were only perceptible at first as the light is in the sky before the moon rises. Then they were steady to see across the ocean which was rough now with the increasing breeze. He steered inside of the glow and he thought that now, soon, he must hit the edge of the stream.

Now it is over, he thought. They will probably hit me again. But what can a man do against them in the dark without a weapon?

He was stiff and sore now and his wounds and all of the strained parts of his body hurt with the cold of the night. I hope I do not have to fight again, he thought. I hope so much I do not have to fight again.

But by midnight he fought and this time he knew the fight was useless. They came in a pack and he could only see the lines in the water that their fins made and their phosphorescence as they threw themselves on the fish. He clubbed at heads and heard the jaws chop and the shaking of the skiff as they took hold below. He clubbed desperately at what he could only feel and hear and he felt something seize the club and it was gone.

He jerked the tiller free from the rudder and beat and chopped with it, holding it in both hands and driving it down again and again. But they were up to the bow now and driving in one after the other and together, tearing off the pieces of meat that showed glowing below the sea as they turned to come once more.

One came, finally, against the head itself and he knew that it was over. He swung the tiller across the shark's head where the jaws were caught in the heaviness of the fish's head which would not tear. He swung it once and twice and again. He heard the tiller break and he lunged at the shark with the splintered butt. He felt it go in and knowing it was sharp he drove it in again. The shark let go and rolled away. That was the last shark of the pack that came. There was nothing more for them to eat.

The old man could hardly breathe now and he felt a strange taste in his mouth. It was coppery and sweet and he was afraid of it for a moment. But there was not much of it.

He spat into the ocean and said, "Eat that, *galanos*. And make a dream you've killed a man."

He knew he was beaten now finally and without remedy and

he went back to the stern and found the jagged end of the tiller would fit in the slot of the rudder well enough for him to steer. He settled the sack around his shoulders and put the skiff on her course. He sailed lightly now and he had no thoughts nor any feelings of any kind. He was past everything now and he sailed the skiff to make his home port as well and as intelligently as he could. In the night sharks hit the carcass as someone might pick up crumbs from the table. The old man paid no attention to them and did not pay any attention to anything except steering. He only noticed how lightly and how well the skiff sailed now there was no great weight beside her.

She's good, he thought. She is sound and not harmed in any way except for the tiller. That is easily replaced.

He could feel he was inside the current now and he could see the lights of the beach colonies along the shore. He knew where he was now and it was nothing to get home.

The wind is our friend, anyway, he thought. Then he added, sometimes. And the great sea with our friends and our enemies. And bed, he thought. Bed is my friend. Just bed, he thought. Bed will be a great thing. It is easy when you are beaten, he thought. I never knew how easy it was. And what beat you, he thought.

"Nothing," he said aloud. "I went out too far."

When he sailed into the little harbour the lights of the Terrace were out and he knew everyone was in bed. The breeze had risen steadily and was blowing strongly now. It was quiet in the harbour though and he sailed up onto the little patch of shingle below the rocks. There was no one to help him so he pulled the boat up as far as he could. Then he stepped out and made her fast to a rock.

He unstepped the mast and furled the sail and tied it. Then he shouldered the mast and started to climb. It was then he knew the depth of his tiredness. He stopped for a moment and looked back and saw in the reflection from the street light the great tail of the fish standing up well behind the skiff's stern. He saw the white naked line of his backbone and the dark mass of the head with the projecting bill and all the nakedness between.

He started to climb again and at the top he fell and lay for some time with the mast across his shoulder. He tried to get up. But it was too difficult and he sat there with the mast on his shoulder and looked at the road. A cat passed on the far side going about its business and the old man watched it. Then he just watched the road.

Finally he put the mast down and stood up. He picked the mast up and put it on his shoulder and started up the road. He had to sit down five times before he reached his shack.

Inside the shack he leaned the mast against the wall. In the dark he found a water bottle and took a drink. Then he lay down on the bed. He pulled the blanket over his shoulders and then over his back and legs and he slept face down on the newspapers with his arms out straight and the palms of his hands up.

He was asleep when the boy looked in the door in the morning. It was blowing so hard that the drifting-boats would not be going out and the boy had slept late and then come to the old man's shack as he had come each morning. The boy saw that the old man was breathing and then he saw the old man's hands and he started to cry. He went out very quietly to go to bring some coffee and all the way down the road he was crying.

Many fishermen were around the skiff looking at what was lashed beside it and one was in the water, his trousers rolled up, measuring the skeleton with a length of line.

The boy did not go down. He had been there before and one of the fishermen was looking after the skiff for him.

"How is he?" one of the fishermen shouted.

"Sleeping," the boy called. He did not care that they saw him crying. "Let no one disturb him."

"He was eighteen feet from nose to tail," the fisherman who was measuring him called.

"I believe it," the boy said.

He went into the Terrace and asked for a can of coffee.

"Hot and with plenty of milk and sugar in it."

"Anything more?"

"No. Afterwards I will see what he can eat."

"What a fish it was," the proprietor said. "There has never been such a fish. Those were two fine fish you took yesterday too."

"Damn my fish," the boy said and he started to cry again.

"Do you want a drink of any kind?" the proprietor asked.

"No," the boy said. "Tell them not to bother Santiago. I'll be back."

"Tell him how sorry I am."

"Thanks," the boy said.

The boy carried the hot can of coffee up to the old man's shack and sat by him until he woke. Once it looked as though he were waking. But he had gone back into heavy sleep and the boy had gone across the road to borrow some wood to heat the coffee.

Finally the old man woke.

"Don't sit up," the boy said. "Drink this." He poured some of the coffee in a glass.

The old man took it and drank it.

"They beat me, Manolin," he said. "They truly beat me."

"*He* didn't beat you. Not the fish."

"No. Truly. It was afterwards."

"Pedrico is looking after the skiff and the gear. What do you want done with the head?"

"Let Pedrico chop it up to use in fish traps."

"And the spear?"

"You keep it if you want it."

"I want it," the boy said. "Now we must make our plans about the other things."

"Did they search for me?"

"Of course. With coast guard and with planes."

"The ocean is very big and a skiff is small and hard to see," the old man said. He noticed how pleasant it was to have someone to talk to instead of speaking only to himself and to the sea. "I missed you," he said. "What did you catch?"

"One the first day. One the second and two the third."

"Very good."

"Now we fish together again."

"No. I am not lucky. I am not lucky anymore."

"The hell with luck," the boy said. "I'll bring the luck with me."

"What will your family say?"

"I do not care. I caught two yesterday. But we will fish together now for I still have much to learn."

"We must get a good killing lance and always have it on board. You can make the blade from a spring leaf from an old Ford. We can grind it in Guanabacoa. It should be sharp and not tempered so it will break. My knife broke."

"I'll get another knife and have the spring ground. How many days of heavy *brisa* have we?"

"Maybe three. Maybe more."

"I will have everything in order," the boy said. "You get your hands well old man."

"I know how to care for them. In the night I spat something strange and felt something in my chest was broken."

"Get that well too," the boy said. "Lie down, old man, and I will bring you your clean shirt. And something to eat."

"Bring any of the papers of the time that I was gone," the old man said.

"You must get well fast for there is much that I can learn and you can teach me everything. How much did you suffer?"

"Plenty," the old man said.

"I'll bring the food and the papers," the boy said. "Rest well, old man. I will bring stuff from the drugstore for your hands."

"Don't forget to tell Pedrico the head is his."

"No. I will remember."

As the boy went out the door and down the worn coral rock road he was crying again.

That afternoon there was a party of tourists at the Terrace and looking down in the water among the empty beer cans and dead barracudas a woman saw a great long white spine with a huge tail at the end that lifted and swung with the tide while the east wind blew a heavy steady sea outside the entrance to the harbour.

"What's that?" she asked a waiter and pointed to the long backbone of the great fish that was now just garbage waiting to go out with the tide.

"Tiburon," the waiter said, "Eshark." He was meaning to explain what had happened.

"I didn't know sharks had such handsome, beautifully formed tails."

"I didn't either," her male companion said.

Up the road, in his shack, the old man was sleeping again. He was still sleeping on his face and the boy was sitting by him watching him. The old man was dreaming about the lions.